The Eye of
Winter's Fury

BOOK THREE

THE EYE OF
WINTER'S FURY

MICHAEL J. WARD

The right of Michael J. Ward to be identified as the author of this work
has been asserted by him in accordance with the
Copyright, Designs and Patents Act 1988.

First published in Great Britain in 2014
by Gollancz
An imprint of the Orion Publishing Group
Orion House, 5 Upper St Martin's Lane, London WC2H 9EA
An Hachette UK Company

This edition published in Great Britain in 2015 by Gollancz

3 5 7 9 10 8 6 4 2

A CIP catalogue record for this book is available
from the British Library

ISBN 978 0 575 09561 8

Typeset by Input Data Services Ltd, Bridgwater, Somerset

Printed and bound in Great Britain by
CPI Group (UK) Ltd, Croydon, CR0 4YY

The Orion Publishing Group's policy is to use papers that
are natural, renewable and recyclable products and made
from wood grown in sustainable forests. The logging and
manufacturing processes are expected to conform to the
environmental regulations of the country of origin.

www.destiny-quest.com
www.orionbooks.co.uk
www.gollancz.co.uk

'There is nothing to writing.
All you do is sit down at a typewriter and bleed.'

ERNEST HEMINGWAY

The Ballad of the North

Winter stands o'er the land
And in her hand, the embers of a life
Taken from him, the named in honour fell
We speak it now,
We sing to her again.

Of steel and bone, and stolen fires bright
Of tresses gold and halls of silver light.
Lay him down, in ice and peak of stone
Till horns sound deep and vengeance brings him home.

Winter blows o'er the land
And in her eye, the fury of his pain
Taken from him, the named in honour fell
We speak it now,
We sing to her again.

H E R O DQ S H E E T

NAME:

CLOAK	HEAD	GLOVES

MAIN HAND	CHEST	LEFT HAND

TALISMAN	FEET	MONEY POUCH

SPEED	BRAWN	MAGIC	ARMOUR	DEATH PENALTIES

HEALTH	
	(see entry 98)

H E R O DO S H E E T

PATH: **CAREER:**

NECKLACE

RING

RING

DEFEATS

SPECIAL ABILITIES:

SPEED _____

COMBAT _____

PASSIVE _____

MODIFIER _____

DEATH MOVE _____

BACKPACK:

H E R O DO S H E E T

SPEED _____ STABILITY _____ TOUGHNESS _____

NOTES: _____

SPEED _____ STABILITY _____ TOUGHNESS _____

NOTES: _____

SPEED _____ STABILITY _____ TOUGHNESS _____

NOTES: _____

NOTES/KEYWORDS:

H E R O [DO] S H E E T

SPEED _____ STABILITY _____ TOUGHNESS _____

NOTES: _____

_____

SPEED _____ STABILITY _____ TOUGHNESS _____

NOTES: _____

_____

SPEED _____ STABILITY _____ TOUGHNESS _____

NOTES: _____

_____

NOTES/KEYWORDS:

Welcome to DestinyQuest!

'A new king will come with death for a crown. Cold will be his heart.
Cold will be his revenge.'
Blood of Barahar

Unlike ordinary storybooks, DestinyQuest puts *you* in charge of the action. As you guide your hero through this epic adventure, you will be choosing the dangers that they face, the monsters that they fight and the treasures that they find. Every decision that you make will have an impact on the story and, ultimately, the fate of your hero.

Your choices, your hero

With hundreds of special items to discover in the game, you can completely customise your hero. You can choose their weapons, their armour, their special abilities – even the boots on their feet and the cloak on their back! No two heroes will ever be alike, which means your hero will always be unique to you. And even better, you can take your hero into battle against your friends' heroes too!

Limitless possibilities, endless adventure

You can play through DestinyQuest multiple times and never have the same adventure twice. With so many options and paths to choose from, the monsters that you encounter, the people that you meet and the loot that you find will be different each time you play. There are numerous hidden secrets to discover, bonus items to collect and unique special abilities to unlock – in fact, every turn of the page could reveal something new for you and your hero.

Discover your destiny …

The next few pages will take you through the rules of the game, outlining the hero creation process and the combat and quest system.

Don't worry, it won't take long – and then your DestinyQuest adventure can begin!

The hero sheet

Let's start with one of the most important things in the game – your hero sheet. This is a visual record of your hero's abilities and equipment. You will be constantly updating this sheet throughout the game, as you train new abilities and find better armour and weapons for your hero. (Note: The hero sheet is also available as a free download from **www.destiny-quest.com**.)

Attributes

Every hero has five key attributes that determine their strengths and weaknesses. These are *speed, brawn, magic, armour* and *health*. The goal of DestinyQuest is to advance your hero from an inexperienced novice into a powerful champion – someone who can stand up to the biggest and baddest of foes and triumph!

To achieve this, you will need to complete the many quests throughout the lands of Valeron. These quests will reward you with new skills and equipment, such as weapons and armour. These will boost your hero's attributes and give you a better chance of survival when taking on tougher enemies.

The five attributes are:

* **Brawn**: As its name suggests, this score represents your hero's strength and muscle power. A hero with high *brawn* will be able to hit harder in combat, striking through their opponent's armour and dealing fatal blows.

    Brawn is the main attribute of the warrior.

* **Magic**: By mastering the arcane schools of fire, lightning, frost and shadow, a hero can command devastating spells and summon fiendish monsters. Heroes that choose this path should seek out the staffs, wands and arcane charms that will boost their *magic* score, granting them even deadlier powers to smite their foes.

    Magic is the main attribute of the mage.

* **Speed**: The higher a hero's *speed* score, the more likely they are to score a hit against their opponent. A hero who puts points into *speed* can easily bring down stronger enemies thanks to their lightning-fast reflexes.

  Speed is the main attribute of the rogue.

* **Armour**: Whenever a hero is hit in combat, by weapons or spells, they take damage. Wearing armour can help your hero to survive longer by absorbing some of this damage. Warriors will always have a high *armour* score, thanks to the heavy armour and shields that they can equip. Rogues and mages will typically have lower scores, relying instead on their powerful attacks to win the day.

* **Health**: This is your hero's most important attribute as it represents their life force. When *health* reaches zero, your hero is dead – so, it goes without saying that you should keep a very close eye on it! Armour and equipment can raise your hero's *health* score – and there are also potions and abilities to be discovered, to help your hero replenish their *health* during combat.

Starting attributes
Every hero begins their adventures with a zero score for *brawn, magic, speed* and *armour*. These attributes will be boosted throughout the course of your adventures. All starting heroes begin with **30 health**.

Equipment boxes
The hero sheet displays a number of important boxes. These boxes each represent a location on your hero where they can equip an item. Whenever your hero comes across a new item in the game, you will be told which box or boxes on the sheet you can place it in. You can only have one item equipped in each box.

Backpack
Your hero also has a backpack that can hold five single items. On your travels you will come across many backpack items, including useful potions and quest items. Each backpack item you come across takes up *one space* in your backpack – even if you have multiple versions of the same type of item (for example, health potions).

BACKPACK:				
Healing +4 health (1 use)	Healing +4 health (1 use)	Stone tablet	Forest dew full heal (2 uses)	Miracle grow +2 brawn (1 use)

Special abilities

The special abilities box, on the right of your sheet, is where you can record notes on your hero's special abilities. Every hero has two special abilities, which they learn when they train a career. Items of equipment can also grant special abilities for your hero. All special abilities are explained in the glossary at the back of the book.

Paths and careers

Your hero starts their adventure as an untrained novice, with no remarkable skills or abilities. Once your hero has gained some experience, however, three paths will become available to you – the path of the warrior, the rogue and the mage. Your hero can only choose one of these paths, and once that decision is made, it can't be changed – so choose wisely. The chosen path will determine the careers and abilities that your hero can learn throughout their adventures.

Your hero's path and current career should always be recorded at the top of your hero sheet, and its special abilities should be recorded in the special abilities box on the right of your sheet. A hero can only be trained in *one career* at a time, but you can swap their career for another one, providing you have found the relevant trainer or reward item. When your hero trains a new career, all abilities and bonuses from the old career are lost.

Gold

The main currency in Valeron is the gold crown. These can be used to purchase potions and other special items whenever you visit a town, village or camp. More gold can be discovered by killing monsters and completing quests.

Quests and monsters

The kingdom of Valeron is a dangerous place, full of ferocious monsters, wild beasts and deadly magical forces ... bad news for some people perhaps, but for a would-be adventurer it means plenty of paid work! By vanquishing foes and completing quests, your hero will grow stronger and more powerful, allowing you to take on tougher challenges and discover even greater rewards.

The maps

The story is divided into two chapters – known as 'Acts'. Each Act has a map, which shows you the locations of all the different quests that your hero can take part in. To select a quest you simply turn to the corresponding numbered entry in the book and read on from there, returning to the map when you have finished.

Choosing quests

Each map will provide you with a number of different quests. Some quests are harder than others. A simple colour-coded system ranks the quests in order of difficulty:

* **Green quests**: These are the easiest quests to complete. Heroes with even the most basic of equipment will still emerge victorious.

* **Orange quests**: Heroes will find these tasks a little more challenging, requiring them to defeat numerous enemies to succeed.

* **Blue quests**: Things get a lot tougher with blue quests. Monsters are more likely to have special abilities and higher attribute scores, meaning your hero will need to be fully prepared and equipped for the dangers they may face.

* **Red quests**: These quests should only be attempted once you have completed the majority of green, orange and blue quests. Your hero will need to use everything they've got to overcome these tough challenges and triumph.

Quests can be done in any order you wish – although note that it is wiser to complete the easier quests (green and orange) before you attempt the harder ones (blue and red). Once a quest has been completed, it cannot be revisited.

Legendary monsters

On each map you will also see some spider symbols. These represent 'legendary monsters': opponents that are tougher than your average foe. Only the bravest of heroes, who are confident in their abilities and have good gear from their questing, should seek out and battle these mighty opponents.

Boss monsters

Each Act of the story has a final boss monster that must be defeated before you can advance the story to the next Act. These boss monsters are represented by the skull symbol on the map.

It goes without saying that these final bosses are no pushovers and should only be attempted once you have fully explored each map and completed most of the quests.

Towns, villages and camps

Every Act of the story has its own town, village or camp, which your hero can visit anytime between quests. They are represented on the map by the building icon. Simply turn to the corresponding page entry whenever you wish to visit. These locations can provide your hero with items to purchase, additional quests, hints and tips and even some career trainers.

It is always a good idea to visit these areas first, whenever you start a new map. The inns and taverns can be a great source of rumour and information regarding the challenges ahead.

Upgrading equipment

The primary goal of DestinyQuest is to equip your hero with better weapons, armour and equipment. These will boost your hero's attributes such as *brawn* and *magic*, and help them to survive longer in battle.

At certain times in the story you will be offered a choice of rewards for your hero. Usually this will be the result of killing a monster or completing a quest, but there are also many other ways of gaining rewards – some easier to find than others.

When you are offered a choice of rewards, you will be told how many items you may pick from the selection. It is up to you to decide which reward/s will be best for your hero. These rewards, such as rings, pieces of armour, weapons and necklaces, will commonly give boosts to certain attributes. Select your rewards wisely to boost the attributes that are the most essential for your hero.

When you have chosen your reward, you write its name and details in the corresponding box on your hero sheet. Make sure to update any attributes that are affected by the new reward. Remember, it is your decision what rewards you take. You can always ignore items if they don't interest you.

Replacing equipment

Your hero can only carry one item in each box. When you choose a reward and your hero already has an item in the corresponding box, the new item *replaces* the old one – and the old item is destroyed. When you destroy the old item, **all attribute bonuses and abilities that it provided are lost**, to be replaced by those from the new item.

Combat

Valeron can be a wild and dangerous place. Most of the creatures you encounter will be hostile and it will be up to you (and your hero!) to battle and defeat these monsters, to emerge victorious.

When you enter into combat, you will be given your opponent's attributes. These are usually *speed*, *brawn* (or *magic*), *armour* and *health*. Some may also have special abilities that you will need to take note of.

The combat sequence

Combat consists of a number of *combat rounds*. In each round of combat you roll dice to determine who hits who and who takes damage. (Note: A die is considered to be a standard 6-sided die.) Once damage has been applied, a new combat round starts. Combat continues until either your hero or their opponent is defeated.

In each combat round:

1. Roll *2 dice* for your hero and add their current *speed* score to the total. This is your hero's **attack speed**.

2. Roll another *2 dice* for your opponent and add their *speed* score to the total. This is their **attack speed**.

3. The combatant with the highest attack speed wins the combat round. If both scores are the same, it is a stand off – the combat round ends (see step 7) and a new one begins.

4. The winner of the round rolls *1 die* and adds either their *brawn* score or their *magic* score to the total, whichever is highest. (Note: monsters will only have one or the other, not both.) This will give you a **damage score.**

5. The loser of the round deducts their *armour* value from the damage score. Any remaining damage is then deducted from their *health*. (If the damage score was 8 and the loser had an *armour* of 2, they would take 6 health damage.)

6. If this damage takes your hero's or your opponent's *health* to zero, they are defeated. If both combatants have *health* remaining, then the combat continues.

7. At the end of each combat round, any damage from passive effects (such as *bleed*, *thorns* and *venom*) are applied to any affected combatants. If you and your opponent still have *health* remaining, then a new combat round begins. Return to step 1.

Example of combat

Sir Hugo has awoken a slumbering serpent and must now defend himself against its venomous attacks.

	Speed	Brawn	Magic	Armour	Health
Hugo	4	7	1	5	30

	Speed	Brawn		Armour	Health
Serpent	6	3		2	12

Special abilities

♥ **Venom**: Once you have taken health damage from the serpent, at the end of every combat round you must automatically lose 2 *health*.

Combat round one

1. Sir Hugo rolls 2 dice to determine his attack speed. He rolls a 🎲 and a 🎲 giving him a total of 6. He adds on his *speed* score of 4 to give him a final total of 10.

2. The serpent rolls 2 dice to determine its attack speed. The result is a 🎲 and a 🎲 making 11. The serpent's *speed* is 6, making its final total 17. The serpent has won the first round of combat.

3. A die is rolled for the serpent to determine its damage score. The result is a 🎲. Its *brawn* score is added on to this, to give a final total of 9.

4. Sir Hugo deducts his *armour* value from this total. This means he only takes 4 points of health damage (9−5=4). His *health* is reduced from 30 to 26.

5. Sir Hugo is also poisoned by the serpent's venom. He automatically takes another 2 points of health damage, reducing his *health* to 24.

Combat round two

1. Sir Hugo rolls 2 dice to determine his attack speed. He rolls a 🎲 and a 🎲 giving him a total of 10. He adds on his *speed* score of 4 to give him a final total of 14.

2. The serpent rolls 2 dice to determine its attack speed The result is a ⚀ and a ⚁ making 5. The serpent adds its *speed* score of 6, making its final total 11. Sir Hugo wins!

3. Sir Hugo rolls a ⚅ for his damage score. He chooses to add on his *brawn* (which is higher than his *magic* sccore). His final total is 12.

4. The serpent has an *armour* value of 2, so takes 10 points of damage. The serpent is left with 2 *health*.

5. Because the serpent applied its venom special ability in the last round, Sir Hugo must now deduct another 2 points from his *health* – reducing it from 24 to 22.

Combat then moves to the next round, continuing until one combatant's *health* is reduced to zero.

Restoring health and attributes

Once you have defeated an enemy, your hero's *health* and any other attributes that have been affected by special attacks or abilities are **immediately restored** back to their normal values (unless otherwise stated in the text). In the above example, once Sir Hugo has defeated the serpent, he can return his *health* back to 30 and continue his adventures.

Fighting multiple opponents

In some combats you will be fighting more than one opponent. When faced with multiple opponents, combat follows the same rules as for single combat – the only difference is that, at the start of each combat round, you must choose which opponent you will be attacking. You must then roll against their *speed* score. If you win the round, you must direct your damage against your chosen opponent (or multiple opponents if you have an ability that lets you do so). If you lose the round, your chosen opponent strikes against you as normal. You must defeat all your opponents to win the combat..

Using special abilities in combat

As your hero progresses through the story, they will discover many special abilities that they can use in combat. All abilities are explained in the glossary at the back of the book.

There are five types of special ability. These are: speed (sp), combat (co), modifier (mo), passive (pa) and death move (dm) abilities.

* **Speed (sp):** These abilities can be used at the start of a combat round (before you roll for attack speed), and will usually influence how many dice you can roll or reduce the number of dice that your opponent can roll for speed. You can only use one speed ability per combat round.

* **Combat (co):** These abilities are used either before or after you (or your opponent) roll for damage. Usually these will increase the number of dice you can roll, or allow you to block or dodge your opponent's attacks. You can only use one combat ability per combat round.

* **Modifier (mo):** Modifier abilities allow you to boost your attribute scores or influence dice that you have already rolled. You can use as many different modifier abilities as you wish during a combat round.

* **Passive (pa):** Passive abilities are typically applied at the end of a combat round, once you or your opponent has taken health damage. Abilities such as *venom* and *bleed* are passive abilities. These abilities happen automatically, based on their description.

* **Death move (dm):** Death moves can be performed when you are faced with multiple opponents. When an opponent is reduced to zero *health*, you may automatically play a death move. These abilities can give you bonuses or allow you to perform a special attack against your remaining enemies. You can only use one death move per combat round. (Note: if an opponent dies as a result of a passive effect, such as *bleed* or *venom*, this can still trigger a death move. However all passive damage for that round must be applied before the death move can be used.)

Damage score and damage dice
Some special abilities will refer to a damage score and others will refer to rolling damage dice. A damage score is when your hero rolls one

die and adds their *brawn* or *magic* to the total (as in the previous combat example). This is the most common means of applying damage to your opponent. Some abilities allow you to roll damage dice instead. Damage dice are simply dice that are rolled for damage, but you do not add your *brawn* or *magic* score to the total. For example, the special ability *cleave* allows you to inflict 1 damage die to all your opponents, ignoring *armour*. You would simply roll 1 die and then deduct the result from each of your opponents' *health*. You do not add your *brawn* or *magic* to this total.

Using backpack items in combat

The outcome of many a combat can be decided by the clever use of backpack items, such as potions and elixirs. From restoring lost *health* to boosting your *speed*, never underestimate how useful these items can be in turning the tide of battle. However, you can only use *one* backpack item per combat round so choose wisely! Also note that every useable backpack item has a number of charges. Once these have been used up, they are gone forever.

Runes, glyphs, dyes and other special items

During your adventures, you will come across a number of *special* items that allow you to add attribute bonuses or additional abilities to the equipment you are already wearing. These items cannot be stored in your backpack and must be used *immediately* when they are found, to add their relevant attribute / ability to a chosen item. Each item of equipment can hold up to three of these special bonuses.

Death is not the end

When your hero dies, their adventure isn't over. Simply make a note of the entry number where you died and then return to the quest map. Your *health* is immediately restored back to full, however any consumable items that were used in the combat (such as potions and elixirs) are gone forever!

You can now do the following:

1. Return to the entry number where you died and try it again.

2. Explore a different location on the map, such as a town or another quest.

You can return to the entry number where you died anytime you wish. If you are having difficulty with a particular combat, then try a different quest, or purchase some helpful potions or items from a local vendor.

NOTE: In some quests, when your hero is defeated, there are special rules to follow. You will be given an entry number to turn to, where you can read on to see what happens to your hero.

Taking challenge tests

Occasionally, during your travels, you will be asked to take a challenge by testing one of your attributes (such as *speed* or *brawn*). Each challenge is given a number. For example:

Speed
Climb the cliff face   9

To take a challenge, simply roll 2 dice and add your hero's attribute score to the result. If the total is the same as or higher than the given number, then you have succeeded. For example, if Sir Hugo has a *speed* of 4 and rolls a [.·] and a [.·'], then he would have a total of 9. This means he would have successfully completed the above challenge.

Take your adventures online!

Join the DestinyQuest community at **www.destiny-quest.com** for the latest information on DestinyQuest books, hints and tips, player forums and exclusive downloadable content (including printable hero sheets, team combat rules and extra bonus quests!).

It's time to begin

Before you start your adventure, don't forget to check that your hero sheet has been fully updated. It should display:

* Your hero's name
* A zero score in the *speed, brawn, magic,* and *armour* boxes
* A 30 in your hero's *health* box

Now, turn the page to begin your adventure ...

Prologue:
Blood and Betrayal

It wasn't like the storybooks at all.

Their pages were filled with tales of high adventure – heroes striving against the odds to win fabled treasures or defeat terrible monsters. Not for them the monotony of travel. No one cared about the wearisome 'getting there'. They skipped the rain and the damp that would freeze you to the bone, torturing you with its incessant drip, drip, drip. The chafing of the saddle, the stink of the horses. The men reeking of wet leather and sweat. The smell of the road.

You glare up at the heavy grey clouds, hanging over you like a shroud. They appear listless. Bored. Failing to deliver the storm that has been brewing for the past seven days. Instead, they spit a despondent shower of drizzle, determined to make your journey as miserable as possible. In that endeavour, they have succeeded.

As has the company.

You glance sideways at the inquisitor, his powerful war horse making your own look like a cart mule. He is a bull of a man, his thick neck corded with veins, his bulging muscles exaggerated by the sculptured plates of white and gold armour. A holy warrior – one of the king's finest. An upholder of truth and justice. If this was like the stories, he'd probably be handsome too, cutting a dashing figure as he rode bravely to war.

But this wasn't like the storybooks at all.

He turns to look at you, his ugly puckered scar crinkling as he furrows his brow. 'You have another question?' he growls, his disdain for you evident. You flinch under that look, knowing what he sees. A spoilt prince. Pampered by comfort and luxury. A prince adorned in gaudily-coloured silks and velvet, with court-fashion lace at the collar and sleeves. No armour for you, save for a padded undershirt. Fine if your assailant had a blunted dagger perhaps, but nothing that was going to stop an arrow or a sword.

So much for royal protection. But then, you're not the one who'd be doing the fighting.

Not like the knights, rattling behind you in their armoured livery, pennants fluttering in the chill wind. Or the king's own guard, in their mail coats and tabards, iron helms catching the drab pale light. You glance back at Molly, hunched sullenly in the back of the supply cart. Your maid. The woman who has nursed you since birth – since your mother passed away. It is a bitter truth that you have more in common with a frail old woman than your armed escort.

You wince with shame. They couldn't even trust you to travel without her. A grown man who needs to be looked after by his nursemaid. 'Molly-coddled', some of the knights had teased. They had every right to. In their eyes you were not a man, just a weak and sickly boy. It wasn't fair.

The inquisitor clears his throat. 'Well?'

You look back at the giant warrior. A veteran of a hundred campaigns. He has seen war in all its grim and nightmarish glory. He has lived it for real, not second-hand through the pages of a book or a bard's whimsical yarn.

'You were at Talanost when it fell, weren't you?' It is a question that has been nagging you for days. The books were still being written of the epic battle between the city's militia and an invading army of demons and monsters. The shadow legion. If anyone was going to tell it as it was, it would be Inquisitor Hort. He was there. On the front lines. 'Is it true that a Nevarin, one of their own, betrayed the legion?'

The warrior's jaw sets hard. He regards you with his usual steely glare – the one you can never hold. You lower your eyes back to the saddle, water dripping off the curls of your fringe. 'I'm sorry. I understand you wouldn't want to talk about it.'

Your cheeks flush as you surrender yourself once again to the rhythm of the road, the rattle of harness and the clump of hooves in mud. It has been another long day of travel and every muscle knows it, knotting in protest as you lurch and bounce in the saddle. Tiredly, you reach for your pouch, knowing that its stash of medicines will help to ease the suffering. By accident, your hand brushes against your sword hilt. You instinctively snatch it back, the enchanted steel burning cold against your skin.

Even the stupid sword hates me.

It had been a gift for your thirteenth birthday. A rare and exquisite weapon, its clawed pommel of blue steel clasped around a heart-shaped diamond. Alone, the gemstone is worth thousands – enough to buy a fleet of ships, a royal palace, a whole army . . . But even that pales into insignificance next to the rest of its craftsmanship. The blade is the finest Assay steel, flame-hardened and etched with a hundred lines of scripture. It was the last blade to be inscribed by Abbot Duran before he passed away, each holy letter draining the last of his fragile health. Duran's Heart, they called it. Some say it was his finest work. His last work. A mighty sword fit for a mighty hero.

Not a spoilt prince.

Angrily, you tug open the pouch and pull out a handful of dried leaves. You stuff them into your mouth, chewing rather than sucking to release their bitter taste more quickly. It takes only a second for the potent magic to kick in – a fiery spark that rushes through your body, starting with your head and then tingling along your spine. You sit rigid in the saddle, shivering as it runs its course, punching fresh energy into your weary limbs. Keeping sleep at bay. Keeping the nightmares away.

'Artemisa Draconis.' The sharp voice slides under your skin, cutting like a knife, ruining the moment. 'Dragon leaf, if I'm not mistaken.'

You look back at the Martyr as she nudges her stallion closer, one delicate white hand resting on the reins. Her hood is pulled down low over her face, its inscribed trim sparkling in the gloom. From the shadows beneath, you catch the flash of her perfect white teeth, curved in an arrogant smile. The one she wears only for you.

You answer with a sullen stare, wishing she would just leave you alone. *You're a prince*, you remind yourself. *Command her to leave you alone.*

'I noticed you haven't slept,' she states. 'Not since we left the capital. That was a week ago.'

'How observant,' you mutter beneath your breath. If only she knew the truth. That you haven't slept – not properly – for nearly five months. Not since the dreams worsened. Now you avoid sleep at all costs. Reading books, taking walks, swallowing the magic . . .

'What is it that you're afraid of, my prince?'

The directness of her question startles you. The hood tilts round, far enough for you to glimpse a single amber eye, wide and staring. It reminds you of an owl. Or one of your father's hunting hawks. 'Did you ever seek out the church for your malady, my prince? There may have been other tonics that could have helped you.'

Other tonics. You can picture what she has in mind. The thought turns your stomach, bringing bile to the back of your throat. Martyrs are regarded as the holiest of priests. Their blood is sacred, running white with the favour of the One God. Holy blood.

You shake your head vehemently, casting an eye over her wiry limbs, jutting out from the soft fabric of her robes. She could be leeching herself right now, the foul worms growing fat on her white blood – a sweet tonic, made all for you. Snorting with disgust, you dig your heels into your horse's flanks, urging it ahead. To your annoyance, she keeps pace, falling alongside you once again.

'It is a shame you never came to see me,' she states softly, her voice barely lifting over the drumming rain. 'I would have liked to have the chance to learn more about you, Prince Arran. After what happened to your brother, Lazlo. I'm in no doubt, such a terrible thing would have given anyone bad dreams.'

You flinch. For a moment you are back in the feast hall. Your father lies slouched in the high seat. A broken man, his mind wasted away by senility. A servant pauses to wipe drool from the king's chin before turning to pour Malden another ale. Malden, your eldest brother – and the king in waiting. He is laughing and joking, relishing the attention he always gets, sharing stories of his innumerable conquests. Reliving the past, before war made him a cripple.

Valeron royalty – what a pretty picture.

Then the soldier arrived, muddied cloak flapping against his boot heels. A man who'd clearly ridden hard, the creases of his face grimed with mud and sweat. Sedge, the king's attendant, moved quickly to head him off. Words were exchanged. Heated at first, then quickly lowering to subdued whispers. The soldier finally acceded to the attendant's wishes, following him towards the royal quarters. You watched them both as they passed your table. Molly had her head resting on your shoulder, snoring loudly. You nudged her away, keeping your eyes fixed on the soldier, convinced there was some grave import to his sudden arrival. He looked over and caught your eye. Just for a second.

That look still haunts you now.

'The Wiccans killed him,' you reply bluntly, fighting to keep the tremor from your voice. 'They didn't spare anyone.' You clutch the reins, twisting the leather in your hands. Lazlo had been your closest brother, a year younger than Malden. He had never been your father's favourite. That was one thing you had in common at least. Lazlo was the wild child, the prankster who never took anything too seriously. His attitude was not befitting of a prince – one who might inherit the throne of Valeron.

It was no surprise to anyone when Lazlo was given Carvel as his protectorate. A backwater town on the edge of the kingdom. Out of sight, out of mind.

But what had been intended as a rebuke turned out to be a blessing. For Lazlo, it was the perfect escape – a release from the politics of court. Freedom to live out his own life, far away from prying eyes. On his rare visits home he would always seek you out, to share stories of his grand adventures, to tell you about the wondrous lands that lay outside of Assay, beyond its high stone walls that shut out the world.

Now he was never coming home.

'The Wiccans will pay for what they did to your brother, Arran.' The Martyr's voice drags you back from your thoughts. 'Their heathen chief, Conall, desires your father's throne.' Her words break into a soft chuckle of laughter. You glare at her, wondering how she could find humour in such a thing. 'Fear not. They are mere savages. Godless and blind, stumbling in the dark.' Her amber eyes twinkle from the shadows of her cowl. 'They are no match for the might of the church.'

Her confidence irritates you. The Wiccans are known to be blood-thirsty warriors, wielding dark and forbidden magics. They are even said to have a demon in their ranks. A monster of legend. If they could outwit Lazlo and sack a fortified town, then they were dangerous.

You turn away, not wanting the priest to see your tears. They are for Lazlo, you keep telling yourself. But deep down, you know they are for you. The spoilt prince.

All your life you've been a prisoner, locked away for your own protection, longing for a chance to see the world – to escape, just like Lazlo. But now, sitting in sodden clothing, chilled through to the very bone, you can't help but crave the warmth of your quarters back home, the familiar smell of tallow and old books, the comfort of a proper goose-feather mattress.

Why me? Of all people, why me?

The request had not come from your father. He was bedridden with another fever. No, it had been Cardinal Rile. 'A chance to prove yourself, boy,' he had said. The cardinal always called you boy, even though you were in your seventeenth year. 'Now is a time for words as well as bravery. A task well suited to you, don't you agree, boy?'

The very next day you were leaving Assay. There was no fanfare or parade, or crowd of cheering well-wishers. But then, what had you expected? They call you the ghost prince, the one that no one ever sees. Always haunting the palace library, poring over dusty tomes, filling your head with fanciful stories. Always reading because you're too afraid to sleep.

They want rid of me. Just like Lazlo. Send me off to the edge of the world . . .

Your destination – Lord Salton's castle. A crumbling military outpost on the Vacherie Delta, its strategic importance long since diminished as borders edged westwards, leaving it to guard stone and dirt and very little else. But now, things have changed. Salton Castle straddles the only pass between the Bale Peaks, a treacherous range of high mountains. And the Wiccans are rumoured to be marching straight for it. By all accounts, the castle is still defensible. But Lord Salton is a coward. He would sooner abandon his charge, taking his household and knights with him, than face down a tribe of savage warriors.

You've been tasked to convince him otherwise. To deliver the king's demand: there is to be no retreat and no surrender. A royal face to sweeten the message.

Salton Castle had to be ready for war.

You brush away the tears, clenching your jaw to stop it trembling. The cardinal was right. You have a duty to perform. It's time to make your father proud – make everyone proud.

And yet, you can't shift the nagging feeling that something is wrong.

As your eyes slide along the procession, you find yourself pondering the cardinal's choice of knights. They had struck you as an odd selection from the start. Their banner sigils denote minor houses – Palfrey, Hanson, Bolivar and Freeman – not the usual nobles that would be enlisted for a royal mission. You also notice that their armour lacks the polish of a true knight. There are no medals or decorations, no sign that they have courageously served their country. Would the cardinal really entrust the defence of a castle to a bunch of hedge knights, unproven in battle?

Thankfully you still have the king's guard to rely upon, a veteran regiment of fifteen soldiers led by Captain Tarlow. Ordinarily, he would never leave the king's side, but the cardinal had insisted. Your safety was now of the utmost importance. You nod and offer the captain a hopeful smile. He scowls back, hawking a gob of spittle into the dirt. The rest of his men share his dour demeanour. No one wants to be babysitting a prince, it seems.

'This will do.' Inquisitor Hort raises a gauntleted hand, calling a halt to the procession.

You look around in confusion. The bleak countryside has not changed all day, steep rock banks and tangled trees and a road little more than a muddy stream. This seems an odd place to set up camp, even to your untrained eye.

There are answering grumbles from Tarlow and his men. The captain glares at the cardinal's knights, who have started to edge closer, surrounding the guards on all sides. Hooves scuff the dirt, harnesses clanking as the barded horses quickly encircle them. You lose sight of Tarlow as a Bolivar knight passes in front of him, blocking the captain from view. The knight stops and turns his head towards the inquisitor, the rain streaming from his oiled helm in liquid rainbows.

'Are we making camp?' you ask irritably, trying to put some authority into your voice. You look from the inquisitor to the knight, demanding an answer.

The inquisitor ignores you, his hard gaze fixed on the waiting knight. He nods his head. You hear the wet-thud of lances hitting the ground – then cold steel hissing free of scabbards. In that same instant, the inquisitor lifts his hand to the warhammer strapped to his back. A cold shiver runs along your spine as he turns to face you.

'Wait! What are you doing? What are . . . ?'

There is the sudden peal of a horn.

The inquisitor freezes, eyes going wide.

Another blast. Deep and reverberating, its echo rattling your very bones. 'What's happening?' You shout to be heard over the thunder of the horn.

Hort twists in his saddle, his warhammer gripped in one hand. He is scanning the trees to the side of the road. 'It can't be,' you hear him mutter.

Your chest tightens with fear, heart thumping in your ears. 'What is it? I don't see . . .'

'Wiccans!' he shouts suddenly, jerking the reins to turn his horse. 'Form up! Form up! We're under attack!'

Only then do you see them, coalescing out of the fog like ghosts, moving fast – leaping over logs and rocks, teeth bared, weapons glinting. And with them a deafening clamour of howls ringing from every direction – closing in on the procession. You spin in circles, your attention darting dizzyingly from one warrior to the next. They look barely human, clad in ragged furs, hair greased and spiked, faces smeared with paint. Or is it blood? One of them is holding a flag aloft, streaming out from behind his clenched fist. You recognise the colours, purple and gold, and the sigil of a goat's head. They belong to Lord Salton.

They took the castle. We're too late.

Then everything happens at once. The inquisitor's warhammer blazes with holy light, its crackling head sweeping round to connect with a snarling axe-man. An eye-wincing crack. The smell of charred flesh. But another has already leapt up onto the back of his horse. The savage's face is a picture of death, his cheeks and forehead banded with white, the eyes circled with black hollows. Daggers flash as they punch into the inquisitor's side, finding the chinks between his armoured plates.

An explosion. Mud and water rain down from the sky. A horse gallops past, nostrils flaring, snorting and whinnying. Another follows, dragging a knight through the dirt, the man's foot still caught in the stirrups. Through the showering debris you see axe blades glittering, hacking through armour and bone, horses toppling to the ground, crushing knights beneath them. Tarlow's guards struggle to manoeuvre against the overwhelming tide of bodies.

Two wiccans race past you, snarling like wolves. They pay you no mind, hurrying towards the knights and guards. It is as if you don't exist – a ghost prince who has truly become invisible. Then you hear another explosive boom, followed by a rush of heat. You spin in the saddle, mouth dropping open when you see the flames from the supply cart billowing up into the grey sky.

'Molly!'

Kicking your horse's flanks you urge it forward, your hand reaching for your sword. In your haste you forget its holy enchantments – words of the One God that seem to recoil at your touch. When your fingers close around the grip, you feel a sharp shock of pain lance along your arm. You jerk backwards and for a moment you lose your purchase on the reins, sliding back off the saddle.

'Arran!' A woman's voice. Cold and brittle.

Hands are suddenly around your throat, nails digging into your flesh – and you are falling.

You land with a splash in the cloying, sludgy mud. For several seconds, you are fighting for breath, your sight blinded by dirt and water. Someone is lying next to you, the mud popping and squelching as they move. You glimpse white robes and a hood. Amber eyes, wide and bright.

You try and pull yourself free but the Martyr pushes you back down, her fingers like claws of iron, digging into your flesh, driving you into the mud with an unnatural strength.

'What . . . ?' You open your mouth, choking as it fills with black fetid water.

She's killing me. The damn priest is killing me.

Your hands ball into fists, pummelling at her sides, legs kicking and squirming. One of your blows scuffs against something hard and cold. A hilt, a dagger. You manage to pull it free from the priest's belt as she shoves you further into the muck.

'Your time is over, prince!'

The stinking waters close over you, distorting sound into a thrum of distant noise. Somehow you manage to surface, muddy spittle bubbling between your teeth as you slide the dagger into the woman's side. You feel it going deep, the blade scraping against bone. A warm rush of blood courses over your fingers.

You drive it in a second time, feeling the Martyr's body jerk, her face only inches from your own. Another spasm. Then the pressure is gone, the strength ebbing from her limbs. Desperately you raise your head, coughing and choking as you suck greedily at the air. The Martyr has become a limp weight, sliding down next to you, dark roses of blood marking her muddied robes. You glance down at the dagger, shocked at what you have done, crimson blood coating you to the elbow.

Their blood is no different to ours after all.

You drop the dagger, struggling to get to your feet. As you start to rise, you see Tarlow only metres away. Dismounted and wounded, he is now fending off a giant Wiccan warrior, a mountain of a man, with long braids of dark hair forming a mane about his shoulders. His bare chest glistens with sweat and rain, and a dizzying array of bright runes that flash and spit in anger.

A sharp, splintering crack.

You jump at the sound. To your left the cart has collapsed, its wood now charcoal black as the flames continue to consume the wreckage. You see no sign of Molly. You stumble towards the blaze, but the heat forces you back, its thick smoke drifting quickly across the road – reducing the battle to shadows darting back and forth, an occasional clank of armour, a harsh clatter as weapons meet.

Then a pained cry drags you back to Tarlow. The captain has stumbled to his knees, struggling to raise his sword with a torn and bloodied arm. The Wiccan stands over him, eyes bulging beneath a heavy brow, sharpened teeth bared and hissing. Then the axe falls. There is a dull-sounding thud. You wipe the grime from your eyes, trying to focus, to make sense of the scene. It is oddly silent. A moment frozen in time. Tarlow leans back, arms outstretched, the axe buried deep in his shoulder. Above him, the giant stands rigid, muscles bunched, the angry fire of his runes making him look more demon than man.

Conall, you gasp. *That must be Conall. Their chief. The one who killed Lazlo.*

The giant grunts as he tugs his axe free. There is a spray of blood then Tarlow topples over, his expression a mask of pained bewilderment. As he crashes into the mud, neck twisted to face you, his dead eyes come to rest on your own.

'No . . .' His stare is like a spear, running you through with its damning accusation. In all your years, you have never known him to leave your father's side. His loyalty was unquestionable. And yet here he is, miles from the capital, lying dead on a road in the northern wilds. He should have stayed with your father, with the throne he was sworn to protect. *It's all my fault.*

The Wiccan warrior throws back his head and issues a mighty roar. The sight of him, so huge and fearsome, like something from another world, another time, fills you with dread.

You are running before you realise it, before you even have a chance to question your actions. Blind fear powers your limbs, filling you with an energy no herb or potion could ever match. Splashing through the mud, you make for the trees, not caring what direction you head in, only that you must save yourself.

Coward! Stupid coward! Your conscience screams in your ears, but the words carry no meaning – no shame. You just want to live. *What else can I do?* On hands and knees you scrabble madly up the hillside, stomach heaving from the stench of smoke and blood. *But I have to go back . . . I should fight . . .* You reach the top of the rise, plunging into the maze of forest. Branches claw at your face, tearing at your clothes. *I have to get away . . .*

You don't see the Wiccan until it is too late. His shoulder hits you in the side, throwing you back against the trunk of a tree. His face is painted in a hideous mask of runes, the musky smell of wet animal clinging to his tattered clothes. He shouts something, barking out the words in a stream of guttural noise. They make no sense to you. Nothing makes sense anymore.

'Please,' you plead, tears streaming down your cheeks. 'Don't kill me. I'll give you anything . . .'

The warrior steps back, wrinkling his nose, glaring at you with a look of disgust. His eyes rove up and down, taking in the sight of your muddied silks and pretty lace. He sees a fool, you realise bitterly. A damn fool.

His gaze settles on your blade, rotten teeth widening into a grin. You look down at the sword's diamond pommel, realising his intent. Of course, he wants Duran's Heart – a trophy worth a kingdom in gold.

'Yes! Yes, take it!' You start to unstrap the belt.

The Wiccan snorts, shaking his head. 'Not give. Fight!' He raises his bloodied axe and takes a step back, giving you room to draw. 'Fight!'

'No . . . please . . .'

'Fight!' He shakes the axe. 'Fight!'

'I can't!' you scream back, snot and spittle flying from your lips. 'I don't know how to!'

The Wiccan recoils at your outburst, momentarily surprised. Then anger quickly returns. 'Craven,' he growls. 'You no warrior.'

You slide to your knees, hitting the dirt. 'No. I am no warrior.' You lower your head, shamed by what you are. A weakling. A prince who can't even defend himself. 'I yield . . .'

As you wait for the axe to fall, you picture Captain Tarlow lying twisted in the mud, his dead eyes glaring back at you. *Did he know? Did he know we were sent here to die?* The Wiccan's boots trudge closer, his animal stink filling your nostrils. He mutters something in his gruff language.

Then darkness.

It is as if a shadow has been cast over you, turning day to night. You look up, aware of a thunderous beat, like giant wings, getting louder and louder. Then the crack of snapping branches. The Wiccan warrior seems equally surprised, craning his neck to study the skies. The axe blade has stopped inches above your head.

'Sanchen!' he growls.

A blue-black shape drops from the heavens, accompanied by a flurry of broken branches and leaves. It lands with a teeth-jarring thump, wings of mottled white obscuring an immense body. Then they sweep back, revealing a nightmarish creature – its body rippling with scales.

A demon prince.

It rises to its full height, over three metres tall, its head crowned by a pair of gold-banded horns. Runed armour clings to its broad chest and shoulders, coating the beast in arcane sigils of dark magic. They smoulder like coals, sending thin columns of smoke spiralling up into the gloom. You cower down at the base of the tree, feeling dwarfed by the size of the monster and its dread aura of power . . .

'Halt!' The demon raises a hand towards you, its dark brow creased with concentration. 'Halt, I command you!'

It takes a moment for you to realise the demon is addressing the warrior. The axe has started to tremble, as if the Wiccan is fighting against something unseen, his muscles straining.

'I told you all, not the boy.' The demon's crimson eyes flick to you. 'Go, Prince Arran. Or this will be your end!'

He knows my name.

The warrior is now grunting and hissing with exertion, his axe edging steadily closer. Whatever magic holds him in thrall, he seems intent on breaking it. And if he does, the axe will complete its downward arc, cleaving your skull in two.

'Make your choice,' the demon hisses.

You quickly find your feet, edging around the paralysed Wiccan and his trembling axe. The demon watches you intently, the rain streaming from his wings and horns. *He saved my life*, you realise suddenly. *He wants me to escape.* You turn away, to look upon the forested valley. It rises abruptly into a series of steep hills, thick with boulders and nettles. In the distance, you can dimly make out a bluff of grey rock, its summit lost to the chill, low-hanging cloud. As if on cue, a peal of thunder breaks overhead, followed seconds later by a pulse of ghoulish lightning. The steady drizzle quickly becomes a deluge, pounding against the earth in thick grey sheets.

Shivering, you turn back to the demon. 'I . . . I have nowhere to go,' you shout, dispiritedly.

The demon gives a roar of fury, more deafening than the storm. 'Fool! The fates have set you on this path.' He gestures angrily towards the valley. 'Do not try my patience. GO!'

The vehemence in his words sets you to running, your feet slipping and sliding through the river of mud. You feel a little foolish, dashing madcap into the forest with no idea where you are headed. But you are alive. And for now, that is both a surprise and a comfort. Holding your hood down over your face, you charge into the stormy tumult, desperate now to put as much distance as you can between yourself and the horrors at your back.

Turn to 11 to begin the first stage of your adventure.

1

You place the plain glass orb onto the podium. (Remove this item from your hero sheet.) After studying the complex carvings at length, you discern pockets of magic focused in three of the outer circles. One pertains to frost, one to earth magic and the last to the darker shadow arts. By activating the runes around a circle, you will be able to call on the spirits that embody that power.

Will you:

Activate the frost runes?	719
Activate the earth runes?	667
Activate the shadow runes?	518

2

Progress through the tunnels is slow and frustrating, your way often blocked by gaping chasms or fallen debris. Often you are forced to backtrack and find alternate routes, other times you have no choice but to jump a gap or dig your way clear, clambering on all fours through narrow openings.

Eventually, after what feels like hours of trekking through the maze-like tunnels, you finally see evidence of daylight – a white brightness edging the hollows of a rock fall. Overcome with relief, you race up to the barrier, fingers clawing at the crumbling stones, pulling them away to clear an opening. Nanuk's strength floods into you, powering your limbs, driving you onwards.

At last, fingers raw and bleeding from the effort, you drag yourself out into the light. Turn to 169.

3

With the diseased bear defeated, you set about searching its cave. Amongst a pile of half-eaten remains you find 30 gold crowns and one of the following items:

Pestilent hide	Matted mukluks	Seeping shawl
(cloak)	(feet)	(head)
+1 speed +2 brawn	+1 speed +1 armour	+1 brawn +1 magic
Ability: corrode	Ability: insulated	Ability: decay

You are also able to salvage a *white fox pelt* and a *flawless emerald*. (If you wish to take either of these items, simply make a note of them on your hero sheet, they don't take up backpack space.)

Your search also reveals a narrow opening at the back of the cave, just wide enough for you to squeeze into. Keen to escape this fetid cave, you push yourself into the tight crevice and grope your way along the ice. After several hundred metres the rift begins to widen, leading you through into another open space. Turn to 397.

4

As you drag the sack through the dirt, something scrapes and catches against a rock. Lifting up the sack, you see that there is a tear at the bottom, causing several sword hilts to poke through. Other items now lie scattered along the trail, having fallen out of the hole. You retrace your steps, stooping to retrieve the stolen equipment.

Amongst the weapons and fragments of armour, you spot a pair of black-enamelled gauntlets, etched with magical runes. You are immediately reminded of the warrior you spoke with in the main hall, who described a similar set of gauntlets that had gone missing.

If you wish to keep these magical gloves for yourself, then you may add the following item to your hero sheet:

Ran's beaters
(gloves)
+1 armour
Ability: charge

If you would rather keep the gauntlets and return them to their rightful owner, then remove the keyword *thievery* from your hero sheet and replace it with the keyword *gains*. When you have made your decision, turn to 383.

5

The next few moments pass in a series of vivid flashes. You see the wolf's jaws snapping inches from your face, his neck stretched taut in an effort to reach you. Bloody froth dribbles over black hair, hot sour breath blasting against your cheek . . .

Yet you are still alive.

In his haste, the alpha has caught himself on a bone, the sharp end now rooted in the animal's side. A bone from a ribcage – the only thing holding death at bay.

You fumble desperately for a weapon, hands scrabbling amongst the dirt and refuse. Then, all of a sudden it hits you – an energy, more powerful than the dragon leaf. It floods into you, pushing itself under your skin, between the bones, inside your muscles. A thunderous roar, bestial and savage, is ripped free from your lips. Fingers swipe through the air, trailing green ribbons of mist, green claws . . .

You have gained the following special ability:

Spectral claws (co): If you take health damage from your opponent's damage score, you can immediately strike back at them, inflicting 1 die of damage, ignoring *armour*. This ability can only be used once per combat.

The claws rake through the wolf's flank, eliciting a hellish shriek. Then there is a deafening crack as the bone splinters. The wolf rolls away, taking longer than he should to find all fours. In places the thick fur has been torn away, revealing deep gashes glistening with blood. The smell of it is intoxicating, a metallic tang laced with a lucid sweetness. You drive yourself forward, snarling like a beast, no longer in charge of your own body, your hands clawing and tearing. Something has control of you, using you to fight back.

If you have the word *sacrifice* on your hero sheet, turn to 37. Otherwise, turn to 54.

6

The tunnel folds into a tight spiral, angling through the trunk until it brings you out onto the gnarled remains of a branch. Turning back to face the tree, you see the crown spreading out above you – a tangle of dark boughs, their pointed tips bunched tight like a regiment of spearmen. From somewhere above, you hear agonised screams – and pleading sobs.

'Rata-rata-tosk!'

The voice startles you. Spinning to your right, you catch a blur of movement racing up the trunk of the tree. It is only when the figure stops that you can make sense of its shape. It looks like an oversized rodent, its fur stippled red and brown, with tall pointed ears and a wide muzzle for a face. Behind its shoulders curls a bushy tail.

'Not come here, rata-rata, not come!' The creature's sharp teeth chatter together as it speaks. A clawed hand reaches for one of the many leather pouches dangling around its waist.

'Wait. Can you help me? I need to find Skoll!'

The creature hisses, its muzzle crinkling back into a scowl. 'Witch keeps him. And I protect, rata-rata-tosk!' He lifts his hand from his pouch, clutching a golden acorn. He throws it down at your feet, the shell splintering into bright shards. From its remains you see a black seedling start to take growth, its thick stem coiling into the air, barbed leaves unfurling.

You back away from it, unsure of its purpose.

With a snigger, the wily squirrel continues to scamper up the trunk, then pauses to look down with a hungry gleam to his eyes. He is clearly waiting to see what you will do next.

You scan the trunk, and its many hand and foot-holds – easy enough to climb. However, you also notice another possible route – a nearby branch you could leap onto. Beyond it, a series of ledges and scraggly vines form a makeshift pathway to the summit.

Will you:

Chase the creature up the trunk?	489
Use the ledges and vines instead?	271

7

The black sludge closes above your head, pushing dank earth into your ears, nose and mouth, burying you in its suffocating embrace. (You must immediately roll on the death penalty chart [see entry 98] and apply the effect to your hero.) Trapped and blinded, you make a last frantic bid for escape, pushing magic into your limbs, bleeding it out in waves of powerful energy.

Then you are falling, tumbling through darkness, the laughter resounding in your ears once again. Turn to 435.

8

Sam produces a pair of picks and sets to work on the lock. Within seconds, the metal chest is open. After Sam has taken his cut of the treasure, you are left with 50 gold crowns. (Remove the *hunters' chest* from your hero sheet.) If you have the *locker* and wish Sam to open it, turn to 641. Otherwise, you continue your journey. Turn to 563.

9

The robed man paces the room restlessly, his fingers playing with his short spike of beard. 'Four weeks you've lain on that bed – and two of those cold without life.'

It takes a moment for his words to sink in. 'Wait, I was dead? That's impossible!' You look to the knight, hoping he will refute such nonsense and offer reason.

'I'm afraid it is true, Arran. We were going to send out a rider, to notify the palace of your passing. But when we came to prepare the body – there was still a life stirring there. Movement. Some nights, it was like you had something wild inside you, trying to get out.'

Segg ceases his pacing, glaring at you with his blue piercing eyes. 'I suspected you were possessed, by some demon from the shroud. But it appears that is not the case.' His stare continues to hold you, as if pushing you to state otherwise, seeking the truth.

'I don't know what happened,' you reply. 'I only remember . . . dreaming.'

'Well, you're awake now,' nods Lord Everard. 'And whatever your malady . . .' He pauses, his eyes taking in the grey pallor of your flesh, 'I will believe it is the One God's work and not the hand of another that brings you back to us.'

Return to 291 to ask another question, or turn to 98 to end the conversation.

10

'Don't even think of coming any closer,' growls the sniper. 'Keep yer distance, or my next shot will take that head clean off yer shoulders.'

Skoll takes hold of his axe, cursing in Skard.

You grab him quickly, before he leads the attack. 'No. It's not worth it, my friend. They have powder weapons – I've seen what they can do, and unless you desire this,' you flick a finger towards your ravaged face, 'I would heed his warning.'

Skoll grunts, but lowers his axe. 'The coward's way. I am a Drokke – a warrior!'

'And better to live as one than die as one,' you add dryly. 'Come. We have more pressing business.'

Not wishing to risk the lives of your companions, you return to your transport and leave the island. (Return to the quest map to continue your adventure.)

11
Prologue quest: Call of the wild

Morning finds you stumbling wearily through the dense forest, its trees still dripping with last night's rainfall. You've had no sleep, relying instead on the potency of the dragon leaf to ease your aches and pains and give fresh vigour to your tired limbs.

The night was a miserable one, spent huddled beneath an overhang of rock, the hard wind battering you with rain. There was no hope of making a fire, not that you'd have known the first thing about making one, so instead you shivered and shook, the cold settling deep into your bones.

It was the longest night you can ever remember. Too fearful of sleep, you chewed on the dragon leaf, its taste both a comfort and a reminder of home. Your thoughts wandered often to the events on the road, the cuts on your neck and face still stinging from the Martyr's attack. She was a holy priest. A follower of the One God. And yet she had tried to kill you – a prince of Valeron.

Then there was the demon. A creature of the underworld; a being of pure evil. He had saved your life, and allowed you to escape. His rumbling voice still rings in your ears – *The fates have put you on this path.*

When dawn's light finally arrived, pushing its way through the leaden clouds, you were still bereft of answers. Instead, the only certainty was that you were on your own, with no one else to protect you. Until now, the forest has proved safe, but you can't help but recall the fireside banter over the previous evenings, the guards sharing chilling stories of the giant wolves that are said to hunt these parts. And the trolls, and the goblins and the . . .

You stop yourself, trying to stifle your fears and focus on the more immediate problem of finding a way home. Above the treetops, the sky is little more than a slate-grey expanse of cloud, diffusing the sun's light and giving no clue to its position. The only landmark you have is the dark smudge of rock in the distance. You assume that must be north and instinct tells you that heading in that direction will only take you into danger. Instead, you strike out towards what you think must be east, keeping to the left of the ridge and hoping that eventually you might find some settlement or sign of civilisation.

East is the way back home.

This choice has led you to a series of steep hills, covered in scraggly bush and silver-barked trees. Stopping to draw breath, you decide to take stock of your meagre possessions. You have enough dragon leaf to last another week. That, at least, is a positive. The sword at your hip is useless, however – an inscribed blade known as Duran's Heart, whose holy enchantments burn at your touch. Wearing gloves or wrapping cloth around the grip have proven equally ineffective.

At least your quilted under-jacket will afford you some protection, and the rest of your clothing, despite being thoroughly sodden with rain and mud, is of good make, and should last the journey.

(You may now add the following items to your hero sheet. Remember to update your attributes to reflect the bonuses from your items. Your hero will now have 2 *speed* and 1 *armour*.)

Leather overshoes	Quilted jacket	Craven's cloak
(feet)	(chest)	(cloak)
+1 speed	+1 armour	+1 speed

Resuming your journey, you discover that the land itself appears to guide your steps. Skirting around the hills, you find yourself following the curve of a dried-up streambed, which winds down into a narrow gully of rock. This makeshift passage drops steeply, forcing you to pick your way past rocks and logs until you come to the valley floor. For the first time, you are presented with a dilemma. To your left, there appears to be a narrow trail, winding up the side of a forested hill. There, amongst the trees, you can spy columns of pillared rock – perhaps remnants of an old building. Ahead of you, the streambed reaches a steep bank, where the ground drops away into a series of ledges, forming a natural staircase down into a thick tangle of trees.

Will you:

Follow the trail to the ruins?	34
Continue down into the denser woodland?	59

12

You push against the door, gritting your teeth against some unseen force. At first you wonder if it is supernatural in origin, but as the crack widens you soon realise it is the result of a strong wind, gusting in from an open balcony.

With effort, you manage to hold it open just wide enough for yourself and Anise to enter.

Like the rest of the tower, the room has been ransacked. There are the remains of several cupboards and trunks pushed up against the right-hand wall, where a few tattered strips of clothing snap and wave like trapped ghosts amongst the broken wood. In the far wall, there is another closed door.

Will you:

Search through the debris?	490
Step out onto the balcony?	325
Leave through the opposite door?	392

13

A man's cries draw you to an archway cut into the tree trunk. Passing through, you find yourself in another winding passageway. The distressful sounds grow louder until you find yourself standing outside a cell, barred by a wall of gnarly roots. Peering between the spaces, you see a Skard warrior held prisoner, his body wrapped in a cluster of branch-like arms extending from the far wall. Your immediate thought is that it might be Skoll, but the warrior is slighter of build, with flame-red hair shaven into runic whirls. He is struggling against the branches, his pale hands reaching forward to try and grab a dagger resting on a plinth only inches away. Each time the warrior's fumbling fingers almost reach the weapon, he is yanked back by the branches.

'Wait – I can free you!' You put your hands to the root bars, trying to prise them apart – but as soon as you apply pressure to the strange roots, you hear a choking gasp from the Skard prisoner as the branches tighten around him. When you remove your hands the branches loosen again, allowing him to breathe.

You look around for another means of opening the cell. In the opposite wall you notice a slight hollow, with a hand-shaped depression set into the back of the hole.

Will you:

Place your hand inside the hollow?	532
Attempt to chop through the barrier?	439
Leave and continue your journey?	6

14

You recognise the game as 'Stones and Bones', which had once been a favourite of your brother Lazlo. It involves players taking turns to pick a stone from a bag, then deciding which stones they keep and which ones to discard in order to create the best 'hand'. A number of games are currently underway along the table.

If you have the word *scripture* on your hero sheet, turn to 464. Otherwise, you return your attention to the taproom. Turn to 80.

15

Blinded by the buzzing, snapping insects, you cease your attack and concentrate on breaking free. Diverting your magic, you pour strength and speed into your craft, urging it towards the far side of the chamber. Luckily, you spy a nearby tunnel. Once inside you aim a blast at the ceiling, causing a cave-in to seal off your escape.

You may have avoided the angry swarm, but their razors and mandibles have caused considerable damage to your transport. (You must lower your transport's *toughness* and *stability* by 4.) When you have updated your hero sheet, turn to 675.

16

You approach the young mage and ask him his name. He recoils slightly as you near, waving the air in front of his face. 'If you must know, my name is Harris. I'm Segg's nephew – so you can't bully me. Okay?'

You slip into the chair opposite, enjoying the mage's discomfort. You pick up the nearest book, studying the title. *Perinold's Runic Ruminations*. Flicking through the pages, you are presented with a dense array of text, punctuated by the occasional arcane symbol.

'That's an original,' the mage glowers, snatching it away from you. 'Have you no clue of its worth?'

'Actually, the original is in the palace library,' you shoot back with a grin.

'Then I got it on loan.' The boy sticks out his tongue.

Seeing that he won't back down, you shrug diplomatically. 'Well, magic really isn't my thing.'

'Really?' Harris frowns, pushing his glasses back up his nose. 'I bet my uncle would disagree. I can feel it around you, really strong . . .' His hand absently goes to the chain around his neck. Dangling on its end is a prism-shaped object, fashioned from onyx or some other dark material. When he sees your eyes upon it, he quickly hides it beneath his collar. 'I'm just the apprentice,' he snorts with derision. 'What would I know?'

Will you:

Ask what he is reading?	105
Ask about the prism?	64
Examine the shelves?	577
Talk to Segg?	328
Return to the main courtyard?	113

17

The blood leads you into a side tunnel, narrow and edged with broken ice. After a hundred metres you come to the remains of some creature; an ugly mass of scales, hair and long pale tentacles. Stepping around it, your eyes are drawn to the far wall. There, frozen into the ice, are a pile of human bodies. It is hard to tell how many – the ice has closed over them, binding the tangled bodies into a solid block. You glimpse faces, coats, mitted hands, a weapon. On one of their coats, a name has been stitched into the leather. *Blair.*

As you back away from the nightmarish sight, your foot hits something. Turning, you watch as a small glass sphere rolls across the ice, clinking into the wall then rolling back. You crouch down to catch it, surprised to feel the unearthly chill emanating from within. (If you wish to take the *frost orb*, simply make a note of it on your hero sheet, it doesn't take up backpack space.)

When you return to the main hall, you find the man waiting for you. 'Well?' he asks.

You shudder, still picturing the frozen faces staring back at you, preserved in expressions of terrible agony. 'Bodies . . .' you stammer. 'They were . . . explorers.'

'I know, I was sent here to find them too.' The man sighs heavily. 'But you saw what I saw. For the ice to take them like that, those explorers must have been there a very long time. Months, I'll wager. Maybe even longer.'

'Months?' You baulk, glancing back at the blood trail. 'But Reah . . . Diggory, they . . .'

'This place isn't right.' He looks around, his face twitching nervously. 'I should have turned back when I had the chance. Maybe we both should have.' Turn to 573.

18

Skidding round a particularly tight corner, the sled loses traction on the slippery ice. Unable to right yourself, its bone frame slams against the tunnel wall, splintering one of its runners and sending you zig-zagging out of control. Your dog-team continues to slog up the next slope, but the steepness of the grade coupled with the drag of your damaged sled slows them to a crawl. Unable to recover, you realise that the infamous corkscrew has beaten you.

You have failed to complete the race and are now disqualified from the tournament. Replace the keyword *rookie* with *underdog*. Return to the map to continue your adventure.

19

You make to leave, but are brought up short when you hear a squelching sound coming from behind you. Spinning round, your eyes sweep across the ring of toadstools, looking for the likely cause. But the noise has gone and there is nothing there – although you are almost sure the toadstools have shifted position, standing a little closer to you.

Another squelch from somewhere behind. A quick look confirms

there is nothing creeping up on you, but again, those toadstools . . .
They look even closer now, their black bodies almost touching as they
form a dark wall around the clearing. Turn to 202.

20

The passageway slopes downwards, sweeping into a gentle curve. The
walls and ceiling are perfectly smooth, without any imperfection or
unevenness. You wonder if this is the work of the ancient Dwarves,
who used their magic to manipulate and sculpt stone into fabulous
structures.

Your eyes adjust quickly to the gloom, allowing you to progress
at a fast pace. The tremors appear to have stopped – for now – but
you are still keen to find a way back to the surface as soon as possible,
rather than become trapped underground.

To your relief the passage soon levels off, widening into a circular chamber. It is bordered by a ring of stone statues, depicting
squat humanoids bedecked in various styles of armour. They all
face inwards, towards the centre of the room, where a large circle of
bronze has been sunk into the ground. A plinth of black stone stands
in the middle of this circle, faintly glowing with magic.

The only exit from the room is provided by another archway.
Rubble spills out of it, suggesting a rock fall in the passageway beyond,
but perhaps it will still prove navigable.

Will you:
Investigate the stone plinth?   110
Continue onwards into the passage?   2

21

You raise Anise's head to the lip of the canteen. 'Here, try some of
this.' You watch as she sups greedily at the water, her thirst forcing
her to drink too fast. She pulls back, wracked with a fit of coughing.

'More,' she manages to gasp, once her breath returns.

Carefully you place the canteen in her trembling hands, helping her to guide it back to her mouth. 'Easy, Anise. Not too quickly.'

You glance over your shoulder, to where Skoll is chewing vigorously on a length of cured meat. He pushes more into his mouth, stuffing it full.

You rise and move toward him, putting out a hand for the bag he clutches to his chest. He glares at you, then grudgingly surrenders the rest of the meat. You snatch it from him and return to Anise, all the time feeling the paladin's eyes watching you.

'How long have you been on the road?' he asks.

'We lost track,' you reply. 'Two weeks, perhaps longer. We weren't prepared for the lack of hunting. The land is so dry and barren.' You break off a small piece of meat and offer it to Anise. 'Careful now. Chew it.'

The sounds from the nearby cave suggest the bird is doing the same, steadily devouring its own meal.

'A hard journey,' the paladin nods. 'I have witnessed the destruction. It spreads far and wide, from the westlands to the Circle Sea. I heard tell that the Holy Lands were the first to fall. Whole mountains gone. Such destruction. Is the cause of it here, I wonder?' He lifts his eyes to the ceiling as if seeking to penetrate the layers of rock, unlock its secrets.

'If I told you, I'm not sure you would believe me.' You tear another strip of meat and give it to Anise, finding comfort in seeing her chew with renewed vigour.

'I had half a mind to seek succour at Bitter Keep,' says Maune, his stare remaining distant. 'I would have liked to have seen my daughter again.'

'Daughter?' You fail to hide your surprise, turning quickly. 'You had a daughter at the keep?'

He smiles. 'Yes, Henna. The posting was her choice. I tried to . . .'

'The keep has fallen.' Your words carry across his own, drawing him to silence. 'I was there. It was taken into the rift, and everyone with it. We,' you gesture to Anise, who is watching the paladin with a worried expression, 'were the only ones to survive.'

Maune frowns, then looks away, his mouth moving, searching for words. He glances sideways at you, raising a finger, trembling. 'Do not lie to me.'

You rise to stand before him. 'I would not lie. I fought by your daughter's side. She held her faith to the end. Her actions, her strength, were what rallied the men. We were attacked by creatures from the underworld – the Nisse. Before the keep was lost we fought them for every stone, every soldier that fell.' You lower your head. 'I'm sorry.'

Maune blinks, tears glistening at the corners of his eyes. Angrily he brushes them away, setting his jaw straight, trying to reassert control over his emotions. 'War has casualties.'

'I know.' You turn your hands over, noting the frost-bitten skin, the jagged scars.

Maune tilts his head, frowning. Then he reaches out, taking the edge of your hood. You flinch, feeling the heat from his inscribed flesh as his arm passes close. It is an effort but you manage to hold your ground, letting him reveal your ravaged face. He drops his hand away, releasing a sharp intake of breath.

'Lord of light . . . .' He touches his cross.

'I must be an affront to your faith.' You avert your eyes, trying to avoid the man's look of disgust and horror. The holy cross sparkles against his breast. 'You are a better man than me, to stay your weapons.'

Maune takes a step back. 'A better man knows to keep his steel in check. A blade cannot make reasoned judgements.'

You pull your hood back over your face.

'There is no light inside of you,' states Maune carefully. 'Neither of you.' He casts his gaze to Skoll, still feasting on the meat as if it was his last supper. 'You have the taint of the shroud. An evil darkness . . .'

From the adjoining chamber there is a sudden, piercing squeal.

'What was that?' Anise asks, alarmed.

Maune is already hurrying into the passage, his sword in his hands. 'Gwen? Gwen!'

You nod to Skoll, telling him to follow. The warrior pushes the last of his meat into his mouth, then draws his axe and races after the paladin. You turn to Anise, helping her to stand.

'Come, we have to move. I can't leave you here.'

'I know.' She staggers into you, putting her head against your shoulder. Wrapping an arm around her, you walk together into the passage – fearing what you may find on the other side. Turn to **405**.

22

The men exchange wary glances. Lord Everard is the first to answer. 'Yes, we heard you were headed out to Lord Salton's castle. We also heard you were ambushed by Wiccans.'

The elderly man raises a gnarly finger. 'Understandably, we thought you dead. And why wouldn't we?' His robes swish around his heels as he paces the room. 'The Wiccans spare no one. They don't see the value in keeping hostages. Rather send their message in blood and ashes.'

Lord Everard frowns. 'Although the palace says otherwise,' he adds stiffly. 'They say you are a hostage. No doubt to rally support for the war.'

You shake your head at that. 'They lie, we were betrayed. I was never meant to reach Lord Salton's castle. I think it was part of a plot. To be rid of me.' You glance between the two men, expecting them to baulk at your claim. But they remain silent. Lord Everard sighs and nods.

'I had suspected that was the case,' he says. 'We have much to tell you, Arran. And some of it will be . . . hard to take.'

Return to 291 to ask another question, or turn to 98 to end the conversation.

23

Your weapons cut a swathe through the nightmarish creatures, their twisted bodies crumbling to dust around your feet. From the remains a ghost of each asynjur rises into the air, their tattered robes fluttering in an unfelt breeze. Then, one by one, they vanish – leaving only black whispers of smoke to trail away into the gloom.

Rummaging through their dusty remains, you discover one of the following rewards:

Sinner's shroud	Eir's treads	Voice of Var
(head)	(feet)	(ring)
+1 speed +1 armour	+1 speed +1 armour	+1 brawn
Ability: bleed	Ability: heal	Ability: blood oath

With the asynjur defeated, you approach the base of the tree. Straight ahead the ground drops into an uneven slope, leading into an earthen tunnel. To your right a series of knotted roots form a makeshift pathway, winding up around the trunk.

Will you:

Enter the tunnel?	418
Follow the winding roots?	372

24

Quest: Tar and feathers

The sky is a vast grey emptiness, barely touched by the dawn light. Frost cracks underfoot, dripping from the links of chain and iron struts – and the hundreds of cruelly-barbed spears that block your way. With a cry from one of the soldiers, there is a grating rumble as some hidden mechanism is activated and the chains clatter back through their ring loops. A moment later and the spear walls are lowered, one by one, like waves of grass, beaten back by the wind. And there, ahead of you, across a mile of iron-worked bridge, is the country beyond the rift. Skardfall.

The cart horse whickers nervously as Kirk leads it across the bridge spanning the eerie emptiness of the Great Rift. He is a short, well-built man, with a pug-nose and permanently disgruntled expression. He reminds you of a pit dog your brother Malden once owned, its face crumpled up into a mass of nostrils and teeth. Further ahead, silhouetted by the light, is a taller soldier, all lean muscle and sharp angles. He looks back at you, his hooked nose the only thing visible beneath his dark hood. Lawson, the other soldiers had called him. A short-tempered man and not one to be easily crossed.

You follow at the rear, with two fresh-faced recruits – Mitch, a young farm boy, enrolled in the army to earn coin for his family. He is thin and gangly, constantly on edge, as if at any moment he might bolt into hiding. Your last companion is the stark opposite. Confident and assured. A female knight fresh from the academy, her burnished armour the only bright thing on this sullen day. Her name is Henna, and aside from the briefest of greetings, she has been content to maintain a dutiful silence.

Looks like you're in for a fun day.

Loaded into the back of the cart are twelve barrels. Everard wants them filled with tar to help bolster the keep's defences. As most of the horses won't stand to be near the acrid-smelling pits, you're going on foot – save for the cart horse, which Kirk insists won't shirk away from anything. He tugs roughly on the reins, muttering curses as he attempts to coax the horse across the bridge. Evidently, heights didn't factor into his decision.

Not the best of starts, but you won't let it dampen your spirits; after all, this is your first chance to get out and explore the untamed wilderness of the north. The land of the Skards.

Once across the bridge, it proves a little disappointing. Bare rock and loose stone litter a featureless plain, occasionally zigzagged by crevasses and impassable ridges. Negotiating it with the cart is both tiresome and frustrating.

After several gruelling hours the land finally dips, bringing you into a valley of wind-sheared pillars and canyons. The ground is smoothed stone, occasionally forming shallow basins of still grey water. Kirk insists this area was once covered by ice, back in the day. But every year, the ice has crept a little further north, leaving channels of ice-melt in its wake.

A cold air gusts along the narrow gullies, pulling at clothes and biting at skin. Its mournful howl is accompanied by the shrieking cries of the birds, circling overhead and nesting along the jagged ledges.

'Petrels,' hisses Lawson, nocking an arrow to his bow.

'Leave them be,' grunts Kirk, glaring up at the pitted rock. 'This is the birdman's territory. Let's not ruffle any feathers, eh?'

'The birdman?' echoes Mitch nervously. His eyes are already darting from side to side.

'Yeah, one of the convicts from Ryker's Island. Went a little crazy, you know. Thinks he can fly or something. Ah, here we go.' Kirk halts in front of the party, throwing back his head to take in a deep breath. 'Smell that?'

You pick up a sweet, pungent oily smell. 'The tar pits?' you venture.

'Indeed, my green-gilled friend.' Kirk flashes you an ugly grin. 'Black gold. Come on, let's get these barrels filled.'

The canyon widens, bringing you to the banks of an immense lake of black tar. Smaller pools lie to either side, several dotted with islands of rock and coarse grass. As Kirk and Lawson start to unload the barrels, you become aware of a grief-stricken howling. At first you wonder if it is a trick of the wind, but the sound only intensifies, reverberating from the walls of the canyon. It sounds like some creature in distress.

'Look, over there!' Mitch is already scurrying down the slope, to where the black tar laps thickly against the pebbled shore. He hops onto a boulder to give himself an elevated view of the lake. You hurry to his side, scanning the black waters until you spot the disturbance. A large, shaggy-haired creature is mired in the tar, beating its arms as it tries to free itself. But each frantic movement only serves to ensnare it further, the sticky tar clinging to its matted hair.

'What is it?' You squint, trying to make out some features. The tar already coats much of the beast, but you get the sense of a muzzled face, a pronounced forehead and two curving horns.

'Yeti,' says Lawson, taking aim with his arrow.

'What are you doing?' gasps Mitch, putting out a hand to stay the intended shot.

'What do you think I'm doing, runt? Putting it out of its misery,' Lawson furrows his brow in concentration. 'It's just a juvenile. Ain't got a hide worth skinning.'

'Don't waste the arrow, Law,' grumbles Kirk, walking over.

'But you can't just leave it!' Mitch looks around frantically, then his eyes fix on the cart. 'We could use a rope. Get the horse to pull it free.'

Henna appears at your side, hand resting casually on her sword hilt. 'It's hardly likely to thank us, is it? I don't fancy a crazy yeti on the loose.'

Lawson lowers his bow, glancing towards Kirk. 'What's it to be?'

The pug-faced soldier grins. 'Let the rookies decide. One vote to save, one to kill. Up to you now, green gills.'

Will you:	
Vote for the beast to be saved?	216
Insist the beast is put out of its misery?	128

25

You ascend a short staircase into a wide, vaulted chamber filled with musty-smelling shelves and stacks. The sight of the familiar library chokes you, bringing back memories of your days as a child, hiding here, lost amongst the many storybooks. You pass between the tightly-packed shelves, your hands running along the spines, leaving a smudge of dust on your fingertips – everything feels real. Exactly as you remember.

You pass the empty tables, passing through a doorway into a small reading room. This had always been your favourite place – the one you came to at night, to read and be alone, to stay awake and avoid the nightmares.

You see yourself, a pale ghost, reclining on the window seat beneath the pitted pane. Moonlight filters in through the glass, joining the amber flickering radiance from the candles on the table. A dozen books lie scattered across it, all your favourite storybooks. Whereas most of them lie open, their pages flicking back and forth in an unfelt breeze, two of them are closed, their titles glowing with a green light of their own.

Drawn to the closed books, you scan their titles, already knowing from their binding and size what volumes have been highlighted to you: *The Astounding Adventures of Skyhawk the Sharpshooter* and *The Magnificent Mind of Theomus the Thinker*.

Will you:

Open *Skyhawk the Sharpshooter*?	767
Open *Theomus the Thinker*?	648

26

You hurry to the centre of the clearing, grabbing the discarded water flask from next to the traveller's body. To your relief it is nearly full, the sound of sloshing liquid audible from inside. Popping open the lid, you put it to your mouth and take a thirsty gulp of its contents.

It isn't water. You turn your head away, preparing to spit it out. But then you pause, realising that its flavour is far from unpleasant – putting you in mind of milk and honey, with the sharpness of cinnamon. You swallow it greedily before taking another mouthful, marvelling at the surge of strength now flowing through your body. Its effects are almost as potent as the dragon leaf.

Congratulations, you have now gained the following backpack item:

Pot of might (2 uses)
(backpack)
Use any time in combat to
raise your *brawn* or *magic*
by 2 for one combat round

As you are about to leave, a glint of something bright catches your eye. Leaning in closer, you see a ring on one of the skeleton's fingers. Its silver band glows with a soft green light, suggesting it could be magical in nature.

Will you:

Take the ring?	116
Leave it with the skeleton and continue?	19

27

The black slush shifts and slides underfoot as you make your way along the alleyway that cuts between high granite hills. Firelight illuminates the mouth of several openings above you, reached by ragged-looking rope ladders. You wonder if some of the populace has resorted to living in caves hollowed out of the rock.

People trek back and forth, picking their way past the rubbish and squalor. As before, you feel ravenous eyes watching you, appraising your gear, weighing up your ability to defend yourself. Hands never stray far from weapons. 'Accident alley', the locals have named it. You can see why.

If you have the keyword *ashes* on your hero sheet, turn to 601.

Otherwise, you may head east towards the docks (turn to 659) or westwards, back towards the compound (turn to 426).

28

The broken door scrapes stubbornly against the floor as you shove it open. Ducking under the low lintel, you enter the room beyond. The area appears to be a storeroom filled with crates, barrels and rotting sacks. Most of the floor is littered with scraps of wood and metal, where someone or something has smashed its way through the room. The ceiling above is panelled wood, covered in green mould and dark stains. At the far end one wall has caved inwards, the stones scorched by an explosion of some kind. The resulting rubble forms a crumbling slope, leading up to a torn hole in the ceiling.

As you scan the store for anything of interest, you become aware of a knocking, tapping sound coming from your right. Anise has already edged past you, holding out the torch towards the noise. As her light sweeps the area, it illuminates a row of crates and barrels. One of the smaller crates is trembling and shifting slightly, as if something inside is beating against the wood, trying to get out.

Will you:

Open the crate?	232
Break open one of the barrels?	156
Climb the rubble to the room above?	272
Retrace your steps and use the stairs?	111

29

You slash and blast at the shrieking monsters, cutting through their leathery wings and sending them spinning away into the abyss. The rest of the flock gather to attack, but with an extra burst of speed you are able to outrun them.

For successfully defeating the terrordactyls, you have gained the following item:

Terrordactyl scales
(special)
Use on a cloak, gloves, boots or chest item
to increase its *armour* by 1

When you have updated your hero sheet, turn to 492.

30

The darkness gives way to light, and the shrieks of the damned. You hit the ground running, your short panicked breaths thundering loudly in your ears. All around you is swirling mist, edged with a shifting green radiance. Shapes waver in and out of focus, some distant, others near, but all indistinct through the foggy dreamscape.

You know you have only moments to hide, to find some place that you can cower in until your body awakens from the nightmare. Sometimes it can feel like minutes, other times hours or even days. The ground underfoot is cold and hard – the blackened soil cracking beneath your feet. Ahead you see a formation of stone, perhaps a building. Its edges shimmer, like a reflection on water. You make for it, your strides lengthening with renewed hope. Shelter, safety . . .

Above you, the clouds boil with fury. A vast seething mass of smoke and lightning. Black droplets of rain hiss down from the scoured sky, poisoned water steaming against the parched sand. It brings no life, only death – like the cold wind reeking of tombs and things turned bad.

I have to wake . . . I have to wake up . . .

You half-glimpse the black shape seconds before it slams into you, its chill touch like a blast of winter air. Then come the claws, sinking deep into your flesh, lancing through your very soul. There is no blood, no wound – instead they leave you with an angry pain like a thousand needles burning in your skull.

'No!' You roar in defiance, spinning over and flailing out with your fists. The shadow reels back, its ghostly features shifting into a mockery of a face. Claws reach for you again, but you are already back on your feet, running – suddenly aware of the cloak pulling against your shoulders, hide-boots crunching through the sand. It is the first time you have come into the dream with your clothes and possessions – or at least shadows of them that feel almost real.

My weapon! Frantically you pull it free from your belt, taking small comfort in the knowledge that, for once, you can fight back.

The stone formation looms out of the mist, a statue of some twisted monster, its many eyes staring sightlessly across the forsaken landscape. There is a narrow fracture at its base, wide enough to wriggle into and hide, but there is no time – the wraith trails after you, hissing and wailing through the dark rain.

With no alternative, you turn to face your fear, raising your weapon to defend yourself. 'You won't take me, demon,' you scream. 'I'm done running from you!'

It is time to fight:

	Speed	Magic	Armour	Health
Nightmare	0	1	0	12

If you manage to overcome this shadowy nemesis, turn to 84.

31

Anise clings to the paladin, relying on him to half-guide and half-carry her through the swirling dust storm. Since leaving the mountain, neither companion has complained nor questioned the mission; both have set their will to the task, doing all that you ask of them. But with the water and food running low you can see Anise's spirit diminishing by the day, her body growing weaker. The paladin seems unaffected by either fatigue or hunger; you assume it is his magic – the glowing script that has been carved into his skin must be somehow nourishing him, keeping him strong. You watch jealously as his strong arms support Anise. He almost looks the hero.

Just like in the storybooks.

'No!'

You jerk round, to see Skoll standing atop the ridge. The burly warrior stumbles back from the buffeting gale, shielding his eyes as he stares ahead at something you cannot see.

Keep it together. You force your numb limbs to action, stumbling and crawling over the last of the rocky scree, the wind growing stronger the higher you climb. Turn to 228.

32

Frustration leads to anger. You can feel Nanuk stirring within you, his impatience becoming your impatience, his desire to end the fight becoming your vented fury. Orrec dances and dodges around you, seemingly unencumbered by his heavy armour. His goading only makes it worse, a haze descending before your vision, your father's voice echoing in your ears.

You've let me down again, Arran. Such a waste. Sometimes I wonder if I fathered you at all.

Ignoring Orrec's instruction, you fall back on brute strength, letting Nanuk's spirit flow into you, dragging a guttural roar from your lips.

It isn't until you are standing over the downed warrior, your weapons at his throat, that you come to your senses. Orrec is looking up at you – no trace of mockery or disappointment in his expression. Only respect. And a little fear.

'Where did you learn that?' He struggles up onto his elbows, wincing with discomfort.

'A book, I think.' You brush the dust from your shoulders, stepping away to let the warrior stand. 'Did I pass?'

Orrec finds his feet, his armour clinking as it settles around his massive frame. 'No one has ever put me in the dirt before. I'd call that a pass, soldier. Welcome to the honoured ranks.'

Congratulations – you have learned the path of the warrior. You may now permanently increase your *health* by 15 (to 45). You have also gained the following special ability:

Upper hand (dm): You automatically win the next combat round (without needing to roll for attack speed). *Upper hand* can only be used once per combat.

When you have updated your hero sheet, turn to 290.

33

You pick your way past the two rusted doors, torn from their hinges. Beyond is a small chamber, once used as a guard room. Three skeletons sit propped in chairs behind a counter, wearing the rotted remains of prison officer uniforms. Their grinning skulls are made eerie by the flickering flames of a naked fire burning its way through refuse dumped in a brazier.

You enter a narrow corridor, bordered on both sides by cells. As your eyes grow accustomed to the gloom, you realise some things are best left to the shadows: crude messages scrawled in filth over the walls; swarms of rats nibbling at decayed remains; prisoners shuffling back and forth, like sleepwalkers lost in a waking dream.

In the distance, a chill scream.

Faces start to appear, leering at you from cells, skin black with dirt, hair greasy and tangled. But you pay them no mind, trying to project a confident air as you advance along the corridor.

'I smells treasure,' croaks a voice to your right.

You risk a glance into the large open cell, its stone floor littered with ragged animal hides and skulls. An elderly man is sat cross-legged on a soiled straw mattress, his lank grey hair hanging like cobwebs over his ghoulish-white face. 'I'm Sam Scurvy,' he slurps, licking at his toothless gums. 'Best thief in Valeron.'

Will you:

Speak with Sam Scurvy?	386
Continue down the corridor?	563
Retrace your steps and leave the prison?	426

34

At the top of the hill you discover a round platform of grey stone, bordered by an outer circle of pillars carved with angular runes. At the centre of the platform stands a single slab of rock, its polished surface decorated with similar markings. A small creature is crouched next to them, studying the glyphs with a keen interest. On hearing your approach it gives a yelp of fright, spinning to face you. Your response is one of equal surprise.

The creature is less than a metre tall, its body thin and gangly like a child's. The head is abnormally large, its bald pate tapering forward into a snout-like nose. From its appearance and size, you suspect it is a fengle – a sub-species of goblin. At least your nights spent poring over bestiaries haven't proved a total waste of time. From what you recall, they are normally cowardly creatures, scavengers for the most part. Perhaps this one might let you go . . .

You raise your hands in a show of submission and start to back away. The fengle's eyes dart to your sword, its yellow eyes widening at the sight of the fist-sized diamond set into the pommel. It licks its lips greedily, long fingers groping towards the rock dagger tucked into its belt.

Before you have a chance to react, the creature rushes towards you, its bare feet splashing through the muddy puddles. Gripped by panic, you try to run but the creature is too fast for you, barrelling into your side and taking you both tumbling to the ground. Luckily, you manage to untangle yourself from its flailing limbs, twisting aside in the nick of time to avoid the thrust of the dagger. When it tries to stab you again, you catch the creature's wrist in your hands, looking to turn the blade away from yourself and back against your assailant. It is time to fight:

	Speed	Brawn	Armour	Health
Fengle	1	0	0	8

If you manage to defeat the Fengle, remember to restore your *health* then turn to 73.

35

It will take you seven turns to climb to the top of the tree (Five turns if you have *ice hooks*.). In each turn Ratatosk throws an acorn, aiming for the hungry mouths below you. You must take a challenge test for each acorn (note: if Leif is with you, he will aid you in destroying the acorns – add 2 to your dice result for each challenge.):

	Speed
Nutcracker	15

If you are successful you have managed to smash the acorn, stopping it from feeding the growth. If you fail, the acorn lands in one of the growth's mouths, making the plant grow even larger. Repeat until one of the following occurs:

If you miss three acorns in total, turn to 159. If you reach the top of the tree (after seven/five turns), turn to 597.

36

Skoll leads the charge, an axe in one hand, magic lighting the other – chopping and blasting through the bodies that block his way. Behind him Anise hollers a defiant cry, swinging her sword to sever heads from bodies, clipping limbs and frozen weapons, leaving a trail of ice and writhing corpses in her wake.

And then there is Maune. A glowing beacon of holiness. The heat from his scripted body sears through the statues' ice armour, exposing their decayed flesh to his brutal strikes. Each movement of his blade, each cut and thrust, leaves another corpse burning, consumed by white flame. Turn to 761.

37

As you close with the wolf, you notice a series of deep cuts around the beast's throat and torso. Evidently the inquisitor made good use of your sword, weakening your savage opponent and buying you a valuable advantage in the coming battle. It is time to fight:

	Speed	Brawn	Armour	Health
Alpha	0	1	0	15

Special abilities
- ♥ **Pack leader:** The alpha rerolls all ⚀ results, accepting the result of the reroll.

🐾 **Wounded**: At the end of each combat round, the alpha must lose 1 *health* from the wounds that it has already suffered.

If you manage to defeat this powerful predator, turn to 298.

38

With the spectral guardian defeated, you may now help yourself to one of the following rewards:

Mammoth mitts	Graven might	Stolen thunder
(gloves)	(cloak)	(talisman)
+1 speed +2 magic	+1 speed +2 magic	+1 speed +4 health
Ability: insulated, heal	Ability: curse	Ability: windblast

When you have updated your hero sheet, turn to 339.

39

The sides of the shaft are pitted with holes and crevices – providing just enough foot- and handholds to make the climb. However, navigating the circular tunnel will not be easy, as you will need to spread your weight between the narrow walls as you push yourself higher up the shaft.

To reach the top, you will need to complete a *speed* or *brawn* challenge, using whichever attribute is highest:

	Speed/Brawn
Risky ascent	9

If you are successful, turn to 83. If you fail, then turn to 323.

You stand over the last of the downed creatures, its strange bulbous brain flickering with magic. Teeth gritted, you drive your weapons through the bloated flesh, turning your head as a bright spray of fluid fountains into the air.

Caul leans on his spear, forcing a grin past his pained exhaustion. 'Those things have been hounding me for days. Never thought I'd see the last of them. I offer you my thanks, friend.'

You kneel next to the creatures' remains. 'If it's all the same to you, I'll settle for a knife.'

Caul tugs one of his blades free, then steps forward to hand it over. 'Ain't much left. I think we can assume they're dead.'

'I know. But I want a trophy.' You set about cutting through the flesh and scales, extracting whatever magic and armour you can find. If you wish, you may now take one of the following rewards:

Tangled tentacles	Scaled pauldrons	Hive mind
(gloves)	(cloak)	(necklace)
+1 speed +1 brawn	+1 speed +1 brawn	+2 magic
Ability: webbed	Ability: shoulder charge	Ability: recall
		(requirement: mage)

When you have updated your hero sheet, turn to 115.

On reaching the top of the tower, little more than a flat stone platform circumventing a peak-slatted roof, you are met by a scene of both horror and destruction. One of the fortress walls has fallen inwards, spilling chunks of rock across the courtyard. The whole west end of the main hall has also collapsed. Dust hangs heavy in the air – and so does the miasma of blood.

Over the wall and through the breach, black-scaled bodies spill into the yard. Reptilian monsters of all sizes and shapes, some wielding mighty swords and axes, others using whatever they can get their hands on – splintered wood, rocks, human body parts . . .

'What are they?' you shout to Segg, who is looking down at the scene with the same wild-eyed disbelief. 'Did they cause the quake?'

'Nisse . . . they're Nisse,' gasps the mage. 'Creatures of the underworld.'

Winged shapes soar overhead, filling the smoke-hued sky with hellish shrieks. You try and follow them as they pitch and dive through the air, swooping on the beleaguered soldiers below. A group of the beasts peel off, their black leathery wings beating the air as they drive their ungainly bodies towards you. They look like spindly lizards, with two webbed feet and a long tail ending in a forked prong.

'Drakelings,' you hear Segg mutter.

The elderly mage raises his hands, fingers pointed skywards. The air shifts, becoming waves of yellow, then amber, then red. Like a shimmering tide, the magic rushes up into the clouds, quickly forming two sleek arcs. As they continue to gain height, they gradually pull back to reveal a long, blazing neck and a bird-like head.

A phoenix.

The firebird dives towards the reptilian monsters, flames billowing from its open beak. It collides with the largest drakeling, sending them both spinning and flailing across the courtyard.

'We must destroy as many as we can!' Segg fires bolts of magic into the oncoming swarm. The nearest flyer is hit, its black wings trailing fire. But still it comes at you, jaws snapping open to vomit a steaming deluge of black bile. You dodge aside, surprised to see the stone where you were standing cracking and popping as it is melted to slag.

'Acid!' you warn Segg. 'Watch yourself!'

You summon magic to your hands, hoping you have the skill to take on these deadly acid-spitting reptiles. It is time to fight:

	Speed	Magic	Armour	Health
Drakeling	3	2	2	20
Drakeling	3	2	2	20
Drakeling	3	2	2	20

Special abilities

♥ **Acid spray**: The drakelings are covering the tower with their deadly acid, leaving you little room to manoeuvre. At the end of the first combat round, roll a die. If the result is ⚀ you have been hit and must take 4 damage, ignoring *armour*. In each subsequent combat round, the chance to be hit increases by 1. In round two, you are hit on a roll of ⚀ or ⚁, on round three, ⚀ to ⚂ and so on.

🔥 **Pyromania**!: Segg and his phoenix cause 2 damage, ignoring *armour*, to each drakeling at the end of every combat round.

If you manage to defeat this monstrous swarm, turn to 520.

42

'You sound both surprised and concerned, my dear.' Sylvie gives you a sideways glance. 'Do you think poor Sylvie can't look after herself – that she needs a man around her home to keep her company? Hmm? Is that what they fill your ears with these days?'

You flounder for an apology, wondering how you might have caused offence. Sylvie's eyes glint mischievously, her lips twitching into a playful smile. 'Ah, you're still such a babe. Grew up behind safe walls, I daresay. You're not ready for the wilds quite yet, are you?'

You find yourself confused at her manner. 'I wasn't given a choice,' you reply sourly.

'Hmm, that's as maybe. Well, seeing as you've asked, I work for the Botany Society. Actually, I used to – before I decided to focus my efforts in other areas. I've had to live in some very remote places, boy, in order to conduct my studies. You learn quickly to fend for yourself when you don't have nothing between you and the great outdoors.'

Sylvie lifts her hand, displaying a band of silver around her wedding finger. 'I was married once. He was a good man. Randal. We were posted here together by the society. Perhaps it was always inevitable we would fall in love.'

'What happened?' You venture. 'If you don't mind me . . .'

'He died,' she interjects, before you can finish. 'It's painful, but it happened and there's nothing I can do about it. Sometimes, the hardest part is learning to let go, to say goodbye.' She looks up, meeting your gaze – then smiles once again. 'Sorry, I didn't mean to snap. I haven't spoken about it for a long time. That's one downside of being alone – no one to talk to. Well, except for the plants.' Her grin widens. 'But they're really not the same now, are they?'

Return to 191 to ask another question, or turn to 207 to end the conversation.

43

You find yourself in a cobwebbed cave chiselled out of the black rock. One wall is lined with barrels, and another contains a rickety-looking wine rack filled with coloured bottles. Stairs at the back of the cave lead up to a trapdoor, which you assume provides access to the main taproom of the Coracle.

If you have the word *Bowfinch* on your hero sheet turn to 148. Otherwise, turn to 380.

44

The lightning bolts lance into your transport, causing serious damage. (You must lower your transport's *toughness* and *stability* by 2.) Thankfully, you manage to reach the far side of the island without sustaining another barrage. With an extra boost of speed, you quickly outdistance the towers' range. Turn to 492.

45

Your weapon splinters the Skard's javelin, your foot catching him in the chest and driving him back to the ground. He reaches for his belt, fingers closing around the black wand. 'Min eld!' he hisses, pointing it towards you.

Then Henna's sword comes slicing down in a brilliant arc of steel. You turn away from the blow, not wishing to see it land.

'Funny,' she pants, dropping to her knees. 'With a face like yours, didn't think you'd be so squeamish.'

You grunt at the joke. 'Is that the last of them?'

She nods. 'I think so. Took down the other hunter. His dogs too.' She winces as she works her shoulders. 'Think I may need a healer, though – and a good bath.'

You take a moment to search what remains of the Skard. If you wish, you may now take one of the following rewards:

Bone smile	Red gutter	Atataq
(necklace)	(main hand: dagger)	(main hand: wand)
+1 brawn +1 magic	+1 speed +1 brawn	+1 speed +1 magic
Ability: reckless	Ability: bleed	Ability: sear

When you have updated your hero sheet, turn to **108**.

46

The einherjar are quick-footed and strong – and more used to fighting on the shifting uneven banks of snow. Despite your strength and magic, you struggle to fend off their brutal attacks. It becomes a battle of attrition, which quickly wears you down. As you fall to your knees in the deep snow, your weapons are knocked from your hands. With nothing left to defend yourself, you resort to clawing and biting, letting Nanuk's spirit rise to the fore.

For an instant you sight the shock on the faces of the warriors, then they back away. Aslev is the first to lower his blood-stained axe. The others look to him, muttering angrily in Skard. Aslev appears to concede to their demands.

'Are you truly what you say you are?' he asks gruffly.

You struggle to find your voice, to find that part of you which is still human. Steadily, you push past the savage, bestial anger – kicking inwardly to reach the surface of your own thoughts, to break past Nanuk's stifling presence.

'I am,' you gasp at last, falling forward onto your hands. 'The ancestor spirit . . . the bear . . . he gives me his power. Sura believed . . . I can save your leader. I just need . . . the chance.'

Aslev offers you his hand and helps you to your feet. Suspicion knits his eyebrows, but there is also admiration in his steely glare. One of the warriors speaks up, barking words in Skard.

Aslev nods. 'We all gave our word,' he says slowly. 'You cannot go back. You will shame us.'

'I can,' you reply defiantly. 'And I will. All I ask is that I am given a chance to prove myself. I will not dishonour the Ska-inuin.' You raise your manacled wrist, its dark magic still flickering in the half-light.

Aslev sighs. 'We will become cursed for this.' He passes his hand over the rune-marked iron. A second later, there is a click as the manacle's teeth spring open. 'We will become nameless, lose our seat in the halls of our heroes.'

You rub at your blackened wrist. 'Gurt cannot judge your worth. He is not the Drokke.'

Aslev grunts. 'I believe it is you who should be afraid of judgement.'

You retrieve your weapons, fists tightening around the grips. 'Perhaps you're right.' You grin darkly. 'Now, come. I have a score to settle.' Turn to 119.

47

You lurch forward, eyes flipping open, hands scrambling for purchase. Your surroundings seem strange, wooden walls and shelves of guttering candles. Light creeps beneath a curtain. From the other side, you can hear a woman whistling merrily to herself. The cabin. Memory suddenly comes flooding back, and with it the unsettling realisation that you were tricked.

You stagger to your feet, still trembling with fear – and the dread cold of that other place. It eats away at your stomach, rooting through you like some malign parasite. You swallow back a wave of nausea, the cooking smells from the main room doing nothing to settle your queasiness.

Fresh clothes have been provided at the end of the bed. You ignore them, instead tugging your damp cloak around your shoulders. After taking a moment to regain your composure, you push back the curtain and enter the main room.

Sylvie is busy with breakfast. You see a pan over the fire, with eggs and bread cooking in goose fat. She looks up as you enter, a smile crinkling the corners of her eyes. It is as if the events of last night had never occurred.

'Did you sleep well?' she asks, flipping over one of the pieces of bread. 'I hope you're hungry. If you don't mind fetching some water from the creek, that would be wonderful. Then I'll get some tea on the boil. There's a bucket out the front.'

Will you:

Ask her why she tricked you?	295
Ask her what she knows about the dreams?	165
Ignore her and leave?	282
Agree to fetch water?	78

48

The immensity of the mountain fills your view, its sheer slopes carpeted in the same red dust that coats the rest of this blighted land. You scan the rocks, looking for a place to set down the ship. Suddenly, there is a shout from the crow's nest. The lookout is gesturing wildly towards the nearest rock face. You try and make out what he is saying, but his words are snatched away by the rushing wind. Instead, you turn your attention to the area he is indicating.

You spot a cavernous opening, previously obscured by a spur of rock. At first you assume the lookout is showing you a means of entering the mountain – but then his words finally carry to your ears. Along with his fear.

'Kraken! Move away! Kraken!'

The attack comes swiftly. You register only a few staccato images – a gigantic beaked snout pushing out of the cave, tentacles surging forward, snapping like whips. Then the ship is rocked to one side, tipping over. A suckered tentacle crashes down across the deck, knocking sailors flying over the rail. There is the crunch as the main mast splinters. More screams. Another tentacle squirms its way between the sails, smashing through anything that gets in its way.

Skoll is struggling against the wheel, trying to haul the ship back on course. Anise rushes to the ship's mounted gun, a malign weapon crafted from the nails of the dead. Spinning it round, she fires on the nearest appendage, peppering it with razor sharp bullets. It withdraws quickly, trailing a shower of ink-coloured blood.

An agonised screech echoes from the cavern.

But the reprieve is short-lived. More tentacles are thrashing through the air, slamming into the deck and crushing sailors to ash. The ship itself is being gradually dragged towards the snapping, toothless maw of the creature. You realise that unless you can free yourself from the kraken's tentacles, you are on course to become its next meal. It is time to fight:

	Speed	Brawn	Armour	Health
Kraken	12	6	7	90(*)
Tentacle	13	8	4	30
Tentacle	13	8	4	30
Tentacle	13	8	4	30
Tentacle	13	8	4	30

Special abilities

🦑 **Under pressure**: If the tentacles are not defeated by the end of the fourth combat round, you are dragged into the jaws of the kraken. This inflicts 4 dice of damage, ignoring *armour*, and reduces the *stability* and *toughness* of your transport by 2. This cycle repeats every four combat rounds until the tentacles are defeated.

🦑 **Thrash it out**: (*) The kraken cannot be harmed until the four tentacles have been defeated.

🦑 **Fire at will**: You may use your *nail gun* ability in this combat. (Note: If your transport's *stability* has been reduced to zero, you can no longer use its associated ability.)

If you manage to overcome the tentacled horror, turn to 238.

49

The moment you step across the threshold the tremors start to subside. You find yourself in a long, vaulted chamber, circumvented by a high balcony. There are no markings or decoration save for a sculptured ceiling showing nine humanoid figures standing at the edges of a circle, arms raised together, hands linked – the pattern reminiscent of an unfurled flower. It is breath-taking in its scale, marred only by the fractures that criss-cross through the stone.

But something else quickly draws your attention.

Statues. Dozens of them, arranged haphazardly across the length of the hall, seemingly without order or design. Some are men and women, others goblin, troll and half-giant . . . Each crafted from the same green stone, glimmering with magic.

As you step cautiously between them, the true nature of their invention is slowly revealed. Each body is contorted, deformed. Some are flailing with arms raised to their faces, others grasping for something, almost pleading. A few are wielding weapons, caught frozen in a swing or a desperate block, captured in a moment of frenzied battle.

You put a hand to one of the statues. A Skard, like many of the other statues, going by his height and brawn. To your surprise you discover the material is not stone, but ice – slick and freezing cold. Worse, you can sense some glimmer of life still flickering from deep within.

You step around the Skard, your gaze falling on the man's face. The mouth is pulled open in a silent scream, nostrils flared, head leaning away – the ice having frozen his features in a fateful instant of death. And yet he is still alive. A single eye tracks your movement, wide and unblinking from the hollow of his frozen skull. You never thought so much pain and suffering could be writ in a man's gaze. The other socket is empty; a pit of cauterised flesh.

Turning, you look into the face of another statue; this one a female knight, clad in plated armour. Through her visor you can see the same agonised expression – and a single eye following you from the depths of its icy prison. The other taken, leaving only a blank hollow.

Another soul trapped in an eternal nightmare.

You draw back, shaking with the horrifying realisation of what has been inflicted on these people. The sentinel's wings . . . adorned with hundreds of eyes . . .

Do you like them?

The woman's voice, scratching inside your mind.

You twist round, tracking the edge of the balcony. A hooded shape is moving there, the body slender, stepping silent as a ghost.

'Melusine . . . ?' You can barely speak, your mind still racing. Skoll had warned you about the witch and her power to turn flesh to ice.

From beneath the folds of her cloak a slender arm emerges, pale as snow. Rings glitter on her long fingers, the red-painted nails tapping absently against the balcony rail. *I wasn't sure you would get this far, Arran.*

'I thought you were a prophet,' you snap, your anger returning.

A soft chuckle, like the tinkling of glass. *Oh, you have much to learn, fledgling. Nothing is certain, only possibilities. I work to ensure my own plans come to fruition. This ending is my choice, not yours.*

'Why . . . ?'

The woman ceases her pacing then turns to face you. In one swift motion, she pulls back her hood. You take an involuntary step backwards, your expression mirroring that of the tortured souls in the chamber. What had once been a face is now a bloated growth of pulpy flesh, distending into coils that curl about her slender neck. A crown sits atop a ridged brow, itself looking as if it was fashioned from skin, with bony hooks that grip like claws. A veil of shimmering light streams out behind her, surrounding her tortured visage in a gossamer halo.

You avert your gaze, fearing to look into the pits of her eyes.

'You are . . . not human.'

Oh, dear Arran. I was beautiful once. A dancer. Every night I would perform the Red Masque at the Scourou Nave. Every night I would exit to a standing ovation, such rapturous applause! Men would shower me with their gifts, they would beg for my attentions. A dancer and a princess. No woman could match my beauty; no performance was ever as spectacular as my own.

You hear the tap of her fingernails as she resumes pacing.

I was traded like a piece of meat. The emperor chose me above all his other daughters to leave my homeland and marry the king of Valeron – all for a bargain, the sealing of a peace treaty; one that barely lasted past my wedding night. Father wanted me there, to spy on my husband – I was a tool, a weapon. For Mordland.

You lift your eyes, watching her move, noticing the graceful sway of her hips, the litheness of her step – the poise of a princess, and a dancer.

Understand this, Arran. Wars are never truly won. There is no end to it, no end to what men will do for power.

'Power? Look at what you have done, Melusine.' You scan the rows of statues, each one a cruel work of pain and suffering. 'Look at what have you done!'

Silence. In the distance you hear another faint rumble. For a moment the ground shivers beneath you.

The woman grips the balcony with both hands. *I bring an end to all things, Arran. I have no regret. No pity. Such emotions were beaten from me, torn away, stolen like every other precious part of me. A ruthless father, a cruel husband. You look upon me with disgust, Arran, but this is everything your world has taken from me.* She pauses, letting the silence grow. *Tell me, prince of Valeron. Has life treated you with any greater kindness?*

You glare back angrily. For a second, you meet her gaze – two pin-pricks of light amidst the darkness of her deformity, blue and penetrating. You look away again. 'I do what I must – to stop this madness.'

And what then – what next for the ghost prince? What will you do when you have saved the world, become the hero? What could possibly follow that – a throne, a kingdom, a petty act of revenge?' Melusine fills your head with her shrill laughter. Sharp and cutting. *Wars are never truly won. I told you that, Arran.*

You pool magic into your fists, preparing to strike.

Melusine raises a hand, and snaps her fingers. *Enjoy the dance, my prince.*

You hear a rustling to your right, a sharp crack, then an echoing thud of something heavy landing. Spinning on the spot, you watch in horror as the crowd of statues start to move, stumbling like zombies towards you. From the balcony you hear Melusine humming to herself, a sad and melancholy tune – in perfect timing with the swaying, erratic movements of the animated statues. It is time to fight:

	Speed	Brawn	Armour	Health
Ice tomb	14	7	16	30
Ice tomb	14	7	16	30
Ice tomb	13	8	16	25
Ice tomb	13	8	16	25
Ice tomb	13	8	16	25

Special abilities

🟣 **Smash it up**: If you win a combat round against an ice tomb, instead of rolling for a damage score you can choose to smash the ice, reducing your opponent's *armour* score by 4 each time.

🟣 **Outnumbered**: At the end of each combat round, you must take 1 damage from each surviving opponent, ignoring *armour*. This ability only applies while you are faced with multiple opponents.

If you manage to defeat these tortured souls, turn to **514**. (Special achievement: If you defeat the ice tombs without lowering their *armour*, turn to **779**.)

50

You pick up the tile and push it into the square-shaped hole. Leaning back, you wait expectantly for something to happen. However, it appears that you have chosen the incorrect rune. As you hurriedly try and prise the tile back out of the grid, you hear a sudden crack of branches followed by another barking cry. If you don't run now, the other fengles will find you! Frantically, you spring to your feet and sprint for the cover of the opposite treeline. Turn to **175**.

51

The bear thrashes wildly with pain. Another blow drives him to the ground, radiating a cloud of dust across the circle. For a moment you hesitate, weapons raised – frozen in the downward motion of a killing blow. Nanuk gives a mewling gasp, lifting his head to lock eyes with you one last time.

Pleading. Begging for life.

You let your weapons fall, screaming and crying all at once, vision blurred. The bear's body evaporates into motes of green light. You toss aside your weapons, raising your arms to draw it in, leaving none of it to waste – knowing you will need all the bear's spirit for what you intend.

You have gained the following bonus:

Body of spirit: You are cured of necrosis. You no longer need to record defeats and suffer death penalty effects. All existing penalties are immediately removed from your hero.

If you are a warrior, turn to 396. If you are a mage, turn to 643. If you are a rogue, turn to 554.

52

'Is tha' the password?' asks the youth, scratching his chin. He glances sideways at his companion, who appears to be mulling it over with difficulty.

'Yeah, yeah ... sounds about right.' The half-goblin shrugs his scrawny shoulders. 'Okay. You're in.' He takes a key from his belt and unfastens the padlock. The gate swings open with an unsettling high-pitched squeal. 'Have a pleasant stay now.' Turn to 33.

53

You clip a boulder, which sends you into a dizzying spiral. Quickly you try and reassert control of your transport, channelling your magic in order to break out of the spin. There is a worrying crunch as you slam into the side of a larger fragment of rock, the force of the collision almost throwing you into the rift. (You must lower your transport's *toughness* by 2.) Luckily, you manage to pull away before sustaining worse damage, dodging the last of the debris to finally make it out the other side. It was a close call. Looking back, you notice that the dragons have also suffered; their large bodies now display numerous wounds. Nevertheless, they are still on your tail and gaining fast. Record the keyword *rocked* on your hero sheet, then turn to 773.

54

You close with the wolf, hoping that your newfound strength will be enough to overcome this powerful predator. It is time to fight:

	Speed	Brawn	Armour	Health
Alpha	1	1	1	15

Special abilities

- 🐾 **Pack leader**: The alpha rerolls all ⚀ results, accepting the result of the reroll.
- 🐾 **Wounded**: At the end of each combat round, the alpha must lose 1 *health* from the wounds that it has already suffered.

If you manage to defeat the alpha wolf, turn to 273.

55

Maune is chuckling to himself. 'Hal . . . Hal Arbuckle.'

Anise glares at him. 'You know that lunatic?'

The paladin rises to his feet, hands raised in surrender. 'Hal, you blind fool, it's me. Take a shot at this and that black soul of yours is headed straight for damnation.'

There is a heavy moment of silence. Then from the tower you hear a cackle of laughter. Maune turns to you, grinning. 'I think we're safe now.'

You follow the paladin into the ruins, where a man is hobbling down a set of worn stairs. He is elderly, dressed in oily leathers and a thick woollen cloak. Grey tangled hair flares wildly around a metal helm, which looks far too small for his head; most probably of goblin-origin – you spot several of their corpses lined against a wall.

The man stumbles towards you, favouring his left leg. The other drags slightly, evidently the result of an old wound. A rifle rests against his shoulder.

Maune moves forward, embracing the old man. 'Hal, my friend.' He quickly casts his eyes around the ruins. 'What happened?'

'Since you saved us from those trolls?' The old sniper shakes his head. 'Bad to worse. We're grounded now, making some repairs. But hope to be airborne soon.' He glances past the paladin, eyeing up the rest of you. 'I don't want any trouble. If yer here to trade, all well and good. But we ain't taking on any extra baggage.'

'Understood,' replies Maune. His eyes find your own, and you read his underlying warning. 'No baggage.'

A crunch of boots forces you to turn. A plump woman approaches from around a wall, a pair of goggles pushed back into her thick russet hair. Her clothes are ragged and weather-worn, their colours faded into an indeterminate shade. One of her hands is bandaged, the other cradles a rifle.

'Belinda, me wife,' says Hal.

Despite the woman's dishevelled appearance, she still manages a warm and friendly smile.

'And that's me brother, Darin.'

You look round, to see a short man with straw-yellow hair turning a piece of meat over a fire. He lifts his scarred face, giving only a swift nod in greeting. Behind him, you see a thicker plume of smoke rising out of a great, wooden gondola – one element of a confusing jumble of parts that reminds you of a beached sailing vessel.

'Oh, that there is *The Free Spirit*,' grins Hal, noting your confused expression. 'Me pride and joy.'

The hull is riddled with an odd array of sails and paddles, all seemingly linked by a confusing network of ropes. Spread on the rocks behind them is a vast leather balloon, its arrow-like shape formed from curved steel rods. They poke out of various ripped holes where the balloon has evidently sustained damage. Patches already cover much of its length.

'Yeah, not so free at the moment,' sighs Hal. 'All thanks to those blasted dactyls. Least they make a good supper.' He lifts his bushy eyebrows, pointing a stubby finger at the meat his brother is cooking.

'If you have supplies, we could trade,' says Maune. 'We're headed north; we'll take whatever you can spare. For a fair price, of course.'

Hal rubs the side of his red-veined nose. 'Well, sure. I got a first aid kit, and a few things I dug up down in those rifts – Dwarven treasures and a few old weapons. I'll trade ya what yer don't need, too.' He gestures to his ruined airship. 'I'll use anything right now, to get her back where she belongs. Come.' Hal leads you into the ruined tower, where a set of sacks and crates have been piled against one of the walls. (Record the keyword *survivors* on your hero sheet.)

Will you:

Purchase first aid supplies?	639
Purchase weapons?	728
Look at the treasures?	674
Trade your own items?	95
Leave?	Return to the quest map

56

When you recover you find that you are still inside the laboratory, but Talia has fled. Next to you is a pouch of gold and a hastily scrawled note: 'Hope I didn't break your heart, honey.' You open up the pouch to find 50 gold crowns inside.

After retrieving your weapons, you begin a search of the lab. Turn to 747.

57

For defeating the rift demon, you may now help yourself to one of the following rewards:

Foreleg stinger	Void	Beeble boom
(main hand: staff)	(ring)	(left hand: wand)
+1 speed +2 magic	+1 magic	+1 speed +2 magic
Ability: sideswipe	Ability: dark pact	Ability: knockdown

When you have updated your hero sheet, turn to 503.

58

You walk through the vast library, stopping occasionally to study some of the books that are on display. The majority appear to be history books. Only a few seem to pertain to magic, which surprises you considering this is Segg's library. Perhaps he keeps his magic books elsewhere.

You find yourself drawn to an area of shelving where the books seem older, most of them displaying loose pages or tattered bindings. Perhaps there will be something here of greater value.

If you have the keyword *secrets* on your hero sheet, turn to 359. Otherwise, your search is once again unsuccessful. You may return to the courtyard (turn to 113) or visit and speak with Segg (turn to 328).

59

You clamber down the stepped slope, eventually splashing down into a shallow mud basin at the bottom of the ravine. Hot and thirsty from your descent, you eye the dark pools of water with a sudden keenness. Sagging to your knees you lean over the nearest one, cupping your hands to take a sip of the water. Its smell, however, forces you to recoil. The water is black with dirt, its surface filmed with a frothy layer of slime. Angrily, you push yourself away and continue onwards, taking more dragon leaf from your pouch to stave off your hunger pains.

Once in the forest, you discover there is no obvious trail to follow. Instead you are forced to weave between the tight press of trees and the gnarly, criss-crossing branches. Scratched and bloodied, you are relieved when you finally stumble out into a wide clearing.

The ground is boggy, the stench of rot even stronger here than it was back at the basin. Around the edge of the clearing a ring of giant toadstools is growing out of the mud, their black-pointed caps giving off a sickly yellow smoke. At the centre of the ring, you can see a scattering of bones and some tattered looking belongings. Evidently another traveller came this way and must have fallen foul of something, but you are not sure what. There looks to be a water flask lying in the mud next to some of the bones. The lid is intact – perhaps it might contain some fresh water to drink. Licking your lips, you ponder your next move.

Will you:

Take a closer look at one of the toadstools?	91
Search the traveller's belongings?	26

60

Between you and Mount Skringskal lies a vast expanse of floating debris, evidently the result of whatever explosion or tremor ripped apart the land. Some magic, possibly seeping out of the dark rift, holds the rock suspended in space, leaving a cluttered maze of obstacles for you to navigate around.

Cautiously, you drop speed to pass through the first of the rock fields, using the opportunity to gain a feel for the handling and flight of your transport. Just as you are starting to gain confidence, accelerating over the last of the smaller, spinning rocks, you are faced by the first of the giant islands. Passing it would pose no problem, but its barren topside is scattered with black towers, each one flickering with magic. You guess they must be some sort of defence, created by the witch to guard against anyone attempting to reach the mountain.

'Watch out!' shouts Skoll.

His warning comes just in time. A bolt of lightning splits the air, crackling outwards from one of the towers. Quickly you dodge aside, managing to avoid the blast – but already you can see other towers powering up their charges.

'Underneath! Take it underneath!' Anise points to the ragged base of the island. You notice winged shapes roosting along the many ridges and crevices; hanging from the rock by their claws. A few have sighted your approach, cawing and screeching in alarm.

Will you:

Attempt to dodge the sentry fire?	**363**
Fly underneath the island?	**387**

61

'You were found north of Whisper Vale, by a trapper from the White Wolf company. He didn't know who you were, else I'm sure he'd have held you ransom for a better reward.' The knight draws a tight breath. 'That was four weeks ago. When you came to us, you were unconscious, feverish. There were wounds – frostbite. You had it bad. We weren't sure we could save you.' He shares a glance with Segg, the crimson-robed man. 'I don't know if it was luck or . . .' He stops to clear his throat. 'You are still with us, Arran. And in these times, I believe that is a mercy.'

Return to 291 to ask another question, or turn to 98 to end the conversation.

62

As your hand settles around the hilt of the enchanted sword a rush of intense cold races up your arm, forcing you to stiffen. The weapon begins to shift in shape, flickering between a two-pronged staff, a short-bladed dagger and the original long sword. You suspect that this ancient artefact is somehow melding itself to its wielder's will.

If you wish, you may impose one of the following forms on the weapon (dagger, sword or staff) – and equip this special reward:

Bifrost	Bifrost	Bifrost
(main hand: dagger)	(main hand: sword)	(main hand: staff)
+1 speed +3 brawn	+1 speed +3 brawn	+1 speed +3 magic
Ability: ice edge	Ability: twin blade	Ability: mental freeze

You may now try and open the chest, if you haven't already (turn to 167), or cross back to the tree and continue onwards (turn to 509.)

63

You spot two men chatting animatedly nearby. One of them is positioning various mugs, plates and pieces of cutlery on the table top to form a map. Both are well-dressed, in thick padded leathers trimmed with fur. One has a set of goggles pushed back into his red-dyed hair. You guess they are both sled racers.

'Stay on the ice, here and here,' says the red-haired racer, moving his finger in a path between two tankards. 'It's tempting to take the snow banks, the obvious short cut. But remember, the snow heats the ice – makes it more brittle. Hides the crevasses, too. Stay on the ice.'

'What about the caves?' asks his companion, pointing to one of the plates. 'I'd normally go top level, less room for passing. But the turning's more difficult. If you get a bottleneck someone's going bye-bye.'

'Agreed. With all the tremors we've been having lately, I'd skirt the caves – miss them out completely. It's a longer route, granted, but less risk of getting trapped or shunted into the walls. I'm playing it safe.'

Will you:

Talk to the barman?	420
Listen to the conversation at the bar?	534
Leave?	426

64

'Oh that thing, it's nothing,' replies Harris, squirming uncomfortably in his chair. 'Something I found in Segg's private library, that's all.'

'Another library?' you ask, intrigued. You glance around at the hundreds of books on show. 'Is this not enough for him?'

The boy chews nervously at his bottom lip, clearly deliberating over his answer. You notice his eyes dart several times to the shelves next to the table. You follow his gaze, seeing nothing untoward.

'It doesn't matter,' says Harris, quickly. 'He'd roast me in an instant if he knew I'd been inside. Secrets are secrets, after all.'

Will you;

Ask what he is reading?	105
Examine the shelves?	577
Talk to Segg?	328
Return to the main courtyard?	113

65

You pick up the box, captivated by its level of craftsmanship. The lid has been painstakingly carved from ivory, its details inlaid with fine silver filigree. The design forms a glittering chain of leaves that march around the edges of the lid, framing its stunning centre-piece – a wolf sculptured in high relief, its head thrown back to howl at the moon.

Excited by what you might find inside, you quickly flip open the lid. Sadly, your hopes of finding treasure are quickly dashed. Its contents are plain and mundane – just some bottles of ink and a black-feathered quill. You doubt you will have much need of such items on your travels, but you recognise that the quill is well-made. Perhaps it will fetch a good price in a local village or town, to help purchase supplies for your journey home. If you wish you may now take the *black feather quill*. (Simply make a note of it on your hero sheet, it does not take up backpack space.)

As your eyes drift back to the bubbling pot of stew, a scrape of boots outside the cabin alerts you to danger. Turn to 102.

66

You urge Skoll to let the creatures go, preferring to focus your attention on the corpses. It appears that each man was killed by a single puncture wound straight to the heart. You cannot fathom how a group of nine men, all hardy-looking and armed with knives and other blades, were clearly taken unawares and each killed in exactly the same fashion.

'This isn't the work of the svardkin,' says Skoll, his brows bunched together. 'Cowardly creatures – scavengers after easy gain.'

'These men were miners.' Anise struggles to lift one of the picks. 'Wonder why they came here?'

'Probably lost their way,' you reply, shrugging your shoulders. 'Like us.'

You search the bodies for anything of interest. Unfortunately, apart from some dry rations and extra clothing, you only manage to salvage 20 gold crowns and a bundle of explosives. (If you wish to take the *explosives* simply make a note of them on your hero sheet, they don't take up backpack space.)

As you finish refastening your pack, you catch a sudden movement at the far end of the cave – a ball of yellow light, darting quickly from side to side. It almost looks like an eye. Before you can alert the others the wisp zips away, heading for a different tunnel to the one the svard-kin took.

Will you:

Follow the yellow light?	**285**
Try and catch up with the svardkin?	**160**

67

After picking your way carefully over the boulders, you start your ascent. At first hand- and foot-holds are numerous, allowing you to progress with relative ease. But then the wind begins to buffet you, blinding you with snow and making your purchase on the slippery ice-wall less secure.

To reach the ledge, you must take a challenge test (note: if you have the ability *ice hooks*, you may lower the challenge total to 8):

	Speed
Scale the ice	14/8

If you are successful, turn to 174. If you fail the challenge, turn to 535.

68

You throw open the door to the cabin, startling Sylvie who is serving up eggs and sausage onto a plate. She drops what she is doing, hurrying around the table. 'Hel's tears, what's got into you, boy? Are you all right?'

'Inquisitor!' you manage to gasp, struggling to catch your breath. 'The one I was with . . . the one I think . . . something is wrong. He is after me.'

Sylvie draws back, eyes widening. 'Please, not the Church. Not here. You can't bring them here!' Frantically, she snatches a cloth bag from a coat hook, then hurries to her worktable. 'You can't stay, not safe.' She sweeps the charms into the sack, then pauses to pick out several of the bottles. 'Take these.' She drops them inside the bag, her hands trembling with fear. 'Take them away.'

Sylvie pushes the sack into your arms.

'What?' You look down at it, confused, then back at Sylvie. 'Is there nowhere for us to hide – anywhere we can go?'

'Not we. You! You're going far away from here!' The woman ushers you to the door. 'I can't have the inquisition sniffing into my affairs. My charms, my magic – they'll have me for a heretic. Be gone!'

Before you can argue, you find yourself back outside the cabin. The door slams closed behind you, followed by the sound of bolts being dragged into place.

You open up the sack and rummage through its contents. You have now gained the following items:

Wytchwood wreath	Clove oil	Crushed mugwort
(necklace)	(2 uses)	(2 uses)
	(backpack)	(backpack)
Ability: protection	Use any time in combat to restore 3 *health*	Use any time in combat to raise your *speed* by 2 for one combat round

You scan the nearby hills, your gaze halting on the menacing silhouette of the inquisitor, lurching towards you like one of the demons from your nightmares. With no other option, you hurry away from the cabin, making for the tangled confines of the forest. Turn to 244.

69

The haft of a blade cracks into your skull, sending you stumbling against the wall. Another blow drops you to your knees. Then everything is darkness. You feel yourself drifting away, the cold of the Norr pulling you into its embrace . . .

Suddenly there is a powerful rush of magic, hitting you head on – driving your spirit back into your dead limbs.

'Nanuk . . .' you gasp.

Your eyes flash open, startling the thief who is about to make off with one of your weapons. He scampers away, leaving you a clear view of the alley. Apart from a few wary onlookers, there is no sign of the ruffians or the monk. Cursing your ill-luck, you quickly check your belongings. All of your backpack items have been taken (remove these from your hero sheet), as well as half of your gold (rounding up). Staggering to your feet, you resume your journey. Turn to 659.

70

You have only gone a little way into the hills before you hear a mewling growl, followed by the rending and tearing of flesh. Drawing your weapon, you advance cautiously, fearing what you may find.

As you crest the hill, you see a body lying sprawled in a circle of flattened grass. It is covered in green-black scales, with bony spines protruding from its shoulders and head. A scrawny-looking wildcat is trying to chew at one of the arms, where the birds have picked clean most of the scales. On seeing you, the animal raises its blood-flecked nose, revealing a set of overlong fangs either side of its jaw. Too late, you realise you have wandered into the path of a sabre-toothed cat – and it doesn't look pleased at having its meal interrupted. It is time to fight:

	Speed	Brawn	Armour	Health
Sabre cub	1	2	0	30(*)

(*) Once the cub is reduced to 10 *health* or less, it will bolt into the grass, fleeing the combat. If you are victorious, turn to 364. If you lose the combat, remember to record your defeat on your hero sheet. You may then attempt the combat again or return to the map.

71

The fight turns from a scrappy one-sided affair into a match of equals, as your magic boosts your strength and allows you to keep time with Barl. You soon realise that the instructor follows the same series of moves, lacking any flair or spontaneity. As a child you would have been impressed with such a display, but now experience has turned you into a hardened fighter.

You read his moves with ease, dodging and ducking to find the openings in his guard. The instructor's quiet confidence is soon reduced to a surly rage, spitting curses as he seeks to get back into the fight. You remain one step ahead, anticipating his predictable retaliation. A desperate lunge leaves him impaled, his jaw dropping open in astonishment.

'Consider today's lesson over,' you sneer, watching as the veteran's lifeless body slips to the ground.

If you are a warrior or rogue, turn to 314. If you are a mage, turn to 591.

72

A service hatch opens in the wall, revealing a display of potions, creams and ointments. You notice that most of the items have parchment labels attached to them, covered in lengthy descriptions.

'What do you recommend?' you ask, struggling to read the labels from where you are standing.

'For you?' There is the sound of someone sucking air between their teeth. 'I'd buy the whole darn shop for that ugly mug of yours. Unless yer treat that frost bite, you'll be short of a few extremities. Fifteen gold each – not bad for a beauty treatment, eh? And same for the spirits, if you wanna put some fire back in yer soul. Makes good paint stripper too.'

You go to grab one of the potions.

'Hey, wait up!' barks the trader, making you jump back in surprise. 'Be sure to read the small print now. I don't do refunds. Once you take it, that's it!'

You may purchase any number of the following, for 15 gold crowns each:

Healing balm	White wolf spirits	Cure all
(2 uses)	(2 uses)	(1 use)
(backpack)	(backpack)	(backpack)
Created in a factory	May induce bouts of	Irresponsibly tested
that may contain nuts	howling and delirium	and environmentally
Ability: pick 'n' mix	Ability: punch drunk	unfriendly
		Ability: cure

You may continue to purchase items from the trader (turn to 151), discuss something else (turn to 685) or leave (return to the quest map).

73

You push the creature away, gagging at the smell of its filthy body and rotting, soiled clothes. As you scrabble free, still shaking from your ordeal, you can't help but feel a momentary pang of guilt. This is the second life you have taken – first the Martyr's and now the fengle. You glance down at the black blood pooling around the creature's body. It had been self-defence, you remind yourself; you had no other choice.

You turn the dagger in your hands. It is nothing more than a jagged splinter of rock, filed to a sharp point. It is crude, but might prove useful in these dangerous woods. You also notice a blue stone attached to a leather cord around the fengle's neck. Pulling it free, you see that it contains the spiral markings of a fossilised shell. The fengle obviously scavenged it, believing it to be special. If you wish, you may now take any / all of the following items:

Shale knife	Fengle's fossil
(main hand: dagger)	(necklace)
+1 brawn	Ability: charm

You turn your attention back to the standing stone, curious as to who would have placed it here and why. However, as you go to take a closer look a series of guttural calls ring out from the trees to your left, accompanied by the sound of feet splattering through wet mud. It appears the fengle was not alone. You glance back at the stone, wondering if you will have time to examine it before the creature's companions are upon you.

Will you:
Stay and investigate the stone?	133
Hurry back into the forest?	175

'Bowfinch,' the woman nods, putting the tankard back. 'All right, but you can pay up front, no way that's going on a tab. You know I only got two bottles, part of the shipment for Lord Eaton's party. If you're lucky, they're still unopened, so I can sell you one – a hundred gold. You got that kind of money? Otherwise, don't waste my time.'

If you wish to purchase a bottle of Bowfinch '55, turn to 334. Otherwise, you decline the offer and turn back to the taproom. Return to 80.

75

The ground gives a violent shudder. Strong enough to almost throw you off balance. Unlike previous tremors, this one does not abate, continuing to rattle and judder as you feel some powerful force start to build.

'What's happening?' You look to Rook, who has stopped in the middle of the passageway, his head cocked to one side. He goes to speak . . .

Then everything is thrown into a tilting, reeling chaos.

From the chapel you hear a splintering crack. You look back to see the statue of Judah riven in two, a deep fissure cutting across his face and chest, severing the lines of scripture carved into the stone.

Rook is already headed for the feast hall, ducking through streams of falling dust. You follow without question, bouncing and scraping from one wall to the next as the ground continues to shift beneath you. When you reach the hall, you see guards hurrying towards the main doors. Several emerge from side passages, still buckling on armour, their dishevelled appearances and bleary eyes suggesting they have just awoken.

The tremors intensify, sending cracks racing through the ground and along the walls. From somewhere in the distance you hear a thunderous crashing of stone. You cover your head, feeling spots of mortar patter down from above.

'We have to get out!' Rook grabs a bewildered soldier, pushing him towards the main doors. 'Move it!' He turns, gesturing to the others. 'Out! Into the yard! Now!'

All of a sudden, the shaking stops. Everyone stands frozen – waiting, listening . . .

Then you hear the distant screams. And a relentless drumming, like fists pounding against a barrier. The soldiers look at one another, confused.

'The wall . . .' Rook looks aghast. 'Something's assaulting the walls.'

One of the recruits snorts. 'Who'd attack us now – in the middle of a quake?'

The drumming continues, now accompanied by roars and screams of a different nature. They sound inhuman. 'That's the wards,' snaps Rook. 'They're being tested, broken. To the walls, men! To the walls!'

He makes for the open doors of the keep, the rest of you following close on his heels. Turn to 152.

76

You push open the door, startling the two undead guards who are feasting on some rotted remains. They lurch to their feet, blood dripping down their grey-mottled chins.

'Flesh . . .' says one, sniffing at the air with a half-decayed nose.

'Bones . . .' grins the other, a pale tongue worming out of its mouth.

With a wheezing groan, the two zombies lumber towards you, one dragging a broken ankle, the other hunched over with its shoulder bone protruding at an ugly angle from its links of chainmail. It is time to fight:

	Speed	Brawn	Armour	Health
Rattle	1	1	2	18
Ruin	2	2	1	15

Special abilities
♥ **Blood brothers**: When the first undead is defeated, the remaining zombie goes into a fit of rage, increasing its *speed* and *brawn* by 1 for the remainder of the combat.

If you manage to defeat the undead guardsmen turn to 448. If you lose the combat, remember to record your defeat on your hero sheet. You may then attempt the combat again or return to the map.

77

You make it through the glacier and onto the home straight – the walls of the prison now less than a mile to the south. Unfortunately, the racer who opted for the dangerous corkscrew is too far ahead to catch, but you can still battle for second and third place with the other competitors.

With a crack of your whip, you urge your dog-team between the nearest racers. Just as you are starting to pass them, your opponents swing their sleds into yours, hemming you in. Unable to manoeuvre out of the bottleneck, you find yourself hurtling towards a break in the ice.

You will need to take a challenge test using your *toughness* attribute:

	Toughness
Break out	12

If you are successful, turn to 519. If you fail, turn to 198.

78

Taking the bucket from the porch, you head to the creek. It proves easy to find, the chattering rush of noise leading you into a wooded dell. Along its base, white-frothed waters dance and splash, carving a zigzagging path amongst the trees. Turn to 155.

79

Along the walls of Ryker's Island, torches flicker like a thousand hungry eyes as the racers take their positions for the final race. To the north, across a landscape scoured by the descent of ice floes, you see the dark mountain known as 'Bleak Peak'. Its summit, little more than a hooked finger of rock, bent like a witch's hat, is every racer's goal – the first to reach the top of Bleak Peak will be announced the winner and receive the prized Winter Diamond.

Your competitors are all experienced veterans, having won through from the previous rounds. You cast your eye along the line of sleds – all bristling with spikes, armour and various mounted weapons. From the walls and inside the compound, you can hear the expectant crowds hollering for their favourites – you are even surprised to hear a few cries for 'ghost', your own racing handle.

Once again, the fur-clad man with the mosaic face takes to the wall, his fingers pointed skywards. 'The Peak has no mercy for fools. The Peak will break those who show fear. Only a true champion will take its crown. Racers ready! Get set . . . go!'

The fire has barely left his hand before the sleds are tearing forward, whips snapping through the air, the howls and snarls of the dog-teams quickly drowning out the hooting cheers from the prison walls. The race for Bleak Peak has begun! Turn to **614**.

80

The taproom resembles a large, high-ceilinged hall, not dissimilar to the great hall at Bitter Keep. But whereas that had been a cold, lifeless space devoid of mirth, the Coracle is bursting at the seams with busy tables, packed tightly together, and heaving crowds – filling the hall with a boisterous mix of laughter, singing and drink-fuelled chatter.

You move through the congested aisles, noting the grizzled features of the Coracle's clientele. You guess most of them must be whalers, going by their wind-burnt faces and ivory piercings.

Ahead of you is the main bar, with mounted heads of bears, muttok and wolves glaring back from its far wall. An olive-skinned woman, her face partly disfigured by a scar, is serving up ale to the thronging masses. To your left, a number of men are sat around a table playing a game. They are holding a number of small round stones in their hands, marked with different symbols. Bets are being made as various players choose and discard stones, then reveal their hands.

Behind the gaming table you spy a doorway leading through to what you assume is a private room. Two rough-looking men in oiled black leathers stand on solemn guard, stopping and questioning those who wish to enter.

Will you:

Watch the gaming table?	14
Try and enter the private room?	123
Talk to the bar woman?	299
Leave?	659

81

'The southerners would like to think them barbarians, with no higher purpose than making war and worshipping heathen gods.' Everard raises an eyebrow, awaiting your response.

'Are you saying that is not the truth?' Every story you have ever heard has painted the Skards as fierce and bloodthirsty warriors, a warning of what becomes of a people when they are driven by their baser instincts. 'The Skards are a threat to our safety,' you persist. 'These very defences were built to keep those savages out of Valeron. They *are* savages, Lord Everard.'

The knight's silence makes you nervous.

'They are hunters,' he states at last, turning his head to meet the rush of the wind. 'They struggle daily against what life chooses to throw at them. Look at this place, Arran. Do you see land for crops, for homes, for a life? The further north you go, where rock turns to ice – where life balances on such a fine edge – that is when you start to appreciate who they really are.'

'You speak highly of them,' you cut in sharply. 'Considering your post, Lord Everard, I would have expected you to hold a grudge, not sympathise with our common enemy.'

Everard bristles at that – you can see it in the set of his jaw, the sudden brightness that flares in those steely eyes. 'Our enemy is whatever chooses to beat down these walls, Arran. Goblins, trolls, demons – and worse. The Skards were our enemy once, just like the others. They were organised, had a strong leader. Death and hardship had taken its toll, so yes, they desired our soft lands of comfort and gluttony. I wonder, who wouldn't? And they'd have won, but for the fact they were routed – lost their leader and, with him, their spirit. So now the tribes are scattered, bickering and fighting between themselves – lost out there in that cruel wasteland, trying to make the best of it, like the rest of us.'

Everard releases a pent-up breath, misting the air.

You nod, by way of apology. 'Indeed. It seems I have much to learn, my Lord.'

'Bah, don't sweat it. You're no different to anyone else,' grunts the knight. 'We all need an enemy, a monster to pit our strength against. You've just got to learn to choose the right fight.'

Will you:

Ask about the Keep's defences?	130
Climb the stairs to the mage tower?	301
Return to the main courtyard	113

82

The frost forge is now yours to use. If you are a warrior, turn to 410. If you are a mage, turn to 394. If you are a rogue, turn to 428.

83

The top of the shaft is covered by a tangled mesh of wood and bark, held together by clods of dried mud and what smells like rotted meat. Grimacing from the stench, you grapple onto the edge of the rock and then push yourself up through the debris.

You clamber out onto solid ground, the blustery wind beating most of the wood and stinking mud from your body. As you look around, half-blinded by the light, you realise that you have emerged inside a giant nest, perched on top of a chimney of rock. Several large eggs lie scattered around you, as well as bones, feathers and some half-eaten remains.

Before you can clamber free, you hear an ear-piercing shriek. A shadow passes overhead, blotting out the light. You look up, just in time to see an immense black-feathered bird swooping down, its blood-stained talons spread wide to grab you. It is time to fight:

	Speed	Brawn	Armour	Health
Roc	2	1	1	25

Special abilities

♥ **Perilous plunge**: If the roc wins a combat round, roll a die. If the result is ⚀ or less, instead of rolling for a damage score, the roc picks you up in its talons, flies up into the air, then throws you back to the ground. This attack causes 5 damage, ignoring *armour*, and lowers your *speed* by 1 in the next combat round. (You cannot use a dodge ability, such as *evade* or *vanish* to avoid this.) If the result is ⚁ or more, the roc rolls for a damage score instead.

If you manage to overcome this bird of prey, turn to **356**. If you lose the combat, remember to record your defeat on your hero sheet. You may then attempt the combat again or return to the map.

84

Your weapon shreds through the ghost's body, drawing out deafening shrieks of pain. Within moments, nothing of it remains but a few wisps of smoke which quickly diffuse into the mist. Exhausted from the fight, you slump against the statue, your relief tainted by the knowledge that there will be more – a lot more.

As if on cue, a shrieking wail rends the air, followed by a whole dirge-like chorus. Then something deeper, more powerful, raises its voice above the din – a thunderous roar suggestive of a monstrous abomination.

You scan your surroundings, trying to gauge which direction they are coming from. This hiding place no longer feels safe. Through the banks of fog you start to see shapes. More shadows creeping across the sand, their black claws grasping towards you. And behind them a giant of darkness, with red burning eyes and a crown of iron spikes.

You turn and run, heading in the opposite direction, letting the strange mist engulf you once again. This is how every dream plays out – you run, you hide, you run . . . The only certainty is that you have to survive.

The landscape changes quickly, becoming a plain of stunted blackened trees and weathered boulders, all sculptured into leering demonic faces. In the distance you can dimly make out a line of mountains, their edges picked out by flickering pulses of green lightning. They are the only notable landmark on this hellish plain so you decide to head towards them, hoping their slopes might offer some protection.

But it seems the dream will not let you escape so easily. As you hurry between the sculptured rocks, you hear a fresh peal of demonic cries. Within seconds they come into view, bright against the green mist. Their bodies blaze like hearth fires, crackling and hissing as they scamper on all fours. There is a whole pack of them, closing in from both sides. You know you can't possibly fight them all, there are too many – maybe twenty or thirty.

'Wake up!' you scream at yourself. 'Wake up!'

You stumble and fall, crashing down onto the cold sandy floor. The nearest group of demons skid past then hurry back, their mouths cracking open to reveal fangs of charred black stone. You cover your face in terror as the heat from their bodies draws close, singeing your clothing. 'Wake up,' you screech. 'WAKE UP!' Turn to 47.

85

It feels like walking against a flood. All around you currents of sand and stone fly past, screaming and howling with angry voices, ripping at your cloak, battering against your armour, whipping you with sharpened lengths. The deluge is blinding, disorienting, filling your vision with a chaotic confusion – as if the very land itself has risen up against you, seeking to thwart your progress.

You stumble onwards. Unharmed. The flying rubble passes through your spirit body, leaving no mark or scratch, nothing but a tingling cold. Only your clothing suffers from the assault: metal now scoured and dented, cloth shredded to tatters. (You must lower a single attribute by 1 on a head, chest or cloak item.)

Your magic keeps you anchored, powering each stride, stopping you from being lifted off into the storm. But it takes every ounce of willpower, pitting your mental strength against that of the wind: two elements fighting for dominion.

The wind shows no mercy, throwing itself against you in endless waves, its own will bent on punishing you. Breaking you.

The old Arran would have given up and let the storm have its way. The old Arran would not have had the strength to endure such might. But you have been forged anew – through pain and sacrifice and death. You meet its fury with your own. Another step and then another.

Just when it feels you have nothing left to give the wind loses its vigour, the walls of sand gradually thinning to a pattering rain. A few more strides and the storm is behind you – its roiling waves curving overhead, like a giant dome.

And beneath it, a city of ruins.

The architecture is both alien and familiar – a collision of different styles, as if its makers worked in isolation rather than unison. Jagged towers and broken-topped halls give way to grand and opulent palaces. Beyond them huge angular edifices rise high as mountains, scraping the very heights of the storm, their immense shadows deep and far-reaching.

You walk along the deserted spaces, the ground dry and cracked, contoured into uneven ripples suggesting the passage of water in times past. Dark lichen crawls out of cracks in walls, creepers hang like dirty cobwebs from arches and bridges. Each building appears hollow, empty. Occasionally, you spy shapes out of the corner of your eye – shadows hovering in doorways and windows. But each time you look they appear to elude you, refusing to be seen.

And then there is the heat. A stifling presence. It rises up out of crevasses and fractures in the rock, expelling an acrid smoke into the air. You cannot fathom what evil is at work beneath your feet – turning this once frozen land into a desert.

You head deeper, the wind still dogging your steps, dragging half-heard voices along the deserted streets. At times you are sure you catch a maddened cry or a peal of laughter, but when you try and discern its source you find yourself wandering lost and confused amidst an ever-branching maze of avenues, their crumbling buildings staring back in vacant silence. Mocking.

Not a city. A graveyard.

And yet, somewhere amongst these forgotten ruins, there has to be the source of the storm. Perhaps the witch herself . . .

You cast out your mind like a net, extending invisible tendrils of magic, feeling for other traces of power. Amongst the buildings there are glimmers, perhaps other souls lost and damned amongst the wreckage – but they are mere candle flames to the sun-sized power that burns intensely . . . right ahead of you.

The street is empty.

You lift your eyes, scanning the walls and rooftops until you spot the creature, squatted on an irregular mass of rubble atop a high tower. It has the appearance of a gigantic fly, black bodied and covered in hair, with six spiny legs splayed out across the rocks. The demon's head comprises a single compound eye, its fractured surface glittering like a dark jewel. It stares out across the ruined city, focused on something distant . . .

The storm.

As you watch, the demon spreads its wings; four immense membranes of midnight black, pitted with white orbs. The wings extend vertically into the sky, rocking back and forth like the sails of a ship – each one moving independently of the others. You feel a prickling against your mind, a sense that . . . you are being watched.

In horror, you realise the true nature of the white orbs. They are eyeballs. Hundreds of them.

One of the wings snaps rigid. From the beast's head three tentacle-like appendages burst out from beneath the main eye, their ends snaking round to face you.

Quickly you race for cover as the street is engulfed in a torrent of oily-black ooze, splatting across the cracked red earth. A second later a jet of fire hits the oil, setting it alight. The heat is other-worldly, a spirit-fire. You scrabble over broken rubble, seeking to put distance between yourself and the searing blaze.

The wings snap round once again, searching for you. Using the debris as a shield you make for a crumbling wall, vaulting off a hunk of masonry to reach the top then jumping again to catch a ledge on a facing building. You draw back into a recess, peering cautiously round its edge, studying the demon's tower.

The interior floors have collapsed, making it impossible to ascend from the ground, but above you an adjoining bridge offers a way across, allowing you to scale the outer walls to the summit. An easy enough climb, if you can avoid being spotted. It is time to fight:

	Speed	Magic	Armour	Health
Sentinel eye	13	8	5	40(*)
Sentinel wings	13	6	7	60
Acid proboscis	12	5	9	30
Oil proboscis	12	5	9	30
Fire proboscis	12	5	9	30

Special abilities

🛡 **Deadly ascent**: This combat is played differently to a normal combat. In order to reach the sentinel you must first scale the tower whilst avoiding its gaze. To achieve this, you must take three *speed* challenges to reach the summit. Any time the result is 19 or less, you have been spotted – and must roll and apply the following damage/effect:

⚀ or ⚁ You are hit by the oil proboscis. This inflicts 1 damage die, ignoring *armour*, and reduces your *speed* by 2 for the next challenge test or combat round.

⚂ or ⚃ You are hit by the fire proboscis. This inflicts 1 damage die, ignoring *armour*. If, in the previous test or combat round, you were hit by oil, this damage is increased to 2 damage dice.

⚄ or ⚅ You are hit by the acid proboscis. This reduces your *armour* by 2 (each time) for the duration of the combat. Once your *armour* is reduced to zero, you must take 1 damage die instead.

If a proboscis has already been defeated, you can ignore its effect and move onto the next challenge.

If the result is 20 or more, you pass the challenge test. Once you have completed three challenges (passed or failed), you have reached the top and can attack the sentinel as normal, rolling for attack speed/damage etc.

🛡 **Blind the eye:** (*) To win the combat you must defeat the sentinel eye by reducing its *health* to zero. However, you can only attack and apply damage to the sentinel eye once the wings and the three proboscises have been defeated. Otherwise, it is immune to all damage effects.

🦋 **Proboscis strikes:** If you take health damage from a proboscis in regular combat, you must also apply its effect (see deadly ascent). For example, if you lost a combat round to the fire proboscis you would take damage from its damage score – and also roll an extra die for its fire effect.

🦋 **Wing buffet:** If the sentinel wings and at least one proboscis are still in play, roll a die at the end of each combat round. If the result is ⚀ or less you are knocked back to the ground and must start your ascent again (see deadly ascent). ⚁ or more, there is no effect. (This ability only comes into effect once you are in regular combat with the sentinel.)

If you manage to defeat this ocular menace turn to **588**.

86
Quest: The Dread Gulf Dare

(You must have the keyword *kitchens* on your hero sheet before you can begin this quest.)

Anise puts a hand on your arm, steering you along the narrow tunnel. You surrender to her direction, no longer able to focus, the pain and cramping in your limbs only getting worse.

'We're almost there,' she insists, her voice pitched low.

You try to answer, but a jolt of pain causes you to bite down on your tongue. All around you the walls glimmer with magic, their holy scripture forming dizzying whorls before your blurred vision. *How did I get talked into this?* Ahead of you, a line of torches splutter blue flames along the low-ceilinged passageway. The bright procession stretches as far as the eye can see.

'I have to go back . . .' you gasp at last, batting at the air. 'The walls . . . the scripture . . . it burns . . .'

'We're here now, shush!' Anise swings you round, to a small arch-way in the wall. You would have easily missed it, still hobbling along the tunnel – to who knows where.

You duck down, entering an even narrower passageway. At its end it opens out into a small room, where a solitary guard is slumped in a chair, head resting on the table. He snores loudly, his breath blowing crumbs across his half-eaten plate of food.

Behind him an iron portcullis has been raised, leaving an open archway to the chill night air.

'Good, the sleep powder has worked,' whispers Anise, moving to one of the torches along the wall. There is a clatter of metal as she struggles to lift it out of the sconce. As you go to help her, the guard murmurs in his sleep, snorting out a long deep breath. For a moment, you both freeze, watching him – waiting until his breathing becomes regular again.

Anise gives a sigh of relief. 'The recipe was one of Segg's,' she says, lifting the torch free. 'He won't rise 'til morning.'

'This was a bad idea,' you reply, gripping your pounding head.

'Oh come on, grumpy.' Anise snatches your arm and turns you to face the open doorway. 'It will be fun.'

You allow yourself to be guided by the kitchen girl, out through the postern gate and onto a ledge of cracked rock. It winds around the edge of the rift, joining with a jagged causeway that criss-crosses its way to a lone tower, standing ominous and silent against the twilight sky.

Where the ledge meets the causeway, you see two figures waiting for you – one holding a torch similar to Anise's. In the circle of blue light, you can dimly make out a scarecrow-thin figure in robes and a taller companion, broad and muscular.

As you near, the robed figure steps forward, pulling back their cowl.

'What the – what you bring corpse-stink for?' The stranger exclaims in a whiney high-pitched voice.

You recognise him instantly as Harris, Segg's young apprentice. The boy clutches a large leather-bound book to his scrawny chest, continuing to glare at you with a petulant frown.

'Hey, you never said *she* was coming!' The taller companion lowers his torch, thrusting it forward to illuminate both your faces. The male is only a few years older than Harris, clad in a thick fur cloak and a weathered coat – both straining to contain his brawny physique.

'I had to,' snaps Harris. 'I needed her to slip the powder to the guard.'

The larger warrior snorts. 'I ain't spending a night with a Skard.'

'You don't have a choice, Brack,' says Harris, glaring up at his companion. 'Or I'll tell everyone you wimped out – you failed the dare.'

Brack looks about to argue, then falls into an angry silence.

'What is this dare?' you ask, looking from one to the other.

'Oh, did your girlfriend not tell you?' pipes up Brack, eyes narrowing at Anise. 'We gonna spend a night – a whole night – out there, across the Dread Gulf.' He turns and points to the lone tower, perched precariously on the spit of rock. 'We're spending a whole night in the Necromancer's Tower.'

Will you:

Ask who came up with the idea?	171
Ask what is so special about the tower?	203
Ask about the book Harris is carrying?	266
Try and convince them it's a crazy idea?	225
Continue to the tower?	297

87

Most of the other racers have also opted to steer clear of the snow. However, in order to avoid the fractures and broken areas of the ice-sheet the sleds are forced to bunch together. You soon find yourself hemmed in on both sides by fellow racers. The competing dog-teams snap and bite at one another, harnesses quickly becoming tangled as the fight grows more intense.

You will need to take a challenge test using your *toughness* attribute:

	Toughness
Grid lock	9

If you are successful, turn to 581. Otherwise, turn to 460.

88

You push open the double-doors and enter the hall. A dozen men are seated at the trestle tables, tucking into bowls of warm porridge.

Most of them look tired, eating in silence. Others lean close, sharing hushed stories, occasionally breaking into low hums of laughter. You suspect these must be the night watch, fresh back from duty. Anise is hurriedly rushing between the men, refilling mugs and clearing dishes. She catches your eye for an instant, then continues to attend the soldiers.

If you have the keyword *gains* on your hero sheet, turn to 277. Otherwise, you see no reason to stay here, so return to the main courtyard. Turn to 113.

89

'Ahh, you do have a kind heart,' says the bard, nodding. 'And for that, you should be rewarded.' She reaches down to her belt and unfastens a pouch of gold, then tosses it to you. Opening it up, you find 50 gold crowns inside.

If you are a rogue, turn to 618. Otherwise, Talia blows you a kiss and then departs, leaving you alone in the secret laboratory. Turn to 747.

90

For defeating the mage, you may now help yourself to one of the following rewards:

Depth plungers	Gulf climbers	Abyssal spike
(feet)	(gloves)	(main hand: dagger)
+1 speed +1 armour	+1 brawn	+1 speed +2 brawn
Ability: knockdown	Ability: barbs	Ability: bleed
(requirement: warrior)		(requirement: rogue)

When you have updated your hero sheet, turn to 141.

91

The palace library held a number of books written by the Botany Society, one of which was filled with sketches of various fungi. You remember that some species are deadly and poisonous, whilst others can prove delicious to eat, and may even have special magical properties. Uncertain as to which category these strange toadstools will fall into, you cautiously edge closer to the nearest one, wrinkling your nose at the sulphurous smoke oozing from its tip. You can't imagine this would be good to eat, but appearances can sometimes be deceptive. Gingerly, you reach out with a finger and prod the toadstool cap . . .

Suddenly the air around you explodes in a mass of whirling, yellow spores. You stumble back, half-blinded by the assault, dimly aware that the rest of the toadstools have started to pump similar plumes of yellow spores into the clearing. Staggering through the haze, you try and spot a means of escape, but your blurred vision has left you disorientated. You knock into one of the toadstools, reeling away from its slimy surface only to blunder into another. They are all around you now, creaking and squelching closer – looking to trap you at the centre of their deadly ring of death.

Desperately, you look around for a means of defending yourself. Next to the scattered bones, you spot a broken branch of willow. With no other option, you hastily pick it up, brandishing it like a club. You have now gained the following item:

Whacking willow
(main hand: club)
+1 brawn

You realise your only chance of survival is to bash your way through the circle of toadstools. It is time to take on the might of:

	Speed	Brawn	Armour	Health
The terrorstools	0	1	1	12

Special abilities

♥ **Spore clouds**: You have been temporarily blinded. For the first two combat rounds only, you must lower your *speed* by 1.

If you manage to defeat these fearsome fungi, remember to restore your *health* to full, then turn to **185**.

92

(You may now remove the keyword *hunted* from your hero sheet.)

You recount your fight with the mammoth and the discovery of Bullet's corpse. Jackson is silent for a moment, his magnified eye pulling back from the peephole. 'Not sure what's harder to believe,' he says softly. 'You taking down a mammoth or Bullet running dry on luck.'

You lift up the metal hipflask that the tracker had been carrying. 'I have proof.'

The eye appears again, pressed up tight against the hole. Jackson gives a sigh. 'Yeah, that's his all right. Bless 'is soul.'

You hear a clink, then a hatch opens to the left of the trader. Resting on it is a small patch of white wolf fur.

'What's this?' you ask curiously, stepping forward to take a better look. The guns scrape against their metal windows as they follow you. 'May I?' you ask, hesitating.

'Go on, it's a trading voucher. My way of saying thank you – for tellin' me 'bout old Bullet.'

You pick up the fur, noticing a wolf's head insignia inked onto the skin's underside. (This is a *White Wolf Trading Voucher*. Simply make a note of the *voucher* on your hero sheet, it doesn't take up backpack space.) The voucher entitles you to one free item from the White Wolf Trading Post (either clothing, weapon or equipment).

If you wish to view available items, turn to **151**. Otherwise, turn to **685** to discuss something else, or return to the quest map to continue your adventure.

93

As you place the last of the wooden pieces into the growth rings a trail of light sweeps around each circle, forming a glowing pattern that radiates towards the centre. There is a sudden rumbling groan, then a tremor, causing the ground to shudder beneath your feet. Warily you back away to the edge of the room, drawing your weapons in readiness. There is another juddering tremor, then the centre circle starts to rise up out of the ground – and to your surprise, you discover it is a part of some monstrous wooden creature. Turn to 681.

94

'There's a hamlet two days to the south,' says Sylvie. 'Three if the weather's fouled up the trails. They're a friendly bunch around there, I make the trip several times a year, to get my paper and inks.' She glances towards the door. 'That sword of yours. You could probably trade it in for a horse or two and enough supplies to see you to the capital – probably convince a couple of the younger farmers to escort you. Sounds like the roads are getting dangerous now.'

You pick thoughtfully at the edge of your bowl. 'That's south. What about north?'

'North?' Sylvie blows out her cheeks. 'Why would you want to go north? Only things you'll find there are bears and wolves – and if they don't get you, the winter will. Think that pretty outfit will keep out the cold?' She shakes her head slowly. 'I don't think you even know what cold is, boy. Real cold. The type that snaps at your fingers and toes, and will steal them off in an instant!' She clicks her fingers, making you jump. 'The north will eat you up and spit you out, boy. Go south. That's what'll get you home the safest.'

Return to 191 to ask another question, or turn to 207 to end the conversation.

'So, what yer got?' asks Hal, peering at your bulging backpack with hungry eyes. 'I'll take whatever odds and ends you're willing to spare. I can always put something to use, patching up me old girl.'

Hal will purchase any of the following items:

Item	Payment (in gold crowns)
Fenrir's fang	100
Giant's backbone	100
Winter diamond	200
Kraken oil	100
Venomous ooze	100
Maggorath's rot	100

You may now purchase first aid supplies (turn to 639), view Hal's weapons (turn to 728), inspect his treasures (turn to 674) or leave and return to the quest map.

96

For defeating the troll, you may now help yourself to one of the following rewards:

Gravel hooks	Spine back	Dusky spurs
(gloves)	(cloak)	(talisman)
+1 magic	+1 speed +1 armour	+1 magic
Ability: barbs	Ability: deflect	Ability: splinters

When you have updated your hero sheet, turn to 141.

97

'I was at Antioch, in Mordland. We'd been pulling back for months, losing ground to the dark templars. I was starting to question my faith.' Maune moves a hand to the cross, hanging from a silver chain against his breast. 'There were demons; too many to count, let alone fight. My brothers and sisters . . .' He stops, his face twisted by a pained memory.

'What happened?' you press, as the silence grows.

He sighs. 'I had a vision, when I was lying in the mud and filth and blood of that place. I thought I would die. I was resigned to it. But the One God in his mercy was not done with me; I still had work to do. He showed me this mountain and the devastation wrought by some darker force, bigger than any we would face in Mordland. I heeded His call – and so I came, travelling the length and breadth of Valeron to reach this . . . mountain.' He looks around with disdain, his nose wrinkling. 'I can sense evil here, but I have yet to find its source.' The paladin's eyes settle on your own, questioning and challenging at the same time.

Will you:

Ask about the markings on his skin?	367
Ask for food and water? (ends the conversation)	433
Attack the paladin? (ends the conversation)	486

98

'I must go home,' you state, looking around for your belongings. 'I must tell my father what has happened.'

'I don't think that is wise,' states Everard, scratching the side of his chin. 'You see . . . while you were out of it, we received news from the capital.'

His grave expression is an ill portent. 'What?' you ask, frowning. 'Is it my father?'

Everard winces. 'Look, there's no easy way of saying this – I would have liked to have waited, until you're—'

'Just tell me,' you snap impatiently.

'He's dead. And Malden too. They were murdered in their beds.'

You hesitate, thinking it a cruel exaggeration – some tavern rumour that has expanded in the telling. But the sombre masks staring back at you tell a different story.

'Mordland spies, so they say.' The robed man steeples his fingers, tapping his chin on them thoughtfully. 'There are some of us who believe otherwise – and your own tale would confirm those suspicions.'

You remain silent, too shocked to answer – your mind still reeling.

Everard sinks into a chair, looking suddenly weary. 'Since the second Shadow War, there has been a faction of the Church that has taken a more aggressive stance. The legion's invasion gave them the excuse they needed, to remind us all of the evils at our door – the evils of magic.' He glances towards Segg, who snorts dismissively. 'The Church's refusal to rebuild the university has angered many. Their desire to launch crusades into Mordland angered your father.'

'I'm the only surviving heir.' The realisation hits you like a thunderbolt. Your brothers, Malden and Lazlo, are now deceased. With no cousins, no nephews . . . .

'Cardinal Rile is acting as regent, for now,' says Everard. 'Until such a time as a new king takes the throne. Some are already denouncing your line as . . . weak. Bad blood.'

You lower your head, shamed by what your family has become. 'What am I to do?' you whisper, studying the vivid veins that branch across your skin. 'I don't even know what I am any more.'

'You'll remain here with us,' says Everard, rising out of his seat. 'To the other soldiers you are nothing more than a stray, brought in with the black fever. Still recovering, I might add – so that will explain your appearance.'

You flinch, putting a hand to your face and wondering what you will find there. 'I can't fight,' you reply, honestly. 'I never had the . . . strength before.' You glance down at the thick muscles bunched along your arms. In places, the skin is mottled with reddish-blue blotches. It reminds you of a corpse you once saw, laid out in the palace mortuary.

(You are now inflicted with *necrosis*. As one of the undead, you cannot die by ordinary means. However, each defeat that you suffer in battle can cause lasting damage to your hero's body. In the *defeats* box on your hero sheet, make a note of each time you lose a combat. For every *five* defeats, your hero must suffer one *death penalty*. When this occurs, roll a die to determine the penalty:

• **Weeping wounds.** In future combats, you must lose 1 *health* at the end of each combat round.

$\boxed{.\,^\bullet}$ **Crippled.** You can no longer use the ability associated with the item in your feet location.

$\boxed{.^\bullet}$ **Head blow.** Each time you wish to use a speed ability in combat you must roll a die. If the result is $\boxed{.\,^\bullet}$ or less, you fail to use the chosen ability. If the result is $\boxed{.^\bullet}$ or more, you can use the ability as normal. If an ability fails, you cannot attempt to use it or another speed ability until the following combat round.

$\boxed{::}$ **Fingerless.** You must immediately destroy an item in one of your ring locations, making the necessary adjustments to your attributes. (Note: If you find a new ring on your adventures, you can equip it as normal in the empty slot.)

$\boxed{\vcenter{\hbox{$\cdot\!\cdot$}}}$ **Nervous twitch.** You can no longer use the ability/abilities associated with the item in your main hand location.

$\boxed{!\,!}$ **Chronic convulsions.** If your *health* drops below 10 in future combats, you must lower your *speed* by 1 for the remainder of the combat.

Each penalty takes immediate effect and lasts until the end of your adventure (or until you have opportunity to remove it) – with the exception of fingerless, which ends once your ring is destroyed. If you roll on the death penalty chart and would receive a penalty that your hero is already inflicted with, you must reroll the die until you receive a different/new penalty.

'You'll be trained,' says the knight firmly. 'For the next few weeks at least, until we can decide what to do with you. That means no special treatment, you'll just be like one of the new recruits. Lucky we had a fresh batch, so you'll fit in fine. Of course, you'll have to drop your name, take on a new identity here. You're a soldier now. Understand?' He crosses a hand to the grip of his sword, drawing it from its scabbard with a ring of steel. 'Kneel before me.'

You do as he asks, too shocked and fearful to say otherwise. Everard lifts his sword and touches you on each shoulder with the flat of his blade. The holy inscriptions spark and hiss, sending a foul-smelling smoke into the air. 'Do you agree to serve?'

'I do.' You lower your head, eyes straying to a cockroach as it wanders in and out of a crack in the stonework. 'I will serve.'

Everard turns his sword over, holding it aloft. The cross of the hilt forms a bright crucifix. 'As the sins of the cursed were once visited upon Judah, so may those sins be heaped upon you should you ever knowingly or willingly violate this solemn vow.' He steps back, gesturing for you to stand. 'Rise, soldier – I now pronounce you a knight of the Last Order.'

Turn to the first map to begin Act 1 of your adventure (see inside front cover). Choose where you want to visit by turning to the entry number displayed next to the shield. As a novice adventurer you may want to explore Bitter Keep first (turn to 113), before embarking on one of the green quests. Good luck!

99

You step away from the pitiful creature, lowering your weapons. 'No tricks,' you rumble, eyeing him suspiciously. 'I already tire of your games.'

The squirrel rolls back to his feet. Then he puts a hand to one of his many pouches.

'Not so fast!' You lunge forward, your weapons finding his throat once again. The squirrel leans away startled, his whiskers twitching.

'I offer no harm, rata-rata. Just a token . . . If I may?'

You nod warily, watching him closely as he pulls open a leather sack. After much rummaging, he produces a large silver acorn. He offers it out to you on the palm of his paw. 'Plant this in soil when you have need of me – and aid will come.'

You glare at the acorn, then back at Ratatosk. 'How do I know it won't summon another one of those monsters?'

'You don't,' he grins, his bristly tail curling over his shoulder. 'That's why it's a token of trust. Take it – I know the Norr like no one else. You may have need of my . . . powers.'

You have gained the *silver acorn* (simply make a note of this on your hero sheet, it doesn't take up backpack space). After pocketing the acorn, you look back at Ratatosk. The squirrel gives a mischievous chuckle, then scampers to the edge of the tree. 'Remember one thing, rata-rata.' His tail swishes to the side as he looks back. 'I am what I am, no more no less. But the witch, rata-rata . . . she has many servants, many faces.' With a peel of chattering laughter, he leaps off into the pale mist. Turn to 616.

100

Your next jump is mistimed, pitching you forward onto your stomach. As you scramble to your feet, three of the dogs successfully make the jump, their slavering jaws looking to tear you to pieces. You must now fight:

	Speed	Brawn	Armour	Health
Pack dog	2	1	1	12
Pack dog	1	1	1	10
Pack dog	0	1	1	10

Special abilities
♥ **Outnumbered**: At the end of each combat round, you must take 1 damage from each surviving opponent, ignoring *armour*. This ability only applies while you are faced with multiple opponents.

If you manage to send these dogs packing, turn to 280. If you lose the combat, remember to record your defeat on your hero sheet. You may then attempt the combat again or return to the map.

101

The prince is light on his feet, moving deftly from stance to stance, parrying your attacks and countering with his own. You quickly lose ground to his skilful onslaught, the green-tinged flames getting closer to your back. To your surprise they give off no heat, only a fierce burning cold. But the fire's pit is deep and sheer, its shaft stretching away to darkness.

'I expected more from you, Arran. A prince with your learning, the best weapon masters, the best tutors.' Sable's dark blade cuts across your cheek. You lean away, slashing for his midriff, but the prince has anticipated your blow, sidestepping it, his boot slamming into your knee. You stagger, thrown off balance.

'So disappointing.' Sable raises his sword, threatening a powerful overhead swing . . .

He gives a strangled gasp, stumbling away. 'Sleet . . .'

You sense him reaching out to the Norr, to his ancestor spirit. You do likewise, pushing your mind into Nanuk's.

You see and taste the dead wolf . . . hanging lifeless in the bear's jaws. Nanuk has been victorious and now his power floods into you, renewed and focused.

Snarling, you leap for the prince, realising that you now have the upper hand. With Sable's wolf defeated, his powers are now weakened. It is time to fight:

	Speed	Magic	Armour	Health
Sable	13	8	7	80

Special abilities

♥ **Might of chaos**: Each time Sable wins a combat round, roll a die to determine the nature of his attack:

⚀ or ⚁ Sable heals himself instead of rolling for a damage score, restoring 5 *health*. (This cannot take him above his starting *health* of 80.)

⚂ or ⚃ Sable rolls for a damage score as normal.

⚄ or ⚅ Sable inflicts a curse on you. This causes three dice of damage to your hero, ignoring *armour*, and stops you playing any speed or combat abilities in the next combat round.

If you manage to defeat the dark prince, turn to 658.

102

The door is nudged open and a woman enters carrying a basket. She is plump and stocky, dressed in a plain wool tunic and heavy overcoat. A fringe of grey hair pokes out from beneath her hood. When she sees you, her face takes on an accusing frown.

'I . . . I didn't mean . . . I'm . . . lost,' you stutter quickly, raising your hands in a show of surrender. Noticing the dried blood on your cuffs, you lower them abruptly.

The woman's eyes move to your sword, her frown deepening.

'I . . . I can explain,' you reply, offering what you hope is your friendliest smile.

'Go on, then,' mutters the woman stiffly. 'Surprise me, but it better be good.'

Will you:

Admit you are a prince who was attacked by Wiccans? 276

Pretend you are a simple traveller in need of shelter? 219

103

As you pull onto the winding pathway that snakes round the mountain you experience a sudden lurch, accompanied by a scraping thud. Twisting in your seat, you see a grapple embedded in the back of your craft, its metal chain stretching back to another racer who is clutching the other end. He is skidding along on the remains of his own sled, which amount to a few boards of wood and a skin of leather.

'Extreme sports, man!' he shrieks, waving his fist in the air.

Your dog-team start to slow, straining against the extra weight of your unwelcome passenger. Unless you can cut them loose quickly, you will be overtaken by the other racers. Not only that – the man has now drawn a wand from his belt, its tip igniting with bright sparks. Cackling with insane glee, he thrusts the wand in your direction, sending a flurry of bolts towards your zigzagging sled.

To break through the chain you will need to take a challenge test using your hero's *brawn* or *magic* score:

	Brawn/Magic
Easy rider	16

If you are successful, turn to 267. Otherwise, turn to 708.

104

The clerk lifts his stock of furs and places them inside a wooden crate. When he turns back to you, he is shaking his head. 'Poor quality, barely worth the shipping. Think all the best trappers must have got eaten up by one of them crevasses that keep appearing. So, what about you, eh? Make it quick, 'cos I'm shutting up shop.'

The clerk will purchase the following items from you:

Items:	Payment (in gold crowns)
White fox pelt	25
Muttok pelt	40
Yeti pelt	60
Sasquatch pelt	100
Mammoth pelt	150
Chipped emerald	30
Flawless emerald	100
Flawless ruby	150

Remember to remove any sold items from your hero sheet. (Note: If you have the *trapper* career, you can increase the value of each pelt by 5 gold.)

If you have a *hunter's chest* and/or a *locker*, turn to 309. Otherwise, with your business now concluded, you decide to leave. Turn to 659.

105

The mage grins, evidently pleased that you have shown an interest – and given him a chance to show off. 'I'm studying perfective and progressive inflections,' he says, patting the open book in front of him. 'They give extra power to runes – I shouldn't really be reading this stuff.' He glances nervously towards Segg's chamber. 'I have a magic reading age twice what it should be – I've already perfected apollonian circles, ones I don't think even graduates of the university could master.' He leans forward, dropping his voice. 'If old Seggie Singed-Pants had his way, I'd still be practising my minor morphemes. You believe that?'

You pass a hand over your head in a sweeping motion. 'What you just said – no clue. Magic is beyond me, I'm afraid.' You pick up another book, flicking through the endless sketches and diagrams. 'I prefer reading stories of adventure – you know, with characters and plot. This is . . . like homework.' You toss the book back onto the table.

'So like Brack,' mutters the boy, shaking his head. 'Learning magic – it's the best adventure ever.'

Will you:

Ask about the prism?	64
Examine the shelves?	577
Talk to Segg?	328
Return to the main courtyard?	113

106

The compound is a confusion of colour, shape and noise, from the brightly-coloured tents and awnings and the bustling throng of people; mostly travellers and sailors, but also high-born visitors, drawn here by the promise of adventure and the spectacle of the sled races. These well-dressed nobles are made conspicuous by their entourages – armed bodyguards and mercenaries, pushing and shoving their way along the tight avenues, one eye on their charges, the other on their belongings.

You head into a less crowded quarter, where the vicious snarling of dogs rises above the chatter and din. A series of wire pens have been set up along one of the walls, maybe fifty or more side-by-side, each holding its own dog-team. There are also kennels, with larger hounds chained to posts, growling and pulling at their restraints.

Next door to the pens, the churned snow has been scattered with greasy odds and ends. A gruff-looking man in oil-stained leathers is currently fixing up a sled with new runners. Behind him a row of finished sleds are lined up on display, all polished to a bright sheen.

'Time's running out! Grab a sled and sign up for the races – you don't want to miss out!'

You turn to see a large wooden board propped up against a ramshackle cabin. A man is currently gesturing to the board, where various names have been scrawled onto stretched parchment. 'Come along, sign up for the season. If you want to win the Winter Diamond, then take your chance on the ice!'

The muddy track continues to meander past the last of the tents, leading into a cleft between two granite outcroppings.

Will you:

107

You shoot out of the tunnel and straight into a dark storm of black bodies and buzzing wings. The insects are giant-sized and frenzied, covered from head to abdomen in ridges of chitinous black armour. A green venom drips from their razor-edged legs, which are already ripping into your transport with a hungry delight.

But they aren't your main concern.

Rising up behind them is a much larger creature, a colossal version of the black-armoured drones but with a bright crimson-hued shell. You suspect it must be the hive's queen. Her sharp mandibles flick back and forth, producing a harsh clacking sound. From the adjoining side tunnels you see more drones pouring into the chamber, evidently answering their queen's summons. It is time to fight:

	Speed	Brawn	Armour	Health
Razor queen	13	11	7	40
Razor swarm	12	10	5	60

Special abilities

🔰 **Queen in peril**: At the end of each combat round, if the queen is still alive the swarm's *health* is increased by 10. (Note: this ability can take the razor swarm above their starting *health*. Once the swarm is defeated, this ability no longer applies.)

🔰 **The swarm**: At the end of each combat round you must take 2 damage, ignoring *armour*. Once the swarm is defeated, this ability no longer applies.

🔰 **Fire at will**: You may use your *nail gun* or *dragon fire* ability in this combat.

If you manage to defeat the deadly swarm, turn to 754. (If you are defeated, remember to record your defeat as normal on your hero sheet, then turn to 15.)

108

With the cart destroyed, you have now lost everything on board. (Remove any collected barrels from your hero sheet. Also remove the keyword *envoy*, if you have it recorded.)

'Guess those thieves got their just deserts,' says Henna, glancing back at the soldiers' bodies.

'We'll send someone back for them,' you reply, your gaze still fixed on the smouldering debris. 'They deserve a proper burial.'

Henna nudges you. 'Hey, at least we can still return with something.' She points to the sack of items, still lying in the dirt. 'Shouldn't be too heavy for you,' she grins.

If you have the word *thievery* on your hero sheet, turn to 182. Otherwise, turn to 221.

109

You leave your chair and approach the nearest bookshelf, running a thumb along the many spines. Most appear to be scholarly works on plants and medicines. 'You have an admirable collection. Some rare books.'

'You're sounding quite the enthusiast,' says Sylvie.

'I grew up around them, that's all.' You shrug, as if it is of no consequence.

'Hmm, actually it was my late husband who was the real collector. But I've needed to keep up with the latest findings for my studies. Not always easy when you're reliant on tinkers and merchants for your supply.'

Your thumb comes to rest on a battered, leather journal. You pull it out, flipping open the pages to reveal a collection of notes and sketches, mostly categorising plant species.

'That was Randal's,' says Sylvie, moving to join you. 'He always was something of an obsessive. There are plenty more of those – I have a trunk full of them in the back room.'

Scanning through the rest of the journal, you stop suddenly on a drawing of a wolf, its eyes staring out at you from the page. 'And this?' You look questioningly at Sylvie, noting her troubled frown. She leans forward and takes the book from your hands.

'He was prone to dreams,' she states softly. 'That's how he met the wolf. Ghost walker.' She strokes the parchment with a distant look of longing. 'He believed the wolf watched over him. An ancestor spirit.'

Your mouth has suddenly gone dry. 'Dreams? What kind of dreams?'

Sylvie snaps the book closed and hands it back. 'Ones best forgotten.'

You return the journal to its resting place, your eyes lingering on the other books. Herbal remedies, plant medicines, potion recipes. 'These dreams . . . He was looking for a cure, wasn't he?' You absently finger the pouch at your belt. 'I've heard dragon leaf can be an effective relief.' You glance her way, curious as to her response.

Sylvie shakes her head, offering you a sad smile. 'A relief, yes. But not a cure.' She takes your arm and guides you back to the table. 'Come, there's more stew in the pot. Time for seconds, I think.'

Return to 191 to ask another question, or turn to 207 to end the conversation.

110

The bronze circle has a patterned motif engraved on its surface, depicting dragons and other creatures of the underworld. There is also a series of magical runes that twist from the edge of the circle to the black stone at its centre.

You cautiously approach the plinth, wary of a trap and unsure of its purpose. The stone stands waist high, smooth and rectangular, without adornment save for a small square depression carved into the top. You assume something must be placed in the niche for the magic to work.

If you have the *stone dragon* in your backpack, turn to 351. Otherwise, you are unable to interact with the structure. With nothing else of interest in the chamber, you decide to continue onwards. Turn to 2.

111

The staircase spirals round, bringing you into a narrow chamber where a pair of wooden shutters bang to and fro in the wind. A small wooden desk is pushed up against a corner of the room, where a figure sits hunched in a chair. They are dressed in a long white night shirt, with a nightcap resting lopsidedly on their head. They make no move to acknowledge your presence.

In the opposite wall, an unlit lantern sits in an alcove, next to an archway that leads through into a curving passageway.

Will you:

Try and speak to the stranger?	404
Continue through the room into the passage?	281

112

You start to close the gap, the racers ahead of you having slowed to a crawl to navigate the high winding ledge. Determined to move up the rankings, you crack your whip, urging your dog-team to quicken the pace – seeking to take the inside line on the next bend and pass one of your competitors.

They glance back, realising your intent, then respond by cutting in front of you, forcing your dog-team to swerve to avoid a collision. Desperately you fight to regain control of the sled and stop yourself from skidding off the edge into the grotto below.

You will need to take a challenge test using your *stability* attribute:

	Stability
The high wire	10

If you are successful, turn to 77. Otherwise, turn to 756.

(If this is your first time exploring Bitter Keep, turn immediately to 137. Otherwise, read on.)

You emerge from the tower, blinking like a new-born in the garish white light. Tugging your hood down low to shield your eyes, you brush past the guards standing station at the foot of the tower and head out into the flurry of quickly falling snow.

To either side of you two high walls of smooth black stone stretch away, widening to form a wedge-shaped courtyard. At its furthest end, the walls meet a tall, rectangular keep fronted by narrow windows and a pair of large double-doors. You assume this impressive building is the keep's main hall, where the soldiers take their meals.

To the left of the hall, the battlements rise via a set of stairs to a higher level, where a round tower stands stark against the pale sky. Everard had mentioned that Segg, the keep's resident mage, had a library and quarters there – and was keen to meet with you as soon as you were able.

Through an archway in the nearest wall, you spy a smaller yard where soldiers are sparring against one another. A gruff-looking trainer moves up and down the drill lines, barking orders and dispensing swift flicks of his leather crop at anyone too slow to follow instruction.

Back in the main courtyard, voices draw your attention. A small group of soldiers are milling around a set of snow-dusted statues. From this distance, it is difficult to discern what has caught their attention.

Will you:

Cross to the main hall?	186
Climb the stairs to the battlements?	168
Enter the training yard?	348
Investigate the statues?	153
Join a quest?	Return to the map

114

You hear a scrabbling sound and a man's grunting coming from behind you. Cautiously, you retrace your steps to see one of the Skards struggling to pull himself onto the plateau. A group of petrels are pecking at his hands, fluttering about his head and cawing. He goes to swat one of them away, his wild swing causing the rock to crumble from underneath him. For an instant he meets your gaze as he scrabbles for purchase, his expression caught between anger and fear. Then he drops in silence, the skittering of stones the only accompaniment to his long fall back to the ground. You peer over the edge to see the hunter's body sprawled in the dust below, his dog-team's frantic barking now reduced to sorrowful whines.

If you have the word *envoy* on your hero sheet, turn to 158. Otherwise, turn to 177.

115

Heading through the tunnels you find yourselves back at the ledge, overlooking the vast gulf and the roaring glacial waters below. Caul eyes the rock walls, looking for another means of re-entering the caves. He shrugs his shoulders in defeat. 'There's nowhere left to go.'

'Not exactly.' You step to the very edge of the outcropping and look over, watching the churning brown waters as they spill past the rocks then drop into the darkness below.

Caul moves to your side, confused by your intent, then gives a startled gasp when he realises what you are proposing. 'That's madness! You'd have us jump?'

'A leap of faith,' you nod, flicking a stone with your boot and watching it spin away into the abyss.

Caul retreats back to the wall, glaring at you as if you've gone mad. 'Let's go back, please. I'd rather take my chances with the flames and lightning.'

Will you:

116

You slide the ring free from the skeleton's finger. Holding it up to the murky light, you see that the band has been inlaid with a row of emeralds, each one intricately carved with its own runic symbol. If you wish, you may now take:

Shine

(ring)

Ability: heal

As you rise to your feet, you freeze when you hear a squelching sound coming from behind you. Spinning round, your eyes sweep across the ring of toadstools, looking for the likely cause. But the noise has gone and there is nothing there – although you are almost sure the toadstools have shifted position, standing a little closer to you.

Another squelch from somewhere behind. A quick look confirms there is nothing creeping up on you, but again, those toadstools . . . they look even closer now, their black bodies almost touching as they form a dark wall around the clearing. Turn to 202.

117

With effort, you manage to pull yourself out of the mud, using the gnarly rungs of the ladder for leverage. The level of the mire continues to rise, but you are able to stay one step ahead of it, climbing higher and higher up the shaft. As you near the top, you spy a nest of woven twigs and leaves cradled in a branch. Inside are a number of potions and a stone rune.

You may now help yourself to any/all of the following:

Flask of healing	Elixir of swiftness	Rune of fortune
(2 uses)	(2 uses)	(special: rune)
(backpack)	(backpack)	Use on any item
Use any time in combat	Increase your *speed* by 4	to add the special
to restore 10 *health*	for one combat round	ability *charm*

You resume your climb, but suddenly the ladder begins to shake and lurch. Looking down, you see that the mud has turned into a pair of giant hands, which have closed around the bottom rung. You try and ascend higher but the hands are pulling the ladder down, its frame creaking and shaking beneath you. The hands give another yank, then you are tumbling into darkness. Turn to 435.

118

Segg's study is deserted, the fire in the brazier reduced to a few flickering tongues of flame. In the wall opposite, where there had once been a bookcase, there is now an open doorway framed by cobwebs. Of the bookcase, there is no sign – making you wonder if it was an illusion all along.

The room beyond is pitch black. You wait a moment for your eyes to adjust. Slowly, you start to make out shapes – each edged with a shifting green light. A pile of books on a table. Candles set in niches around the curving walls. A chair and the outline of a man.

You walk into the centre of the room, eyes fixed on Segg. His robes shine bright, the rubies and other adornments gilded with a piercing green glow. You nod your head, wondering if the mage can see you as well as you can him. 'Segg?'

'I see you have the gift.' The ghostly figure nods his head, then raises the fingers of one hand. A whoosh of heat passes around the room, lighting each of the candles in turn. As it sweeps round you, the room is steadily filled with a soft flickering light.

Segg is seated in a high-backed chair, hunched forward slightly to scrutinise you with his shrewd, blue eyes. His long pale fingers play with the ends of his beard. 'Impressive. You are a natural.'

'I didn't do anything,' you reply, confused. You glance warily at the candles as their flames sputter and then appear to grow brighter.

'Most mages can't do what you do – not without many years of study and exercise, not without drawing from a kha. For you, the shroud is simply a part of your being. Magic is natural to you, like breathing.' He pauses, eyes flicking to your still body. 'If you'll excuse the expression.'

'Was that the test?' You put an edge to your voice, already feeling impatience.

'Oh no, this is the test.' Segg makes no movement, save a slight nod of his head. From three of the candles next to him, the flames roar up in a showering column – then fall back into the room, taking on the shape of humanoid creatures. They remind you of the demons from your dreams, their bodies fashioned from pure dancing flame. Moving on all fours, the sprites stalk towards you.

'What is this?' You draw your weapons, raising them defensively.

'Magic is about concentration,' says Segg, casually settling back into his chair. 'You can't be distracted. You need to focus.'

One of the sprites lunges for you, narrowly missing your leg by inches. You look down to see smoke curling from your charred breeches.

'The candles are the source of the demons' power.' The mage gestures lazily to the points of flame around the room. 'Snuff them out – using your mind.'

'My what? I'll give you a piece of my—' You dodge aside, letting a spear of flame pass by your ear.

'Concentrate!' Segg leans forward in his chair, shaking a clenched fist. 'Focus!'

The sprites have started to circle you like hounds, their bodies sparking brighter as they steal more of the fire from the surrounding candles. It is time to fight:

	Speed	Magic	Armour	Health
Fire sprite	2	2	2	12
Fire sprite	2	2	2	12
Fire sprite	2	2	2	12
Candles (*)	–	–	–	16

Special abilities

- **After burn**: At the end of every combat round, each surviving sprite automatically inflicts 1 damage, ignoring *armour*.
- **Black out** (*): If you win a round, instead of rolling for a damage score against a fire sprite, you can attempt to snuff out the sixteen candles. Roll two dice to determine how many candles you are able to put out. Once all the candles are put out, the sprites no longer benefit from the *after burn* ability, and their *magic* and *armour* are reduced by 1.

If you are able to defeat Segg's elementals, then turn to 229. Otherwise, you may repeat the combat or choose a different trainer (return to 369 to make your choice.)

119

You kick open the doors of the longhouse, the bar splintering under the force. A quick gesture upends the table, sending it flipping over. Plates rattle across the wooden slats, greasy food splattering across the wall. Gurt watches slack-jawed, gripping the sides of his chair as you advance to stand before him.

'I want an audience with the asynjur,' you demand.

'Nonsense!' huffs the bloated warrior, blowing out his cheeks. 'Take him. What are you standing there for?' He tries to lean past you, motioning frantically to the four Skards. They fold their arms, watching him stoically. 'Wha— What is this?' he gasps.

'I won't ask again.' You take a step towards him, causing the man to flinch backwards into his chair. He gropes past his fat belly, struggling to find the pommel of his sword.

He stops, his eyes catching your raised brow. Carefully he lifts his hands into the air. 'If you think Syn Hulda will give you a warmer greeting, then be my guest.' His cheeks bunch around an ugly smile. 'Take him to the hall,' he snaps, addressing the Skards. 'Let's see what Syn makes of this upstart fool!' Turn to 521.

Segg is silent, listening attentively as you describe the dreams. You feel a little foolish, talking of nightmares and demons. In the cold light of day, they always seem like some child's fantasy – hazy and indistinct, the details only half-remembered. But even now, you can still feel the cold and the fear of that place – and the presence of the bear, watching over you like a silent guardian. 'In the end, I used dragon leaf to avoid them. I found it in some old book on herb-lore.' Your gaze shifts to a row of bottles, lined along a shelf. 'I suppose I got my wish at last. Now, I don't need sleep – at least, my body no longer seems to crave it.'

'Interesting,' he says after a moment's thought. 'It would appear to occur when your mind is relaxed. Sleep, yes – but I imagine you could travel there if you used the correct meditative techniques.'

'Travel?' You baulk.

'In mind, not in body. I have read of such things – the Skards have shamans, mages that can dream walk. They use potions and other means to meditate and travel to the shroud – the place that you have seen. But, I must admit, I have rarely heard of such a thing south of the rift. Old blood, perhaps.'

'You don't seem at all surprised,' you say, with a hint of disappointment.

'Surprised, me?' Segg spreads his arms wide, chuckling to himself, while the flames turn somersaults in the air. 'Do you really think there's anything left to surprise this old mage?'

Will you:	
Ask about learning magic?	342
Ask about your strange condition?	234
Return to the library?	353

You pick up the tile and push it into the square-shaped hole. Leaning back, you wait expectantly for something to happen. However, it appears that you have chosen the incorrect rune. As you hurriedly try and prise the tile back out of the grid, you hear a sudden crack of branches followed by another barking cry. If you don't run now, the other fengles will find you! Frantically, you spring to your feet and sprint for the cover of the opposite tree line. Turn to 175.

122

On reaching the cave, you turn and look back towards the far shore. The dogs are mired in the tar, forming a collection of bobbing heads, fighting against the gloopy undertow. One of the Skard hunters is now making his way across the stones, paying no heed to the fate of his dog-team. With an axe in one hand and a knife in the other, it is clear that revenge is at the forefront of his mind. Turn to 344.

123

As you step up to the guards, one of them moves to head you off, putting his palm to your chest to draw you to a halt. 'Hey, where you think you're going? This is a private party – Lord Eaton's. Guests only, so unless you've got an invitation, you ain't getting in.'

If you have the *party invitation*, you may hand this over and enter (turn to 253). Otherwise, you have no choice but to return to the taproom. Turn to 80.

124

The hand moves quickly, leading you on a frantic chase as it tries to find a hiding place amongst the boxes and barrels. To catch the hand, you will have to pass a *speed* challenge:

	Speed
Catch the hand	9

If you are successful, turn to 398. Otherwise, turn to 357.

As the pool gets deeper you are forced to swim out to the remaining items, gritting your teeth against the biting pain. (Add two *defeats* to your hero sheet.)

You struggle to focus, your surroundings blurred by the thick noxious smoke. No longer caring what you might find, you reach out blindly for the nearest treasure. (Roll a die. On a ⚀ or ⚁ result, you may take the fang, on a ⚂ or ⚃ result you may take the ring, on a ⚄ or ⚅ result you may take the dimensional aperture):

Fenrir's fang	**Faith healer**	**Dimensional aperture**
(backpack)	(ring)	(special: unique)
A sharp canine tooth	+1 brawn +4 health	Doubles the size
from a giant wolf	Ability: heal	of your backpack –
		allowing you to
		carry 10 items

Unable to endure the pain any longer, you decide to make for shore. Turn to 303.

You plough through the powdery snow, your sled bouncing over the waves of hidden rock and ice. As you progress, the hummocks become steeper and sharper, the roughness of your passage putting your sled in serious danger of becoming wrecked.

You will need to take a challenge test using your *stability* attribute:

	Stability
Wave rider	9

If you are successful, turn to 422. If you fail, turn to 531.

'A traveller, you say.' The woman appears unconvinced. 'And tell me, why would you be travelling these parts? For the scenery?' She raises her eyebrows.

'Not a traveller, a merchant,' you correct quickly. 'But I was set upon by bandits, back on the road. I was the only one to get away and . . .'

'The only one? Who were you travelling with?'

You wince, cursing your slip up. 'I met some others. We thought we'd travel together, for safety.'

'Didn't do you much good now, did it?' The woman huffs, then she nods to your sword. 'Tell me, did you steal that sword or were you taught to use it? A fine blade for a boy like you.'

You glance down at the holy sword, Duran's Heart – the named blade that was gifted to you for your thirteenth birthday. 'I . . . it . . . I found it, yes. On one of the men who attacked us.'

'A holy blade. And does that belong to the man also?'

Her eyes shift to the dried blood coating your sleeve. You look away, avoiding her glare. 'He was . . . one of the bandits,' you stutter, knowing the lie is written all over your face.

The woman shakes her head with a frown of disappointment. 'You are a fool to think I'd believe your story. You are but a child. A thief, no doubt. One who got caught out, and now plans to rob me blind.' She puts her basket down next to the chopping block, then rests her hands on the curved handle of the wood axe. 'Are you good with that blade, son? You had better be . . .'

'No wait!' You raise your hands imploringly. 'I'm no thief. You can have the sword – I can't even touch the cursed thing.'

For the first time, the woman exhibits surprise. 'Is this true?' she gasps.

Too late, you realise what you have done, blurting out your secret with no mind to the consequences. To confess such a thing is almost tantamount to treason. 'I can only touch the scabbard,' you reply honestly, seeing no point in spinning out another lie now you've gone this far. 'The inscriptions . . . if I put even a hand to them, they . . .' You struggle for the words.

'Reject you?' the woman supplies thoughtfully.

You nod, trying to gauge her reaction. This secret is one you have only shared once before, with your nursemaid Molly. And you doubt she'll be telling anyone now . . .

'You're no witchfinder, then,' the woman's brow creases. 'Perhaps there is some truth in what you say after all.' Make a note of the word *pauper* on your hero sheet, then turn to 256.

128

You give the nod to Lawson, who nocks an arrow and takes careful aim. A few tense seconds pass before he fires his shot. It thuds cleanly into the beast's forehead, throwing it backward into the tar. The thick waters ripple out from the body, then fold back in, sucking the creature down into the inky depths. Within moments, there is barely a disturbance on the surface of the lake.

Mitch shakes his head, then gives you a hurt look. 'How could you?'

Before you can reply, Henna jumps to your defence. 'It would only have brought more of them,' she says briskly. 'You heard it. That thing was making more noise than those pestering birds.'

Mitch glowers sullenly. 'Still don't make it right.'

'Come on kids, we got work to do.' Kirk ushers you away from the shore, back towards the cart. 'Time to get our hands dirty.' Turn to 263.

129

You flick to the back of the book, comparing the glossary of markings with those that have been carved into the stone figures. It appears that they are Titans, and the runes are the individual marks that represent their names. However, there are – according to the book – supposed to be nine Titans, but only eight are shown in the carving.

'One's missing,' you state, cross-referencing the marks in the book against those on the wall. 'Here it is . . . Fafnir.'

The moment you utter the name, the portal glows brighter – then bursts into a blinding light, forcing you to cover your eyes. When the piercing radiance finally diminishes, you see that the oval portal has disappeared. Water rushes out of the space beyond, near to freezing, almost knocking you over with the force of its passage, carrying broken fragments of pottery and other debris with it.

The torrent quickly subsides as the water spreads out across the room and into the adjoining passages, leaving you ankle deep in floating wreckage.

'Think this was a storeroom,' says Caul. He ducks his head into the newly-opened cavity. It is small, although a rock fall at the rear of the chamber may have cut off deeper sections. You can see a number of empty shelves lining the walls, which must have once held the pots and other items now floating around you. A steady stream of water trickles from a crack in the store-room's ceiling.

'Disappointing,' sighs Caul, scrunching up his face. 'Thought there might have been some chests of gold, at least.'

You search through the wreckage, looking for anything that might be salvageable. To your relief, there are a few sealed pots that appear to have survived intact. If you wish, you may now take any/all of the following:

Drake scales	Titan blood	Fixing infuser (1 use)
(special)	(special)	(backpack)
Use on a cloak, chest,	Once used,	Use at any time
gloves or feet item	permanently gives	to remove one
to increase its	you the ability	death penalty from
armour by 1	*might of stone*	your hero

You also find a *plain glass orb*. If you wish to take this item, simply make a note of it on your hero sheet, it does not take up backpack space. Once you have finished picking through the debris, you re-join Caul and head out of the chamber. Turn to **494**.

130

'I'm afraid what you see today is merely a shadow of our former strength. Back when I joined the order, we were trained as cavaliers.

We'd ride out across Glory Bridge and take the fight to our enemies – goblins and trolls, mostly, but the Skards also, when they wanted to test us.' Everard points to an iron bridge, spanning the rift. Lines of angled spears have been set in rows across its length, forming a painful mile of death to anyone foolish enough to set their might against it.

'But I'm afraid your father never considered the north a threat.' Everard glances at you warily. 'I never judged him for it – perhaps he had good reason. But our coffers are low and our equipment is less than it was. Soldiers don't come here to ride out across the Glory Bridge anymore, they come here if they've got nowhere else to go. This really is the end of the road.'

A statement you can well believe.

Your gaze sweeps along the ragged line of battlements, fronted by a tiered succession of curtain walls. A few lone guards are visible along the walkways – little more than ants in comparison to the vastness of the fortifications. 'There's something I don't understand, though.' You gesture towards the rift. 'Goblins and trolls, they're creatures of the underworld. If they can't take the keep – why don't they just tunnel underneath it?'

Everard smiles knowingly. 'That's every smart rookie's first thought. These walls go deep – and I mean deep. Serious magic at play. I understand a hundred White Abbots gave their lives to inscribe the walls of this place. Their life blood, their magic, is in every stone. Anything evil tries to break through . . .' He chuckles and shakes his head. 'I've heard the screams. It's not pretty.'

Will you:

Ask about the Skards?	81
Climb the stairs to the mage tower?	301
Return to the main courtyard	113

131

For defeating the mighty yeti, you may now help yourself to one of the following rewards:

Wild mojo	Freeloader's hide	Dreadlock armbands
(ring)	(chest)	(gloves)
+1 magic +1 armour	+1 speed +1 magic	+1 speed +2 magic
Ability: critical strike	Ability: crawlers	Ability: lash

You have also gained a *sasquatch pelt* (simply make a note of this on your hero sheet, it doesn't take up backpack space). When you have updated your sheet, turn to **631**.

132

Without the book, you have no knowledge of the rules and feel uncertain about giving the guard advice. This game is clearly for high stakes – and if you make the wrong move, you dread to consider the consequences.

If you wish to try and help the guard anyway, turn to **335**. Otherwise, you can refuse to aid the guard and await the outcome, turn to **321**.

133

At the foot of the stone there is a carved grid, filled with a number of strange symbols and markings.

On closer inspection, you discover that one of the symbols is missing. Four square tiles lie next to the stone, which you assume the fengle must have found. Perhaps one of these tiles is meant to be placed in the grid to solve a puzzle.

The other fengles are getting closer, their cries getting louder and more urgent. You realise that you will only have a chance to try one symbol before you will need to make a run for it. But which one will you choose?

Will you:

Choose the triangle rune?	181
Choose the diamond rune?	213
Choose the pentagon rune?	121
Choose the hexagon rune?	50

134

You place the 'one of snakes' on the discard pile and pick a new stone from the bag. You have gained the 'four of stars'.

You have the following stones:

The monk takes his turn, then waits for you to make your next move.

Will you:

Play your current hand?	734
Discard the three of snakes?	612
Discard the one of crowns?	646

135

You charge past the soldiers, ducking and weaving between the flying debris. As you close on the mage the hooded creature pulls a wand from its belt, sending bolts of lightning streaking towards you. It is time to fight:

	Speed	Magic	Armour	Health
Geomancer	4	3	2/5(*)	35

Special abilities
- **Stone shower**: At the end of every combat round, the flying shards cause 2 damage to your hero, ignoring *armour*.
- **Stone shield**: At the start of the third combat round, the geomancer will cast *stone shield*, hardening its robes into a rock-like armour. This will add 3 to your opponent's *armour* but lowers their *speed* by 1 for the remainder of the combat.

If you manage to defeat this stone-flinging mage, turn to 251.

136

Reah brightens at the mention of the word. 'They were the very reason we came here. You see, when you look closer at the Dwarven histories, the older tablets found at Dur Andrel and Dour Gaun, there is frequent mention of the giants of Urd. That's what the Dwarves called the surface world.'

'I have read of such things,' you reply, casting your mind back to the palace library. 'But they're not real. A hundred arms, fifty heads? A bedtime story to scare children.'

Reah shakes her head. 'A storyteller's fancy. These creatures existed. They have many names – Titans, frost giants, jotun. The Skards speak of them with reverence; they believe their ancestors once walked beside them, as equals.'

'What has this got to do with the caves?' you interject, still sounding sceptical. 'You thought you'd find Titans there?'

'We did,' snaps the male, his brow creasing in anger. 'There are structures, buildings, inside the caves.'

'Dwarven,' you snort. 'There are Dwarf ruins everywhere in Valeron.'

The woman nods. 'They share some common magic in their craft, yes. But these structures are different to anything I have ever seen before. We know that the Dwarves used something known as Titan blood in their magic. It gave them the ability to turn matter into stone. There are countless references in their texts to those who had been gifted with this blood – they named themselves Titans, in honour of those who came before. I wonder if there's more to this, something we've yet to find. These original Titans – the jotun, frost giants – they could predate the Dwarves, predate anything we have yet discovered.'

Will you:

Ask about the rock that was found?	264
Ask about the man in the tent?	332
Ask how you might help? (starts the quest)	146

137

Everard escorts you to a draughty, cobwebbed room at the top of one of the keep's towers. 'I think it's best you have your own quarters,' the knight explains, moving to the window and pulling back a pair of wooden shutters. Grey light spills into the room, bringing with it a chill wind, laced with dancing snow. Thankfully, it appears the storm of the previous night has abated. 'You're still recovering,' states Everard, 'and prone to night fevers – that's the story we're sticking to. At least this way you won't be in the barracks with the other soldiers.'

'You said no special treatment,' you say glumly, eyeing the room's sparse furnishings. Just a pallet bed, a bucket and washstand, and a clothes chest underneath the window. The fireplace opposite has not been lit in an age, its grate filled with a heap of cold ashes.

Everard nods. 'One step at a time, my prince.'

'I'm not a prince any longer.' You step towards the washstand – and the mirror, balancing on the shelf above it.

'You're right.' Everard sighs. 'We all need to play along, until such time as we can decide our next move. I will leave you – come find me if you need . . . want to talk.' He bows stiffly, then leaves the room, closing the door behind him.

You shuffle up to the mirror, using the palm of your hand to clear away the thick coating of dust. Then you lean in close.

The face looking back at you bears no resemblance to the one you remember. Instinctively, you step away, horrified – then a perverse curiosity drives you back for a second look.

Your face is drawn, even more so than it was before, sagging off your bones and accentuating the hollows of your eyes and cheeks. The skin has a grey-green sallowness, dry like leather, and is branched with dark roots around the lips, nose and eyes.

You hold your stare, gazing into the glassy, colourless orbs that glare back at you. It is as if the life spark has gone out – and what is left is just ashes, like those lying dark and cold in the grate. Putting a hand to your hair, you tug at the gnarly strands and watch as they fall loose into the washstand, exposing the smooth scalp beneath. You stifle a sob, hand reaching for the shaving blade next to the mirror.

'I'm a prince no longer,' you whisper, pushing back what remains of your hair and passing the blade across the scalp. Minutes later and the washstand is filled with black curls of hair – your head now shaven to a smooth dome.

Next, your attention shifts to the chest. Lifting open the lid, you discover your previous belongings, some fresh clothing, a sword and several items of grey leather armour. You assume these are basic army issue that all recruits receive. If you wish, you may now equip any/all of the following:

Waxen leathers	Dutiful watch	Sentinel handwraps
(chest)	(main hand: sword)	(gloves)
+1 brawn	+1 brawn +1 magic	+1 brawn +1 magic

As you go to leave the room, you pause for a moment, eyeing the mattress and the warm-looking furs strewn across it. In times past, such a sight would have been cruel torture, its comfort promising much-needed rest, but also the dreaded night terrors . . . Now, such tiredness and cravings have gone. Instead, you are left with an icy numbness.

What's happened to me?

You close your eyes, sensing the bear's presence still lurking at the back of your mind, in the darkest pit of your being. His strength leaks into you, and with it the freezing chill that stills your heart. You glance down at your muscular body, its broad chest unmoving, without breath or life. You wonder if your strange connection to the beast is the only thing keeping you alive.

Shivering, you turn and leave – determined to find distraction from your melancholy thoughts. Turn to 113 to begin your exploration of the keep.

138

You are unable to interact with the spirit. With nothing else of interest in the room, you take the unlit lamp (make a note of the word *lamp* on your hero sheet) and then continue into the next passageway. Turn to 385.

139

Caught by one of the spinning fists, you are thrown backwards into a snow drift. You struggle to rise, the powdery granules pulling at you like quicksand. With an eldritch screech the beast surges forward, raising its arms to bring them down in a crushing blow. Desperately you try and break your weapons free – your eyes held fast by the rapidly descending fists . . .

A guttural cry.

Desnar slides beneath its swing, thrusting a dagger into the creature's chest. As the beast rears back he follows up with a second strike to its neck, connecting with something vital and sending the beast's body exploding outwards in a billowing cloud of snow and ice.

The battle is over.

Desnar throws a curse into the chill wind, his long braids of hair flapping loose about his shoulders. He turns his head, sparing you a cursory glance; disappointment is written in every line of his weathered face. 'Weak,' he grunts. Turn to 208.

140

You clamber ashore, using an overhanging branch to help drag yourself out of the thick mud. As you lie, cold and shivering, on the banks of the mire, you turn to watch the snake's body slowly sink beneath the surface. You were lucky to have survived – and as you glance around at the bone-covered clearing, it becomes clear that the snake's previous victims were not so fortunate.

Once you have recovered, you decide to search through the remains. As you suspected, there are some human bones as well as animal – possibly lost travellers like yourself, who blundered into the mire. Picking through their belongings, you find 5 gold crowns, a leather cap and a plain silver ring, which you may now take:

Murk loop	Forest cap
(ring)	(head)
Ability: vanish	+1 armour

Your muscles ache and your body is tired. All you want to do is lie down and sleep, to curl up and pretend you are back home – back in the safety of the royal palace. But you are too fearful to rest; you must keep moving in the hope of finding a proper shelter. After chewing more of the dragon leaf to bolster your strength, you head up the bank and back into the forest. Turn to **161**.

141

The jubilation is short-lived. More of the creatures are flooding into the yard through the breached walls, like a swarm of rats escaping a fire. The reptile warriors seem unstoppable, their bodies hardened by scales or coated in stone armour. Behind their ranks, Dwarf-sized mages in tattered robes fashion monstrous creations from the very rubble of the keep, mashing them together into crude mockeries of warriors. Elsewhere you see the rock itself turned to liquid, drawn through the air by dark magics to form fists and hammers, slamming into the remnants of the keep's defences.

You struggle through the melee, dodging and parrying the incoming blows, trying to keep on the move. Once again, your thoughts turn to Anise. Perhaps she has already fled the keep – the only sensible choice, and one you consider taking yourself.

A white warhorse barrels through the thronging bodies, resplendent in plated barding, while its armoured rider hacks at the reptilian monsters, taking off heads and limbs with a butcher's precision. 'For Valeron! For Glory!' The voice manages to resonate across the yard, despite the confines of the rider's helm. It is unmistakably Everard. A horn bounces at his side, glowing with scripture.

'To me! Rally, men, rally!' The horse rears up on its hind legs, the steel-shod hooves smashing down to crush the scaled bodies beneath. The rider turns in the saddle, scanning the battlefield. Then his eyes alight on you. Tugging on the reins, he turns his horse, urging it forward. 'The prince,' he calls. 'Defend the prince!'

It takes a moment for the words to sink in – to realise that your identity has now been revealed to the surrounding soldiers.

'Prince?' You look to your side, to see a female knight glaring at you with suspicion. You barely recognise Henna. Blood spatters her face and speckles her once bright armour. She is shaking visibly from exhaustion, half-dragging her dust-caked sword through the dirt. 'You never said you were a prince!'

Before you can answer, Everard breaks from the throng, his horse tearing up mud and stone as he circles around you. 'The prince! To the prince! This is Arran – the heir to the throne of Valeron. The blood of Leonidas. Prince Arran!'

Henna's shakes her head in disbelief. 'It can't be.'

'I'm sorry, I couldn't tell . . .' Your words falter, your attention now caught by a figure staggering through the mist. A thin girl with flamered hair. Her torn dress hangs off her scrawny shoulders, exposing pale skin, scuffed and bleeding. She is gripping a kitchen knife in trembling hands.

'Anise!'

She doesn't hear you, staggering as if in a daze, oblivious to the soldiers and monsters locked in combat around her. You push back into the melee, desperate to reach her – but then you hear a deafening, monstrous rumble. A terrifying, gut-wrenching noise.

'One God protect us.' Everard lifts the horn to his lips, blowing a single brazen note. You follow his gaze to the shadow crawling over the remnants of the keep wall. Its size is difficult to comprehend, dwarfing everything – blotting out the sky as it rears up then smashes down, tearing through the walls' foundations like they were paper. Your first impression is that of a beetle, with a shiny chitinous shell and thin splayed legs. But then you realise this is a much darker creation. The head is a gaping hole, a tunnel lined with hundreds of circles of teeth. And above the mouth a bony crown sweeps back, the spiked ridges flickering with magic.

'Hold fast!' Everard blows another note on the horn. 'Believe in the light. Have faith!'

You watch in horrified amazement as the beast's armoured plates shift apart, like the dark petals of a flower opening to the sun. From between the exposed cavities black fleshy pillars emerge, each one bulging as if seeking to expunge something inside. Then, as one, the spiracles launch an oily black substance into the air. It falls like rain, landing indiscriminately – a hot acid that burns through armour, stone, flesh.

'Rally men! Hold fast!' Everard fights to control his bucking horse, a glob of acid sizzling through his helm. He tugs it free, casting the melted metal away. 'Form up. We can take it down!'

The frightened soldiers are holding back, cowering beneath their shields as the acid spatters around them. Henna shifts beside you, taking the grip of her blade in both hands. Then she starts forward alone. You hear her uttering the words of a prayer, her sword blossoming with white light.

You look again for Anise, but she is gone – perhaps taking cover amongst the rubble. The ranks of monsters are thinning now, melting into the ruins. It strikes you as odd that they are not pursuing the battle. There seems a sudden urgency to their flight, as if they have a sense of forewarning, a knowledge that something bad is about to happen.

Or perhaps they know their demon will finish the work that they have started.

Turning back, you see Henna still advancing across the emptying courtyard, dwarfed by the monstrous immensity that towers before her. Her courage moves something inside you.

Gritting your teeth, you hurry forward, falling into step beside the young knight. She glances your way, offering a tight smile. An unspoken thank you.

'My prince.' You turn to see Everard following on foot, with the rest of the soldiers fanning out beside him. You see Rook and trainer Orrec amongst their ranks. Everard bows his head. 'We stand together.'

As you near the giant monster, you notice its crown of spines start to glow brighter. A moment later and your head is pounding with a blinding agony, like hot knives being driven into your skull. The line of soldiers wavers, a tirade of grunts and curses coming from beneath their helms.

'Fight it!' hisses Everard to his men, frowning against the pain. 'It's trying to weaken us!'

Henna raises her glowing sword, then charges forward with a defiant cry. You follow her lead, your own magic forming a shimmering halo around you. It is time to fight:

	Speed	Brawn	Armour	Health
Gargax crown	5/3 (*)	2	2	20
Gargax thorax	5/3 (*)	2	2	30
Gargax legs	3	1	2	20

Special abilities

- **Nip 'n' tuck**: If Gargax's legs are reduced to zero *health*, the head and thorax *speed* are reduced to 3 for the remainder of the combat. If the thorax is destroyed, the *acid rain* ability no longer applies. If the crown is destroyed, you no longer suffer from *mind fumble*.
- **Acid rain**: At the end of each combat round, you must take 2 damage, ignoring *armour*.
- **Mind fumble**: You cannot play any speed or combat abilities while you are inflicted with *mind fumble*.

If you have any tar barrels recorded on your hero sheet, you can use them at the end of a combat round. Each tar barrel causes 1 damage to all opponents, ignoring *armour*. You can use up to four barrels per combat round. (Remember to remove any used tar barrels from your hero sheet.)

If you manage to defeat this demon of the underworld, turn to **445**.

142

It takes half an hour to load the last of the barrels onto the cart. Once the task is complete, you step back, muscles aching from the hard labour.

'All in and ready to go,' says Kirk, wiping his brow. 'We did good today.'

The team managed to fill *12 barrels of tar*. (Make a note of this on your hero sheet then turn to **315**.)

143

Branch and bark scatter across the chamber as you chop through the last of the saplings to reach the elusive Ratatosk. With every step, the dark magic pouring out of the splintered remains fills you with a new-found vigour. You have gained the following special ability:

Shadow thorns (dm): Summon barbed roots to rip and tear at your opponents. This causes 1 die of damage to each opponent (roll once and apply the same damage to each). *Shadow thorns* can only be used once per combat.

Ratatosk tries to scamper past you, but his many wounds have taken their toll. Your foot catches him in the side, sending the rodent tumbling back against the wall. Before he can recover, your weapons cross at his throat.

'Spare me,' he snorts breathlessly. 'You have power . . . to defeat . . . the witch. I see it, rata-rata-tosk.'

'Why should I spare vermin like you?' Your weapons press deeper, cutting into the skin. Ratatosk flinches, his eyes shifting nervously from side to side.

'I help you,' he rasps. 'I know secret ways. I show you, like I showed her . . . trust me.'

'You're asking me to trust you, after what you've done?'

The squirrel licks its teeth with a pale tongue. 'I only do what I have to,' he grins weakly. 'Nature teaches us . . . to adapt and survive, rata-rata-tosk.'

Will you:

Spare the creature's life?	**99**
Finish him and take his treasures?	**727**

144

The guard removes the one of hearts from his hand and places it face down on the discard pile. He reaches into the pouch and takes another stone at random. He has now gained the two of stars:

The guard rubs his chin thoughtfully. 'Hmm, just a fool's pair,' he whispers out of the corner of his mouth. 'Let's hope it is enough to win.' Turn to 570.

145

'Ah, my plants.' Sylvie rolls her eyes, giving a whimsical sigh. 'I don't know where I'd be without them. So much to learn, so much to discover.' She walks over to the window, where a purple-flowering plant is growing among thorny shrubs. 'Plants are like teachers. Take this one, for instance. The death rattle.' Her fingers caress the purple, bell-shaped flowers.

'Death rattle,' you echo in surprise. 'Odd name for a flower.'

'It's actually a parasite,' she replies. 'It gains its nutrients from other plants. It takes what it needs, and then it kills them.' Her fingers drift to the barbed shrub that surrounds the flowers. 'But not the dwarf thistle. The thistle has spines that offer protection, keeps predators away. So the death rattle lets it live, to benefit from its natural defences, leeching only what it needs to keep them both alive. The two co-exist as one.'

Sylvie looks back at you, the firelight dancing in her eyes. 'But you're right, everything comes to an end eventually. The death rattle, by its very nature, is the more aggressive of the two. It can't help itself. And when it finally oversteps its bounds . . .'

'It kills the thistle.' You finish her sentence, glancing back at the bright shock of purple blossom growing amongst the dark thorns. It is hard to imagine something so beautiful being so deadly. Sylvie nods and returns to the table.

'You should take a greater interest in the world around you, boy. Nature tells us a story, teaches us valuable lessons. That's why I dedicated my life to its study.'

Return to 191 to ask another question, or turn to 207 to end the conversation.

146

The man steps forward, lowering his eyes. 'We are not fighters – we are explorers. Our best men and women went into those caves. We all knew the danger – the risk they were taking. But I know Blair, our leader – he would have taken every precaution.' He lifts his gaze, the hollows beneath his eyes giving him a ghoulish visage. 'Please, will you go look for them?'

You regard the pair, taking in their haggard features, the blue-tinged lips, the glassy and staring eyes. Like ghosts. You doubt they have eaten properly for weeks, and from the look of their meagre supplies the outlook is bleak. But there is still something in their eyes, a spark of hope, perhaps – a stubborn reluctance to give up on their companions. Maybe that is all that is keeping them alive.

'Yes,' you find yourself saying, before you have even thought it through. 'I'll see if I can find your team – bring them back.' You offer out your hand. The man takes it quickly into his frost-bitten fingers, his grip surprisingly firm.

'I am Diggory,' he grins, displaying rotted stumps for teeth. 'Please, bring us peace.'

You nod awkwardly, then look to Reah.

The woman is silent. She bows her head and walks to stand outside the tent. Then she starts to hum a song. A slow, sorrowful tune that seems to rise and sigh with the wind. You don't catch the words, but the rhythm is familiar – you can picture a mourner at your mother's funeral, their black veil rustling in the wind. They were singing. A song of loss and farewell.

After giving the man a last reassuring nod you start into the canyon, wondering what you will encounter in these mysterious caves. Turn to 361.

147

Rutus loses his footing in the wet slush, forcing his intended blow wide of its mark. As he goes to re-balance himself, you drive your shoulder into the warrior's chest, your momentum taking you both down in a tangle of limbs. Swords forgotten, you end up in a frantic wrestling match, looking to grapple each other into an inescapable lock. Thankfully, your newfound strength proves its worth and soon Rutus is gasping for air – begging for release from your choking hold.

'Well, this one's got some teeth,' says the trainer, his admiration beaming in his smile. 'I'd let him go now, he's turning blue.'

You release your grip, the anger in you finally beginning to subside. It isn't until you wipe the spittle from your mouth that you see the other men watching you with a sense of unease.

'You smell like a dog, and fight like one too.' Rutus rubs his throat, where red welts are already starting to show. 'Man, where'd you learn to fight like that – the pit?'

You stagger to your feet, then offer out a hand for Rutus. He glares at it, scowling. 'Keep your paws to yourself,' he rasps, his voice still raw from his beating. With a pained grunt, he levers himself back up, then retrieves his sword from the churned-up mud.

'Come on ladies, back to work!' The trainer cracks his riding crop against his boot. 'Stop gawking, Henson.' As the men fall back into their sparring lines, the trainer glances your way, nodding his head in respect. 'Not a bad show,' he says. 'But don't let it get to your head.'

For your victory over Rutus, you have now gained the following special ability:

Intimidate (mo): Use to reroll all dice for attack speed, for both yourself and your opponent. You must accept the rerolled results. You can only use *intimidate* once per combat.

Record the keyword *brawler*. (If you previously had the keyword *baited*, you may now remove this from your hero sheet.) Turn to 113 to revisit the main courtyard or 168 to climb the stairs to the battlements.

148

You methodically slide the bottles out of the racks, turning them round to read their labels. To your relief you manage to uncover a full bottle of the infamous Bowfinch '55, which Gurt asked you to find. Carefully you wrap this item in a cloth and place it inside your pack.

Congratulations! You have acquired a bottle of *Bowfinch '55* (simply make a note of this item on your hero sheet, it does not take up back-pack space. You can also remove the keyword *Bowfinch* from your hero sheet.)

Make a note of paragraph number 190. When you wish to return to Gurt and hand over this rare item (to continue the red quest, *The Hall of Vindsvall*) turn to 190 at any time.

You may now search the cellar (turn to 380) or leave (turn to 80).

149

Your tarred shoulders are now covered in the birdman's feathers. You may upgrade your *cloak* item to the following:

Tar and feathers
(cloak)
+1 speed
Ability: immobilise, charm

When you have updated your hero sheet, turn to 114.

You head round the side of the cabin, looking for any clues as to the whereabouts or identity of its owner. The vegetable patch you spied earlier has certainly been well-tended, with neat rows of cabbages and radishes, and pea plants growing around a small trellis. An axe rests on a chopping block nearby, with several stacks of split wood piled next to it, covered by a leather awning.

As you pass around the back of the cabin, the wind stirs a solitary beech tree, sending the chimes in its branches tinkling and spinning, their bright beads catching the leaden light. Beneath its boughs a pen has been built, housing a group of chickens, clucking and scratching at the mud. The top of the wooden fence has been woven with thorny vines, reminding you of the charm that you saw on the door.

Everything points to a careful and hard-working owner – someone who clearly takes pride in their home as well as being mindful of the necessary precautions. You eye the sharp thorns on the chicken pen, wondering what type of predator they are designed to keep out.

'Excuse me?'

The voice makes you jump, having been certain you were alone. You turn to see a woman striding down the hillside with a covered basket nestled under one arm. She looks stocky, although her saggy tunic and heavy overcoat may be exaggerating her build. The woman stops by the chopping block, the axe not far from her reach. 'Can I help you?' she enquires, her tone remaining neutral. A gust of wind whips at her hood, pushing it back to reveal a fringe of greying hair.

'I . . . I didn't mean . . . I'm . . . lost,' you stutter, suddenly not sure what to say.

You can feel the woman's eyes appraising you with suspicion. First the sword, then the blood on your cuffs. You realise you must look a puzzling sight, your once expensive clothing now weathered and torn. 'I can explain,' you reply, offering what you hope is your friendliest smile.

'Go on then,' mutters the woman stiffly. 'Surprise me, but it better be good.'

Will you:

Admit you are a prince who was attacked by Wiccans? 226
Pretend you are a simple traveller in need of shelter? 127

151

'Want, want,' Jackson mutters. 'Everyone wants. What do I look like, a darn charity? What I got costs gold and you earn that by good honest workin'.'

'I have gold,' you reply sharply. 'What do you have?'

There is a piggish snort from the other side of the wall. 'Gold, I got gold he says. Did your mama send you out with a shopping list, eh?' Another series of honking snorts, which you assume passes for Jackson's laughter.

'Do you have . . . *anything*?' you ask, frowning with impatience.

'This is a trading post, 'course I got things. I got weapons, clothing and essential equipment, all standard White Wolf issue – all approved by the company. Prices are fixed, so don't try any of that hagglin' nonsense or I'll skewer that tongue of yours with Mildred and Hetty. Yer hear me?'

You glance at the two crossbows, nodding warily.

'Good. I'm also willing to hire out space, give you one of me lockers. Ain't nowhere safer to keep your valuables. I protect 'em likes they were me own.'

Will you:

Ask to view the weapons?	566
Ask to view the clothing?	262
Ask to view the equipment?	72
Purchase a storage locker?	707
Discuss something else?	685

You push past the soldiers milling in the archway. As you break through their lines, you skid to a halt, suddenly realising the reason for their hesitation.

You are met by a scene of both horror and destruction. One of the walls has fallen inwards, spilling chunks of rock across the courtyard. The whole west-wing of the keep has also collapsed. Dust hangs heavy in the air – and the miasma of blood.

Over the wall and through the breach, black-scaled bodies spill into the yard. Reptilian monsters of all sizes and shapes, some wielding mighty swords and axes, others using whatever they can get their hands on – splintered wood, rocks, human body parts . . .

'What are they?' you hear one of the soldiers shout. 'Did they cause the quake?'

A cloud of winged shapes sweep across the courtyard, filling the smoke-hued sky with hellish shrieks. You try and follow them as they pitch and dive through the air, swooping on the beleaguered soldiers below. From one of the nearby towers you see spears of fire streaking through the air, slamming into the winged reptiles and sending them burning to the ground. A flash of crimson from the tower's steeple confirms that it is Segg – the keep's resident pyromancer.

All of a sudden you are being jostled and pushed as soldiers rush past you to meet the advancing horde. Explosions continue to tear through the wall, showering dust across the yard and spreading confusion. A nearby monster sprints forward, its scaled body cracked by veins of rippling fire. From its flared nostrils, smoke gouts in thick black plumes. A soldier heads it off, driving his sword into its body. The monster gives a snickering hiss, almost like laughter, as it drags itself up the blade, pushing the steel deeper into its scaled flesh. The soldier struggles to tug the weapon free, but the monster's claws already have him, gripping him close in a fatal embrace.

Then the monster explodes. You spin away, ducking down as blood and bone, dust and metal fall like rain. When you look back, there is nothing left save a smoking crater. Three more of the creatures have jumped down off the wall and are hurrying towards the hall. You look around for support, but the surrounding soldiers are all locked in combat. It is now up to you to defend the keep from these exploding monstrosities. It is time to fight:

	Speed	Brawn	Armour	Health
Ember wild	3	2	2	20
Ember wild	3	2	2	15
Ember wild	3	2	2	15

Special abilities
♥ **Combustion**: When an ember wild is defeated it immediately explodes, inflicting 4 damage to your hero, ignoring *armour*.

If you manage to defeat these hot-blooded horrors, turn to 537.

153

The three statues tower over the soldiers, each one a depiction of a reptilian-looking humanoid with spiked crests running along their arms and back. One of the soldiers is being egged on by his companions, while he draws a moustache and beard on the largest of the statues using a piece of charcoal.

'Can't believe they got this far,' mutters one of the younger men. 'Do you think there's going to be more?'

An older veteran with pepper-black hair shrugs his shoulders. 'I'm more concerned by the men we lost. Seven body bags in the chapel and all down to these three.'

There are hoots of laughter from the others as the soldier with the charcoal steps back from his creation. 'Looking better already!' he chortles.

You approach the veteran, who is the only one not amused by the prank. 'What happened?'

He glares at you in surprise, wrinkling his nose. 'Hey, you're the one who . . . Allam's teeth, yer look like death.'

You offer him a shrug of your shoulders. 'Don't worry, it's not contagious.'

The soldier leans away, plainly unconvinced. 'Well, seeing as you asked, these things scaled the wall the other day. Took eight men to finally stop 'em. Soon as they was wounded, the monsters turned to stone, used it like armour to defend themselves.' He points to a sword, half-protruding from the torso of one of the beasts. 'Segg calls it Titan blood or something. He's always muttering strange things that one, full of fancy ideas. I just see it plain – these things are strong. And if there's more of 'em, then we're in trouble.'

The other soldiers seem undaunted by the strange creatures; the prankster is now attempting to climb onto the largest and straddle its shoulders.

'Cut it out, Filch,' growls the veteran. 'Show some respect, will yer – we got good men dead 'cos of these.' He turns and walks away, shaking his head. Filch waves him off, his enthusiastic motion forcing him to lose his balance. He slips from his perch, hitting the ground to a further roar of laughter.

You may now:

Enter the main hall?	**186**
Climb the stairs to the battlements?	**168**
Investigate the training yard?	**348**
Join a quest?	**Return to the map**

154

Your way is clear to the other side. Reaching the wall, you start to climb the interwoven tentacles, using them as a ladder. Higher and higher you rise, until you spot a shelf of rock jutting out above you. The knot of tentacles crawls across its underside, sweeping over its lip and disappearing from sight.

Those last few metres present you with a scary ascent, your weight solely suspended by your spectral claws. Groaning in agony, you finally drag your pain-racked body over the ledge and lie there, gasping – the heat still pressing close on all sides, unwilling to give you a moment's respite.

You rise, swaying slightly as you try and gain a sense of your surroundings. The tentacles continue to wind past you, as do hundreds of others, all coiling and weaving over each other to meet the gigantic brain-like mass that fills the cavernous space.

This must be the demon. Cerebris.

There is no obvious shape or form to its body, if indeed it has a body at all. The fleshy folds seem stacked on one another, leaking a foul green pus that fills the air with a corpulent stench. Crimson veins criss-cross beneath the surface of its translucent skin, occasionally blossoming with a fiery light as parts of the bloated mass swell and deflate.

Weapons ring into your hands. You advance towards the demon, wondering – hoping – that you have the strength to penetrate its bulbous form and end whatever life lurks within.

The ground starts to shiver – another tremor building. You quicken your pace, eyes scanning the creature for any sign of weakness. Halfway along its glutinous bulk you spy a glowing red sphere, bulging between creases of pus-coated flesh. It beats with a fell energy, radiating waves of searing magic – bright as a sun.

The demon's heart. Its kha.

You leap onto its lower haunches, stepping over the ridges of flesh to draw nearer to its heart. Tendrils of frost spiral along your weapons, coating them in hard ridges of barbed ice.

'It ends here!' You throw back your arm, preparing to pierce the heart . . .

A muffled scream draws you up short.

You spin round, so fast you almost fall – your soul drawn to the sound of that voice, as surely as a moth to a flame.

'Anise!'

She hangs in the witch's outstretched hand, the woman's pale fingers gripped around the underside of her chin. A dry clicking comes from the girl's throat as she struggles to breathe, sucking desperately at the air. Her throat is one dark bruise, extending up the side of her face. An eye is swollen shut, dried blood caking her hair. The breeches she wears are torn, the ragged material stuck around a nasty wound.

You are too late, Arran. The witch's scratchy voice rakes through your mind. Anise tries to struggle, to break free of the woman's grip, but her arms are pinned to her side by some magic. *Tell me, how does it feel when hope crumbles, when all you once coveted is finally taken away? Look at me, Arran. I want to see that pain – the pain of knowing you have lost everything.*

You find yourself moving, stalking closer – rage building.

Melusine raises her other hand, revealing a long wand-like sceptre, white and sharp as a fragment of ice. She teases it against the girl's throat, forcing her to buck and whimper at its touch.

Anise. What a sweet name. A rose, caught between two thorns. The wand continues its slow caress, each stroke drawing a broader line of crimson. Cutting deeper.

You cry out, steps faltering. 'Don't do this!'

A piercing laughter. *You plan to save the world, Arran. You can't even save a life. You couldn't even save your own.*

'Let her go.' Your eyes narrow in warning.

Or what, Arran? What will you do? Her deformed visage is hidden behind a crowned veil, but you can feel the icy heat of her gaze beating through it. *The last seals weaken. When they break, the world serpent will be released. Everything will be brought to ruin, and yet you stand here begging me to save a single life?*

The wand presses deeper, forcing out a gurgling scream. *Do you need her, Arran – to hold your hand when the end comes?*

You tense, judging the distance – preparing to strike. 'I said . . .'

Yes, let her go.

The witch snaps back her arm. You see a fountain of blood, bright against bruised flesh. Then Anise is falling, crumpling silently to the ground. The witch steps over her body, the veil peeling back of its own accord. Your eyes meet – and in that horrifying instant it is as if the world has already ended, exploding in a freezing torrent of pain.

Screams.

It takes a moment to realise they are yours.

The agony is all-consuming – a fierce cold that overwhelms your own.

It stiffens your limbs, cracks your jaw rigid, pushes inside your mind . . . tightening like a vice. Only a desperate last effort of will saves you – your predatory instinct surging up to defend itself. Screams become guttural, spitting roars.

Painfully, like tearing skin from ice, you manage to avert your gaze . . .

You take a slow and heavy stride, your body feeling like a corpse again. Leaden, unresponsive. You look down, still shaking . . .

A green ice has started to form around your legs, seeking to entrap you like the tortured souls in the hall. Gritting your teeth you expel a burst of magic, splintering it to pieces. Freedom leaves you stumbling off balance; but you quickly recover, turning your stagger into a desperate charging lunge. It is time to fight:

	Speed	Magic	Armour	Health
Melusine	14	8	10	100

Special abilities

🍷 **Petrifying gaze**: Roll four dice at the end of each combat round. For each ⚃ or ⚅ result, you must take damage equal to the roll, ignoring *armour*. For example, if you rolled two ⚃'s and a ⚅ you would take 16 damage. All other results are ignored. If you have an ability that lets you reroll dice (such as *charm*), you may use this ability to affect the outcome.

🍷 **Fimbulwinter**: If you have the Titan shield, Fimbulwinter, you only take damage from each ⚀ result you roll for petrifying gaze. For example, if you rolled three ⚀'s, you would take 3 damage. All other results are ignored.

🍷 **Insulated**: If you have the *insulated* ability, you can reduce Melusine's damage score by 3 (Note: this does not affect Melusine's *petrifying gaze*).

If you manage to defeat the witch, turn to 706.

155

You walk down to the banks of the stream, looking forward to washing away the grime from the past few days. However, as you kneel beside the waters, you catch movement out of the corner of your eye. Further down the bank, a man is lying on his belly, splashing water on his face. He wears no armour, just a tattered white tunic and breeches stretched taut over hard muscle. Apart from a dagger in his belt, he carries nothing else of note. As you ponder what to do next, the man pushes himself back up and then looks your way. Surprise hits you both as your eyes meet and recognition dawns. The puckered scar, the hard chiselled features. It is Inquisitor Hort. The holy warrior who was meant to be your bodyguard.

He starts towards you, wincing as he shifts his weight, favouring his right leg. 'Arran!' he hisses, fumbling for the dagger. 'May the One God curse you and your family! I will finish what I was sent here to do!' He limps closer, his eyes gleaming with fury.

Will you:

Confront him about what happened on the road?	287
Run back to the cabin?	312
Run into the nearby woods?	244

156

The rotted wood crumbles away as you break open the lid. For a second you are presented with a writhing mass of worms and maggots, pushing their way through hunks of rancid grime – then the overwhelming stench hits you, forcing you to reel away, your stomach heaving.

'Ugh! What is it?' Anise is already back in the corridor, covering her nose with her arm. She waves for you to join her as the room starts to fill with a foul-smelling green vapour.

'I don't know, but it smells bad.' As you stumble half-blind through the cloud of mist, you are almost thankful that your body is still able to react to such a stench.

Some life left in me after all . . .

'Come on!' Grabbing your arm, Anise hurries back to the stairs that lead to the next level of the tower. Make a note of the keyword *methane* on your hero sheet, then turn to 111.

157

(Note: You must have completed the orange quest *The bitter end* before you can access this location. If you have visited this location before, turn to 106.)

The frozen ice creaks worryingly beneath your feet, offering a cruel and constant reminder that you are no longer walking over land.

Should the thin ice break, you would plunge through into the freezing depths of the ocean. It is an unsettling thought – but the trapper had assured you that this was the only way to reach Ryker's, an island only accessible by foot when the waters are frozen.

Ryker's Island. It had been a penal colony once, where the worst criminals in the kingdom had been confined. The hangman's noose should have been their punishment, but your father's predecessor – King Hark – had been a church man. He believed every soul was worth saving.

Even mine? you wonder bitterly.

According to Everard, there had been an uprising some time ago – the prisoners had broken out of the prison, but instead of fleeing back to the mainland they had remained at the island, forming their own ragtag community. You can understand why. As the ice groans beneath your feet, the heavy skies clouded with snow, you can't imagine a more remote place to live. Far away from authority – far away from the church and the King's army. Who would want to bother with a prison, out here in the middle of nowhere?

As you press onwards, the land turns from ice to hard-packed snow. Edges of black rock begin to cut through the customary whiteness: a comforting assurance that you have finally reached dry land.

Ahead, a dark shape looms menacingly out of the haze – a high wall of black iron. Torches flicker at regular intervals along its spiked length, their light catching on the barbed wire frills that curve cruelly against the bleak skies. This is truly a prison, built to keep the world out as much as to keep those within confined behind its walls.

Your eyes scan the expanse of smooth dark metal, looking for a gate or a doorway. Then you hear a voice from high above.

'Who goes there? You a damn Skard?'

You look up to see a man leaning over a section of the wall. His long hair streams in the wind, a thick cloak bunched around his shoulders.

'Not a Skard,' you reply, raising your hands. 'A trapper – come to sell furs. I seek shelter.'

You hear a squeal of rusted metal, then part of the wall swings inwards, revealing a previously hidden doorway. Relieved, you start towards it, but back away again when you see two men marching out, both holding oil lamps. One is short and wiry, stinking of drink. The other is taller and heavier, his wind-burnt face illuminated by the wash of light. Both have bands of red cloth tied around their upper right arms.

'He smellsh like a Skard,' drawls the thin one, slurring his words.

They look warily around, as if expecting you to be accompanied by others. The man from the wall is still watching.

'Just stick 'im and take his stuff,' he shouts down. 'Leave the body for the wolves.'

The smaller guard licks his lips nervously, his eyes flicking to your weapons. 'Easy for you to say, Bert,' he shouts back. 'You wanna come down 'ere and try?'

You pull back your hood. Both men draw away with startled gasps. The heavier-set guard is the first to speak.

'Hel-fire, what happen' to ya? How long yer been out there?'

'A long time,' you reply, knowing that your frost-bitten, deathly countenance must paint a ghoulish picture. 'I ask only for shelter. I am no Skard. Please . . . ?' It pains you to beg these men, but after days of solitude on the ice the sudden desire to be amongst people is almost overwhelming. Perhaps you crave a reminder of what life was like – news from home, the life you left behind.

'Agreed,' nods the thin man, moving aside. 'Me head's too pickled to be fightin' and arguin'. Come on, Gupp, let the man inside.'

The giant complies with a surly grunt, leaving you free to enter the settlement of Ryker's Island. Turn to 288.

158

You remember Kirk's words when you discovered the body lying in the grass – 'if there was anything of value, the birdman will have got it now.' Perhaps there is a secret stash of treasures hidden away somewhere in the eyrie.

It doesn't take long to find – a large nest perched on top of a flat boulder, fashioned from mud and twigs, and other things you'd rather not think about. Inside, wrapped in the remains of a mouldy cloak, is an assortment of odds and ends.

As well as 50 gold crowns, you may also take any/all of the following:

Bristle band	Brave deeds	Stone dragon
(ring)	(special: feather)	(backpack)
Ability: agility	Use on a head or chest item to increase its *brawn* or *magic* by 1	A stone-carved idol of a ferocious dragon

When you have updated your hero sheet, turn to 177.

159

The vines hook around your legs and waist, pulling you towards the gigantic plant. Angrily you tug your weapons loose and begin hacking at the thick tentacles. Just as you are about to be fed to the hungry mouths, you manage to sever the last of the vines – twisting at the last moment to avoid a lunging set of teeth.

The reprieve is short lived. A rustling crack alerts you to another growth of vines, spreading and twisting out of the plant's bulbous stem. With barely a chance to recover, you are forced to duck beneath the flailing onslaught whilst your weapons swing blindly to keep the snapping mouths at bay. Clearly, this plant is gripped by a frenzy, and will stop at nothing to gobble you up! It is time to fight:

	Speed	Magic	Armour	Health
Jogahh	8	9	10	80

Special abilities
♥ **Spit it out!**: If you win a combat round, instead of rolling for damage you can dive into one of Jogahh's mouths and attempt to remove an acorn. Roll a die – on a result of ⚁ or more, you have successfully removed the acorn, lowering Jogahh's *speed*, *magic* and *armour* by 1. If the result is ⚀ or less, you fail – and must automatically take 4 damage (ignoring *armour*) from Jogahh's acidic secretions. You may remove up to three acorns over the course of the combat.

If you manage to defeat this virulent growth, turn to 562.

160

The svardkin have led you into a winding maze. The pathways are tight and narrow, twisting and crossing back on themselves in an infuriating manner. Soon you have lost all sense of direction. Of the svardkin there is no sign – and no tracks in the ice to follow.

'We should go back,' pants Anise. 'Whatever they had isn't worth breaking our necks over.'

Skoll gives a disgruntled snort. 'Agreed, we didn't come here to chase after svardkin.'

You try and retrace your steps back to the main cave, but the twisting maze has left you disorientated and lost. After several tiring hours, you finally emerge from the tunnels into a larger cavern dominated by a pool of melt water. You decide to make camp on its banks and resume your journey once the others have rested. Turn to 467.

161

The trees eventually thin, giving way to hills blanketed with rocks and wildflowers. Back in the open, the wind now returns in force, buffeting against your stubborn advance. Its chillness lashes with a bitter sting, forcing you to hug your cloak protectively about your body. By now, there is little warmth or comfort to be gained from your sodden clothing. Instead their wet folds chafe and cut at your skin, while the blisters on your feet make every footfall an eye-wincing agony.

You swallow back the tears, determined not to give into despair. And yet, hope is fading fast, as is the grey sullen light. It will be dark soon and with it comes the dreadful prospect of another night spent out in the open. If only Lazlo was here, or Captain Tarlow. They would know how to build a shelter, make a fire, hunt for food. You know nothing of living and surviving outdoors. The dragon leaf will only last for so long. And when that runs out . . .

You clamber up a rise of boulders to get a better view of your surroundings. Part of you wonders if heading back into the forest would be a safer idea – at least there you have some shelter and a better chance of foraging for food. A night spent out in these bleak open hills, especially if another storm rolls in, will offer nothing more than misery and hunger.

As you scan the hills, your attention is caught by a thin column of smoke rising into the sky. Its source is obscured by another ridge of boulders. Your first reaction is relief – surely it must be a campfire, and that means warmth and food. But then, you also realise it means the presence of strangers. Will they be friendly? They could even be Wiccans, sent to finish the bloody business they began on the road.

You decide it would be foolish not to take a closer look. Scrambling down the boulders, you hurry across the intervening moorland to reach the opposite ridge. As you pass around its moss-covered rocks, your heart leaps with joy when you see a log cabin nestled at the bottom of the slope. It looks homely enough, with vegetables arranged neatly in a garden, firelight flickering between the window shutters, wisps of cooking smoke rising from its chimney.

Without hesitation you hasten towards it, your stomach rumbling at the thought of warm, cooked food and proper shelter. You pay little mind to who the cabin might belong to – or whether they would be willing to share their home. *I'm a prince,* you remind yourself. *They have to offer me succour. It's the king's law.*

As you near, you see the front door is decorated with a thorny-looking wreath – some charm, perhaps, to ward away danger. You knock, but there is no answer. After knocking again, you reach for the handle of the door. You pause, wondering if it is right to enter a stranger's home uninvited. A brief tug confirms that the door is unlocked.

Will you:

Open the door and enter the cabin?	196
Take a look around the outside?	150

162

The very air seems to vibrate as a cold shadow stretches across the courtyard. It is accompanied by a rumbling thunder clap – drowning the cries of the bewildered onlookers. Your eyes are drawn upwards, to the immense black cloud of falling rubble. Segg's tower. In horror, you realise the whole building is collapsing, its peaked steeple spinning through the debris, flames licking around its edges.

There is chaos as soldiers and monsters run for cover. You make for the main hall, hoping the doorway will provide some safe haven, but a sudden tremor causes you to stumble and fall. One of the ember wilds streaks past you, arrows and weapons protruding from its body. Bright blood spatters across the stone . . . sizzling and smoking.

'No!' You struggle to your feet, looking around for support. 'Stop it! Stop it before . . .'

The creature hurls itself against the wall . . . and explodes. The resulting blast wave blows you backwards, through dust and smoke and screaming bodies. Turn to 320.

163

Your weapons slice through the moth's wings as if they were paper, dragging the creature to the ground. Once prone, the moth has no defence against your attacks, its bright dust pumping into the air in a last desperate effort to blind you. It is too little, too late.

You step away from the remains of the insect, noticing that its dust is now sticking to your clothes, sparkling like glitter. You have now gained:

Spectral dust
(special)
Use on a cloak, gloves, boots or chest item
to add the special ability *deceive*

Anise retrieves her torch, the blue flames hissing and sparking as they catch the dust still whirling through the air. 'My people call them death lights. They bring ill-luck to those who see them.'

'No kidding. I figured that out when the thing tried to eat me.' You stoop down next to the body of the moth, studying one of its broken wings. The thin membrane still pulses with a silver light, forming some kind of runic pattern or map. If you wish you may take the *moth wing* (simply make a note of it on your hero sheet, it does not take up backpack space).

When you re-enter the chamber, you are surprised to see the door to your left creaking open of its own accord. From the room beyond you hear a man's voice, raised in anger. 'No! I will not serve you, Zabarach! I will not!' There is a cry of pain, then the sound of metal scraping across stone. You share a look with Anise, before tentatively edging towards the next room. Turn to 548.

164

'Good, good,' grins the thief. He opens out his patched-cloth bag, tilting its contents towards you while his eyes rove shiftily from side-to-side. Rummaging through the proffered items, you discover a tattered dirt-stained book, a makeshift knife fashioned from a chunk of granite, and a bundle of shimmering grey cloth. 'Only twenty gold apiece,' says the man, shaking the bag. 'Hurry up or we gets in trouble, yes?'

You may purchase any of the following for 20 gold crowns each:

Stones & Bones	Prison break	Great escape
(backpack)	(main hand: dagger)	(cloak)
The ultimate strategy guide (game of the year edition)	+1 speed +1 brawn Ability: first blood	+1 speed +2 health Ability: getaway

To continue chatting to the thief, return to 288. To explore the rest of the compound under your own steam, turn to 106.

165

'You assume I know something, then?' Sylvie flips an egg, leaning back as the fat spits in the pan. 'All I know is what Randal told me or I've managed to deduce from my studies. There's an old Skard word, Norr. It means crossing, the state between waking and sleeping. Some minds are able to dwell there, to walk that place as a spirit body.'

'Norr?' You frown, trying to recall ever having heard the word.

'It's the thin line, the meeting place between our world and the shroud – the realm of magic.'

You feel the cold in your stomach intensify. 'The shroud.' You have always been forbidden from mentioning such a thing. To the Church it is a blasphemous evil, a hell where demons and other malign spirits dwell. 'I . . . I never knew. No one ever told me. They can't have known.'

'It's a rare affliction, boy.' Sylvie meets your troubled gaze. 'I'm sorry.'

You close your eyes to stop the room from spinning, still giddy from the dream. 'This can't be happening to me . . .' Instinctively you reach for your pouch, relieved to find it is still attached to your belt. You have enough dragon leaf to keep the dreams away, for a while at least . . .

'That won't help you.' Sylvie puts a hand to her hip, the other pointing with her knife. 'That is the coward's way. You need to become stronger, boy. The mind is like a muscle. It must be exercised. Avoiding the dreams will only make it worse.'

Will you:

Ask her why she tricked you?	295
Leave the cabin?	261
Agree to fetch the water?	78

166

Using the rocks for cover, you wait to ambush the hunter, hoping the element of surprise will help you to defeat the bigger and stronger Skard. After a tense wait, you hear the scuff of boots outside the cave. Then a musty animal stink wafts past you as a shadow edges along the tunnel wall. You grip your weapons tightly, waiting for the hunter to come into full view. His broad shoulders scrape the rock, his hair hanging in a matted, greasy curtain across his face. He doesn't see you until it is too late. Confined by the tunnel walls, he staggers back, struggling to raise his axe and knife as you launch into him with a flurry of strikes. It is time to fight:

	Speed	Brawn	Armour	Health
Hunter	2	2	1	30

Special abilities

🛡 **Element of surprise**: In the first two combat rounds, the hunter's *speed* is reduced to zero.

If you manage to best this savage hunter, turn to 317. If you lose the combat, remember to record your defeat on your hero sheet. You may then attempt the combat again or return to the map.

167

The aura of dread around the chest is palpable, the runes growing brighter and more restless as you draw near. Your own distrust is heightened by Nanuk's agitation – even though your spirit link is weak you can sense the bear huffing and snorting, his teeth bared in warning. Nevertheless, curiosity has got the better of you.

Putting your hands to the lid of the chest, you lift it open. You flinch, having fully expected some sort of magical trap or curse, but the lid creaks back easily enough – leaving you free to lean over and take a look inside.

For a brief instant you feel as though you are teetering on the brink of a vast chasm of darkness – an abyss of midnight black. Then two shadowy hands reach out from the gloomy depths, grab you by the shoulders and pull you into the chest.

You are dragged headfirst along a dark shaft, the walls writhing with hundreds of shadowy hands, all pushing and groping as they guide you deeper and deeper into the dark. Then all of a sudden you are falling, your cries stifled by the thick, oppressive air. You land on a damp, spongy surface – the floor of a murky chamber. Hands continue to stretch and grasp from the black walls, a mournful chorus of wails echoing all around.

You draw your weapons, eyes desperately searching for a way out. The wailing stops and there is silence.

Free me, whispers a voice. A woman's. Young and frightened.

You look round frantically for the source. Then your eyes alight on a monstrous face, pushing itself out of the far wall. A young girl's, once beautiful, perhaps – but now twisted and distorted into an evil mask of malign hatred. The head continues to stretch towards you, its long neck little more than a few threads of shadow distending behind it.

The mouth widens, revealing a dark maw filled with hundreds of similar faces, all grinning evilly, their teeth filed down to dagger-sharp points. You try and back away but the walls have closed in, the ghostly hands pushing you towards the snapping, hungry faces. It is time to fight:

	Speed	Magic	Armour	Health
Pandora	7	5	5	50
Helping hands	5	4	4	25

Special abilities

● **Helping hands**: You must reduce your *speed* by 1 for the duration of this combat. Once the helping hands are defeated, this ability no longer applies.

● **Pandora's pain**: At the end of each combat round you must take 2 damage, ignoring *armour*. Once Pandora is defeated, this ability no longer applies.

You must defeat both Pandora and the helping hands to win the combat. If you manage to defeat this headstrong horror, turn to 284.

168

(If this is your first time visiting the battlements, turn to 223. Otherwise, read on.)

On reaching the walkway, you are buffeted by the strong winds gusting in from across the broken wasteland. Lord Everard stands alone at the wall, cloak whipped back from his broad shoulders, his expression pensive.

Will you:

Speak with Lord Everard?   209
Climb the stairs to the mage tower?   301
Return to the main courtyard?   113

169

You grope across a pebbled slope, still half-blinded by the stark brightness of the outdoors. Stones and pebbles shift beneath your weight, some skittering away to form rippling streams. Near at hand, coarse yellow grass blows flat in the wind, while ahead of you a field of scoured boulders skirts the edge of a jagged fissure..

With a grunt you drag yourself a little further down the slope, your strength ebbing into a numb exhaustion. For a fleeting second, as your eyes flutter closed, you see Nanuk silhouetted against the green of the Norr landscape. He paces back and forth, restless – waiting. It would be so easy to let yourself go . . . to return to the dream.

A hissing snarl. Footsteps crunch.

You startle awake as three figures sharpen into focus, marching straight towards you up the slope. Their outlines are wide and brawny. They move with purpose, their clawed hands gripping wicked-looking cleavers. As they near the harsh light catches on their bodies, highlighting scales and teeth.

You scrabble frantically for your weapons, realising that these are the same horrors that assaulted the keep; some mockery of human and reptile, with evil faces distended into elongated snouts. You back up the slope, crab-stepping with weapons held ready. But the creatures' attention is caught by something else . . . above you . . .

A white shape blurs through the air, slamming into the lead creature and sending it flailing backwards. As it crashes down, you see a bone javelin protruding from its forehead.

You duck down, casting a quick glance past your shoulder. Beyond the rock fall, a shelf of cream-coloured rock juts several metres above you. Whoever threw the javelin must be on top of the escarpment and out of sight.

The clatter of steel and a scuffling of feet.

'Ara vantar!'

Suddenly, two bodies come hurtling over the edge of the rock shelf, tangled together. They land heavily, scraping and rolling their way down the slope. A scaled creature and a man. Dust and stone is kicked into the air, limbs ploughing furrows into the ground as they wrestle with each other, both a match in size and brawn.

Another cry. To your left, a giant of a man drops down onto the slope, half-skidding on the loose stones. Dressed in furs and hide, with a mane of thick hair hanging past his shoulders, he looks more animal than human. A gruff roar escapes his lips as the giant springs forward. He barrels into one of the remaining monsters, leading with a bone-spiked shoulder. They both go down in a heap of fur and scaled flesh.

The last monster turns to aid its fallen companion, kicking out at the giant before he has a chance to react. The blow sends the hunter lurching backwards, the bone knife in his hand skating away down the slope. Hissing in triumph, the creature makes another leap for him, its rusty cleaver raised high above its head.

A rattling clink.

The reptile seems to hang in the air for a second, then gives a surprised shriek as it is dragged backwards in a spray of blood. A third hunter, shorter than the others, with a shaven head and weasel-like face, is gripping the end of a chain, its links wrapped around his gloved arm. The other end appears to be sunk into the creature's back by some type of claw-like spear.

With extraordinary strength, the smaller hunter drags the monster towards him, then races around behind a boulder. The creature slams against the side of the rock, just as the hunter reappears, dragging the chain with him. He leaps over the struggling monster and pulls the chain tight across its neck. With a deft movement of his hands, he locks the two lengths of chain together, leaving the monster bound to the rock, choking and gasping for air.

You rise to your feet, transfixed by the battle – looking from one fight to the next, unsure where to focus your efforts. The three hunters are putting on an impressive show, looking more than a match for their larger adversaries. To your left, the giant-sized hunter is now straddling his downed opponent, whose body has hardened to stone. Unperturbed, the hunter has a rock in both hands and is smashing it repeatedly into the monster's face, sending splinters and stone-dust flying in all directions.

Further down the slope, the first hunter is punching tooth-like daggers into the side of his assailant. His arms and chest are coated in gore. The monster kicks its legs, claws trying to find purchase around the man's throat, but the hunter leans away, laughing as if it was all a game. The daggers rise and fall a final time. Dark blood trickles between the pebbles.

'Trek ni vedi!' The shaven-headed hunter has brandished an axe, the blade looking like a flanged bone. His arm swings back and forth, blood spraying to either side. Then he stands back, holding the monster's severed head before his grinning face. 'Trek ni vedi!' He turns and waves it at his companions.

The first hunter hawks then spits a shower of bloody froth into the dirt. He goes to wipe his mouth on his sleeve, but jerks away when he sees the gore smeared all over it. He gives it a tentative sniff, then a thoughtful lick, grimacing with revulsion a moment later. 'Slabra ki.'

His gaze shifts across to his fellow hunters.

That's when he catches sight of you, his blue eyes narrowing. 'Utkik! Unda varlden!' He quickly rises to his feet, the two bloody daggers still gripped in his ham-sized fists. As he advances you notice the birth mark on his face, almost like a red claw discolouring the left cheek. A necklace of bones rattle and clink against his broad chest.

But what you notice most is the look in his eyes.

The three hunters are clearly Skards – and you doubt they will show you any mercy.

Will you

Stand your ground and fight?	355
Attempt to flee?	313
Drop your weapons and surrender?	443

170

The knife is small and easy enough to conceal. You have gained the following item:

Pruning knife
(left hand: dagger)
+1 magic
Ability: first cut

You contemplate investigating the carved box, but the crunch of boots outside the cabin alerts you to danger. Turn to 102.

171

'I did,' Harris proclaims, looking pleased with himself. 'To date, and I know this for a fact,' he waves a finger through the air, as if lecturing to students, 'no-one has made it through a full night. The last one to try was Borgant Hull. Poor fellow.'

'What happened to him?' you croak, not sure you want to know the answer.

'Oh, he's dead,' replies Harris, shrugging his shoulders. 'Went quite mad, I believe.'

Brack scratches at his blond hair, no longer looking so sure of himself. 'And he was a soldier?'

'No, he was a coward,' states Harris, twitching with irritation. 'Don't worry, we'll be fine. After all, we have you to protect us, don't we, Brack?'

The burly warrior beams back, squaring his broad shoulders in acknowledgment of the praise – evidently not picking up on the note of sarcasm in Harris's words or the boy's mocking grin. (Return to 86 to ask another question or turn to 297 to continue on to the tower.)

172

You make a snap decision and veer to the left, scraping past the walls of the cleft to emerge in a shadowed gorge. The air here is cold, the wind keening eerily along the sharp, angular rock walls.

You throw yourself into a headlong sprint, heedless of the uneven ground and scattered rubble, which could twist or snap an ankle with ease. The noise of the dogs behind you is getting louder and more insistent. You can picture their ugly faces, the strong jaws and teeth . . .

'Move!' you scream at yourself. *Don't look back.*

The jagged walls zigzag back and forth, eventually throwing you against a wall of impassable rock. The only way forward is to climb. You look up at the daunting rock face, rising fifty metres or more to the grey sky above.

To climb the wall you will need to complete a *speed* or *brawn* challenge, using whichever attribute is highest:

	Speed/Brawn
Canyon climb	9

If you are successful, turn to 333. If you fail the challenge, turn to 194.

173

The barman snorts with amusement, then startles when he realises you're being deadly serious. 'Bowfinch? Blimey, that'll set you back a pretty penny, especially out here. Do yer think the likes of this rabble carry that kind of money?' He gestures to his shabby-looking clientele. 'Listen. Your best bet is to try the Coracle, down at the docks. There's some party going on there, a rich lord showing off his money. Maybe the Coracle's stocked its cellar with something more than bilge water.'

Will you:

Ask about work?	469
Take a seat in one of the alcoves?	634
Listen to the conversation at the bar?	534
Leave?	426

You drag yourself onto the ice shelf, battling against the furious wind that seems intent on pulling you back. Your cloak snaps through the air as you struggle to your knees, covering your face to shield it from the snow and ice borne up on the currents.

The opening is a wind tunnel – a wide shaft that stretches back into the innards of the mountain. Water trickles down the walls, sculpting the ice into smooth, dripping candles. Some almost seem to hold a shape – like hands reaching out, grasping towards you. Similar formations hang from the ceiling, all angled in the direction of the wind.

Head bowed, you crawl forwards into the tunnel, each inch that you gain a torturous effort. It is as if the very mountain itself is trying to expel you from its presence.

Then you hear the voices. Moans. Whispers. A pained cry, carried on the wind.

You look up, to see a mist coalescing around the dagger-like stalactites. Lightning flashes – and for a moment ghostly faces are illuminated amongst the smoke, their features drawn and twisted into demonic horrors. A keening wail echoes from their open mouths.

You watch transfixed as the misty coils wrap around the hanging ice, tightening and constricting like snakes. There is a dreadful cracking sound as the stalactites come loose. Ice showers down into the passageway, followed by a whistling rain of deadly spikes. By some miracle you manage to twist aside, saving yourself from becoming impaled. But the wind catches you off guard, lifting you off your feet and sending you tumbling back along the passageway.

Desperately you reach out, spectral claws lancing from your fingers to scrape and then dig into the wall. You barely have a chance to steady yourself before the wailing mist is streaking down towards you, its broiling fists gripping daggers of ice. It is time to fight:

	Speed	Magic	Armour	Health
The Keening	4	4	3	50

Special abilities

🛡 **Stalactite splinters**: At the start of every third combat round, the keening mist showers you with fragments of ice. You must roll six dice. For each ⚀ or ⚁ result, you must automatically take 4 damage, ignoring *armour*. If you wish, you can spend a *speed* point to avoid any / all damage from the six rolls (your *speed* is restored at the end of the combat.)

🛡 **Wind fall**: The wind is battering against you, driving you back towards the edge of the ice shelf. If the keening is not defeated by the end of the seventh combat round, you are sent hurtling out into the snow-whipped skies. This automatically loses you the combat.

If you manage to defeat this chilling opponent, turn to 352. If you are defeated, you are thrown back out of the cave. Record the defeat on your hero sheet, then return to 361.

175

You push desperately into the forest, not daring to look back in case you see the angered fengles in hot pursuit. Instead, you try and focus on the path ahead, working hard to maintain your footing as the tangled roots and loose stones threaten to send you tumbling. The ground soon dips, forming a downward slope. As the angle steepens, your downward momentum causes you to pitch forward, sprawling head over heels down the slope to land with a loud smack in a thick pool of mud.

You splash and kick, struggling to find purchase on the pool's bottom. Gradually, you manage to right yourself, relieved to discover that the mud isn't as deep as you thought – the sludgy waters only reach to your waist. However, your problems are far from over. A sharp serpentine hiss sounds inches from your ear. With a startled cry, you flinch away, covering your face with your arms. The imagined strike never lands. Instead you feel something long and slippery slide past your legs, then begin to coil around your body.

Steadily, you lower your arms, eyes now fixed on the scaled head bobbing back and forth above the water. Transfixed by its glittering eyes, you watch as its wide jaws hiss open, sending a forked tongue flickering between sharp fangs. Panic suddenly drives you to action. Frantically, you reach for your dagger, realising that you are now trapped in the clutches of a giant mud snake. Unless you can defeat it quickly, the snake's venom will soon overpower you. It is time to fight:

	Speed	Brawn	Armour	Health
Mud snake	0	1	0	14

Special abilities

♥ **Mud bath**: You must lower your *speed* by 1 for the duration of this combat.

♥ **Weak venom**: If you take health damage from the snake, roll a die. On a ⚀ result you are inflicted with *venom* and must lose a further 2 *health* at the end of each combat round for the duration of the combat. If you roll ⚁ or more, the venom has no effect. Once inflicted with venom, there is no need to roll in future rounds. You can use your *charm* special ability if you wish, to reroll the venom result (remember, you can only use each *charm* ability once per combat).

If you manage to defeat the mud snake, remember to restore your *health* then turn to 140.

176

The spirit vanishes and the medallion with it. Anise nods with approval. 'Good riddance,' she says to the now-empty space where the spirit had once been. 'Come on, let's get to the roof before any more ghosts decide they want to play.' Turn to 195.

177

You cross to the other side of the eyrie, where a slope of tumbled boulders leads you back down to the canyon floor. From here, you backtrack through the narrow gullies, determined to discover what has become of the cart and your companions. Turn to **391**.

178

You enter a steamy kitchen, where a red-faced cook is beating and stretching dough. He raises a floury hand as Anise scampers past. 'You've forgotten Segg's wine again, girl,' he snaps briskly. 'You know what the old fool's like when he doesn't get his wine.'

The cook does a double-take when he sees you hovering by the doorway. ''Ere, what d'you want?' He waves you away, sending a cloud of flour billowing across the table. 'I swear, we got no more, I tell you. We're on basic rations – if you want suckling pig or venison I suggest you turn round and ride south, good and hard now.'

Anise smiles when she sees you have followed her. 'Segg sent him for the wine,' she states, her eyes glinting mischievously. 'Come on then, don't keep him waiting.' She gestures for you to join her by a copper pot heating next to the fire.

The cook mutters something, then returns to kneading the dough.

'So, what did you come here for – to poke fun at me like the others?' She picks up a ladle and starts stirring the mulled wine. Without giving you a chance to answer, she nods over to some shelves. 'Get one of those bottles, will you? The big one – Segg likes his wine.'

'Are you really a Skard?' you ask, reaching for the bottle.

'Are you really a dream walker?' she answers back playfully.

You freeze in mid-action. 'What did you say? Dream what?'

'I saw you, when they brought you in. Who else d'you think does all the fetching and carrying around here? Getting water, fresh bandages, medicines . . . Stupid Harris is just plain lazy, so Segg relies on me.'

Her eyes appraise you for a second. 'Of course, back then you were all skin and bone. Not like now.'

'I still don't know—'

Anise blows out her cheeks, looking exasperated. 'Just bring me the bottle and hold it. You can do that, can't you?'

You grin. 'Are all Skards so bossy?'

'I'm not a Skard,' she glowers, slamming a funnel into the neck of the bottle. 'I was cast out. To them, I have no name. Without a name, I am nothing.'

'Your name is Anise.' You watch as she ladles the wine into the funnel.

'That's the name Everard gave me.'

You watch as she continues to fill the bottle, noticing her small mannerisms – the way she chews her bottom lip when she is concentrating, bunching her shoulders whenever she lifts the ladle. Everything she does appears careful and meticulous. 'Stop looking at me!' she snaps. 'Do they not have girls where you come from?'

You wonder if your dead, pallid skin is capable of blushing. The thought brings you back to reality with a jolt – suddenly making you self-aware of the large and ungainly body you now inhabit. The bottle slips in your hand. You catch it, but some of the red wine spills onto your fingers. It burns, more than it should.

'Clumsy me,' you hiss through the pain.

Anise takes the bottle from you, swapping the funnel for a cork. 'Don't worry, all done.' She brushes the stray curls from her eyes. 'Thank you.'

'What for – holding a bottle?'

'For talking to me like I'm not a kitchen rat.' She gives you one of her lop-sided smiles, then turns away quickly. 'I should be going. Much work to do. I'll take this to Segg – yes, that's what I'll do.' Flustered, she hurries away, slipping past the cook, who rolls his eyes in exasperation.

(Make a note of the keyword *kitchens* on your hero sheet.)

Will you:

Return to the hall and talk to the lone soldier?	**308**
Leave and return to the courtyard?	**113**

179

Black scars criss-cross the snow as the remaining racers weave between the splintered wreckage of crashed sleds. Light quickly turns to shadow, the land rising up to form a vast mountain, blotting out the sky with its dark immensity. Bleak Peak.

A narrow pathway winds up around the mountain's face, spiralling all the way to its lofty summit. To reach it, some racers have opted for the snow-covered foothills whilst others have driven onto a slope of ridged ice – a route that offers a quicker means of gaining the mountain's winding track.

Will you:

Risk the ice slope?	524
Head across the snow hills?	749

180

You pull back your cloak, revealing the bear necklace – the halstek – that marks you as leader of the bear tribe. There is a mixture of astonishment and anger from the assembled warriors. Gurt continues to pick meat from his bone with a nonchalant air.

'Who did you kill for that?' he asks, before filling his mouth yet again.

'Taulu gave me this necklace,' you state warily, glancing at the Skards. 'Before he died. He entrusted me with it. Desnar, his brother challenged me for the right to wear it – to lead the bear tribe. We underwent vela styker and I proved the victor.'

Gurt shakes his head. With a flick of his hand, he gestures to the warrior beside you. Before you can stop him, the Skard grabs the necklace and rips it free, scattering the bones and claws across the table. You reel back in shock, feeling the manacle bite hard into your arm as Nanuk fills your mind with a demented howl.

'No . . . you cannot . . .'

Gurt stares at you from beneath his brows. 'My patience is wearing thin. And you're ruining a good meal.'

Will you:

Agree to fight the einherjar?	318
Pledge your allegiance to Gurt?	200

181

You pick up the tile and push it into the square-shaped hole. Leaning back, you wait expectantly for something to happen. However, it appears that you have chosen the incorrect rune. As you hurriedly try and prise the tile back out of the grid, you hear a sudden crack of branches followed by another barking cry. If you don't run now, the other fengles will find you! Frantically, you spring to your feet and sprint for the cover of the opposite treeline. Turn to **175**.

182

As you drag the sack through the dirt, something scrapes and catches against a rock. Lifting up the sack, you see that there is a tear at the bottom, causing several sword hilts to poke through. Other items now lie scattered along the trail, having fallen out of the hole. You retrace your steps, stooping to retrieve the stolen equipment.

Amongst the weapons and fragments of armour, you spot a pair of black-enamelled gauntlets, etched with magical runes. You are immediately reminded of the warrior you spoke with in the main hall, who described a similar set of gauntlets that had gone missing.

If you wish to keep these magical gloves for yourself, then you may add the following item to your hero sheet:

Ran's beaters
(gloves)
+1 armour
Ability: charge

If you would rather return the gauntlets to their rightful owner at a later date, then remove the keyword *thievery* from your hero sheet and replace it with the keyword *gains*. When you have made your decision, turn to **221**.

183

Your feet become tangled in the bloodied canvas. Losing your balance, you drop to the ground – a mishap that quickly becomes a blessing. The yeti's next swing sweeps overhead, exposing its body to a counter strike. You take the opening without a second thought, driving your weapons hard through the fur and fatty tissue to puncture whatever vital organ you can reach. You keep pushing until you feel the beast's body go slack, then you release your grip, rolling away as the enormous yeti topples forward.

There is a sticky-sounding splat.

You find yourself face down in a treacle tart. Grimacing, you scoop the goo from your eyes, spitting out a mouthful of pastry. 'Some party,' you remark dryly.

If you are a warrior, turn to 440. If you are a mage, turn to 131. If you are a rogue, turn to 561.

184

The troll slams its hammers against the ground, sending a shockwave ripping through the stone of the keep. Soldiers are thrown up into the air by the force of the blast, including several of the reptilian monsters.

For a brief moment, the battlefield is obscured by stone dust.

Then a dark shape rushes past you.

Rook is sprinting towards the troll, his cloak now tattered ribbons whipping back from his shoulders. He sends knives spinning towards one of the scaled warriors. Several thud deep into its chest but appear to do little harm. Without slowing, he skids underneath the creature's sword swing, drawing another dagger to hamstring it as he slides past. The reptilian stumbles then falls. Before it can recover, you take off the creature's head with a well-aimed swing of your weapon.

Rook rolls to his feet, giving you a brief nod. 'Still alive?'

'Barely,' you grunt, spitting dust from your lips.

The ground has started to tremble again – but this time the cause is evident. The troll is lumbering towards you, flanked by two of the tall warriors. As they approach you notice their scaled flesh shimmer, then start to change colour – going from blue-black to a cold grey.

'Stone blood,' hisses Rook. He motions to a group of guards on the inner wall. They move to the edge, holding buckets which you assume contain tar. One member of the group has a lit torch, waving it in answer. It is time to fight:

	Speed	Brawn	Armour	Health
Nisse troll	4	3	3	20
Nisse warrior	3	2	2(*)	15
Nisse warrior	3	2	2(*)	15

Special abilities

🛡 **Petrifying peril**: The warriors are coating themselves in stone. At the end of each combat round, their *armour* is raised by 1 – up to a maximum of 5.

🛡 **Regeneration**: The troll heals 2 *health* at the end of each combat round. Once the troll is reduced to zero *health*, this ability no longer applies. (This cannot take the troll above its starting *health* of 20.)

🛡 **Outnumbered**: At the end of each combat round, you must take 1 damage from each surviving opponent, ignoring *armour*. This ability only applies while you are faced with multiple opponents.

If you have any tar barrels recorded on your hero sheet, you can use them at the end of a combat round. Each tar barrel causes 1 damage to all opponents, ignoring *armour*. You can use up to four barrels per combat round. (Remember to remove any used tar barrels from your hero sheet.)

If you manage to defeat your opponents, turn to 427.

185

You swing out blindly, your makeshift club sending chunks of toadstool flying in all directions. Eventually you find an opening and push forward, the edge of the forest dimly visible through the rotting haze. But, just as you are about to reach the safety of the tree line, one of the toadstools shuffles into view. Without slowing, you swing your arm back and deliver a punishing whack with your club. There is a satisfying explosion of pulpy flesh as the remains of the toadstool shower down around you, coating your clothing in sticky goo.

You have gained the following bonus:

Death cap fungus
(special)
Add 1 *armour* to a chest, feet
or cloak item you have equipped

At last, your way is clear. You plunge into the forest, stumbling and tripping over roots and stones in your haste to escape. Only when you finally drop to your knees, half-blinded by sweat and sticky toadstool slime, do you pause to take breath.

Looking back, you are relieved to see that there is no sign of pursuit. After taking a moment to recover, you continue onwards through the tangled undergrowth, determined to put as much distance as you can between yourself and the peculiar ring of toadstools. Turn to **161**.

186

(If you have the word *fractured* on your hero sheet, turn to **88**. Otherwise, read on.)

You push against the wide double-doors, their hinges creaking and groaning as they slowly open out onto the great hall. To your surprise it is a grander chamber than you had expected, although still a pale imitation of the royal court back at the palace.

Two rows of trestle tables run the length of the hall, framed on either side by frosted-glass windows and fluttering house banners. At the opposite end, stairs lead up to a high table where you assume Everard and his top-ranking officers take their meals.

A gust of wind follows you into the hall, sending the nearby torches fluttering in their sconces. 'Shut the door,' grumbles a nearby soldier, waving his mug in your direction. He is plainly a grizzled old veteran, his craggy pock-marked face made rougher by his thick tangle of hair and beard.

Further along the same table, a group of young recruits are talking and laughing. One of their number, a blond-haired male with arms as thick as barrels, is recounting some tale of battle, making stabbing gestures with his leg of mutton.

Will you:

Talk with the lone soldier?	308
Join the recruits?	199
Leave and return to the courtyard?	113

187

Your eyes are drawn to the flames licking around the coals. Most of the acolytes are standing around the fire, their attention focused solely on the ritual. You dart from pillar to pillar, seeking the best angle for your attack, then – praying that your aim is true – you toss the explosives into the fire.

They tumble across the coals in a shower of sparks. There are a few gasps of alarm, then suddenly the cavern is lit by a bright explosion, sending rock and bodies flying through the air. With weapons drawn, you are already moving forward, striding through the smoke, slashing and cutting at the staggering acolytes that get in your way.

'What's happening?' The woman shrieks. 'It's impossible . . .'

You emerge out of the dust, stepping over the scattered coals. The female and two of her coven have survived the blast. You meet her cold glare with a twisted grin.

'I like to defy the odds.'

'The fool! Insidious has failed us!' The woman draws out her wand, aiming its spiked head towards your chest. 'I will not make the same mistake!' It is time to fight:

	Speed	Magic	Armour	Health
Coven matriarch	11	7	5	40
Coven acolyte	10	6	4	30
Coven acolyte	10	6	4	30

Special abilities

🟣 **Matriarch's malice**: The matriarch has magical wards carved into her skin. While the Matriarch has *health*, you cannot use modifier abilities during this combat.

🟣 **Dark mending**: At the end of each combat round, each opponent will heal themselves for 2 *health*. This cannot take them above their starting *health* and once their *health* is reduced to zero, this ability no longer applies.

🟣 **Outnumbered**: At the end of each combat round, you must take 1 damage from each surviving opponent, ignoring *armour*. This ability only applies while you are faced with multiple opponents.

If you manage to defeat these villainous mages, turn to 523.

188

A set of worn stairs brings you to a narrow landing, with an open window at either end. In the wall facing you are two doors, both looking identical. From behind the door on your right you can hear the chinking of armour and a muffled grunting noise.

Will you:
Take the left door?   12
Take the right door?   76

189

'Race one is across the shattered sea,' explains the organiser. 'Thirty racers, split into two rounds of fifteen. The top five racers in each round go through to the final. Understand? Good – let's get you onto the ice.' Turn to 222.

The Skard sentries escort you back into the longhouse. Gurt grimaces with disappointment as he lifts his eyes from his bowl of stew. 'You're back, to waste more of my time.' He licks his fingers, pushing the last of his meal aside. 'I've told you, you ain't getting an audience with the asynjur . . .'

You pull the bottle of Bowfinch from your pack and then roll it down the table. Gurt splutters in surprise, almost lifting up the table as he struggles to lean forward, snatching the bottle before it drops off the edge.

You fold your arms, waiting.

Gurt empties his mug over the floor then, after shaking it free of dregs, proceeds to fill it with wine. He sniffs the contents suspiciously then tips the mug back, gulping it down. When the mug is dry he slams it back down onto the table, giving an appreciative belch.

'Well?' you enquire.

Gurt pours another cup, licking his red-stained lips. 'You're a persistent little hound, I'll give yer that.'

You have gained the following special ability:

Dogged determination (mo): You may reroll any/all of your hero's speed dice, accepting the result of the rerolled dice. This ability can only be used once per combat.

Gurt waves his mug through the air, sloshing wine down his sleeve. 'All right then. Take him to the hall. Let's see what Syn Hulda makes of my lapdog!' Turn to 521.

191

You slump into the nearest chair, giving a sigh of contentment. It is good to feel safe and warm again. While Sylvie stirs the pot, you take a moment to study her. Clearly she is an outdoors woman, used to fending for herself. There are no airs or graces to her appearance, the tangles in her grey hair and the patches on her clothing testament to a make-do attitude. Her build is stocky, with broad shoulders and a plump roundness to her figure. A far cry from the noble women at court – thin and pale as porcelain, dressed in sweet smiles and elegant dresses, no different to a toymaker's doll.

You glance down at your own clothing, torn and muddied – the lace on the sleeves hanging loose in several places. *What would those fine ladies think of me now?*

Sylvie takes a bowl and ladles out some stew, then places it on the table. You wait expectantly for some cutlery, but the woman has already moved on to serving her own portion, before taking a sip from the edge of her bowl. 'Hmm, delicious.'

Evidently court manners have no place here. With a shrug, you grab the bowl in both hands and bring it to your lips. You take a gulp of the hot meaty stew, then notice Sylvie's eyes regarding you with interest, presumably waiting for your verdict. 'It's good,' you lie. The truth is, the stew is watery and over-spiced, with a fatty residue that clogs in the throat. Not what a prince like you is used to. But you are famished, so you greedily take another mouthful. 'It's perfect,' you add, struggling to swallow a lump of gristle.

While you continue to eat, your attention drifts to your surroundings. Books and scrolls appear to take priority in the main room, along with the bewildering menagerie of plants. A small work table is set against the far wall, scattered with twigs and leaves, and a number of half-finished charms.

Will you:

Ask why she chose to live in this remote place?	42
Ask about the plants?	145
Ask about the charms?	239
Ask about the books and scrolls?	109
Ask for directions to the nearest settlement?	94
Finish your meal (ends the conversation)?	207

192

The race organiser furrows his brow. 'What you doing, showing your face here? Everyone saw you crash and burn out on the ice. I got no time for losers – now get gone!' He waves you away, tutting the whole time. Return to 106.

193

Taking Caul's advice, you head back through the chambers and passages to arrive at the trapped corridor. You opt to go first, throwing yourself into a full-on sprint. Fire roars all around you, the glyphs sparking with magic as your boots strike the stone. To survive the 'corridor of doom' you must pass a number of *speed* challenges. Each challenge you successfully complete allows you to move to the next challenge on the list.

If you fail a drake fire challenge you must immediately take 10 damage, ignoring *armour*. You may then move onto the next challenge. If you fail a lightning challenge, you are knocked back to the previous challenge on the list, which you must pass again to proceed:

	Speed
Drake fire	12
Lightning rune	13
Drake fire	12
Lightning rune	13
Drake fire	14
Lightning rune	13

If you still have *health* remaining after completing all of the challenges then you have reached the end of the corridor. Turn to 637. If you lose all your *health*, you must count this as a defeat on your hero sheet. You may then try the challenge again.

194

Your newfound strength is a bonus, but not enough to make up for your lack of climbing experience. You have barely made it five metres before you lose your footing and fall, plummeting back to the ground in a flurry of dust and stone.

You scramble to your feet, just as the dog-team comes skidding round the corner. Trapped against the wall, you have no choice but to fight:

	Speed	Brawn	Armour	Health
Pack dog	2	1	1	12
Pack dog	1	1	1	10
Pack dog	0	1	1	10

Special abilities
♥ **Outnumbered**: At the end of each combat round, you must take 1 damage from each surviving opponent, ignoring *armour*. This ability only applies while you are faced with multiple opponents.

If you manage to send these dogs packing, turn to 236. If you lose the combat, remember to record your defeat on your hero sheet. You may then attempt the combat again or return to the map.

195

At the rear of the chamber you discover a rectangular depression cut into the wall, where an iron ladder rises up to the inky night sky. Holy inscriptions have been etched along the sides of the shaft, now mostly worn away or painted over in arcane whorls of grime and blood.

Anise is first onto the ladder, hurrying up the metal rungs to the top. She disappears over the edge, then a second later beckons you to follow.

Climbing the ladder, you find yourself on the roof of the tower. The wind is fierce, stabbing at you with its cold daggers, whipping back your cloak and forcing you to stagger. Ahead, you can see the ghost of a knight, standing on the edge of the battlements. There is a wild look to his eyes as the wind sweeps back his long auburn hair.

'Rinehart?' Anise shouts the name over the roaring gale, her expression more baffled than fearful.

The knight looks back at you, the ghost-light flickering in his pained glare. 'Do not stop me! I betrayed my family, betrayed my vows.' He takes another step, his feet on the very edge of the stone, his balance wavering as he looks down at the vertiginous drop. 'My brother . . . he can never forgive me for what I did!'

If you have *Mott's medallion* and wish to offer it to the knight, turn to 533. Otherwise, turn to 343.

196

You lift up the latch and push open the door. The interior of the cabin is awash with warmth and light, cast from the roaring fire that blazes in the hearth. An iron cooking pot rests on the hearth's lintel, a cloud of steam rising from its bubbling contents.

Tentatively, you call out again, to check if anyone is home. There is no answer.

'Suppose I should make myself at home,' you grin, stepping inside and leaving the door to close behind you.

The main room of the cabin is small and cluttered, dominated by a wooden table covered in pots, plants and jars of herbs. The opposite wall is lined with shelves, where books and scrolls are pushed into every available space.

Hungrily, your mind wanders back to the cooking pot. Surely no one would mind if you just helped yourself. As you start towards the fire you notice a small table, tucked underneath the window. The top is covered with twigs, leaves and herbal mixtures – and several half-worked charms.

Intrigued, you cross to take a closer look, wondering if there is anything here that might be useful. Rummaging through the freshly-picked wood litter, you recognise burdock root and sage, and strips of cherry bark. Most of the herbs and mixtures are medicinal in nature, simple cures and tonics for everyday ills. Of greater interest is the small carved box, resting next to a sheaf of papers. You also spot a black-handled knife that has been used to shave the bark. A series of runic symbols glow along its iron blade.

Will you:	
Take the knife?	170
Open the box?	65
Refuse to tamper with someone's belongings?	102

A drum beat resounds across the camp. Sura turns her head, her grey eyes falling on the small group that is gathering. 'It is time,' she whispers.

You follow the old woman into the crowd. Men and women move reverently aside for the old woman – for you, they give glares and gruff curses. Your back prickles from the imaginary knives you can picture sinking into your flesh.

'They do not want me here,' you hiss at Sura. 'I should go . . .'

Sura ignores you, coming to a halt at the centre of the circle. The drum beat falls to silence. For a time, the only sound is the low despondent moan of the wind. Desnar steps forward, his black hair now braided and tied back by a leather band. He is followed by a shorter man, thin and wiry, with a long drooping moustache tipped with red dye. In his hands he holds a spear and a bone knife.

Sura speaks in Skard, her voice raised to the assembled crowd. Then her eyes flick to you.

'By nightfall we will have a chieftain. The two of you will take the blood test. Only one may wear the halstek.' Sura nods to the Skard holding the spear and the knife. He takes a step forward, offering them both at arms length. Sura moves aside, gesturing for you to approach the man. 'As you challenge one of our own, southlander, you have the right to decide the test. The spear is the test of the hunter. A chieftain must provide for his people. Without the hunt, we are nothing.'

'And the knife?' you croak, nervously.

'The test of the warrior. The fighter. A chieftain should have the strength to lead. The strength to best his enemies in battle.'

> Will you:
> Choose the spear?   629
> Choose the knife?   488

Unable to react in time, your sled skids sideways across the snow, ploughing into a steeped bank. You are thrown up into the air, your sled flipping over and dragging your yelping dog-team with it. By some miracle you manage to twist out of your fall, spectral claws extending from your fingertips. They scrape along the edge of the crevasse, throwing up a flurry of white splinters until they finally find purchase, stopping you from plunging into the ice-cold waters.

You may have avoided taking a dip, but unfortunately you have failed to complete the race. You are now disqualified from the tournament. Replace the keyword *rookie/veteran* with *underdog*. Return to the map to continue your adventure.

199

As you approach, several of the recruits turn their heads, watching you with interest. The blond-haired warrior continues to jab and swing his mutton, until he realises he is no longer the centre of attention. Grumpily, he shifts round in his seat, his eyes narrowing when he sees you.

'What in Hel's fire is that?' he gawps, looking you up and down.

'Something with more brains than you, Brack,' grins the lone female of the group. She is perched on the edge of the table, feet resting on the bench. Of all the recruits she is the most well-groomed, resplendent in plate armour that has been polished to a high sheen. Her auburn hair is close shaven, given her a boyish look. A scar along her cheek does nothing to diminish her natural beauty. 'It's our handsome new recruit.'

Her comment draws sniggers from her companions. You can well believe that your appearance is nothing short of peculiar – with pale, rheumy eyes and skin mottled with broken veins and bruises. But being the outsider is nothing new to you.

'If that's what the fever does, oh man . . .' Brack rips a piece of meat from the leg, chewing it noisily with a half-open mouth.

'Actually, for me – it's probably an improvement,' you shrug, playing along with the joke. It appears to work, eliciting more laughter from the soldiers.

'I'm Brack,' grins the blond-haired warrior, holding out a ham-sized fist.

You look at the proffered limb, then back at him, confused.

'Touch fists, man. Show respect.'

Awkwardly you make a fist and knock it against his own. Brack seems pleased with the gesture, nodding and ripping another chunk of meat from his mutton bone. 'That's Henna,' he says, jerking a thumb at the girl. 'I'm teaching her good table manners, ain't I, lady?'

The female nods her head in a more civil greeting. 'Brack is our resident jester. He just forgets to wear the bells.'

Brack licks grease from his fingers, grinning. 'Don't listen to her, she's from the academy. All posh and proper like, not like us rough boys, eh?' He punches one of his companions on the arm, a thin-looking lad with braids in his hair. His sinewy arms are covered in various tattoos. He grins at Brack, nodding eagerly – evidently keen to please.

'This is Jarrow,' says Brack, tossing his bone into the other boy's bowl. 'He don't say much, which is why I like him. So, what about you then, fever man? What yer got to say for yourself?'

You are about to answer, when your attention is caught by a red-haired kitchen girl, collecting empty plates from a nearby table. She looks anything but pretty, with a squared jaw and pinched nose, and a lip made crooked by a scar.

And yet you can't take your eyes off her – perhaps it is the way she carries herself. Sure and confident.

Brack is the first to notice. He makes a rumbling at the back of his throat, then spits in the girl's direction. 'Damn Skard,' he growls. 'The only good Skard is a dead 'un, that's what my pa used to say.'

Jarrow shrieks with laughter, an unsettling noise in the sudden uneasy silence.

The girl looks your way and offers a half-smile, before turning quickly and heading back to the kitchens.

'Her name is Anise,' says Henna. 'I understand they found her when she was a babe. Her people left her to die . . . out on the ice fields.'

Brack smirks. 'And I can see why. Fetch me more meat, girl!' He shouts after her. 'Stupid Skard. If I had my way . . .' He puts a hand to his dagger. 'What you say, Jarr?'

The younger lad gives another of his hyena laughs. Henna rolls her eyes, pushing off from the table. 'Suddenly, I don't like this company,' she sighs. 'I'm heading off for duty.'

Will you:

Follow Anise into the kitchens?	178
Talk to the lone soldier?	308
Leave the hall and return to the courtyard?	113

200

The rune-carved manacle continues to sap at your strength, draining your magic and leaving you weak and nauseous. You drop to your knees, out of exhaustion rather than submission, but it is a gesture that pleases Gurt.

'The dog has learnt to beg.' He sucks the last of the tender meat from his bone then tosses it at your feet. You glare down at the greasy item, then lift your eyes to meet his wide expectant grin. 'There are scraps on that bone, don't let it go to waste.'

You glare back at Gurt, then at the grinning Skards. Taking the bone, you make a show of pulling at the remaining fatty strands, forcing them down your dry, dead throat. Finally you suck out the soft marrow, before tossing the clean bone aside.

Gurt sniggers like a cruel child. 'Good, now you're going to perform a new trick. I tell you what I want and you go fetch. Simple enough for you?' He lifts his tankard, taking several noisy gulps. Then he slams it back onto the table with a rumbling belch. 'This so-called beer tastes like barrel water. What I want is something more refined, more suited to my standing.' He wipes the foam from his lips, then knocks the tankard away with his fingers. 'Normally I get supplies from the trappers, but they're thin on the ground. So, you can go to Ryker's. They'll have shipments in for the winter months. Get me a bottle of Bowfinch, the '55 vintage.'

You stare back at the man with genuine surprise. 'You want me to get you a bottle of wine? Is this how you test my courage?'

Gurt slams his fists on the table, rattling the pots. 'Courage? I'm seeing how far you want to go to make a bigger ass of yourself. These are my terms. If you don't like them, you know what you can do. Now, remove this . . . thing.' He waves a hand at you, turning his head in feigned revulsion.

You are dragged out of the hall, your cries of agony resounding in your ears. Once you are back on the snow fields the manacle is removed from your arm, then the two warriors melt back into the pale mist. You are left lying in the snow, clutching at your burnt flesh, teeth still gritted against the pain.

You realise that the only way to gain entrance to the Hall of Vindsvall is to please the vile Gurt. Surely it can't be that difficult to get hold of a bottle of Bowfinch '55. (Make a note of the keyword *Bowfinch* on your hero sheet. Then return to the quest map to continue your journey.)

201

The fight soon descends into an inelegant scrap, both of you slipping and sliding on the churned-up snow. A lucky opening finally presents itself – and with a snarl you drive your weapons through the man's torso, pinning him to the alley wall.

You sheathe your weapons, then quickly search the man's corpse – already sensing the previously timid onlookers moving closer, hungry for any spoils. You manage to grab a money pouch (you have gained 30 gold crowns) and two *muttok pelts* (simply make a note of these on your hero sheet, they don't take up backpack space). You may also take one of the following:

Without prejudice	Avianators	Blood scent
(gloves)	(head)	(ring)
+1 speed +1 brawn	+1 speed +1 magic	+1 brawn
Ability: savagery	Ability: finesse	Ability: bleed
	(requirement: mage)	

Remove the word *ashes* from your hero sheet. You may now head towards the docks (turn to 659) or the compound (turn to 426).

You step towards the edge of the circle, hoping your fears are unfounded. However, as soon as you come within range of the toadstools, they start to shuffle forward, their black caps belching clouds of spores into the air.

Desperately, you look around for a means of defending yourself. Next to the skeleton you spot a broken branch of willow. With no other option, you hastily pick it up, brandishing it like a club. You have now gained the following item:

Whacking willow
(main hand: club)
+1 brawn

You realise your only chance of survival is to bash your way through the circle of toadstools. It is time to take on the might of:

	Speed	Brawn	Armour	Health
The terrorstools	0	1	1	12

Special abilities

🛡 **Spore cloud**: At the end of each combat round, roll a die. If the result is ⚀ or less, you are caught in a blinding cloud of spores, reducing your *speed* by 1 for the next combat round only. If you roll ⚁ or more, you have avoided the spores.

If you manage to defeat these fearsome fungi, remember to restore your *health* to full, then turn to **185**.

203

'It's a colourful history, to be sure,' says Harris with apparent relish. 'It used to be a watchtower, manned by guards from the keep. Now it's strictly out of bounds. No one is allowed to go there.'

'With good reason, I am sure,' you interject.

Harris snorts. 'Yes, something bad happened there. I found out about it in one of Segg's books.'

'I know I'm going to regret asking this,' you sigh. 'So, why is the tower out of bounds?'

'It was over-run by creatures from the rift,' answers Harris. 'There were guards trapped inside – some powerful magic surrounded the tower, stopping anyone from entering or leaving. With no chance of rescue, the guards holed themselves up in a storeroom, tried to survive. But the dark things still found them . . . pounding and beating against the door. It was only a matter of time before the creatures broke in, and set to the guards with their claws and teeth.'

Anise shivers, pulling her cloak tighter around her body. 'That's a horrible story.'

Harris looks over at her with an upraised eyebrow. 'You think that's the end? The guards were dying one by one – horribly, screaming and crying as they were torn to pieces. Only one remained, a mage. He resorted to the forbidden arts in a desperate attempt to save himself. He used necromancy. He raised his fallen companions from the dead and turned their corpses against the enemy.'

Harris's eyes flick to you, taking in your mottled, grey-flesh. 'Somehow, he was able to break the magic that surrounded the tower. When the soldiers finally managed to get inside, they found a blood bath – but no survivors.'

'This was a long time ago, right?' Brack is still smiling, but you sense his anxiety.

Harris clicks his tongue. 'Stop interrupting, you buffoon. In the years after, it was clear that there was something wrong with the tower. Things kept happening, strange occurrences – soldiers going missing, reports of strange sounds, many refusing to set foot inside. Then, the necromancer returned. A shadow of his former self, but somehow alive once again, as if the tower itself had willed it. Only three soldiers were brave enough to go against him. Two brothers, Mott and Rinehart – and a cavalier, Caeleb.'

'Oh, and I bet this ends well . . .' Brack pulls a playful face, still pretending to be amused rather than scared.

Harris shoots him an irritated look. 'No, it didn't. The necromancer killed Mott and raised him back from the dead. Rinehart was forced to kill his own brother, then, driven mad by what he had done, he threw himself from the roof of the tower.'

'And the necromancer?' asks Anise, breathless from the suspense.

'Caeleb was successful in ending the mage's life. He was the only one to return. A week later, he resigned from his post. Some say he was never the same man again. Since then, the tower has been left to rot and ruin – the perfect dare for anyone who thinks they're brave enough to spend a night within its walls.' (Return to 86 to ask another question or turn to 297 to continue on to the tower.)

204
Quest: The winter caves

(NOTE: You must have completed the orange quest *The bitter end* before you can access this location.)

The nights have grown longer, the days shorter. Time has lost all meaning – days, weeks – you can no longer be sure if it has not been a lifetime. The landscape has become a vast white emptiness, stark and brilliant to your now-sensitive eyes. During the day it is often unbearable, forcing you to hunker down and await the night, when your heightened vision can dress everything in a muted green.

A ghost world.

At times you wonder if you have left Valeron altogether; somehow slipped into the dreamscape of the Norr. The veil between the two seems thin. The lure of that other place is a constant craving.

Hood pulled low, you trudge on, the ice matting your furs and armour. You cannot feel the cold – you cannot feel anything anymore, not even the pain of loneliness or the yearning sickness for home. No cold, no pain. And yet, your body still bears the ravages of the north – red and yellow patches of frostbite, darkening in places to a blue-blackness; blisters from the burning ice; double-vision from the glare that you cannot shut out . . . You wonder what the pain might feel like if you still had your humanity. Instead, your body feels nothing but a dead weight, dragging you down – anchoring you to this forsaken world.

You have no need of shelter. No need of sleep. Instead, when the pull of the Norr is at its strongest, you hunch into your furs, leaving the whip-sharp wind to do its worst. Eyes closed, you drift off – reaching out with your mind, touching that other presence and letting it pull you away. To the dreamscape. There the land is a twisted shadow, where lost spirits howl and demons stalk. But there is always Nanuk. Waiting for you. Protecting you.

On each journey you feel your link with the real world weakening, like a rope that has frayed and is down to its last fibres. If it wasn't for Nanuk perhaps it would snap altogether, severing you from the life you once knew. But the bear always sends you back – guiding your spirit into that cold-dead body, leaving you squirming and kicking as your muscles spasm, coming alive in fervent protest. And so you awake to darkness and set out once again, ever onwards into the white-green void – a lone figure, detached and drifting . . .

The near-endless plains give rise to rockier highlands, where frozen ridges push up through the splintered ice. These jagged formations grow increasingly larger, until you find yourself dwarfed by their clipped peaks. The wind, now funnelled along makeshift valleys, carries a desolate, mournful keen.

There have been no signs of life for days, possibly weeks. So it comes as a jolt when you turn down another steep-walled channel and see two figures standing outside a ragged-looking tent. Before you have a chance to pull back, you see that you have already been spotted – one of the pair is waving their hand, beckoning you over.

One thing the north has taught you – always be wary of others.

You approach with your hands resting on your weapons, quickly sizing up your opponents, looking for strengths, weaknesses . . . possessions that might prove valuable. The dawn light picks out the woman's smile as she watches you advance. Like her companion, she is dressed in a thick fur-trimmed jacket reaching to her knees, hands tucked inside lobster-shaped mittens. The other figure is tall and broad-shouldered – a middle-aged man, with thin brown hair and a straggly beard. He tugs a glove off with his teeth, his bared hand moving to a knife at his belt. He hesitates, seeing your weapons and knowing that he is badly outmatched.

Inside the small tent, fashioned from leather and furs, you see a third member of the group – a red-haired male, almost wasted to bone. He tosses and turns beneath a covering of blankets, murmuring in his sleep or some pained delirium.

'Oh, fortune smiles!'

Your eyes flick back to the woman. Her grin is still fixed to her face, as if it was frozen there by the wind. Up close, you see she is about the same age as the man. A stitched label on her jacket reads: *Reah*. 'Will you help us, stranger?' she asks eagerly. 'We are desperate – and all alone out here.'

Will you:

Ask what they are doing in the canyon?	237
Ask about the man in the tent?	332
Ask how you might help? (starts the quest)	146

205

You cross to the other side of the rock, where a slope of tumbled boulders leads you back down to the lake. From here you quickly backtrack along the shore, determined to discover what has become of the cart and your companions. Turn to 391.

206

Searching the remains of the fire giant, you find 100 gold crowns and one of the following rewards:

Gjoll's hammer	Swathe of scales	Deep-ice dredgers
(main hand: hammer)	(cloak)	(feet)
+2 speed +4 brawn	+2 speed +2 armour	+2 speed +3 armour
Ability: stagger	Ability: deflect	Ability: heavy blow

When you have updated your hero sheet, turn to 705.

207

You knuckle your tired eyes, stifling a yawn. It would be so good to give in, to finally go to sleep and sate your body's craving for natural rest. But you can't. You fear what happens when you sleep – a fear that drives you immediately to your pouch, seeking more dragon leaf. However, you pause when you notice Sylvie watching. Something in her look makes you reconsider.

'Would you like a night cap?' she smiles. 'Probably high time I tested my home brew on someone other than myself. It'll help you sleep.' Sylvie gets out of her chair and heads over to a cupboard.

'No, I'm fine,' you protest. 'Please, I don't need any help.'

Sylvie returns to the table carrying two small cups and a leather gourd. 'Of course,' she grins. 'Silly me. You could probably sleep standing on your feet with all you've been through.'

You continue to shake your head, realising she has misunderstood your meaning. 'Please, I can't . . .'

The woman rolls her eyes. 'It isn't that bad, honest.' Removing the stopper, she fills the cups and then pushes one toward you. 'Try it anyway. It'll put some fire in your belly, chase out that cold.' Her look is expectant – almost challenging.

You take the cup, peering at the clear liquid inside. It smells of aniseed. 'I suppose I could,' you concede, not wishing to offend. You raise the cup in a toast, 'Long live the king!', then knock back the contents. It isn't until you swallow that you feel the heat of the liquid. It makes you breathless, choking for air.

'Strong, isn't it?' grins Sylvie. You notice her own cup is still on the table, untouched.

Then the room starts to spin, the shadows whirling into a dizzying blur. 'I feel . . . what have you done?' You grip the table, trying to steady yourself – to find some anchor as the room continues to pitch and roll.

'It's a mild toxin, nothing more. Like I said, it will help you to sleep.'

'No, you . . . don't understand!'

You feel the woman's arms around you, strong and firm, helping you to stand. 'Now, I've got a spare bed made up – always keep it ready for strays such as yourself.' Sylvie guides you towards the curtain, pulling it back to reveal a small room with a pallet bed on a wooden frame. A beaded curtain in the opposite wall leads to a further room, which you assume is her own quarters. 'In the morning, we'll sort you out some clothes. I still have a few of Randal's things. You're of a similar build, I think.'

Sylvie continues to twitter to herself, as if nothing was untoward. You grapple at her, trying to break away, but you are so sick and dizzy you have no strength. Weakly, you find yourself falling onto the bed, the ceiling lurching and rocking.

'Please,' you beg, eyes now widening in fear. 'The dragon leaf . . . the dragon . . .' Your hand fumbles for your pouch.

'No, you won't be needing that my dear.' Sylvie's hand settles over your own, gently pushing it away. 'You trust me. You need to trust me.'

Her words grow fainter as your eyelids close, the exhaustion finally taking you. 'No,' you whisper. 'You can't . . . let . . . me . . . sleep.'

Then you are sinking through walls of darkness, your mind travelling to that other place – the one you most fear. Turn to 30.

208

With the monsters defeated, you run to the boy's side. His body is broken, ribs protruding from bruised flesh. Putting fingers to his throat, you feel for a pulse – but there is nothing. Snow is already settling over the body, clinging to the wet blood and shrouding him in white.

You go to pick up the body, looking round for Desnar. To your surprise, the Skard is standing over the carcass of the wolf. He glances your way, shaking his head. 'He nameless,' he grunts. 'We leave for land. This we take . . . feast, yes?' He puts a hand to his mouth, moving his jaw to mimic eating.

'He was your son!' you protest, surprised and angered by the Skard's lack of compassion.

Desnar picks up the forelegs of the wolf and begins dragging it through the snow. 'Help or silence,' he growls. 'Himruk gone. He nameless now.'

You rise to your feet, pausing for a moment to look into the boy's dead eyes. *Nameless*. The word pulls at a memory. Anise, the kitchen girl from Bitter Keep.

'I'm not a Skard,' she had told you, defiantly. 'I was cast out. To them, I have no name. Without a name, I am nothing.'

You wonder what act she had committed, what crime had forced her to follow a similar path to Himruk – to be disowned by her tribe, her own family . . . You picture her face, the red curls of hair falling around her crooked grin. Her emerald-green eyes bright with mischief.

You give a wavering sigh, tilting your head to let the snow gently kiss your cheeks. Anise is gone. Just like all the others. You'll never see that smile again, hear her voice, feel the warmth of her breath . . .

No! You clench your fists with a snarl. *I'm a fool. There is no going back . . .*

You turn into the savage wind, welcoming its sudden fury. *No going back. Not ever . . .*

Following the bloodied trail, you catch up with Desnar. The snow is now falling thick and fast, reducing your visibility to less than a metre. You are impervious to the cold, but Desnar is not. A scarf is now pulled tight across his face, frost sparkling from his brows and hair. He is clearly struggling now with the weight of his burden, but too stubborn to give it up. Grabbing the wolf's hind legs, you help lift the beast. Desnar looks back, nodding with silent approval.

Together you struggle through the blustery storm, your faith resting in the Skard's ability to find his way home. Turn to 769.

209

You join Lord Everard at the wall. He mumbles a passing greeting, his gaze remaining fixed on the white horizon.

'Admiring the view?' you ask with a wry smile.

'More the weather,' he says, frowning. 'It's been a while since we saw snow here.' He scratches the back of his head. 'I wonder if that's a good omen – or a portent that something worse is on its way.'

'Perhaps I brought the winter with me.' You peer back at Everard, eyes glinting from beneath your hood. He regards you thoughtfully, and for a moment you sense the uncertainty in his look.

'Maybe you did,' he says, his frown etched a little deeper. 'These are strange times, no doubting that.'

(If you have the word *trader* on your hero sheet, turn to 286.)

210

The passage presents an intimidating series of twisting, winding bends – most of which have become partially covered in fallen rock and ice. Your fellow racer is clearly an expert, navigating the undulating curves with ease. For a novice like yourself, however, it is proving a hazardous endeavour.

You will need to take a challenge test using your *speed* racing attribute:

	Speed
The corkscrew	12

If you are successful, turn to 571. Otherwise, turn to 18.

211

The chapel is reached by a short corridor from the main hall. The heavy oak door creaks inwards, revealing a long vaulted chamber, more a church than a chapel. A single row of stone pews lead to a raised altar, where a statue of Judah looks down from his Mordland cross, a crown of thorns resting on his brow.

Candles flicker in niches along the wall, illuminating the holy scripture that has been inscribed into the grey stone of the seats, the altar, the high walls. You cannot understand the words, but you know they are taken from Judah's scripture, holy words, designed to empower those who follow the light.

You feel them pressing against you, needling into your skin. It starts as a slight discomfort, quickly becoming something more severe, a pounding pain in your head, an aching in your muscles. You are about to turn and leave when something hits you hard between the shoulders.

You spin round angrily, following the bounce and thud of an object off to your right. When your eyes catch up with it, you see an apple rolling in the dirt.

Smug laughter rings down from the rafters.

Lifting your gaze, you see Rook seated on a wooden beam, his legs swinging back and forth. He shines another apple on his sleeve, watching you from beneath his dark hood. 'If that had been a knife, you'd be dead.'

'I think you're a little late for that.' You put your hands to your weapons, surprised at how sluggish your movements feel; the pain in your limbs has grown sharper and more insistent.

Rook pushes off from the beam, his black cloak swirling back from his shoulders as he drops into the chapel, landing with a graceful flourish. He straightens, pushing back his cloak to take a bite of his apple. He grins, stepping around you as he eats, watching with playful eyes. 'You made two mistakes. The second you made here, when you gave me an easy target.'

'And the first?' You glower, feeling your anger rise.

'By coming here in the first place.' He takes another bite of the apple, then tosses the core over his shoulder.

'Shouldn't you show more respect?'

Rook moves his hands to his left breast, unfastening the clasp of his cloak. 'I could say the same of you, corpse-walker. How does it feel, having those holy words crawl underneath your skin? They don't like you, do they? It is in their nature to repel those who are impure.'

'Is this your lesson?'

'One of them.' Rook lets his cloak drop from his shoulders. Underneath, his grey jerkin is sleeveless, his slender arms bunched with hard muscle. Somehow, two daggers have found their way into his hands. You see another five or six protruding from his waistband. 'Don't let your enemy choose the fight. Here, in this place, you are weaker. I have the advantage.'

He circles you again, the candlelight making an oily rainbow of his greased-back hair. 'I fought with your brother Malden. He was a man you could follow, willingly. Without question.'

You picture your eldest brother for a moment – the brave hero who everyone looked up to. Even when he was a cripple, lounging in your father's throne, a wine cup in hand, words slurred and confused, he still had everybody's ear.

'War did him no favours,' you reply curtly.

Rook bends close, voice dropped to a whisper. 'I'm not going to teach you to be like him.' He leans back, squaring his shoulders.

'You want me to be an assassin, is that it?' You look him up and down with derision.

'Draw your weapons.'

You do so, gladly – despite the pain racking your body.

'I've seen you train,' says Rook, spinning his daggers. 'I know your mind is sharp. But your body is what holds you back. You haven't learnt to move with grace – to feel the dance.' He darts in close, looking to strike, then spins away, an effortless leap taking him onto one of the pews. 'Don't follow me with your eyes, fool. Follow me with your steel – your strides. Come on!'

He springs from the pew, his heel catching you in the chest. The blow sends you stumbling back, swiping at his shadow, cutting through dusty air. 'Dance!' You feel a boot against the back of your knee. It throws you off balance, dropping you to the ground. That's when the anger really hits – erupting inside you, pushing away the throbbing pain. You whirl to face him, a rumbling growl echoing around the chamber. By instinct you raise your weapons, deflecting the knife intended for your shoulder. A second whistles past your ear.

'Better!' Rook pulls another knife from his belt, flipping it between his hands. 'Come on then, corpse-walker. Let's see what you got.' It is time to fight:

	Speed	Brawn	Armour	Health
Rook	4	2	2	35

Special abilities

🖤 **Rook's talons**: At the start of each combat round, take a speed challenge to avoid Rook's throwing knives. If the result is 10 or more, you have passed and take no damage. If the result is 9 or less, you have been hit and must lose 4 *health*.

If you are able to defeat Rook, then turn to **412**. Otherwise, you may repeat the combat or choose a different trainer (return to **369** to make your choice.)

212

You place the 'four of hearts' on the discard pile and pick a new stone from the bag. You have gained the 'three of crowns'.

You have the following stones:

The monk decides to play his hand. Turn to **718**.

213

Quickly, you select the tile and push it into the square-shaped hole. The moment it settles into place, the glyphs give a pulse of greenish light, then the stone starts to move. You back away in surprise, watching in bewilderment as the top half of the slab revolves and pivots aside, revealing a secret cavity carved into the lower section.

You lean forward, excited by what you might find inside. However, instead of gold or some exciting magical treasure, you discover nothing more than a plain-looking rock resting on a square of tanned leather. You reach inside and pick it up, surprised to find that its dark surface is vibrating slightly. Veins of emerald branch through it, glowing softly like the runes carved into the standing stone. If you wish, you may now take:

Stardust
(talisman)
Ability: charm

A nearby cry forces you back to your feet. Quickly, you pocket your find and hurry for the cover of the trees, not wishing to be discovered by the fengle's companions. Turn to 175.

214

Your sled is unable to withstand the merciless pounding of the rough terrain. First one of your runners snaps, then the sled itself is flipped over, smashing to pieces against the hard ice.

You have failed to complete the race and are now disqualified from the tournament. Replace the keyword *veteran* with *underdog*. Return to the map to continue your adventure.

215

You learn from Aslev that the einherjar are an ancient order of warriors, sworn to protect the Drokke and the Hall of Vindsvall. Their magic comes from the Dwarves – the ability to carve enchanted horns to channel their spirit into powerful spells and charms.

If you wish, you may now equip the following item:

North wind
(left hand: horn)
+2 speed +2 brawn
Ability: windblast
(requirement: warrior)

The einherjar has the following special abilities:

Sound the charge! (sp + co): (requires a horn in the left hand) Roll an extra die for your attack speed. If you win the combat round, you may also roll an extra die for your damage score. This ability can only be used once per combat.

Rallying call (co): (requires a horn in the left hand) Instead of rolling for a damage score you can issue a rallying call. This instantly restores 6 *health* and raises your *brawn* by 2 for the next combat round only.

You may now return to the map. When you are ready to re-join Skoll and Anise, select the Boss Monster encounter (the skull icon) to begin the next stage of your journey.

216

You help to unhitch the horse from the cart. It is a strong shire horse, probably used to pulling ploughs before it ended up at the Rift – a detail you suspect Mitch noticed, being a farmer. Using a length of rope from the cart, Mitch fastens one end around the horse and makes a noose with the other. After several failed attempts he manages to lasso the flailing beast, the rope settling across a shoulder and hooking underneath an arm.

'Got some skill, this kid,' says Kirk, spectating from a nearby rock. He chews on some dried meat, then tosses it to Lawson. 'Might just work, this. But keep an arrow ready. If things go berserk . . .'

Lawson chuckles, ignoring Mitch's angered glare.

'Come on!' the boy urges. 'We can do this.'

The horse takes the strain and begins to heave up the slope. At first the yeti pulls back in resistance, driven by its panicked efforts to free itself – but against the rope and the tar, its strength is soon spent.

Slowly but surely, the tar-covered yeti is dragged onto the shore. Mitch punches the air, grinning like he just won the Capital Games. You back away, wary of what the creature might do.

'It's dead,' says Henna, a hint of irritation in her voice.

'It certainly ain't moving,' says Kirk, pushing himself back up. 'Stick it with an arrow, Law, just to be sure.'

Mitch steps closer to the beast. 'Wait, I don't think . . .'

The arrow leaves the bow and thuds into the shaggy body. There is an almighty roar as the yeti rises up, arms swinging round, black tar showering through the air. You hear an eye-wincing crack. Mitch goes sailing back, his neck twisted at a funny angle. He crashes down amongst a tangle of grass and rock.

Before anyone has a chance to go to his aid the yeti is rearing up, beating its chest with two enormous fists. Then it is charging towards you, its mouth opening wide to reveal a frightening chasm of yellowed fangs. It is time to fight:

	Speed	Brawn	Armour	Health
Tarred yeti	1	2	1	25

Special abilities

♥ **Treacle tar**: Each time the yeti wins a combat round and causes health damage to your hero, you must lower your *speed* by 1 for the next combat round only.

♥ **Outnumbered**: Your companions add 2 to your damage score for the duration of this combat.

If you manage to overpower this ferocious monster, turn to 350. If you lose the combat, remember to record your defeat on your hero sheet. You may then attempt the combat again or return to the map.

217

You back away from the creature's remains, a hot sensation burning along your limbs. Where the creature's claws have dug into your flesh you see that the skin has become angry and red, as if infected by something.

'Rift rot,' says Anise grimly. 'That can be nasty.'

You already feel your limbs weakening, a wave of sickness making you feel dizzy. 'Can it be cured?' you rasp, rubbing at the swellings.

'You'll need healing,' she says. 'And I doubt we'll find any of that around here.'

You have been infected with the following disease:

Rift rot (pa): In future combats, you must lose 1 *health* at the end of each combat round for the duration of the combat. Rift rot can only be removed by drinking a health potion or using an item / ability that restores *health*. Once removed, you will no longer suffer its effects in combat.

Nursing your wounds, you cross the room into the adjoining passageway – more determined than ever to escape this cursed tower. Turn to 379.

'Ryker was the prison warden, that's how this place got its name. Then the prisoners broke out, took it over. Once the dust settled and they finally stopped beatin' on each other, they chose a leader. They called him Ryker, just like the warden. It's a title now more than a name. Think there've been two, three Rykers in all.'

'And he's inside the prison?' You gesture to the pinnacle of rock rising up into the sky. Through the snow and haze, you can dimly make out tiny flickers of light.

'Ah, the prison,' the thief rubs his hands together nervously. 'A dung heap of bad ones; yer think this is the worst of it, think again. Aye, we be thankin' the maker, they keep themselves to themselves. You always knows a Ryker man by the red band around their arm. No-one messes with them folk, not even the whalers.'

To continue chatting to the thief, return to 288. To explore the rest of the compound, turn to 106.

219

'A traveller, you say.' The woman appears unconvinced. 'And tell me, why would you be travelling these parts? For the scenery?' She raises her eyebrows.

'Not a traveller, a merchant,' you correct quickly. 'But I was set upon by bandits, back on the road. I was the only one to get away and . . .'

'The only one? Who were you travelling with?'

You wince, cursing your slip up. 'I met some others. We thought we'd travel together, for safety.'

'Didn't do you much good now, did it?' The woman huffs, then she nods to your sword. 'Tell me, did you steal that sword or were you taught to use it? A fine blade for a boy like you.'

You glance down at the holy sword, Duran's Heart – the named blade that was gifted to you for your thirteenth birthday. 'I . . . it . . . I found it, yes. On one of the men who attacked us.'

'A holy blade. And does that belong to the man also?'

Her eyes shift to the dried blood coating your sleeve. You look away, avoiding her glare. 'He was . . . one of the bandits,' you stutter, knowing the lie is written all over your face.

The woman shakes her head with a frown of disappointment. 'You are a fool to think I'd believe your story. You are but a child. A thief, no doubt. One who got caught out, and now plans to rob me blind.' She reaches into her basket and pulls out a knife. 'Are you good with that blade, son? You had better be . . .'

'No wait!' You raise your hands imploringly. 'I'm no thief. You can have the sword – I can't even touch the cursed thing.'

The woman takes a step back. 'Is this true?' she gasps.

Too late, you realise what you have done, blurting out your secret with no mind to the consequences. To confess such a thing is almost tantamount to treason. 'I can only touch the scabbard,' you reply honestly, seeing no point in spinning out another lie now you've gone this far. 'The inscriptions . . . if I put even a hand to them, they . . .' You struggle for the words.

'Reject you?' the woman supplies thoughtfully.

You nod, trying to gauge her reaction. This secret is one you have only shared once before, with your nursemaid Molly. And you doubt she'll be telling anyone now.

'You're no witchfinder, then,' the woman appears to visibly relax. 'Perhaps there is some truth in what you say after all.' (Make a note of the word *pauper* on your hero sheet, then turn to 249.)

220

After several hundred metres, the floor of the shaft falls away into a slope of broken ice. Water pours out of several depressions in the wall, forming bright rivulets as they thread their way between the smoothed slabs.

You drop onto the slope, your feet immediately skidding on the wet ice. Flung onto your back, you slide down the water-scoured chute, landing in a tumble of limbs at the foot of the rubble. After brushing the wet ice from your clothes, you examine your new surroundings. Turn to 397.

You hoist the sack onto your shoulders, hoping that Everard will appreciate the return of his missing equipment. As the sun starts to dip towards the horizon, you leave the canyon and head back to the keep. (Make a note of the keyword *trader* on your hero sheet.) You may now return to the map to continue your adventure.

222

A morning haze still smokes across the ice as the tournament racers take their positions outside the prison walls. Beneath your sled's runners the sheet is thin and fractured, creaking and snapping constantly as if it might give way at any moment. Only a few feet below the ice, you can see the ocean water rushing past in a trailing flurry of bubbles – promising a swift end to those unlucky enough to fall through.

Spectators line the wall, hooting and hollering for their favourite racers. From inside the compound, similar cries are also audible. Above your head, the yellow globes of the 'canaries' zip back and forth, feeding back images to the crowds in the prison.

Next to you, a female racer with blue-dyed hair is waving at the passing globes. She catches your eye and smiles. 'You a newbie?'

You shrug your shoulders, confused.

'Cute.' She snaps a pair of goggles over her eyes, then takes up her dog whip. 'Well, no going back now. This is it, honey. The dash for the cash.'

'Racers ready!'

You twist round to see a fur-clad male standing on the wall, his face a mosaic of red and black markings. He raises his arm above his head, fingers pointed towards the pale sun. 'Burn it up, people! Get set . . . GO!' He looses a fireball into the sky, its vivid scarlet tail soaring up and over the ice.

Then the crisp air is shattered by the crack of whips and the scraping of sled runners as the dog-teams swarm out across the ice, hurtling forward like bullets shot from a flint-lock. The race is on!

For the first few minutes, you try and relax into the motion of the sled, barking commands to your dog-team as Leeta had instructed. The speed is exhilarating, but the ice is slippery and rent with fissures. Ahead of you, a sled is flipped up and over by one such fracture, the rider and his dog-team sent spinning through the air in a tangle of harnesses and splintered wood. The other racers break around the wreckage, their eyes set solely on the course ahead: a circuit of the frozen ice plain that circumvents Ryker's island.

You career across the brittle ice, trying to maintain a steady line and keep your distance from the nearest sleds. Already several of the racers have broken away to take an early lead, whilst you remain neck-and-neck with the rest of the pack.

Suddenly, you notice a couple of sleds veer off the main course, their riders choosing to take a short cut over a ridged area of snow banks. If their gamble pays off, they will close the distance on the leaders.

Will you:

Cut across the snow banks?   126
Stay on the ice?   87

223

On reaching the battlements, you lean out over the nearest wall to view the landscape. For a moment you teeter on the edge of vertigo, your mind reeling from the scene before you.

'Impressive, isn't it?' Everard steps beside you, placing his gloved hands on the snow-wet crenulations.

You have read many books about Skardland and the area now known as Skardfall. In ages past, a great cataclysm ripped through the land, tearing it into impassable stretches of crevices and chasms. You had never expected to see it – but now you have, you realise that no description or artist's painting could ever capture the raw and over-powering majesty of the Great Rift.

'Meet mother nature,' grins Everard. 'A cruel parent, to be sure.'

You are silent, still struggling to take in the immensity of the canyon, its walls dropping away into an ominous pitch black. Beyond the shattered ridges and deep-scoured trenches, there lies a bleak country of hills and valleys. The snow has started to dress the higher terrain, but the rest of the land remains bare and brown, devoid of life.

'This is the first snow we've had in nearly a year,' Everard continues. 'Trust me, this isn't cold, boy. Not like what the north used to be like. But things are changing. Weather's been getting warmer. Look, there – see those rocks?'

You follow his finger to the opposite side of the rift, where gnarly columns of rock arch over the dark abyss. 'I've seen icicles hanging off those, long as these here walls.' Everard snorts, shaking his head. 'That was back in the day, when all we had to worry about were Skards and—'

Everard stops, frowning. 'Agh, here we go again.'

You look sideways at him, confused. Then you feel it – the wall has started to vibrate. From an incessant humming beneath your palms it quickly becomes a violent tremor, shaking the foundations of the keep. You are thrown against the wall, gripping its side to maintain your balance. Across the rift you hear stones grating and moving. Plumes of thick, grey dust shower into the darkness.

Then the rumbling ceases and a heavy silence descends.

'They're getting worse,' sighs Everard. He leans over the wall, eyes searching the rift. 'Started a couple of months back – minor quakes. Segg's convinced they're the start of something bigger.' He looks over, smiling at your bewildered expression. 'Don't worry, Bitter Keep has stood through a lot worse. Nothing's going to be moving this one, I promise you that.'

Will you:

Ask about the Skards?	81
Ask about the Keep's defences?	130
Climb the stairs to the mage tower?	301
Return to the main courtyard?	113

224

Your goal in this quest is to successfully cross the rift and reach Mount Skringskal. To achieve this, you will need to overcome a number of obstacles and challenges. Your transport (either the *Naglfar* or Nidhogg) will take damage during the crossing, reducing their *speed*, *stability* and *toughness*. These attributes can help your hero in combat, so it is in your interest to ensure that they stay as high as possible. The attributes provide the following bonuses in combat:

Tactical manoeuvres (co): If your transport has a *speed* of 5 or greater, you may use *tactical manoeuvres*. This allows you to avoid taking damage from your opponent/s in a single combat round and increases your hero's *speed* by 2 for the next combat round only. This ability can only be used once per combat.

Armour plating (pa): For every 2 points of *toughness* that your transport has remaining (rounding down), you may increase your hero's *armour* by 1 for the duration of the combat. (If your transport had a *toughness* of 9, you could increase your *armour* by 4.)

If your transport's *stability* is reduced to zero, you can no longer use your transport's combat ability (either the *nail gun* or *dragon fire*).

When you are ready to begin, turn to 60.

225

'So, spending the night in a haunted tower . . .' You tap a finger against your chin, thoughtfully. 'No one else thinks this might be a bad idea?'

Anise slaps you on the shoulder. 'Stop it! You're worse than Jitters Jackson.'

'Who?' you ask in bemusement.

'He works the trading post north of here. Sometimes I go with Everard. I can still speak a little Skard.'

'Jitters is a Skard?'

'No, silly, Jitters works for the White Wolf Company – the Skards go there from time to time to sell pelts and meat. Jitters is so scared of everything, he's barricaded himself inside his own fortress. You rarely even see him.'

'A mad fool is what he is,' sniffs Harris. 'Come on, I'm getting cold. We're doing this – so no more complaining.' (Return to 86 to ask another question or turn to 297 to continue on to the tower.)

Tired and miserable, you decide to tell the truth. The woman listens to your story in silence, her expression unchanging. As you draw to its end, choosing to omit the part about the strange demon, a hint of irritation creeps into your voice. Why doesn't this woman show any concern or alarm? She didn't flinch when you described the bloody massacre on the road or the very fact that you are a crown prince of the realm.

Your words falter to silence, waiting expectantly for a response.

The woman regards you for a moment longer, then gives a dismissive snort. 'I've heard some tall tales in my time, boy . . .'

'It's true,' you implore, feeling your anger surge once again. 'Would I have this if I was just some . . . some commoner?' You lift the scabbard at your side, showing her its jewels and the holy inscriptions on the hilt. 'This is Duran's Heart. A named blade, given to me on my thirteenth birthday.'

The woman takes a step closer, but her eyes linger on your face rather than the blade. 'You could have stolen it.'

Her accusation startles you. 'I'm no thief! You can have the sword – I can't even touch the cursed thing.'

For the first time, the woman exhibits surprise. 'Is this true?' she gasps.

Too late, you realise what you have done, blurting out your secret with no mind to the consequences. To confess such a thing is almost tantamount to treason.

'I can only touch the scabbard,' you reply honestly, seeing no reason to spin a lie now you've gone this far. 'Since I was given it, the inscriptions have always . . .' You struggle for the words.

'Rejected you?' the woman supplies thoughtfully.

You nod, trying to gauge her reaction. This secret is one you have only shared once before, with your nursemaid Molly. And you doubt she'll be telling anyone now. *I have to get home. I have to tell them what happened . . .*

'You're no witchfinder, then,' the woman's brow creases. 'Perhaps there is some truth in what you say after all.' Make a note of the word *prince* on your hero sheet, then turn to 256.

227

The knight has you beaten, his sword raised for a killing blow. But before he can bring it down, you hear a cry. Anise charges into view, using her torch as a weapon to batter against the knight's dark armour. With an angry hiss he turns to face her, thrown off balance as he tries to swat her away with his sword. The girl's distraction gives you the perfect opening. Quickly, you drive your weapon between Mott's armour, pushing deep into whatever spectral body resides within.

When the weapon is withdrawn, the knight goes staggering back, the pieces of black plate dropping one by one to the ground. Once the suit is lost, you are left with the ghost of a young man, dressed in the true armour of a Valeron knight. Angrily, he tosses the sword aside as if it suddenly disgusts him, then his glowing eyes fix on you.

'My brother . . .' He holds out a gauntleted hand. From its end dangles a bright medallion, hanging from a gold chain. 'Take it and be at peace, brother.'

You realise that the knight is still trapped in the past, believing that you are his brother Rinehart – the one who was forced to kill him by the evil necromancer. Anise moves to your side, helping you to stand. 'Have nothing to do with it,' she says, scowling at the proffered medallion. 'This place is full of tricksters and evil.'

The outline of the ghost starts to flicker and fade, returning to whatever half-world it came from. Of the other spectre, there is no sign, although you are certain you have not seen the last of him.

Will you:
| Take the medallion? | 252 |
| Refuse the spirit's gift? | 176 |

228

The air is thick and heavy with sand. You can feel the solid particles cutting and tearing at your dead skin. Ahead of you a surging wall of crimson wind rushes across the plain, forming an impenetrable barrier.

Skoll snatches a skull from amongst the rocks, bleached white by the fury of the storm. He swings back his arm, then throws the skull into the midst of the churning, fast-moving tempest. The skull barely reaches its outer edge before splintering into jagged fragments – snatched away by the wind in the blink of an eye.

Skoll continues to glare at the whirling sand, then tilts back his head and howls. A bestial, dirge-like outpouring of despair – a sound to rival that of the raging storm.

Anise is beside you, eyes narrowed over her scarf. 'This wind is an act of sorcery. There must be some way to break its spell.'

You stagger against a boulder, barely able to support yourself on your exhausted legs. 'Look at it – what hope do we have?'

Skoll bares his teeth – and starts forward.

He gets only a few metres before he is forced back, his exposed flesh cut and bleeding from the bite of the spinning debris. 'Beriliv bak, hurt nasar!' He spits his curse into the face of the storm.

'We could wait,' insists Anise. 'For the others – the Ska-inuin will come. Perhaps our combined might . . .'

Skoll spins on her, his eyes bright with an angered madness. 'They will not come!' He gestures back to the wasteland. 'They did not heed my call.'

'There is still time,' Anise implores. 'The land is not what it once was – their passage will be difficult.'

Skoll snorts and spits again. 'Ska-inuin have proven weak. We are done for. It is over!'

You push off from the boulder. Tentatively, you approach the storm.

Whipped-up chunks of debris clatter against your armour, tearing at cloth, raking across your cadaverous skin. You feel no pain, but you know if you took another step – and then another – you would simply be torn to pieces.

'No flesh or bone can pass . . .' You step back, your gaze drifting to Anise. The girl glares back at you with a mix of desperation and confusion.

'Is this the end?' she asks, almost challengingly. 'If we stop now, we have failed.'

'Bah. I will not be weak,' snarls Skoll. 'I will not lie down and die!'

'You won't have to.' Your words are softly spoken, and yet some-how carry over the keening gale.

The Skard's scowl grows deeper. 'Magic will not avail us.'

A sacrifice will have to be made, boy. Only you will be able to choose, life or death.

The spinner's words. Their sudden meaning pierces you like a blade. 'The sacrifice. It's me.'

Your companions look at you, baffled.

It was never the paladin. I am the sacrifice.

Anise suddenly grabs you by the arm. 'What are you saying? Please, Arran. Don't!'

You close your eyes, casting your mind towards the Norr, reaching for its magic – for Nanuk. His spirit has grown weaker – you have taken much from the bear, burning through his reserves of magic like a flame melting at tallow. But the bear has more to give. You reach out again, moulding your will into a spear-head. *I need your magic, Nanuk. I need all of it, if I am to become what I must.* Turn to **668**.

229

The sprites fall to your weapons as the final candle flame winks out. The room is thrown into darkness, the dusty air filled with smoke and the acrid stench of sulphur. Slowly the edges of your surroundings sharpen into focus, tinged by the same brilliant light as before.

Segg starts to raise his fingers, to relight the candles. You pre-empt him, sending a wash of magic spiralling around the room. One by one, the candles ignite, each capped with a bright green flame. Their deathly pallor illuminates Segg's surprised expression.

'Impressive,' he states, raising an eyebrow. 'I'd say that brings your training to an end.'

Congratulations – you have learned the path of the mage. You may now permanently increase your *health* by 10 (to 40). You have also gained the following special ability:

Recharge (dm): You regain a speed or modifier ability that you have already used in combat – allowing you to use it again. *Recharge* can only be used once per combat.

When you have updated your hero sheet, turn to **388**.

For defeating the entire coven, you may help yourself to 50 gold crowns and one of the following rewards:

Ritual end	Shade's vice	Necropolis stalkers
(main hand: dagger)	(ring)	(feet)
+2 speed +2 brawn	+1 brawn	+2 speed +2 magic
Ability: eviscerate	Ability: mortal wound	Ability: poison cloud
(requirement: rogue)	(requirement: warrior)	(requirement: mage)

When you have updated your hero sheet, turn to 523.

231

You flee back into the trees, the sound of brutal carnage and the inquisitor's roars of pain providing all the incentive you need. Your own wounds stab with pain, forcing you to stagger as the trees and branches blur into a haze.

For a second – a heartbeat – you feel yourself slipping away, to that dark place you have always dreaded. You can feel its chill inside of you, its black hooks pulling you in, dragging you back to the dreams, the nightmares . . .

'No!' Somehow you manage to find your pouch, hands fumbling as you push the dragon leaf into your mouth. Biting down on the bitter leaves, you feel their familiar warmth surge through your body, forcing away that dreaded chill.

And for a while, they numb the pain.

Grappling through the wall of branches, you emerge on the banks of a fast-flowing stream. Ahead, a lip of granite juts out into the white-frothed shallows, forming a series of pitted stones that stretch to the far bank. You splash into the waters, almost losing your footing as the force of the rushing tide churns around your ankles. Clambering onto the nearest rock, you use it as a stepping-stone, hopping from one surface to the next, until you have reached the far bank.

A sudden howl lifts over the roar of the water, followed by a chorus of wails.

You glance back, startled to see a group of wolves sitting by the shoreline. Their heads are tilted back, calling to their pack mates.

You are running once again, dragging your now flagging limbs up the slope and back into the forest. The ground is harder here, ridged with bands of stone. Through the wiry tree-limbs, you spy high walls of grey rock. The air hangs heavy with musk and decay.

You break from the trees, stumbling into a wide clearing – hemmed in by a tumble of slate boulders. Bones litter the floor, hundreds of them – small ones, large ones, skulls, spines. They crack underfoot as you turn in a slow circle, scanning the rocks and the trees behind you. Another howl rends the air, but you cannot determine the direction.

Then you see them, slinking out from the undergrowth, heads hung low, tongues lolling from between glistening canines. You back up into the bone-strewn ravine, realising that the wolves have you trapped, penned in by the walls of stone. Another step and something pushes hard against your back; you half-turn to see the broken rib cage of some enormous animal poking out of the mud, its bones picked clean, shining bright in the gloom.

A deep, reverberating growl.

Your eyes lift to the nearest wall of slate. Standing on the topmost rock is a huge black shadow, its body seemingly swallowing the light. Only the creature's eyes seem to hold any semblance of life, golden orbs smouldering with hunger.

You realise this must be the alpha male, the leader. You stare back at him, too afraid to move, too afraid to do anything but wait. Already you can feel the warmth of the dragon leaf starting to fade; tiredness and pain begin to return with a vengeance.

It's over . . . too tired to fight it . . . too tired . . .

Your eyelids flutter. Unconsciousness, darkness . . . you hear the dreams calling, whispering, growing stronger; the coldness of that other place settles around you like a shroud.

You lurch forward dizzily, slipping on loose bones, just as the wolf kicks off from the rock and springs into the air. Turn to 5.

Using your weapon you prise open the lid, jerking back in surprise when you see a skeletal hand scuttling around inside the box, grasping and clawing to get out.

'Ugh, that's disgusting,' cries Anise, pulling a revolted expression.

The hand suddenly makes a leap for the edge of the box, its bony fingers closing around the rim. Then, with another hop, it lands on the floor, skittering across the ground like a spider.

Will you:

Try and catch the hand?	124
Ignore it and open a barrel?	156
Climb the rubble to the room above?	272
Retrace your steps and use the stairs?	111

Your weapon splinters the Skard's javelin, your foot catching him in the chest and driving him back to the ground. He reaches out, fingers closing around the black wand still lying in the dirt. He mutters a curse as the wand starts to glow.

Then Henna's sword comes slicing down in a brilliant arc of steel. You turn away from the blow, not wishing to see it land.

'Funny. With a face like yours, I didn't think you'd be so squeamish,' grins the female knight, lifting her bloodied sword to rest against her shoulder.

Mitch crawls out from hiding, covered head to foot in dust and grime. 'Is he dead?' he asks nervously, staring at the corpse as if it might leap up at any second and attack.

'Without a head, I'd say it's a safe bet,' you reply grimly.

'Is that the last of them?' He looks anxiously to Henna.

She nods. 'I think so. Took down the other hunter. His dogs too.' She winces as she lowers her sword. 'Think I may need a healer though – and a good bath.'

You take a moment to search what remains of the Skard. If you wish, you may now take one of the following rewards:

Bone smile	**Red gutter**	**Atataq**
(necklace)	(main hand: dagger)	(main hand: wand)
+1 brawn +1 magic	+1 speed +1 brawn	+1 speed +1 magic
Ability: reckless	Ability: bleed	Ability: sear

When you have updated your hero sheet, turn to 360.

234

'I should probably offer you an apology.' The elderly mage sighs, running a hand through his fine, white hair. 'I was concerned for your well-being. You have to understand that.' He lifts his eyes to look at you, both pity and regret written on his lined face. 'This . . . what happened to you, I have seen its like before.'

You shift uncomfortably, waiting for him to continue.

'Powerful mages can store a part of their essence, their soul, in an object. This can allow them to return to their body – even after death.'

'I am no mage,' you protest. 'I don't see how—'

Segg waves you to silence. 'That's just one way; one that I have seen myself. But you – I feared that you had something else inside of you, something that wanted to use your body. That is why I thought it better we . . .' His eyes flick to the flames, crackling in the brazier. His message is clearly understood.

'But something changed your mind.' You press him cautiously, the heat in the room suddenly feeling more oppressive.

'Everard believed in you, even when I did not. And now, I harbour no doubt that you *are* Prince Arran. That makes you the sole remaining heir to the throne of Valeron.'

You snort dismissively. 'Do you really think they would welcome me back with open arms – kneel and swear allegiance to *this*?' You glare down at your transformed body, the firelight making the pallid skin look even more alien. 'Perhaps you should have burned me, stopped me before—'

'Enough of that!' Segg fixes you with a fierce-eyed stare, the fire in the room flashing high in anger. 'Command respect, Arran, and the people will follow. Do not pity yourself or what you have become. This is a second chance for you – use it wisely.'

Will you:

Ask about learning magic?	342
Ask if he knows anything about the dreams?	120
Return to the library?	353

235

You dart past Willow's scratching claws then feint in the opposite direction, wrong-footing her. Too late, the sprite's eyes widen – realising her mistake. The whirling swarm of leaves slice straight into her, cutting through the bark-skin body and shredding her wings to ribbons. She stumbles to her knees, amber sap bubbling from her many deep wounds. Before she can recover you raise your weapons, reverse their blades, then spear them into the sprite's wounded form – pinning her to the ground.

The creature's body cracks and crumbles, then spills across the ledge in a spray of amber and splintered wood. You may now help yourself to one of the following rewards:

Willow wrap	Nature's foil	Sprig steps
(chest)	(main hand: dagger)	(feet)
+1 speed +2 brawn	+1 speed +2 brawn	+1 speed +2 magic
Ability: counter	Ability: gouge	Ability: quicksilver

With your way now clear, you race up the walkway towards the summit of the colossal tree. Turn to 597.

236

You slump against the rock, your limbs aching with exhaustion. But it is not over yet. The crunch of stones announces the approach of one of the Skards. You stagger to your feet, eyes fixed on the narrow tunnel.

After several tense moments, the hunter appears around the corner, an axe in one hand and a bone knife in the other. His matted hair hangs across his face, framing a twisted sneer of contempt. With a bestial roar, he leaps over the bodies of his fallen dogs, looking to exact his brutal revenge. It is time to fight:

	Speed	Brawn	Armour	Health
Hunter	2	2	1	30

If you manage to best this savage hunter, turn to 317. If you lose the combat, remember to record your defeat on your hero sheet. You may then attempt the combat again or return to the map.

237

'We were part of an expedition . . . *are* part of an expedition,' corrects the woman. She makes a gesture behind her, to the widening canyon. 'We came to investigate the caves to the north. There is evidence of a much older structure. We believe it has some connection with the Titans.'

You look back to the single tent – and the few boxes and sacks of supplies coated in thick sheets of ice. 'How many of you are there?' you ask, frowning.

'There were nine of us,' says the man briskly. You notice that his hand has not left his knife. The fingers are trembling, blackened by frostbite. 'We were due to return to the coast, take our ship back to the mainland, but then one of our team found the rock. So we . . .' He trails off, a sudden despair evident in his baleful eyes.

The woman, Reah, takes over. 'The rock is unlike anything we have seen before. Our leader went back in, with four of our team – to try and find a way into the deeper caves, to see if we could find out more. They didn't come back.'

Will you:

238

The tentacles hang uselessly from the beast's bulbous body, streaking the rock with an oily film. You continue to rain blows against the head, your magic blasting through the thick pulpy flesh. The kraken gives a last mournful-sounding wail, then it slumps to the floor of its cave, ink oozing from its shattered mouth.

Congratulations! For defeating this monstrous beast, you have gained the following special reward:

Kraken oil
(backpack)
You don't want to let
this one slip away!

You sail past the kraken's body, making for an opening that leads inside the mountain. The *Naglfar* has taken a beating, but the ship is already healing itself thanks to the dark energies that bind it together. The sailors once again clamber over the rigging, trapped in their endless existence as slaves to the corpse ship.

Once the landing platform is extended, you gesture for Anise and Skoll to leave the ship. Before joining them, you turn to the first mate. He pushes his dreadlocks aside, revealing a disfigured face, his nose and mouth dragged askew by a terrible scar. One eye stares back, the other is an empty hollow.

'Was good sailing with yer, Cap'n,' he grins crookedly.

You pat the conch. 'We will still have need of the ship. Listen for my call.'

The sailor salutes you. 'You're our captain now. One of us.'

You glance past his shoulder at the other crewmen, all dutifully watching you with an earnest trust. Their faith in you is almost touching – filling you with an odd sense of pride. Nodding farewell to the assembled crew, you turn and follow the others into the mountain. (Return to the map to continue your journey.)

239

'It's something I dabble in from time to time,' Sylvie shrugs. 'Just taking what nature provides and enhancing it.'

'Enhancing it?' You lean forward with interest. 'Do you mean magic?'

Sylvie gives your comment a dismissive wave. 'Bah, if you want to name it so. A few petty runes, a simple incantation or two. I'm not entirely sure my work always has the desired effect, but the charms prove popular to passing tinkers who then sell them onto the towns and villages. In return I get the delicacies I wouldn't otherwise see. Spices, pastries, honeycomb. I do have something of a sweet tooth, I'm afraid.'

Return to 191 to ask another question, or turn to 207 to end the conversation.

240

For besting Desnar and becoming leader of the bear tribe, your bond with Nanuk's spirit has strengthened. You have also gained the following special ability:

Pain barrier (mo): Heal yourself for the total passive damage inflicted to a single opponent in the current combat round. (For example, if an opponent was inflicted with *bleed* and *disease*, you would be able to heal 3 *health* – 1+2). This ability can only be used once per combat.

When you have updated your hero sheet, turn to 721.

The guard removes the two of moons from his hand and places it face down on the discard pile. He reaches into the pouch and takes another stone at random. He has now gained the four of stars:

Next, the hooded ghost discards a stone from his own hand and takes another from the bag. A cold, cackling laughter comes from the shadows of his cowl as he studies his new hand.

'What should I do now?' whispers the guard. 'I have a fool's pair. It might win me the game.'

Will you:

Trade in the one of hearts?	424
Trade in the three of stars?	441
Show your hand?	517

Time spent investigating the disturbance means that some of the barrels have not been filled. Once the cart has been loaded up, you count eight filled barrels out of the original twelve.

'Could have been better,' grumbles Kirk, wiping his brow. 'But no matter, some is better than none, eh?'

The team only managed to fill 8 *barrels of tar*. (Make a note of this on your hero sheet then turn to 315.)

As you are about to start up the slope, you spot a glimmer of something from the corner of your eye. Ducking down to avoid being seen, you crawl over to the edge of the cave where rubble covers much of the wall. Half-buried beneath the rock fall is the skeleton of some humanoid creature. You carefully pull away a few of the stones, to reveal their hand – clasped around a large green gemstone.

Evidently, the goblin scavengers must have missed this rare treasure. If you wish to take the *flawless emerald* simply make a note of it on your hero sheet, it doesn't take up backpack space.

The goblins remain focused on their leader, who is grunting and cursing as he struggles to reach whatever object has caught his eye. You decide to leave them to it – hurrying up the slope and into the tunnel. Turn to 2.

244

You push through the trees, purposefully steering yourself away from the wider trail into the denser woodland. Within minutes you have lost all sense of direction, your way impeded by the thick undergrowth and clawing limbs of the forest. You doubt the wounded inquisitor could find you in these tangled wilds, but your fear urges you onwards, deeper and deeper into the thicket.

You don't see your attacker until it is too late – a furred body springs agilely from out of the trees, locking onto your back and dragging you to the ground.

You try and swat the creature away, feeling claws dig through your jerkin, lancing you with pain. A muzzle swings into view, fangs flecked with hot spittle.

A wolf. Somehow, you manage to find your feet, despite the weight of the animal. With a cry of exertion, you hurl yourself back against the nearest tree, ramming your attacker. The beast gives a yelping growl, but its claws only dig deeper, its hold on you tightening.

You fall to the forest floor, the wolf dragging you down, its jaws now worrying at your cloak, trying to lock onto something solid. Then a bright arrow of light cuts through the air, exploding next to you in a blinding flash. Suddenly, the weight is gone; a high-pitched whine rends the air.

You turn to see the wolf bolting into the undergrowth, half-running and half-loping – one side of its body a smoking ruin. But the relief of your sudden rescue is short-lived. Painfully you twist back to look upon the inquisitor, his raised fist still glowing with bright magic.

'Should have left you to the wolves,' he scowls. 'But I'll finish this myself.'

You glimpse shadows at the corners of your vision, flitting between the trees. A trick of the light, perhaps – or just a product of your pain and fear. You ignore them, your attention remaining fixed on the inquisitor. 'Who gave the order – was it Cardinal Rile?' You spit out the name accusingly. 'Did he ask you to do this – to lead us out here, to kill Tarlow and the others?'

'A perfect plan,' nods the inquisitor, tugging the dagger from his belt. 'We weren't expecting the Wiccan, but that's all for the better. I'll make this look like their work, not ours.' He advances towards you, boots crunching through the sudden silence.

You struggle to your knees, the movement making you dizzy with pain. 'The inquisition . . . you call yourself holy – protectors of the weak!' You force back a wave of nausea, half-choking on the bitter bile. 'I thought . . . you stood for goodness – for purity. And here you are, wanting to kill a prince! Call me a coward, then – a craven. What does that make you, oath breaker?'

Something in your words halts the warrior. His brow furrows, making a V of his punctured scar. 'The Church still stands for good,' he mutters. 'I must do what I was ordered.'

'Please, you don't have to—'

The warrior lunges, looking to grab you with his free hand. Too late, his eyes shift sideways – to the wolves, darting past the trees. Two of them, bigger than the last, spring on top of him in a blur of fur and teeth. Desperately, the warrior twists and spins, trying to stop them gaining leverage, but their heavy bodies are already latched tight to his, dragging him down to the forest floor.

Will you:

Go to the inquisitor's aid?	330
Use this chance to escape?	231

You place the 'one of crowns' on the discard pile and pick a new stone from the bag. You have gained the 'three of crowns'.

You have the following stones:

The monk takes his turn with an almost wearisome air, tossing the stone that he picked back onto the discard pile. You wonder if he's already got a winning hand or is simply bluffing. It is now your move.

Will you:

Play your current hand?	593
Discard the one of snakes?	762
Discard the four of hearts?	628

246

You can smell blood and carrion before you even enter the chamber. A giant eagle is ripping at a corpse with its talons, pulling stringy lengths of meat away in its sharp beak. The creature bristles with surprise as you enter, its head flicking back, tilting quickly from side to side.

It stands its ground, wings flapping golden feathers through the air as it emits a guttural series of screeches and hacking squeals. A clear warning.

Skoll's eyes are wide, moving from the mangled corpse to the bird and back again. The rumbling from his stomach betrays the course of his thoughts – you wonder if it is the bird or the meaty corpse that holds the most appeal.

Then you notice the saddle and harness, piled in the corner. And next to them, a backpack.

You glance around cautiously, reminding yourself of the layout of the chamber. It is small, more of a natural cave than the carved, angular halls that comprise most of the mountain. An opening to the east leads out onto a short ledge, then the empty blackness of the rift. The chill, cold wind blasts at you from the dark, filling your ears with its keening cry.

At the opposite end of the chamber, behind the eagle, is a slope of rock angling around the edge of the cave to a doorway above. It is there you see the light, shining white and solid around a shadowed figure.

'What is it, Gwen? Found something to feast on at last?'

The figure strides confidently into the chamber. A short man, his build muscular and hard. A white cloak hangs off his broad shoulders, flapping around black boots spattered with mud. He stops when he sees you.

'Gwen, you've got yourself a pair of admirers.'

'Who are you?' rumbles Skoll, his hunger making him short on manners.

The man resumes his descent of the slope, his eyes darting between you and the Skard. The light hangs like an aura around him. It isn't until he gets closer that you realise it is coming from his skin: hundreds of jagged lines glowing across his face and shaven scalp – and the flesh exposed between his gloves and the sleeves of his ermine jacket. The light gives off an angry heat, one you find both oppressive and daunting . . .

Just like the sword my father gave me, you remind yourself. *Holy magic.*

'You're a paladin.' The word is spat like poison from your lips.

The man puts a hand to the hilt of his scabbarded sword. 'Yes.'

His cold, grey eyes are the mirror of the eagle's, now standing silent and watchful as it ruffles its feathers. 'My name is Maune – and I am a paladin of the seventh circle. You speak of my calling as you might an enemy; someone who has caused you ill. I am only your enemy if you give me reason to be.' He gives Skoll a sharp look. 'I am a holy man. A devout servant of the One God.'

Skoll is fingering his axe. You can tell he is weighing up his options. Food and water dominate his thoughts, not sharing pleasantries. You shift your attention to the man's pile of belongings. A number of canteens are strapped to the outside of his pack. No doubt he also has food stashed inside.

247

Wishing to avoid a confrontation with the hunter, you hurry deeper into the cave. The opposite tunnel forms a twisting pathway, at times only wide enough for you to squeeze through sideways. After much pushing and scraping, you find yourself stumbling into a tight circular chamber, small enough to touch both walls from its centre. You have reached a dead end – but the shaft is less than twenty metres high, and at its summit you can see daylight, filtering between a mesh-like structure. Against the brightness of the sky, it is difficult to tell what is causing it.

Back along the tunnel you hear grunting and the scuff of boots. The hunter is still after you.

248

You manage to hold your position, the treacherous edge drawing further and further away. With your attention still locked on your fellow racer, you almost fail to spot another of your competitors sweeping in ahead you. It is a dark-skinned woman with long snow-white hair billowing from beneath her spiked helm. With one hand on the grip of her sledge, she leans back to flip open the lid of a basket.

'Your funeral, pal!' The racer you were tussling with suddenly swerves away – just as the woman pushes over the basket, scattering its contents wide over the snow and ice. The black shards of metal are plain to see, their barbed points threatening to lame your dogs and ruin your sled.

To navigate through the caltrops, you will need to take a challenge test using your *speed* racing attribute:

	Speed
Caltrop chaos	12

If you are successful, turn to 179. Otherwise, turn to 647.

249

'A witchfinder? Gosh no!' You are astonished the woman would even consider you a member of their order – a group of feared swordsmen, renowned for their bloodthirsty methods of bringing witches and other sinners to justice.

'Please,' you beg, determined now to press your advantage. 'You can take the sword – it's yours. Inscribed by a White Abbot. It'll fetch a good sum of money – and the diamond too. Please, just some food and shelter – please?' Hearing your own desperation shames you. Lowering your eyes, you let your shoulders slump.

Stupid fool. This sword could buy this whole damn cabin – a thousand cabins. And I offer it willingly for some supper and a blanket . . .

The woman gives a chuckle. 'Indeed, how could I resist such a generous offer?'

You glare back sullenly, wondering if she mocks you. But her beaming smile seems genuine enough. 'I am Sylvie and this – as you have already seen – is my humble abode.' She crosses to the table, pushing empty plant pots aside to make room for her basket. 'Your sword,' she states, meeting your gaze. 'Will you take it out of my home? Just leave it on the doorstep, if you would.'

You nod quickly, unstrapping the scabbard from your belt and placing it outside the door. When you return, Sylvie has removed the blanket from her basket, revealing freshly-picked mushrooms.

'Here, take a seat.' The woman pulls out a chair, then quickly removes the spiked plant that had been left there. 'Unless you'd rather change first. Those clothes must be wet through, you'll catch your death.' She nods to the side-room. 'I have some old clothes . . .'

'I'd rather eat,' you smile ruefully, eyes fixed on the pot heating next to the fire.

'Dinner it is, then.' Sylvie pulls back her hood and removes her coat, hanging it next to the fireplace. She then proceeds to busy herself by taking mushrooms from out of the basket and chopping them to add to the stew. Turn to 191.

250

Resting inside the jaws of a giant skull, you find a man huddled in fur blankets. You hurry over, believing him to be still alive. It isn't until you kneel beside him, noticing the vacant eye sockets and half-missing nose, that you realise the man is dead. A coating of opaque ice covers most of his body, preserving much of his flesh and clothing.

A silver hipflask is clutched in one of his gloved hands. You manage to break it free, turning it round to discover a small inscription near its base. It reads: *Bullet. Aim true and stay lucky.* You realise this must be the trapper that 'Jitters' Jackson told you about. (Replace the keyword *tracker* with the word *hunted.*)

If you are a rogue, turn to 547. Otherwise, return to the quest map to continue your adventure.

251

There are cheers from the nearby soldiers as your weapons slice through the mage's robes. For a moment you glimpse the creature's face beneath the hood – a snake-like visage, decayed and scabrous as if plagued by some disease. Then the body crumples to the ground, the once animated stones pattering down around it.

If you are a warrior or rogue, turn to 90. If you are a mage, turn to 346.

252

Before the spirit fades, you reach out and take the medallion. The chain is cold to the touch, its gold and ivory disc displaying an insignia of a griffon, carved in high relief.

'Leave it behind,' insists Anise, still grimacing with disgust. 'I'm not about to trust anything in this tower.'

You lift up the chain, letting the medallion spin back and forth, catching the light from the torch. (If you wish to wear *Mott's medallion*, simply make a note of it on your hero sheet, it does not take up an item/backpack space). Then turn to **195**.

253

You hand over the invitation for inspection. (Remove the *party invitation* from your hero sheet.) The guardsman nods then moves aside, pocketing the invitation. You pass through the doorway into a short corridor that opens out into a lavish room. It is full of smoke and chatter, and finely-dressed men and women.

As you pass through the room, you catch snatches of conversation. Much of the chatter appears to be focused around diamonds and an upcoming mining contract. There are also some concerns expressed over the recent quakes.

'Everything was shaking,' gasps a woman, fanning herself as if she might faint at any moment. 'Even my necklace broke. Took poor Charles an age to find all those pearls.'

'But it is something of an adventure, Lord Eaton,' guffaws a young dandified male, his laced cuffs flapping through the air as he waves his arms. 'Who'd have thought we'd be rubbing shoulders with whalers and other such low-lifes? It's positively screaming scandal.'

You flinch at the man's prim manner and flamboyant clothing, reminded of your own days back at court – back when you were a weak, sickly prince mollycoddled by a nurse.

Distracted by your thoughts, you accidentally bump into someone – a tall man in a blue velvet coat and high-necked shirt. His grey eyes regard you with disdain.

'Who are you?' he asks stiffly, leaning away as if from a bad smell. 'Are you one of the servants?'

Before you can reply a woman slides her hand into the man's arm and tugs him away. 'Oh Fromarc, come and tell the others your story. The baron and the troll, it's my favourite.'

'Oh, if you insist, Lady Hawker,' he grins, his eyes captivated by her own. They walk off together, leaving you to sigh with relief.

Next to you a man is slouched in a high-backed chair, clearly sleeping off his drink. He has a red strip of cloth tied around his upper right arm. You also note the sleeve of his jerkin is rolled up, displaying a tattoo.

Ahead of you is another doorway, with a tall dark-skinned guard blocking the way. He has his arms folded across his broad chest, eyes levelled ahead with a gruff obedience. An ivory plaque next to the doorway displays a carved image of a bottle.

Will you:

Take a closer look at the man's tattoos?	662
Approach the cellar?	724
Leave the party?	80

254

Reaching into the snow, you pull out a glowing shard of ice. Its surface vibrates with a powerful energy, sending streamers of magic arcing around your fist.

'What is this?' You glance at Skoll, who is helping Anise down from the rock.

'The heart of an elemental,' he grins. 'Take the magic. It will make you strong.'

You feel a sudden rush of numbing cold as Nanuk reaches into you, taking control of your body. Before you can stop him, you find your fingers tightening around the shard. The frozen glass begins to crack, its sharp edges cutting deep into your hand. Then the whole shard shatters – releasing a bright plume of magic into the air. The glittering motes are hungrily absorbed by your dead body, bolstering its strength and healing your wounds.

You have now gained the following bonus:

Elemental infusion: You may permanently increase your *health* by 10.

You may also remove one death penalty effect. When you have updated your hero sheet, turn to 617.

<h1 style="text-align:center">255</h1>

'Ah yes, I should thank you for bringing in the ... specimen.' Segg inclines his head, his bright blue eyes roving across the jars and bottles on a shelf. All appear to contain various organs and body parts, suspended in some kind of vinegary liquid.

You grimace at the grisly display. 'Did you learn anything?'

Segg walks over to one of the jars. 'My studies have only served to raise further questions.' He lifts up the jar, shaking it to send a series of black scales spinning around the murky water. 'These are drake scales – a sub-species of dragon. But I've not seen any creature like this. It is almost as if ... it was made. Created somehow. I'd go as far as to say, this might have once been human. A Skard, perhaps.'

'But why are they here?' You glance back at the shelf – your gaze fixing on a large jawbone resting inside a bowl-shaped bottle. The teeth are almost the size of your hand. 'Do you think there are more of these things?'

'The Skards have many tales of the old times. There is one that refers to a Dwarf city, deep beneath the ice. They say the Dwarves and the ancient Skards were locked in a constant battle – a war against demons from the underworld. The only way they could survive was to take on the strength of their enemies, become the very demons that they sought to destroy. They became Nisse.'

'Nisse.' You repeat the word, struggling to make sense of it. 'Is that Skard?'

The mage nods. 'It means cursed.' He returns the jar to the shelf, setting it between a floating forefinger and what looks like a blackened, human heart. 'In answer to your question, Arran – could there be more of these? I fear the answer is yes. But what we should really be asking is this – why now? After thousands of years, why would the Nisse choose this moment to return?'

(Remove the word *envoy* from your hero sheet. Return to 328 to continue your conversation with Segg.)

256

'A witchfinder? Gosh no!' You are astonished the woman would even consider you a member of their order – a group of feared swordsmen, renowned for their bloodthirsty methods of bringing witches and other sinners to justice.

'Please,' you beg, determined now to press your advantage. 'You can take the sword – it's yours. Inscribed by a White Abbot. It'll fetch a good sum of money – and the diamond too. Please, just some food and shelter – please?' Hearing your own desperation shames you. Lowering your eyes, you let your shoulders slump.

Stupid fool. This sword could buy her whole damn cabin – a thousand cabins. And I offer it willingly for some supper and a blanket . . .

The woman gives a chuckle. 'Indeed, how could I resist such a generous offer?'

You glare back sullenly, wondering if she mocks you. But her beaming smile seems genuine enough. 'I am Sylvie.' She turns, gesturing to the log cabin. 'And this is my humble abode. Nothing special, I might add, but it serves me well enough.' When the woman looks back, her smile has faded. 'You will leave your sword on the doorstep, understand me? Now, come – let's see if we can't put some meat on those bones.'

You nod quickly, unstrapping the scabbard from your belt as you follow her to the front door. Turn to 269.

257

The ledge brings you to the entrance of a large circular chamber. Carved into the stone floor are a number of circles, arranged in an arcane pattern around the edge of the room. Lines and whorls twist away from the outer motifs, snaking towards a central circle where a podium of black stone rests inside a ring of runes.

Caul draws back, sniffing the air as if detecting some unpleasant odour.

By contrast, you find the complex work fascinating. There is a residue of magic still locked in the circles' design, one which you may still be able to put to use.

You follow the complex patterns, trying to ascertain their nature. Segg taught you some basics but the rest seems to come to you instinctively, as plain as reading words on a page.

'These are used to call spirits,' you declare, following the path of one of the spiralling whirls. 'I think they are summoning runes and those,' your eyes drift to the runes surrounding the podium, 'are words of binding.'

Caul is still hovering by the doorway, looking shiftily around the room. 'I don't care what it does – is it safe?'

'Oh yes,' you reply, with a dark grin. 'For now . . .'

If you wish to place a weapon or item of equipment on the central podium, turn to 403. If you have a *plain glass orb* and wish to place it on the podium, turn to 1. If you would rather not tamper with this strange magic, you may leave the chamber and continue on your way. Turn to 732.

258

Rutus folds his arms, looking down at you with a smirk. 'Had enough, dog?'

You are too busy rolling around in the slush, gripping your stomach where his punch had landed. Clearly, strength is no substitute for experience.

'It's the maids for you,' snorts the trainer, gesturing with his crop to a line of straw practice dummies. 'You can dance with them a while, until you're ready.'

'Could have gone worse,' grins Rutus, offering out his hand. 'Guess the fever took more than your looks, eh?'

You ignore his gesture, pushing yourself back to your feet. 'Next time,' you promise, meeting his gaze.

'I'll be ready,' he replies guardedly. 'You know where to find me, rookie.'

You watch him join the rest of the men, jealous of their comradeship and back-slapping. Feeling once again the outsider, you march over to the practice dummies, determined not to run and hide like you always have in the past. Straw and wood go flying as you hack and chop at your target, secretly wishing it was Rutus and the cheers were all for you. (Record the keyword *baited* on your hero sheet.)

When you are ready to leave the yard, turn to 113 to revisit the main courtyard or 168 to climb the stairs to the battlements.

259

The guard removes the two of moons from his hand and places it face down on the discard pile. He reaches into the pouch and takes another stone at random. He has now gained the two of stars:

The guard is still grinning to himself. 'Queen's wave again,' he whispers to you. 'I'm sure we've won this.' Turn to 570.

260

For defeating the captain, you may now help yourself to one of the following rewards:

Naglfar anchor	Whelk walkers	Cross bones
(left hand: grapple)	(feet)	(cloak)
+2 speed +3 brawn	+2 speed +2 armour	+2 speed +2 brawn
Ability: knockdown	Ability: haste	Ability: malice

When you have updated your hero sheet, turn to 479.

261

After reclaiming your sword, you leave the cabin and head out to the creek. It proves easy to find, the chattering rush of noise leading you into a wooded dell. Along its base, white-frothed waters dance and splash, carving a zigzagging path amongst the trees. (Make a note of the keyword *blade* on your hero sheet, then turn to 155.)

262

A service hatch opens in the wall, where you can see a tray filled with various wolf-skin garments. You are surprised to see a glimmer of magic around them; evidently the materials have been imbued with some minor enchantments, which probably even Jackson isn't aware of.

'How much?' you ask, leaning cautiously over the line to take a closer look.

'Sixty gold,' snaps Jackson. 'Top quality company threads those, so don't you be turning your nose up at 'em. Too good for the stinking likes of you, I wager.'

The following items are available for 60 gold crowns each:

White wolf mitts	White wolf treads	White wolf jerkin
(gloves)	(feet)	(chest)
+1 speed +1 armour	+1 speed +2 brawn	+1 speed +2 magic
Ability: frost guard	Ability: sidestep	Ability: insulated

You may continue to purchase items from the trader (turn to 151), discuss something else (turn to 685) or leave (return to the quest map).

263

Filling the barrels is a dirty, stinking and laborious task. First, the thick tar is scooped into smaller buckets, which are then used to pour it into the seemingly bottomless wooden barrels. Once the barrels are full, Kirk twists a lid into place and then he and Lawson roll them back to the cart.

After an hour you are dizzy from the stench, the protective leather gloves doing little to keep the tar from getting on your skin and over your clothes. Henna spends most of her time muttering about her armour and how long it will take to clean. Then eventually even she falls quiet, focused on getting the grim task completed.

With half the barrels filled, Kirk nudges Lawson then nods towards the far side of the canyon. Lawson gives an answering nod, then goes to retrieve his bow and quiver from the nearby rocks.

'You girls okay for a while?' Kirk removes his gloves and drops them onto a rock. 'Me and Lawson got some business to do. Just scouting out the canyon, you know. Soldier stuff.' He taps the side of his nose. 'So, you noobs stay together. And don't talk to strangers, okay?'

Before anyone can argue the two men are gone, laughing and joking to each other – leaving you behind to fill and transport the rest of the barrels to the wagon.

An hour later and your patience starts to sour. 'If they don't return soon we'll be here until nightfall.'

'I'm lodging a formal complaint,' Henna scowls, watching in disgust as the tar drips from her gloves. 'I didn't sign up for this.'

You tip another bucket of sludge into the barrel, half-choking on the overpowering stench. 'Sooner we're done, sooner we can go home.'

As you reach down to refill your bucket, a sudden chorus of shrieks alerts you to the nearby hills. A group of petrels have taken flight from a thicket of long grass, squawking overhead as they wheel across the lake.

'What spooked them?' Henna goes to draw her sword, then hesitates when she remembers the gloop on her hands. 'Oh, let's ignore it. I'm sure it's nothing.'

You scan the hills, fearing there may be a hidden predator using the tall grass for cover. Or perhaps it's just your imagination getting the better of you.

Will you:

Decide to search the hills?	70
Continue to fill the barrels?	306

264

The woman ducks into the tent and returns with a bundle of leathers clasped between her mitted hands. You take the bundle and peel back the cloth. Inside you discover a black shard of rock, smooth as glass, with veins of green branching beneath its surface.

'We don't exactly know what it is,' says the woman, looking back at her companion. 'A type of metamorphic rock, not unlike marble. Its dense structure suggests a strong heat source, possibly magma. I suppose it could have been brought to the surface following the cataclysm.'

'Or brought here from elsewhere,' mutters the male, gazing skywards.

'This is magic,' you reply, touching the stone and watching as the green veins pulse, brightening then dimming once again.

'It has some . . . energy, yes,' Reah says uncertainly. 'We can't be sure if there is something else trapped within the sample – it may even be a living organism.' Reah takes the stone from you, wrapping it tightly in the leathers. 'I'd rather you didn't get too close. We don't know what we're dealing with yet.'

Will you:

Ask about the Titans?	136
Ask about the man in the tent?	332
Ask how you might help? (starts the quest)	146

265

You gesture to the bearded man in the blue velvet coat. 'I'm here on Baron Fromark's orders. He says he'll be most honoured to cover any costs.'

The guard glares at you for a moment, then with a huff he moves aside. You nod in thanks then hurry past him, taking a short set of stairs down into the cellar. Turn to 43.

266

'The book?' Harris looks down at it, momentarily confused – as if he'd forgotten he even had it. 'Yes . . . I . . . I took it. One of Segg's, he won't miss it. Was just left lying around.' He moves a hand across the cover, tracing a brass motif with his fingertips. 'A book of spells. That's it.' He nods to himself, seeming more certain. 'I thought it might be useful.'

'Ain't nothing useful in one of them,' scowls Brack, leaning away as if the book might suddenly bite him. 'I don't even touch the things. Ugh!'

Harris tucks the tome back under his arm. 'Hmm, why does that not surprise me, Brack?' (Return to 86 to ask another question or turn to 297 to continue on to the tower.)

267

You cut through the chain, taking a smug satisfaction in seeing the boisterous racer go tumbling away in a flurry of snow. Focusing back on the track, you see the nearby racers swerving erratically.

Rocks and thick chunks of ice have broken loose from the mountainside and are now raining down across the track. You suspect one of your competitors may have used magic or some other weapon to start the rock fall. Your only hope of survival is to ride through the chaos as quickly as possible.

You will need to take a challenge test using your *speed* racing attribute:

	Speed
Rock fall	14

If you are successful, turn to 716. Otherwise turn to 756.

268

With the spectral guardian defeated, you may now help yourself to one of the following rewards:

Swift tusk	Mammoth tresses	Forget-me-knot
(main hand: sword)	(cloak)	(necklace)
+1 speed +3 brawn	+1 speed +2 brawn	+1 speed +1 brawn
Ability: deep wound	Ability: malice	Ability: exploit

When you have updated your hero sheet, turn to 339.

269

You follow Sylvie into the cabin, relieved to feel the rush of heat the moment you are through the door. A fire crackles in the hearth, sending dancing shadows across the walls.

'Make yourself at home.' Sylvie offers you a smile.

The main room of the cabin is small and cluttered, dominated by a table covered in pots, plants and jars of herbs. Most of the walls are taken over by shelves, where books and scrolls are pushed into every available space.

Sylvie makes room on the table for her basket, lifting back the blanket to reveal a number of freshly-picked mushrooms. She catches your eye, then gives an apologetic sigh. 'Sorry, I wasn't expecting guests. Here, take a seat.' The woman pulls out a chair, then quickly removes the spiked plant that had been left there. 'Unless you'd rather change first. Those clothes must be wet through, you'll catch your death.' She nods to a side-room. 'I have some old clothes . . .'

'I'd rather eat,' you smile ruefully, eyes fixed on the pot heating next to the fire.

'Dinner it is, then.' Sylvie pulls back her hood and removes her coat, hanging it next to the fireplace. She then proceeds to busy herself by chopping mushrooms, before lifting the lid from the pot and adding them to its bubbling contents. Turn to 191.

270

The herd has fled southwards but one muttok has remained behind, standing its ground – the grey-haired giant with the barbed antlers. Lowering its head, the beast springs into a full-on charge, driving itself at Desnar. The Skard waits until the last possible moment then leaps aside, driving his javelin straight through the back of the beast's neck. The muttok hurtles onwards for several metres, kicking up a flurry of dust and snow, then it starts to stagger. Desnar takes another javelin and marches after it, waiting until the beast has fallen onto its forelegs before sliding the second javelin through its midriff. The beast gives a gargling screech, then falls limp at his feet.

'Vic tarnik!' The Skard pulls a knife from his belt, grinning from ear to ear. He crouches next to the downed animal, hacking at the magnificent antlers until they come free. Then he rises to his feet, holding up his trophy in bloodied hands. 'Vic tarnik!'

You bow your head in defeat, accepting that Desnar has bested you in the challenge of the hunt. Turn to **578**.

271

Ducking beneath the plant's flailing creepers, you race towards the edge of the broken branch and take a running jump . . .

For a heart-stopping second you glimpse the vertiginous drop below you – over a mile of twisted limbs, dagger-sharp leaves and tangled roots – then you are scrabbling for purchase on the branch, spectral claws pushing out of your fingers to slide deep into the bark.

With effort, you manage to drag yourself onto more solid ground. Looking back, you see no sign of the scurrilous rodent – you assume it must have scrambled up into the thick canopy of branches. After taking a moment to compose yourself, you study the ledges and vines that stretch before you.

I can do this.

You run and leap once again, snatching hold of the stringy lianas to propel yourself across to the first ledge. You land in a run, maintaining your momentum as you jump for the next growth of vines. You only just make it, your hands sliding down their slippery dew-coated surface before you finally secure a hold.

Carefully you drag yourself up the tree, hand over hand, until you reach a higher ledge. With a grunt of exertion you swing yourself onto the gnarly outcropping, using your feet to help lever you to safety.

A quick glance confirms that the worst is now past. The ledge you are on winds its way round to the summit of the tree, less than a hundred metres above you.

You breathe a sigh of relief.

That's when you hear the banshee-like wail coming from behind you.

As you turn you sense a shifting in the air, a buzzing flash of movement. You drop to the ground, just in time, as a storm of bright daggers blur past in a rustling roar. Lifting your eyes, you see a strange fey-like creature hovering overhead – a woman, with tree-bark skin and black butterfly wings humming above her shoulders. She moves her hands in a curving arc, weaving some sort of spell.

You glance back, realising that she is controlling the daggers – they sweep round, like an angry swarm of bees, and start back towards your position. As they near you realise that they are actually leaves, but hardened into deadly-sharp points. You throw yourself aside as they hurtle across the ledge, several thudding deep into the bark of the tree. Another wail rends the air. You draw your weapons, spinning to face the devilish creature as she dives towards you, fingers grasping for your throat. It is time to fight:

	Speed	Magic	Armour	Health
Willow	7	5	4	70
Leaf blades	6	4	2	25

Special abilities

- **Blade storm**: At the end of each combat round, you must automatically take 4 damage, ignoring *armour*, from the whirling leaf blades. Once the blades are reduced to zero *health*, this ability no longer applies.
- **Natural order**: The leaf blades are immune to *bleed* and *venom*.

Once Willow is defeated, the leaf blades are also automatically defeated (if they still have *health*). If you manage to overcome this winged fiend, turn to 235.

272

You have emerged in a large, rectangular chamber, its walls, floor and ceiling covered in thick growths of fungus. As you step away from the hole, you hear an unsettling creak beneath your feet. Looking down, you see that the floorboards have become warped and rotted. You wonder if they will still be capable of supporting your weight. To your right, an open doorway leads through to a narrow corridor.

'Careful,' whispers Anise.

You take another step into the room, wincing as the wood groans and cracks. Then another, distributing your weight as best you can. Anise carefully shadows you, her pool of torchlight slowly filling the room.

A sudden rush of movement alerts you to danger.

You swing round, eyes following a dark shape as it drops from the ceiling.

'It's a riftwing!' Anise shrieks, ducking behind your back. 'Watch out!'

The creature resembles a cross between a goblin and a bat, with black leathery wings and peaked furry ears. From beneath its flayed nostrils, you see two rows of needle-like teeth steadily opening wider.

With a hiss, the monster lunges for you. Reacting on instinct, you manage to catch one of its spindly wrists, stopping its taloned fingers just shy of your throat. The other limb ends in a scarred stump, battering uselessly against your chest. As the two of you stagger back against the wall, you notice one of its wings is hanging loose from its back, the membrane torn. The creature must have been in a previous fight, which has left it injured and weak. It is time to fight:

	Speed	Brawn	Armour	Health
Riftwing	2	1	1	28

If you manage to defeat this winged fiend turn to 217. If you lose the combat, remember to record your defeat on your hero sheet. You may then attempt the combat again or return to the map.

273

The alpha male lies at your feet, its body broken and torn as if savaged by some wild animal. The rest of the wolves scamper into the trees, leaving you alone at the centre of the blood-spattered clearing.

You may now choose one of the following rewards:

Alpha's tooth	The howling
(left hand: dagger)	(cloak)
+1 brawn +1 magic	+1 speed
Ability: dominate	Ability: savagery

When you have made your decision and updated your hero sheet, turn to 338.

274

(Note: You must have completed the orange quest *The bitter end* before you can access this location. If you have visited this location before, turn to 374.)

You brush the flakes of snow from the map and study it again. The symbol shows a wolf's head, or at least an admirable attempt at one, designed to match the stamp on the back of the leather hide. *The White Wolf Trading Company.* Once again, your eyes scan the featureless banks of snow that stretch as far as the eye can see. There has been no real landmark to navigate by for several days – instead you have been guessing your orientation from the position of the sun, when it deigns to show itself through the swirling whiteness. You could be miles off course, left wandering this howling wasteland until your frost-bitten body finally decides to give up. A small part of you no longer cares.

Keep moving. Just keep moving.

It feels as if that has been your mantra since the attack on the road.

But everywhere fate has led you, only chaos and upset have followed. You hope that this time will be different. Perhaps some friendly company and news from home is all the tonic you need to boost your flagging spirits.

It is darkening towards evening when you finally see the lights. At first you wonder if it is merely a mirage. Your eyes have become crusted with snow and ice, your surroundings fogged by the wind-swept snow. It is easy to imagine shapes and colours, to see things that aren't there. You blink, rubbing a hand across your face, then stare once again. Lights just ahead – only a few hundred metres away. A rise of hills must have previously obscured them from view. You quicken your pace, dragging your numb limbs through the thick drifts of newly fallen snow, wanting nothing more than to escape the wind, the snow, the ice . . . to have something solid underfoot at last.

The light comes from a pair of oil lamps, hanging outside a low-slung building fashioned from what looks like sheets of metal. As you step closer, you realise it is more of a bunker than a building, its rusted iron walls extending back into a rocky hillside.

You knock on the front door, which displays a white wolf daubed in paint. There is no answer from inside – and yet you can see light framing the edges of the door. With a shrug of your shoulders, you push it open and step in. A bell chime tinkles as the door opens inwards, revealing a large metal room, the walls and ceiling covered in brown blotches of rust.

A white line has been painted a few feet back from the opposite wall. After stamping the snow from your boots you cautiously start to cross the room, pushing your hood back from your face. 'Hello? Anyone home?'

You hear a distant banging, some angry muttering. Suddenly two metal panels flip open at chest height, and the nozzle of a musket is pushed out of each.

'Whatya want?' growls a man's voice from behind the wall.

You find yourself judging the height of the person, your eyes coming to rest on a small glass-covered peep-hole. An eye is pressed against it, distorted into a huge staring orb.

'I only came to—' You take a step forward.

'Back up! Don't cross the line!' The voice snaps. There is a rattling clink from somewhere to your left. You glance sideways, spotting the crossbow that is now hanging down from the ceiling by a complex set of pulleys and strings. To your discomfort, the weapon is pointed straight at you.

With hands raised, you step back behind the line. 'Are you open for trade, supplies?'

'Might be,' grunts the voice. 'You gotta permit? Ain't seen the likes of you before – got the height for a Skard, but yer speak too proper. I'm Jackson, clerk of the White Wolf Trading Company. Now, don't you be trying any funny business now – you can see I taken all the necessary precautions.' As if to underline the point, you hear another rattle and a thud, this time to your right. Another crossbow has dropped down from the ceiling, its bolt trained at your head.

(If you have the keyword *hunted* on your hero sheet, turn to 92.)

Will you:

Ask to see his wares?	151
Ask about trading?	327
Ask about his 'precautions'?	549
Ask if he has any news?	450
Trade items? (requirement: permit)	730
Leave?	Return to the map

275

After an hour of trekking eastwards you finally spy a cave opening, little more than a narrow cleft in the side of the glacier. A strong musty odour of decay seeps from within – you feel Nanuk's uneasiness, his pacing back and forth.

'What is it?' you whisper to yourself, drawing your weapons.

Nanuk responds with a reverberating growl, his mind pushing into yours, his strength cording your muscles. You have never known him to react in such a way.

Cautiously, you advance into the tunnel. There is spoor on the ground: droppings and claw marks. Some animal must have made its home here. A few metres in the tunnel becomes a wider cave, the ice giving way to black rock. You notice veins of magic glowing beneath its surface, just like the shard that Reah showed you.

The stink comes from the corpses. Human and animal. And the decaying creature that is shuffling at the back of the cave – a polar bear, or something that may have once passed for one. Its white fur is matted with pus, weeping from the sores and lesions that cover its body. As the animal turns its muzzle, sniffing at the air, you see that is obviously blind – the pupils of its eyes have whitened to a milky haze.

The bear senses you, lifting its head to emit an ear-shattering roar. Then the savage giant bounds towards you, its huge claws ripping through the ice. It is time to fight:

	Speed	Brawn	Armour	Health
Doomta	5	3	3	60

Special abilities

- **Blind rage**: At the end of the fourth combat round, the bear will go into a berserk rage. This lowers its *speed* by 1 but raises its *brawn* by 3 for the remainder of the combat.
- **Disease**: Once you have taken health damage from Doomta's damage score, you must lose a further 2 *health* at the end of each combat round, ignoring *armour*.

If you manage to defeat this corrupted predator, turn to 3.

276

Tired and miserable, you decide to tell the truth. The woman listens to your story in silence, her expression unchanging. As you draw to its end, choosing to omit the part about the strange demon, a hint of irritation creeps into your voice. Why doesn't this woman show any concern or alarm? She didn't flinch when you described the bloody massacre on the road or the very fact that you are a crown prince of the realm.

Your words falter to silence, waiting expectantly for a response.

The women regards you for a moment longer, then gives a dismissive snort. 'I've heard some tall tales in my time, boy . . .'

'It's true,' you implore, feeling your anger surge once again. 'Would I have this if I was just some . . . some commoner?' You lift the scabbard at your side, showing her its jewels and the holy inscriptions on the hilt. 'This is Duran's Heart. A named blade, given to me on my thirteenth birthday.'

The woman takes a step closer, but her eyes linger on your face rather than the blade. 'You could have stolen it.'

Her accusation startles you. 'I'm no thief! You can have the sword – I can't even touch the cursed thing.'

The woman's frown returns. 'Is this true?'

Too late, you realise what you have done, blurting out your secret with no mind to the consequences. To confess such a thing is almost tantamount to treason.

'I can only touch the scabbard,' you reply honestly, seeing no reason to spin a lie now you've gone this far. 'Since I was given it, the inscriptions have always . . .' You struggle for the words.

'Rejected you?' the woman supplies thoughtfully.

You nod, trying to gauge her reaction. This secret is one you have only shared once before, with your nursemaid Molly. And you doubt she'll be telling anyone now.

'You're no witchfinder, then,' the woman appears to visibly relax. 'Perhaps there is some truth in what you say after all.' (Make a note of the word *prince* on your hero sheet, then turn to 249.)

277

The bearded warrior is tearing at a hunk of meat. He stops eating as you approach, his mouth hanging open with half-chewed food.

'Thought you might want these.' You place the gauntlets on the table, then await his response.

Ran finally closes his mouth, chewing and swallowing his food. After wiping his fingers on his jerkin, he lifts up one of the gauntlets to inspect it. He nods, his smile widening. 'Where did you find 'em?'

'It's a long story,' you reply, glancing warily at the other soldiers. 'Maybe best not to ask too many questions.'

'The thief?'

'Has learnt their lesson.'

Ran leans back, fumbling for something by his waist. After much grunting, he drops a small leather pouch onto the table. 'That's some of me earnings and a little keepsake. Take it. Least I can do.'

You pick up the pouch, opening it up to find it filled with gold. You also spot a plain copper ring amongst the glittering coins. 'No, you keep this . . .'

Ran puts out his hands, shaking his head. 'Won't hear another word. I like to reward honesty – trust me, not much of that around 'ere. Me, I'm just content with a full belly and a pillow for me head. Now shoot, before I change my mind.'

You have gained 50 gold crowns and the following item:

Constant copper
(ring)
+1 brawn +1 magic
Ability: watchful

After thanking the soldier, you leave the hall and return to the courtyard. Remove the keyword *gains* from your hero sheet, then turn to 113.

278

You find yourself in a small, cobwebbed chamber lit by an eerie green orb of light. It slowly circles the room, illuminating shabby-looking shelves and cupboards and piles of wooden boxes and trunks. The air is thick with dust and the stale stench of decay.

A quick search reveals that this space is some kind of store-room. As well as mildewed books and some chipped stone tablets covered in runes, you also find various arcane objects – wands, staffs and charms – and a few musty items of clothing, which you assume must be enchanted in some way. Clearly, Segg must have collected these over the course of his lifetime; perhaps some were pilfered from the dark creatures that have assailed this keep.

Aware that you might be discovered at any time, you hurry your search for something useful. Three items catch your eye: a book of spells, written onto sheets of flayed human skin; a pair of black boots frosted with ice; and a stone tablet, its pock-mocked surface crawling with dark runes of death and necromancy.

You may now choose up to two of the following items:

Jeeper's creepers	Little nippers	Tome of Necromancy
(left hand: spell book)	(feet)	(backpack)
+1 speed +1 magic	+1 speed	Use at any time to
Ability: wither	Ability: silver frost	remove one death
		penalty from your hero

When you have made your choice, you quickly pull on the book levers to flip the wall and return to the main library. From here, you may enter Segg's quarters and speak with the mage (turn to 328) or return to the courtyard (turn to 113).

279

'Oh, they're prospectors,' explains the thief. He lifts his chin, scanning the tops of the tents. 'Ryker's clever, been using them to check out the rifts and tunnels, check what's safe before he sends his men in. Look, over there.' He tugs on your arm and points to a pair of elegantly-dressed gentlemen with scented pomanders held to their noses. Behind them, hovering at shoulder height, are two globes of yellow magic.

'Miners used to have canaries with 'em. If there's danger, bad air and stuff, then the canaries would keel over and die. That's how the mages got their name. Ryker gets 'em to scout out the caves; they send in those yellow things, like eyeballs; they see what's going on, then somehow what they see gets sent back to the mages.' He taps the side of his head, rolling his eyes. 'Crazy magic, eh?'

You glance back at the white sheets tethered to the wall. 'Interesting, but what's that got to do with the sled races?'

The man whistles through his black teeth. 'Think we gonna watch out there in the cold?' He shakes his head. 'The canaries follow the racers, then we sees the pictures – just like a moving painting, right there.' He points to the stretched sheets. 'Like we said, Ryker's calling it big sheet entertainment. Wouldn't want to miss any of the action now, would we?'

To continue chatting to the thief, return to 288. To explore the rest of the compound. Turn to 106.

280

With the dogs defeated and their pack mates struggling in the mire, you are free to cross to the other side unhindered. You pause at the mouth of the cave, looking back towards the shore. One of the Skard hunters is hurrying towards the first of the stones, an axe in one hand and a knife in the other. Of his companions, there is no obvious sign. Turn to 344.

281

Ignoring the strange ghost, you take the unlit lamp (make a note of the word *lamp* on your hero sheet) and then continue into the next passageway. Turn to 385.

282

Without speaking you head for the door, not wishing to remain here a moment longer. But Sylvie's voice brings you up short, you pause on the threshold.

'I'm sorry,' she says.

'You should not have done what you did.' You glance back over your shoulder, your eyes narrowed with anger. 'You don't know what it's like.'

'No, you're right, I don't.' Sylvie steps away from the sizzling breakfast, her face etched with concern. 'Randal had the gift also. And the moment I saw you, I just knew.'

'How? How did you—?'

'I sensed the magic within you. But not like a mage – not one who chooses to use it, takes it and moulds it to their will. No, with you it's different. It is like the magic is just a natural part of you. As it was with Randal.'

Anger turns to surprise. 'Do you know what these . . . these dreams are? Why me?'

'All I know is what Randal told me or I've managed to deduce from my studies. There's an old Skard word, Norr. It means crossing, the state between waking and sleeping. Some minds are able to dwell there, to walk that place as a spirit body.'

'Norr?' You frown, trying to recall ever having heard the word.

'It's the thin line, the meeting place between our world and the shroud – the realm of magic.'

You feel the cold in your stomach twist into knots of fear. 'The shroud.' You have always been forbidden to mention such a thing. To the Church it is a blasphemous evil, a hell where demons and other malign spirits dwell. 'I . . . I never knew. No one ever told me. They can't have known.'

'It's a rare affliction, boy.' Sylvie meets your troubled gaze. 'I'm sorry.'

You close your eyes to stop the room from spinning, still giddy from the dream. 'This can't be happening to me . . .' Instinctively you reach for your pouch, relieved to find it is still attached to your belt. You have enough dragon leaf to keep the dreams away, for a while at least . . .

'That won't help you.' Sylvie puts a hand to her hip, the other pointing with her knife. 'That is the coward's way. You need to become stronger, boy. The mind is like a muscle. It must be exercised. Avoiding the dreams will only make it worse.'

Will you:

Still insist she tricked you and leave?	261
Agree to fetch water for breakfast?	78

283

Guards spill into the room, their torches pushing back the shadows. You raise an arm, shielding yourself from the sudden brightness, struggling to focus. Dark shapes blur past, bodies smelling of sweat and the winter's cold.

A hooded man shifts into view, his face made sharp by the flickering torchlight. It is Rook, one of Everard's soldiers. He is speaking to you, but it takes a moment before the sounds wash in.

'Speak to me – what happened?' His tone is clipped, used to getting answers.

You notice some of the guards circling you, weapons drawn. Others are inspecting the bodies. Of the men that surround you, their distrust is evident.

'Anise?' The word catches in your throat. You start forward but an arm holds you back.

'She's fine,' says Rook. He moves in front of you, piercing blue eyes flashing beneath his hood. 'It's over now. It's over.'

A blanket is put around your shoulders, its coarseness scratching at your neck and arms.

'Move aside,' someone orders. Bodies brush past you again. More words are spoken, gruff and commanding, but you are no longer listening. A white noise roars in your ears – becoming screams, the necromancer's laughter.

'This tower is out of bounds!' A single voice drags you back. You open your eyes to see a flurry of crimson robes sweeping into the room. 'One God, protect us!' Segg takes one look at the destruction and then begins gesturing frantically to the guards. 'Seal this place! Seal it now. We must leave!'

The elderly mage hurries to your side, full of concern. 'Are you all right? Are you hurt?'

'It was a dare,' you reply weakly, too numb to feel anything. 'To survive the night.' Your eyes drift to the open doorway – where the first light of dawn is creeping steadily across the stonework.

Record the keyword *fractured* on your hero sheet, then return to the map to continue your adventure.

284

The grasping hands drive you into the creature's mouth, where the devilish heads snap and bite at your clothing, piercing through to the flesh beneath. Nanuk sends his strength into you, pooling magic into your clawed hands. With a bestial roar, you drive your bolstered spirit energies into the maw of the beast – turning your head away from the brightness of the blast. Screams fill your ears; a deafening dirge-like crescendo.

Silence. You blink.

You are crouched next to the open chest. The runes have vanished, as has the dark aura. You cautiously peer over the rim, to discover that the interior is now an ordinary chest. Resting inside are two glowing artefacts – one a pale orb, the other a painted figurehead of an angel. If you wish, you may now take any/all of the following:

Pandora	Spirit of hope (1 use)
(backpack)	(backpack)
A painted figurehead	Use any time in combat
of an angel	to restore 10 *health*

You may now examine the sword, if you haven't already (turn to 62), or cross back to the tree and continue onwards (turn to 509.)

285

You round a corner, skidding to a halt as you come face to face with a thin, middle-aged man in tattered blue robes. His wide staring eyes peer at you from between long locks of tangled hair. The yellow light buzzes around his head like an angry fly, then winks out in a puff of smoke.

'No!' The man shrinks away from you, looking terror-stricken as he cowers up against the wall. The ice in front of him is marked by a line of runes. You sense their magic is weak, their carving looking rushed and ill-planned. Behind the frightened mage is a wall of rock – trapping him in a dead-end.

'Leave me! Leave me!' he shrieks. His eyes flick wildly from side to side as Skoll and Anise appear at your shoulder. 'I am protected! See!'

You lift your hands from your weapons. 'It's okay, I'm not here to harm you. What happened?'

'Harm? What more harm could you do?' he snaps with derision.

'You were with the miners?' asks Anise gently.

The mage stifles a sob. 'It wasn't me. I didn't do it! I'm not to blame!'

'Then who is?' snaps Skoll impatiently. His tone puts fear back into the man's eyes.

'We . . . we didn't see the trap until it was too late. A charm spell . . . an enchantment. They fell asleep, I couldn't wake them. Then the others came . . . the ones with the hoods. And . . . and . . .' The man bites his bottom lip, a sudden defiance flaring in his eyes.

'You're safe now,' says Anise, edging forward. 'Come, you must be famished. We have food.'

The man gives an angry hiss, stabbing at you with a quivering finger. 'Don't you come any closer,' he demands. 'They sent you, I know they did. You want me to sleep, just like the others. Then you'll kill me. But . . . but I'm not sleeping – no, not ever!'

Skoll merely grunts at his threat. 'This one has gone mad. Best we leave. There is nothing we can do.'

Will you:

Step across the line of runes?	572
Leave the mage and resume your journey?	750

286

(Remove the word *trader* from your hero sheet.)

You tell Everard the full story of what happened by the tar pits, including the part about the soldiers trading weapons and armour to the Skards. Everard listens in silence, fingers tapping against the wall. When you have finished, the knight shakes his head sadly.

'No one likes a tell-tale, Arran. Least of all me.'

You startle in surprise. 'Excuse me?'

'Yeah, I had my eye on those boys. I knew what they were up to.'

'They're dead,' you reply bluntly. 'And you don't seem to care.'

Everard swings to face you, the colour rising in his cheeks. 'You may be a prince, Arran – our future king – but don't tell me what I should or should not be thinking. I care about a lot of things, my prince. I care about this keep and I do care about my soldiers. But if some choose to play with fire, then they're gonna get burnt.' He pauses, eyes narrowing. 'And they got burnt, didn't they? End of story.' He turns back to the wall, armour clinking as he rests his arms against the stone.

You sense that pursuing the topic would be unwise – and yet you can't help but feel disappointment at the man's reaction. 'I'm sorry. Clearly I misjudged you.' The statement hangs poignantly in the air as you march away, feeling his gaze needling like daggers into your back.

Will you:
Climb the stairs to the mage tower?　　　　301
Return to the main courtyard?　　　　　　113

287

You stand your ground, holding yourself still as you watch the inquisitor hobble nearer. Out of his armour he looks more like a common thug than a holy warrior. And all the more menacing for it.

'What . . . happened?' Your words are little more than a hoarse croak. You swallow, then repeat the question with more authority. 'Why did you stop us on the road? I demand an answer!' You can still picture the dark look that had taken him as he reached for his warhammer. His eyes spoke of murder. As they do now.

'You were sent here to die,' snarls the inquisitor. He summons a ball of white fire into his open hand, letting the smoke curl around his fingers. 'That was my order, my test of faith.'

You stumble backwards, stung by his admission. Tears rise, unbidden to your eyes. 'No, there's a mistake . . .'

'Indeed, one I intend to set right.' His voice grows harder still. 'You've had every chance – every chance.' With a snarl, he hurls the ball of flame through the air. It slams into you with the force of a punch, winding you and sending you flying onto your back. For several seconds, you are coughing and gasping, your nostrils filled with a sulphurous smoke. When you can focus again, the inquisitor is standing over you; a giant obliterating the sky.

'Why wouldn't you make something of yourself?' He turns the dagger, its blade catching the muted morning light. 'Even Malden, cripple Malden, is more a man than you'll ever be.'

'You sound like my father,' you snort disdainfully. 'Did he order this?'

The inquisitor's brow creases, puckering his red scar. 'The king? Ordering me from his sick bed? No, lad. The Church is the only authority now. To purge this realm of all evil and waste. The throne is weak. It is time for a new—'

Your foot slams into his knee, drawing out a snarl of pain. You kick again, driving hard into his wounded leg. Then you are scrabbling in the dirt, twisting yourself back onto your feet and running.

'Fool!' snarls the warrior. 'You can't run from me! There's nowhere for you to hide!'

Will you:

Run back to the cabin?	312
Run into the nearby woods?	244

288

You are met by a garish blaze of tents and temporary structures, and the cloying stench that accompanies people and animals. Gagging, you quickly push Nanuk's magic away, leaving your senses dulled to the stench of dirt, sweat and degradation.

A hand settles around your shoulder. 'We sees a new arrival, yes?'

You jerk away from the man's grasp, but hesitate when you see the thin emaciated figure smiling back at you. His wasted body is swaddled in soiled blankets and a tattered cloak, the hood of which has frayed to almost nothing. A bag hangs off one scrawny shoulder, patched with various coloured cloths. 'Welcome to the top of the world,' he sniggers, his fingers pinching your arm as he guides you along the aisle of tents. 'We shows you round, yes?'

'Who are all these people?' you ask, confused. 'Why're they here?'

Most of them appear to be in poorer shape than the man at your side, hunkered down in layers of fur and clothing, looking like corpses awaiting the undertaker. You receive mean, suspicious stares – and covetous glances at your weapons and clothing. Between the tents, ragged children scamper and play, throwing snow balls at one another. Elsewhere you hear snatches of music and laughter coming from an array of luxurious pavilion tents, their banners and flags billowing in the wind.

'The sled races,' says the man, pulling you to a halt and pointing back towards the wall. You see a series of white canvas sheets hanging down from the spiked crenellations. 'Big sheet entertainment – Ryker's got the canaries involved. It's gonna be spectacular!' He opens out the palms of his hands, waving them in the air while he makes a series of whooshing noises.

'Sled races..?' You turn your head, suddenly drawn by the barking din of pack dogs. Across the jumbled wave of tents, you spy a line of kennels and pens. 'Can anyone enter?'

You feel the man's hand on your arm again. 'Forget that for now, good sir. We might have something for you, if you'd be interested. Yes? Few things we accidentally ... acquired. So, we'd settle for a very good price, just to move them on, if you gets what we're saying, hmm?'

Will you:

Ask to see the thief's wares?	164
Ask about the 'canaries'?	279
Ask about the prison?	218
Explore the compound on your own?	106

289

You make a snap decision and veer to the right, building momentum as you sprint along the banks of the lake. Then you leap, hitting the edge of the first stone awkwardly, your heavier and more muscular body confusing your balance. The surface of the stone is slick with tar but luckily you manage to right yourself, just as the dogs bound madly towards the shoreline in hot pursuit.

To cross the remainder of the stones you will need to complete a *speed* challenge:

If you are successful, turn to 122. If you fail the challenge, turn to 100.

290

The ground gives a violent shudder. Strong enough to almost throw you off balance. Unlike previous tremors, this one does not abate, continuing to rattle and judder as you feel some powerful force start to build.

'What's happening?' You look to Orrec, whose eyes are now on the main courtyard.

'This is bad . . .'

A splintering crack tears through the air. You look back to see the statue of your father riven in two, a deep fissure cutting across his scowling face. The ground continues to shake.

Orrec grabs you and starts running for the main courtyard. A tower door opens and guards spill out, most of them still buckling on armour, their dishevelled appearances and bleary eyes suggesting they have just awoken.

The tremors intensify, sending cracks racing through the ground and along the walls. From somewhere in the distance you hear a thunderous crashing of stone.

'Get to your positions!' Orrec grabs a bewildered soldier, pushing him towards the main yard. 'Move it!' He turns, gesturing to the others. 'Out! Positions, now!'

All of a sudden, the shaking stops. Everyone stands frozen – waiting, listening . . .

Then you hear the distant screams. And a relentless drumming, like fists pounding against a barrier. The soldiers look at one another, confused.

'The wall . . .' Orrec frowns, listening. 'That's the holy inscriptions . . . the abbots' magic.'

The drumming continues, now accompanied by roars and screams of a different nature. They sound inhuman. 'Allam's teeth!' Orrec starts running for the main yard. 'Something's trying to break the wards. We're under attack! To the walls, men! To the walls!' Turn to 152.

291

Your body goes from lightness to heaviness. You try and move, but something is holding you down. There are voices. A confusion of noise.

I tell you, I saw it. Look, his hand . . .

Impossible. He can't still be alive.

Let me see. Stay back!

You hear a scuffle of boots.

Arran? Arran? Do you hear me? You try your best to surface, to reach out towards the sound of that voice.

Another speaker. *He's dead. Leave it be. It's just a spasm. A reflex action.*

Silence. You slide back into the dream, your fingers sinking deep into matted fur. The bear grunts, his bright eyes shining back at you from the chill darkness. You try and read his expression, understand what he seeks to tell you – but the whispering at the back of your mind is foreign, incomprehensible.

Look, there's movement.

One God protect us. He's alive.

The bear's eyes have merged into a blinding tunnel of light. You blink, trying to look away. Your body feels heavy again, as if it has become stone: impossible to move. Voices.

We should end this. It is an abomination.

I won't have it. Such an act would be treason.

No, it would be a mercy.

The light grows brighter still. You squirm away, buffeted by its heat, desperate to find the comfort of darkness once again – but the Norr has gone, and your eyes are wide open . . . refusing to close.

'Will you get that thing out of my face!'

The light swings away as a man leans in close, his pale skin wrinkled with age. A golden earring flashes with jewels. 'Tell me your name. Tell me your name, boy.'

You go to draw breath, but there is no air. Gasping, you lurch forward, startling the man who quickly jerks out of your way. You sit up in bed, hands grappling at sheets. Then your muscles cramp, an excruciating pain like nothing you have ever known before. Unable to breathe, you kick and squirm.

'Hold him!' booms a commanding voice.

You roll off the bed, slamming down onto a hard stone floor. For a second, you catch sight of your hands. Large and brightly veined, the skin almost translucent. Then another convulsion throws you onto your back, leaving you bucking and writhing like a fish out of water. Dimly, you sense shapes moving around you – a glint of armour, a swish of crimson robes. Hands reach out and lift you up.

'Tell me your name!' A voice hisses in your ear. 'Else we will end your life, demon.'

You can hear wind and rain battering against a nearby window. The shutters rattle angrily, as if desperate to fly open and let the storm sweep inside.

'Arran!' you croak hoarsely. 'I'm Prince Arran!'

Somehow, you manage to break free of your captor. You stumble away, hitting a wall, lurching from one surface to the next. As you move, your body feels different. Muscles pull against the thinness of a nightshirt. Along your arms, corded veins throb with a vibrant energy.

Full of life, and yet – your chest remains heavy and still. Unmoving. Again you suck hungrily for air, trying to push something into your lungs. Instead a wheezing rattle tumbles from your cracked lips.

You put out a hand to steady yourself, struggling to focus on the shapes coalescing in the flickering lantern light. 'What . . . what has happened to me?' you rasp.

'Arran, calm down. You're in shock.' The deep voice belongs to a thick-set man, dressed in brightly-polished armour. His hair is cropped close to his head, peppered with grey.

'Who was your father? Answer me?' The persistent questions come from a thinner man, the elderly one with the earring. Crimson robes spill from the golden circlet around his neck, sparkling with rubies.

'The king . . . my father . . . Leonidas . . .' Your throat is dry and sore. The words cut you like daggers.

'Enough!' The armoured knight raises a hand. 'We can safely assume this is no demon.'

The red-robed gentleman scowls, his distrust still evident.

Your eyes flick to the third. A wiry man, his face hidden by the shadows of his cowl. He stands with his back against the door, arms folded across his chest. Daggers and knives protrude visibly from his belt. His manner exudes a deadly confidence.

'This does not sit well with me,' the rogue drawls from the shadows. 'This is necromancy.'

'I won't hear it,' snaps the armoured knight, waving the hooded one to silence. 'Prince Arran. We are honoured by your presence.' He pushes back his cloak, then drops to one knee, head bowed low. 'And we are at your service.' With reluctance, the crimson-robed man and the hooded one both dip their heads in reverence, but their refusal to kneel is made plainly evident.

For a moment, the only sound comes from the creak of the shutters and the gale venting its fury on the other side. A stray breeze brushes past you, ruffling through your unruly fringe. Trembling, you put a hand to your head, feeling the matted curls of hair, the coldness of your scalp. Cold like death. You draw your hand away, startled when you see clumps of loose hair still tangled between your fingers.

The knight looks up, kindness – or perhaps pity – written on his face. 'You have been through a lot, my prince. I understand you must have questions – as we do ourselves.'

'Who . . . who are you?' You force the words past the soreness in your throat.

'I am Lord Everard,' states the man in armour. He rises to his feet, before gesturing first to the crimson-robed gentleman and then to the rogue. 'And this is Segg and Rook. Both sworn to Bitter Keep – to its rocks and mortar, and to the blood of the Last Order. For Valeron and its king, we serve.'

'King?' Rook shakes his head and turns away. 'There is no king.' He pulls open the door and leaves, his black cloak trailing after him like a living shadow. The door clatters closed of its own accord.

The Last Order. You have the heard the name many times – a group of hardy soldiers who defend the walls and castles along the Great Rift, protecting the kingdom from the monsters and barbarians of the north. You had always pictured it as a remote place, far from anywhere, on the very edge of the world – where civilisation meets the chaotic, frozen wastes of Skardland. The Last Order. So-called, because no one ever comes back.

You glance down at your body – now a slab of thick-set muscle. Gone is the thin, weakling prince. In his place, something else has been dragged into life. Something different. Something changed.

Will you:

Ask how you came to be here?	61
Ask about what happened to your body?	9
Ask what they know about the attack?	22
Ask to go home (ends the conversation)?	98

292

You awake to cramping muscles. Unable to support yourself, your legs give way and you fall – slamming hard against the ground. Beneath you, the wooden floorboards are rattling as they knock against each other, their foundations rocked from side to side. All around you, the air is thick with dust and ice – the groaning and shuddering of the hall a grim reminder of what occurred at Bitter Keep.

'Anise,' you manage to gasp through locked teeth.

You try and rise but are thrown sprawling back onto your stomach.

There is a scream from somewhere behind you, then the sound of earth being ripped apart.

With effort, you manage to shut out the confusion – relaxing your body, pushing the magic into your dead limbs, bringing them steadily back to life.

With a brutish roar you spring to your feet, weapons drawn and ready.

Through the ice you can see Skoll, seated on his throne. You can feel the heat, the magic, emanating from his body. The frozen walls are starting to crack, accompanied by a thunderous boom as the half-giant's awakened power pummels against his prison.

'Arran! Help us!' A young girl's voice.

You snap round, looking for its source.

'Arran!'

Your sharp eyes penetrate the dusty fog, settling on Anise and the white-haired einherjar Aslev. Both are struggling to move debris aside to rescue a trapped warrior. He is pinned to the ground, his legs and arms tangled around the body of the wooden statue.

'Allam's teeth, what are you doing?' A familiar, flabby face leans out of the rubble, barking orders angrily. 'Use your axe,' spits Gurt. 'Come on, you fools, try harder!'

You start towards them, but a warning from Nanuk draws you up short – a raw snarl that diverts your attention to an open doorway.

Three crimson-robed women are hurrying through it, their skirts bunched in their fists. They are followed by a fourth, moving with slower, more confident strides, her slender body dressed in a glittering gown of frost-blue silk. Charms and trinkets flash amongst her braided white hair. Syn Hulda.

The tremors subside, but their fury is now written on the asynjur's face. 'What is this?'

Another crack of ice.

The woman's eyes widen as they look upon Skoll's throne. Deep fissures are now forking outwards from the entombed warrior – crumbling the ice and breaking it apart. 'It can't be,' she chokes in horror. 'He returns!'

Her furious gaze sweeps across the hall, alighting on you with a chill look of hatred. 'Fools! I will have your souls for this! You are all traitors – and you will be destroyed!'

The asynjur throws back her head, a fierce blue light radiating from her eyes. 'Now, look upon me – and fear!'

Her pale skin hardens to ice, her body bulging as it begins to grow, splitting through the seams of her gown. Horns slide outwards from her brow, curving and branching to form a pair of barbed antlers. There is a snapping of bones, the ripping of muscle. You watch transfixed as the beast's legs fold back on themselves, toes curling inwards to become cloven hooves.

Syn Hulda has transformed herself into a demon.

The other asynjur share your horrified amazement, backing away from the terrible apparition. As one, they begin to chant a spell – some enchantment to ward themselves from this evil. But they are too late.

With a snarl the demon raises a clawed hand, sending spears of frost lancing into each of the mages. Their shrieks are deafening as flesh turns to ice, their bodies distorting and reshaping themselves into devilish monsters. They drop onto all fours, scampering to their mistress's side. She pats at their frozen manes with a loving affection. 'Ah, loyalty – so rare and precious a thing.' Her frosted lips crack into a fang-toothed smile. 'You will kneel before me too, southlander. Or suffer the same fate!'

Desperately, you look back to the throne. The ice continues to crumble and melt, but Skoll is still trapped inside and unable to aid you. Anise scoops up a discarded sword and starts forward but Aslev snatches her arm, pulling her back.

'Let me go!' she snaps angrily. 'We can fight!'

'Don't you dare turn your back on me!' splutters Gurt, kicking his legs feebly in the air. 'Free me, now. That is an order!'

Aslev grinds his teeth, clearly torn by some internal struggle. 'The hall is lost,' he says gruffly. 'We should rally the others.'

'To Hel with the others!' roars Gurt. 'Now get me out of here!'

Anise continues to wrestle against Aslev. 'The hall is not lost!' she asserts, tears welling in her eyes. 'Remember your duty! The einherjar are sworn to protect the Drokke!'

Aslev looks to you, questioningly.

'Stay back!' you command, waving them away. 'Aslev is right. Fetch aid – summon the others!' You spin to face the grotesque demon, hoping to buy time for your companions to escape. With weapons raised, you advance towards the former asynjur.

'What is this?' snorts the demon. 'A show of courage from the young whelp? Too foolish and stubborn to know when to kneel before your betters.'

You bare your teeth in a snarl. 'I am the last blood of King Leonidas, a crown prince of Valeron – and I kneel before no-one!' Magic ignites the air, sparking around your enchanted weapons. From the Norr, you feel Nanuk's spirit wash into you, filling you with a primal strength. You tense, ready to attack . . .

'Wait!' You hear the scuff of boots as Aslev races to your side. 'You will not face this evil alone, prince of Valeron. I am an einherjar – and this is my hall to protect.'

Anise takes position at your other shoulder, glaring at you past a hard frown. 'Leave it to a woman to talk sense,' she scowls. 'Think you're the only one with a score to settle?'

The einherjar lifts an ivory horn to his mouth, then blows a single shrill note into the air. Its piercing blast awakens something deep inside you. Your body pulses, your powers quickening.

You meet the warrior's gaze – and in that briefest of moments, you share a connection: a kinship.

'For Valeron!' you cry.

'For Skardland!' calls Aslev, raising his axe.

'Free me, you fools!' screams Gurt.

Then together the three of you charge the demon, your battle cries joined by the frenzied clash of iron and magic. It is time to fight:

	Speed	Magic	Armour	Health
Syn Hulda	8	5	10/4(*)	80
Frost hound	7	4	3	15
Frost hound	7	4	3	15
Frost hound	7	4	3	15

Special abilities

- **Sound the charge!**: For the first two rounds of combat your *speed* is increased by 2.
- **Ice skin**: (*) Syn Hulda has an *armour* of 10. Once her *health* is reduced to 40 or less, her *armour* is lowered to 4. (Note: Syn Hulda is immune to any abilities that would ordinarily lower her *armour*.)
- **Ice fangs**: At the end of every combat round you must take 1 damage, ignoring *armour*, from each frost hound still in play.
- **Ice breaker**: When a frost hound is reduced to zero *health*, its body explodes into fragments of jagged ice. Each hound causes 5 damage, ignoring *armour*. (If you have the *insulated* ability, this damage is reduced to 2.)
- **Ice prison**: Roll a die at the end of each combat round. Once you have rolled three ⚁ results, Skoll will have freed himself from his ice prison and will join you in combat. He will immediately heal you, restoring 6 *health*, and increase your damage score by 2 for the remainder of the combat.
- **Body of ice**: Your opponents are immune to *bleed*, *decay* and *venom*.

You must defeat Syn Hulda and the three frost hounds to win the combat. If you are successful, turn to **568**.

'Look, the dog's come sniffing back,' shouts Rutus, stepping out of line to face off against you. 'Ready for another fight, or you just here to play maids' lapdog?' He jerks a thumb towards the straw target dummies.

The other soldiers halt their training, watching the confrontation with interest. The trainer folds his thick arms across his chest. His voice rings out loud and crisp in the chill morning air. 'Well, I think we have ourselves a grudge match. Careful there, Rutus. This one looks hungry.'

The soldier grins, revealing several missing teeth. 'Yeah, I'm beating this dog back down to the ground. Ready to eat some mud, rookie?'

You are both handed swords, then proceed to circle each other warily. It is time to fight:

	Speed	Brawn	Armour	Health
Rutus	3	1	1	45

Special abilities

🛡 **Training yard**: You cannot use any special abilities or backpack items in this combat.

🛡 **I yield**: Once Rutus is reduced to 10 *health* or less, roll a die at the start of each combat round. On a roll of ⚅ or more, he yields to you, winning you the combat. Otherwise, the combat continues as normal.

If you manage to defeat this skilled soldier, turn to 147. If you lose the challenge, turn to 258.

294

Unable to break free from the growth, you are dragged inside its snapping jaws. You must immediately roll on the death penalty chart (see entry 98) and apply the result to your hero. Remember, you may be given an opportunity later in your adventures to remove this effect.

You drop back to the ground, a shower of black blood spattering the dirt. It takes a moment to realise that it is seeping from your own wounds. Anise moves to stand over you, holding her magical torch above her head. The growth seems to recoil from the blue flames, its cruel mouth now emitting a pitiful whine.

'Are you okay?' she asks, her voice shaking with fear.

You pick yourself up, staggering as you find your balance. 'I've been better.'

'You're bleeding.'

You brush her hand away. 'I'm fine, please . . .' Blood soaks your sleeve and your jerkin, and yet you feel no pain. It is as if the skin underneath is numb – dead, like a corpse.

Anise studies you a moment longer, chewing her bottom lip nervously. Then she raises her torch and turns away. 'Okay, you're right – let's keep moving.' Turn to 366.

295

'Tricked?' Sylvie straightens in surprise, her brow creasing as if pondering the question. 'Well, I suppose I did. But it was for your own benefit.'

'My own benefit?' Your hands grab the back of the nearest chair, gripping it tight to stop them from trembling. 'Do you even know what it's like when I sleep? You can't possibly—'

'You travel,' replies Sylvie, matter-of-factly. Her attention turns back to the breakfast.

You start to sound an answer, but find yourself stammering instead, your thoughts tangling in a jumbled confusion.

'The moment I saw you . . . I just knew,' Sylvie continues. 'And I can't tell you why. I sensed the magic within you. But not like a mage – not one who chooses to use it, takes it and moulds it to their will. No, with you it's different. It is like the magic is just a natural part of you. As it was with Randal.'

'Your husband?' you croak, still feeling sick.

'It's old blood,' she replies, nodding. 'He thought he was the only one. I thought it too, until I laid eyes on you. I had to be sure.'

'You knew! Then that makes what you did . . . it only makes it worse!' You push the chair away, knocking it into the table. 'You knew what would happen!'

'I did.' Sylvie breathes a guilty sigh. 'But you can't keep running from it. You have to learn to master that power, before . . . it masters you.'

Will you:

Ask her to tell you what she knows about the dreams?	165
Leave the cabin?	261
Agree to fetch the water?	78

296

You notice a number of treasures tangled up in the drake's parasitic tentacles. If you wish, you may now take one of the following rewards:

Dark matter	Lurid shroud	Titan's touch
(main hand: wand)	(chest)	(gloves)
+1 speed +2 magic	+1 speed +1 magic	+1 speed +2 magic
Ability: vortex	Ability: anguish	Ability: arcane feast

You hope, with the death of the corrupted Titan, the explorers and Caul are now finally at peace. After giving the frozen trapper a final nod of farewell, you head into the glacial tunnels – following them back to the surface. (Return to the quest map to continue your adventure.)

297

As you near the tower, you are almost disappointed by its plainness. No grinning skulls or ghostly apparitions, just an expanse of grey, crumbling rock and dark empty windows. There isn't even a warning sign saying 'turn back now'.

'It looks cold,' says Brack, shivering in the wind.

You can't help but agree. The wind carries a bitter edge, moaning and howling from the rift below. The torches sputter, sometimes dimming to mere embers – but their magic somehow keeps them alight.

'A shame they don't give off any heat,' says Anise, putting a hand close to the blue flames.

'Quit complaining,' snaps Harris, stepping towards the front door. He procures a small key from his robes and inserts it into the lock. There is a loud click followed by a teeth-grating squeal as the boy pushes against the heavy oak. Slowly, it opens inwards, then Harris is gone – swallowed by the darkness inside.

You follow, emerging in a large oval chamber. There are no windows, only plain stone walls scabbed with creeping mould. The torchlight continues to waver and dance, filling the space with an assembly of shadows, stretched and distorted like the ghoulish monsters you were expecting to find.

As the light shifts across the room, you are presented with a few mouldy sheets lying in one corner and an overturned copper pot in another. In the facing wall there is a door of wood and banded iron.

Anise hands you the torch, then proceeds to unfasten a small sack from her belt.

'What's that – you brought us supper?' snorts Brack.

'As a matter of fact, yes,' says Anise. 'What did you bring, just the empty space between your ears?' She opens up the sack. 'I got some cakes – and this.' She throws a small flask to the warrior, who catches it, glaring at it as if it were a draught of poison.

'You expect me to drink anything you've made?' He removes the stopper then sniffs the contents. Looking undecided, he takes a drink, spitting it out a second later. 'It's disgusting.'

'That's two-hundred-year-old Assay brandy. Too strong for you?'

Brack sneers, then takes another gulp. Swallowing this time. 'Hmm, it's okay,' he concedes, with a disgruntled frown. 'Least it's warm.'

'Speaking of which, we should try and find some wood.' Harris is standing in front of a disused fireplace, its recess filled with netted cobwebs. 'If we could light a proper fire, the night will pass a lot easier. What do you say?'

You find his eyes looking straight at you. 'Me?' You glance towards the closed door that leads deeper into the tower.

'I'll go with you,' smiles Anise, sensing your uncertainty. She tosses the sack to Harris, then takes the torch back. 'I'm not scared of shadows and ghost stories.'

'Wait,' you raise your hands for attention. 'Shouldn't we stay together? I've read a lot of stories, and believe me – it's always the ones that go off and leave the group that end up . . .' You wince, leaving the sentence unfinished.

'And what of those left behind?' grins Harris. You notice that he is fiddling with something around his neck – a prism of black glass. Its smooth faces flash bright as they catch the torchlight.

Brack takes another swig from the flask, blowing out his cheeks. 'This stuff should keep us all right, I'd say.' He catches Anise's jubilant smile. 'Only drinking it out of courtesy, mind. Don't think I like it, Skard.'

'Come on,' Anise tugs on your arm. 'Let's take a look around.'

As you move towards the door, you notice Harris is now wearing a pair of spectacles and is poring over one of the pages in his spell book. Around his neck the black prism starts to glow, suffused with its own inner light.

'Hey, what . . .' You go to question what the mage is doing, but Anise gives you another sharp tug. The next thing you know, she is throwing open the door and bundling you through into the narrow corridor beyond.

As she follows behind, the door suddenly slams shut with a deafening crack, hitting her on the back and throwing her forward. You catch her as she bumps into you, the two of you shaking in the corridor as you stare at the closed door.

'Did . . . did you do that?' you whisper.

Anise shakes her head, her breath escaping in short gasps.

A light flickers under the door, green then purple. There is a loud bang and a scream. You think it might have been Brack. You rush to the door, pulling against the handle – but it won't move. It feels like some force, some pressure, has a hold on it, stopping it from opening.

'Harris! Brack!' You slam your shoulder repeatedly into the wood, but it is hard and tough – reinforced by studded iron bands. It stands firm, leaving you stumbling back, rubbing your grazed shoulder.

Another scream, then the door rattles. The flickering light grows brighter, then winks out.

There is silence. Anise stifles her sobs behind the palm of her hand.

For seconds, maybe even minutes, you both wait – ears straining to hear anything from the room. You think you detect footsteps, pacing back and forth.

'Harris?' you call. There is no answer.

You shift round in the tight passage, looking at the way ahead. In the glow of the torchlight you see the corridor continue for several metres before ending in another door. This one is hanging off its hinges, the shredded wood looking like it was ravaged by some beast.

To your left, an archway leads through to a set of stairs, leading up into darkness. From somewhere above, you hear a persistent banging noise, like a door being opened and closed.

'There should be a signal fire at the top of the tower,' says Anise, still trembling. 'If we can light it, perhaps the guards will see it from the walls.' She looks at you imploringly, then back at the closed door behind you. 'I think we should do that – keep moving.'

Will you:

Climb the stairs?	111
Head past the broken door?	28

298

The alpha male lies at your feet, its body broken and torn as if savaged by some wild animal. The rest of the wolves scamper into the trees, leaving you alone at the centre of the blood-spattered clearing.

You may now choose one of the following rewards:

Duran's shard	Alpha's tooth	The howling
(main hand: dagger)	(left hand: dagger)	(cloak)
+1 magic +1 brawn	+1 brawn +1 magic	+1 speed
Ability: bleed	Ability: dominate	Ability: savagery

When you have made your decision and updated your hero sheet, turn to 338.

It takes a while to catch the woman's attention amidst the clamouring crowd of customers. When she finally hurries over to you, she appears flustered and impatient. 'Come on then, what's your poison?' she asks brusquely, reaching for an empty tankard. 'Though by the looks of it, you swallowed some already.'

If you have the word *Bowfinch* on your hero sheet, turn to 74. Otherwise, you decline the drink and turn back to the taproom. Return to 80.

300

All of a sudden, the Skard is staggering away from the cart, grunting in pain. He drops the wand, its bright glow fading to black. At first you cannot see the cause of the warrior's distress, then you glimpse a bright flash of steel from beside one of the wheels. The Skard gives an angered cry, then tumbles back into the dirt, gripping his bloody leg.

He doesn't see the scrawny boy crawling back into the shadows – but you do.

Mitch! You realise the young recruit must have hidden under the cart when the Skards attacked. His intervention may have just saved the day.

Drawing your weapons, you charge out of hiding towards the injured Skard. As you do so, you hear a woman's battle cry and the clatter of plate armour. Henna comes bounding over the rocks to your left, her two-handed sword raised high above her head. Together, you may stand a chance against this powerful Northman. It is time to fight:

	Speed	Brawn	Armour	Health
Igluk	2	2	1	40

Special abilities
- **Hopping mad:** Igluk has been wounded by Mitch's dagger. The Skard automatically loses 1 *health* at the end of each combat round, ignoring *armour*.

Watch my back: Henna adds 2 to your damage score for the duration of this combat.

If you manage to defeat this ferocious warrior, turn to 233. If you lose the combat, remember to record your defeat on your hero sheet. You may then attempt the combat again or return to the map.

301

A set of weather-worn stairs wind around the edge of the tower, bringing you to a rusted iron door. You contemplate knocking, but decide in the end to simply push it open. Once inside the tower, you are surprised to find yourself stepping into an opulent library, its marble floor lined with wooden tables, each one lit by a solitary candle. The walls are high, with several tiers of shelving all groaning under the weight of books, stone tablets and scroll cases. Wheeled ladders rest at intervals around the room, allowing access to the higher shelves.

As you pass along the rows of tables, you realise that the room is impossibly large – too big to fit inside the confines of the tower. Clearly, some magic is at work.

At the end of the library, past a rune-etched archway, you see Segg – the crimson-robed mage – seated in front of an iron brazier. Shadows dance and wheel around the walls of the side-chamber, cast by the bright glow of the flames.

Will you:

Explore the library?	353
Speak with Segg?	328
Return to the main courtyard?	113

302

For besting Desnar and becoming leader of the bear tribe, your bond with Nanuk's spirit has strengthened. You have also gained the following special ability:

Spirit call (co + pa): Instead of rolling for a damage score after winning a round, you can summon a bear spirit to fight by your side. The bear spirit causes 2 damage at the end of each combat round to one nominated opponent. This ability can only be used once per combat.

When you have updated your hero sheet, turn to 721.

303

You drag yourself out of the slime, your clothes and armour steaming from its deadly toxins. (You must lose one attribute point from an equipped item.) After taking a moment to recover from your ordeal, you press on into the tunnel. Turn to 468.

304

You throw open the door to the cabin, startling Sylvie who is serving up eggs and sausage onto a plate. She drops what she is doing, hurrying around the table. 'Hel's tears, what's got into you, boy? Are you all right?'

'Inquisitor!' you manage to gasp, struggling to catch your breath. 'One of the bandits . . . the ones that ambushed me on the road. He's still alive – he's after me.'

Sylvie's face becomes a scowl of anger. 'I knew it! Harbouring a thief – I should have known this would bring me ill luck.'

'Wait!' You look around frantically, your mind racing with fear. 'Is there nowhere to hide – anywhere we can go?'

'Not we. You! You're going far away from here!' The woman ushers you to the door. 'I can't have the inquisition sniffing into my affairs. My charms, my magic – they'll have me for a heretic. Be gone, thief!'

Before you can argue, you find yourself back outside the cabin. The door slams closed behind you, followed by the sound of bolts being dragged into place.

You scan the nearby hills, your gaze halting on the menacing silhouette of the inquisitor, lurching towards you like one of the demons from your nightmares. With no other option, you hurry away from the cabin, making for the tangled confines of the forest. Turn to 244.

305

You squeeze your toes over the edge of the rock, feeling the chill wind from below gust around you. With arms stretched to your sides you give Caul a last cursory glance, offering a nod of encouragement – then you launch yourself into space.

You have no fear of death – after all, you are already dead, your body just a cold vessel for your trapped soul. Nevertheless, as you go tumbling past the roaring waters, you feel a sudden fear take hold. Below you there is only darkness, with no sign of its end.

As you continue to tumble through the void, you notice a distant light twinkling against the darkness. It quickly grows bigger, fragmenting into a dazzling expanse of radiance, dancing and shimmering in kaleidoscopic patterns.

Water, you realise. An immense pool, its surface rocked by the force of the waterfall crashing down into its centre.

With no means of slowing your descent, you watch as the roiling waters rush up at speed, their foaming waves offering scant warning of the dangers that may lurk beneath.

To survive the fall you will need to take a *speed* challenge:

	Speed
Leap of faith	10

If you are successful, turn to 345. If you fail the challenge, turn to 442.

306

As you are finishing up the last barrel, a clinking of armour alerts you to the returning soldiers. 'Well, lookee here.' Kirk runs his eyes across the row of barrels, impressed that you have completed the task. 'Nice work, rookies. Now, let's get these loaded onto the wagon.'

Henna flicks tar from her gloves, her anger made plain. 'Care to let us in on your little adventure?' she asks sharply. 'It's not standard practice to leave untrained—'

'Oh relax.' Kirk cuts her off, putting an edge into his voice. 'Tar first, talk later.' Turn to 142.

307

The camp is only minutes away, so close you are surprised that you missed it. A tribute to the Skards' skill at concealing their numbers. Past a rise of high-peaked snow berms you come upon a dozen shelters, carved from blocks of hard-packed ice. Against the whiteness of the wastelands, they are almost invisible.

There are no cooking fires to alert unwanted attention. Instead you see chunks of raw meat being handed around a circle of men sitting cross-legged at the centre of the camp. The carcass of an animal lies in the snow nearby, where a woman is cutting slivers of meat and placing them onto the crimson-stained snow.

You smell the sharp tang of blood and the odour of unwashed bodies. Several children are playing at the edge of the camp. Noting your arrival, they go running amongst the shelters whistling and calling. Within seconds you see men and women emerging from their ice homes. The men in the circle look round with interest but continue to eat, pulling at the stringy meat with sharpened teeth. Only one stands at your approach. A tall, lithe-bodied man, his long black hair swept back over his shoulders. He has bright, keen eyes and a look about him that suggests a surly confidence – and guile.

There is a racking sob. A woman staggers towards you, an arm covering her mouth. Feet crunch through the snow as a man pushes past her, his red hair knotted into horn-like bands. You realise they must be Imnek's parents. The warrior from the lake carefully places the body into the father's arms. They exchange glances, then the father turns and carries him away; no words are spoken.

Sura stands before the circle of men. She stamps her staff into the ground, then speaks in Skard. You notice the men in the circle shifting to look at you, their eyes locked on the bear necklace.

The black-haired Skard is trembling, his fists clenched at his side. His cool demeanour has dissolved into a look of animal-like rage. You tense, sensing that your meeting may have already turned sour.

Sura puts out a hand, as if willing him to calm. But the Skard is inconsolable. He surges forward, fingers bent like claws. You barely have a chance to raise your hands, summoning magic to your palms, before the agile warrior is upon you – snatching the necklace from around your neck.

Your magic blows him backwards, sending him somersaulting through the air to crash down amongst his men. They are immediately on their feet, axes and spears clattering to attention.

The dark-haired Skard throws back his head, blood coating his teeth. The necklace is gripped tightly to his chest. 'I am blood of Taulu. I am leader!'

Sura points a gnarled finger at you. 'This one has an ancestor spirit. I see it in his eyes. You know the ways of our people, Desnar. You must take the test.'

The Skard wipes the blood from his lips, glowering at you with contempt. 'Vela styker? With a southlander?' There are angry mutterings from his entourage of warriors.

'Do you fear losing, Desnar?' The woman's eyes gleam bright beneath her furred hood. 'Taulu gave this one the halstek. He has a right to vela styker.' She puts out her hand, palm upwards, and gestures to the Skard. 'Do not test my patience.'

'Demons take you, witch.' Desnar shoulders through his men and puts the necklace into her hand. 'This clan is mine. No one can match me.'

'Then you have nothing to fear.' The woman's bony fingers snap closed around the necklace. 'Vela styker it is. I suggest you prepare for dawn light.' She shifts round, a mischievous smile twisting the corners of her mouth. 'And that goes for you too, southlander. Come with me.' Turn to 358.

308

(If you have the keyword *gains* on your hero sheet, turn to 277.)

'May I?' You straddle the bench opposite the soldier, holding out a hand in friendship. He glares at it distrustfully, taking another gulp from his mug.

'Not seen you before,' he grunts, wiping froth from his beard. 'Yer remind me of that shifty-eyed Rook. Seems more new faces every damn day.' He glances sideways at the soldiers further along the table, grinding his teeth together noisily. 'Listen to 'em. Think they could take on the whole north, the way they talk.'

'But new blood's got to be good,' you venture. 'I daresay this keep needs as many able men as it can get.'

The soldier snorts, stabbing a wedge of cheese with his knife. 'Depends though, don't it? Depends who you can trust.'

You lean forward, trying to ignore the stench of beer and sweat. 'Go on.'

The soldier takes a bite of cheese, working it around his mouth thoughtfully before swallowing with a gulp. 'Things been going missing. I ain't alone in noticing – a sword here, a helmet there, nothing that might cause serious concern. But now me gauntlets have gone. I keep them in me bed locker. No one touches 'em save me. And someone's taken 'em.'

'Can't you get replacements? I'm sure—'

The soldier glowers at you, pouring another cup from his clay jug. 'Listen, pup. Me gauntlets were me father's, and his father's before him. Proper Dwarven iron, magic, like. They're worth a heap of coin – the most precious thing . . . the *only* thing . . . me family has in way of a fortune.'

'And you suspect someone here of stealing them?' You frown, finding it hard to believe that a soldier would steal from another soldier.

The man downs his mug, then proceeds to fill it again. 'I reckon it's that Rook. Shifty fellow. Sharpshooter and all that, always showing off. Don't like the way he looks at people, like he's better than 'em. I reckon he's up to something. And I don't trust it.'

You remember back to the hooded rogue, who you met briefly when you first awoke. 'I didn't get the impression he trusts many people,' you add, nodding.

The soldier is quiet for a second, before releasing a noisy and foul-stinking belch. 'Me name's Ran, short for Randolph. You find anything, you be coming straight to me, right? Especially if you find those gauntlets. I'll pay yer a finder's fee, I promise yer that.'

'I'll keep an eye out,' you reply, rising from your seat. 'See what I can discover.' (Make a note of the keyword *thievery* on your hero sheet.)

Will you:

Talk to the recruits?	**199**
Leave and return to the courtyard?	**113**

309

You wonder if the clerk has a means of opening the container/s. He waves them away with a nonchalant frown. 'Go see Sam Scurvy – up at the prison. He's the best thief . . . I mean locksmith, at Ryker's. He'll get those open for you.'

If you wish to trade with the clerk, turn to 104. Otherwise, with your business now concluded, you decide to leave. Turn to 659.

310

Underneath one of the fallen weapon racks, you discover some interesting items: a spear, a rusted helm and a pair of scuffed leather gloves. If you wish, you may take any/all of the following:

Knight's reach	Plague mitts	Broken pride
(main hand: spear)	(gloves)	(head)
+1 speed +1 brawn	+1 magic	+1 armour
Ability: quicksilver	Ability: rust	Ability: retaliation

If you haven't already, you may now watch the ghost's game (turn to 414), or leave and continue your journey (turn to 188).

311

You stand with your back to a wall of grey mist, while ahead of you rises a nightmarish mockery of the great tree Yggdrasil. The scoured bark is charcoal black, its sap a poisonous green leaking from the many hollows and cracks that rake its vast heights. Dark boughs scratch at the broiling clouds, twisted and malformed, their withered leaves curled and blackened. Yggdrasil was a celebration of majesty and beauty – but this creation is its malformed shadow, corrupted and dying.

You look around but there is no sign of Nanuk. This is the first time, since you were joined, that you have travelled to the Norr and not had him at your side. You reach out, sensing for him – grasping for a glimmer of his presence. There is a faint echo of the bear's spirit at the furthest limits of your awareness, but it is distant; somehow cut off by the wall of dank fog that rolls across the black sand.

You are alone.

Resolved to your fate, you draw your weapons and stride towards the tangled roots. As you near, five figures detach themselves from the shadows. They look almost human, but their bodies have been twisted out of shape, as if the bones have been snapped and reformed into devilish silhouettes. They shuffle towards you, moaning in tormented agony, their black bark-like skin coated in venomous thorns. You assume these creatures were once asynjur – shamans sent here to find Skoll – but they have fallen to the taint of this nightmarish place. It is time to fight:

	Speed	Magic (*)	Armour(*)	Health
Asynjur	6	5	5	20
Asynjur	6	5	5	20
Asynjur	5	5	5	15
Asynjur	5	5	5	15
Asynjur	5	5	5	15

Special abilities

💜 **Crowd control**: For every asynjur that is defeated, the remaining asynjur have their magic and *armour* lowered by 1 each time.

💜 **Shadow thorns**: At the end of each combat round, you must take 1 damage (ignoring *armour*) from each asynjur that is still alive.

If you manage to defeat these tormented mages, turn to 23.

312

You scramble out of the dell, making a bee-line for Sylvie's cabin. A quick glance over your shoulder confirms that the giant warrior is loping after you, but thankfully his injured leg is slowing him down. With a burst of speed you clear the nearby ridge, changing course to follow the curve of the hills. You doubt the cabin will provide much refuge or safety, but right now in this hostile wilderness it seems your only choice.

If you have the word *prince* on your hero sheet, turn to **68**. If you have the word *pauper* on your hero sheet, turn to **304**.

313

You look around frantically for an escape route but the other two Skards have moved closer, penning you in. With no other choice, you turn and sprint for the rock shelf. It stretches about three metres above you, but by vaulting onto the rock wall then making a leap for the shelf, you manage to grapple your fingers onto its edge.

But before you can haul yourself up, you feel a blow to your side. Then a heavy weight dragging you back to the ground.

'Int sa sabet!'

You twist round, reaching for your weapons. The Skard warrior stands over you, nostrils flaring, eyes wide like some blood-crazed beast. 'Fegis!' He spits.

You swing at him, struggling to put any strength behind the blow. His boot kicks your weapon aside. Then he drops onto your stomach, knees first, his daggers blurring with unnatural speed. One punches you through the shoulder, another into your side. You hear a sickening ripping sound – then smell something foul. Another blow across the face, perhaps an elbow.

He clambers off you, snorting back snot and spittle. 'Fegis,' he grunts again, shaking his head. He turns and gestures to the shaven-headed hunter. 'Slur den.'

The other Skard saunters towards you, his axe resting back on his shoulder.

Add two *defeats* to your hero sheet. Then turn to 656.

314

For defeating Instructor Barl you may now help yourself to one of the following rewards:

Aggressor's mantle	Assault grips	The drill
(cloak)	(gloves)	(left hand: sword)
+2 speed +2 brawn	+1 speed +2 brawn	+2 speed +3 brawn
Ability: barbs	Ability: piercing	Ability: bleed, gouge

When you have updated your hero sheet, turn to 444.

315

Kirk leans back against the side of the cart, arms folded, legs crossed – looking for all the world like he has nothing better to do than take in the air. 'Now, I probably don't need to say this, kids, but we're a team, right? And what happens on duty stays on duty, you take my meaning?'

You glance at Henna then back at Kirk. Your evident look of confusion draws a chortle from the pug-nosed soldier.

'Where did you go?' asks Henna, frowning. 'You just left us to . . .'

'We were leaving a little marker. For a friend. So he'd know it was safe.'

'Friend?' Your eyes narrow suspiciously.

'Look, I just need you kids to keep tight-lipped, okay? No one is going to get hurt. It's just a little trade, a bit of dealing on the side. You know?'

'I don't think I do.' Henna draws herself straight, resting her hands on her hips. 'Has this been authorised by Everard?'

'He don't need to know,' mutters Lawson, the brim of his cowl lifting to reveal grey glittering eyes. 'So keep that pretty mouth of yours shut.'

An uneasy silence falls. Kirk breaks it with a nervous chuckle. 'Okay, okay. Everyone relax, let's not make a big thing of this. Better we stick together and—'

The noise of barking dogs draws him to silence.

You look around, trying to place the source. Your gaze falls on an area of the canyon where weathered pillars cast long shadows across the broken ground.

Three men are moving between them. Even from this distance, they look tall and muscular, clad in animal fur and hide.

'Skards,' gasps Henna. She goes to draw her sword but Kirk places a hand on her arm as he edges past her.

'Don't.'

Two of the men are struggling to keep a rein on their brutish pack of dogs. The animals are snapping and slavering to break free, tugging against their restraints until their corded necks are bulging.

The two dog-handlers hold back to the shadows, the wind sweeping their matted hair across their faces. The third continues to approach, carrying himself with a self-assured grace, like an animal prepared for the hunt.

He stops several metres from the cart. Blue eyes, like tundra ice, look to each of you in turn. Weighing you up, seeing how you measure. When your eyes meet, you are the first to look away, a queasiness pulling at your stomach as you take in the man's unsettling array of hooked javelins, strapped to his back.

'Hawt.' The greeting is guttural, like an animal cry.

Kirk echoes it, with none of the same gusto. 'You brought friends,' he says, leaning on tiptoe to view the growling dog-teams. 'I've always been a bit of a dog man too. Man's best friend and all that. The faithful hound, always looking out for . . . his . . .' He drawls into silence, swallowing nervously. 'Yes, well let's get to business. Law.'

The hooded soldier walks to the back of the cart, reappearing moments later dragging a sack. Its many bulges and ridges, and the clunk of metal, suggests it is filled with a multitude of objects. The sack is placed down in front of the Skard.

'Some good items there – good steel. Pair of gauntlets I think might be Dwarven.'

The Skard curls his upper lip, glaring at Kirk.

'Yes, yes, allow me.' He stoops down to open the sack, pulling out two plain-looking longswords. You are in no doubt these items have been stolen from the keep's armoury. The Skard takes one of the swords, testing its weight, turning the blade over in the leaden light. He puts a thumb to its edge, grinning when he sees it draw blood.

'Good,' he says simply, nodding.

'And . . .' Kirk spreads his arms wide, in a beckoning manner.

The Skard looks down at him, the shadows cutting grim lines around his sneer. He shakes his head. 'No. Nothing. Not have anything.' His words are hesitant, struggling with the language. But they carry command. Finality.

Kirk gives Lawson a sideways glance. You feel Henna at your side shifting uneasily. Her hand is on her sword.

'We have a deal,' says Kirk, licking his dry lips. 'I give you iron and steel, you bring me some of those magic stones, like you did before. Then I sell 'em on and we're all happy.'

The Skard shrugs and turns away, as if signalling the meeting is at its end.

Kirk starts forward, reaching out desperately. 'Wait, we had a—'

You didn't see the Northman move. But the eight inches of steel sticking out of Kirk's neck did not get there by accident. The Skard glares at him, teeth clenched, as he twists the blade. Kirk's gargling screams echo around the canyon. Then the body drops to the ground with a wet-sounding slap.

For a moment, you feel only stunned disbelief.

A sudden rush of air blasts past your ear. You stagger sideways, disorientated. When you look back Lawson is standing there, an arrow still nocked to his bow. But his mouth is open, eyes fixed on the javelin in his chest. With barely a cry, he topples backwards.

'Run!'

It is Henna's voice, but you barely hear it over the baying of the dogs. They have been released from their restraints and are now sprinting straight for you on their short but powerful legs.

You turn, slipping on a loose stone, grateful for your mishap as another javelin skims your back by inches. You stagger into the side of the cart, pushing off from it into a full-on sprint. The dogs are right on your heels, their teeth snapping for a hold. There is no time to stop – you have to find a means of escape.

To your left you spot a narrow cleft, forming a tunnel into the maze-like canyons. Ahead of you and to the right, there is the black lake of tar. A series of rocks criss-cross its surface, leading to a cave on the opposite bank.

Will you:

Cross the tar pit to reach the cave?	**289**
Head into the gullies and canyons?	**172**

316

You are halfway across the cave when you suddenly hear a squeal from one of the goblins. The small one with the shield has spotted you, pointing a stubby finger in your direction.

The other goblins are pulling rusty knives from their belts. All except for the leader.

'Me arm – it's stuck!' The largest goblin leans back, boots sliding in the dirt as he tries desperately to free himself. His companions hang back, torn between attacking or helping their struggling leader.

'Wha' yer waitin' for?' He growls. 'Just stick 'im!'

The three goblins hurry to attack, while their leader continues to grunt and curse as he tries to pull his arm free. It is time to fight:

	Speed	Brawn	Armour	Health
Grubnose	3/5(*)	3	3	25
Goblin	3	3	2	16
Goblin	3	3	2	12
Goblin	3	2	1	10

Special abilities

🟣 **Stick 'im!**: At the end of each combat round, you must take 1 damage ignoring *armour* from each surviving goblin (not including Grubnose).

🟣 **Grr, 'tis ain't fair**: (*) Grubnose has his arm stuck. He will still be able to attack and defend, but will do so with a *speed* of 3. At the start of the fourth combat round, Grubnose will have freed his arm – raising his *speed* to 5 for the remainder of the combat.

If you manage to defeat these motley scavengers, turn to 583.

317

The battle is over in a matter of seconds, a life ended in brutally short fashion. You stand over the corpse, wanting to feel something – regret, elation. But all you are left with is a cold numbness in your limbs. You glance down, watching a trail of black blood ooze from a shallow wound in your arm.

What am I becoming?

You go to take a breath, but your chest remains tight and constricted. Instead you end up choking, your throat cutting like razors as you spit out a foul-smelling bile. You wipe it against your sleeve, trembling . . . frightened.

It is some time before you are able to calm yourself – to focus on the matter at hand. *Have to get back. Find the others.*

Kneeling next to the corpse, you scan the body for anything of use. The axe blade is dulled and thick with rust, but the bone knife looks sharp and serviceable. You also notice a shimmer of magic around the hunter's white-fur boots – and an iron ring, etched with runes. You may now take one of the following rewards:

Flenching knife	White vixen	Hunter's eye
(left hand: dagger)	(feet)	(ring)
+1 brawn	+1 speed	Ability: sneak
	Ability: evade	

With your pursuers defeated, you decide to head cautiously back to the cart. Turn to 391.

318

You eyes scan the four Skard warriors, then return to Gurt. 'I would hardly call those fair odds,' you rasp, clenching your fists as your magic continues to ebb away.

'Agreed, few men could match a single einherjar in battle – let alone four,' sniggers Gurt, sucking the last of the meat from his bone.

'No, you misunderstand me . . .' You lift your manacled hand, the chain rattling against the table. 'I can defeat your warriors. But you have me chained. Is that how you fight your battles?'

Gurt slams his fists on the table, rattling the pots. 'Take him out! Remove him! Teach him what it means to cross the einherjar!'

You are dragged forcibly from the hall. Once you are back on the snow fields the four warriors surround you, pulling axes from their belts. They exchange words in Skard – their tone questioning, uncertain. The white-haired warrior, Aslev, barks a command – then they set about you, kicking and hacking with their weapons.

You feel a sudden rush of strength as a primal hoarse-throated roar is ripped from your lips. Nanuk's spirit flows into you, fighting the magic of the rune-carved restraint. Your weapons fly into your hands, then you are twisting and dodging the incoming attacks, your bestial snarls rending the air. With nothing to lose, you turn on the einherjar. It is time to fight:

	Speed	Brawn	Armour	Health
Handler	7	6	4	40
Einherjar	7	5	4	40
Einherjar	7	6	4	35
Einherjar	7	5	4	30

Special abilities

🪶 **Bow to your will**: Once an einherjar is reduced to 10 or less *health*, they surrender and kneel – taking no further part in the combat.

🪶 **Chain of command**: You are weakened by the black iron manacle. This reduces your *speed* by 1 and your *brawn* and *magic* by 4 for the duration of the combat. If you defeat the handler (by reducing them to 10 or less *health*), you break free of the chain – restoring your attributes.

🪶 **Outnumbered**: At the end of each combat round, you must take 1 damage from each surviving opponent, ignoring *armour*. This ability only applies if you are faced with multiple opponents.

If you manage to defeat these Skard heroes, turn to 354. Otherwise, remember to record your defeat on your hero sheet, then turn to 46.

319

You unfasten the gold clips on your scabbard and hand the weapon to Hort. 'I think this is more fitting for a holy warrior, don't you?'

He smiles at that, taking the grip and sliding the sword free with a ringing echo of steel. As he does so, the sigils along its blade burst into billowing white light, coming alive at his touch.

The wolf snarls, drawing back, its eyes narrowing to slits of glittering amber.

'This is a mighty weapon,' grins the inquisitor. 'And it will make a glorious end.' He drops into a low stance, dagger in one hand and the sword in the other. 'Run, Prince Arran,' he whispers. 'I will buy you time. My debt to you is repaid.'

There is a roar from the darkness, then the wolf springs forward, its black body slamming into the warrior, fangs and steel slicing through the air. (Make a note of the keyword *sacrifice* on your hero sheet, then turn to 231.)

320

You are rolling and crashing over sharp rock. Oddly, there is no pain, your dead body little more than a rag-doll, poked and punched, cut and sliced. You hear a bone crack, a pressure against your throat; an arm bends awkwardly, not responding to your efforts to move it. Dust fills your nostrils, pushing its way into your dry throat.

Blinking, you look around. Everything is a fine powdery dust, forming thick clouds hanging in the air. Through it, you glimpse ragged shapes – stumbling, staggering. A horn rings out in the distance.

You manage to struggle to your feet, one arm hanging useless at your side. A rib is showing through your jerkin, coated in black blood. It is an odd and bewildering sight.

I should be dead.

As if in response, your body's numbness is replaced by a burning cold, rushing along the length of your spine. It prickles down your legs, across your shoulders, pushing its way beneath your skin. You sense a powerful presence feeding you with its strength.

Nanuk.

Your arm snaps back into its socket, the bones scraping together beneath the bruised flesh. The exposed rib splinters and then crumbles like chalk, the tiny fragments lifted away on the chill wind. Beneath the remnants of your clothing the open wound closes, the black blood replaced by a puckered scar.

Then the coldness subsides, leaving you numb and empty once again.

You stumble through the haze, your foot knocking into the body of a soldier. He stares up at you vacantly, his pale face freckled with blood. A jagged stone protrudes from his chest, having pierced straight through his breastplate.

Looking round, you see a smoking mound of rubble where there had once been a building. Everard had boasted that Bitter Keep could endure anything – standing proud until the ending of the world. Perhaps that time has come. Turning away, you set your sights on the far-side of the courtyard and the ringing sounds of battle. Turn to 376.

321

A number of turns are played, in which each opponent discards a stone from their hand and takes another one at random from a black pouch. Finally, the guard nods to himself, as if certain of a win. Nervously, he places his stones face up on the table, revealing his hand. Then he sits back, awaiting his opponent's response. Turn to 570.

322

Mech leads you into his workshop, which is little more than a run-down wooden shack overflowing with junk. After kicking away some of the mess, the man proceeds to fish out a number of items for your inspection – a box of torn metal plates, some vats of gloopy whale grease and a pot of bright yellow dye, faintly glowing with magic.

If you have a sled, you may purchase any of the following upgrades for 40 gold crowns each:

Greased runners:	+1 speed	+1 stability
Armour plating:	+2 toughness	
Go-faster stripes:	+2 speed	

An upgrade can only be applied to each sled once. (Note: If you replace an existing sled with a new one, all upgrades that have been applied to the old sled will be lost. Each sled must have its own set of upgrades.)

You may now view the available sleds (turn to 432) or explore the rest of the compound (turn to 106).

323

Your newfound strength is a bonus, but not enough to make up for your lack of climbing experience. You have barely made it five metres before you lose your footing and fall, plummeting back to the ground in a flurry of dust and stone. It seems you have no other choice but to fight the hunter – hoping that the narrow tunnel shaft will give you an advantage against him. Turn to 402.

324

The muttok elder lies dead at your feet. Crouching next to the body, you begin cutting away at the beast's magnificent antlers. After considerable effort they finally come free in your bloodied hands. Rising to your feet you hold up your trophy, revelling in Desnar's look of shamed defeat.

Congratulations, you have bested the Skard in the challenge of the hunt. If you wish, you may now equip the following item:

Stag's crown
(head)
+2 brawn +2 magic
Ability: barbs, charm

You have also gained a *muttok pelt* (simply make a note on this on your hero sheet, it doesn't take up backpack space). Record the word *triumph* on your hero sheet, then turn to 578.

325

The balcony is surrounded by a waist-high wall, punctuated by thin crenulations. In daylight, you imagine the view over the rift and the surrounding country must be spectacular – but now, on this moonless night, you are presented with an inky impenetrable darkness. You look back towards the keep walls, noting the small bobbing lights moving back and forth – the guards walking the battlements. They seem to hang suspended in the blackness, tiny and small against the great cold expanse.

A flutter of wings jolts you from your thoughts.

Before you can turn something slams into your back, knocking you into the wall. For a second you are half-blinded by a sudden bright light, your ears filled with a loud buzzing.

'Get away from him!' screams a voice.

You see blue flames trail through the air as Anise waves her torch at your assailant, forcing them back. The intervention buys you time to gather your wits, although you are still convinced your eyes are playing tricks on you.

Through a glittering cloud of dust, you see a giant moth hovering over the balcony. The creature's wings are translucent like veils, but seem to glow with their own inner light, illuminating the silver veins that bulge from the creature's body – and the sharp teeth glittering from its skeletal head.

The moth's kicking legs knock the torch from Anise's hands, sending her scurrying back into the tower. Before you can follow, the creature swoops towards you, a dusty powder showering from its wings. It is time to fight:

	Speed	Magic	Armour	Health
Death moth	2	2	0	30

Special abilities

🛡 **Spectral dust**: Each time your damage score causes health damage to your opponent, you are blinded by the moth's dust. This reduces your *speed* to zero for the next combat round only.

If you manage to overcome this winged horror, turn to **163**. If you lose the combat, remember to record your defeat on your hero sheet. You may then attempt the combat again or return to the map.

326

Aslev emerges from the hall, bowing his head to the both of you. 'My Drokke. There is the matter of the einherjar. We should choose a new Seff to lead us.'

Skoll slaps you between the shoulder blades. 'I believe this is our Seff.'

'Me?' you bristle with surprise. 'I am not a Skard . . . I couldn't . . .'

'Neither was that half-man,' sneers Skoll, waving towards the hall. 'It is done. It is decided. Aslev, do you honour this?'

The warrior is already beaming with approval. 'Of course! My men would gladly follow. If our Seff would learn our ways, then I will teach him.'

Skoll pats the einherjar on the shoulder. 'Good. Now, enough talk. Warming a throne for a hundred years has left me with a hearty appetite. I declare a feast, then we may gossip like the crones – and make plans for war.'

He turns to you, his yellowed grin bulging an array of scars. 'Will you share my table, Bearclaw? We cannot go to war on empty stomachs.'

You raise your hands in rebuttal. 'Thank you, Drokke. But my condition . . . I fear I no longer have a taste for it.'

Skoll shrugs his shoulders. 'Then attend to your business, my friend. Two suns from now, I will be heading north. To Mount

Skringskal. And I will need you at my side. You are a mighty warrior – and a shaman. The ancestors have chosen you above all others. It is a sign. Perhaps I see you becoming a Drokke one day. You understand this?'

A hand slips into your own, squeezing your fingers tight. You look round to see Anise, her pale skin freckled with blood. You push her tangled locks aside, meeting her gaze.

'You will come back, won't you?' she breathes nervously.

You take a moment to unpick your thoughts, to settle your emotions. When next you speak, you know it is as a man – not the child you once were. 'I have always been a ghost, Anise. Someone who never mattered. I was betrayed. The people I thought I could trust left me for dead by a roadside. They wanted to take everything from me – they *have* taken everything.' You feel Anise's hand against your cheek. The tenderness of her touch makes you flinch, your tortured visage mirrored cruelly in her eyes, reminding you of what you have become. 'I am a monster now. I know that. Every day, I am losing my humanity – I do not know if I deserve saving . . .'

Anise goes to withdraw her hand, but you snatch it back – pressing it tight against your cheek. 'But, I have been given purpose. You are my people now. And I will fight for you. Not as a prince, but as a Skard.'

'Bearclaw,' whispers Anise. She leans forward and puts her lips to your own.

'Bearclaw!' shouts Skoll, raising a fist into the air. 'Winter comes to our land – but we still have fire in our hearts. Remember this day, my friends. This is the day of my return, when the Ska-inuin will rise and take our lands back from the witch.' Golden light blossoms around his fingertips, forming a blazing beacon against the darkening skies. 'Winter comes, and with it our vengeance!'

If you are a warrior, you may speak with Aslev and learn the einherjar career (turn to 215). Otherwise, you may now return to the map. When you are ready to re-join Skoll and Anise, select the Boss Monster encounter (the skull icon) to begin the next stage of your journey.

'What, suddenly yer a trapper now? You can't trade with me unless it's all official-like. I need to put you on the books, see, and issue you with a permit.'

'Go ahead.' You fold your arms, teeth grinding with annoyance.

'There's a service charge,' replies Jackson, rattling his guns at you. 'Five gold. Then yer can trade.'

'I have to pay you so that I can . . . sell to you?' You play through the statement in your head, looking for the logic.

'Listen, brains. Where else you gonna trade – Ryker's? You won't get better prices for your fur than 'ere at White Wolf. And the bonus is, we won't try to kill yer.'

You glance at the musket barrels.

'Well, only if you do something . . . excitable.'

You may purchase a *White Wolf Hunting Permit* for 5 gold crowns. (If purchased, simply make a note of the permit on your hero sheet, it doesn't take up backpack space.) This item verifies you as an official trader and will allow you to sell items to the White Wolf Trading Post.

Will you:

Trade items? (requirement: permit)	730
Discuss something else?	685
Leave?	Return to the map

328

The heat in the room is stifling, forcing you to involuntarily draw back. Segg continues to stare into the fire, its dancing patterns reflected in his eyes. It isn't until you draw a nervous cough that the mage blinks and appears to come to his senses. With a flick of his hand the flames diminish, becoming little more than thin bright tongues, licking around the coals.

'Do come in,' he smiles, gesturing to a chair by the wall.

'It's a little hot for me,' you reply awkwardly, still feeling the heat of the room burning against your cold skin.

'Ah yes, your condition. That would explain it.' The mage rises from his seat, grimacing as he straightens his back. 'I'm glad you came to see me, Arran – I want you to take a look at this.' He walks over to a desk and pulls out a book from underneath a collection of papers. He opens the book to a certain page, marked by a scarlet ribbon, and then hands it to you.

The page is covered in strange glyphs and markings – magic, you quickly surmise.

'Tell me what you see,' insists the mage, stepping back and watching you expectantly.

'Gibberish,' you reply flatly. 'I don't really—'

'Look harder!' he snaps. His irritation causes the flames in the brazier to leap a little higher.

You stare at the runes – following the intricate spirals of their form, the way they interlink, the hidden patterns created by the lines and spaces. At the back of your mind you feel the tug of that other presence – that other place. From mere scratches of ink, the scrawls quickly become glowing sigils of green light, burning into your eyes, into your brain.

'It's a spell.' You pass your hands over the runes, knowing instinctively which ones need to be made complete, tracing lines and shapes, forming a union.

A flurry of sparks lift from the page, startling you. With a gasp, you drop the book to the floor, stepping away from it in fear. 'What . . . what did I do?'

Segg cracks a smile. 'Proved to me you have what it takes, Arran.' He folds his arms, the jewels on his sleeves catching the firelight. 'You have a natural talent for magic, boy – I'm surprised no-one has ever told you that before.'

Will you:

Ask about learning magic?	342
Ask about your strange condition?	234
Ask if he knows anything about the dreams?	120
Return to the library?	353

(If you have the word *envoy* on your hero sheet, you may turn to 255.)

You hand over the ten gold crowns (deduct this amount from your hero sheet). 'Good, good!' The man pulls a stub of charcoal from his belt and steps up to the board. 'So, what name are yer going for? Something flashy . . . something that sounds like, well, like a crazy ice sled racer!'

You pull a frown, then a name comes to you; one the other children always used to tease you with around court. 'Ghost,' you reply. 'Call me ghost.'

The man gives an impressed snort. 'Hmm, I like it.' He adds the name to the bottom of the list. 'Now, just visit me before each race, so I can check you in. Oh, I almost forgot . . .' He darts into his cabin, emerging a few seconds later with a cracked sheet of leather. 'These are the rules. Take a gander.'

You snatch the leather from his hand, already seeing that it is blank and unmarked. You turn it over a couple of times, then look back at the man. He is chuckling to himself, his grin almost splitting the sides of his narrow face.

'There are no rules,' you sigh, delivering the punch line.

'Oh, you better believe it,' he sniggers. 'Don't think for a second these people want to see a fair fight – and don't think the other racers are gonna care either. No rules. So, watch yourself – and give a good show.'

(Record the keyword *rookie* on your hero sheet.) To begin round one of the tournament, turn to 189. If you would prefer to race at a later time, then turn to 106 to continue your exploration of the compound.

330

You scrabble to your feet, sobbing from the pain. The inquisitor needs your help, and you are not about to leave him behind to die, despite his betrayal. You draw your weapon and charge the nearest wolf, its back exposed as it arches over the warrior's body, head rolling back and forth, tearing into flesh and bone.

Your weapon does likewise, beating and stabbing at the beast, until it breaks its hold. The wolf springs round, lips peeling back from bloodied fangs. You swing again, your actions led by panic rather than bravery, hitting it squarely on the nose. The wolf flinches away, then races back into the forest.

Its companion does likewise, a length of bloody cloth clenched between its teeth.

You stand over the inquisitor, trying not to look at the extent of his wounds, knowing that the man is surely done for. No holy magic or healing is likely to save him.

Hort looks up at you, squinting in the half-light. He holds up a crimson-stained hand. You take it, helping him back to his feet. The warrior staggers against the nearest tree, his tunic hanging in ribbons from his broad chest.

Then you hear it. A rumbling growl – a sound so deep it sets your bones to shaking. Hort nods to something over your shoulder. Slowly, you turn, hands gripped to your weapon, to see a pair of amber eyes staring back at you from the snarled thicket. They are set within an immense pool of darkness. The sharp stench of blood is joined by something fouler, reeking of death.

The giant wolf takes a step forward, breath misting and steaming from its enormous muzzle. It pauses, watching you both. Waiting.

'Go,' whispers Hort, raising his gore-soaked dagger. 'It's the pack leader. I'll do what I can. Go.'

You turn, meeting his gaze. Before you can answer, he shakes his head.

'Don't think me a hero,' he scowls. 'But you've taught me enough this day. Now run.'

If you have the keyword *blade* on your hero sheet, turn to 319. Otherwise, turn to 231.

331

You sever the last of the devilish roots, dodging aside as the monster's body drops to the ground with a rattling din. Amongst its skeletal remains, you spy a number of enchanted items. If you wish, you may now take one of the following:

The equaliser	Macabre mantle	Marionette string
(ring)	(cloak)	(necklace)
+1 brawn +1 magic	+1 speed +1 armour	+2 magic
Ability: reaper	Ability: gut ripper	Ability: boneshaker

When you have updated your hero sheet, turn to **509**.

332

'Jerico,' sighs the woman, following your gaze. 'When the rest of our team didn't return, we went looking for them. There was a fresh fall of snow; we didn't see the crevasse until it was too late. Jerico fell in – but we managed to save him. He has broken ribs; there might be bleeding on the inside. Without a medic . . .'

'Have you not tried to get aid?' You look from Reah to her male companion, who is still regarding you with a sullen, suspicious glare. 'Are you waiting for a rescue team? The sea is frozen, winter is coming . . .'

'Don't we know it,' snaps the man. 'We took shelter in a cave nearby but it became unsafe. Better to take our chances here. We sent our youngest south, he still had strength. He took most of what we had left – struck a course for Bitter Keep. We thought they would come for us. But nothing . . .'

You shake your head. 'Bitter Keep is no more. Your friend – I have seen no sign.'

Reah puts a gloved mitt to your arm. 'Please, we cannot leave here until we find out what happened to the others. They went into the caves – we won't know peace otherwise.'

Will you:

Ask what they are doing in the canyon?	237
Ask how you might help? (starts the quest)	**146**

333

You clamber up onto a dusty plateau, where columns of rock cut a ragged outline against the sky. Their careful arrangement gives the impression of something man-made, perhaps the remains of a temple or a once-grand amphitheatre.

You pass between the high pillars, listening to the singing and cawing from the hundreds of nests perched precariously on the scarred stone. Much of the ground is crusted with droppings, the wind carrying its stink to your nostrils. There are also broken shells and feathers, and some brown straggly weeds, miraculously clinging to life in this barren place.

'No . . . not come here.'

The voice is faint, barely a whisper. For a moment, you wonder if you imagined it. Then you catch movement out of the corner of your eye. A brief blur of white, the patter of feet. When you try and follow it, you are left staring at empty corridors of rock, a few white petrel feathers gusting through the air.

'No, not the eyrie.'

Another flurry of footsteps. You hurry around the nearest pillar, again finding no-one.

'My place. This is mine.'

'Who are you?' You spin angrily, tired of the game.

Squatted on a rock is a man – at least you think it is a man. His clothes are covered in hundreds of feathers, stitched into the fur. Long strips of leather hang down across his bowed legs, dressed again with feathers to give the appearance of wings.

He makes a clicking sound at the back of his throat, head twitching. 'Eyrie for the birds,' he rasps, his words thin and strained, like someone for whom language has become foreign. 'Not for stinking carrion.'

You spread your palms, backing away. 'I'm just passing through,' you reply guardedly.

The man's age seems indeterminate – his face a mask of grime and sweat, the wild hair caked in mud. 'This the birdman's home,' he huffs, flicking his head back. 'Protect the nest. The eggs. The birds.'

He scoops up a rock, flinging it in your direction. You dodge it easily, leaving it to shatter against the wall behind you. When you look back, the birdman has gone. Suddenly, you hear the scuff of footsteps to your left. You swing round just in time to catch the birdman as he bounds into you, a pair of clawed knives gripped tightly in his fists. You must now fight:

	Speed	Brawn	Armour	Health
Birdman	2	1	2	20

Special abilities

🦃 **Spitting feathers**: If you win a combat round, roll a die. If the result is ⚀ or less, the birdman swipes you with his feathered wings, knocking you back. This prevents you from rolling for damage. The combat round ends and a new one starts. If the result is ⚁ or more, you can roll for damage as normal.

If you manage to cull this crazy ex-convict, turn to 421. If you lose the combat, remember to record your defeat on your hero sheet. You may then attempt the combat again or return to the map.

334

Congratulations! You have obtained a bottle of *Bowfinch '55* (simply make a note of this item on your hero sheet, it does not take up backpack space. You can also remove the keyword *Bowfinch* from your hero sheet. Remember to deduct 100 gold crowns.)

Make a note of paragraph number 190. When you wish to return to Gurt and hand over this rare item (to continue the red quest, *The Hall of Vindsvall*) turn to 190 at any time.

You may now remain in the taproom (turn to 80) or leave (turn to 659).

The guard displays his hand to you. The guard has the following stones:

In the centre of the table is a black velvet bag, containing the remaining stones that have yet to enter play. It is the guard's turn to discard one of the stones in his hand and take a replacement from the bag. 'What shall I do?' he asks worriedly, scratching his balding pate.

Across the table, the hooded ghost waits for your move in deathly silence.

Will you:

Discard the one of hearts?	480
Discard the two of moons?	241
Discard the one of stars?	417

336

The very air seems to vibrate as a cold shadow stretches across the rooftop. You turn, just in time to see the last of the drakelings rushing in, its entire body aflame. Segg gives an anguished cry, throwing up his arms. Then the immense beast smashes into the side of the tower.

You are thrown through a thunderous whirlwind of dust, freefalling as the spiked rooftop pitches after you, tearing through the smoke-smeared skies. You hear screams from below, the sound of rocks pummelling the earth. A reptilian body sweeps past you, its tail smacking into your chest and knocking you into a dizzying spin. You put out your arms, trying desperately to halt your fall. Turn to 320.

Legendary monster: Sasquatch

It appears you weren't the only one to gate-crash the party. Another guest goes flying overhead, cutting the air with a deafening squeal. A violin follows – then some plates and a goblet. A freshly-roasted pig brings up the rear. From the pavilion tent, the screaming intensifies as people struggle to beat their way out, wigs and bonnets askew in the mad scramble to escape.

Five minutes earlier, you had been drawn to the clearing by the sound of music and merriment. Inside the tent a table had been laid for dinner, groaning under the weight of the fruit and meats served up out of the vast array of picnic hampers. The guests, a gaudy array of Valeron nobles, laughed and gossiped in refined comfort, picking daintily at their tiny servings, whilst occasionally clapping the efforts of the string quartet.

You had watched from the tree-line, wary of the dogs lying next to the sledges – and the armed guardsmen patrolling the perimeter. It may have been an ill-advised decision to hold a party in the middle of a wild forest, but clearly the nobles hadn't come completely unprepared.

That is, until the hunting team arrived back. Running out of the trees, screaming at the top of their lungs. One of their number was stumbling, blood soaking through his breeches. Another was casting wild glances past his shoulder.

Then the yeti came, kicking up a great flurry of snow, a nine-foot giant of shaggy brown hair. Its huge fists scooped up the stragglers with ease, tossing them over its broad shoulders as if they were little more than twigs. They broke in a similar fashion too, bones cracking noisily as they rolled and tumbled through the treetops.

The musicians finally heard the screaming. Their melody ended in a screech of strings.

It has been pandemonium ever since.

Party-goers are now hurrying towards one of the sledges, elbowing and shunting each other to secure a space. In their panic, they don't see the beast until it is too late. The yeti snatches up the entire craft, dogs and all, then with a single twist of its huge shoulders hurls the sledge back into the forest. Jingling harnesses accompany the whimpering howls of the surprised hounds.

The other dog-teams are wise enough to break for the trees, chased by the guests desperate to catch a ride. They never make it, as the yeti drags the entire tent off its supports, swinging the canvas round like a giant club, cracking through bodies and smashing the sledges to smithereens. A few of the guardsmen who haven't already lost their resolve and fled attempt to encircle the beast – but they can't get close enough to draw blood. The yeti picks them up in its leathery paws, then tosses them away like a toddler mad with its toys.

You can understand the beast's rage. Blood seeps from a puncture wound in the yeti's left shoulder. Beneath its ribcage you can see the broken shaft of a spear. The brash hunters thought they could best this mighty creature – perhaps take its valuable pelt as a trophy. Out here, in the frozen wilds, there are no second chances.

You draw your weapons and step into the clearing, prepared now to finish the job – and put this beast out of its painful misery. It is time to fight:

	Speed	Brawn	Armour	Health
Sasquatch	8	7	4	60

Special abilities

- **Swat back**: If you lose a combat round, roll a die. On a [1] or [2] result, the Sasquatch attacks as normal. If the result is [3] or more, its mighty paws swat you backwards. This immediately inflicts 2 dice of damage, ignoring *armour*. It also sets up a *ground smash* (see below).
- **Ground smash**: If the Sasquatch uses *swat back*, you must immediately take a *speed* challenge to dodge its follow-up attack. If the result is 14 or less, you are hit and must take a further 1 dice of damage, ignoring *armour*. If the result is 15 or more, you dodge the attack.

If you manage to defeat the enraged yeti, turn to 183.

You don't remember much of the fight, but you can still taste it. The blood clogs your senses, as does the presence pushing at the back of your mind. For an instant, a shadow wavers across the ground, a broad immensity of darkness – a silhouette of a bear.

You blink, not sure if what you are seeing is real or just one of the dreams. The rocks and the trees start to blur – smudged with a green luminescence.

I'm dreaming? No, perhaps I'm dying . . .

You blink.

Stones crunch and skitter away. You are stumbling through the forest, lurching from one tree to the next, a residue of your former strength helping to keep you upright. But you know it is a futile effort – with the wounds you have sustained, the blood you have lost, there is no doubting that you will die out here, alone in this vast, indifferent wilderness.

You blink.

Hands grope over black rocks and sand. You feel the icy cold of the other place wash over you. Painfully you lift your head to see a swirling maelstrom of cloud above, flecked with bursts of ghoulish lightning. The dream. You are back in the dream.

You blink.

The scene remains. A bleak wasteland of blackness. Columns of rock rise up to claw at the sky, forming endless corridors of clutching fingers. And between them, the stray shadows watch. The demons. They stretch closer, their wraith-like forms sweeping over the wind-tossed sand. You are too weak to run, too weak to defend yourself.

Let it end, just let it end.

Then you feel a sudden rush of air – a black body goes barrelling past you, swiping at the shadow demons, ripping through their bodies. A gravelly roar thunders back from the rocks, as the immense beast rears up on two hind limbs, the orange glow from his deep-set eyes shining like lanterns in the dark. The shadows recoil, screeching and crying, leaving you unharmed.

The beast drops onto all fours and turns his head. The wind tussles through a thick mane of hair, rippling over broad shoulders and across his back. A giant grizzly of a bear. *Nanuk*. The word is whispered in your mind.

'Nanuk. Is that your name?'

The animal edges forward, nudging his muzzle against your chest. You stroke the thick, dark fur, feeling its warmth – the first comfort you have felt in this cold, nightmarish place. The bear shifts himself beside you, curling around you protectively, letting you snuggle into his fur.

In that moment, you suddenly feel whole again – as if a broken part of yourself has been returned and mended. You keep a tight hold of the animal, leeching strength from your bond, wondering if you will ever awake from the dream – or if this is how it will be, for all eternity. Turn to 291.

339

Searching through the graveyard, you find a *mammoth pelt* (simply make a note of this on your hero sheet, it does not take up backpack space) and the following item:

Bone dust
(special)
Use on a cloak, gloves, boots or chest item
you have equipped to add the
special ability *fear*

If you have the keyword *tracker* on your hero sheet, turn to 250. Otherwise, return to the quest map to continue your adventure.

340

Black smoke trails into the air as the fire takes quickly, snapping hungrily at the dry timber.

'Min eld, Min eld in Gava!' The Skard warrior raises his arms to the sky, his barking laughter an odd accompaniment to the roaring flame.

At the front of the cart, the panicked horse bucks and rears, pulling frantically against its harness. The fire is now eating along the leather cords, edging closer to the fear-stricken animal.

Suddenly, there is movement from the boulders to your left. A woman's cry echoes back from the canyon walls as Henna runs out of hiding, her two-handed sword raised high above her head. Ignoring the Skard she charges towards the horse, bringing her sword down in a series of desperate swings, severing the harness. As the last cord snaps, the horse bolts for freedom.

The warrior strides towards Henna, presenting a mountain of muscle, his teeth bared. Somehow a javelin has made it into his hands, slipping effortlessly from the bindings at his side. He lifts it up, preparing to throw it.

You charge forward, calling out to divert his attention. He spins on you, his cold eyes narrowing to splinters of hatred – then you shoulder into him, taking you both spinning and flailing through the thick black smoke. It is time to fight:

	Speed	Brawn	Armour	Health
Igluk	2	2	1	40

Special abilities

🛡 **Watch my back**: Henna adds 2 to your damage score for the duration of this combat.

If you manage to defeat this ferocious warrior, turn to 45. If you lose the combat, remember to record your defeat on your hero sheet. You may then attempt the combat again or return to the map.

341

'A-ha, our ice ghost returns,' grins the organiser, patting you on the shoulder. 'Are yer ready to get racing?' (If you have the keyword *rookie* on your hero sheet, turn to 189. If you have the keyword *veteran* on your hero sheet, turn to 529.)

'My father always frowned on magic – he was an army man, believed in steel and faith.' You stoop to pick up the book, brushing the dust from its red leather cover. 'He had an advisor, Avian Dale. He once told me I might have the talent, but I don't think I really listened – perhaps I didn't want to.'

'Avian Dale,' the mage nods, taking back the book. 'Understandable that your father would want to shelter you from magic. He had the Church forever at his back, a formidable power and some might say, a domineering one – I doubt he would want a royal son to be practising the forbidden art.'

'It's not exactly forbidden though, is it?' You gesture to the spell books, scattered across the desk. 'Providing one learns to control it – then there's no harm.'

Segg drops the book onto his chair, staring at it for a long time. When he speaks, the flames flutter wildly in the brazier, sweeping across him in bands of shadow. 'The Church has strong views when it comes to magic. They believe it should be controlled, for all our sakes. Better for it to be seen than hidden away and go underground. That is why they permitted the University to be built in Talanost. So mages could learn to master their powers. Magic is dangerous, have no doubt about that. In some ways, I agree with what they did.' His eyes stray to the fire. 'But I fear times are changing. The shadow war – the destruction of Talanost, Wiccans ranging across our countryside, rumours of a new emperor in Mordland. All these are fuel for their holy fires, to condemn us all as heretics.'

'You aren't really selling the whole magic thing,' you reply, smirking. 'Do you want to teach me this or not?'

Your bluntness draws Segg from his reverie. A crooked smile twitches his lips. 'The impatience of youth, eh? Just like Harris. Yes, you have a natural talent, boy – powerful, I'd say. But you're not quite ready yet. Some careful study, and – yes.' He nods approvingly. 'I think I could make something of you, boy.'

343

The knight lifts his arms to his side, his heavy cloak writhing and flailing in the buffeting gale.

'No!' You start forward, looking to stop him. But you cannot reach the knight in time. He steps off from the wall, plummeting from sight in the blink of an eye.

You grab hold of the battlements, leaning over the edge to watch as the ghost's light is swallowed by the darkness.

'There was nothing you could have done,' says Anise, joining you at your side. 'They're ghosts, reliving the past.'

'Perhaps the medallion . . .' You shake your head, torn with regret.

'They will not find peace, not in this place.' Anise turns back to the rooftop, eyes scanning the dirt and debris. 'We must think about the living. Harris and . . .' She stops suddenly, her words cut short. You look around, confused by what has caught her attention. Then realisation dawns.

'No signal fire . . .' The girl looks to you in bewilderment. 'What are we going to do now?' Turn to 560.

344

You duck into the cave, the low ceiling forcing you to stoop. After several metres the tunnel mouth widens, lifting to form a dome-like impression. The surface of the rock is pitted with hundreds of holes and channels, some wide and dripping with water, others little more than narrow fractures. A few open out to the sky above, filtering shafts of pale light into the chamber.

The opening is cluttered with boulders and loose stone – but once past the rubble, the ground is smooth and even. On the other side you see another tunnel-like opening leading deeper into the rock.

Will you:

Hide and ambush the hunter?	166
Head deeper into the cave?	247

345

You flatten out into a dive, putting arms straight, arrowing your fingers, trying to make yourself as small and sleek a missile as possible. Nevertheless, you hit the pool with a painful thwack, bones splintering and muscles ripping free of their tendons as you plunge into its dark bubbling depths. (You must roll once on the death penalty chart and immediately apply the effect to your hero. You must also lose one backpack item.) Then turn to 696.

346

For defeating the mage, you may now help yourself to one of the following rewards:

Brimstone brow	**Pebble dash**	**Shingle stone**
(head)	(cloak)	(chest)
+1 magic	+1 speed +1 magic	+1 speed +1 armour
Ability: lightning	Ability: haste	Ability: might of stone

When you have updated your hero sheet, turn to 141.

347

Desnar watches the frantic carnage with surprise and then admiration, barking encouragement as you decapitate the last of the abominable horrors.

Amongst the churned and bloody snow, you discover a number of treasures glowing with magic. You wonder if these strange objects may have been responsible for animating the ghoulish snow monsters. If you wish, you may now take one of the following rewards:

Scarlet scarf	Rune of midwinter	Frosty's fingers
(cloak)	(special: rune)	(necklace)
+1 speed +2 brawn	Use on any item to	+2 magic
Ability: distraction	add the special ability:	Ability: cold snap
	frost burn	

When you have made your decision, turn to 208.

348

(If this is your first time visiting the training yard, then read on. If you have the keyword *brawler* on your hero sheet, turn to 780. If you have the keyword *baited*, turn to 293.)

The air rings with the dull thwack of wooden training swords as soldiers ebb and flow in lines through the wet slush, testing each others' defences. The trainer is a head taller than any man there, his massive frame made more imposing by the polar bear pelt that hugs his broad shoulders. He flicks his riding crop at a soldier as he passes, baring his bright teeth in anger. 'Tighter, Henson! I've seen goblins show more initiative. Read your opponent, watch their footing. But don't dance. We ain't maids a-wooing. See an opening and take it!'

You fold your arms, studying the warriors from the side-lines, admiring their dedication and endurance. When the trainer notices you, he cracks the riding crop, calling a halt. He strides towards you, a mountain of muscle and sinew.

'What we got here, then?'

You feel all eyes upon you – and suddenly you regret coming to the yard. Too many questions, too many chances that you might be discovered.

'This, my friends, is what I call a survivor.' The trainer turns to address his men, his arm snapping out to level the crop at your chest. 'The black fever. That's an enemy that don't care to dance. It don't do anything but kill. And it does it well. Do you know how many survive the fever?'

He is met with blank expressions. A few are already glaring at you, as if your very presence is somehow meant to be an insult.

'None,' says the trainer, looking back at you with his tight white smile. 'You should be dead. Henson, give him a sword. A proper one.'

The soldier does as he is told, taking a steel blade from a nearby stand and tossing it toward you. As you snatch the grip deftly from the air, you find yourself marvelling that you can actually lift it. Back at the palace you had always struggled with even the lightest of blades, wearing your tutor's patience thin. But now it feels perfectly weighted in your hands. You make a few cutting motions through the air, hearing it zing.

I might even get away with this.

'Big fella, aren't we?' snaps the trainer, circling around you. 'What training you had?'

You stammer for an answer, feeling the grins and side-glances from the other soldiers. 'I was a bodyguard,' you lie. 'Life has been my teacher, sir.' *Yes, that sounds good.*

'Rutus!' The trainer calls to one of the soldiers. He steps forward, a young man about your age, short but strong, his muscles glistening with sweat from the morning's sparring. 'Get a sword and show this one what life has to teach us, sir.' He calls out the last word in a mocking tone.

You glare at him angrily, feeling something stir in the pit of your stomach, a roar that you want to release. For a brief moment you sense the bear from your dream, somehow by your side, urging you on, filling you with his strength.

The guard comes at you fast, cutting his blade through the air with no fear of the consequences. His first strike knocks your sword from your grip, followed quickly by a boot to the groin. You find yourself rolling in the dirt, gasping in pain.

There are hoots of laughter from the soldiers. Rutus spits into the dirt, then raises his arms in victory. 'That's life,' he shouts, to more applause.

With a look of undisguised disgust, the trainer heaves you to your feet. 'Get back at him,' he hisses through his teeth. 'At least make a fight of it.'

You grab your sword as Rutus turns to face you. 'Oh, you want another kicking, dog? I'll give you one!'

He charges again, coming at you side on, looking to simply barrel through you and take you down. But this time you are ready for his attack and refuse to be humiliated once again. It is time to fight:

	Speed	Brawn	Armour	Health
Rutus	3	1	1	45

Special abilities

❤ **Training yard**: You cannot use any special abilities in this combat.

❤ **I yield**: Once Rutus is reduced to 10 *health* or less, roll a die at the start of each combat round. On a roll of ⚁ or more, he yields to you, winning you the combat. Otherwise, the combat continues as normal.

If you manage to defeat this skilled soldier, turn to 147. If you lose the challenge, turn to 258.

349

You manage to wrestle free of the growth, dropping back to the ground with half of the decayed skeleton on top of you. Desperately, you kick it away, the jaws still snapping hungrily from its mouldy innards.

'In future, look and not touch,' says Anise, her back pressed against the wall.

'Agreed.' You clamber back to your feet. As you do so, you notice a small metal box lying in the dirt. It must have come free when you pulled the body down. The box is heavy, despite its size, made from a cobalt-blue steel. Cracking open the lid, you discover several stubs of flint inside. When the flint is struck against the steel, it creates a spark – ideal for lighting fires.

You have now gained *flint and tinder* (make a note of this on your hero sheet, it doesn't take up backpack space). Using your newfound item, you quickly set to work, lighting the candle inside the lamp you found. (Replace the keyword *lamp* with the keyword *flame* on your hero sheet.) Stepping carefully around the remains of the skeleton, you press on into the tower. Turn to 366.

350

The fight is a panicked frenzy – mostly spent dodging the yeti's powerful arms as they are swung back and forth looking to hit anything in range. You manage to land a few lucky blows, as do your companions. Eventually, after a tiring ordeal, the beast staggers then slumps to the ground, the tar steaming off its arrow-riddled body.

You immediately hurry after Henna, who is running to where Mitch was thrown. When you catch up, the knight is already turning away, shaking her head. You look past her to the crumpled body.

The boy is dead. Killed either by the Yeti's attack or the rock that broke his skull. There is no bringing him back.

'Ah, that's a shame,' sighs Kirk, talking as if it was an everyday event. 'We'll get him on the cart. Take him back once we're done.'

You bow your head, tortured by the knowledge that it was your decision that led to this.

'Don't let it worry you. Accidents happen out here.' Kirk hands you a knife. 'Least take a trophy home.' He jerks a thumb in the direction of the shore. 'Might be tarred, but that'll only make it warmer, eh?'

If you wish, you may now take the following item:

Tarred shoulders
(cloak)
+1 speed
Ability: charm

Make a note of the keyword *resolve* on your hero sheet. Then turn to 263.

351

The size of the depression immediately puts you in mind of the statue that you found in the birdman's eyrie. You take it out of your pack and push the statue's base into the angular hollow (remove the *stone dragon* from your backpack). There is a loud click as it drops into place, fitting the hole perfectly. The eyes of the dragon start to flicker, then settle into a pale green glow.

The ground shudders. You grip the pedestal, sure that you are experiencing another quake. A second tremor rattles you, vibrating through the stone and the bronze circle you are standing on. Then you hear a thud, the whistle of something moving fast, a clatter of metal then a dull rumbling coming from somewhere below.

Your stomach gives a sickening lurch as the bronze platform starts to lower, scraping and squealing against the accumulation of dust and grime. It drops quickly, taking you down into a shaft of smooth stone. After it has gone fifty metres or more the platform grinds to an abrupt halt. It continues to judder violently, screeching in protest as if seeking to break through some form of obstruction.

You look around at the shaft. The walls are smooth, making a climb back to the cave impossible. Then your eyes alight on an opening to your left, where the platform meets the rock. You scramble over to it, realising that it is the entrance to a passageway, but whatever is obstructing the platform is stopping the lift from lowering far enough to make it properly accessible. There is a chance you could squeeze yourself through the tight opening.

As the thought comes to you, the lift shakes and then starts to rise, taking you back up to the cave.

Will you:

Quickly try and slip into the passageway?	499
Leave it and return to the main cave?	483

352

Your enchanted weapons draw shrieks of agony from the ghost-like shapes. With each frenzied strike the incessant wind appears to grow a little weaker, until you are finally able to stand your ground, cutting through the mist and stilling its wail to silence.

After taking a moment to recover from your ordeal, you press on into the mountain.

Further along the tunnel you discover a body sprawled on its stomach. The creature appears humanoid, covered in a thick, bristly white fur. A fallen stalactite has pinned it to the ground, having passed straight through its lower torso. Blood stains the ice.

With a mighty shove you manage to push the body over, surprised to discover that the creature is a giant ape. In life it would have stood a head taller than you, its shoulders at least twice as wide. There are ugly scars cutting across its face – one eye-socket is empty, displaying only a blackened hollow.

You lean closer, looking for anything that might explain its origins. There is evidence of some advanced intelligence – a sparkling ring adorns one finger, while a dented chest plate is attached by threaded sinews around the beast's neck and waist. Your hand settles around the broken stalactite, pulling it free. There is some dark magic still coursing within the ice. If you wish, you may now take one of the following items:

Aldo's ruin	Primate plate	Frost fang
(ring)	(chest)	(left hand: dagger)
+1 brawn +1 magic	+1 speed +1 armour	+1 speed +2 magic
Ability: deceive	Ability: reckless	Ability: frostbite
		(requirement: mage)

You also spot a glass sphere, resting on the ground nearby. Purple flames are trapped within it, crackling and sparking as they pulse with energy. (If you wish to take the *shadow orb* simply make a note of it on your hero sheet, it does not take up backpack space). When you have updated your hero sheet, turn to 220.

353

(If you have the keyword *fractured* on your hero sheet, turn immediately to 58.)

The library is almost as impressive as the one in the royal palace. You believe you may have finally found a home away from home – somewhere you can be alone . . .

'Ugh! What's that terrible stink?'

You spin round, to see a young boy seated at one of the tables. You hadn't spotted him before, hidden behind a stack of books. Several lie open in front of him, their neat rows of runed glyphs sparkling against the yellowed parchment. 'You smell worse than Brack, and that's saying something.'

The boy looks no older than thirteen, dressed in plush green robes trimmed with white fur. His face is narrow and pale, dominated by a pair of gold-rimmed spectacles resting on the end of his nose. He continues to glare at you, with a look of obvious distaste – as if you have invaded his own personal space and he wants you to leave.

Will you:

Talk to the mage?	16
Ignore him and look for a book?	577
Talk to Segg?	328
Return to the main courtyard?	113

354

The last Skard falls back into the snow, blood seeping from his many wounds. You stand over him, noting that he is the white-haired warrior who Gurt referred to as Aslev.

He bows his head, as the others have done.

You put your weapon to his neck, then lift his chin. 'You will bow to no one. Come with me.'

He shows his teeth in warning. 'We gave our word,' he hisses. 'You cannot go back. You will shame us!'

'I can,' you reply defiantly. 'And I will. All I ask is that I am given a chance to prove myself. I think I've made a promising start, don't you?'

For defeating the einherjar, you may now help yourself to one of the following special rewards:

Dark mail coat	Habrok's perch	Rune of weakening
(chest)	(head)	(special: rune)
+2 brawn +1 armour	+1 speed +2 magic	Use on any item to add
Ability: iron will	Ability: focus	the special ability *curse*
	(requirement: mage)	

When you have updated your hero sheet, turn to 119.

355

You choose to fight, digging your heels into the ground and preparing to meet the Skard in battle. His companions hold back, watching with a mix of amusement and interest as their burly companion bounds straight into you.

There had been a plan in your mind – a set of moves, a feint to the left, a low blow to the right, wrong-foot him, then quick slices to the chest and arms, where his defences seem weakest. Perhaps Nanuk will pour his magic into you, giving you the fatal edge . . .

But such plans are quickly smashed out of you as the Skard sends you flying back into the rock shelf. You don't even get a chance to recover. A dagger punches through your shoulder. Another into your stomach. You hear a sickening ripping sound – then smell something foul. Another blow across the face, perhaps an elbow.

He clambers off you, snorting back snot and spittle. 'Fegis,' he grunts, shaking his head. He turns and gestures to the shaven-headed hunter. 'Slur den.'

The other Skard saunters towards you, his axe resting back on his shoulder.

Add two *defeats* to your hero sheet. Then turn to **656**.

356

The bird is relentless in its attacks, driven by a natural instinct to protect its eggs. But luck favours you, as a wild swing pierces its feathered body, delivering a killing blow.

The bird crashes down onto the nest, narrowly missing you by inches. It seems the pursuing Skard was less fortunate, however. From the rocks below, you hear a momentary scream, then a loud bone-cracking thump. He must have been trying to climb out of the shaft when the bird hit him.

From this height, you don't rate his chances.

For your victory over the giant roc, you may now take one of the following rewards:

Butcher's bill	Dashing talons	Virile plumage
(head)	(gloves)	(chest)
+1 brawn +1 magic	+1 brawn	+1 magic
Ability: bleed	Ability: sideswipe	Ability: charm

If you are wearing the *tarred shoulders*, turn to **415**. Otherwise, turn to **205**.

357

The hand dashes between your legs, disappearing amongst a stack of crates. For a moment, you contemplate hurling them aside – anything to get at that annoying limb – but Anise's sigh of impatience draws you away.

'Chasing hands . . .' The girl gives you a wearisome look. 'Somehow, I don't think that's going to get us out of here, is it?'

Will you:

Open one of the barrels?	**156**
Climb the rubble to the room above?	**272**
Retrace your steps and use the stairs?	**111**

358

Night has fallen – and with it comes a frigid wind, blasting across the camp, forcing you to stagger against its fury as you follow Sura into one of the ice homes. Inside, you are surprised by its immediate warmth. A number of stone lamps flicker on a bed of leathers, casting golden shadows across the tight-packed walls.

You suspect this is Sura's home. There are charms and other magical trinkets set out on ice shelves. In one corner you see several carved staffs half-wrapped in bear furs. A simple pallet bed, some horned cups and a leather sack filled with clothes complete what you assume are the woman's worldly belongings.

'Sit.' Sura motions to one of the furs spread across the ground.

You take your seat, awkwardly aware of the tightness of the space.

Sura lowers herself with a groan onto the pallet bed, a hand to her back. When she catches your look of concern, she gives a wheezing chuckle.

'Not seen an old lady before, son?' She settles onto the bed, setting her staff aside to rub at her legs.

'You speak common . . . well,' you stammer, wondering if you might cause offence. 'I mean, the Skards I have met – they have difficulty . . .'

'Think us all savages, then?' The woman grunts, putting a hand beneath one of her fur sheets and pulling out a bag. 'Might surprise you, but we've taken your kind in before, in times past. They taught us the tongue. We don't gut *all* you southlanders on sight.'

You grimace, not entirely comfortable with the compliment.

'Why?' you ask, watching as the woman opens up the bag.

Her eyes fix on you, then narrow. 'Why what?'

'Why bring me here? I am an outsider. Who was that . . . that warrior who challenged me?'

'That was Desnar, who made himself leader in Taulu's absence. They were brothers.'

'So he challenges me?' You snort, shaking your head. 'I don't want to be part of these games. I'm not after power. He blames me for Taulu's death – but he can have the stupid necklace. I don't want it.'

'You don't?' Sura sounds disappointed. She tips the contents of the bag into the palm of her hand. A black flaky herb that gives off a sour smell. 'But Nanuk has chosen you. One of the great ancestor spirits of our tribe.'

You roll your eyes, giving the woman a pained expression. 'Please, I told you – I am not interested. I am not a leader, look at me . . .'

Her eyes remain fixed on your own. 'I am. And I see the bear spirit in your eyes. Unusual for a man to have the magic, and so strongly. You are a shaman, like myself. You could lead, but you need to find your strength. You need to find . . .' She leans forward, prodding your chest with a gnarled finger. 'Your heart.'

'It's dead,' you snap, brushing her hand away. 'I'm dead. Can't you see that?'

The woman shrugs her scrawny shoulders, then proceeds to push the herbs into a small bone pipe. 'I see you have questions, south-lander.' With a flick of her fingers, she sends a green flame dancing from her fingertips. It ignites the herbs, filling the shelter with the aroma of cinnamon and wood smoke. 'So ask away, and let Sura answer.'

Will you:

Ask about the shaman's magic?	688
Ask about the bear necklace?	545
Ask what 'vela styker' means?	587
End the conversation?	575

359

As you glance along the dusty spines, you begin to spot names that seem oddly familiar. You say them to yourself, repeating them in rhyme, trying to place where you have heard them before. Then you remember – the ghost in the tower, who scratched out the strange message on the table. The words are the surnames of various authors: *Pendegost, Frayling, Augur* and *Volst*.

You reach for each book in turn, surprised to discover that they are false spines, hinged on some sort of hidden lever system. As each book is pulled in sequence, there is a dull click. Suddenly the room starts to spin, as the section of wall revolves round on a hidden plat-form, taking you into a secret chamber. Remove the keyword *secrets* from your hero sheet, then turn to 278.

360

Thanks to Mitch's intervention, the barrels of tar were saved from the Skard's fire. (You should have a note of how many barrels you managed to fill. Keep this, as it may be important later.) Turning the cart around, you prepare for home – and probably a lot of questions.

'Guess those thieves got their just deserts,' says Henna with a sigh. 'Never thought soldiers would stoop so low.'

'Hey, wait up! Can someone help me out here?' You both turn, to see Mitch struggling after you with the sack of stolen equipment.

If you have the word *thievery* on your hero sheet, turn to 4. Otherwise, turn to 383.

361

The walls of the canyon part like grey-white curtains, presenting you with a vast expanse of ice and razor-edged rock. Ahead, through the haze of powdery snow drifting like smoke across the silent wasteland, you see what can only be 'the caves'. They loom tall, a double-peaked mountain formed by two glaciers pushed together. Its uneven slopes are pitted with nooks and fissures, many of which bleed waterfalls of ice, their spear-like prongs glistening in the dawn light.

You approach with caution, acutely aware of the crevasses that zigzag through the ice. There are no snow bridges to hide them, but the crossing is still slow and treacherous. Beneath your feet, black rock can be glimpsed through the many inches of ice. In some places there is only a frozen emptiness; each pop and crack of the ice sets your teeth on edge.

After an hour of carefully navigating the fractured plain, you come to the foot of the mountain. A mound of tumbled rock covers nearly half-a-mile of its base. You wonder if the main entrance had been somewhere behind it, trapping the other explorers inside.

You crane your neck, shielding your eyes as you take in the ridges and ledges that protrude from the ice-covered walls. Above one area of rock-fall, about forty metres up the face of the mountain, you can see an icicle-dripping shelf and what looks like an opening behind it. The climb would be difficult, but the shelf appears to be the only reachable means of entering the caves.

Alternatively, you could trek around the base of the mountain, looking for an easier way inside.

Will you:

Attempt to climb to the rock shelf?	67
Look for an alternative entrance?	275

For defeating the ancient wind demon, you may now choose one of the following rewards:

Hailstorm	Tundra span	Grips of the gale
(left hand: glass sword)	(cloak)	(gloves)
+2 speed +3 brawn	+1 speed +2 armour	+1 speed +2 brawn
Ability: piercing	Ability: windfall	Ability: haste

When you have made your decision, return to the quest map to continue your adventure.

363

You maintain your current heading, accelerating across the top of the island. The air hums and crackles around you as the towers charge up their blasts – then suddenly jagged strips of lightning surge forth, tearing towards your transport. In order to avoid these deadly strikes, you must take a challenge test using your transport's speed:

	Speed
Fire in the sky	14

If you are successful, turn to 711. If you fail the challenge, turn to 44.

364

With the cat gone, you are free to inspect the strange corpse. Whatever this creature was, there is no obvious sign of how it met its end. A box lies in the grass next to an outstretched claw. The lid has been smashed open and whatever was inside has been looted.

You hear the crunch of stones behind you. Turning, you are relieved to see Kirk and Lawson. 'What you found?' asks Kirk, stepping around the body. 'Oh, one of the scalies. Bunch of these attacked the Keep the other day. Tough as nails, gave us a real beating.' He crouches down to pick up a feather from the ground. 'Hmm, if there was anything of value, the birdman will have got it now. Nothing comes and goes around here without him knowing.'

'Segg might be interested,' you glance at each of the soldiers. 'He could study it. Find out more?'

Lawson grunts. 'Yeah, crazy fool would probably like that.'

'All right, enough gawking.' Kirk tucks the feather behind his ear. 'Let's get this back to the wagon and get those barrels on board.' Make a note of the word *envoy* on your hero sheet. Then turn to 242.

365

Tankards and chairs go flying as two ale-soaked men punch and grapple with each other, spitting drunken curses. Their boots scuffle back and forth across the sawdust-covered ground, neither able to land a decisive blow. The rest of the patrons continue to drink and converse, unconcerned by the unruly display of violence; clearly brawls and drunkenness are the norm around here.

You push through the fetid press of unwashed bodies, keeping your hands tightly clutched to your backpack and gold pouch. More than a few eyes and hands have moved in their direction, but quickly draw back when they catch your chilling gaze.

You find a space at the bar, a makeshift arrangement of planks and barrels soaked with ale and grease. Putting your back to the counter, you take in the size of the place. As its name suggests, the Jailhouse Rock has been hewn out of the granite peak, resembling more a vast cavernous chamber than a building. Wooden walkways form a haphazard web-work up and down the walls, leading to side rooms and alcoves. Most are obscured by a filthy haze of smoke.

Will you:

Talk to the barman?	420
Take a seat in one of the alcoves?	634
Listen to the conversation at the bar?	534
Leave?	426

The mould covering the walls gets thicker and more virulent, forcing you to pick your way past drooping growths and snarled roots. Eventually you both emerge in a large rectangular chamber.

The floor, ceiling and walls are all covered in the same decaying mould.

As you step into the room, you hear an unsettling creak beneath your feet. Looking down, you see that the floor is wood rather than stone – the floorboards warped and rotted. You wonder if they are still capable of supporting your weight. To your right, an open doorway leads through to a narrow corridor.

'Careful,' whispers Anise.

You take another step into the room, wincing as the wood groans and cracks. Then another, distributing your weight as best you can. Anise shadows your movements, her pool of torchlight slowly filling the room.

A sudden rush of movement alerts you to danger.

You swing round, eyes following a dark shape as it drops from the ceiling.

'It's a riftwing!' Anise shrieks, ducking behind your back. 'Watch out!'

The creature resembles a cross between a goblin and a bat, with black leathery wings and peaked furry ears. From beneath its flayed nostrils you see two rows of needle-like teeth steadily opening wider.

With a hiss, the monster lunges for you. Reacting on instinct, you manage to catch one of its spindly wrists, stopping its taloned fingers just shy of your throat. The other limb ends in a scarred stump, battering uselessly against your chest. As the two of you stagger back against the wall, you notice one of its wings is hanging loose from its back, the membrane torn. The creature must have been in a previous fight, which has left it injured and weak.

If you have the word *methane* on your hero sheet, turn to 497. Otherwise, turn to 371.

'That is holy scripture.' You nod to the glowing lines etched into the man's skin. You cannot imagine the pain and the commitment of those who would endure such an act, all for the devotion of their god. 'Tell me, how many inscribers died to give you that shiny coat?'

The paladin flinches at your scorn. 'It is necessary if we are to fight in His name. The inscribers are as dedicated as we are. They give their lives willingly.'

You snort.

'Do you have reason to fear the Church?' Maune takes a step forward, leaning his head to try and peer at your face. 'You are a wayward child, I can see that. And keeping company with a northern savage.'

It takes a moment for Skoll to react, an angry growl issuing from his lips. He moves to attack but you manage to put an arm out, urging restraint. 'Do not rise to it,' you intone slowly. Your attention returns to Maune.

'The Church has wronged me and my family,' you reply. 'I have lost everything. Your god is not one of mercy or compassion.'

Maune eyes you levelly, his emotions masked by a stern exterior. 'Men are corruptible. The holy light is not.'

Will you:

Ask what he knows of Rile's betrayal?	507
Ask Maune why he is here?	97
Ask for food and water? (ends the conversation)	433
Attack the paladin? (ends the conversation)	486

'The many weigh heavier than the few.' You take Skoll's hand, finding some small amusement in the pain caused by your chill touch, its cold sending fingers of frost crackling across his knuckles. He hoists you to your feet, then averts his gaze.

'You did not have to become this.' He glowers, rubbing his smarting hand. 'We could have found another way.'

You retrieve your weapons. 'What's done is done, remember? Now we must avenge those we have lost.' Your gaze turns to the yawning chasm. 'Do you know where this demon is – the one we must destroy?'

He nods. 'We need only follow these.' He gestures to the stippled tentacles, branching through the stonework. 'Come, this way.'

You follow the Skard along the ledge until you are directly beneath one of the appendages. Its trunk-like form stretches across the gulf, forming a crude but navigable bridge. Skoll holsters his axe then starts climbing, using the cracks in the wall to lever himself higher. Then, with a grunt, he leaps onto the tentacle, straddling it like a horse. The appendage holds, its ends tethered deep into the rock to either side.

You can feel the heat emanating from the tentacle's cracked skin, but with no other choice you scale the wall and join the Skard. He seems unperturbed by the molten blood flowing through the beast's innards, but for you its heat scolds your spirit-body, like a thousand hot needles piercing beneath your skin.

'Let's be quick,' you gasp.

Skoll finds his balance then starts across the void, his eyes set firmly on the other side. You are halfway across when a sudden, shrieking clamour forces you to turn.

A host of shadowy demons are crawling up out of the darkness. Their shape and number are indistinct – at times they seem many, humanoid in shape, then they merge and become one, flowing together into a single confusion of grasping limbs.

The shadows move with speed, flowing around the tentacle like some virulent disease. They are headed straight for you.

Skoll draws his axe and nudges back past you. 'Go.'

You look at him in confusion.

'They come too quick. I hold them. Go.'

The Skard does not wait for your answer. He strides towards the surging darkness, limbering his shoulders, making practice cuts with his axe. You doubt he can possibly fend them all off.

As if sensing your hesitation, he calls back. 'The many weigh heavier than the few. Now run, or I'll kick you there myself!'

You bow your head in farewell, then turn and follow the Skard's instruction, hurrying to the other side. Turn to **154**.

369
Quest: The bitter end

It feels good to breathe again. To enjoy the rhythm of your body, the throbbing beat beneath your breast. Odd you could miss something so normal and everyday – and rediscover its joy here, in this place of creeping shadow and dead things, where you feel more complete. More human.

At your side sits the bear. His name presses against your mind once again – Nanuk. He seems diminished now, not as large and imposing as he once was, as if part of his being is now within you. Muscles ripple along your arms where once there had been only skin and bone. You feel the power in every fibre of your being – not just a physical strength but something older, more primeval.

The dreamscape shimmers around you. Norr. The bear forms the word for you as he brushes up against your legs, letting you stroke the soft fur between his ridged shoulder blades. Simply touching him sends shimmering light branching across your fingertips. His magic. Your magic.

Oneness.

The stonework of the fortress stands stark against the green, but wavers in and out of reality as if clinging to a thin thread of existence – a shadow. Your eyes sweep back across the walls and towers. They are both familiar and unfamiliar, twisted a little, misshapen at the edges. It is as if the builder had been given a plan of the keep and then, part way through, had given in to madness, turning his creation into some tortured mockery of its intended purpose. This is the shadow of Bitter Keep. Somehow its presence pushes through the veil into this world – the one of spirit.

For days you have walked the silent battlements with only Nanuk for company. The silence is welcome – the solitude also. The demons have come many times, as they always do. Frightening nightmares from out of the wasteland. They have left you wondering if they are shadows of something too, damned spirits like yourself that have been trapped here so long that their humanity has become lost.

Each time the demons come, Nanuk sees them off with tooth and claw. And now you fight by his side as an equal. No longer the weak and sickly prince that you once were. Magic courses from your finger-tips, strength powers your strikes. In battle you feel at one with Nanuk – as if your minds have become joined, a union that goes deeper than anything you have experienced before. It is tempting to stay here in the dream . . . walking the walls of the shadow keep forever.

Just breathing. In and out. Feeling alive once again.

'Arran!'

The voice wakes you to the familiar pains and cramps. Sitting cross-legged in your room, you open your eyes to a piercing light. Then you find yourself clawing at the ground as your muscles spasm, the sinews snapping taut like rope. You clamp your teeth together, spitting and snorting, resenting being brought back from your med-itations – back to this mockery of a body. A dead weight. A dead corpse.

Everard strides across the room to the open window. 'Allam's teeth, it's like a morgue in here.' He pushes the shutters closed against the chill wind, his gaze shifting to the fireplace that has never been lit. 'Do you not feel the cold, boy?'

You wait for the muscles to relax before levering yourself to stand, using the bed for support. 'No,' you reply, the word burning in your throat.

'Segg is worried about you. He says you are spending longer,' Everard throws you a hard look 'meditating, or whatever you do. I doubt it's healthy for you, Arran. You have responsibilities. Running from them will not solve anything.'

'Running?' You stare across the cold room, eyes adjusting to the gloom. The slatted light competes with the hard lines of Everard's face. 'What would you have me do?' You glance down at your trem-bling hands, black and bruised.

The knight grimaces, thinking. 'We need to get you away from here. Either across land to the south or charter a ship. Perhaps Ryker's Island.'

'The prison?' You have heard many stories of that dread place – a forgotten outpost on the coast of the frozen north, where your father's predecessor had housed the worst of the worst – the criminal elite. King Hark had been a church man, a devout follower of the One God. He believed that even the darkest wrongdoer was capable of repentance – if given enough time for reflection. And where better to do that than a remote prison with no chance of escape, surrounded by miles of ice flats and frozen sea?

'Not any longer,' sighs Everard. 'There was a uprising some time ago, the inmates seized control. I thought you would have known. The prison is more an outpost now. A pit of murderers and scoundrels, for sure, but also traders and hunters. Some would even go as far as to call it . . . civilised.'

'And where then?' you ask with some bitterness, not sure you like your life being mapped out for you, pushed from one place to the next at someone else's discretion.

'Well, that really depends on you, doesn't it?'

'Me?' You startle in surprise. 'You mean, do I want the throne? To try and win it—'

The room shudders then lurches. You stumble into the bed, which is rattling on its iron posts. Everard backs into a corner, bracing himself as the tremor continues, filling your ears with a resounding bellowing roar. You expect it to stop at any moment, like they always do – but this one lingers a little longer. Stone shifts, dust showers from the ceiling.

Then it is over, leaving silence in its wake.

'They're getting worse.' Everard steps away from the wall, brushing the dust from his shoulder plate. 'At this rate, no one will need to attack the walls, they'll just step over them.'

Your eyes linger on the elderly knight, the previous conversation still working through your mind. 'Cardinal Rile now rules in my absence. My people think me dead or captured by the Wiccans. Do you really think I have a chance of returning – of winning support?' You take a step closer, arms wide by your sides. 'The people of Assay would sooner welcome Conall and his Wiccan dogs, than . . . this.'

'You're still the heir.'

'Saying it means nothing.'

'No, it's about believing, Arran.' Everard steps closer, meeting you with his steel-grey eyes. 'I believe you can lead, Arran. Not because of what you are now, but because of what you were.'

'A weakling?' You move your jaw, hearing it click

Everard snorts, shaking his head. 'You have not known strength before. You know what it is to be weak – yes. You know what it is to be the underdog. That is a quality that most of our leaders lack.'

'And having been the underdog will win me back my throne?' You laugh, a hacking dry rasp.

'No.' Everard grits his teeth, grinding them back and forth. After taking a deep breath, he turns and starts towards the door. He hesitates with his hand on the latch. 'I came here to deliver a message. Well, three in truth. I judge you are ready for some proper training – and I'm not alone in that. Segg believes you have a talent for magic and would like to tutor you further. Trainer Orrec, on the other hand, fancies you as a soldier of the keep and awaits you in the yard.' The latch clicks back and Everard opens the door.

'You said there were three.'

'Oh yes.' Everard glances back. 'If guile and shadow are more to your tastes, then Rook will meet you in the chapel.' He grins to himself before leaving.

Will you:

Visit Segg to learn the path of the mage?	118
Train with Orrec to learn the path of the warrior?	459
Meet with Rook and learn the path of the rogue?	211

370

Searching through the wreckage, you find one of the following items:

Soul mirror	Night whispers	Spirit charger
(necklace)	(talisman)	(head)
+1 speed +2 brawn	+1 speed +5 health	+1 speed +2 brawn
Ability: darksilver	Ability: immobilise	Ability: recovery

When you have updated your hero sheet, turn to 755.

371

You throw the riftwing back across the room, buying yourself enough time to ready your weapons. When the creature comes at you again, shrieking and jabbering with rage, you are able to meet its attack with steel and magic. It is time to fight:

	Speed	Brawn	Armour	Health
Riftwing	2	1	1	28

If you manage to defeat this winged fiend, turn to 217. If you lose the combat, remember to record your defeat on your hero sheet. You may then attempt the combat again or return to the map.

372

The walkway hugs the contours of the tree, delivering you to a tunnel-like opening in the trunk. Stepping inside, you find yourself in a high-ceilinged chamber, its gnarly walls pitted with hundreds of hollowed tunnels. Shafts of light spill from these tiny openings, illuminating the pale-winged moths that flutter and dance through the dusty air.

As your eyes steadily grow accustomed to the light, you hear a deep rustling from above. Scanning the ceiling, you spot a giant shape crawling across the knotted wood. It is a moth, like the others that dwell here – but this one is nearly ten times their size, its pale translucent wings as large as a ship's masts.

You watch as it scurries over to a position on the far wall, where its wings snap open to cover several of the openings. To your surprise the light passes through the wings, forming glistening patterns on its silky membrane. These patterns are shadowed on the floor of the chamber, where dazzling circles of rainbow light are now converging.

The pattern shifts and changes, rising up into motes of dust which quickly coalesce into the shape of a Skard warrior. His features are indistinct, little more than shimmering colours, washing back and forth in rainbow hues – yet his dangerous intent is clear. He moves towards you with a light-footed grace, his arms distending outwards into two bright blades of light. Then, with a hollering roar, he charges. It is time to fight:

	Speed	Magic	Armour	Health
Rainbow warrior	6	4	5	50
Red aspect (*)	5	4	3	20
Green aspect (*)	6	5	5	20
Blue aspect (*)	7	5	6	15

Special abilities

♥ **Spectrum of spirits** (*): At the start of the *third* round of combat, the rainbow warrior transforms into his red aspect. You must defeat the red aspect before you can return to attacking the rainbow warrior again. After another *two* rounds of combat, if the rainbow warrior is still alive, he transforms into his green aspect. Again you must defeat the green aspect before you can return to attacking the rainbow warrior. After a further *two* rounds of combat, the rainbow warrior (if still alive) transforms into his blue aspect. Once this is defeated, you may return to attacking the rainbow warrior for the remainder of the combat. (Note: aspects can only be damaged if they are in play. While an aspect is in play, the rainbow warrior is immune to all damage.)

♥ **Colour of magic**: Your opponents are immune to all passive effects, including *bleed*, *barbs*, *disease* and *venom*.

If you manage to defeat this multi-coloured villain, turn to 423.

373

Talia drops into the chair opposite. For a moment, you both exchange a wry grin. 'You came back,' she says, removing her hat and flicking out her hair. 'Does this mean we can finally get down to business?'

If you wish to take Talia up on her offer, then remove the word *covert* from your hero sheet and turn to 585. Otherwise, you return to the taproom. Turn to 365.

374

'Back again,' grunts a familiar voice from behind the barricade of iron. 'Least I don't need to remind you o' the rules. No funny business, now. Remember, I taken all the necessary precautions.' He sticks the barrels of his muskets through the holes in the wall. 'See, I'm all loaded up and my fingers are mighty twitchy today.'

(If you have the keyword *hunted* on your hero sheet, turn to 92.)

Will you:

Ask to see his wares?	151
Ask about trading?	327
Ask about his 'precautions'?	549
Ask if he has any news?	450
Trade items? (requirement: permit)	730
Leave?	Return to the map

375

The acolytes' attention is focused on the ritual. You move quickly, sliding around the pillar and advancing towards their exposed backs.

Nanuk. You open up your mind, letting the bear's strength pour into you.

Spectral claws flash from your fingers. You punch through the two acolytes standing closest to you, killing them before they even have a chance to react. Then your weapons ring out of their scabbards, your advance barely slowing.

One of the acolytes turns. And gives a cry of alarm.

The woman spins, her eyes widening then narrowing to slits of rage. 'Insidious was a fool!' she snaps. 'We will not make the same mistake! Kill him!' It is time to fight:

	Speed	Magic	Armour	Health
Coven matriarch	11	7	8	40
Coven acolyte	10	7	4	30
Coven acolyte	10	6	4	30
Coven acolyte	9	6	4	20
Coven acolyte	9	6	4	20

Special abilities

🍷 **Matriarch's malice**: The matriarch has magical wards carved into her skin. While the Matriarch has *health*, you cannot use modifier abilities during this combat.

🍷 **Dark mending**: At the end of each combat round, each opponent will heal themselves for 2 *health*. This cannot take them above their starting *health* and once their *health* is reduced to zero, this ability no longer applies.

🍷 **Outnumbered**: At the end of each combat round, you must take 1 damage from each surviving opponent, ignoring *armour*. This ability only applies while you are faced with multiple opponents.

If you manage to defeat this dark gathering, turn to 230. If you are defeated, remember to record your defeat on your hero sheet. If you wish, you may return to an earlier point to select a different option (providing you meet the item requirement.) Turn to 627.

376

The fight already seems lost. Through the swirling dust clouds, all you can see is death and carnage. The lizard-like monsters are everywhere, their massive swords cleaving the air, hewing down soldiers as if they were stalks of corn. One guard races towards you, screaming. Then his eyes roll back into his head and he topples forward, an axe protruding from between his shoulder blades.

You wonder if Anise is still alive. Desperately, you scan the wreckage, looking from one body to the next, half-hoping and half-dreading what you might find. Another soldier backs into you, flighty with panic. Your attempts to communicate are lost, your words drowned by the roars and screams. Everything is chaos.

You hurry across the courtyard, hoping to find Everard or a high-ranking officer. Instead, your way is blocked by two pockets of battle. To your left, soldiers are trying to scale a mound of rubble to where a short creature in hooded robes has its hands raised to the sky. Their advance wavers as chunks of rock fly up from the surrounding rubble, smashing into the soldiers and forcing them back. One guard takes a splinter in the neck, dropping to his knees, an arc of crimson spraying from the wound. The hooded creature gives a sibilant hiss, each gesture of its clawed hands ripping more stone from the pile to shower the beleaguered soldiers.

To your right, three reptilian warriors are hacking and slashing at anything that gets in their way. Behind them looms a mountain of scaled muscle – a giant troll-like beast with glittering black orbs for eyes. In each of its barrel-sized fists is a stone hammer, crawling with dark runes. Similar markings adorn its curving horns and the iron ring dangling from its snot-encrusted snout.

Will you:

Attack the mage?	135
Fight your way past the troll?	184

377

For defeating the captain, you may now help yourself to one of the following rewards:

Crow's nest	**Barnacled eye**	**Tidal chaser**
(left hand: totem)	(head)	(main hand: staff)
+2 speed +2 magic	+2 speed +2 magic	+2 speed +4 magic
Ability: murder	Ability: decay	Ability: wave

When you have updated your hero sheet, turn to 479.

378

The girl is a determined fighter. Unable to block her frantic attacks, you take a blow to the head. The next thing you know, you are falling backwards – the cold ice rushing up to meet you with a thwack! The landing is painful, but not as painful as watching your sled pull away. The girl gives a victorious wave as she guides your craft round the final bend, passing between the fluttering banners that mark the finish line.

Without a sled you have been disqualified from the race – and receive no prize. Blue Angel is the official winner of the ice sled tournament, leaving you with nothing but a bruised ego. Replace the keyword *veteran* with *underdog*. Return to the map to continue your adventure.

379

The decay only gets worse, carpeting every surface in sight until you are stumbling through a constricted tunnel of green fungus. In the room ahead, you see something moving – a nightmarish mass of fetid mould, its bulbous peak scraping the ceiling. Various items are caught up in the folds of its corpulent flesh, including a broken shield, a sword and a dented helm. You suspect this creature is the source of the pestilence that has spread throughout the tower.

With a sense of impending dread, you enter the room – its only exit blocked by the rotting mound. As your boots sink into the muck that surrounds it, the creature starts to tremble and shake. Suddenly a pair of skeletal hands burst out from its body. They are followed by a grinning skull, then a mould-encrusted ribcage.

The skeleton makes a grab for you, its bony fingers settling around your arms and gripping them like iron. As you try to fend off your bony assailant the mould starts to produce festering tentacles, each one ending in a slime-dripping mouth. They creep towards you, branching and multiplying into hundreds of snapping maws while the skeleton continues to hold you fast, stopping you from escaping. It is time to fight:

	Speed	Brawn	Armour	Health
Moulder	2	2	1	18
Skelly	2	1	1	10

Special abilities

🟣 **Many mouths of Moulder**: At the end of each round that Moulder is still alive, roll a die. If the result is ⚀ or less, you must lose 1 *health* from the beast's deadly tentacles.

🟣 **Skelly's grip**: You must lower your *speed* by 1, until Skelly is defeated.

If you manage to defeat this putrid duo, turn to 476. If you lose the combat, remember to record your defeat on your hero sheet. You may then attempt the combat again or return to the map.

380

Next to one of the beer barrels you find a sleeping drunk, his clothes dirtied and tattered. He is lying in a pool of spilt ale, drool dripping from his mouth. Every so often he gives a loud snort, mumbling to himself in his sleep.

Tied to his belt is a purse of gold, which you may take if you wish. (The purse contains 20 gold crowns.) If you have *Hergest's Hauntings* in your backpack, turn to 406. Otherwise, with little else of interest in the cellar, you decide to leave and return to the taproom. Turn to 80.

381

You take the acorn that Ratatosk gave you and push it into the soil. At first, nothing seems to happen. Then, as the cold stinking sludge slides up around your neck, you hear a loud popping, cracking sound.

Suddenly wiry branches start to rise up out of the earth, splitting and forking as they climb up the shaft. Within seconds you are looking at a makeshift ladder, offering a possible escape route from the slimy mire. However, the pull against you is strong, dragging you deeper and deeper . . .

You will need to pass a *speed* challenge:

If you are successful, turn to 117. If you fail, turn to 7.

382

You hand the carved staff back to Sura, then approach the Skard. He lifts his chin defiantly at you, an ugly scowl pulling at the myriad of scars that cut across his face.

'Framlin das!' he spits, his nose wrinkling as if from a bad smell.

You look down at him. A growl rumbles in your throat.

For a tense moment, you wonder if a fight will ensue. But Sura quickly intervenes, speaking something in Skard. Her tone is brusque, commanding. The warrior furrows his brow, then mutters a grumbling curse before spitting into the snow. He turns away, showing you his back.

You give Sura an uncertain glance. She regards you with her usual unreadable expression. 'Wait,' she breathes.

You hear the clink of iron. The man is unfastening something, his abrupt movements making his anger evident. He holds out the weapon, refusing to look your way, saying nothing.

'Go on,' insists Sura.

With a shrug, you take it from him, surprised by its lightness as you coil it into your hands. On one end is a leather arm band, which evidently tethers the chain to your body. You proceed to fasten it around your arm, tightening each of the many straps that hold it in place.

'Thank you,' you reply, wondering if the Skard will understand. 'Will you teach me . . . ?'

The man tilts his head, looking back at you from the corner of his eye. With a contemptuous sneer, he marches over to the mound of snow. Once there he replaces the bone targets, then steps away to a safe distance.

Pulling back your arm, you spin the chain above your head, feeling the weight and rhythm of its clawed end. Then you let fly, releasing the links – trying to keep your aim as straight as possible. Your first few attempts land wide of the mark, drawing mocking laughter from the Skard. But you persist at the task, pouring your magic into the weapon to help guide its course. Gradually, you start to hit the targets, your speed and aim improving – until you are not only able to hit them, but also snatch them up out of the snow with the cupped claw, drawing them back into your waiting palm.

Sura chuckles with approval. 'Good. If we're not to make a shaman of you, at least we gain a reaver.'

The Skard shakes his head, spits again into the snow then heads away, shoulders hunched – clearly looking defeated by your impressive show.

You have gained the following item:

Bleak reach
(left hand: grapple)
+2 speed +2 brawn
Ability: hooked
(requirement: rogue)

The reaver has the following special abilities:

Take the bait (co): (requires a grapple in the left hand.) If you win a combat round, you can attempt to grapple your opponent with the link chain. Roll three dice and add the *speed* modifier of your grapple to the result. If this total is equal to or more than your opponent's *speed*, you are successful. This immediately inflicts damage to your opponent equal to your total (three dice plus the *speed* modifier), ignoring *armour*. It also reduces their *speed* by 2 for the next round of combat only. This ability can only be used once per combat. If you fail, you cannot roll for a damage score and the combat round ends. (You may use abilities that let you reroll dice to try and alter the outcome of your result.)

Spirit breaker (co): Once you have successfully used *take the bait* (see above), you can play a spirit breaker. This can be used in any subsequent combat round, instead of rolling for a damage score. This inflicts three damage dice, ignoring *armour*, and reduces your opponent's *armour* by 2 for the remainder of the combat.

When you have updated your hero sheet, turn to 197.

You help lift the sack onto the back of the cart. As the sun starts to dip towards the horizon, you leave the canyon and head back to the keep. (Make a note of the keyword *trader* on your hero sheet.) You may now return to the map to continue your adventure.

Caul spits into the palm of his hand, then holds it out. 'Looks like you can handle yourself,' he grins, nodding to your weapons. 'I'd wager we'd be a good match for whatever these caves decide to throw at us. I'm in.'

You take his hand and shake it. 'Good. We should start by finding your belongings. Which way should we go?' You look around, scanning the chamber for exits.

Caul steps past you, heading for a narrow opening in the far wall. 'This way, but stay sharp. There's death here, my friend – things gone bad.'

You follow his lead, hands clamped tightly to your weapons. 'I don't fear death,' you reply bluntly. 'It's the living I'm more concerned with.'

Caul glances back at you, the green light reflected in his eyes. 'Oh, you think so?' He flicks his dagger into his hand, then heads into the tunnel. 'You're in for a few surprises.' Turn to 765.

As the passageway curves to the right, you notice a yellow-green lichen covering the walls, snaking between the cracked stonework. It grows denser as you continue, until you finally come upon a thick growth spread across the ceiling with the skeleton of a guard hanging suspended within it. The mould has almost entirely covered his body, creeping over his sagging skull and pushing into the vacant eye sockets. You sense a strong magic around the growth.

Will you:

Search the dead guard?	465
Leave him and continue onwards?	366

386

'Got any nice boxes?' he asks, his rheumy eyes looking over your person. 'I can open anything – no lock can keep ol' Sam Scurvy out. But know this – I take half of what's inside. That's ma price.'

If you have a *locker* and wish to open it, turn to 641. If you have the *hunters' chest* and wish to open it, turn to 8. Otherwise, you decline Sam's offer of help. Turn to 563.

387

You go into an immediate dive, taking yourself out of range of the towers' defences and putting you straight into the path of the winged creatures. As they near, you realise they are much larger than they first appeared, with teeth-lined beaks and long bony crests that sweep back over their scaled bodies. Cawing and shrieking, the devilish birds set upon you in a berserk rage. It is time to fight:

	Speed	Brawn	Armour	Health
Terrordactyl	12	12	9	35
Terrordactyl	12	12	9	35
Terrordactyl	12	12	9	35
Terrordactyl	12	12	9	35

Special abilities

🛡 **Dive bomb**: Each time a terrordactyl rolls a double for its attack speed you automatically lose the round, even if your attack speed was higher. For the remainder of the round you cannot use combat or modifier abilities.

🛡 **Fire at will**: You may use your *nail gun* or *dragon fire* ability in this combat.

If you manage to survive this aerial assault, turn to 29. (If you are defeated, remember to record your defeat as normal on your hero sheet, then turn to 506.)

388

The ground gives a violent shudder, strong enough to almost throw you off balance. Unlike previous tremors, this one does not abate, continuing to rattle and judder as you feel some powerful force start to build.

'What's happening?' You look to Segg, who is clutching the arms of his chair with white-knuckled hands.

The mage's answer, if he ever gave one, is lost to the groaning and shuddering of the walls. You start for the exit, but the ground shifts underfoot, throwing you back across the room. The candles fall from their alcoves, hot wax spattering across the ground. A table shatters, books spill onto the ground, their covers ripping. All of a sudden you are in a familiar darkness once again. You try and focus, but everything is shaking around you. Over the din you think you hear an explosion, then a gut-wrenching crack. You cover your head, half expecting the ceiling to come in, to be buried underneath a deluge of rock.

A moment of silence. The quake has stopped . . .

Then you hear the screams. And a relentless drumming, like fists pounding against a barrier.

'The wall . . .' Segg is clambering to his feet, his outline sparkling green in the darkness. 'Something's assaulting the walls.'

You frown, still confused. 'What do you mean?'

'That's the sound of the wards – they're being tested, broken.'

For a moment you envision the high walls of the keep and the holy writing etched into the rock. What manner of creature would throw itself against them, enduring such pain?

A grating rumble makes your stomach turn. You hug the floor, fearing another quake. Instead, a doorway in the opposite wall slides open, filling the room with a bright white light – daylight.

'To the roof,' says Segg, passing through the opening and out onto a narrow balcony. A set of stairs wind away out of sight, presumably to the top of the tower. You follow without question, half running and half stumbling through the dust and debris. Turn to **41**.

389

For defeating the witch, you may now help yourself to one of the following rewards:

Gorgon's gaze	Glacial orbit	Death cycle
(talisman)	(necklace)	(ring)
+1 speed +2 brawn	+1 speed +2 brawn	+2 brawn
Ability: petrify	Ability: piercing	Ability: cleave

When you have updated your hero sheet, turn to **538**.

390

With the spiders defeated, you run to the boy's side. He is squirming in pain, his limbs leaving churned furrows in the snow. Pushing back his hood you see that his skin is filmed with sweat, his eyes already glazing over – their life fading.

His body shudders and then lies still.

As you lay him to the ground, you hear a man's guttural roar. Before you can react you feel hands grab your jerkin, then you are tumbling backwards, a weight dragging you through the snow. A woman's voice calls out – but the words are drowned by the smack of cold water closing around you. Hands are suddenly around your throat, tightening, pulling you down.

For a second your attention catches on the fern-like plants at the bottom of the lake, the tips of their feathery fronds glittering with globules of light. At least one mystery has been solved. As for the other . . .

You twist and kick, loosening your assailant's grip just enough to pull him around. You stare into the angered face of a Skard warrior, his long braided hair billowing through the water like a medusa's snakes. Bubbles spill from his nose and mouth as he goes to reach for you again, his intention evidently to drown you in the freezing waters.

But you can't drown the dead.

You clamp hold of his arms, surprising the Skard. Grinning, you watch as he starts to buck and wrestle, the frigid cold of the water quickly stealing whatever breath he still had left.

The scene offers you a moment of curious reflection: to watch a man's life ebbing away before your very eyes. To see his fear. To know that you have bested him – that you have been proven the victor.

It would be so easy just to hold on. To see it through to the end.

No. I am better than this.

You release his arms, watching as he goes kicking upwards. You follow, breaking the surface of the light-flecked waters. The Skard has dragged himself onto the shore, coughing and shivering, his clothing waterlogged. Behind him you see the boy who ran from the spiders, his eyes glaring at you with a mixture of fear and anger. By his side stands a woman, bent with age, her face weather-worn and creased. A few white whiskers protrude from her upper lip. In her gnarled hands she holds a staff, carved from bone and wrapped with dyed leathers.

'Verka! Verka!' The boy is pointing at you, tugging on the woman's sleeve. She nods, her grey eyes narrowing.

The Skard warrior has tugged a knife from his belt, turning to face you with teeth bared. You merely watch him with a cold detachment as you rise up out of the lake, using your magic to lift you back to the shore. As you alight on the rocks you look down at the gathering of Skards, awaiting their next move. Your hands settle warily on your weapons.

Only then do you realise that they are all staring at your chest – and the necklace of bear claws that Taulu gave you before he was killed.

'You have what belongs to us,' says the woman, her voice unusually deep and resonant for one so frail-looking. Her use of the common tongue also surprises you. 'How did you come upon such a thing? Did you kill him?'

You step down from the rocks, forcing the boy to skitter away. The woman holds her ground, the warrior edging closer to her, his hand still tight around his dagger. 'Taulu gave this to me. I did not end his life. That was down to another – one he called the witch.'

The warrior's eyes widen. He looks nervously at the woman, awaiting her response.

'Smurt Imnek!' hisses the boy, finding his confidence again. He stabs a finger at you. 'Smurt Imnek!'

You glance at the woman.

'He says you killed the boy. His name was Imnek, second son of Vierlod Eddervun.' The woman nudges one of the spiders with the end of her staff. 'Is this true? Speak of what happened.'

You recount your discovery of the boys and the fight by the lakeside. The woman translates to her two companions. When you mention the second boy running, the warrior's face darkens with anger. He rises to his feet, pushing his dagger into his belt. Then he grabs the child roughly, gripping him by his ear. The boy gives a whimpering cry of pain. Words are exchanged, the man obviously berating the boy for his cowardice.

The woman cuts over them, giving a sharp order. 'Pul tista dek. Imnek it fader.'

The male hisses, then quickly acquiesces to her command, stooping to pick up the dead boy.

Satisfied, the woman's grey eyes shift back to you. 'I am Sura of clan Bear. You will come with us.' She speaks in the same authoritative tone that she used for the warrior. 'You will meet with Taulu's brother. You will do this.'

The woman doesn't wait for a response. She turns and heads up the bank, moving with the surety and stride of someone half her years. The warrior follows, spitting into the snow at your feet. His evident distrust is shared by the boy, who stays close to the man's side, glowering at you with a sulky frown.

You glance up at the darkening violent-streaked skies. It seems the tranquillity of twilight is over – and a storm is on its way. Stepping over the corpses of the spiders, you trail behind the three Skards as they head out over the snow-whipped plains. Turn to 307.

391

From your vantage point, you can see the cart and one of the Skards standing next to it – the tall warrior who spoke with Kirk. There is no sign of the other hunter or his dogs, which provides some small relief.

While you debate your next move, the Skard pulls a short wand-like object from his belt. He steps closer to the cart, holding it out towards one of the barrels. Suddenly, the end of the wand ignites, glowing with a brilliant red flame. In alarm, you realise his intentions – he is going to set fire to the cart and the barrels of tar!

If you have the word *resolve* on your hero sheet, turn to 340. Otherwise, turn to 300.

392

As you cross the chamber, the door suddenly creaks open of its own accord. From the room beyond you hear a man's voice, raised in anger. 'No! I will not serve you, Zabarach! I will not!' There is a cry of pain, then the sound of metal scraping across stone. Gripping your weapons, you edge slowly into the next room. Turn to 548.

393

Clumps of rotted meat litter the cavern floor. Searching through the remains of the mutated creature, you find one of the following items:

Entrapment	Green mile	Longest yard
(ring)	(feet)	(left hand: grapple)
+2 brawn +2 magic	+1 speed +2 magic	+2 speed +3 brawn
Ability: immobilise	Ability: sidestep	Ability: barbs
		(requirement: rogue)

Talia has pulled her scarf back over her nose. Returning to one of the worktables, she snatches up a sheet of parchment and begins to roll it up.

'What's that?' you ask with annoyance. 'What's really going on here, Talia?'

The bard's eyebrows knit together. 'I told you, Mandaleev was a chemist. I got what I came for, now let's go.'

You grab her arm as she walks past you. 'What's in those canisters? Are they dangerous?'

Talia struggles against your grip, then appears to surrender, slumping her shoulders. 'Okay, sweet pea. I was hired to obtain a formula for the virus that Mandaleev was working on. It's a weapon, a very deadly and powerful weapon. But I don't care about that – I care about my own life and making a better one for my daughter. So, if you would be so kind.'

'Daughter?'

'Yes, I'm getting paid a handsome fee for this, honey. Enough that I don't have to risk my neck again. Trust me, disappearing has its price. And those,' she nods to the canisters, leaking yellow smoke into the cave, 'are probably what Mandaleev hoped would transport his virus. Look, relax. I'm going to lock this place up. No one will ever know.'

Will you:

Insist Talia destroys the chemical formula?	752
Let Talia take the chemical formula?	89

394

You can use the forge to craft your own magical weapons. For each weapon, you will need a special backpack item. If you have the required item/s, you can make the associated weapon:

Blighted blaster	Northern legacy
(left hand: wand)	(main hand: staff)
+2 speed +3 magic	+2 speed +4 magic
Ability: charm	Ability: charm
(requirement: Fenrir's fang)	(requirement: giant's backbone)

These weapons can then be improved using further items from your backpack. (NOTE: When an item is used, it must be removed from your hero sheet. Items can only be used once.) The bonuses include:

Item	Bonus (added to chosen weapon)
Winter diamond	special ability: *wind chill*
Kraken oil	special ability: *agility*
Venomous ooze	special ability: *blind*
Maggorath's rot	special ability: *decay*

You may return to the frost forge any time between quests, to craft items or add abilities (make a note of this entry number on your hero sheet). Return to the quest map to continue your adventure.

395

For defeating the rift demon, you may now help yourself to one of the following rewards:

Crimson kernel	Nadir	Maxilla mortis
(talisman)	(left hand: sword)	(ring)
+1 armour	+1 speed +1 brawn	+1 brawn
Ability: critical strike	Ability: rust	Ability: gouge

When you have updated your hero sheet, turn to 503.

396

The rush of cold is sudden and fierce, punching through your chest, freezing your heart and stealing your very last breath. It fills you, numbs you, a coldness so intense that it burns the stone beneath your feet, cracking it to frozen splinters.

If you wish, you may now learn the glaciator career. The glaciator has the following special abilities:

Ice mantle (pa): You may permanently raise your *armour* by 2. You are also immune to any effects/abilities that would lower your *armour* in combat.

Brittle edge (pa): Each time an opponent wins a combat round and rolls for a damage score, your opponent immediately takes 2 damage, ignoring *armour* (whether they cause health damage or not).

When you have made your decision, turn to 677.

You find yourself in a large cavernous chamber illuminated by an eerie green light. It seeps through the cracks in the walls and ceiling, where you glimpse veins of black rock set back into the ice. As you advance warily, weapons drawn, you pass a number of cathedral-like pillars, stretching all the way to the domed ceiling above. They are arranged in regimented rows, suggesting that they were sculptured with a purpose in mind. You examine the nearest one, noticing rune-like glyphs glowing just beneath the surface. Their meaning escapes you.

The vastness of the space is daunting. In places the ceiling is pitted with melt holes, many of which stretch away to distant circles of daylight above. Some appear to channel the wind, filling the chamber with a chorus of ghostly moans. A fear creeps along your spine. Several times you glance over your shoulder, feeling like someone – or something – is following you. But each time you look for any sign of a pursuer, you are presented with nothing more than green-lit ice.

Jumping at ghosts. You berate yourself and head onwards, determined to find some clue as to what happened to the missing explorers.

A noise forces you to turn yet again.

This time you see a man, slumped on the ground, his back resting against one of the pillars. He is huddled in thick furs, his blonde hair matted across his ashen face. Both hands are pressed tight against one of his thighs. A smear of blood trails back around the pillar.

You immediately run to his side.

'What happened?' You kneel next to him, looking down at the leg. You rummage in your pack, wondering if you have anything that may help.

With a hiss the man lifts his hands, a dagger flicking into one of his bloody palms. He holds it to your throat, a wheezing snicker gasping from his mouth.

'Think you'd trick me, eh? You another ghost, come to try your luck?'

You glance down at his leg – there is no wound there. Clearly the blood was not his own.

'I think I was the one who was tricked,' you reply guardedly, meeting the man's pale eyes. 'I'm no ghost – I came looking for explorers. Were you one of them?'

The man appears confused for a second, his gaze dropping to your armour and weapons. 'Is this true?' he rasps, his hand shaking as it grips the dagger.

You nod as best you can with a blade to your throat. 'Tell me what happened here. The blood . . .'

The man lowers his dagger with a sigh. 'Go look for yourself.'

Will you:
Trust the man and follow the bloody trail?	17
Ask him to tell you instead?	466

398

You finally manage to corner the hand between two boxes. Grabbing a sack, you open it out just as the hand makes a leap for you, the ivory fingers balling into a fist. Quickly, you close the sack, holding it out at arm's length while it bulges and shakes. After several minutes of frantic movement, the sack finally hangs still – the hand evidently admitting defeat.

'You're not actually keeping that, are you?' asks Anise, sounding thoroughly disgusted.

'Why not? It might come in handy!'

She shakes her head.

If you wish, you may now take the following item:

Clackers
(backpack)
A skeletal hand
with a mind of its own

You turn back to the dusty storeroom, contemplating your next move.

Will you:

Open a barrel?	156
Climb the rubble to the room above?	272
Retrace your steps and use the stairs?	111

399

Searching the remains of the fire giant, you find 100 gold crowns and one of the following rewards:

Windshear horns	Dragonbone vest	Entropy
(head)	(chest)	(main hand: sword)
+2 speed +2 armour	+2 speed +2 brawn	+2 speed +4 brawn
Ability: piercing	Ability: counter	Ability: deep wound

When you have updated your hero sheet, turn to 705.

400

Skoll strides over to the curving wall of branches, where you notice two objects tangled up amongst the snaking limbs. He rips away the makeshift barrier, freeing the objects. Noting your bemusement he holds them up, one in each hand. Both are made of dark iron and have a single round edge; the rest appears broken, ending in jagged points.

'Fimbulwinter,' states the warrior. 'It was a shield, forged by the Titans. I hoped to find the last piece here, but it has gone. Instead I found the witch – and this . . . trap.'

'Then how do we find the missing piece?' You look past the warrior, to the opening he has made by tearing apart the branches. You can see a distant column of red light, spearing up into the broiling clouds. 'What is *that*?'

Skoll follows your gaze. 'The Well of Urd. A break between worlds – our realm and the shroud. The Titans hold it closed; they sacrificed their spirits to keep it so, but the witch has found a way to weaken their power, if only for a brief time.'

You tilt your head, taking in the turbulent sea of cloud. 'She is summoning demons from the shroud?'

Skoll nods. 'To aid her in freeing the world serpent – the creature that will destroy our realm. You know little of this task. Why did you come here?'

'Sura,' you answer, after a brief pause. 'A shaman. She believed in you – that you would reunite the tribes.'

'And you were crazy enough to listen to a shaman?' He grunts with amusement. 'Come.' He stuffs the fragments of the shield under his arm. 'Whatever your cause, it can wait. We must return home – to Vindsvall.' Turn to 292.

401

Rummaging through your pack, you pull out the players' guide. You quickly flick through its pages, reading up on the rules of the game. (Make a note of entry number 776 – you can refer to this entry at any time to study the rules of 'Stones and Bones'.) When you are ready to play, turn to 511.

402

After a tense wait, you see dirt-stained fingers grappling along the tunnel wall, followed by an arm and shoulder, then an angry sweat-soaked face. With a snarl the Skard struggles to free himself, hand fumbling for his knife. Seeing your chance you charge forward, weapons slashing at the prone warrior. It is time to fight:

	Speed	Brawn	Armour	Health
Hunter	2	2	1	35

Special abilities
🛡 **Tight spot**: In the first two combat rounds, the hunter's *speed* is reduced to zero.

If you manage to best this savage hunter, turn to 317. If you lose the combat, remember to record your defeat on your hero sheet. You may then attempt the combat again or return to the map.

403

(Decide which weapon/item of equipment you will place on the podium.) After studying the complex carvings at length, you discern pockets of magic focused in three of the outer circles. One pertains to frost, one to earth magic and the last to the darker shadow arts. By activating the runes around a circle, you will be able to call on the spirits that embody that power.

Will you:

Activate the *frost* runes?	455
Activate the *earth* runes?	569
Activate the *shadow* runes?	595

404

You approach the figure warily, weapon drawn. As you near, you are surprised to see that the man has no physical body, only a translucent green shimmer outlining his features. A ghost. He is leaning over the table, his hand passing back and forth across the wood. He appears to be writing, his lips mouthing something you cannot hear. There is no paper on the table and the man has no writing instrument, and yet he seems intent on his task, moving his hand in a series of erratic motions, no doubt forming letters that you cannot see. Despite your attempts to communicate with the ghost, he remains oblivious to your presence.

If you have a *black feather quill*, turn to 472. Otherwise, turn to 138.

405

Maune's grief-stricken howl is the first sound to greet you as you enter the chamber. He stands over the remains of the dead eagle.

Its head has been severed clean from its shoulders. A trail of blood streaks across the dust, leading up the slope and through the doorway above.

Skoll looks back at you, shrugging his heavy shoulders. 'We're not alone. The wolf you saw . . . it could be another shaman.'

You open out your consciousness, feeling for Nanuk. There is a hazy impression of the wolf, still circling the bear. Its teeth are like shards of midnight, the one yellow eye shining with a bestial cunning. Each time the bear takes a swing, the wolf springs back. Teasing. Mocking.

The same corruption you smelt on the wolf lingers in this chamber. 'Yes, they were here.'

Maune staggers to his feet, drawing the sign of a cross above the mangled remains. 'One God, give us strength. Give us light.'

'We already have our path.' You nod to the blood-spattered earth. 'They want us to follow.'

'Gladly.' Maune pools fire into his fist, then hurries up the slope. Skoll is right behind him. You start to follow, but a stab of pain forces you to stagger. Wincing, you grip your forehead.

'Nanuk . . . ?'

Again, you quest out for the bear – only to be met by claws, teeth and the coppery taste of blood. The two animal spirits are now locked in deadly combat, thrashing through the sand.

'What is it?' Anise puts a comforting hand on your arm, squeezing it tight. 'We should stay with the others.'

Will you:
Follow Maune and Skoll?	**693**
Return to the Norr and aid Nanuk?	**619**

406

You feel a sudden vibration against your back. Removing your pack, you look inside to discover that the book *Hergest's Hauntings* has started to glow with a ghostly white light. You pull it out and flick through the pages, until you arrive at a section labelled Ryker's Island. Following the author's directions, you uncover a hidden niche behind one of the beer barrels. You crawl into the space, scrabbling over loose rock and animal droppings, to eventually find yourself in a tight crevasse that runs alongside the cellar.

Here, tucked between two rocks, is a metal chest. You crawl forward and pull it free. Flipping open the lid, you discover a pile of gold coins and a large fist-sized ruby hidden inside. (Congratulations, you have gained 50 gold crowns and a *flawless ruby*. Simply make a note of the ruby on your hero sheet, it doesn't take up backpack space.)

Elated with your finds, you retrace your steps and return to the taproom. Turn to 80.

407

The Skard glares down at you, his scars twisting around his ugly smile. For a moment you see your father standing there, judging you, pitying you for your weakness. Your brother Malden, even as a cripple, mocking you for being a lesser man. Inquisitor Hort, Desnar, Captain Everard – all standing in judgement, weighing your worth, and finding you lacking . . .

Not any more.

You knock his hand away, your leg swinging round to take the Skard in the side. Your blow barely moves the heavy half-giant, but it was only a feint. Magic blooms in your fist, the chill frost of the Norr crackling around you.

Then you expel it with a scream of rage.

The blast almost lifts Skoll off his feet. He wobbles backwards, grunting through the pain. He recovers frighteningly fast – coming at you before you have barely found your feet. You duck beneath his wild swing, hands reaching out for your fallen weapons. They lift up from the ground, slapping into your open palms – just in time to block his follow-up strike. Your weapons tangle with his axe.

You wrestle back and forth, the Skard's strength bearing down on you, forcing you against the wall. Suddenly, his hand is around your throat. You grin back at him, leering, as his fingers pass through your ghostly spirit, finding nothing tangible to hold. Snarling, he draws back his hand, fingers blackened with cold.

You free your weapons, swinging blindly, the force of your magic stoving in his chest plate. He staggers, but is somehow able to get his axe back around. You see its edge, enchanted with runes. Unable to avoid the blow in time, the axe slices across your shoulder, leaving a bright line of scolding agony.

'You still feel pain, ghost!' Skoll presses his attack with renewed vigour.

Desperately you fend off his whirling axe, aware that you have now become turned in the melee. Each blow knocks you closer to the rock's edge, and the precipitous drop to the darkness below. It is time to fight:

	Speed	Brawn	Armour	Health
Drokke	14	7	8	100

Special abilities

🛡 **Northern grit**: Skoll is immune to any abilities that reduce his number of speed dice (such as *curse*, *knockdown* and *webbed*).

🛡 **Berserker frenzy**: Once Skoll's *health* is reduced to 50 or less, he goes into a frenzy. This lowers his *speed* by 1 but increases his *brawn* by 4 for the remainder of the combat.

If you manage to defeat this ferocious Skard, turn to **558**.

408

The wooden guardian has been defeated. You may now help yourself to one of the following special rewards:

Thorn tongue	Fierce amber	Knotted cowl
(left hand: grapple)	(left hand: glass sword)	(head)
+2 speed +2 brawn	+2 speed +3 brawn	+1 speed +1 brawn
Ability: lash	Ability: coup de grâce	Ability: webbed

With little else of interest in the room, you decide to continue onwards. Turn to **13**.

409

You take the lantern and throw it into the hole.

'Run!' Grabbing Anise, you hurry into the adjoining passage, just as an almighty explosion shakes the tower. You hug the wall as wood and mould go flying past you in a billowing cloud. When the air finally begins to clear, you see that you have blown a smoking hole in the previous room, exposing the charred remains of the storeroom below. You doubt there is anything left worth salvaging.

With the creature defeated, you step over the burnt debris and continue along the passageway. (Remove the word *flame* from your hero sheet, then turn to 379.)

410

You can use the forge to craft your own magical weapons. For each weapon, you will need one or two special backpack items. If you have the required item / s, you can make the associated weapon:

Icewind cleaver	Warped edge
(main hand: axe)	(left hand: sword)
+2 speed +4 brawn	+2 speed +4 brawn
Ability: charm	Ability: charm
(requirement: Fenrir's fang and giant's backbone)	(requirement: giant's backbone)

These weapons can then be improved using further items from your backpack. (Note: When an item is used, it must be removed from your hero sheet. Items can only be used once.) The bonuses include:

Item	Bonus (added to chosen weapon)
Winter diamond	special ability: *ice edge*
Kraken oil	special ability: *agility*
Venomous ooze	special ability: *blind*
Maggorath's rot	special ability: *decay*

You may return to the frost forge any time between quests, to craft items or add abilities (make a note of this entry number on your hero sheet). Return to the quest map to continue your adventure.

411

You notice a number of treasures tangled up in the drake's parasitic tentacles. If you wish, you may now take one of the following rewards:

Gram	Ridillvar	Volsung
(left hand: sword)	(head)	(chest)
+2 speed +2 brawn	+1 speed +1 armour	+1 speed +2 armour
Ability: furious sweep	Ability: watchful	Ability: silver frost

You hope, with the death of the corrupted Titan, the explorers and Caul are now finally at peace. After giving the frozen trapper a final nod of farewell, you head into the glacial tunnels – following them back to the surface. (Return to the quest map to continue your adventure.)

412

Rook is beaten back by the speed of your attacks, his feet tangling in the black cloth of his discarded cloak. A kick to the knee sends him sprawling to the ground, his knife skittering across the flagstones.

'I gave you that one,' he sniffs, dabbing at the cut on his lip.

You sheathe your weapons, barely able to stand as the holy inscriptions continue to sap at your strength. 'If this sermon's over,' you rasp, clutching the back of a pew for support, 'can we go somewhere more agreeable?'

Rook rolls to his feet, scooping up his cloak in the same fluid motion. 'Indeed, I think you more than deserve it.'

Congratulations – you have learned the path of the rogue. You may now permanently increase your *health* by 5 (to 35). You have also gained the following special ability:

Scarlet strikes (dm): Automatically inflict damage equal to the total *brawn* of your main hand and left hand weapons to all remaining opponents, ignoring *armour*. *Scarlet strikes* can only be used once per combat.

When you have updated your hero sheet, turn to 75.

413

The skeleton key fits the lock perfectly. Flipping open the lid, you are met by the welcoming sight of gold! You have gained 100 gold crowns. You also discover a secret compartment, which offers up a *chipped emerald* (simply make a note of this on your hero sheet, it doesn't take up backpack space). After pocketing your finds, you leave the clearing and continue your journey. Return to the map.

414

You circle the table, watching the two ghosts. The guard is muttering to himself in dismay, casting furtive glances between his hand of stones and his hooded opponent. There are no bets being placed and no money on the table – you sense there is more at stake here than just a game of stones. You try and see under the hood of the robed ghost, but the cowl hangs low, hiding the ghost's features in shadow. A skeletal hand protrudes from one of the sleeves, gripping its stones in a tight fist.

As you lean over the guard's shoulder to study his stones, he suddenly turns his head, his eyes focusing on you for the first time. 'Can you help me, stranger?' he begs, eyes pleading. 'I have to beat him. If I lose again, my soul will be his!'

If you have the book *Stones & Bones* in your backpack, turn to 510. Otherwise, turn to 132.

Your tarred shoulders are now covered in the roc's feathers. You may upgrade your *cloak* item to the following:

Tar and feathers
(cloak)
+1 speed
Ability: immobilise, charm

When you have updated your hero sheet, turn to 205.

Maune gives you a sharp look. 'You're asking me to believe the demon's lies? He called you Arran, but it cannot be . . .'

Claws punch out from your fingers as you advance towards the paladin. You have come too far to falter now. The paladin's magic will cleanse the fires – restore balance, as the Titans would have wanted.

War has casualties.

'We have to do this.' Your eyes flick to the paladin's sword, then his open hand. Sizing up his defences, his weapons.

Maune lifts his chin, standing proudly. Resolute. 'If you truly are my king, I'm sorry.'

He blurs forward.

The paladin's magic is anathema to you. It burns like the face of the sun, peeling back your dead flesh, driving spears of pain into your skull. You can barely block his sword, the blow sending you reeling back, the bone of your arm splintering under its force. His fist, bright with holy scripture, glances off the side of your head.

You see only light, blinding you with pain. (You must immediately apply one death penalty effect to your hero, see entry 98.)

Through the piercing haze, you see the paladin towering above you – his scowl distorting the lines of scripture carved into his skin. Holy words, taken from Judah's sacred texts. Holy words that spell your death.

'One God, forgive me.' Maune lifts back his arm, angling his sword . . .

A scuffle of feet.

The paladin backsteps as Skoll swings his axe down with a savage roar. Maune catches the crescent blade in his sword's teeth, continuing to swing wide to pull the axe from the warrior's grip. Exactly what the Skard had intended.

The axe was never meant to land. A ruse.

The kick to the chest, however . . .

You watch the final moment play out – oddly silent, save for a scuffle of boots on stone.

Maune teeters on the edge, arms flapping by his sides, then he simply drops from sight. There isn't even a scream. Instead the flames roar with a sudden vigour, reaching higher into the dawn skies. The green becomes flushed with white, the two colours seeming to whirl and coil about each other, as if in some fateful conflict – then the fire rushes forth in flames of the purest blue, the runes around its edge blossoming into silvery hues of light.

A fierce cold fills the chamber.

Ice creeps and sparkles from the pit's edge, spreading like the branches of a tree across the stone floor. Its cold crispness is palpable on the air, snapping around the columns, dressing the statuesque figures in coats of frost.

The transformation takes less than a few moments.

The dead, red earth is gone. Ice sparkles now from every surface, reflecting the blue-white flames that dance from the pit.

'The frost forge,' whispers Skoll with reverence. He drops to one knee beside you, his head bowed. 'The Titan magic lives again.'

You crawl to its edge, scooping up part of the broken shield in your shaking hands. 'Fimbulwinter,' you gasp hoarsely.

Skoll helps you to stand, his eyes carefully averted from the ruin of your face. He picks up the other pieces of the shield. 'We need only hold them in the fires. The magic will remake what was broken.'

A hand on your arm.

You glance sideways, surprised to find even that small movement so difficult. Your eyes feel like lumps of grit, scraping in their sockets.

Anise is at your shoulder, her own gaze focused on the flames. 'We do this together.'

Each of you holds a shard of the shield, extending them into the fire, pushing the pieces together and holding them. The cold heat from the flames licks around the dull metal, suffusing its broken, jagged edges with a soft glow of magic. It ripples across the surface, forming a network of thin veins meeting at its centre in a pale orb. An eye.

'It is done.'

You remove the shield from the fire. To your surprise it feels almost weightless, the metal now faded to a glass-like translucence.

'Fimbulwinter,' smiles Skoll. He removes his hand and Anise follows suit, leaving you holding the shield. 'The Titans lend their aid to our cause.'

Congratulations. You have forged the mythical Titan shield, Fimbulwinter. (Make a note of the keyword *resolute* on your hero sheet.) You have also gained access to the frost forge's magic for the remainder of your adventure. Turn to 82.

417

The guard removes the one of stars from his hand and places it face down on the discard pile. He reaches into the pouch and takes another stone at random. He has now gained the four of stars:

Next, the hooded ghost discards a stone from his own hand and takes another from the bag. A cold, cackling laughter comes from the shadows of his cowl as he studies his new hand.

'What should I do now?' whispers the guard. 'I have a Queen's Wave. This could win me the game.'

Will you:

Discard the one of hearts?	144
Discard the two of moons?	259
Show your current hand?	517

418

The tunnel opens up into a cavernous hollow. Thick vine-like roots hang like stalactites from the ceiling, dripping a steady stream of green-coloured ichor into a pool at its centre. The gloopy substance bubbles and smokes, occasionally belching clouds of toxic steam into the air.

As you approach the edge of the pool, you notice a number of items trapped in the thick green slop. Your boot accidentally lands in a puddle. You draw it back quickly, watching with revulsion as the toxic liquid begins to eat away at the leather, filling your nostrils with an acrid stench.

You back away from the pool, your eyes straying to the tunnel opening at the far side of the chamber. It offers a route onwards, winding away into the innards of the tree.

Will you:

Wade out into the toxic pool?	527
Skirt its edges and continue onwards?	468

419
Legendary monster: Tekksertok the Terrible

You skid down the slope, hoping the valley below will provide shelter from the coming storm. As the ground levels off you find yourself stepping between a myriad of alien shapes breaking out of the low-lying mist. At first you mistake them for ice sculptures, carved by the persistent wind. Then you realise they are bones. Hundreds of them, all resting in teetering structures, like tombstones in a graveyard.

Nanuk pushes into your mind, warning you of danger.

What is it? I don't . . .

Then you sight the creature between the cupped bones of an enormous ribcage. It moves slowly, the ground crunching beneath its weight. As the creature passes your position you can hear its laboured breathing, each exhalation rattling the surrounding structures and sending loose bones skittering across the ice.

You ready your weapons, advancing cautiously towards the beast. The mammoth's body reaches over four metres high, covered in long tresses of grey-black hair. The head is rounded, like a knight's helm, its ridged plate sweeping down past two coiling tusks to form a long leathery trunk. The beast continues to snort great deep breaths as it strides ponderously through the graveyard.

You creep closer, entranced by both the sadness and majesty of this ancient animal, wondering if it has come to this place to die – to finally re-join the spirits of its ancestors. Nanuk pulls at your mind once again, urging you to flee. You cannot understand the cause for such alarm . . .

Until you are hit from behind and sent flying through the air, smashing through several mounds of bones before skidding across the ice. For a moment your vision is blurred, distorting the immense shape that towers above you.

Tekksertok! The word burns in your mind, filled with impressions of pain and terror.

Desperately, you scrabble to your feet, eyes fixed on the ghostly form of the giant mammoth – almost twice the size of the one you have already seen. You realise this behemoth must be a spirit guardian, a protector of this sacred site.

The mammoth throws back its head, the long trunk raised to deliver a thunderous boom. Then the beast drops forward into a full-on charge, clearly intending to gore you with its enormous tusks. It is time to fight:

	Speed	Brawn	Armour	Health
Tekksertok	9	6	4	70

Special abilities

- **Tusk punch**: If Tekksertok rolls a 🎲🎲 for his damage score, he performs a tusk punch. This adds a further two dice to his damage score (3 in total) and reduces your *speed* by 1 for the next combat round only.

- **Trunk whack**: If you roll a double for your attack speed (before or after a reroll), you are hit by the mammoth's trunk. This causes 2 dice of damage, ignoring *armour*, and also lowers your *armour* by 1 (each time) for the duration of the combat.

If you manage to defeat this monstrous mammoth, turn to 540.

420

You raise a hand to get the barman's attention. He sidles over, tucking a scruffy looking cloth into his belt. 'Well, ain't you the pretty one?' he smirks, admiring your armour and weapons. 'A nice show . . . better calibre than the usual merc.' His gaze shifts back to your face, mouth still twitching with amusement. 'Shame about the looks, though – what happen, you try to chew the face off a glacier?'

Will you:

Ask about work?	469
Ask what he knows about Ryker?	692
Ask what he has for sale?	709
Take a seat in one of the alcoves?	634
Listen to the conversation at the bar?	534
Leave?	426

421

The man fights with a berserk frenzy, shrieking and hollering like one of his birds – yet he is weak and malnourished, and easily overcome. As you stand over his ragged body, you catch sight of the dark blood oozing from a gash along your arm. To your surprise, there is no obvious pain.

What am I becoming?

You go to take a breath, but your chest remains tight and constricted. Instead you end up choking, your throat cutting like razors as you spit out a foul-smelling bile. You wipe it against your sleeve, trembling . . . frightened.

It is some time before you are able to calm yourself – to focus on the matter at hand. *Have to get back. Find the others.*

Kneeling next to the corpse, you search the body for anything of use. You may now take one of the following rewards:

Feathered fronds	Birdman's hook	Petrel pelmet
(gloves)	(main hand: dagger)	(head)
+1 brawn +1 magic	+2 brawn	+1 magic
Ability: feint		Ability: focus

If you are wearing the *tarred shoulders*, turn to 149. Otherwise, turn to 114.

422

After navigating the ice humps, your sled drifts back in pursuit of the other racers. Suddenly you hear a deafening crack, then one of the other sleds disappears from view – plummeting through a break in the ice. You have only seconds to react, in order to lead your dog-team safely around the deadly fissure.

You will need to take a challenge test using your *speed* racing attribute:

	Speed
Ice breaker	10

If you are successful, turn to 471. If you fail, turn to 198.

423

You cut bright ribbons from the spectral warrior, darting agilely around his slashing blades. With each blow you hear an ear-piercing screech rending the air – whether from the warrior or the moth itself, you cannot be sure. As the warrior weakens you step past his guard to deliver a killing blow, driving your weapons through the remains of his tattered body.

The final death cry comes from above – an eldritch scream that echoes back from the gnarled walls of the room. You look up to see the moth's body hardening and then crumbling, becoming a cloud of thick grey dust. The particles shower down through the dazzling haze, sparkling like yuletide glitter.

Of the warrior, nothing now remains, save for a rainbow of light sparkling above a rare treasure. You may now help yourself to one of the following:

Mother wing	**Rainbow raiment**	**Colours of the wind**
(cloak)	(chest)	(feet)
+1 speed +1 armour	+1 speed +1 brawn	+1 speed +1 armour
Ability: heal	Ability: blind	Ability: sidestep

If you are carrying the *moth wing*, turn to 704. Otherwise, the room offers nothing of further interest. Cautiously, you cross the beams of light and continue onwards. Turn to 509.

424

The guard removes the one of hearts from his hand and places it face down on the discard pile. He reaches into the pouch and takes another stone at random. He has now gained the two of stars:

He can barely hide his excitement as he shows you the stones. A full house and two crowns is a strong hand. It is now time for his opponent to make his move. Turn to 555.

425

A shriek. A body tumbles past you. You try and grab it, but a sudden lurch of the creature's body spoils your aim, your spectral hand closing round empty air. 'Anise!'

You watch helpless as she rolls along the beast's snaking body, falling further and further away ... Until she is suddenly snatched up by a giant fist. You follow a thickly knotted arm, muscles bulging as they tense, taking her weight – to find another figure clinging to the back of the demon, their other arm wrapped tightly around one of its spines. A burly Skard, blond hair whipped back behind his stone-grey helm. His face is bloodied, caked with filth and dust, and yet you can still make out the criss-crossed ridges of gnarly tissue that line his features.

'Skoll!' The word is barely given voice before it is ripped away by the roaring gale.

The warrior's brow creases as his eyes strain against the brightness and the blasting chill of the wind. 'Luck of the ancestors,' he calls back. 'Together at the end.'

He swings Anise, allowing her to grab a nearby spine. She hugs it tightly, gasping for breath, her eyes shut tight with fear.

Skoll looks back at you and grins, cracking the filth that cakes his face. 'Let us make this a fight worthy of the ballads.' Turn to 777.

426

Torches flicker from sconces along the granite walls, their light trickling along the rivulets of filth and melted snow that run down the track. Here, the mood is solemn, your footfalls echoing back from the stony confines of the ravine. You feel eyes on you the whole time, not only from the occasional passer-by but also the groups of men and women skulking in the archways and alcoves.

Buildings have been carved into the rock – some look little more than squats, with graffiti daubed on walls and refuse piling up outside their doors and windows. One structure is a little grander than the rest, its hollows echoing with music and laughter. A tattered bed-sheet hangs crookedly from an upper-storey balcony, painted with the smeared words 'Jailhouse Rock'.

To your left a sloping pathway tracks around the edge of the outcropping, leading to its summit. A frost-coated skeleton sways back and forth from a noose, a wooden sign clutched in its frozen fingers. It points along the pathway, the scrawled letters spelling 'Prison'.

To your right, past the noise and light of the Jailhouse, the track narrows into a tight alley, reeking of decay and squalor. It leads down to the docks, where you can dimly make out the masts of ships silhouetted against the rust-stained sky.

Will you:

Head towards the prison?	557
Enter 'Jailhouse Rock'?	365
Turn down the alley?	27
Explore the compound?	106

427

The troll looms over you, hammers raised above its horned head. You doubt you will be able to move fast enough to avoid the incoming blow. But the hammers never fall. Instead the troll jerks round, staggering sideways. You notice a ragged shape hanging from its back by a pair of daggers.

With a snorting growl the troll swings round again, trying to shake off its tormentor. Rook scrambles up onto the monster's shoulders, then plunges his daggers into the nape of its neck. He somersaults away, leaving the beast to stumble woozily, blood fountaining across its back.

For a moment, all eyes are focused on the beast – awaiting the inevitable, willing its end.

The air is split by an agonised roar as the troll teeters forward, then begins to fall. You race out from beneath the widening shadow, hearing the rush of air getting stronger. There is a thunderous boom, followed by a wave of stinging grit. Once it has passed, you look back to see the immense creature lying sprawled at the centre of a ruined crater. Rook steps around its edge, brushing the grime from his clothing.

'Another one bites the dust.'

If you are a warrior or a rogue, turn to 470. If you are a mage, turn to 96.

428

You can use the forge to craft your own magical weapons. For each weapon, you will need one special backpack item. If you have the required item, you can make the associated weapon:

Deathmist needle	Warped edge
(main hand: dagger)	(left hand: sword)
+2 speed +4 brawn	+2 speed +4 brawn
Ability: charm	Ability: charm
(requirement: Fenrir's fang)	(requirement: giant's backbone)

These weapons can then be improved using further items from your backpack. (Note: When an item is used, it must be removed from your hero sheet. Items can only be used once.) The bonuses include:

Item	Bonus (added to chosen weapon)
Winter diamond	special ability: *ice edge*
Kraken oil	special ability: *agility*
Venomous ooze	special ability: *blind*
Maggorath's rot	special ability: *decay*

You may return to the frost forge any time between quests, to craft items or add abilities (make a note of this entry number on your hero sheet). Return to the quest map to continue your adventure.

429

You push the stones aside, freeing the banner. As you lift it up, you see that the cloth is still bound to an iron cross-piece. Searching amongst the rest of the debris, you find a rusted support bolted to the stone. The wind continues to pound against you, making every effort twice as hard. It is several minutes before you are able to push the end of the pole into the support. Then you step away, gesturing for Anise to light the frayed edge of the banner using her torch. But, to your dismay, the magical fire does not catch. At first you assume it is just the wind, then you remember that the blue flames don't give off any heat. 'It's no good,' says Anise, stepping back from the banner, her shoulders slumped in defeat. 'We failed.' Turn to 580.

Seethe lies sprawled across the rocks, his breath rattling in his throat. The savage wounds he has sustained have finally taken their toll. You slip your mind free from Nidhogg, letting the dragon resume control of his own body – to deliver the final death blow to his own brother, who chose to side with Melusine and let his kind be enslaved to her will.

With the deed done, you jump down from the dragon's back to re-join Anise and Skoll. Both are still speechless from the spectacle they have witnessed. You simply nod with exhaustion, sagging against the rocks to regain your power; feeling every inch of your heavy, dead weight.

For defeating the elder dragon, you have gained the following special reward:

Venomous ooze
(backpack)
Freshly squeezed from the
glands of a corrupted dragon

A narrow pathway zigzags up the side of the mountain, leading to an angular doorway carved into the rock. Anise and Skoll have already started towards it. You pause, turning back to the dragon. His wounds are extensive, much of his body raked and burnt. And yet, there is a semblance of a smile on the dragon's face.

Thank you. You have given me what I desired most.

'Revenge.' You nod. 'I know its craving well.'

The battle is far from over. When you have need of me . . .

You pat the horn that hangs at your waist. 'I know. We will fight again, my friend, I promise.'

You share a parting nod before heading after the others, your eyes drawn to the glowing peak high above. (Return to the map to continue your journey.)

Claws leap from your fingertips as Nanuk guides your hands, urging you to a point to the right of the demon's scaled back. You rip into the hard flesh, pulling apart bone and tissue to reach the frozen heart. Tearing it free, you hold the trophy aloft, its frosted blood dripping down your arms.

If you wish, you may equip the demon's heart and learn the valkryn career:

Syn's heart
(left hand: unique)
+2 speed +2 magic
Ability: silver frost
(requirement: mage)

The valkryn has the following special abilities:

Frost hound (dm): (requires Syn's heart) When you defeat an opponent, you can transform the corpse into a frost hound. The hound will immediately attack another single opponent, inflicting 2 damage per round (ignoring *armour*) for the duration of the combat. You can only use this ability once per combat, to summon a single hound.

Crystal armour (mo): (requires Syn's heart) Instead of rolling for a damage score, you can cast *crystal armour* to coat yourself in barbed ice. This raises your *armour* by 3 and also inflicts 1 damage to all opponents at the end of every combat round. Once *crystal armour* is cast, if you lose a combat round and are unable to avoid your opponent's attack (by using dodge abilities such as *sidestep* or *vanish*), then you must roll a die:

⚀ or ⚁: Your crystal armour is shattered, inflicting 4 damage to your hero.

⚂ or ⚃: Your crystal armour is shattered, but you suffer no damage.

⚄ or ⚅: Your crystal armour is unharmed.

(Note: If your crystal armour is shattered, you no longer benefit from its ability/powers for the remainder of the combat.) When you have made your decision, turn to 602.

432

'Well, I got three left, as yer can see.' The man folds his arms, looking proudly along the row of sleds. 'I'll cut you the best deal I can, but I'll be straight with yer – there's no one else gonna be selling sleds in Ryker's – so you can love it or lump it, your choice.'

If you wish, you may purchase one of the following sleds (Note: you may replace an existing sled with a new one, but all sled upgrades will be lost):

	Speed	Stability	Toughness
Northern light (100 gc):	2	2	1
Tundra runner (180 gc):	2	4	2
Glacier's edge: (240 gc):	2	5	3

(Remember to record the details of your sled on the second part of your hero sheet.) You may ask about sled upgrades (turn to 322) or explore the rest of the compound (turn to 106).

433

Your eyes dart to the paladin's stash, and its promise of food and water. Life for Anise. You drop your weapons by your side, letting your anger subside.

'I see you have supplies,' you gesture to the pack. 'We are hungry. We have another with us, a girl. We desperately need food and water.'

Skoll glares at you questioningly, probably sensing some ruse on your part. His hand is still gripped tight around his axe.

You catch his eye. 'For Anise,' you whisper.

The paladin nods. 'I have little, but enough to restore your party's strength. If I may?' He is still watching the Skard, awaiting his reaction.

'Thank you.' Your words are meant for the both of you. Your insistent stare is only for Skoll.

The warrior grumbles something next to you, some curse in Skard. But there is no conviction to it. His shoulders are slumped, resigned to surrender.

'Food,' he sighs. 'One meal.' His eyes flick to the bird. 'Then that cursed thing can eat me for all I care.'

Maune moves towards his pack, patting the bird as he passes. 'Come. Let us attend to your needs, then. The One God provides for all.' Turn to 21.

434

You squeeze through the narrow space, your eyes adjusting quickly to the gloom. Thankfully, the tremors appear to have stopped – for now.

After several hundred metres, the crack widens into a rubble-strewn opening. Clambering over the rocks, you freeze when you hear voices from the cave ahead. Cautiously, you creep forward to get a better view.

You have emerged in a natural cave, with a high ceiling dripping with glowing stalactites. A group of goblins are gathered around an area of rubble to the left of the cave. The largest is grunting with exertion as he squeezes his arm between a space in the rocks.

'I is almost there,' he mutters, sweat and grime glistening on his yellow-green skin.

Two of the smaller goblins are trying to pull away the surrounding stones, without a great deal of success. A fourth is cowering underneath a dented shield, casting wary glances at the ceiling.

Across the other side of the cave is a slope leading up to another tunnel. Reaching it shouldn't be too difficult with all the rocks and boulders strewn across the room.

Will you:

Surprise and attack the goblins?	**567**
Attempt to creep past them?	**493**

435

You crash down onto hard-packed earth, sending clouds of red dust billowing into the dry air. Spitting out a mouthful of dirt, you roll over onto your back, eyes scanning across crimson skies and the torn wreckage of your surroundings. Flames lick around the burnt hulks of metal machines, their shape and function alien to you. Oily waters lap close to the sandy shore, its wide span overshadowed by a broken bridge, its twisted girders bent like broken fingers.

'Wake up!' you croak, coughing on the dry dust. 'All I need to do is wake up.'

A noise. A clatter of metal.

Long spindly fingers close over the torn wreckage. Then a pair of pale arms twist into view, pulling a thin body behind them. The demon is little more than a skeleton, its skin drawn tight over ragged bone. There is no face. Instead, a wedge-shaped mask of mirrored metal is nailed to its head – smooth and featureless, save for your own terrified visage staring back at you.

'She won't thank me for this,' hisses the now-familiar voice. 'But your soul is too tempting. Too delicious. Playtime is over, and now it's time to feast!'

You hear the crash of shifting debris. Frantically, you glance to your right, to see two ugly, scaled brutes clambering onto one of the wrecks. They have wide toad-like faces, their fat bodies bubbling with giant pustules. You watch in revulsion as the pustules grow bigger, then one of them bursts, depositing a squirming reptilian creature onto the soil. Another breaks open, releasing a second. These small parasitic horrors rise up on bowed legs, tongues licking between sharp fangs. More are starting to appear, squirming to free themselves from their toad-like hosts.

You drag your attention back to the demon. It is crawling towards you, its mirror-like mask reflecting the tortured landscape. 'Look, look and see,' the demon jeers. 'The end of all worlds, the end of everything!' It is time to fight:

	Speed	Magic	Armour	Health
Insidious	10	6	6	70
Seeper	10	5	5	20
Seeper	10	5	5	20
Parasite	9	4	3	8
Parasite	9	4	3	8

Special abilities

🟣 **Endless tide**: At the start of each combat round after the first, each seeper will produce another parasite, with the same stats as above. If a seeper is reduced to zero *health*, they can no longer produce parasites – but any parasites already in play will continue to attack.

🟣 **Sinister arts**: Each time you take health damage from Insidious you must sacrifice an unused ability of your choosing or else take an extra 5 damage, ignoring *armour*. A sacrificed ability cannot be used for the remainder of the combat.

🟣 **Parasitic pests**: At the end of every combat round, you must take 1 damage, ignoring *armour*, from each parasite currently in play.

To win the combat, you must defeat all opponents (including any parasites currently in play). If you are able to defeat this menacing horde, turn to 771.

436

You feel a buzzing sensation emanating from your backpack. Opening it up, you discover that the book *Hergest's Hauntings* has started to glow with a ghostly white light. Quickly, you flick through the pages until you arrive at a section labelled Ryker's Island. Following the author's directions, you uncover a loose stone in one of the nearby cells. By pulling it out of the wall, you reveal a secret crawl space.

You scramble along the tunnel, until it widens into a jagged cleft of black rock. The floor is panelled with iron, leaking sickly-yellow vapours through open vents. The putrid smoke seems to be coming from a hidden room below. Despite your best efforts, the grilles cannot be removed. Instead, you focus on the cleft itself.

Ahead is an area that looks like a nest. Dirty rags and gnarled bones form makeshift bedding, on top of which are various pilfered items, some looking half-chewed. As you are about to investigate further, you hear the pattering of tiny feet behind you . . .

A swarm of white rats are scampering over the rocks, their albino-red eyes glowing with an insatiable hunger. Each rat has a number stamped on their hind-quarters, suggesting they might have once been test rats. Frantically, you ready your weapons and prepare to take on the frenzied host. It is time to fight:

	Speed	Brawn	Armour	Health
Test rats	5	4	2	20
Test rats	5	4	2	20
Test rats	5	4	2	20

Special abilities

🛡 **Disease**: Once you have taken health damage from a rat's damage score, you must lose a further 2 *health* at the end of each combat round, ignoring *armour*. (You can only be inflicted with *disease* once.)

🛡 **Outnumbered**: At the end of each combat round, you must take 1 damage from each surviving opponent, ignoring *armour*. This ability only applies while you are faced with multiple opponents.

If you manage to defeat these vile vermin, turn to **491**.

437

The necromancer's bones lie strewn across the room, his robes hanging in tatters from your hands. You are still dazed, having little memory of the fight save for fleeting, savage images – teeth biting, nails clawing, fists battering and punching. Somehow the bear was inside you. Its ferocity, its rage had taken over.

You stand, trembling, watching as the cloth slips from your black, bruised fingers.

Whatever power once had a hold of you, it has now drawn back to the recesses of your mind. In its absence, you are left with an aching emptiness – a death-like cold that no heat is able to dispel.

For your victory over the necromancer, you may now help yourself to one of the following rewards:

Lich's gaze	Dread mantle	Grave light
(head)	(cloak)	(ring)
+1 magic	+1 speed +1 brawn	Ability: blind
Ability: insight	Ability: fear	

When you have updated your hero sheet, turn to 283.

438

'Think I'd fall for that one?' growls the guard, snatching you by the collar. 'He ain't got a tab 'ere, Eaton ain't payin' for the party. And you're a dirty liar.'

There are gasps and cries from the party-goers as they watch the guard drag you back into the taproom of the Coracle. He gives you a final shove before turning and heading back into the private room. It appears your attempt to get inside the cellar has failed. Turn to 80.

439

You hack at the wall of roots, severing them with ease. However, as each root comes apart you hear the creak of the branches tightening around the imprisoned warrior. You desperately hasten your efforts, pulling the last of the roots away to push yourself through the gap and into the cell.

But you are too late. The branches have snapped closed around the warrior. His head lolls back on his shoulders, his body hanging lifeless within its thorny prison. As you watch, the warrior's corpse starts to fade – his spirit breaking up into fractured shards of dark light. Within seconds there is no trace of the prisoner, save the gnarled branches that once held him captive.

You turn back to the pedestal – but of the dagger, there is no sign. Evidently it was just an illusion to torment the poor warrior. Searching the cell, you find nothing else of interest. With no other option, you leave and continue your journey. Turn to 6.

440

For defeating the mighty yeti, you may now help yourself to one of the following rewards:

Braveheart mantle	Chest beaters	Big foot
(cloak)	(chest)	(feet)
+1 speed +2 brawn	+1 speed +2 brawn	+1 speed +1 brawn
Ability: savage call	Ability: knockdown	Ability: rebound

You have also gained a *sasquatch pelt* (simply make a note of this on your hero sheet, it doesn't take up backpack space). When you have updated your sheet, turn to 631.

441

The guard removes the three of stars from his hand and places it face down on the discard pile. He reaches into the pouch and takes another stone at random. He has now gained the two of stars:

The guard rubs his chin thoughtfully. 'Still a fool's pair,' he whispers out of the corner of his mouth. 'Let's hope it is enough to win.' Turn to 570.

442

You hit the pool with a painful thwack, bones splintering and muscles ripping free of their tendons as you plunge into its dark, bubbling depths. (You must roll twice on the death penalty chart and immediately apply the effects to your hero. You must also lose one backpack item.) Then turn to 696.

443

You let your weapons fall to the ground, raising empty palms in a show of surrender. Your action surprises the Skard, who hesitates in his advance, his brow furrowing as he looks down at your discarded weapons. One of his companions shouts something, drawing a barking laughter from the other.

'Fegis!' The hunter echoes their name-call, spitting with derision.

You shake your head, trying to indicate you don't understand.

He steps forward, raising his boot and kicking you in the leg. It drops you to the ground with a painful crunch. When you try and rise, he pushes you down again with the heel of his boot.

'Fegis . . .' he grunts again, shaking his head. He turns and gestures to the shaven-headed hunter. 'Slur den.'

The smaller Skard saunters towards you, his axe resting back on his shoulder. Turn to 656.

444

The palace walls start to flicker and fade, slowly washing away to reveal a void of darkness. All around you the laughter echoes once again, a snickering cruel sound.

'Enough of this!' you bellow in challenge, backing away from the creeping blackness. It is closing in from all sides, eating up the stonework until you are left standing on a rapidly-diminishing island. Your words are met by another peal of laughter.

This way.

A woman's voice. Soft and gentle.

You turn, surprised to see a white rift of light slowly opening against the dark void, spreading wider and wider until it has formed a glowing portal.

This way. The voice becomes more insistent.

The darkness continues to rip away at the stones. Looking down, you are shocked to see the edge is formed out of fingers, hundreds of them, raking the ground with sharp nails, tearing through the very fabric of this dream.

You look back to the light – and make a snap decision. Quickly, you race to the edge of the island and throw yourself out across the abyss. With legs kicking to maintain your momentum you make the distance, hitting the portal of light and passing through into a blinding radiance. Turn to 713.

445

Working together, the keep's defenders whittle away at the demon's defences, gradually slowing and weakening it. Once the beast is on its last legs, Henna delivers the killing blow – sinking her glowing blade into the creature's brain. A blast of noxious air and bile is blown out of the creature's mouth as it breathes its last, then a welcome silence follows.

A lone soldier raises his fist into the air. 'For Valeron!' he calls defiantly. 'For Glory!'

His mantra is quickly picked up by the surviving guardsmen, accompanied by an echoing clamour of victorious cheers. If you are a warrior, turn to 553. If you are a rogue, turn to 395. If you are a mage, turn to 57.

446

You place the 'three of snakes' on the discard pile and pick a new stone from the bag. You have gained the 'two of moons'.

You have the following stones:

The monk decides to play his hand. Turn to 593.

Quest: The bear necessities

Twilight can last for hours in the north, the pale light of day giving way to green and blue hues then slowly darkening to a vivid purple. In those hours, there is almost a serene beauty to the expansive, snowy plains – a tranquil calm before the night comes, and with it the inevitable blizzards that sweep across the ice, unleashing their cruel fury without remorse.

Twilight, when there is a moment of peace, a time when you can almost appreciate the wonders of the landscape. Like the lake that stretches out before you, its sparkling waters aglow with dancing lights.

You veer from your intended course, keen to discover what phenomena might be responsible for the peculiar display. However, a splash and a disturbance on the water forces you to duck for cover, falling into a crouch behind a mound of wind-blown snow.

The sound of children laughing.

You raise your head, quickly scanning the banks of the lake. Two boys are crouched by the water's edge, both clad in thick animal furs. They appear captivated by the same lights sparkling up from the lake's depths – one holds a spear and is prodding its shaft into the water, goaded by his companion.

They must be Skards. Both look no older than ten – the child with the spear is the brawnier of the two, with dark brown hair braided into plaits. The other is red-haired and freckled, giggling as he points to the swirling motes of light.

Distracted, neither child has spotted the predators moving quickly across the rocks behind them. Three multi-legged creatures, each a metre in length, resembling white-translucent spiders. You leap up and shout out a warning.

Both boys look up, mouths falling open in surprise. They don't see the first spider pounce. It lands on the ginger-haired boy, its legs wrapping around his chest. He screams and squeals as the mandibles pierce through his leathers.

The other boy starts forward to aid his friend, but draws back when he sees the other pair of spiders dashing in. He throws his spear in haste, missing his target. Left unarmed, he turns and runs, ignoring his companion's screams.

You race around the lake, fearing you may be too late to save the boy's life. The two spiders immediately turn and scuttle towards you, their mandibles dripping with a blue-tinged poison. The third quickly releases the Skard's limp body, then rushes to join its companions. It is time to fight:

	Speed	Brawn	Armour	Health
Water spider	5	4	3	20
Water spider	5	3	3	20
Water spider	5	3	3	20

Special abilities

🦋 **Paralysis**: If you suffer health damage from a spider's damage score, you cannot use special abilities in the next combat round (passive effects that are already in play will continue to do damage).

🦋 **Outnumbered**: At the end of each combat round, you must take 1 damage from each surviving opponent, ignoring *armour*. This ability only applies while you are faced with multiple opponents.

If you manage to defeat these multi-legged monsters, turn to 390.

448

After a frantic battle, you finally stand over the zombies' remains. Instead of feeling elation at having survived another battle, your mind is troubled by yet more nagging doubts. You prod one of the bodies, noting the grey pallor of its dead skin and the black blood that pools around your feet. Their condition is not unlike your own – bodies without a life, without a heart. You squeeze at a cut along your arm, watching as a similar black blood oozes between your fingers.

'Perhaps I will share their fate,' you whisper to yourself.

Anise steps past you, shaking her head. 'What magic could have done this?' The blue light from her torch illuminates the true extent of the grisly scene. 'These men should have been left in peace, not made to live like animals.'

You look away from the cadavers, not wishing to be reminded of what you might become. Instead you focus on the rest of the room. Next to the right hand wall is the broken remains of a table and what might have been a chest. Amongst the debris, you discover a black-bladed axe – its edge still sharp and untarnished – a wand fashioned from bones that hum with magic, and a pewter tankard with an inscription on the bottom that reads: *Sore head, like lead, come morning I'll dread – now drink, don't think, another let's sink.*

You may now take one of the following rewards:

Decapitator	Rattle and hum	Last orders
(main hand: axe)	(left hand: wand)	(talisman)
+1 speed +1 brawn	+1 magic	Ability: punch drunk
Ability: cleave	Ability: boneshaker	

A door in the opposite wall creaks open of its own accord. From the room beyond you hear a man's voice, raised in anger. 'No! I will not serve you, Zabarach! I will not!' There is a cry of pain, then the sound of metal scraping across stone. Gripping your weapons, you edge slowly into the next room. Turn to 548.

449

With a deafening screech, the wraith's body shatters into a shower of ice crystals. You step back, watching as the tiny fragments splinter across the floor, joining the jagged pieces of stone from the broken mirrors. Caul whistles through his teeth, shaking his head.

'I don't want to say I told you—'

'Don't.' You fix him with a cold stare, pushing your weapons back into their bindings.

Caul's lips slowly twist into a smile. 'Just glad you're on my side.' He steps around the debris, where you notice a number of items glowing faintly with magic. 'Least this detour wasn't a complete waste. Now these I certainly ain't touching, but I'm sure it won't stop the likes of you.'

You may now take one of the following rewards:

Wraith shard	Whispering shroud	Phantom menace
(left hand: dagger)	(chest)	(necklace)
+1 speed +2 brawn	+1 speed +1 magic	+1 brawn +1 magic
Ability: silver frost	Ability: curse	Ability: phantom
(requirement: rogue)	(requirement: mage)	

With nothing else of interest in the chamber, you head back along the tunnel and take the stairs down to the cave. Turn to 474.

450

'It's late and I got duties to attend to.' Jackson gives a snotty-sounding sniffle. 'Me good lassie's waiting for me, all sweet and promisin' like. Sleek black body, '87 vintage.' A hacking laughter resounds from behind the wall. 'One of the perks of the job. Highland Black. Whole crate right next to me and it ain't getting drunk on its own. So, wag that tongue of yours and get on with it.'

Will you:

Ask about getting home?	508
Ask about places of interest?	463
Tell him about what happened at the keep?	559
Ask if he has any work?	624
Discuss something else?	685

451

You attempt to confuse the guards. 'But today isn't Dilain,' you complain, frowning. 'What was yesterday again?

The half-goblin looks to his young companion, shuffling his feet nervously. 'You remember, Hub? I dunno, think that was Sol. But that would make today Ullir.'

'So what was the password for Ullir?' you ask quickly, hoping to catch them off guard.

To fool the confused duo, you will need to pass a *speed* challenge:

If you are successful, the bumbling guards provide you with a password allowing you into the prison (turn to 33). Otherwise, they are not fooled by your ploy. You promise to return at a later date. Turn to 426.

452

'Look around you.' Skoll gestures to the ruined hall and the crevasses running through the glacier. 'Jormungdar is an ancient demon, trapped beneath the ground. With every passing winter the magic that holds the serpent prisoner is weakening. What we have seen is only the start – one day, it will break free.'

You close your eyes, trying to stem the sudden tide of memories – the images, the faces, the many lives that were lost that fateful day at Bitter Keep. 'We never knew . . .' you rasp hoarsely, the words sticking in your throat. 'We were never prepared . . .'

'Our people are the same. We wake each morning to know the land is ours. We believe it will be here for our children and their children, and those that come after . . . ' Skoll casts his eyes across the blue-washed ice. 'It has always been the witch's plan to free the serpent. She wishes only to destroy; to break the land and leave it to ruin.' He steps to the edge of the glacier, the wind tugging at his fur-trimmed cloak. 'Look and remember, Bearclaw. This is all we have. When the land is gone, we have nothing.'

Return to 602 to ask another question or turn to 326 to end the conversation.

453

You push the stones aside, freeing the banner. As you lift it up, you see that the cloth is still bound to an iron cross-piece. Searching amongst the rest of the debris, you find a rusted support, bolted to the stone. The wind continues to pound against you, making every effort twice as hard. It is several minutes before you are able to get a flame to catch – and then to grow, lighting up the frayed banner fabric.

Anise helps you to lift the standard, pushing the end of the pole into the old support. Then you step away, watching as cinders swirl up into the night sky, the standard slowly engulfed by the roaring flames. Turn to 580.

454

For defeating the captain, you may now help yourself to one of the following rewards:

Mako's bite	Diving bell	Captain's coat
(main hand: axe)	(head)	(chest)
+2 speed +3 brawn	+2 speed +2 armour	+2 speed +2 brawn
Ability: revenge	Ability: pain sink	Ability: overpower

When you have updated your hero sheet, turn to 479.

455

Raising your hands, you trace the circular patterns with your fingers, connecting the lines and whorls with the magic that now flows through you. The runes start to flicker and then glow, illuminating a trail to the centre circle, where white-blue energies crackle above the podium. For a brief moment you glimpse some creature trapped within the bright maelstrom – a thin and spindly humanoid, its pale limbs coated in jagged icicles – then it is gone. The energy sparks out and the runes dim.

When you walk over to the podium you discover that your item is now covered in a layer of frost, sparkling with hook-like barbs. (Congratulations! Your chosen weapon/item of equipment now has the *thorns* ability.) When you have updated your hero sheet, turn to 684.

You scrabble in the dust for the final key then lunge towards the door, ducking to avoid a snapping snake head. Pushing the key into the lock, you are relieved to hear a gratifying click. The blustery smoke vanishes – the snakes dispersing into harmless wisps. Then a crack of light splits the door, widening as the panels swing open, revealing a small cavity and three podiums of rock. On each one is a treasure and a glowing tablet of stone.

You may now take one of the following items:

Thought knots	Robes of meditation	Sage's key
(cloak)	(chest)	(talisman)
+2 speed +1 brawn	+2 speed +2 magic	+1 speed +5 health
Ability: trickster	Ability: recall	Ability: evade

You may also choose one of the following runes:

Rune of winter	Rune of protection	Rune of shadows
(special: rune)	(special: rune)	(special: rune)
Use on any item to	Use on any item to	Use on any item to
add the special ability	add the special ability	add the special ability
silver frost	*iron will*	*vanish*

Once you have updated your hero sheet, turn to 444.

457

The woman draws your attention instantly, her feathered hat bobbing above the heads of the nearby patrons. Likewise her coat of bright crimson, embroidered with golden thread, provides a striking contrast to the drab shades of grey and brown.

'Talia! My Talia!' A young man, his face flushed with drink, reaches out drunkenly to grab her waist. 'Give us a song – a love song, what d'ya say?'

The woman is plump and middle-aged, her locks of brown hair

paling to grey. Nevertheless, she moves with a light grace, swinging her hips away from his groping fingers. 'Not today, sweet thing,' she chirps playfully.

His face sours. 'Then come here and give us a kiss. I'll pay yer a coin for it – and maybe you'll give me a second for free once you seen what I got to offer.'

'Save it for the docks, my dear,' she winks, waving a hand dismissively through the air. 'I hear they're less choosy there.'

The crowd parts for the woman, a few of the men affecting a slow shuffle as they gawp at her ample cleavage heaving against her bodice.

'Oh, put your tongues away,' she jibes, stepping up to the bar. 'At least let a lady have a drink in peace.' Talia removes her hat and places it on the counter, then proceeds to arrange her dishevelled hair.

Eyes turn back to the young man, who has risen from his bench and is staggering towards her. Two of his mean-looking friends move to join him, hands on their knives. They spread out behind the woman. The young man affects a confident saunter as he edges closer.

'Why you turn your back on me, honey?' he drawls, putting his arms round her waist. 'That ain't no way to greet an old friend, is it?' He presses against the woman's back, his head nuzzling into her neck.

'Oh, Wren. How I've missed your ways . . .' Talia lifts a hand to his head, her long fingers playing affectionately with his long greasy hair. A heartbeat. Then her fingers tighten, pulling his head to the side and forcing him to yowl in pain. As deftly as before, she spins round, performing a pirouette, whilst a sword flashes out from the scabbard beneath her coat. Its blade is transparent, like glass, etched on both sides with silvery runes.

'You'd like a song, would you?' she smiles, her head tilted playfully.

Before the ruffian can reply, the woman has brought her sword to her lips. From her mouth comes a sound like a high reverberating hum. You notice the glasses on the table next to you start to rattle across the boards, their contents sloshing back and forth. Back at the bar the woman holds her sword aloft, its blade vibrating with a high-pitched whine.

'Damn witch,' hisses Wren. He rocks on his feet as he attempts to draw his sword. His friends watch in dismay, then slowly start to back away.

Talia moves quickly, her wrist flicking round in a dazzling blur of brightness. You hear the ping of shirt buttons and a rip of cloth. The woman steps away, leaning her head to the side to admire her handiwork. The man's shirt has been cut open, flapping around his protruding beer belly. Angrily, he draws his sword and makes a reckless stab in her direction. Somehow the woman is already moving, darting past his attack, her own blade still humming with energy. Again, a series of fast strokes cut the air, leaving a dizzying after-glow in their wake.

The man stumbles into the bar as his breeches fall down around his ankles.

Talia sheathes her sword, her gaze dropping to his soiled long johns. She cocks an eyebrow. 'Well sweetie, that's a real disappointment for a lady.'

The taproom fills with a raucous laughter. The woman takes a bow, basking in the applause, while her assailant glares at his companions, who are also hooting and applauding.

'Bloomin' bards!' The young man stoops to pull up his breeches then staggers awkwardly away, muttering under his breath.

The barman slams a mug of ale onto the counter. 'There you go, Talia. Good show.'

'Haven't lost my touch, dear,' she grins, taking the mug. 'And another for my friend.'

The barman glances round, confused. 'Friend?'

Talia's eyes scan the room, then settle on the alcove where you are sitting. 'Over there,' she smiles, pursing her lips. 'I've a little business to attend to.' She snatches up her hat then makes for your table, ignoring the inquisitive stares. Turn to 731.

458

Chunks of rock whip past you as you guide your transport into the thick of the rock belt. Your mind link allows you to use your magic to make the necessary adjustments to speed and bearing. Within moments you are wheeling and diving past the deadly particles, trying to maintain your speed whilst avoiding the worst of the debris.

To successfully navigate the rock belt, you must take a challenge test using your transport's speed:

If you are successful, turn to 746. If you fail the challenge, turn to 53.

459

When you reach the training yard you find Orrec alone, resting against the pedestal of a statue. As you approach, your eyes wander to the stone-carved figure. You have never really studied it before, your attention usually focused on your sparring partner or the target dummies arranged along the opposite wall. The carving depicts a middle-aged man, resplendent in plated armour, a hunting hawk on one hand and a sword in the other. The royal crest is emblazoned on the man's chest and mirrored in the lattice-work of his crown.

'Glad you could make it.' Orrec straightens. 'In truth, I had my doubts you would come.'

Your eyes remain fixed on the statue – returning your father's stare. You can't help but admire the workmanship. Whoever made it knew your father. The look of conceited disdain in his eyes, the scowl around the puckered lips. Perfect and chilling.

'Well, I didn't drag you here for the conversation.' The warrior snorts a laugh, folding his thick arms as he looks you up and down.

'I'm sorry,' you apologise, tearing your eyes away from your father's disapproving stare. 'I'm here to train. Although I feel your efforts are wasted.'

'You do?' The warrior frowns. He takes a step closer, the light refracting off his highly polished armour. It is the first time you have seen him dressed in anything but pelts and leathers. The armour is ornate and of an unfamiliar design. The shoulder guards are long and ridged, the mail skirt flared and hanging below the knee. The tips of his boots curve upwards, reminding you of a court jester's motley. 'I've watched you improve. There is no doubting you have strength. Endurance, too. Few can go a whole day against the maids without drawing a sweat.' He motions with his eyes to the practice dummies. 'But straw and wood are one thing, flesh and blood is something else.'

You follow him as he circles you, aware that you are the only man in the keep to match him in height and size. 'There's something missing with you,' he says, eyes narrowing. 'Combat has a rhythm. With you, I sense your mind and body are not as one. They are divided – working in opposition.'

You flinch, aware that his insight is probably closer to the mark than he intended.

'Shall we?' He steps away, drawing a sword from the scabbard at his waist. The blade is short and thin, looking comically small in the hands of such an imposing figure. You draw your own weapons. After bowing heads, you begin to spar.

You find yourself lying in the mud several seconds later, the flat of his blade having knocked you near unconscious. You put a hand to your cheek, feeling the cold stickiness of your black blood. Orrec seems unconcerned, waiting for you to get back up.

'You're too stiff.' He moves quickly around you, forcing you to turn, keeping you off balance. 'You need to learn to bend, shift your shoulders and your hips. Connect your thoughts with what your body is doing. Watch me – see what I do.' He darts in with his sword, his blade cutting a blurred line. You duck your head back just in time to avoid the blow. When you offer out a return swing, he dodges to the side, leaving you to cut through empty air. 'Good. That's better. Now, step it up – show me what you've got!' He backs away, nodding for you to come at him again. You glance up at your father's face, feeling his bitter disappointment spearing into your soul, telling you *you're no good*. Spitting into the dirt, you shift your focus to Orrec, determined to prove them both wrong. It is time to fight:

	Speed	Brawn	Armour	Health
Orrec	3	2	3	40

Special abilities

🖤 **Swift steps**: If Orrec wins a combat round and causes health damage to your hero, your opponent's *speed* is raised by 1 for the next combat round only.

🖤 **Sixth sense**: If you play a speed or a combat ability, roll a die. If the result is ⚀ or less, Orrec has evaded your move and its effects are ignored (the ability is still counted as having been used). If the result is ⚁ or more, you may play the ability as normal.

If you are able to defeat Orrec, then turn to 32. Otherwise, you may repeat the combat or choose a different trainer (return to 369 to make your choice.)

460

Your sled has taken a serious battering from the rough crossing. You must permanently reduce your sled's *stability* rating by 2. When you have updated your sheet, turn to 471.

461

'Skoll has been our Drokke for a hundred winters. He led our people – the Ska-inuin – against your walls of stone, to take the lands to the south, to leave the north behind us.'

'No Skard has ever taken the walls of Bitter Keep,' you add, with a hint of pride.

'Oh, he would have,' says the woman with a fierce certainty, 'but we had a greater enemy at our back. The witch.' Sura makes a quick gesture in the air – a ward or ritual, perhaps, to see away bad spirits. 'She steals our winter, puts the fires of Hel into our world. Below us the serpent sleeps, and she seeks to awaken it.'

'A serpent?' You pull an incredulous frown.

Sura's expression becomes hard. 'Do not mock me, boy. Have you not felt it, seen it with your own eyes? The shifting of the land, the shaking of the mountains?'

You fall silent, your mind flashing back to that fateful day at Bitter Keep – the terrible scenes of death and destruction as it fell into the rift. 'Yes,' you croak at last. 'I saw it.'

'Skoll tried to stop her, many winters ago. But she is strong, helped by powerful spirits from the other side. In defeat, he sought the Norr, the spirit world – to find a way to defeat her.'

'He failed . . .' You read the sadness in her tone.

'Yes . . .' Sura takes a deep breath. Her eyes roll back into her head, until only the whites are showing. 'He is lost to us,' she rasps. 'His spirit calls to us, oh it calls . . . in the sigh of the winds, the cry of the tern. But he does not know the way home. He cannot return, his body is without spirit, it is empty . . . cold.' The woman gives a sudden, heaving gasp. She blinks, trying to refocus. 'Where . . . where was I?'

'You were telling me about Skoll.' You lean back, wafting the potent smoke away.

'Ah, yes.' The woman's eyes brighten suddenly. 'He is a mighty warrior, the greatest. Skoll will always be Drokke. He sits at Vindsvall, his body frozen in the ice. The Frost Father. And with him, the Kronas. The crown only a Drokke can wear.'

'*Frozen?*' you gasp.

'A Drokke must die in battle,' she replies sharply. 'Or a curse will befall the people.'

It takes a moment for her words to sink in. 'Wait, so no one else can unite your tribes?'

'A sad truth.' Sura turns her neck, letting the bones crack. 'The Asynjur – the shamans – search for his spirit, but no one has found him. We fear the witch has trapped his soul. And she will not give him back to us.'

Will you:

Ask about the bear necklace?	545
Ask what 'vela styker' means?	587
End the conversation?	575

462

For defeating the abomination, you may now help yourself to one of the following rewards:

Golden feather	Troll's blood (1 use)	Drake thorn
(special)	(backpack)	(special)
Use on a totem, staff or wand to increase its *magic* by 1	Restore 2 *health* at the start of every combat round for one combat	Use on a sword, glass sword, axe or dagger to increase its *brawn* by 1

When you have updated your hero sheet, turn to 733.

463

'What's there to know? Point yourself in any direction and you're gonna find snow and ice and mountains. If you're crazy enough to go North, well, eventually you're gonna hit the North Face. That's a mountain range, tall and impressive enough to warn you that yer at the end of the darn world. That's when sensible people turn back. No one passes the North Face and lives to tell the tale. Particularly if the wicked witch gets you.'

'The witch?' you ask with sudden interest. 'What do you know about the witch?'

There is a grunting snort from behind the wall. 'I was kidding. Just a stupid Skard tale – the white witch who lives in a palace of ice. They think she's a bad 'un – the one to blame for every little problem they ever had in their lives. Pitiful. You know, I think the cold does something to their brains.'

Will you:

Ask another question?	450
Discuss something other than news?	685
Leave?	Return to the map

464

You spot the monk that Talia told you about seated at the end of the table. He is a large man, likely an impressive sight in his youth but now muscle has turned to fat, his flabby face blotched with broken veins from too much drink. He is surrounded by empty kegs and bottles, his heavy-lidded eyes struggling to focus on the stones he is holding. Nevertheless, as he scatters them across the table, revealing their many carved symbols, it appears he has won the game. His opponent mutters a curse, watching sullenly as the pile of gold is scraped towards the monk's half of the table.

As the loser gets up and re-joins his companions, you slip into the now vacant seat. Your eyes settle immediately on the small black book hooked to a chain around his neck – a holy book, its cover inscribed in white-glowing script.

'Would you care to play?' you ask, returning the stones to the bag.

The monk scratches his shaven head, stifling a belch. 'You got gold?' he grunts, struggling to focus his bleary eyes. 'Twenty gold on the table, then we play.'

'I want to raise the stakes,' you reply, nodding to his book. 'I want to play for that.'

The monk puts his hands to his book protectively. 'This is precious,' he slurs, rocking in his chair.

'You've had a lucky night.' You glance down at the monk's winnings – a sizeable hoard of gold. 'I'm sure your luck will hold.'

The monk shrugs his big shoulders. 'Fifty gold to play,' he snorts. 'And my bet is the book.'

If you have fifty gold crowns and wish to stake it on a game, then turn to **574**. Otherwise, you have no choice but to return later. Turn to **80**.

465

You reach up, pulling away the mouldy fronds to get at the soldier's body. As you do so, the growth suddenly expands outwards, forming long root-like tentacles that lock around your arms. Anise screams as you are lifted towards a widening set of jaws that have appeared through the guard's ruptured armour. To break free, you will need to pass a *brawn* or *magic* challenge (using whichever attribute is highest):

	Brawn/Magic
Fungalot's fangs	8

If you are successful, turn to **349**. Otherwise, turn to **294**.

'Not the trustin' sort either,' the man grins, seeming impressed. 'If you'd followed that blood, it would have taken you to the remains of a creature. Ran into a whole darn pack of 'em, chased me out of the deeper caves. Weird-looking things they were, with tentacles and teeth. I'll admit, I don't fright easy, but those critters . . .' He shakes his head, blowing out a sigh. 'Thought I'd try and lose 'em, but one clearly wasn't giving up the fight. So had to rely on my knife. Dirty work it was.'

'Impressive,' you nod, noting he has no wounds of his own.

'Yeah, well,' he shrugs. 'My bravery ain't the point. It's what I saw in the cave. Bodies. Maybe half a dozen. All frozen tight, covered in ice.'

'The explorers!' Your eyes widen. 'I was sent here to find them.'

'You and me both.' The man sighs heavily. 'But for the ice to take them like that, those explorers must have been there a very long time. Months, I'll wager. Maybe even longer.'

'Months?' You baulk, glancing back at the blood trail. 'But Reah . . . Diggory, they . . .'

'This place isn't right.' He looks around, his face twitching nervously. 'I should have turned back when I had the chance. Maybe we both should have.' Turn to 573.

467

After another lacklustre meal of raw meat and dried moss, Skoll and Anise settle down to sleep. You keep watch as you always do, no longer needing food or sleep. Exhaustion quickly takes them both into fitful dreams. They toss and turn, murmuring inaudibly. You find yourself thinking back to the miners' bodies. Nine men, armed and strong, left for dead in these caves.

You lay a fur blanket across an ice-coated rock, then sit to watch over the others. It gives you a sense of pride that you can perform this small task – allowing them to recharge their energies for the next day's march.

The cold of the Norr creeps into you, beckoning you to leave your body and draw yourself away. You resist, shaking your head. *No, Nanuk. I have a duty.*

The pull becomes stronger, like hands closing around your mind, pressing it tight. You struggle against it, sensing that it isn't Nanuk. Some other presence has a hold of you. Before you have a chance to defend yourself, you feel your mind sliding away. *No! I must watch . . . I must protect the others . . .*

Your eyes flash open.

Cold air rushes into your lungs. Your heart thumps against your chest as your body awakens to its shadow of a life. Quickly, you leap to your feet, kicking up a flurry of fine black sand. All around you the haunted landscape of the Norr shimmers into view, lit by the bright flashes from the broiling clouds above.

A roar of warning.

You turn, to see Nanuk bounding towards you. The bear is wounded, one of his back legs oozing magic from several deep cuts. He twists round, looking back the way he came. There, gliding over the black sand, you see three wraith-like spectres clad in tattered robes. They give a piercing shriek, their clawed hands distended towards you.

Nanuk answers with a deep-throated roar, his own claws raking the sand in readiness. You draw your weapons, relishing the chance to fight side-by-side once again. It is time to fight:

	Speed	Magic	Armour	Health
Night terror	9	6	4	40
Night terror	9	5	4	30
Night terror	9	5	4	30

Special abilities

🖤 **Shiver strike**: If you take health damage from a night terror's damage score, you must lower your *speed* by 2 for the next combat round only.

🖤 **Terror incarnate**: At the end of every combat round, you must take 1 damage from each surviving night terror, ignoring *armour*.

🖤 **Bear power!**: Nanuk adds 2 to your damage score for the duration of this combat.

If you manage to defeat this terrible trio, turn to 501.

468

The tunnel bores up into the trunk of the tree. It is difficult to discern what fashioned the passageway – some parts look like they were gouged out of the wood by claws and teeth while other sections are perfectly smooth, suggesting some form of magic may have been used in its crafting.

The tunnel becomes steeper, until you are forced to use a dangling trail of roots to help you climb an almost vertical wall. You find yourself scrabbling out of a hole into a wide chamber. The ceiling and walls are covered in thick knotted roots, some the size of cathedral columns. They look like they have woven themselves together, criss-crossing each other as they wind down to the floor.

The rotting remains of a creature lie scattered nearby. It is almost skeletal, the flesh having been picked away to leave bare bones threaded with sinew. As you pull yourself out of the hole, you hear a creaking and groaning from above. Looking up, you give a horrified gasp – a set of roots are uncoiling themselves from the ceiling. Slowly, they lower themselves towards the rotted creature, curling around the bones and the sinewy threads that hold it together.

With a rattling crack the roots lift themselves into the air, the creature's body rising up with them. You watch in astonishment as the roots shift and re-arrange themselves, causing the monster's rotted limbs to twitch like a marionette. A root snaps around its head, lifting it forward, while another tugs open its mouth, revealing sharp glistening fangs. Then the rest of the roots buck and jump, sending the arms and legs dancing madly as the grisly puppet pirouettes towards you. It is time to fight:

	Speed	Magic	Armour	Health
Roots	7	5	–	–
Danse macabre (*)	–	–	4	100

Special abilities

🛡 **Danse till you drop!**: (*) In this combat you roll against the roots' *speed*. If you win a combat round, the roots will drop Danse Macabre, allowing you to strike against the skeleton for *two* combat rounds (hits are automatic; there is no need to roll for speed). After two rounds, the roots lift the skeleton up once again, meaning you must win another combat round before you can strike twice against the skeleton.

🛡 **Hip-hop bones**: At the end of each combat round you must take 2 damage, ignoring *armour*, from the flailing roots and bones.

🛡 **Body of bone**: Danse Macabre is immune to all passive effects.

If you manage to defeat this body-popping horror, turn to 331.

469

'Well right now, all eyes are on the sled races. Money to be won there if you have the bottle. Otherwise, trading furs if you can get 'em. Although . . .' He glances furtively at the nearby patrons, then leans forward against the bar. 'Bet you noticed the big wigs flaunting it around Ryker's. Not all those stuck-up oafs are here for the races – there's some serious business going down. I hear talk of diamonds, mining operations, contracts and all that.' The barman nods his head, eyes gleaming. 'Ryker's might be the pimple on Valeron's ass, but it's gonna get mighty popular soon. Mark my words.'

Will you:

Ask what he knows about Ryker?	692
Ask what he has for sale?	709
Take a seat in one of the alcoves?	634
Listen to the conversation at the bar?	534
Leave?	426

470

For defeating the troll, you may now help yourself to one of the following rewards:

Discord	Grit sting	Flint sparks
(main hand: hammer)	(gloves)	(feet)
+1 speed +2 brawn	+1 brawn +1 armour	+1 speed +1 brawn
Ability: after shock	Ability: counter	Ability: lightning
(requirement: warrior)		(requirement: rogue)

When you have updated your hero sheet, turn to 141.

471

There are four racers ahead of you. Three are speeding towards an immense glacier breaking up out of the ice. A jagged fissure at its base provides a narrow opening, which you assume must offer a safe means through this daunting obstacle. The other racer has opted to take the longer route, avoiding the glacier altogether by going around it.

Will you:

Enter the glacier?	**764**
Go around it?	**695**

472

You slide the shaft of the quill between the ghostly fingers. To your surprise, the hand grips the implement with a tight pressure and starts to scratch words into the rotted wood. You lean over the ghost's shoulder to read what he is writing. As soon as he is finished, the hand passes back to the start, tracing the same letters again, each movement cutting a little deeper into the wood. Eventually you can make out four words: *Pendegost, Frayling, Augur, Volst.*

You glance at Anise, wondering if they mean anything to her. The kitchen girl shakes her head, looking equally confused. Whatever message the ghost is trying to communicate, its meaning is lost to you. (Record the keyword *secrets* on your hero sheet.)

With nothing else of interest in the room, you grab the unlit lamp (make a note of the word *lamp* on your hero sheet) and then continue into the next passageway. Turn to 385.

473

The wooden guardian has been defeated. You may now help yourself to one of the following special rewards:

Nettle touch	Quill cover	Blood bloom
(gloves)	(head)	(main hand: wand)
+1 speed +1 magic	+1 speed +1 magic	+1 speed +2 magic
Ability: barbs	Ability: splinters	Ability: regrowth

With little else of interest in the room, you decide to continue onwards. Turn to 13.

474

The cave is large and dome-shaped, its walls glittering with veins of green rock. Caul immediately runs over to a canvas pack and a collection of weapons that have been discarded on the ground. He takes up a spear, eyeing it almost reverently.

'Together again at last,' he grins. 'And here's me seven sisters.' The trapper crouches next to his pack, pulling a strap of knives from underneath it. He puts an arm through the leather thong, pulling it down across his chest. He pats the knives, grinning like a child at Yuletide. 'Take what you want.' Caul nudges the pack with his boot. 'All yours.'

You look at him, confused. 'But these are yours . . .'

Caul shrugs his shoulders. 'In this place, I'd rather stay light. If you want to burden yourself, then go ahead.'

You step around the pack to the examine the trapper's equipment. As well as a selection of skinned hides there is also a second spear, a pair of paddle-shaped snowshoes and a set of gloves. If you wish, you may now help yourself to one of the following:

Hrotnar	Snowshoes	Foxtail bracers
(main hand: spear)	(feet)	(gloves)
+1 speed +2 brawn	+1 speed +1 armour	+1 speed +1 brawn
Ability: impale	Ability: sideswipe	Ability: cunning
(requirement: warrior)		

Inside the pack you find a *muttok pelt*, a *yeti pelt* and a wrap of *seal blubber* (if you wish to take any of these items, simply make a note of them on your hero sheet, they do not take up backpack space.)

Caul is already making for a tunnel in the opposite wall. As you move to follow, you notice a line of grooves cut into a smoothed area of floor. Your eyes trace their pattern – a winding spiral that twists towards a centre point, where a raised serpent's head has been carved into the stone. You realise that the grooved spirals form its coiled body.

Caul is waiting for you by the entrance to the tunnel. 'Leave it,' he growls impatiently. 'There's something I want to show you – this way.'

Will you:

Examine the snake's head?	**676**
Follow Caul into the tunnel?	**775**

475

You hear the stamp of hooves and a snorting bellow. The herd has fled southwards but one muttok has remained behind, standing its ground – the grey-haired giant with the barbed antlers. Lowering its head, the beast springs into a full-on charge, the spiked tips of its antlers aimed straight for your chest. It is time to fight:

	Speed	Brawn	Armour	Health
Muttok elder	6	4	4	50

Special abilities

◗ **Head rush**: Any round in which you do not play a speed ability, you are automatically caught by the elder's antlers. These cause 4 damage, ignoring *armour*. (This is in addition to any further damage the stag may cause, if it wins the combat round.)

If you manage to defeat the lord of the herd, turn to 324.

476

You twist your weapon into the skeleton's ribcage, using it as leverage to rip the bony monster from its prison. There is a sucking, squelching pop as the skeleton finally comes free, its once-animated bones rattling lifelessly to the ground, no longer powered by the magic of the mould-beast.

With the skeleton defeated, you set about cutting through the remaining tentacles, finally driving your weapons and magic into the ruptured hole where the skeleton had once been. The resulting explosion sends clods of mould and dirt flying in all directions. You twist away as it spatters across your clothes, filling your nostrils with the reek of decay.

'Lovely,' grimaces Anise, standing with arms held to her side, looking down at the muck now coating her from head to foot.

'Mould bath,' you grin sheepishly. 'It might grow on you.' After wiping the grime from your eyes, you set about searching through the creature's remains. As well as 30 gold crowns, you also find one of the following rewards:

Perish	Rotted shield	Crawling cap
(main hand: sword)	(left hand: shield)	(head)
+1 speed	+1 armour	+1 brawn +1 magic
Ability: decay	Ability: slam	Ability: parasite

When you have updated your hero sheet, turn to 525.

477

Leeta becomes increasingly animated as she shows off her collection of dog toys – a grisly array of whips, spiked collars and what she terms 'incentives'. 'Look, look, this is my favourite. Meat on a stick,' she laughs, lifting up a wooden pole. You note the frozen carcass dangling from one end, unsure if it is animal or human. 'Stick this in front of their little faces and you'll be rocketing across the finish line. Cute, huh?'

You may purchase any of the following upgrades for 40 gold crowns each:

Barbed whip	+1 speed
Spiked collars	+1 toughness
Meat on a stick	+1 speed

(Note: You can only buy each item of equipment once. Remember to make the necessary adjustments to your hero sheet.) You may now view the lead dogs (turn to 502) or explore the rest of the compound (turn to 106).

478

Three of us. There were always three of us. That was balance. The woman shakes her head, her eyes unfocused as she recollects a memory. *I am Kismet, the spinner. I create the threads, the lives. Gabriel was the weaver, set the course of each and every fate. And Aisa . . .*

The woman stops, her normally serene features suddenly twitching with anger. *She was the cutter. The ender of life. For all things must come to an end.*

'Where are the others now?' You look around at the dazzling weave, bright against the void. You see no sign of anyone else. Instead, there is only a feeling of emptiness. A sadness. The woman has started to scratch at her head again.

Aisa's desire was too strong. Not happy, not contented to end lives. She wanted to end the plan, the work. She wanted to destroy the weave. The woman twists her head to look at you, blood seeping from the fresh cuts above her brow. *Aisa created Hel. The chaos, the shroud. It touches all worlds. Seeks to engulf them. Swallow them. I watch the threads die. Hundreds. Thousands. More. I hear the music soften. I hear it.*

You watch and listen, no longer sure if this woman speaks the truth or is spouting some crazed nonsense; just another spirit trapped here like yourself, driven insane by solitude. 'And what of Gabriel?' you venture, playing along with this peculiar story.

He had to restore balance. Eight worlds gone, only one left to save, only one. Dormus. He gave everything he was, the loves, the sacrifices, the tears, the very essence of being. He put himself in you, in every thread that still existed and every thread that was yet to come. He shared his light and his love. He took his choice, his power over destiny, and gave it to each and every one of you.

Your gaze strays to the web, a million strands all converging and bisecting in a bewildering array of shapes. There seems no pattern or form to the weave, just a mayhem of chaotic confusion.

Yes, you see it too. There is no plan. No plan! The woman taps manically at the sides of her head. *He only made it worse. No symphony now. Only noise. A disharmony. Sometimes I wish. I wish it would just end!*

(Return to 713 to ask another question or turn to 760 to end the conversation.)

479

Congratulations! You have gained the *captain's conch*. This gives you control of the *Naglfar*. (Simply make a note of this item on your hero sheet, it doesn't take up backpack space) Your ship has the following attributes (record these on the second part of your hero sheet):

	Speed	Stability	Toughness
Naglfar	7	8	10

If you have the *Pandora* in your backpack, you can reattach the figurehead to the ship, restoring the vessel to its former glory. This will increase the ship's *speed* and *toughness* by 2. (Remove the *Pandora* from your backpack.) Once your hero sheet is updated, return to the map to continue your adventure.

480

The guard removes the one of hearts from his hand and places it face down on the discard pile. He reaches into the pouch and takes another stone at random. He has now gained the four of stars:

Next, the hooded ghost discards a stone from his own hand and takes another from the bag. A cold, cackling laughter comes from the shadows of his cowl as he studies his new hand.

'What should I do now?' whispers the guard. 'I have a Queen's Wave. This could win me the game.'

Will you:

Discard the two of moons?	541
Show your current hand?	517

481

'I keep seeing 'em, always lurking at the edges. Shadows you never get a proper look at. Even heard their whispering.' Caul snorts, giving a nervous laugh. 'I know. When I hear myself, I think I'm losing it too, all kinds of craziness going through my head right now. You see . . .' He drops his voice, flicking a nervous glance over his shoulder. 'Those explorers, back in the canyon. This place got me thinking. What if . . . you know.' He nods his head, grinning with yellow-stained teeth.

'I'm not sure I do,' you reply, confused.

'I once heard a story, over at Ryker's. Of a spirit that haunts the coast. A drowned sailor. Those that saw him said he was searching for something – something he lost. Theory is, he's trapped here until he finds what he's looking for. Some think it's a treasure, others his dead crewmates.'

'Are you saying . . .' You pause to swallow, feeling your throat constrict. 'Reah and the others were . . . ghosts?'

Caul leans back, the green light etching strange patterns across his grimy face. 'This place plays tricks on you. I ain't trusting nothing no more.'

Will you:

Ask what he knows about the caves?	498
Ask if he has any weapons or supplies?	609
Ask if he will accompany you?	384

482

To your surprise you spot another figure clinging to the back of the demon, their arms wrapped tightly around one of its spines. A thickly-muscled man, blond hair whipped back behind his stone-grey helm. His face is bloodied, caked with filth and dust, and yet you can still make out the criss-crossed ridges of gnarly tissue that line his features.

'Skoll!' The word is barely given voice before it is ripped away by the roaring gale.

The warrior's brow creases as his eyes strain against the brightness and the blasting chill of the wind. 'Luck of the ancestors,' he calls back, readjusting his grip on the slippery spine. 'Together at the end. Let us make it a fight worthy of the ballads.' Turn to 777.

483

Not wishing to risk injury by going for the opening, you let the platform carry you back to the cave. With nothing else of interest in the chamber, you decide to leave via the passageway. Turn to 2.

484

Using the *chemist's notes* (you may remove this item from your hero sheet), you are able to make your own deadly potions and powders. However, their effects aren't always reliable!

If you wish, you may now learn the chemist career. The chemist has the following special abilities:

Chaotic catalyst (co): Instead of rolling for a damage score, you may douse your opponent in a volatile concoction. Roll a die to discover the result:

⚀ or ⚁ Your opponent heals 6 *health*.

⚂ or ⚃ Your opponent is inflicted with *venom* and must lose 2 *health* at the end of every combat round for the duration of the combat.

⚄ or ⚅ Your opponent takes 4 damage dice, ignoring *armour*. Any opponent who is next to them on the combat list (above and below) takes 1 damage die, ignoring *armour*.

This ability can only be used once per combat.

Dry ice (co): Use this ability instead of rolling for a damage score to shroud the battlefield in swirling smoke. At the beginning of each subsequent combat round, roll a die:

⚀ or ⚁ You must lower your *speed* by 1 for the current round.

⚂ or ⚃ No effect.

⚄ or ⚅ Your opponent/s must lower their *speed* by 2 for the current round.

With little else of interest in the laboratory, you decide to leave the prison. Turn to 426.

485

With no means of igniting the gas, the riftwing clambers back out of the hole then charges at you once again. It is time to fight:

	Speed	Brawn	Armour	Health
Riftwing	2	1	1	28

If you manage to defeat this winged fiend, turn to 217. If you lose the combat, remember to record your defeat on your hero sheet. You may then attempt the combat again or return to the map.

Your eyes narrow to slits of rage. The paladin has suddenly become the representation of everything bad that has happened to you – the betrayal by the roadside, your death, the cursed body you are now forced to inhabit . . . . He has become your target.

You shift your body, edging yourself into a battle stance. Skoll reads your movement, his muscles tensed. You share a brief glance, noting the grim smile on his ragged face.

Then together you move.

The fight is over in moments. But the outcome is a little different to what you had expected. The paladin moves with a speed that is frighteningly quick, the light blurring his body into a dizzying streak. The blast takes you in the stomach before you even know it is coming – a ball of holy energy that burns with the heat of a thousand fires. It blows you off your feet, punching you into the far wall. Dusty rock crumbles around you with the force of the impact. You crumple to the ground, cradling the burns, flinching with each burst of pain. (You must immediately apply one death penalty effect to your hero, see entry 98.)

Skoll fares no better. The Skard is suffering more than you thought, his actions lacking their usual strength. His charge is more of a stagger, the axe whipping through empty air as the paladin deftly moves around each blow. Then Maune draws out his sword, a short blade notched with angular teeth. They catch the Skard's axe, twisting it out of his grasp. Maune's other hand snaps out, fingers catching around Skoll's throat. There is a flash of light then the Skard is stumbling back, his skin smoking with heat.

The flat of the blade whips down, striking across Skoll's chest. On any ordinary day, the half-giant would have shrugged off such a blow. But tired and starved as he is, the strike is enough to send him sprawling to the ground beside you.

To his credit he recovers quickly, rolling over and snatching up his axe once again. However the eagle, who had previously been content to watch the encounter with a cold indifference, suddenly leaps across the space, wings stretched wide. Its neck darts forward, beak snapping only inches from the Skard, forcing him back against the wall.

Your eyes flick back to the nearby pack, and its promise of food and water. Life for Anise. You drop your weapons by your side, raising your hands.

'Forgive us, please,' you gasp, still wincing from your burns. 'We are hungry, tired. We have another with us, a girl. We need food and water. Please.'

The paladin barks a command and the bird draws back, still hissing at you with suspicion. 'I did not take you for thieves. If only you had asked, I would have gladly given.'

'I'm asking now,' you insist.

Skoll grumbles something next to you, some curse in Skard. But there is no conviction to it. His shoulders are slumped, resigned to surrender. He uncurls his fingers from around his axe. 'Food,' he gasps between breaths. 'One meal. Then that cursed bird can eat me for all I care.'

Maune sheaths his blade. 'Come. Let us attend to your needs, then. The One God provides for all.' Turn to 21.

487

You place the 'three of swords' on the discard pile and pick a new stone from the bag. You have gained the 'two of moons'.

You have the following stones:

The monk decides to play his hand. Turn to 593.

488

You point to the knife. There are some approving grunts from the crowd, but Desnar looks far from happy. His lips twitch with nervousness, his shifty glare reminding you of a cornered animal.

'Blas lamna sur gas!' Sura motions impatiently to the warrior.

Desnar grudgingly offers out his right hand. The moustachioed Skard puts the bone blade to his palm and cuts a deep line.

'Your hand,' says Sura, nudging your arm.

You mimic Desnar's gesture, watching impassively while the same blade is drawn across your own palm. You don't feel anything – neither the touch of the bone or the pain of its passing. Your dead flesh remains numb to it all. Instead you scan the faces in the crowd, taking some small pleasure from their shocked gasps as they watch the congealed black blood ooze out of the wound.

Desnar sneers, stepping forward to grasp your hand. His action takes you by surprise, and at first you flinch, drawing back – but then you realise this is part of the ritual. You clasp hands firmly, gripping tight. You glare into each other's eyes, both tightening your grip, locked together in a silent show of strength. Desnar grinds his teeth, his eyes narrowing. You can almost feel his bones about to snap . . .

With a hiss he pulls away, making a flourishing gesture to mask his surrender.

'Hallret!' He barks furiously.

A Skard hurries to his side, placing a staff into his bloodied hand. It is an impressive looking weapon, fashioned from white wood, with a pair of forked antlers as its headpiece. He raises the staff above his head, turning to the crowd.

'Vic tarnik!' he chants.

The words are echoed by several of his men, but with little gusto. Most of the crowd remain intent on you, their expressions a mix of curiosity and suspicion.

'What happens now?' you whisper to Sura. 'Do we fight here?'

The woman shakes her head. 'You decided the test. Now Desnar will choose the fight. Follow him.' She bows her head. 'May the ancestors be with you, southlander.'

'Wait – you aren't coming with us?' You look around at the watchful crowd.

Sura frowns. 'This is a test, a feud between yourself and Desnar. Only one of you will return with victory. This is the test of the fighter. One of you must submit – or die.'

The crowd part, leaving you a clear path to the edge of the camp where the ocean of snow sweeps away in rippled waves. Desnar gives you a sly grin, then starts out into the bleak wasteland. You give Sura a hesitant nod, then follow after the Skard. Turn to 702.

489

The black plant is spreading quickly across the broken branch, its thorny stem starting to sprout a number of crimson buds. Quickly, you dodge past its flailing vines and start to climb the trunk. Ratatosk gives a shriek of anger, then begins fishing in his pouch again.

You have almost reached his position when he tosses another seed through the air. It spirals past you towards the growth. You risk a glance over your shoulder, to see that the buds have blossomed into a hungry set of carnivorous mouths. One of them reaches up and snaps the seed from the air. As the plant swallows it there is a thunderous ripping, creaking noise as its stem bulges outwards, sprouting more vines and leaves.

You realise that the seeds must be helping the plant to grow.

'Rata-rata-tosk!' sniggers the squirrel. Then it scampers further up the tree, its bushy tail twitching back and forth. Angrily, you start after it, struggling to stay one step ahead of the grasping vines that are spreading up the trunk. Turn to 35.

490

Amongst the broken wood, you find a number of mildewed, moth-eaten clothes. Some appear to carry magical enchantments, their thread and trims glittering with a faint green light.

If you wish, you may now take one of the following rewards:

Night shirt	Day glow wraps	Storm shoulders
(chest)	(gloves)	(cloak)
+1 magic	+1 brawn	+1 speed
Ability: charm	Ability: radiance	Ability: charge

You also find a key, fashioned from a finger bone and a grisly array of teeth. If you wish to take the *skeleton key*, simply make a note of it on your hero sheet, it does not take up backpack space.

Suddenly, the door to your left creaks open of its own accord. From the room beyond you hear a man's voice, raised in anger. 'No! I will not serve you, Zabarach! I will not!' There is a cry of pain, then the sound of metal scraping across stone. Gripping your weapons, you edge slowly into the next room. Turn to **548**.

491

With the rats defeated, you are free to examine the nest. Amongst the bones and dirty bedding you find 30 gold crowns and two of the following items:

Chemist's notes	Tome of necromancy	Red pills (3 uses)
(backpack)	(backpack)	(backpack)
A tattered book of	Use at any time to	Use at any time to heal
recipes and formula	remove one death	4 *health*
(requirement: mage)	penalty from your hero	

With little else of interest in the cleft, you crawl back into the cell and resume your journey. Turn to **661**.

492

You pass between two giant islands, dodging the fragments of rock and earth that spiral around them. One of the larger pieces spins past you, revolving its underside into plain view. Anise is the first to call an alarm, urging you to take notice.

Two huge dragons are clinging to the rock. Most of their black scales have rotted away, leaving only bared ribs and gangrenous tissue exposed. One of them cranes its bony neck around, leering at you with a skull-like face.

Then a scream fills your ears, a horrible unending screech.

Moving as one, the two dragons drop from the rock, their tattered wings unfolding to catch the thermals. Their ancient bones crack and groan as they twist their bodies, levelling themselves out into a full-on pursuit.

'Keep going!' shouts Skoll, ducking to avoid a torrent of green-tinged flame. 'We'll never survive an open battle!'

The dragons snap and claw at your rear, seeking to knock you from the skies. In desperation, you look around for a means of escape. Straight ahead a criss-crossing wall of magic has been woven between islands, forming a spider-like web. You suspect it to be another of the witch's traps, but it might offer you a slim chance of losing the dragons.

'There!' Skoll points to your left. 'Head for that!'

A mass of rock and dust glitters in the half-light, all turning and spinning through a deadly orbit. The dragons are large and less agile than your craft – you may have a better chance of navigating the rock belt. Even so, it will be a dangerous test of skill.

Will you:

Ride through the magical web?	536
Navigate the rock belt?	458

493

To pass the goblins without being seen, you will need to pass the following *speed* challenge:

	Speed
Creepy crawly	10

If you are successful, turn to 243. Otherwise, turn to 316.

494

As you descend deeper into the mountain, you become aware of a thunderous roar echoing in the distance. It grows steadily louder, until a turn in the passageway brings you to an open ledge. You step out cautiously to find yourself looking out across a vast chasm, cleaving the mountain in two. Brown glacial waters rush below, bouncing and crashing past a field of boulders to finally drop away into a billowing curtain of angry noise, its destination lost to the inky darkness.

Across the other side of the gulf, you can see a myriad of ledges and open doorways carved into the black rock. You can even make out towers and other structures extending out over the abyss, connected by bridges and winding pathways.

An underground city.

'Quite something, isn't it?' Caul shouts over the roar of the water.

You realise that this must have been what Reah and the others were looking for – evidence of a lost civilisation. Dwarf. Titan. Perhaps both.

Wrenching your gaze from the distant city, you turn your attention to more immediate concerns – such as how to progress. There are no bridges or means of crossing the gulf. Instead, your only way forward is a narrow ledge, sweeping down from where you are standing to another doorway in the rock wall, situated at a lower elevation. Trying to ignore the precipitous drop and the churning waters below, you carefully make your way along the tight path, with Caul bringing up the rear. Turn to 257.

495

The man slides out from beneath the sled, wiping his hands on his apron. 'Name's Mech. You needing repairs?' He notices you admiring the three sleds behind him. 'Ah yeah, I worked up quite a few damaged racers in my time, made them good as new. Doubt even a Skard runner could pull faster than these beauties.' He tugs at one end of his thick moustache, cracking the ice frozen to the bristles. 'I got a deal with Leeta at the kennels. Buy a sled and you get a free dog-team. One of the racers gone missing – think he ended up, you know . . .' the man gives a click of his tongue, whilst drawing a finger across his throat. 'One man's misfortune is another man's gain, as they say.' He shrugs his shoulders. 'So, you interested in buying a sled – or maybe one of me upgrades, to give yer an edge in the tournament?'

496

Maune gives you a sharp look. 'You're asking me to believe the demon's lies? He called you Arran, but it cannot be . . .'

Skoll steps away, letting you approach the startled paladin. You stand before him, letting his eyes search your own. 'I know it must be hard to believe. I was betrayed by the church; they murdered my father, my brother. I would have shared the same fate; I was meant to share that fate . . .' A shudder runs through you, remembering back to the roadside and the frightened naïve boy who was lost to the wilds. 'Everything was taken from me. Everything.' You glance at Skoll, who is watching intently from beneath a clenched brow. 'But not my humanity.'

The Skard startles. 'Bearclaw. We have to do this!'

You turn squarely to face him. 'No, we don't. We are better than that. I am better than that.'

There is a clink and scrape of metal. Maune has fallen to his knees, his sword resting across his outstretched palms. A show of fealty and submission.

'My king. The One God has led me to your side.'

You catch Skoll's scowling retort.

'We will fight the witch together, my friend,' you insist. 'With faith and steel, and magic. We will be remembered as heroes, Skoll. Not as murderers or cowards. My father was a soldier, a great warrior. But he was a weak man. I will not be my father.'

Your gaze holds Skoll's, daring him to challenge you. His eyes shine with anger, his mouth twitching, fingers flexing around his axe. You are on the edge of summoning your spectral claws. Nanuk's magic is almost palpable on the air, flickering about you.

'This is an ill decision,' mutters the Skard, dropping his eyes. He turns his back on you, and says no more.

An arm slides around your waist, taking you by surprise. You twist round, finding Anise staring up at you, a tired smile turning her lips. 'No, you made a brave decision. And one worthy of a king.'

Maune stands, sheathing his blade. 'I will lay down my life for you, my king. And if needs be, fight to retake the throne you lost.'

You nod in thanks. 'Henna would be proud of her father.'

The fires of the forge continue to rage green, flaring angry claws at the brightening dawn skies. Without the shield, you realise you will be at a disadvantage when facing the witch queen Melusine. This is her victory – but as your eyes sweep back to the paladin, a veteran warrior of countless crusades, you wonder if you may have gained something greater. (Make a note of the keyword *repentance* on your hero sheet.) Return to the quest map to continue your adventure.

497

You lift the creature into the air and hurl it across the room. With an angry squeal, the riftwing slams into the opposing wall then drops through the hole into the room below – where you suspect the green gas is still escaping from the open barrel. If you have the keyword *flame* on your hero sheet, turn to 409. Otherwise, turn to 485.

498

'Never even knew they were here.' Caul shrugs. 'I was following yeti tracks, thought I'd get me some nice hides to add to my collection. Then I found the explorers, like I said. They seemed to think this place was important; something to do with Titans.' He pauses, his gaze following a vein of rock that branches through the ice. 'Seems plain to me this place ain't anything natural. Could be riches here – treasure, if we can get deep enough.'

Will you:

Ask if he has any weapons or supplies?	609
Ask why he thought you were a ghost?	481
Ask if he will accompany you?	384

499

You swing your legs into the opening, pushing yourself forward as quickly as you can. To complete the manoeuvre, you will need to pass a *speed* challenge:

	Speed
Race against time	10

If you are successful, turn to 610. If you fail, you manage to make it through, but not without suffering a serious injury. You must roll immediately on the death penalty chart (see entry 98) and apply the penalty to your hero. Once you have updated your hero sheet, turn to 610.

500
Quest: The Hall of Vindsvall

The storm has abated. In its wake a crystalline mist hugs the white landscape, throwing your surroundings into an indistinct haze. You stagger onwards, the effort excruciating. Next to you, the two Skards are impassive to your suffering, their thick polar boots crunching through the mantle of snow, setting a pace that you struggle to maintain.

They had come out of nowhere. Not even Nanuk had sensed their presence – or perhaps he chose not to alert you. Two warriors. Their furs stitched with plates of black iron, snaked with runes. You had raised your hands in surrender, asking to be taken to the Hall of Vindsvall.

Then they snapped the manacle around your wrist.

The pain still draws sobs from your lips. Pain the like of which you had long forgotten – an itching, burning sensation that boils beneath your skin. Dark spumes of smoke rise from the burnt flesh where the manacle rubs, its rune-worked chain coiled in one of the warrior's fists. If you fall behind he yanks on the shackle, tugging you forward – drawing further cries from your frost-cracked lips.

They do not slow. When you beg for release, you are met by the same blank stares through the visors of their winged helms. No concern or remorse. The warriors simply stride ahead with the same determined purpose, seemingly knowing their direction even though you have spotted no discernible landmark or even the sun.

When you finally sight the longhouse it is a blessed relief. You can make out white-timber walls, braced with beams of a darker wood. A carving of an eagle looms overhead, its wings spread wide as if taking off in flight. It guards the impressive doorway, two large double-doors of the same pale wood as the rest of the hall, carved with branching runes that sparkle with a silver light – like patterns of frost on a window pane.

One of the warriors unslings a horn from his shoulder, raises it to his lips and blows a single short note into the frigid air. There is the sound of a wooden brace being lifted, then the doors swing inwards. Without ceremony, the two warriors advance into the room – the chain-handler dragging you between them.

You were expecting an expansive chamber, stretching back beneath wooden beams. Instead you find yourself in a much smaller room, dominated by a long table. Braziers line the walls, filling the room with a thick heat. It only serves to heighten the stench of sweat and dampness.

Two warriors stand at the head of the table, flanking a high chair where a repulsive toad-like man sits hunched over a platter of meats. Other bowls and dishes surround him, all full of rich foods swimming in grease.

The man is laughing, evidently having just shared a joke or anecdote. The warriors behind him, both tall and muscular Skards, continue to stare straight ahead. Their helmets are removed, tucked under their arms, displaying faces that are weather-worn and scarred. The warrior on the left glances your way, his snow-white hair sparkling like silver in the firelight.

You almost detect a smile, as his gloved hand tightens around his sword-grip.

The seated man looks up with a grunt, the mirth fading from his eyes. 'What in the name of . . .' He pauses, swallowing. 'You look like you were spat out the gates of Hel.'

'Perhaps I was,' you hiss, your teeth clenched from the pain. One of the warriors grabs you by the shoulder and pushes you forward.

You stagger against the table, grabbing hold of its edge to support yourself. The snickering laughter from the seated man only serves to stoke your fury. You lift your eyes, taking the measure of this stranger.

His frame is massive, a bulging mass of bloated flesh that struggles to even fit into the chair. Above his neck folds, the man's paunchy face is surrounded by a wild mass of black hair, like a thunderous cloud. Grease and spit drip over his chin, where a short black beard sprouts unevenly from the pockmarked skin. Piggy eyes and a ruddy cauliflower nose complete the repulsive portrait.

'You aren't a Skard,' you say sluggishly.

'No, but I am a man,' he grins, his hand finding its way into one of the bowls. 'Which is more than I can say for you.' He scoops a chunk of pickled fish out of the oil and pushes it into his greasy mouth.

'I was sent here by Sura, a shaman of the bear tribe. She believed ... I believe that I can help your leader.' You look around at the faces of the men. The Skards are exchanging glances, but the man at the table merely belches, then a deep laughter rolls out from his enormous belly.

'A hag's errand!' He snorts, then wipes a sleeve across his spit-flecked lips. 'I am Gurt Bloodaxe and I lead the einherjar – the fated warriors who guard the Hall of Vindsvall. You are not fit to stand before me. You are not even fit to beg for the scraps from my table. Take him away!'

The Skard handler pulls on your chain, but you struggle to resist.

'I was told to come here!' you snap furiously. 'I have a power ... I can help the asynjur. I can help rescue Skoll!'

The man's eyes bulge. 'Is this some dare? Some joke?' He glances darkly at the white-haired warrior next to him. 'Aslev, do you seek to mock me?'

The Skard frowns, his body straightening. Clearly the accusation has stung him.

You decide to press on. 'I am a shaman ... I have the powers of your asynjur ...' You grimace as the iron manacle bites deep into your flesh, driving you almost to your knees. You can feel your magic ebbing away, being drained by the hungry runes worked into its metal. 'Release ... me, let me show you.'

Gurt leans forward, his rolls of fat bunching against the edge of the table. 'You believe you can succeed where a hundred asynjur have failed?' His wobbling paunches make it difficult to tell if he is smiling or scowling. 'Skoll sits the high chair, frozen in the ice. A relic. A reminder of glory days long past. There is no going back.'

You notice the Skards looking again at one another, sharing questioning glances. The white-haired warrior, who the man referred to as Aslev, shifts uneasily. His hand continues to clench and unclench around his sword.

Sensing their anger you try a different tack, addressing the warriors. 'Listen to me . . . I am here to help your people. The Ska-inuin. Your tribes are broken . . . separated . . . they wait for a new leader to bring them together. Make them strong. They need a Drokke.'

The Skards merely glare at you, looking affronted by your words. The chain-handler's eyes flick to the man at the table, awaiting a command.

'They follow me,' drawls Gurt, dipping a hunk of salt bread into a meaty bowl. 'I didn't always look this way, see. Back in the day I could fell a troll with one swing of my axe. I earned my name – I earned my title.' He shovels the bread into his mouth, juices running over his pot-chin. 'They gave their word,' he continues, chewing on his food. 'Skards are hot-headed, by Hel's teeth everyone knows that, but when they swear allegiance – they cannot break their vow. Else, they believe the spirits will curse them – and their bloodline.' His eyes shift nervously around the table, looking at the Skards as if daring them to challenge his words. Satisfied, his eyes roll back to you.

'So, you see,' he grunts, patting his enormous belly. 'I am the gatekeeper. No one enters the Hall of Vindsvall without my say. No one has audience with Syn Hulda without my say. So, I'll give you one last chance to impress me. Or else I'm having my loyal subjects,' he gestures to the four warriors to emphasise his words, 'drag you back out in the snow and kick those corpse teeth out of that ugly face of yours.' He reaches for a leg of meat from his platter, glaring at you as he rips a greasy chunk from the bone.

Will you:

Show your bear necklace? (If you have the keyword *triumph*)	180
Agree to fight the Einherjar?	318
Pledge your allegiance to Gurt?	200

501

With Nanuk you feel whole again. The two of you move in harmony, your thoughts flowing together, every action becoming natural and instinctive. The night terrors are powerful spirits, but against your combined might they are hopelessly outmatched. Within minutes they are left lying across the sand, their mouldered robes still flapping in the wind.

You may now help yourself to one of the following rewards:

Oblivion hood	Band of suffering	Dreamer's cord
(head)	(ring)	(necklace)
+1 speed +2 brawn	+1 brawn +1 magic	+1 speed +1 magic
Ability: decay	Ability: thorns	Ability: focus
(requirement: rogue)		

The euphoria fades and quickly your attention turns to Nanuk. But your surroundings are fading, and the bear with them.

'Nanuk?' You reach out, but your knuckles bruise against stone. A dark laughter fills your ears, malicious and cold. Looking round, you see walls and pillars rising up out of the sand. Within seconds you find yourself in a wide corridor of white marble, lined with gilt-framed paintings. Regal faces stare back at you with dead eyes. All unnervingly familiar.

'The palace,' you gasp.

'No place like home,' whispers a voice in your ear.

You jerk aside, your weapons spinning round to catch your tormentor. But they meet only air, turning you to face the length of the corridor. To your left is an archway, leading through into the palace gardens. Further along and to the right, an open oak door beckons you to one of your favourite haunts – the library.

Will you:

Enter the gardens?	**635**
Go to the library?	**25**

'Some riders don't bother with a good alpha,' explains Leeta, peeling her bloodied mitts from her hands. 'But then, they don't make it very far. Dog-teams will buckle under the pressure, bicker amongst themselves. A leader will help you keep them in line. Here, take a look at these three.'

You follow her to a row of smaller pens, where three hounds are snapping and snarling at each other. If it wasn't for the wire-netting dividing them, and the chains straining around their thickly-muscled necks, you could well imagine the dogs ripping each other to shreds.

If you wish, you may now purchase a lead dog for your dog-team:

Marrow wind (80 gc):	+2 speed	+2 toughness
Gruntus (120 gc):	+2 speed	+3 toughness
Sid Savage (175 gc):	+3 speed	+4 toughness

(Note: You can only have one lead dog at a time. You may replace lead dogs whenever you want by purchasing a new one from Leeta. Remember to update your hero sheet with any changes.) You may now view the dog equipment (turn to 477) or explore the rest of the compound (turn to 106).

The next tremor comes without warning, building quickly into a ground-hammering quake. Everything becomes blurred as the world tilts and shudders, throwing you one way and then the other, the sound of moving stone rumbling in your ears.

Everard knocks into you, his eyes darting round frantically. Cracks have started to branch through the courtyard, some widening into dark fissures. Nearby, a wall slides away from view as if dropped suddenly from all existence.

'Take this!'

You turn to see Everard removing a pin from his cloak. He presses it into your hand.

'What token is this?' You look at it, confused – a silver pin, fashioned in the shape of a hound.

'Safe passage,' he shouts. 'Wear it!'

You slide the pin into the cloth of your jerkin, nodding back at him.

Then the ground pitches, rising up into a steep incline. Rocks, tiles and splintered wood bounce and slide past you, joining the grating explosion of noise that is getting louder and more deafening. Bodies, both dead and living, are dragged past as the ground rolls over on itself, presenting a dark abyss below.

You scrabble for purchase, hands scraping across the rough stone. Your eyes are set on the grey sky above, the lip of the rock moving against the backdrop of ragged, dawn-lit clouds. Screams and wails are audible above the din. *Don't look down . . .*

You hand settles around something hard and leathery. A wing. You grip it tight, your descent halted, legs kicking and flailing in the dusty air. Gritting your teeth, you manage to drag your other hand onto the dead creature: one of the flying reptiles that first assaulted the keep. Its body is pinned to the earth by a black spike, possibly from one of the tower steeples. You hang onto it for dear life.

The world shudders, the roaring only getting louder. You sense the earth shifting again, starting to fall back into the crevasse. You make the mistake of looking down, your stomach lurching as you see the stone crumbling away, falling into the darkness.

You tighten your grip on the creature, aware of a sickening ripping sound coming from its dead body. Your added weight is pulling against the spike, threatening to tug it loose and send you both tumbling into the abyss.

'No!' You grapple against the creature, trying to secure a better hold – but gravity is intent on dragging you down . . .

Another squelching crunch; muscle and bone tears away from the spike.

Nanuk! Nanuk!

You feel a stirring in your mind. Then the familiar cold of the Norr rushes in – as it did when you were healed. But this time it moves straight through you, flowing out of your body and into the corpse of the drakeling. A wing flutters. Webbed feet scratch at the stone. Just a reflex action, perhaps . . . No, the head is moving, the beak snaps open, and from its ragged lungs comes a terrifying screech. In horrified alarm, you realise that your magic has brought the monster back to life. Its body is ravaged, innards half-hanging out of terrible wounds. Bones protrude from a broken neck, but still it is alive, shrieking like a nightmare become real.

Its frantic movements dislodge the spike. For several gut-wrenching seconds you are in free-fall, arms gripped around the beast. Then its wings snap open and you are flying, buffeted on the searing thermals rising from the pit. The flight is ungainly, diving and rolling in a sickening series of spins, the membrane of one wing flapping uselessly in the wind. And yet the drakeling is managing to stay airborne, taking you through the blinding dust and out into the rift.

'No!' You will the monster to turn around, to take you south – back across the keep. 'Nanuk! Turn south!' Nothing seems to work – no thought, no amount of pulling and tugging will make the drakeling deviate from its course. Instead, you feel powerless; an unwitting passenger, clutching tight to the frightened beast as it struggles across the black void that yawns beneath you. Turn to 528.

504

For defeating the witch, you may now help yourself to one of the following rewards:

Sepulchre snare	Valediction	Oblivion helix
(cloak)	(main hand: dagger)	(ring)
+2 speed +2 brawn	+2 speed +4 brawn	+2 brawn
Ability: choke hold	Ability: cruel twist	Ability: curse

When you have updated your hero sheet, turn to 538.

505

The knight fights with a maddened fury, his relentless strikes forcing you to the edge of the tower, where a section of the battlements have crumbled away. As he goes to deliver what he intends to be the final blow, you dodge aside, using your strength and weight to hurl him over the side.

You almost follow him over, but Anise grabs a hold of you, pulling you back.

'Thank you,' you manage to croak.

'Don't mention it,' she gasps, her quick breaths frosting the air.

Together you lean over the edge, watching as the falling light is swallowed by the darkness.

'You couldn't change it,' says Anise, noting your silence. 'There was nothing you could have done to save him.'

You turn, searching for the medallion. It is still lying in the dust where you dropped it, but now its appearance has changed – the chain and disc have become blackened and charred, giving off a sickly-yellow smoke. If you wish, you may now take:

Knight's end
(necklace)
+1 brawn +1 magic
Ability: corruption

Anise is suddenly tugging at your sleeve, gesturing wildly at the wind-blown rooftop. 'No signal fire ...' she cries in exasperation. 'What are we going to do now?' Turn to **560**.

506

You manage to outrun the terrordactyls, but not before their claws and teeth have left their mark. Your transport has suffered serious damage in the assault. (You must lower your transport's *toughness* and *stability* by 2.) When you have updated your hero sheet, turn to **492**.

507

'Have you received news from the capital?' you ask icily. 'I understand the king has been deposed.'

Maune looks at you askew. 'I was in the city for a time. I was under the impression Mordland spies were responsible for the king's death, and that of his son.'

'His son?' You try and rein in your anger, fists clenching tighter around your weapons.

'Malden. The king in waiting. A good man. His wounds were ill-deserved, his death more so.'

You bow your head, taking a moment to compose yourself. 'He had another son.'

'Oh, the ghost prince.' Maune sounds indifferent. 'He was taken by the Wiccans. There was fear he might be used as a bargaining piece, but such schemes are beyond the minds of . . .' his eyes flick to Skoll with contempt. 'Hill men.'

'And Rile?' You lift your eyes. 'What of him?'

Maune frowns. 'He is a Cardinal, blessed by the holy light. He does his duty, as must we all in these dark times. People need a leader, if only until a new king is chosen. Although those that claim such a blood right have been found . . . lacking. At least with Rile on the throne the Church has a stronger standing at last.'

'Convenient,' you shoot sharply.

Maune takes a breath before answering. 'If you had ever seen Mordland, boy, you would understand what is at stake. Their land is heathen, given over to false gods and demon worship. Their true faith however, is only reserved for their emperor; a twisted man both bloody and cruel. The holy light is all we have, to keep such evil from our borders. The king didn't believe . . .'

'The king didn't believe in launching more crusades,' you interject tersely. 'So think, Maune. Why would Mordland have him killed?'

The paladin starts to answer, then checks himself. He gives another sigh. 'Mordland will do anything to weaken our kingdom, to spread panic and chaos. They underestimate us.' The paladin's light flares bright about his body. 'Most of our enemies do.'

Will you:

Ask Maune why he is here?	97
Ask for food and water? (ends the conversation)	486
Attack the paladin? (ends the conversation)	433

'Home?' Jackson scoffs incredulously. 'You seriously think yer getting to the mainland this side of winter? I tell you, I should shoot you now and put you out of yer misery. The sea east of here is all froze up. No traffic at all, unless you try for one of the whaling vessels. But even those are probably holed up at Ryker's or already headed back south.'

'What about overland?' you ask, starting to feel despondent. 'There must be a way.'

'Yeah, there's a bridge at Bitter Keep.'

'There *was* a bridge at Bitter Keep,' you correct.

'Ah, well I'd say you'd need to grow a pair of wings then, smart guy. How else you crossin' that rift?'

Will you:

Ask another question?	450
Discuss something other than news?	685
Leave?	Return to the map

509

You push through a wall of trailing roots to discover another opening. This leads you into a winding tunnel, which snakes erratically through the trunk of the tree. A foul-smelling green ichor seeps from the walls and ceiling, forming sizzling puddles that slowly eat away at the wood and dirt. In some sections the acid has burnt through entirely, forming deep pits that stretch away into the bowels of the tree. You navigate these with care, to avoid slipping into the deadly channels.

At last the tunnel curves and then widens into another vast chamber, again carved from the bole of the tree. The ground is perfectly flat and smooth, revealing the banded growth rings that radiate from the centre. A number of hollow depressions have been cut into the various rings, some containing wooden pieces, others left vacant. You notice a pile of chopped wood in a corner of the room. Investigating these you discover that they are all circular cross-sections of trees, containing different numbers of growth rings. You wonder if these might allude to some sort of arcane puzzle.

You sort through the cross-sections, spreading them out on the ground in front of you. There are pieces with the following number of growth rings: 2, 15, 17, 21, 23, 53 and 72 rings. You assume these are to be placed in the vacant holes, following a pre-ordained pattern.

Decide where you want to place your seven numbers. The numbers that you place over the symbols must be totalled to give you a final answer to the puzzle. If you think you have solved the puzzle, turn to the appropriate numbered entry to discover if you were correct. If you are wrong, or unable to solve the puzzle, then you decide to ignore this odd distraction and continue onwards. Turn to 13.

510

Rummaging through your pack, you pull out the book that you found in Segg's library. You quickly flick through its pages, reading up on the rules of the game. (Make a note of entry number 776 – you can refer to this entry at any time while carrying the book, to study the rules of 'Stones and Bones'.)

When you are ready to play, turn to 335.

511

After several rounds of choosing and swapping stones, you end up with the following hand:

The monk waits for you to make your next choice, slurping noisily from his next mug of ale.

Will you:

Discard the one of snakes?	134
Discard the three of swords?	650

512

You manage to break away from your opponent, passing the finish line in fourth place. This qualifies you to enter the final race. However, you only receive 60 gold crowns for your fourth place ranking. (Replace the keyword *rookie* with the word *veteran*.) Return to the map to continue your adventure.

513

Your hands move across the console, activating the runes and throwing the orb's magic against your advancing opponents. They stumble through the onslaught, their enchanted stonework blasted and pummelled by the energies channelled against them. As the surviving statues near your location, you vault over the balcony and charge into the fray, using your own weapons to finish off their crumbling forms.

Amongst the smoking rubble, you discover glowing fragments of stone imbued by the magics that have been unleashed. If you wish, you may now take one of the following special rewards:

Frost nexus	Earth bond	Shadow hex
(talisman)	(talisman)	(talisman)
+2 magic	+2 brawn	+2 brawn
Ability: blizzard	Ability: resolve	Ability: blind strike
(requirement: mage)	(requirement: warrior)	(requirement: rogue)

When you have updated your hero sheet, turn to 737.

514

Rage consumes you, delivering your blows with a savage zeal. Bodies fall. Ice showers across the ground. A small part of you finds comfort in the destruction – each death a release for the tortured souls trapped by the witch's magic.

But your foes are many – pressing in constantly, giving you no room to manoeuvre. Magic spills in waves from your body, blasting the statues with a wrathful fury, sending severed limbs spiralling through the air. It seems you have the upper hand – until a troll shoulders into you, throwing you back against the wall. Before you can recover, another statue – a Skard warrior – wraps his thick arms tight around you, dragging you into a crushing embrace. The troll charges in again, a frozen club raised above his sharp-tusked head . . .

But the blow never lands. Instead the arm explodes, splintering into fragments of ice. Another explosion sends the troll staggering, a spear-tip protruding from its chest. You hear a man's bellowing cry from the far side of the hall. A flash of steel whips past your face, clunking dully into the face of the Skard behind you. He is flung back, his grip loosening – just enough for you to break free, spinning round to deliver the killing blow.

You turn again, to see more of the statues falling and shattering against the ground. (If you have the keyword *repentance* on your hero sheet, turn to 36. Otherwise, turn to 682.)

515

The wooden guardian has been defeated. You may now help yourself to one of the following special rewards:

Verdant cape	Canopy cover	Werewood claws
(cloak)	(head)	(gloves)
+1 speed +3 brawn	+1 speed +1 brawn	+1 speed +2 brawn
Ability: unstoppable	Ability: overpower	Ability: gouge

With little else of interest in the room, you decide to continue onwards. Turn to 13.

516

You slip the robes over your armour, tugging the cowl down to hide your face. Then you step out from the pillar, moving forward with head bowed, arms by your side.

The acolytes' attention is focused on the ritual. As you near, one of the men turns, glancing at you with dark eyes. 'You're late,' he hisses, ushering you to take your place alongside the others.

You move past him, aware that you are now surrounded by the enemy.

Nanuk. You open up your mind, letting the bear's strength pour into you.

Spectral claws flash from your fingers. You punch through the two acolytes standing beside you, killing them before they even have a chance to react. The woman starts to turn, eyes widening. You drive both fists into her, retracting them in a shower of blood. She drops like a stone, the poker rattling across the ground.

Then you spin to face the remaining three acolytes: young and startled apprentices. For a moment, you wonder if they will run – but on seeing their mistress fall, a bitter fury overtakes them. They stand their ground, cruel daggers flicking into their gloved hands. It is time to fight:

	Speed	Magic	Armour	Health
Coven acolyte	10	7	4	30
Coven acolyte	10	6	4	30
Coven acolyte	9	6	4	20

Special abilities

🛡 **Dark mending**: At the end of each combat round, each opponent will heal themselves for 2 *health*. This cannot take them above their starting *health* and once their *health* is reduced to zero, this ability no longer applies.

🛡 **Outnumbered**: At the end of each combat round, you must take 1 damage from each surviving opponent, ignoring *armour*. This ability only applies while you are faced with multiple opponents.

If you manage to defeat these villainous mages, turn to 523.

517

You urge the guard to show his hand. He nods in agreement, placing his stones face up on the table in front of him. 'There, beat that!' he grins triumphantly. Turn to 570.

518

Raising your hands you trace the circular patterns with your fingers, connecting the lines and whorls with the magic that now flows through you. The runes start to flicker and then glow, illuminating a trail to the centre circle, where purple energies crackle above the podium. For a brief moment you glimpse some creature trapped within the bright maelstrom – a writhing ball of shadow, with tentacles whipping out through the air – then it is gone. The energy sparks out and the runes dim.

When you walk over to the podium you discover that the elemental is now trapped inside the orb, filling it with a powerful magic. (Congratulations! You have now created a *shadow orb*. If you wish to take this, simply make a note of it on your hero sheet, it does not take up backpack space.) Turn to 684.

519

You manage to shunt one of your opponents aside, narrowly avoiding the crevasse. Recovering quickly, you pull away from the other racers, passing the finish line in second place.

Congratulations! This qualifies you to enter the final race. You also receive a prize of 150 gold crowns for your second place ranking. (Replace the keyword *rookie* with the word *veteran*.) Return to the map to continue your adventure.

520

Blood and acid steam from the melted remnants of the tower platform. Behind you, one of the drakelings lies sprawled across the slatted tiles, its body speared on the roof spike. From between its curved serrated teeth, black bile continues to dribble – eating away at the stones and mortar.

For defeating the drakelings, you may now take one of the following rewards:

Corroded boots	Drakeling claw	Dark-scale skin
(feet)	(left hand: wand)	(chest)
+1 speed +1 magic	+1 speed +1 magic	+1 speed +1 armour
Ability: acid	Ability: wave	Ability: heal

When you have updated your hero sheet, turn to 336.

521

You feel a touch on your arm. It is Aslev. He nods to a pair of double doors at the opposite end of the room. You give Gurt a final contemptuous glare, then move to follow Aslev and the other Skards. When the doors are flung open, you are surprised by the sudden bite of coldness that floods into the hall, sending the brazier flames flickering. You had been expecting another, grander chamber – instead the doors have opened out onto a wind-swept hillside, the banks of snow rising steeply into the flaky mist.

'This way,' says Aslev. He makes a sharp turn to the right, climbing a set of wooden stairs half buried by the snow. They rise steeply, taking you around a pinnacle of dark rock, which soon gives way to a rough wall of ice. The steps are uneven and slippery, forcing you to deliberate over every step, the chill emptiness to your left reminding you of the sheer drop to the ground below.

The stairway becomes a stippled ridge, carved out of what you assume is a vast glacier. You spy large root-like protrusions breaking out of the ice-wall above, their spindly lengths snaking away into the haze. It isn't until you pass beneath an overhanging limb that you realise they actually are roots – their wood of the purest snow-white. As you ascend the last of the stairs the wind drives hard against you, howling across the vast plateau. Here the mist is reduced to a few ragged streamers, clinging around the tangled roots of the biggest tree you have ever seen.

It stretches into the blue, winter skies, its colossal branches sparkling with crystalline leaves. From the pale bark an icy slush oozes out of the cracks and fissures, forming a multitude of dripping candles, their tips hardened to icicles. The size of the tree would overshadow even the highest towers of Bitter Keep – its topmost canopy is almost lost to view, the bright leaves twinkling like distant stars.

'Yggdrasil,' states Aslev, glancing back at you. 'And the Hall of Vindsvall.' He motions you towards a building carved out of the tree itself. It is a longhouse, similar to Gurt's at the foot of the glacier, but this is twice the size, the wood decorated with intricate gold sculptures. You can see arched windows and stairs cut into the trunk, suggesting that the hall extends back into the hollows of the tree.

The doors of the hall stand open. You are marched into a vaulted chamber, its floor, walls and ceiling all carpeted with a fine silver frost. An immense pit has been dug into the centre of the hall, where a fire crackles and spits around the base of a wooden statue. By all reckoning, the flames should have consumed the figure – a long-haired warrior, brandishing a spear and a shield – but the pale wood appears untouched by the heat.

Past the fire you come to the foot of a set of wide stairs, which lead up to an immense dais. There, part of the natural tree protrudes into the hall, its sap funnelled into a vast teardrop that covers the surface of the dais. Inside the ice, distorted by the glistening sheen, is a high-backed throne – and seated on it is a half-giant, powerfully-built, with long hair spilling out from beneath a pronged stone-grey helm. A war-hammer rests across his knee, a shield propped against the chair. He sits frozen in the ice, looking perfectly serene – perfectly preserved.

You realise it must be Skoll, the leader of the Skards, whose spirit is lost in the Norr. The asynjur have frozen his body, to protect it from the ravages of time and starvation.

The sound of voices breaks you from your thoughts.

Your gaze shifts to a woman as she moves into view from around the ice-cropping. Her skin is as smooth and pale as that of the tree, a coppery silk gown clinging tightly to her lithe body. She steps grace-fully in bare feet, the ground sparkling with frost wherever she steps. Her age is indeterminate, the face betraying no crease or wrinkle, but her hair is snow-white, falling across her shoulders in two woven plaits.

The Skards immediately fall to the their knees, heads bowed. 'Syn Hulda,' they intone reverently.

The woman's attention is focused to the side of the hall, where you see another einherjar. His hands are clamped tightly around a young girl, struggling to restrain her.

'No! I won't leave,' the girl cries angrily. 'Why won't you listen to me? My mother was right – the ice must be broken! Skoll is dead!'

You step forward, squinting from the brilliance of the enchanted light. The girl is thin, her skin tight to her bones, making her emerald-green eyes all the brighter. Matted strands of ginger hair hang over her face, partly covering the bruise rising on her cheek.

You blink. Your mind races.

The girl is wearing a coat too large for her, and baggy breeches tucked into seal-skin boots. As she kicks and struggles against her captor, your eyes meet hers.

'Anise . . .'

The girl wriggles out of the Skard's grasp, throwing herself towards you. The next thing you know her arms are flung around your body, holding you tight – the firmness of her embrace taking you by surprise.

'Anise.' You gently brush away her hair, uncovering the smile that so captivated you back at the keep – the bright eyes, aglow with fire. Then her lips find yours. It as if your soul has been reawakened. Your senses bleed outwards, filling your dead body. Something flutters in your chest, coming alive if only for the briefest of seconds – your heart beating, lungs shivering. As you break away you suck in a long delicious breath, tasting the scent of her hair, her body, her warmth . . .

'How . . . How is this possible?' you gasp, searching her wide eyes. 'The keep . . .'

'I looked for you,' she sobs, tears running unchecked across her bruised skin. 'There was so much . . . death. I was lost. Then . . . Everard's horse . . . I rode across the bridge, before . . . before . . .'

Rough hands close around her, dragging the girl away. 'No!' she screams, kicking and punching. The einherjar drags her back across the dais, ignoring her maddened protests.

The moment she is gone you feel your body shudder, the fingers of ice clenching around your heart once again, stilling it cold. Dead.

'Take your hands off her!' you growl angrily, drawing your weapons. You start forward but the woman intervenes, stepping between you. She regards you with sharp, cobalt eyes.

'What is this?' she asks politely, her gaze flicking quickly to Aslev. The Skards remain kneeling while Aslev recounts your audience with Gurt and your desire to help free Skoll.

'Nonsense, I can't possibly allow it,' she replies, her tone smooth and confident. 'This is a sacred hall – and I will not have . . . death brought here.'

You bristle with rage. 'Sura sent me – why won't you people listen?'

Syn arches her back, startled by your outrage. 'You are truly some wild animal,' she says in a tight voice. 'I do not have the time or the patience to tame you.'

The woman's cold calmness only incites your rage further. A growl issues from your lips as you leap for her, but hands settle around your arms, pulling you back. Aslev and one of the other einherjar grip you tightly.

'Let me go!' you hiss sharply.

'You're doing this all wrong,' whispers Aslev.

'Throw them both from this hall,' says the woman, turning her long pale neck to regard Anise. 'The dogs need feeding. And they are not as choosy of their meat as I.'

'No!' You snarl, trying to break free. 'I came here to save you – to help defeat the witch!'

The woman's head snaps round, looking you straight in the eye. 'The dogs will rip the lies out of you, corpse-walker.' The stillness of her face makes her words all the more chilling.

She turns and walks away, her supple body moving gracefully across the frosted floor.

'Damn you!' you spit, struggling again to free yourself.

Aslev pushes his face close to your own. 'Stop!' he growls.

You glance at him, teeth clenched. 'Unhand me, or I swear I will not be responsible . . .'

'Just wait – and calm yourself.' Aslev removes his hands from you, then intercepts the other einherjar who is struggling to drag Anise from the chamber. Words are exchanged – both Skards look back towards the dais. The woman has departed, having exited through an archway at the back of the hall. Aslev nods then hurries back to you, glancing back towards the arch. 'Do what you have to do,' he states quickly. 'You will get one chance at this. If you have the . . . power you say you have, then now is your time.'

You break from the other warrior's grip, glaring at him angrily – then you look to Aslev. 'Is this another trick?'

The white-haired Skard flushes with anger. He stabs a gloved finger in your direction. 'Listen and understand, southlander. We endanger our lives and our names for this. Now, do what you must – enter the Norr.'

'No, please . . .' Anise runs to your side, pulling on your cloak. 'We should go from here. There is nothing you can do.'

You turn to her. 'What did you mean, when you said your mother was right?'

Anise looks surprised by the question. 'She was an asynjur. Syn had her executed for speaking out. My mother knew they couldn't save Skoll – keeping him frozen here, like this, only keeps our people from choosing a new Drokke. Don't you see, I think this is what she wants. Syn Hulda . . . she is not what she seems. I am sure of it.'

'Is that why you are nameless?' You put a hand to her cheek, your thumb wiping away her tears.

The girl nods, lowering her head in shame. 'I was cast out . . . Syn has made it known to all. My family, my bloodline is cursed.'

You look past her shoulder, meeting Aslev's gaze. You exchange a knowing look. He steps forward, his hands settling around her arms. Anise glances round, then struggles against his grip. 'What . . . what are you doing?' she snaps.

'I have to do this,' you whisper tenderly. 'I will come back, I promise.'

'No!' Anise wrestles to free herself. 'It's too dangerous!'

You approach the wall of ice, your gaze settling on the distorted image of the half-giant Skard seated on his frozen throne. *Nanuk.* You close your eyes, placing the palms of your hands against the cold ice. You let its frigid chill flow into you, numbing your mind, your senses. *Find the other asynjur. Take me to them.*

Sounds drift away one by one. Slowly, you erase the world around you, letting your spirit lift free of your dead body, rising up to become one with the dream-world of the Norr. Turn to 311.

522

You place the 'one of crowns' on the discard pile and pick a new stone from the bag. You have gained the 'two of moons'.

You have the following stones:

The monk decides to play his hand. Turn to 593.

523

You cut Skoll and Anise free of their bindings. The warrior slumps to his knees, still groggy from whatever charm spell the coven used to entrap them. Anise throws her arms around you, holding you tight.

'Where did you go?' she whispers. Her fingers stroke your new armaments, brought back from the Norr and still smouldering with dark magics.

'Just exorcising a few demons,' you smile thinly.

Skoll finds his feet, staggering slightly until he regains his balance. Pushing hair out of his eyes, he offers you a bemused grin. 'Rescued again. This will do nothing for my standing.' He scans the bodies, then makes towards a pile of belongings stacked on a wooden pallet. He has spied his helmet and his pack. He starts towards them, then pauses, glancing back.

'First time north of the face, you should take in the view.' He nods to the wide tunnel across the other side of the cave, its black walls edged by the brightness of daylight. 'I'll get the rest of our gear.'

You follow Anise up the tunnel, her hand inside your own as you step out onto the shelf of rock. Below you, a plain of melting snow breaks into a rust-coloured wasteland dotted with jagged peaks and ridges. A dead land, mirrored by the listless yellow sky, its wide expanse dotted with floating islands of rock. They hang in the sky like dark clouds, their undersides dripping with dust and a foul decay.

The sight is both breath-taking and haunting.

Anise tightens her grip on your hand. 'This is it, the last stage of our journey.'

You nod, keeping silent, the spinner's words weighing heavy on your mind. *A sacrifice will have to be made, boy. Only you will be able to choose, life or death.*

You turn to look upon Anise. So beautiful, despite the firm set of her features, skin as delicate and white as egg shells. 'I won't let any harm come to you, I promise.'

Tears leak from the corners of her eyes. 'I know.'

You take Anise in your arms and hold her close. (Return to the Act 2 quest map to continue your journey.)

524

You soon discover the challenge of the slope is not the slipperiness of the ice, but the ridges and razor-backed rocks that protrude from its surface. Your sled bounces and swings across the hard ground, its runners threatening to break at any moment.

You will need to take a challenge test using your *stability* attribute:

	Stability
Bone breaker	12

If you are successful, turn to 103. Otherwise, turn to 214.

525

Another set of stairs brings you to what you assume was once a barracks. The shattered remains of bunk beds occupy the left and right-hand walls, joining rusted weapons and shields that have spilled out of several toppled weapon racks.

In the centre of the room is a square wooden table, which appears to have escaped the rest of the devastation. Seated at it are two ghosts, one a guard clad in rusted plate and chainmail, the other a tall hooded figure swathed in mottled black robes. Both of them seem intent on playing a game involving small runic stones. The guard looks to be losing, his ghostly-green expression one of fear and dismay as he studies the dice-sized stones in his hand. You enter the room warily, fearing that they may attack or sound an alarm – but both of the ghosts remain focused on their game, oblivious to their surroundings.

Will you:

Watch the game?	414
Search the debris?	310
Leave and continue?	188

526

You opt to go first, throwing yourself into a full-on sprint. Fire roars all around you, the glyphs sparking with magic as your boots strike the stone. To survive the 'corridor of doom' you must pass a number of *speed* challenges. Each challenge you successfully complete allows you to move to the next challenge on the list.

If you fail a drake fire challenge, you must immediately take 12 damage, ignoring *armour*. You may then move onto the next challenge. If you fail a lightning challenge, you are knocked back to the previous challenge on the list, which you must pass again to proceed:

	Speed
Drake fire	12
Lightning rune	13
Drake fire	12
Lightning rune	13
Drake fire	14
Lightning rune	13

If you still have *health* remaining after completing all the challenges then you have reached the end of the corridor. Turn to 637. If you lose all your *health*, you must count this as a defeat on your hero sheet. You may then try the challenge again, or opt to find an alternative route (turn to 672).

527

Lured by the thought of treasure, you slide down the slope into the sludgy slime. To your relief, you only sink up to your waist in the foul substance, but its acidic properties are slowly eating away at your clothing and flesh and corroding your weapons. (You must lose one attribute point from any two of your equipped items.)

You press on into the pool, moving as quickly as the thick sludge will allow. With great effort, you manage to reach the first of the bobbing objects – all glowing with a faint green residue of magic. If you wish, you may take one of the following items:

Nightspeed's shoe	Symbiotic scales	Poisoned acorn (2 uses)
(talisman)	(chest)	(backpack)
+5 health	+1 speed +1 armour	Use instead of rolling for
Ability: haste, charm	Ability: evade	a damage score to inflict
		venom on one opponent

You must now decide if you will risk heading deeper into the pool to grab more items (turn to 736) or wade back to shore and leave the chamber (turn to 303).

528

The drakeling struggles to maintain its course, dipping lower into the rift.

'Come on! Faster!' You try and urge the creature to greater effort, but you sense the magic failing – slowly drawing itself back inside you, leaving the coldness of the grave to take hold of the creature once again.

A sheer wall of rock veers to your left as the drakeling gives its last breath, then starts to plummet. To your surprise, the fall is short and abrupt, ending with the crunch of bones – thankfully, the drakeling's. You have crashed onto a narrow ledge, jutting out from the side of the rift. In the wall facing you are two openings. One looks like it was carved by design, with a cracked archway stretching across the entrance. The other looks like a fresh opening, little more than a jagged crevice, most likely caused by the recent quakes.

You turn and look back across the mile of emptiness to the far side of the rift. A dust cloud hangs heavy in the air, obscuring what was once the keep. From the chunks of stone still spilling into the abyss, you doubt anything of the structure now remains. Even the bridge, which once spanned the gulf, is now crumbling and coming away from the rock, its shattered parts spinning end over end, oddly silent as they are swallowed by the bottomless void.

The way home – lost forever.

Another tremor shakes the ground, almost causing you to pitch forward into that same darkness. You quickly step away from the edge, your attention shifting back to the two openings. Perhaps one will provide a safe path back to the surface.

Will you:

Slip into the crevice?	434
Head underneath the archway?	20

529

'It's the final race – and the stakes are high. Only ten competitors left, the best of the best, and Ryker's got a real challenge in store. Bleak Peak – the mountain that takes no prisoners. Have your wits about you, kid, because there can only be one winner – and unless you got the guts and the cunning to beat the opposition, you're gonna be eating dirt.' Turn to 79.

530

You half expected the camp to be bustling with activity, but it is oddly quiet – only a few men and women are trudging through the snow, attending to their chores. You see Desnar leading a small entourage towards the edge of the camp. He is carrying a spear of bone in one hand and a leather pack in the other. At his side you see the boy from the lakeside who had run to fetch the others.

'What's happening?' You look to Sura for an explanation.

'He was Himruk, first son of Desnar. He was a coward and so he is stripped of name. The nameless have no place in our tribe.'

You watch as Desnar hands the spear and pack to his son. Then he draws back his hand – and slaps the youth hard to the ground. The warrior barks something in Skard, then kicks the boy until the child finds his feet again. Motioning to the icy wastes, Desnar and his men watch impassively as the boy wipes away his tears, then sets his gaze to the horizon.

'What will become of him?' You watch the child stagger away through the snow, the wind whipping his braided hair. He looks so young – too naïve to be braving the harsh wilderness alone.

'He will die,' says Sura flatly, with no hint of remorse. 'Or he will hunt and survive – and come back a man.'

'You are a harsh people,' you remark with distaste.

'This is a harsh land. Now follow me.' Sura leads you to the opposite edge of the camp, where a large animal hide has been stretched across the ground, tied to what look like mammoth tusks. Runes have been daubed onto the hide in various coloured dyes, forming a circular arrangement.

'I will teach you the ways of the asynjur,' says Sura, gesturing for you to stand in the circle. 'If your magic is strong, then we can make a shaman of you – strengthen your link with the Norr.' Sura paces around you, eyeing you like an exhibit in the palace museum. 'But you have a rare strength. What I saw last night . . . I could focus your mind to pull Nanuk into you, like the were-warriors of old. To channel his energy, to shift your body into your spirit animal.'

You grimace at the woman, finding neither idea particularly appealing. As she continues to pace your eyes fix on one of the Skard warriors, practising a deadly set of manoeuvres with a hooked chain. It is similar to the one you saw Ninvuk use when you were attacked by the Nisse. A row of bones have been set up in the snow several metres away. The Skard is using the chain to whip each bone into the air, his skilful movements guiding the chain with startling precision.

'The hook and claw,' Sura nods, noting your interest. 'Used by the pirates of Rowan and Vaidskrig. Some of our people have mastered its use. A most deadly weapon, in the right hands.'

Will you:

Learn the shaman career (requirement: mage)?	686
Learn the were career (requirement: warrior)?	607
Learn the reaver career (requirement: rogue)?	382
Decline learning a new career?	197

531

Your sled has taken a serious battering from the rough crossing. You must permanently reduce your sled's *stability* rating by 2. When you have updated your sheet, turn to 422.

532

You decide to place your hand inside the hollow. The moment your fingers and palm settle against the cold dark wood, you feel a sharp pain. Instinctively, you snatch back your hand, nursing it to your chest. To your horror, you see teeth-like fangs protruding from around the handprint, several of which are now flecked with blood. Slowly, the fangs sink back into the bark.

Looking down at your hand you see that the teeth have punctured you, the ruptured flesh already puffy and bubbling with a deadly green poison. You have been inflicted with the following curse:

Curse of frailty (pa): You must lower your *health* by 5 until you next roll a double in combat.

You glance back at the cell, where the Skard is struggling once again to reach the dagger.

Will you:

Try using something from your backpack?	710
Attempt to chop through the barrier?	439
Leave and continue your journey?	6

533

You remove the medallion from around your neck and offer it to the knight. A golden light flickers around its edge, throwing stark shadows across the rooftop.

The knight spreads his arms, tensed and ready to jump – then he catches sight of the medallion. His expression darkens almost instantly. 'What is this?'

He steps down from the battlements, tugging his sword free from its scabbard. 'You have my brother's medallion – the mark of my family.' His voice cuts clear through the wind, deep and resonating.

'Take it!' You shout hoarsely, struggling against the dryness in your throat. 'Your brother forgives you!'

The knight shows no sign of having heard you – as if your words have been torn away by the keening gale. Anise clings to your side, fearful of the man's haunted demeanour.

'Put it away,' she cries. 'I told you, no good will come of this!'

'You are the necromancer's work!' sneers the knight with disdain. 'My brother is dead. I killed him with my own hand! There is no forgiveness for what I did!'

Before you can stop him, the knight's pace quickens into a full-on charge. You drop the medallion, quickly drawing your own weapons to defend yourself. It is time to fight:

	Speed	Magic	Armour	Health
Rinehart	2	2	2	35

If you manage to overcome this grief-stricken ghost turn to **505**. If you lose the combat, remember to record your defeat on your hero sheet. You may then attempt the combat again or return to the map.

534

Three scruffy-looking men are seated at the bar, smoking rolls of tobacco and knocking back mugs of ale. You overhear snatches of their conversation.

'Good thing he got the money to entertain all them pimped up highballers, I wouldn't want to be footing the bill.'

'He ain't, I told you,' sighs one of the other men. 'I heard ol' Baron No Mark is paying for everything. Only way he can get a piece of the action.'

'No Mark?' The third speaker almost chokes on his ale. 'That's rich coming from the likes of you, Sykes. That No Mark, as you call 'im, runs most of the mines down south. He's the man for the job and everyone knows it, but he can't move his operations here without coin – and without Ryker's nod. He gotta suck up to the big guys this time, and you bet he hates every minute of it.'

Will you:

Talk to the barman?	420
Take a seat in one of the alcoves?	634
Leave?	426

535

You lose your grip and fall, hitting the rocks at the bottom of the mountain. (You must count this as one 'defeat' on your hero sheet.) Angrily you struggle to your feet, using your one responsive arm to balance yourself. The other hangs limply at your side.

With a defiant growl you butt your shoulder into the wall, locking the bones back into place. After flexing your fingers, you glare stubbornly at the mountain, contemplating another attempt.

Will you:

Try the climb again?	67
Look for an alternative entrance?	275

536

Pulses of lightning flicker across the magical weave, promising a deadly shock to anything that catches on its criss-crossing strands. Undaunted, you continue to accelerate towards the web, tilting your craft in order to pass through one of the narrow spaces.

To avoid hitting the web, you must take a challenge test using your transport's speed:

	Speed
Spider and the fly	13

If you are successful, turn to 596. If you fail the challenge, turn to 768.

The last creature has you pinned against the wall as you drive your weapon deep into its chest, teeth gritted as the steel slides past scales and bone. Steaming blood boils out from the wound, thick and viscous like molten magma. You kick the creature away, leaving your weapon in its chest – then dive for cover as its body starts to glow brighter, smoke rising from its nostrils and eye sockets. With a wet-sounding boom the body explodes, showering the wall of the keep with a spray of glittering blood. Your weapon skitters across the ground to rest next to you, still glowing with heat.

You have gained the following:

Ember touched
(special)
You may add the special
ability *sear* to your main
hand or left hand weapon

For defeating the ember wilds, you may now help yourself to one of the following rewards:

Rift spike	**Warded scales**	**Scarlet crest**
(left hand: dagger)	(chest)	(left hand: axe)
+1 speed +1 brawn	+1 speed +1 brawn	+1 speed +1 brawn
Ability: sweet spot	Ability: might of stone	Ability: heavy blow
(requirement rogue)		(requirement: warrior)

When you have updated your hero sheet, turn to 162.

538

The chamber continues to shudder violently. Scrabbling through the dust, your hands settle around the witch's wand. Clutching it tight, you lurch drunkenly to your feet, eyes shifting to the demon.

Chunks of rock rain down from the ceiling, bouncing over the mass of corpulent flesh. The demon's veins burn bright with fire, its heart pulsing faster and faster, looking like it might explode at any moment, bursting out of its pus-leaking chamber.

'Die!' you scream – filling that single word with all your hate and pain, and anger. Your arm snaps back then flings the wand through the air, your magic guiding its trajectory straight into the heart. There is a flash of bright, blue light.

A wall of noise crashes over you, its force knocking you backwards. A booming wail, so loud and deafening that it dwarfs the thunder of the devastation around you.

Then the heart blackens, frost crawling across its bloated mass. The livid veins fill with ice, turning blue as their fires are quenched. From the tentacles you hear the crackling of frozen flesh, their dead skin crumbling away to form a dead white ash – leaving only the frost-blackened body behind, its life expelled by the full onslaught of your wrath.

The demon is dead.

A rustle of falling dust – and everything is still.

You stumble wearily across the chamber, wanting desperately to weep – but your spirit body denies you even that final reprieve. 'Anise . . .' You fall by her side, grabbing her pale, cold hand. You wince, releasing it when you see the frost-blackened marks left by your fingertips.

She is already dead, staring up at the dawn light, its soft radiance creeping through the shattered dome of the chamber.

If you have the keyword *repentance* on your hero sheet, turn to 699. Otherwise, turn to 586.

539

To your surprise, you come out on top – your dog-team having maimed several of your opponent's lead hounds. You quickly pull away, crossing the finish line in first place!

Congratulations! This qualifies you to enter the final race. You also receive a prize of 200 gold crowns for your first place ranking. (Replace the keyword *rookie* with the word *veteran*.) Return to the map to continue your adventure.

540

The enraged beast throws itself into a desperate charge. You roll aside just in time, leaving the mammoth to plunge headfirst into a heap of skeletal remains. Quickly, you circle round the immobilised beast, raining blows to its flanks and rear, until it is finally brought crashing down – showering you in ice and bone dust.

If you are a warrior, turn to 725. If you are a mage, turn to 38. If you are a rogue, turn to 268.

541

The guard removes the two of moons from his hand and places it face down on the discard pile. He reaches into the pouch and takes another stone at random. He has now gained the two of stars:

He can barely hide his excitement as he shows you the stones. A full house and two crowns is a strong hand. It is now time for his opponent to make his move. Turn to 555.

542

As you approach the mountain you feel Nidhogg shifting course, re-exerting his control. At first you assume he is taking you in to land, but then you spot the jagged outcropping he is headed for. A creature lies sleeping on the rocks, a pair of leathery wings folded across its immense, reptilian body.

Another dragon. Larger than any you have encountered before.

'Nidhogg – stop!' You try and take command, but the dragon is resisting. Unable to alter your course, you are forced to watch helplessly as you draw closer and closer to the beast.

The fading sunlight shimmers across endless rows of emerald-green scales, layered to form a bright mantle of armour. Their shadowed contours highlight the muscled curves of its powerful body, tapering back over hundreds of metres into a coiled tail of dizzying spirals.

Awe turns to fear . . . then rage. Your link with Nidhogg makes you party to his feelings, and his surge of hatred is almost overwhelming.

Seethe!

Nidhogg is headed straight for his nemesis, a blustery roar issuing from his mouth. The other dragon lifts his horned snout, displaying a single slanted eye which sleepily widens into glowing crimson.

Brother. I have been expecting you. The voice is a sibilant hiss. *I knew Melusine would never break you. Not like the others. Always the stubborn one. Always the fool.*

Seethe releases his hold on the rock, his wings remaining tight to his body as he stretches into a dive. Nidhogg doesn't slow or deviate from his path – the two dragons are careering straight towards one another, their collision inevitable.

'Nidhogg! No!' Desperately you try and regain control, but the dragon has blocked you from his mind, leaving you beating against an impenetrable wall.

The two enemies crash together in a tangle of bodies, tails lashing furiously, claws raking and tearing through flesh. Blood showers around you like rain.

You betrayed us. Your own kin! Nidhogg's jaws clamp around the other's neck, fangs scraping over scale and bone.

You cannot win, little brother. Her magic has made me stronger.

The mighty green digs his claws deep into Nidhogg, twisting his heavier body and dragging you straight into the side of the mountain. You jump free, sliding and rolling through a flurry of red dust to finally land on a narrow plateau jutting from the mountain's face. Anise and Skoll tumble next to you, quickly finding their feet as the two dragons continue to wrestle and claw in the dirt. The green already has the upper hand, pinning Nidhogg to the ground, belching a steaming spray of acid over his body.

The black dragon squirms in pain, his hacking, guttural cries echoing back from the mountain's gullies. His mind barriers fall – and then you feel his pain.

You collapse to your knees, gripping your head as the searing heat rushes through you, threatening to burn away your very being.

You can dimly hear Anise's voice somewhere close. 'Arran? Arran, what is it? What's wrong?'

'It's Nidhogg.' Skoll shakes you, pulling you to your feet. 'They are still bonded. They share each other's pain.'

Another wave of agony spears into your mind. You can taste the dragon's blood, the smell of sulphur rising from his burnt flesh. A hot blinding flash. Then the dragon's consciousness starts to fade, his life force ebbing away.

Skoll shakes you again, as if trying to wake you from a bad dream. 'Break the link. You must let go!'

'No!' You shove the warrior aside, staggering towards the two flailing shapes. With each faltering step, your strength returns. Another stride and you are running. You leap onto the nearest of Nidhogg's wings, using it to gain height, scrambling across the burnt scales to straddle his ridged spine. Your weapons ring from their scabbards as you meet your adversary's crimson gaze.

Seethe throws back his head with a mocking laughter. *Oh, how you have fallen, little brother. To rely on a human to fight your battles.*

Quickly, you reach out with your magic, taking control of Nidhogg's body.

You are weak! Seethe slashes down with his claws, but you are already moving, guiding Nidhogg's actions. Together, you twist aside, whipping a razor-sharp tail across Seethe's belly. The green lurches back, surprised by the retaliation.

Nidhogg gives a throaty roar, his vigour returning. *This is not weakness, Seethe. This is loyalty. Let us remind you of what that means, brother!* It is time to fight:

	Speed	Magic	Armour	Health
Seethe	13	8	9	100

Special abilities

- ❤ **Poison spray**: At the start of every combat round, Seethe sprays poison. This inflicts 1 die of damage, ignoring *armour*, and reduces Nidhogg's *stability* and *toughness* by 2.
- ❤ **Fire at will**: You may use your *dragon fire* ability in this combat.

(Note: If Nidhogg's *stability* has been reduced to zero, you can no longer use his associated ability.)

If you manage to defeat this corrupted dragon, turn to 430.

543

You notice a number of treasures tangled up in the drake's parasitic tentacles. If you wish, you may now take one of the following rewards:

Fafnir's fury	Ghost	Lamentation
(main hand: dagger)	(head)	(ring)
+1 speed +2 brawn	+1 speed +1 brawn	+2 brawn
Ability: decay	Ability: veiled strike	Ability: fear

You hope, with the death of the corrupted Titan, the explorers and Caul are now finally at peace. After giving the frozen trapper a final nod of farewell, you head into the glacial tunnels – following them back to the surface. (Return to the quest map to continue your adventure.)

544

Skoll crouches down, then begins to draw lines in the snow. 'There were nine. Old Gods from the time before time.' He makes nine strokes with his finger. 'They taught the dwarves the magic. The same magic they gave to my people.' He starts to draw a circle around each line, one after the other. 'The Titans grew old and frail, so they made new bodies out of stone. Then they put their spirits inside, making them immortal.'

Skoll leans back, looking down at the nine circles. 'Then came the cataclysm, when the earth shook. A great demon from the underworld had awakened – Jormungdar. The serpent's coils tore through the land. It would have destroyed everything, but the Titans and the Dwarves built a prison. They used their magic to trap Jormungdar inside, deep within the ground. But to make something so large, so strong, came with a cost. The magic ripped a hole in our realm, a door to the shroud. The Well of Urd. To stop the demons coming through, eight of the Titans sacrificed themselves.' Skoll crosses out eight of the circles. 'They hold the demons back to this very day, giants of stone that can never move or break from their task.'

'And the ninth?' you ask, noting the final uncrossed circle.

'If all the Titans had sacrificed themselves, the well might have been closed forever. But Fafnir did not help his kin. He desired life, to remain ever-living.' Skoll breathes a sigh as he brushes away the marks. 'My people sing ballads of his deeds, fighting side-by-side with the Dwarves against the evil that came from the underworld. They are good songs, but I do not know the truth of them. I fear the choice that Fafnir made, to betray the other Titans, may have doomed us all.'

Return to 602 to ask another question or turn to 326 to end the conversation.

545

'Every tribe has a chieftain – and the chieftain wears the halstek, the symbol of our ancestors.' Sura's gaze drifts to one of the staffs lying amongst the blankets. Its ivory top-piece has been carved to resemble a bear's head, its jaws stretched wide in a vicious snarl. 'Desnar has challenged you for the halstek. Without it, he cannot truly lead us.'

'Then he can have it,' you raise your hands in submission. 'I don't want to lead. Who would follow me? Desnar is a Skard. He should have it.'

Sura is silent, regarding you thoughtfully as she tongues her gums. Then she speaks. 'You are a dull blade, southlander. No good to anyone. But we can sharpen you, yes.' She nods, her eyes continuing to appraise you. 'Desnar is not a man to respect. He is hard. He is cunning. But he does not have what you have . . .' The woman leans close, her eyes lifting to meet your own. 'Nanuk.'

Will you:

Ask about the shaman's magic?	688
Ask what 'vela styker' means?	587
End the conversation?	575

546

If you know the password, then assign a number to each letter based on its position in the alphabet (a=1, b=2, c=3 and so on). Total the individual numbers and turn to the relevant entry number. If you are successful, read on. Otherwise, you have given the wrong password. You can either try and bluff your way through (turn to 451) or leave and return later (turn to 426).

547

A few metres from Bullet's corpse, you find a selection of traps and knives scattered across the ice. A quick inspection confirms that they are still serviceable. Evidently these must have been the trapper's tools – and with their previous owner now deceased, there is nothing stopping you from laying claim to these grisly items.

If you wish, you may now learn the trapper career. The trapper has the following special abilities:

Best laid plans (pa): Before a combat starts, decide which type of trap you will lay (you can only lay one trap per combat). Roll a die to give you a trigger number:

* **Snap jack:** Your trigger number is the number of rounds your trap will take to snap closed. (If you roll a ⚄ then your trap will activate at the start of the fifth combat round.) When it does, a single opponent of your choosing automatically takes 10 damage, ignoring *armour*.
* **Cluster mine:** Your trigger number is the number of rounds your trap will take to go off and the maximum number of opponents affected. (If you roll a ⚂ then your trap will set off on the third round and affect three opponents.) Each affected opponent of your choosing takes 1 damage die ignoring *armour*, and their *armour* is then reduced by 1 for the remainder of the combat.

Vital artery (co + pa): Instead of rolling for a damage score after winning a round, you can use *vital artery*. This inflicts 1 damage die to a single opponent, ignoring *armour*, and does a further 1 point of damage at the end of each combat round for the duration of the combat. You can only use this ability once per combat.

As a trapper you also receive a bonus of +5 gold crowns when selling hides (you will be reminded of this bonus at the appropriate times). When you have made your decision, return to the map to continue your adventure.

548

Fragments of armour swirl up off the dusty floor, whipped along on bright currents of magic. They spin and twirl toward the centre of the room, where the ghost of a man stands, arms and legs extended – squirming and struggling as the armour snaps into place around his body, suiting him in plates of black iron.

'No . . . Zabarach! I will not serve you!'

A helm slides over his face, muffling his words. Then a sword settles into the palm of his hand, its blade igniting with dark flames.

You glance at Anise, then back at the knight – wondering if you should stay or run. Suddenly the door behind you slams closed, the force of its movement almost rattling it off its hinges.

'You are mine!'

A spectral figure rises over the knight's shoulder, clad in billowing robes. Long locks of white hair flow back from the man's scalp, stirring back and forth as if submerged beneath water. 'Mott, you serve me.' He points to you with a gnarly finger. 'Now go, my servant – and slay the brother who betrays us!'

The knight obeys, striding purposefully towards you, red orbs of hatred burning between the visor of his helm.

'They're ghosts, trapped in the past,' cries Anise, tugging on the door, trying desperately to open it. 'Remember Harris's story – Mott and Rinehart were brothers. Rinehart had to slay his brother!'

Evil laughter fills the room as the undead knight continues to advance, his magic sword sputtering flames of cold shadow. It is time to fight:

	Speed	Magic	Armour	Health
Mott	3	2	1	25

Special abilities

🛡 **In dark service**: Once Mott is reduced to zero *health*, roll a die. On a result of ⚀ or more, he rises from the dead, regaining 10 *health*. If he is defeated a second time, this ability no longer applies.

If you manage to overcome this accursed knight, turn to 227. If you lose the combat, remember to record your defeat on your hero sheet. You may then attempt the combat again or return to the map.

549

'I'm the sixth clerk they sent 'ere. First two only stuck it for one week, the third went a bit crazy. As for the others . . . well, no one knows exactly what happened to the others. Think there was some . . . altercation with the Skards.'

'So you've taken to barricading yourself in?' You wave a hand over the iron-panelled wall. 'Is trading really that dangerous?'

'You ever met a Skard?' Jackson shakes his muskets, his eye looming large against the glass peep hole. 'I got weapons back 'ere, food, equipment, gold. The trappers are fine; they're civilised – well, as civilised as anyone gets out 'ere. But the Skards . . . They ain't ones for small talk. They don't wanna trade, they just wanna take – like the world owes 'em something. I ask you, do I look like I'm handin' out charity?' He pauses, as if expecting an answer – then continues regardless. 'Last trading post was stripped down – everything gone. Them Skards will steal anything that ain't nailed down. But Jackson don't go running, snivelling like some goblin runt. I'm sticking it out – ain't no one taking this trading post from me.'

Will you:

Attempt to break in?	740
Discuss something else?	685
Leave?	Return to the map

You brush the girl's eyelids with your fingertips – closing them for the last time. Despite everything she has endured, there is a comforting look of peace about her. 'I wish I could be with you.' Leaning close, you kiss her forehead, a web of frost sparkling across her skin. Then you rise and walk away.

You have gained the title *The Mourner* and the following special ability:

Tormented soul (mo): You may sacrifice 4 *health* to instantly restore a speed or combat ability that you have already used. This ability can only be used once per combat.

You may now return to the map or advance to the final boss monster encounter by turning to 717.

551
Quest: Angels and demons

Light radiates through the translucent walls of ice, casting a sparkling sheen across the frozen floe-channels and tumbled-down slabs; the light a reminder of a world that exists outside these caves. It is a torment rather than a comfort.

Since ascending the ancient stairway that led into the North Face, the caves and tunnels have been unending. Skoll was sure you would encounter goblins and other dark creatures on your journey, but so far you have discovered nothing – save for a growing sense of unease, heightened by solitude.

Tempers are frayed and starting to show.

With little else to occupy your thoughts, you have found yourself resenting your physical bulk more and more. Every movement is now a sluggish effort, as if your brain – your spirit energy – is struggling to drive the body that you are forced to inhabit. Your dead limbs feel heavier than usual. Many times you stagger on the slippery ice, bumping arms and shoulders against the tight walls. Sometimes you wish for a stab of pain – a sign of life. Instead, there is only the dull numbness. It is an effort not to draw your spirit away and leave your body behind; return to the Norr. You desperately crave its freedom – to be back with Nanuk.

Skoll and Anise have grown closer. You can see it in their furtive looks, the way they huddle close at night, sharing their bodies' warmth. They are still human – they share that bond. You wonder what Anise sees when she looks upon you. Unlike them, you are numb to the cold and have no defence against its bite. They quickly feel the pain and know to warm themselves, or huddle deeper into their furs. You have no such warning. The ice constantly eats away at you, turning more of your pale flesh to a charcoal black.

You watch them.

Sometimes the jealousy is too much to bear. Listening to them. Talking. Laughing. Whispering.

On a few occasions, when Anise has noticed your pensive glares, she has reluctantly moved to join you – an uncomfortable silence ensuing. Once you tried to lighten the mood by asking for some lessons in Skard, believing it would bridge the divide. But you've never had a tongue for languages, and picking up the guttural words proved difficult for you. Frustration quickly led to anger – and the lesson ended with the two of you arguing. Skoll has been respectful enough to keep his distance, but there is often challenge in his eyes. And a wariness.

Deeper and deeper you go.

On day four, you find the bodies.

They are human, dressed in foul-stinking furs. You count nine, arranged in a rough circle, surrounded by their few motley belongings. Amongst the packs and rolls you spot several picks and hammers. Several of the men have a red cloth-band tied around an upper arm.

Two creatures are crouched next to a body, trying to tug a belt loose to get at a pouch. At first you mistake them for goblins, but their skin is as translucent as the ice, their big round eyes pale and milky.

'Svardkin!' hisses Skoll. He drops his pack, tugging an axe free. 'Get away from them, thieves!'

The two creatures startle, then make a dash for the safety of a nearby tunnel. You notice one of them is clutching a cloth bundle to its chest. Evidently, they have pilfered something from the miners.

Will you:

Stay and examine the bodies?   66

Chase after the svardkin?   778

552

A woman is walking around the pens, feeding the dogs from a bucket of fatty entrails. You call her over, nodding to the larger hounds tethered next to the kennels. 'Are these for sale?'

The woman tips her bucket, emptying the last of the sloppy remains next to one of the hounds. It pounces on the gristly meat, its sharp canines ripping at it hungrily.

'Sure, if you've got a sled – I have a few good alphas that'll lead your dog-team.' The woman raises her gloved mitts, splattered with grease and blood. 'My name's Leeta. I would shake your hand, but . . .'

You nod with an understanding grimace. 'What else do you have for sale?'

'The races are tough,' she sighs, blowing out her cheeks. 'The riders run their dogs ragged, some don't make it to the end. It's a fine line, getting the most of out of 'em – but I can help you there. I got whips and collars, whole load of dog toys to keep your team ahead of the pack.'

Will you:

Purchase a lead dog? (requirement: sled)   502

View the dog equipment?   477

Explore the rest of the compound?   106

553

For defeating the rift demon, you may now help yourself to one of the following rewards:

Bristle backbone	**Crackdown**	**Dusk needles**
(chest)	(head)	(cloak)
+1 speed +1 armour	+2 brawn	+1 speed +1 brawn
Ability: thorn armour	Ability: charge	Ability: impale

When you have updated your hero sheet, turn to 503.

554

The rush of cold is sudden and fierce, punching through your chest, freezing your heart and stealing your very last breath. It fills you, numbs you, a coldness so intense that it burns the stone beneath your feet, cracking it to frozen splinters.

If you wish, you may now learn the soul thief career. The soul thief has the following special abilities:

Mind flay (co): Instead of rolling for a damage score, you can cast *mind flay*. Roll 1 damage die and apply the result to each of your opponents, ignoring their *armour*. For each opponent that takes damage, you may restore 2 *health* to your hero. This ability can only be used once per combat.

Heart steal (pa): Whenever you use *piercing* or *deep wound* in combat, you may automatically roll an extra die for damage.

When you have made your decision, turn to 677.

555

The hooded ghost opens its fist and lets the stones roll onto the table. They all land face up, displaying a perfect house and a crown. 'Royal Hoard,' whispers a voice from beneath the cowl.

The guard looks at the symbols with a sly grin, then places his own stones, one by one, onto the table. As each stone is displayed the hooded ghost leans a little closer to the table, bony fingers gripping the table-edge. 'No, it can't be.'

The guard displays a matching Royal Hoard, but his hand beats his opponent's, with a higher house and the two of crowns.

'You cheated! You cheated!' The hooded figure stands, his dark form seeming to stretch and grow larger. Bony hands reach for the guard, the cowl finally falling back to reveal a grinning skull.

Undaunted by his foe, the guard raises an arm – summoning a magical sword to his hand. Leaning away from the grasping fingers, he drives the shimmering blade through the mottled robes, eliciting an ear-piercing shriek from the ghoulish skeleton.

'I win!' He grins, withdrawing the blade and watching in triumph as the robes slide empty to the floor. 'Game over.'

He turns to you, then points past your shoulder with the tip of his sword. You follow the line of the blade to a cobwebbed corner of the room. Suddenly, a pair of stones start to lift out from one of the walls, flipping outwards to reveal a secret alcove. 'Your reward,' he replies. 'For Valeron. For Glory.' Then he tilts back his head, eyes focusing on something unseen – and vanishes from sight.

'Treasure! Look!' Anise is already crossing the room to the alcove. 'There's potions here!'

You hurry to join her, eager to discover what rewards the guard has left behind. As well as 40 gold crowns, you may also take any/all of the following items:

Pot of healing (2 uses)	Four of stars	Pot of speed (2 uses)
(backpack)	(ring)	(backpack)
Use any time in combat	+1 brawn +1 magic	Use any time in combat
to restore 4 *health*	Ability: charm	to raise your *speed* by 2
		for one combat round

You may now search the room, if you haven't already (turn to 310) or leave through the open doorway (turn to 188).

Legendary monster: *Naglfar* the Corpse Ship

Birds rise up out of the gully; ragged-looking vultures with barely a scrap of meat on their bones. They wheel overhead in wide circles, their hoarse cries announcing the approach of the *Naglfar*.

You are crouched on a narrow tongue of rock, overlooking the canyon. A dry wind beats about your face, driving more stinging ash and dust into your eyes. You rub at them angrily, only making the discomfort worse. Blinking, you try and refocus.

The bow of the ghost ship swings round the gully, moving into plain sight. Green mould and barnacles cling to its massive bulk – itself a horrific creation, fashioned from the nails of the dead, or so Skoll believes. Swirling tides of magic surge beneath its prow, making the craft appear to hover above the ashen ground.

The ghost ship shimmers like a desert mirage: something caught between worlds, sailing the thin divide that separates life from death. Thirteen night-black sails bunch in the wind, each one displaying thirteen skulls. Thirteen, the number of the curved beaks carved into its lofty crow's nest, each spitting spectral flames into the hellish sky.

Thirteen. Unlucky for some.

The ship's hull has been ruptured, leaving a deep gouge running along most of its port side. A green glow seeps from this ghastly maw, illuminating the ground like a gruesome search light. Its brightness leaves the ship's carved figurehead in shadow, but its malign silhouette – a wailing horned demon – is unmistakably chilling.

Naglfar. The whaling vessel that brought the witch north and was wrecked off the coast hundreds of years ago. Whether it was anger or revenge that guided her actions, or even some twisted gratitude, the witch has raised the ship from the ocean – crew and all – to forever sail over her blighted wasteland; damned for all eternity.

You want that ship.

It drifts closer, creaking ominously as it rocks back and forth on unseen currents. The captain stands rigid at the wheel, while crewmen scurry across the deck and through the rigging; performing the same tasks they once did in life. Before they were drowned in the cold waters of the North Sea.

You rise, grimacing at the discomfort from your cramping muscles. Your deterioration is worsening – you glance down at your hands, trembling like an old man's. Part of your face is now rotted to bone. You can feel the wind fingering the spaces, pulling against the last threads of sinew.

Another corpse for the corpse ship, you reflect dourly.

The ship passes beneath your position. You lean over, eyes scanning back to the rocks at the far side of the gully. Skoll is moving forward, swinging a grapple above his head. Then he lets fly. A dark line streaks towards the ship, then there is a deafening crunch as the barbed head breaks through the lower stern. The *Naglfar's* bow lifts skyward as the vessel lurches back, pulling against the rope. The other end is bound tight to the largest boulder in the rock-pile, anchoring the ship in place – directly below you.

Spectral claws flash from your fingertips. Then you are running for the edge, springing off at the last moment, magic flickering around your limbs as you power yourself towards the main mast. You reach it with ease, claws ripping into the mouldy fabric of the sail. Startled cries sound from below. You drop quickly, hitting the deck. The nearest sailor, his bloated body partly encrusted with coral, takes a swing at you with his cutlass. You elbow him in the face, smashing through rotted bone, then gut him with your claws. His body turns to grey ashes, carried away on the wind.

You spin sharply, a blast of magic racing from your hands. It slams into the gunner on the poop deck, who had been training a crossbow on Skoll. The charge hits him in the side, blowing ash into the air as he explodes.

You continue to move swiftly, relying on magic to power your limbs. A flick of your hand throws a nearby net over the starboard rail. Anise breaks from cover beneath the ship, snatching the knotted ropes to use as a ladder.

The captain stumbles past his surprised crew, a whale-bone leg tapping noisily against the deck. The tattered remains of an admiral's coat hang off his bony limbs, the shoulders decorated with fronds of black seaweed. Beneath the shadows of a tri-horned hat, you spy a single eye of burning fury. The other is covered by a barnacled eye-patch.

'I'm taking your ship,' you state firmly, baring your weapons.

The captain pats at a conch shell hanging around his neck. Some sign of his status, you suspect. The crew look from you to the captain, then back again – seemingly awaiting an order, or perhaps undecided who they should be following.

The captain's jaws creak open, revealing black stumps for teeth. 'I am Captain Caverdos and this is the *Naglfar*. My ship.' With startling speed he whips a bright cutlass from his belt, holding its point towards your throat. 'While I carry this conch, the crew answers to me, and only me – savvy?' He glances around at his mesmerised crewmen. 'What yer waitin' for – the tide to take us? Ten bloated leeches for the first one to bring me 'is head!'

The crew draw their swords and daggers. Behind you there is a crack as a trapdoor is thrown open and a burly half-giant pulls himself up from below. Gripped in his meaty fist is a club fashioned from part of a shark's jaw.

'But there's more of 'em,' whines one of the sailors. He points to Anise, who has now clambered onto the deck, her short sword ringing out of its scabbard. Skoll swings over the rail to join her, a wicked battle axe in each hand. There is a moment's tense silence as both sides eye one another.

Then the captain gives a blustery snort of rage and charges – his attack finally inciting his cowardly crewmen into action. It is time to fight:

	Speed	Magic	Armour	Health
Captain	11	8	8	60
Mako	10	6	6	40
Sailor	10	6	6/3(*)	15
Sailor	10	6	6/3(*)	15
Sailor	10	6	6/3(*)	15

Special abilities

🛡 **All hands to the deck**: At the start of each combat round after the first, a new sailor (with the same stats as those above) joins the combat.

🛡 **Aura of command** (*): While the Captain is alive, the sailors have an *armour* of 6. This is reduced to 3 if the Captain is defeated.

🛡 **Mako's bite**: For each ⊡ your hero rolls for attack speed (before or after a reroll), you are caught by Mako's shark axe and must take 4 damage, ignoring *armour*. If Mako is defeated you can ignore this ability.

- ◆ **Mutiny on the *Naglfar*.** The crew of the ship have a morale of 15. When this is reduced to zero any surviving crew will immediately surrender, winning you the combat. Each sailor you defeat reduces the crew's morale by 1. Defeating the Captain will reduce morale by 5 and defeating Mako will reduce it by 3. The combat must continue until the crew's morale is reduced to zero.

- ◆ **Overwhelmed**: Skoll and Anise are keeping the crew distracted, but time is against you. If a combat round ends with seven sailors in play (after passive effects have been applied), then you have automatically lost the combat.

If you manage to incite a mutiny and take over the ship, turn to **745**.

557

The slope curves round the bluff, exposing you to the freezing bite of the cruel north wind. You ascend several hundred metres before arriving at a high wall of iron mesh topped with barbed wire. Beyond the wall is a dark stone building, looming ominously against a rust-stained sky.

Ryker's prison.

Two guards are standing outside a padlocked gate, wearing the same red-cloth armbands as those on the outer wall. One looks like a half-goblin, short of stature with a pug nose and a jutting lower jaw. His companion is a gangly youth with a dark fuzz of beard and a ring through his nose. Both look nervous as you approach.

'Gotta gi' us the daily password,' croaks the half-goblin, pointing a clawed finger at you.

'Wha' day is it?' asks the youth, his face twisted with concentration.

'I dunno, make one up. Don't matter, does it?'

'Third day o' of the week – password for Dilain,' proclaims the youth brightly, looking pleased with his decision. 'Either tell us or you can't come in. Plain and simple, just like us, eh, Zurg?'

Will you:

Try to outwit the guards?	451
Provide them with the password?	546
Leave?	426

558

Sensing victory, Skoll throws himself into a barrage of blows, scream-ing out a guttural cry with each savage swing. You catch them against your weapons, boots scraping the very edge of the rock. A couple land, the runed blade scolding like hot irons. But you keep your focus – watching, feeling his rhythm.

The axe lifts – ready to swing one final time. You dodge aside at the last moment, using your speed to twist round behind him. Angrily, he swings blindly, the weight of his axe carrying him after you. His momentum leaves him staggering off balance, closer to the edge . . .

He catches your eye, the anger gone – replaced by a frightened shock. Stone crumbles, he teeters back . . . Instinctively, he reaches out, grasping for you.

'Bearclaw!'

Dropping your weapons, you go to grab his hand. But you are too late. Your cold fingers brush against his own, which then slip away before you can form a grip.

He disappears from sight in a rustle of leather and cloth.

You are left holding a ring: a knotted braid of white hair, banded with twists of iron and ivory. If you wish, you may now take:

Cold blood
(ring)
+2 brawn +2 magic
Ability: heal, insulated

When you have updated your hero sheet, turn to 626.

'Earthquake . . . yeah, let me think . . .' You can hear Jackson sucking at his lips. 'Rings a bell. Thought I just had a bout of the shakes. Or was that the day I cracked open the crate of Assay Brandy? Hmm, perhaps so.'

'You mean you didn't even feel it? It took down the whole keep!'

'I had to mend a few shelves. Some broken bottles. Think my ceramic duck got broke. That was a present from a sweetheart. Or was it my mother? Hmm.'

You shake your head in exasperation, realising that you are unlikely to get much out of Jackson's drink-addled brain.

> Will you:
> Ask another question? 450
> Discuss something other than news? 685
> Leave? Return to the map

560

What might have once been an iron brazier is now a twisted length of iron, rolling back and forth in the wind. Desperately, you look around for an alternative – your eyes finding a tattered banner, pinned down by chunks of stone from a ruined section of wall.

Perhaps you could light the banner and use it to signal the guards.

If you have the keyword *flame* on your hero sheet, or are carrying *flint and tinder*, or have the *Atataq* wand equipped, turn to 453. Otherwise, turn to 429.

561

For defeating the mighty yeti, you may now help yourself to one of the following rewards:

Clawed tatters	Hair ball	Pine prowlers
(chest)	(necklace)	(feet)
+1 speed +2 brawn	+2 brawn	+1 speed +2 brawn
Ability: gut ripper	Ability: choke hold	Ability: sneak

You have also gained a *sasquatch pelt* (simply make a note of this on your hero sheet, it doesn't take up backpack space). When you have updated your sheet, turn to 631.

562

Heads and vines go spinning away into the mist as you hack and slash through the barbed jungle. At last, weapons dripping with gloopy sap, you stand over the trampled, broken remains of the creature. Where the original seed had landed you discover a glowing black sphere, still pulsing with magic. If you wish, you may now take the following item:

Heartwood
(talisman)
+1 armour +3 health
Ability: resolve

Your attention shifts back to the tree – and the agonised screams still rending the air. Of the scurrilous rodent there is no sign – you assume it must have scrambled up into the thick canopy of branches. Sheathing your weapons, you start to ascend the knotted bark once again, determined to reach the tree's summit. Turn to 597.

563

The corridor turns a ninety-degree corner, leading you down another line of squalid cells. If you have the book *Hergest's Hauntings* in your backpack (and haven't already used it at this location), turn to 436. Otherwise, you continue along the corridor. Turn to 661.

Flickering orange light spills from the cracks in the walls, illuminating the fleshy tentacles that snake like roots through the rock. They are everywhere now, some so large that they block off entire passageways. Each one gives off a torpid heat, forcing you to tread warily, avoiding their touch.

You pass through the shattered remains of buildings, their walls and floors tilted at unnatural angles. You cannot be sure if they fell here from the surface, dragged to these depths by the shifting plates of earth, or if they have lain here for generations – relics of a bygone age.

At last, squeezing out of another tunnel, you find yourself on a ledge, overlooking a vast gulf – almost as wide as the great rift in Skardfall. Your eyes scan the sheer walls, where more tentacles wind over each other, reaching down towards the fire-flecked darkness below.

A scream.

Further along the same ledge, you see another opening – and a black-robed acolyte crawling on all fours, blood soaking his robes. 'Please no,' he begs, looking back fearfully. 'I will help you – please . . .'

A giant of a man strides from the darkness of the tunnel, and plants his axe in the man's back. You hear a fleshy thud and the crack of bone. The robed mage doesn't even give a cry or whimper. He simply slumps face down into the dirt.

'Vadick lott, nefigger!'

The giant puts his foot to the man's back, tugging his axe free in a spray of blood. Matted hair hangs across his face, a crowned helm hanging askew. He pauses, looking down at the dead mage, then he turns to face you, dark brows creased over his cunning, bright-blue eyes. In the crimson half-light, his face is like a demon's – crisscrossed with livid scars, turning his skin into a grisly patchwork.

'Skoll . . .' You grip your weapons uncertainly.

The Skard blinks and leans forward, as if trying to see past some fog. Then he gives a bellowing laugh, lowering his axe. 'Bearclaw.'

'Where is Anise?' You look past him to the tunnel that he emerged from. There are no voices, no footsteps.

Skoll shrugs his shoulders. 'I left her. We haven't time.'

It takes a moment for his words to sink in. 'Left her? What do you mean—'

Skoll turns away, his eyes roving across the gulf. 'We have to find the demon.'

Snarling, you surge forward, barrelling into the Skard and driving him against the wall. Such is the force and speed of your strike, the warrior is too surprised to retaliate.

Your faces meet, mere inches apart.

'Where is she? Tell me where she is.'

'I am Drokke. Take your hands—'

'Where is she – ANSWER ME!' you scream. The Skard grits his teeth as a dark frost starts to coat his body, spreading like an intricate spider's web.

'There was a rock fall. I pulled her free, but it did no good. She could not walk – she would only have slowed me down.'

You shake your head disgustedly. 'She was hurt? Tell me how to find her.'

'The tunnel is gone. There is no way back.'

The pain twists through you. 'No . . .'

Gagging with grief, you stagger back. Your foot knocks into the dead mage. For the briefest of moments, you are distracted . . .

'Nerock Ta!'

Skoll whirls, striking you with his fist. It catches your helm, knocking you sideways. Then the flat of his axe slams into your chest. You are sent flying onto your back, skidding across the rock.

'I am a Drokke!' he shouts, spittle flying from his lips. 'Know your place.'

Still shocked, you take a boot heel to the side. The Skard towers over you, radiating anger. 'She was nameless. No better than a southlander.'

'Anise was one of us,' you rasp.

'Us?' He bares his teeth in a snarl. 'You are not of the Ska-inuin. I fight for my people. To save them. The many weigh more than the few. It is our way.'

'I still fight for your people,' you snap coldly. 'As did Anise.'

Skoll growls.

You flinch, waiting for his next strike.

Instead, he offers out a hand. 'Enough! Past deeds will stay my fury. Take it – time runs from us. We go find the witch and end this. The girl is gone. Forget her.'

Will you:

Punish the Skard?	407
Accept his hand and continue onwards?	368

565

Ignoring Caul's protests you lead the way into the narrow passage, the trapper following reluctantly behind. The whispering steadily grows in volume, until harsh guttural words resound from the black stone walls. It reminds you of the Skard language, but distorted somehow – broken by pauses and strange inflections.

'We should go back!' hisses Caul angrily. 'Can't you hear it?'

You squeeze out of the passage into a round chamber of polished black stone. Hanging from the ceiling, by what looks like tendrils of leather or skin, are three triangular shards. They are crafted from the same black stone as your surroundings, but glow with a spectral light. You approach the nearest, the whispering now raised to an angry deluge of hissing curses. As you gaze into the stone's mirrored surface, you see your pale visage staring back at you. The image quickly distorts – the face and body lengthening to become a ghostly white shroud.

Before you can draw back, a pair of hands reach out of the mirror. They grab hold of your cloak, bunching it tight, then drag you towards the stone. You flinch, expecting to hit its hard surface, but instead you feel a cold tingling as you pass straight through . . .

You find yourself in a mirror image of the chamber, its edges wavering as if they are partly illusion. The three shards now hang suspended around you. In each of their dark planes, a distorted image of Caul beats furiously against them – desperate to break in.

Vintern tar dul! Vintern tar dul!

The voice echoes around the chamber, louder now than ever before.

A cold blast of air. You look behind you to see a wraith-like apparition coalescing at the centre of the room, its ragged body coated in wraps of tattered fur. From the creature's attire and its long braided hair, you assume it was once a Skard – before some ancient magic trapped it in this arcane prison. With a shrieking howl the spirit drifts towards you, its taloned hands reaching for your throat. It is time to fight:

	Speed	Magic	Armour	Health
Ice wraith	5	3	4	40 (*)
Mirror shard	–	–	2	14
Mirror shard	–	–	2	14
Mirror shard	–	–	2	14

Special abilities

🖤 **Mirror, mirror:** The wraith can add 1 to its damage score for each mirror that currently has *health*. (If you have the *insulated* ability, you can ignore this damage bonus.)

🖤 **Fractured spirit:** (*) The wraith cannot be harmed until the three mirror shards are destroyed (but can still attack you if you lose a combat round). Once the mirrors are destroyed, the wraith can be attacked and damaged as normal. Caul will also be able to come to your aid, adding 2 to your damage score for the remainder of the combat.

🖤 **Soul glass:** The mirrors are immune to *bleed* and *decay*.

In this combat you roll against the ice wraith's attack speed. If you are successful, then you may strike against a mirror shard – or the wraith, if all three mirrors have been destroyed.

If you manage to defeat this spectral menace, turn to 449.

566

A service hatch opens in the wall to reveal three weapons, each chained and padlocked to a metal frame.

'The fire wand is new this season,' says Jackson. 'The spear is a discontinued line, so you won't see many of them around. Collector's item, and you heard it 'ere first. The claw – well, that speaks for itself, don't it? I seen Skards scale whole mountains with those backscratchers.'

The following items are available for 60 gold crowns each:

Spit roast	Ice claw	Tindersticks
(main hand: spear)	(left hand: fist weapon)	(main hand: wand)
+1 speed +2 brawn	+1 speed +2 brawn	+1 speed +2 magic
Ability: skewer	Ability: mangle, ice hooks	Ability: immolation

You may continue to purchase items from the trader (turn to 151), discuss something else (turn to 685) or leave (return to the quest map).

567

You leap over the rocks, surprising the cowering goblin. He lowers his shield a fraction too late, your weapon piercing through his ragged leather armour. As the goblin goes squealing to the ground, you turn to face the others.

'Me arm – it's stuck!' The largest goblin is trying desperately to free himself while his two smaller companions look on, torn between running or staying.

'Wha' yer waitin' for?' growls the leader. 'Just stick 'im!'

The two goblins pull rusty knives from their belts then hurry to attack, while the leader continues to grunt and curse as he tries to pull his arm free. It is time to fight:

	Speed	Brawn	Armour	Health
Grubnose	3/5(*)	3	3	25
Goblin	3	3	2	16
Goblin	3	3	2	12

Special abilities

🛡 **Stick 'im!:** At the end of each combat round, you must take 1 damage ignoring *armour* from each surviving goblin (not including Grubnose).

🛡 **Grr, 'tis ain't fair:** (*) Grubnose has his arm stuck. He will still be able to attack and defend, but will do so with a *speed* of 3. At the start of the fourth combat round, Grubnose will have freed his arm – raising his *speed* to 5 for the remainder of the combat.

If you manage to defeat these motley scavengers, turn to 583.

568

Skoll's warhammer glows with golden light, each spinning blow sending the hounds flying across the wrecked hall. Your own weapons beat and pummel at Syn's frozen armour, weakening her magical defences. At last she stumbles to her scaled knees, head bowed.

'Have mercy,' she hisses.

You stay your weapons, hesitating . . .

Then the demon lifts its cold-blue eyes. You catch the malign smile splitting the malformed face – and too late you realise your fatal mistake. The demon lunges, teeth and claws reaching for your throat. Then a hellish scream fills your ears.

You blink, wondering if it is your own pained cry you hear – but no, the demon's claws are grasping futilely in the air, the body seized by violent convulsions. The creature arches its back, the head twisting round to snap at something it cannot reach. A sword. It has been driven into the back of the demon's neck, angled straight into its spine. Anise gives the blade another push, teeth clenched as every ounce of her remaining strength is put to the task. You hear the cracking of bone and the liquid noise of muscle and tendons being severed. Then the demon flops forward, the light in its eyes fading to darkness. Anise glares down at the corpse.

'That was for my mother,' she spits.

For defeating the demon, you have gained 50 gold crowns and one of the following rewards:

Winter of woe	Coldheart cinch	Seed of Yggdrasil
(ring)	(necklace)	(talisman)
+1 brawn +1 magic	+1 speed +1 brawn	+1 speed +4 health
Ability: freeze	Ability: mangle	Ability: regrowth

If you are a mage, turn to 431. Otherwise, turn to 602.

569

Raising your hands you trace the circular patterns with your fingers, connecting the lines and whorls with the magic that now flows through you. The runes start to flicker and then glow, illuminating a trail to the centre circle, where blue-black energies crackle above the podium. For a brief moment you glimpse some creature trapped within the bright maelstrom – a spinning tornado of dust and rock, with two crimson jewels for eyes – then it is gone. The energy sparks out and the runes dim.

When you walk over to the podium you discover that your item is now rattling against the stone, quivering with the pent-up force of the earth elemental. (Congratulations! Your chosen weapon/item of equipment now has the *knockdown* ability.) When you have updated your hero sheet, turn to 684.

570

The hooded ghost opens his fist and lets his stones roll onto the table. They all land face up, displaying a perfect house and a crown. 'Royal Hoard,' whispers a voice from beneath the cowl. 'You lose.'

The guard looks at the symbols in horror, his mouth hanging open. 'No . . . it can't be . . .' Then suddenly he starts to tremble and convulse, his hands going to his throat. You watch dumbfounded as he is lifted up out of his chair, feet kicking above the ground. 'No! Please!' he manages to gasp. 'No!'

The hooded figure stands, his dark form seeming to stretch and grow larger. Bony hands reach for the choking guard, the cowl finally falling back to reveal a grinning skull.

There is a scream – then both ghosts vanish.

You look to Anise, still shocked by what you have witnessed.

'I suppose that could have gone better,' she sighs, turning one of the stones over in her hand. Its face displays two grinning skulls. 'Doubt things will end any better for us, unless we reach that signal fire.'

You may now search the room, if you haven't already (turn to 310) or leave through the open doorway (turn to 188).

571

You break out of the corkscrew, hot on the tail of the lead racer. The walls of the prison are now less than a mile to the south. With none of the other competitors in sight, you realise that you are in second place and have a chance of taking first!

Cracking your whip, you urge your dog-team alongside the other sled, looking to overtake. To your surprise, the other racer turns out to be the girl with the blue-dyed hair. She blows you a kiss before swinging her sled into yours, the runed spikes cutting jagged strips out of your frame. Lines cross as the dog-teams snap and tussle with one another – both sleds locked in a desperate scrap for pole position.

You will need to take a challenge test using your *toughness* attribute:

	Toughness
Pole position	13

If you are successful, turn to 539. If you fail, turn to 694.

572

You step across the line of runes. As you suspected, the man is clearly panic-stricken and sleep-deprived, and the magic protection he thought he had created amounts to little more than a snap of lightning, which causes you no ill-harm.

Seeing that his magic has failed, the mage lunges past you. You manage to grab an arm, but the spindly man squirms free of your grip. Skoll doesn't even attempt to obstruct his escape, moving aside to let the mage past. He catches your eye and merely shrugs his shoulders.

Against the wall, where the man had taken refuge, you discover a small bundle of objects. As well as 20 gold crowns, you find one of the following:

Divining rod	Backhanders	Tremor guard
(main hand: wand)	(gloves)	(chest)
+2 speed +3 magic	+1 speed +1 armour	+1 speed +2 brawn
Ability: insight	Ability: lightning	Ability: reckless

In silence you head back into the tunnels, your mind still turning over the mage's words. Perhaps you are not as alone in these caves as you first thought. Turn to 750.

573

'I'm Caul Flenchard, trapper for the White Wolf Company.' The man wipes his bloody hands against his leather coat. 'I chose to stay on for the winter – get me some good winter hides, swell the coffers then drink it dry at Ryker's. Was a good plan, 'till I stumbled on those explorers in the canyon – like lost children they were, no clue of the risk they'd taken on, staying here for the winter. Seemed convinced their team were still alive . . .'

You frown. 'Odd, they never mentioned you. How long have you been here?'

Caul puts a hand to his brow. 'Can't say as I rightly know. Time has a way of losing itself around here – a week, perhaps.'

'A week?' Your raise your eyebrows in surprise. 'Have you not tried to leave? I found a way in, just over . . .'

The trapper shakes his head. 'I want to know what's going on here. I went deeper, but got chased out by a bunch of monsters.' He glances down at his blood-stained hands. 'I ain't ready to quit.'

Will you:

Ask what he knows about the caves?	498
Ask if he has any weapons or supplies?	609
Ask why he thought you were a ghost?	481
Ask if he will accompany you?	384

574

You place the gold on the table (deduct fifty gold crowns from your hero sheet). The monk shakes the bag and then chooses five stones. You follow his lead, hoping that you have the skill and knowledge to best this expert player.

If you have the book *Stones & Bones* in your backpack, turn to 401. Otherwise, you will have to rely on guesswork and luck to win the game. Turn to 511.

575

The smoke makes you feel dizzy. Shapes become indistinct, blurring at the edges. You try and stand but your hands fumble uselessly at your sides. Sura is chanting something, a mantra that fills your head with a pounding pain. Nanuk is growling and seething – you feel him raking claws through the air, trying to resist her power as he is tugged from the Norr, his spirit spilling into your body.

The last thing you remember is a roar coming from your own lips. Something raw and powerful, and animal-like. Then you fall backwards, sinking into a sea of soft furs. They are comforting, warm ... and so you close your eyes and let the darkness take you.

You awake with a start, sitting bolt upright, your hands reaching for a weapon. Sura is still watching you from her pallet bed, even though you see grey light stretching into the shelter from the tunnel's opening. It is morning.

'I slept?' You shake your head, trying to clear it of the dull ache that hammers behind your eyes. 'I don't remember travelling ... I usually ...'

'Relax, boy.' Sura gives you a reassuring smile. 'I merely called forth your ancestor spirit. I spoke with him.'

'Nanuk?' You peer closer at the old woman, wondering if you misheard her – looking for some hint of mockery in her smile.

'He saved your life,' she states, pushing herself up off the bed. She gives a tiny groan as her old bones crack and settle. 'I did not know you were a chieftain of your own people.'

'A prince,' you snort. 'My own people betrayed me.'

'You desire revenge.' The woman edges past you to pick up one of the staffs.

'I do?' You raise a questioning eyebrow.

'That's why he saved you. You still have work to do, southlander. Take this.' Sura hands you the staff, then proceeds to retrieve her own. 'Follow me, and don't ask Sura so many questions. We don't have much time. Understand? Now, move yourself!'

She slaps your back with her staff, forcing you to your feet. You are happy to oblige the woman – eager now to escape the stuffy confines of the shelter. Ducking through the opening, you step out into the piercing light of day. Turn to 530.

576

Searching the remains of the fire giant, you find 100 gold crowns and one of the following rewards:

Volatile chains	Gaoler's key ring	Girdle of flame
(gloves)	(ring)	(chest)
+1 speed +3 magic	+1 magic +1 armour	+2 speed +3 magic
Ability: shock blast	Ability: shackled	Ability: immolation

When you have updated your hero sheet, turn to 705.

577

You walk over to the nearest set of shelves, scanning the rows of spines for anything that catches your eye. After some deliberation, you pick out three books – certain they will help pass the time during your stay at the keep.

The first is titled *Stones & Bones*, and contains rules and tactics for playing the popular game of the same name. Lazlo had once tried to teach you to play, but either you had never fully grasped the rules or Lazlo was too skilled a player, as you never won a single game.

The second is *Hergest's Hauntings*, which contains a collection of maps and sketches of various buildings and other locations. A footnote at the start of the book explains that the author is dead, but this predicament has not hampered their ambitions – in fact, being a ghost has made it remarkably easy for them to snoop around places they wouldn't otherwise get to visit.

The final book is a *History of Skardland*. It is mostly a collection of oral tales, rumoured to have been passed down through generations of Skards, but there is also a section at the back of the book dedicated to 'Makers' Runes'. You aren't clear what these are, but they look interesting.

'Hey, corpse stink!' The boy calls over to you. 'You know you can only take two books out of the library, right? Don't think of taking more – Segg has a charm on the door. Last time I tried it I got boils on my . . . well, you don't want to know. Couldn't sit down for a week, just embarrassing!'

If you wish, you may now take up to two of the following:

Stones & Bones (backpack)	Hergest's Hauntings (backpack)	History of Skardland (backpack)
The ultimate strategy guide (game of the year edition)	No lock, no door, no wall can stop me	The essential bluffers' pocketbook of the North

Turning away from the shelves, you contemplate your next course of action.

Will you:

Talk to the mage?	16
Speak with Segg?	328
Return to the main courtyard?	113

The walk back to camp drags into an awkward silence, neither of you speaking or acknowledging one another. Instead you let Desnar lead the way across the sparkling white plains, your earlier footprints already erased by the fast-falling snow.

'Fader! Fader!'

The voice startles both of you. From atop the hills, a child stumbles into view. He is waving with one arm – his glove and sleeve covered in blood. Your first thought is that the boy has been injured, but then you see the carcass of the animal he is dragging behind him – a white wolf, twice his size. A broken spear protrudes from the animal's haunches.

You look back at Desnar, surprised to see the Skard beaming with admiration. 'Himruk!'

But the moment is fleeting. The smile is lost in a horrified gasp – his voice suddenly raised in warning. 'Himruk! Sno nada!'

Your gaze shifts to the boy – and the mound of snow rising up behind him. Too late, Himruk turns, sensing the danger at his back. The behemoth continues to rise, the powdery snow lifting and then falling back to form two trunk-like arms and a peaked head. There is a wailing screech as snow is sucked inwards, forming a huge gaping maw.

'Himruk!' Desnar races forward, but is unable to reach the child in time. You hear the crack of bones as the snow giant brings its fists down, crushing the boy beneath their weight. Then, with another screech, it lifts a barrel-sized leg out of the snow and drags itself forward. You draw your weapons, hurrying to aid Desnar as he attempts to take on the might of the abominable snowman! It is time to fight:

	Speed	Brawn	Armour	Health
Abominable Snowman (*)	6	4	4	70
Snowman (*)	5	4	3	15
Snowman (*)	5	4	3	15
Snowman (*)	5	3	2	15

Special abilities

♥ **'I get knocked down, but I get up again . . .':** (*) For every 20 *health* the Abominable loses, a snowman rises up from the remains and joins the combat. You must defeat all four opponents to win the combat.

- ♥ **Snow joke**: You must take 1 damage at the end of each combat round from each opponent currently in play. (If you have the *insulated* ability, you can ignore this damage.)
- ♥ **Father's fury**: Desnar adds 2 to your damage score for the duration of this combat.
- ♥ **Made of snow**: Your opponents are immune to *bleed*, *decay* and *venom*.

If you manage to overcome the abominable snowman, turn to 347.
If you lose, record your defeat on your hero sheet and turn to 139.

579

'You come here often, honey?' Talia steps from the shadows, hands resting on the pommels of two scabbarded swords. Her crimson coat hangs open, revealing a tight lace bodice flickering with embroidered runes. 'Do you have the book? Good – then let's get this party started.'

She moves quickly to the lowest step, reaching down to turn a previously hidden circular wheel. You hear a groaning, followed by the sound of rushing water passing underneath the stone floor. There is a clang, then the swish of ropes and a clatter of a pulley. Talia glances round at an area of wall seconds before it starts to rise smoothly into a hidden recess.

A rough-hewn tunnel is slowly revealed; a thin yellow mist curls languidly between the swaying cobwebs. Talia pulls a scarf from her belt and proceeds to tie it around her face, covering her nose and mouth. 'Try not to breathe too much,' she says, heading past you and into the tunnel.

'Not exactly a problem,' you reply dryly, drawing your weapons.

After a hundred metres the tunnel ends in a carved archway, beyond which is a large cavernous chamber. You can see tables littered with flasks and test tubes, a row of pallet beds, and a multitude of metal canisters, all leaking the sickly yellow smoke.

Talia halts before entering, her eyes scanning the archway of stone.

Lines of scripture have been carved into its panelled border, pulsing faintly with a soft white light. You draw back, feeling the heat of the holy magic prickle against your dead skin.

Seemingly oblivious to your discomfort, Talia turns and holds out her hand. 'The book, sweetie.' You relinquish the tattered volume and proceed to watch as the woman flips through the pages, her eyes scanning the print and then the words around the arch. (Remove *Judah's Book of Canticles* from your hero sheet.)

At last she gives an elated gasp. 'Here it is, the missing words of the canticle. Okay, let's try it.' She takes a step back, then gestures to the archway as if addressing an audience. 'As by man came death, and by man the light of His truth will shine again.'

There is a moment's silence, then the scripture flickers and fades, leaving only dark stone around the archway. Talia glances back at you, shrugs her shoulders, then steps through. When nothing seemingly untoward happens, the woman urges you to follow. Turn to **741**.

580

A black smoke starts to rise up from the stone around your feet, the air suddenly stinking of ashes and something else – an ancient, decaying evil. 'What's happening?' Anise turns on the spot, watching as the sooty tendrils are lifted up on the wind.

A ghostly laughter fills your ears.

Then you are falling. It is as if the ground has been swept away from you, swallowed by a vast abyss of darkness. You hear Anise scream, but you cannot see her – wind batters against you as you are spun like dust in a whirlwind, spinning round and round, faster and faster . . .

You hit the floor hard. Bones crack. Your mouth fills with a foul-tasting bile and fragments of tooth. You spit them out, scrabbling to your feet, aware that the ground is wet and slippery. An acrid stench fills your nostrils – sharp and sweet.

Blood.

You are back in the entrance chamber. Your eyes follow the crimson streaks as they sweep away, forming a dazzling pattern of circles and runes. Standing at their centre is a man – or what might once have been a man, before death and time had their way. He is corpse-thin, clad in cobwebbed robes, black as midnight. Of his face, there is little left – only a few tatters of skin sagging off yellow bone, a single eyeball.

Harris lies at the creature's feet, eyes staring vacantly at the ceiling. Dried blood and bruises cover his neck, where a chain looks to have constricted itself, choking him. On the end of the chain is the black prism.

'What . . . what's happened?'

A girl's voice. Anise. You turn to see her lying near the wall, holding her head woozily. Not far from her are the remains of Brack. You look away in revulsion, the source of the blood now clearly apparent.

'Welcome,' whispers the robed corpse.

You draw your weapons – your first thought to protect Anise.

'Ah, so impetuous.' A chill laughter echoes around you. 'Just like Harris. And he served me so well. I pulled the strings and he danced, brought me here so I could be free once again.' The single, half-rotted eyeball twists in its hollow socket, gazing down at the prism resting on the dead boy's chest. 'And you will serve me too.'

'Think again!' You start to charge – then suddenly you hit something, hard as stone. An invisible barrier. It closes around you, pressing hard against your cadaverous body. Desperately you struggle to break free, but your limbs have become frozen; too heavy to move.

'Interesting.' The necromancer folds his arms, the bones creaking and scraping together. 'You are already almost a corpse. Fit to serve me.'

At the back of your mind you hear a roar – a primal anger desperate for release. You try and move again, but your body is refusing. It feels like a dead weight, hanging cold and useless, a prison for your mind. You want to scream, but your jaw is clamped shut.

'Perhaps a little display is in order,' chuckles the dark mage, 'to prove to me your newfound allegiance.' His single eye flits to Anise, who is struggling to stand, her ragged dress streaked with soot and grime.

Your body starts to move, like a marionette. The motions are jerky and abrupt, legs and arms pulled painfully against your will as they snap into position, driving you forward towards Anise. As your arms are lifted and your weapons catch the ghost-light sparkling around the dread necromancer, you realise his intentions.

Anise backs against the wall, watching your advance with terror in her eyes. 'No, please,' she whispers, shaking. 'Don't do it. Fight it!' Her words seem distant to you, like echoes rippling back from another time and place. But her face remains vivid, every detail pin sharp – screaming at you to stop. Anger . . . fury . . . fear.

These are emotions you know. You can feel them surging through you, pushing strength into your limbs, your mind pulling open in a thunderous snarl of rage. For an instant you glimpse the bear – the strange creature that you met in the dreamscape, your guardian. His amber eyes fill your vision, his vitality and power passing into you.

'No!' You spin round, your body now your own again, wrested free from the necromancer's magic. Without hesitation you throw yourself against the mage, hearing bones snap as you crash together. Then a bolt of magic streaks into your side, throwing you back to the ground. When you look round the necromancer is hunched over, an arm bent back at an unnatural angle. The light that once glowed around him now seems diminished.

'Fool!' The mage straightens, his bones sliding back into place. With a wheezing breath he raises a hand, his wrinkled fingers distending towards you. 'If you will not serve me in death, then you will suffer the same fate as I did. Imprisoned within the soul stone!'

There is a bright flash of light – and suddenly you find yourself surrounded on all sides by black panes of glass, each perfectly smooth, mirroring your anguished face into an endless infinity. Somehow, you know what has happened, even though your mind is still struggling to comprehend it. The necromancer has trapped you inside the black prism. Unless you can escape, you will never be able to defeat him. It is time to fight:

	Speed	Magic	Armour	Health
Necromancer	3	2	2	10 (*)
Prismatic prison	0	0	3	20

Special abilities

♥ **Prison break**: You cannot attack or deal damage to the necromancer until you have broken out of the prison. Your attacks against the prison automatically hit (the prison has no *speed*). Once the prison has been reduced to zero *health*, it is destroyed and you are freed.

🌱 **Soul surge**: For each combat round you spend in the prison, the necromancer grows in power, gaining 5 *health* at the end of each round that you are trapped. Once the prison is destroyed, the necromancer no longer gains *health* – and you can attack him as normal.

🌱 **Glass walls**: The prison is immune to all passive effects, such as *barbs* and *bleed*.

🌱 **Guards, guards!**: If you lit the tower's banner, guards will join you in your fight against the necromancer, raising your damage score by 2 for the remainder of the combat. You only gain this bonus once you have broken out of the prison.

If you manage to send this villain back to the grave, turn to 437. If you lose the combat, remember to record your defeat on your hero sheet. You may then attempt the combat again or return to the map.

581

To your relief your dogs prove vicious fighters, whilst the sled itself manages to withstand the constant knocks and bumps from the other racers. Gradually, you manage to pull away from the pack and start to gain ground on the leaders. Turn to 471.

582
Boss monster: Avalanche

(Note: You must have completed the red quest *The Hall of Vindsvall* before you can start this challenge.)

Skoll is standing alone at the foot of the glacier, his head tilted as if listening to the wind. Behind him, a full backpack rests against a rock – with various ropes, spears and knives bound to it by loops of sinew. A breeze stirs the fur of his hood, pushing it back to reveal a dark helm fashioned from rune-carved stone – the symbol of his status. The crown of the Drokke.

He shifts his stance as you approach, extending his forearm to the sky. Scanning the clouds, you spot a bird circling overhead. Its white feathers and jet-black crest remind you of a tern, but its size hints at a much larger bird of prey. With a hacking screech the bird sweeps down on its great wide wings, alighting gracefully on Skoll's gloved arm.

'Ah, Habrok,' grins the half-giant. He scratches affectionately at the soft white down beneath the bird's throat. 'After all these years. I have need of you, old one. The time has come.'

The bird flicks its head, turning a single beady eye to the Skard. You feel a flow of magic between the two. Communication, you sense. Like your own bond with Nanuk.

'Take my message to the chieftains of the tribes. They will come to Vindsvall and see the shattered hall; the broken throne that was my prison. They will know I have gone north and they will follow.'

The bird gives an answering caw, then spreads its grey-feathered wings and lifts into the sky. You watch as it wheels above you in ever-widening circles before streaking southwards.

Footsteps crunch, dragging your attention back to the glacier. Aslev approaches, his white horn and rune-carved axe bouncing at his hip. Beside him is Anise, wincing as she shoulders a heavy pack, its weight forcing her to bow her back.

You look to Skoll, startled. He reads your expression, answering with a smile and a shrug of his shoulders. 'She would not listen to me.' He regards her thoughtfully, the fondness in his gaze not going unnoticed.

'I'm ready,' she states boldly, glaring at you with a challenging stare.

'Anise . . .' You shake your head. 'Please, stay at the hall . . .'

She rolls her eyes in exasperation. 'And have me sing songs while I wait for my beloved to return? Is that what you expect of me?'

You start to answer, but she shakes her head. 'Don't. I'm stronger than you think I am – and I'm coming with you.'

Skoll slaps you on the shoulder. 'See, she will not be turned.'

Aslev bows before you both. 'Drokke. Seff. What is your duty for me?'

Skoll unstraps his hammer and holds it out to the einherjar.

'Take it,' Skoll insists. 'For the chieftains will need to believe I have returned. This is my great-grandfather's warhammer. He named it

Surtnost, the troll-bane, for it was the weapon to smite the mightiest of their kin. Surtnost has never left my side. It has a glamour, a magic. It will always return to its master. And you will bring it to me, with the chieftains at your side. Understand?'

Aslev takes the weapon in his palms, his eyes widening as he looks upon it with reverence. 'A . . . a mighty gift, my Drokke. I will guard it with my life.'

'No,' grins the half-giant. 'The hammer will guard *your* life.'

Aslev lifts his gaze with a worried frown. 'What if the chieftains do not come? It has been many years. They may not believe . . .'

Skoll gives a surly grunt. 'Then they are cowards and they will die nameless. All of them. Come, Bearclaw. We go north.' He stoops to pick up his pack. As he hefts it onto his shoulders, you notice the fragments of the shield poking out of the top-flap.

'What about the third piece?' you ask. 'Without it we cannot remake the shield.'

Skoll puts his hands to the straps, tugging them down. 'The weaver will have the answers.'

You look to Anise, who appears equally baffled. 'The weaver, right. And, where do we find this weaver-person?'

'We don't,' grins the warrior. 'They will find us.'

He nods to Aslev, then turns to face the newly-risen sun, its pale light edging the scars running down his cheeks. 'When I see you again, Aslev, it will be the end of days.' He glances back with a mischievous smirk. 'Don't be late.'

'My Drokke.' Aslev falls to one knee, head bowed. 'May the ancestors go with you.'

Skoll flashes you the same smile, then together the three of you begin your long journey northwards. Turn to 703.

583

You search the goblins' bodies. Their armour and weapons are mismatched and of poor quality, possibly filched long ago from various corpses or victims. However, a few items catch your eye. The leader has a leather pouch tied around his neck. You open it up to find 40 gold crowns inside. He also has a gourd fastened to his belt, containing a thick oily liquid. The cap on his head, while plain and grubby, has a faint glimmer of magic about it.

You may take any/either of the following items:

Goblin grog (2 uses)	Grubnose's smart cap
(backpack)	(head)
Use any time in combat to	+1 brawn +1 magic
restore 4 *health*	Ability: trickster

You turn your attention to the rock fall. Peering through the space where the goblin had his arm, you see the half-covered face of a statue peering back at you. The one visible eye is fashioned from a bright green emerald. You reach in and pull it free without too much trouble. Sadly the gemstone is chipped in several places, possibly through the goblins' attempts to prise it out.

If you wish, you may take the *chipped emerald* (simply make a note of it on your hero sheet, it doesn't take up backpack space.) With nothing else of interest in the cave, you leave via the tunnel. Turn to 2.

584

A sudden lurch. You feel yourself being lifted, legs kicking through empty space. Above you, powerful wings beat against the air.

'Stop struggling,' hisses a voice, barely audible over the cracking, booming crescendo of splintering earth. From below, great plates of rock are thrown up into your path, whilst spinning stone and masonry whip past at speed. Somehow your winged rescuer is able to weave their way through the confusion, as if possessing some innate sixth sense.

An archway looms ahead, cut into a high wall of stone. For a moment you are headed straight for it, then an abrupt turn takes you hurtling away – just in time, as a cart-sized boulder smashes into the wall, obliterating everything in a cloud of dust.

A series of rocky ledges stream past, blurring into a dark streak.

'Let me go!' You grab the wrists of the creature – its claws having hold of your jerkin. Cold fire races from your fingertips, searing into its flesh. You hear a snarl of anger.

'Let me go,' you intone again.

Black stone rushes up to meet you. The impact is sudden and hard; one that would surely have broken every bone in your body. Instead, you feel the shudder of the impact, then the disorientating sensation that you are sliding backwards. The ground is tilting, rising up like the prow of a ship meeting the surge of a wave. Once again you try and grapple for a hand-hold, but the stone is smooth as glass. From below you, a terrible heat hammers against your body. It fills you with pain.

Wings sweep across you again. A clawed hand settles around your arm. 'Do you want to be saved, fool?' booms the voice.

Without waiting for an answer you are lifted up as the stone crumbles and drops away beneath you, falling into a fiery void. You are rising, wings beating either side of you, filling your head with thunder. Then you are travelling at speed along a widening crevasse, its dark walls dropping away with a menacing, grinding din. Another sickening lurch and you are ascending still further, towards a wide shelf – where you are finally released, left to roll and tumble across the rock.

You come to rest on your back, dizzy and disorientated., The demon has alighted on a nearby boulder, his silver-flecked wings folding back to reveal black-scales and runed armour.

You start to draw your weapons, then hesitate. The demon has made no move to attack you. He simply watches you, as if waiting for something.

Recognition to dawn.

'You! You're the one who saved me from the Wiccans.'

The demon shrugs his broad shoulders, spiked with bone. 'A means to an end. Come.' He flexes his wings then kicks off from the stone, gliding across a slope of rubble to another plane of rock above. As you follow him up the slope, you realise you can no longer see the sky or the ruined city; you are underground. It must be utterly dark, but your eyes can see as perfectly as day.

You scrabble after the demon, scaling the rubble to find yourself at the edge of a vast, cathedral-like chamber. The walls are perfectly smooth, rising up to form an immense multi-faceted dome above. Green light dances across the dark stone, illuminating the eight giant statues that stand silent at the centre, facing inward to where a pool of emerald radiance shimmers and dances.

You pull yourself up, looking around for the demon. His winged shadow whirls across the heads of the statues – then there is a crunch as the beast lands at the very edge of the pool. Green light dances along his curved horns, picking out the sharp bones jutting from his arms and elbows. A spiked tail flicks back and forth.

You approach the circle, passing the skeletal remains of sorcerers, their black robes curled in tatters around half-melted bone. Crystal fragments crunch underfoot, giving voice to the only sound in the silent chamber.

'What is this place?' You step over another body, moving to inspect the nearest statue. Each one stands over six metres tall – humanoid in shape save for the narrow sweep of their heads, curving back into immense pronged ridges. The stone is black and smooth, like obsidian, and veined with mineral hues of iron and copper. A silvery runic band spirals down from their broad shoulders, winding around their torso and limbs like a cobwebbed cloak.

Tentatively you put a hand to the surface of the stone. It is deathly cold to the touch. And yet, just like the witch's statues, you sense a life beating deep within – weak, like a dying flame.

The statues form a circle, arms raised, palms held outwards, bodies leaning in as if pushing against an immense weight. Your eyes follow the line of their blank, staring eyes to the whirling pool of green light.

'The Well of Urd,' you gasp, remembering what Skoll had told you. 'These are the Titans – they sacrificed themselves to hold back the demons, to stop them from using the well to enter our world.' You glance back at the burnt remains of the mages.

'A scholar, then,' growls the demon, sounding impressed.

'What happened here?' You kick at one of the bones.

'A lot of bad things,' he replies darkly.

'Enlighten me.'

'Very well. Melusine used her magic – and that of her coven – to weaken the Titans. They were able to pull demons through. One in particular – Cerebris. He is the demon who is destroying the seals of Jormungdar's prison.' The dark angel raises his molten eyes towards the domed ceiling. 'For six hundred years he has been growing, spreading, digging deep into the earth. His magic weakens the seals: powerful wards that the Titans and dwarves crafted an age before.'

'Why did you bring me here?' You step warily towards the glowing pool.

'Are we talking in the grand sense – or for my own selfish whim?' The demon's lips curl back, revealing a crescent of white fangs. 'I needed you to do one thing for me. Something I couldn't do myself.'

In the distance you hear another tremor, tearing through the innards of the underworld. Your thoughts turn to your companions, and what may have become of them.

Anise . . .

'You will see her again.' The demon catches your eye.

You snarl, hands moving to your weapons. 'Enough games! Why am I here? Answer me, demon.'

'Demon?' The creature snorts. 'Not so long ago, I was just like you, Arran. Not a prince, no – but I had my humanity. What you see is through no choosing of my own.'

'You sound like the witch! Blaming others for your misfortunes.'

The demon bristles. 'I saved your life. Have you forgotten?'

'I died. Did you forget that, too?'

'I put you on the path – ensured your destiny would come to pass.'

'Riddles!' You tug your weapons free. 'Tell me why I'm here!'

The demon gives a rumbling growl. 'Because you're special. Does that please you? No one else could have made the sacrifice. To give up everything – to pass through the eye of the storm. Without you, I would never have been able to reach the well.'

You shake your head, bewildered. 'That's it? You used me . . . just to kill the sentinel?'

There is another distant echo, of crashing rock and earth being rent asunder.

'Your fate shines bright, Arran. You have a greater purpose to serve.' The demon edges closer to the green pool, the shimmering radiance picking out the silver veins of his wings. 'I'm simply here for vengeance. That same cold desire as you, Arran. Someone took something from me – an artefact of great power. His name is Lorcan. And this will lead me straight to him.'

'How?' You gesture to the stone Titans. 'You would try and break their magic?'

The demon scoops his hand into the pool. He holds it out before him, letting the green light spill between his fingers. 'No. The Titans' magic is a barrier. It stops the creatures of the shroud from travelling into our world. But the magic will not deny someone achieving the opposite.'

Your mind fumbles for his meaning. 'Wait, you mean this is a gateway – you intend to *enter* the shroud?'

The demon stretches its wings. 'To find Lorcan, yes.'

You peer down into the swirling depths, feeling the familiar cold of the Norr rising up from its vaporous currents. It is almost enticing . . . an escape . . . freedom.

For a moment you feel your spirit being tugged towards it, joining with the chill waters, submitting to their undertow, letting them drag you down and down, back to the Norr . . . 'No!' You stagger back, fighting the compulsion. 'You can't. You'll die.'

'Ah, such touching concern.' The demon forms a mockery of a smile. 'Yes, I will die, eventually – that fate is written. And you're going to save the world.' His eyes fix on you with a steady gaze, so bright that the rest of his face is cast in shadow.

'No, stay! Help me. We must stop this demon – Cerebris. The witch. I cannot face them alone!' You resent the note of fear in your voice, but the loss of your companions and the pressing isolation of this underground realm has left you feeling suddenly vulnerable.

'Alone.' The demon holds your stare. 'That is the future I have seen. If I interfere, that weave will come undone – and she will win. I cannot allow that.'

You feel your anger rise again. 'Then go. Run – chase this Lorcan. I hope he's worth it!'

The demon watches you for some moments, holding back an unspoken thought. Then he releases a sigh. 'When this is done, do not pursue vengeance. Seeking to win back the throne of Valeron . . . It will not bring you peace, Arran. I am sorry.'

Rock crumbles beneath the beast's claws as he kicks off into the air, wings beating for a brief instant – then he drops, passing from sight beneath the pool's shimmering surface. There is no disturbance, not even a ripple to hint at his passage. For some minutes you stare at the whirling currents of light, the demon's last words replaying in your mind.

It will not bring you peace, Arran. I am sorry.

The earth shifts and rumbles, dislodging a shower of dust from the domed ceiling. The tremor passes quickly, but it is enough to remind you of your purpose.

Turning away from the pool, you look around for the nearest exit. A jagged fissure in the nearby wall leads through into a rubble-strewn passageway. You make for it immediately, your thoughts now turned to the fate of your companions. Turn to **564**.

585
Quest: Weird science

'Good.' Talia reaches into her cleavage and pulls out a tight roll of parchment. She then proceeds to unravel it across the table-top, using mugs to anchor it down. You lean forward with interest, realising that it is a map – a series of floor plans, painstakingly detailed with measurements and elevations.

'That's the prison,' you state, craning your neck to admire the detail.

'Yes, it is. These are the original architect's plans – the only copy that exists. See this,' she taps a finger on an area of the map, where a smaller floor plan has been drawn below the main one. 'This is a secret basement, underneath the prison. I don't think anyone knows of its existence – certainly not Ryker or the inmates. It was even a secret to the prison guards.'

'What's down there?' you ask quickly, your curiosity aroused.

Talia glances round the taproom nervously, then leans in. 'You know how the prison break started? One of the inmates went crazy – broke out of the medical wing. Crazy enough to smash through walls, rip bars from cells, kill a lot of guards. We're talking superhuman strength. A mutant.'

You nod, urging her to continue.

'This prison was a front, for medical experiments. I don't think our former king knew about it, he thought he was doing a good thing housing prisoners here, hoping they might repent their sins. But the Church had other ideas. To them, these prisoners were already damned – lost souls. They used them as meat, test subjects for various covert experiments. The chemist assigned here was Viktor Mandaleev.

He studied and taught at the University in Talanost before he was shipped to this hel-hole.'

'He was experimenting on prisoners?' You frown.

'Indeed. His work had become very ... specific. He had what some might term an obsession. To create the perfect soldier. A super-human.' Talia's eyes drift back to the map. 'That basement holds a lot of answers, and I need to get to them.'

'Where do I fit into all this?' You shift nervously in your seat. 'Surely Ryker will have found and taken anything of worth; he runs the prison.'

Talia shakes her head. 'I told you, no one else knows about this. Past the medical wing, there is a door that leads to a storeroom. That's empty now, yes. And getting that key wasn't easy.' Talia breaks off, her fingers tracing a ring of fading bruises around her neck. 'In the storeroom there's a set of stairs – and a hidden mechanism. It opens a secret door.' She taps an area of the floor plan where a corridor stretches away from an apparently solid section of wall. 'So far, so good. But then Viktor left a final obstacle. A doorway warded with holy scripture. The words are part of Judah's teaching, a canticle. I believe the only way to pass through unscathed is to recite the end of that canticle.'

'I'm not a Church man,' you sigh, settling back into your chair. 'I can't help you.'

'Neither am I,' grins Talia. 'But it just so happens there's a monk here. He gambles and drinks down at the docks – I suppose his religious sensibilities are a little questionable these days. Alas, I know he has a book of scripture. Keeps it with him all the time.'

'You're resourceful. I'm sure you could work that seductive charm of yours ...' A smile steals across your lips.

Talia grimaces. 'I've tried. I don't think I'm to his taste. I even tried gambling to win it, but he's too good a player. I'm also ... conspicuous, as you have already pointed out. I don't want his blood on my hands.'

'You want me to kill him?' You flinch in surprise.

The woman shrugs her shoulders. 'I need that book. I don't really care how you do it. There's a lot at stake here. I believe there could be all kinds of chemicals down in that basement. It's an accident waiting to happen.'

'Don't tell me you're doing this out of some environmental concern,' you smirk dubiously.

Talia answers you with a hard stare. 'Get me the book and I'll reward you. Meet me in the prison, past the medical wing. I'll be waiting.' The woman snatches up the map and begins to roll it back up. 'I'm counting on you, honey. Don't let me down.' (Record the word *scripture* on your hero sheet.)

Will you:

Talk to the barman?	420
Listen to the conversation at the bar?	534
Leave?	426

586

'No . . .' Your hands clench into fists, sending magic crackling through the air. 'Not her – she did not deserve this!'

By force of habit you reach out for Nanuk, begging for his aid. But your desperate plea goes unanswered. Now there is only a chill hollow where the bear's spirit had once shone. The loss of Nanuk only makes the pain worse, driving home an overwhelming sense of loneliness. Failure.

'If only I could give you life.'

The words spark a memory. In your mind's eye, you are back at Bitter Keep. Another tremor rips through the courtyard. Walls are collapsing. Everything is breaking up. The ground tilts wildly towards the sky, sending rubble and bodies tumbling into the darkness. Your hands flail for a handhold, settling around the corpse of a drakeling. You remember fingers pressed tight to the scaly skin. A flood of energy, passing through you.

New life had been pushed into the drakeling's body – a mere shadow, yes. But still a life. One that saved your own, on that fateful day.

Is such a thing . . . possible?

Your hand is already moving, fingers reaching for the girl's throat. Then you stop, drawing back. It would not be Anise. You would create an aberration, a walking corpse – no different to what you yourself were, once upon a time. But the pain of loss is unbearable. The pain of missing her . . . Surely any life is better than none?

Will you:

Use your magic to raise her from the dead?	**689**
Leave her to rest in peace?	**550**

587

'Vela styker. A blood challenge – a test. To decide who will be chief.' Sura says it matter-of-factly, as if it is of no consequence. But her words startle you all the same.

'Blood challenge! To lead your tribe?' You look around wildly, suddenly feeling penned in by the confines of the ice shelter. 'I can't lead anyone – I should be going. I am not meant . . .'

'Hush, boy.' Sura chuckles softly, a fond smile creasing the lines of her face. For a moment her kindly expression, the crinkling around the eyes, reminds you of your old nurse, Molly. 'I will train you,' says Sura, her tone resuming its usual seriousness. 'I see you have the power. With my help, I can teach you how to use it.'

Will you:

Ask about the shaman's magic?	**688**
Ask about the bear necklace?	**545**
End the conversation?	**575**

588

After severing the demon's wings you focus your attacks on the eye, smashing through its magical barrier to penetrate the soft, oily tissue beneath. Black ichor sprays from its many wounds as you slice and blast with unrelenting fury, your attacks bolstered by your heightened magic.

The creature dies in silence, its legs twitching feebly in the air.

Then you feel it. An immense rush of calm, like a deeply-held breath finally released. The spinning vortex above you starts to recede, folding back on itself in angry waves until the evening sky is finally revealed, flecked by curtains of pink and violet light.

The storm continues to ebb – rolling and tumbling through clouds of rock and dust until nothing is left but a thin haze, hugging the contours of the outer city and the wasteland beyond.

The demon has been defeated, and with it the source of the magical storm. Your companions will now be able to enter the city unharmed.

If you wish, you may now take one of the following rewards:

Storm eye	Sentinel wings	Spirit fire
(ring)	(cloak)	(talisman)
+2 brawn +2 magic	+2 speed +3 health	+1 speed +5 health
Ability: windblast	Ability: haste	Ability: sear

When you have updated your hero sheet, turn to 653.

589

You tentatively place one foot onto the bridge, the colours swirling and pooling around your boot as it presses against the surface. To your surprise the bridge proves firm underfoot, having the consistency of a soft carpet. Confident that the crossing will be safe, you follow the glittering span over to the floating island – a bare chunk of rock and earth that looks as if it was ripped free from the ground.

At the centre of this odd anomaly is a pedestal – and hovering above it, revolving slowly on an invisible axis, is a magnificent two-bladed sword. The hilt and handle are fashioned from a cobalt-blue metal, inlaid with black gemstones. The blades are rapier thin, sparkling with a fine coating of hoarfrost.

Behind the pedestal, there is a black iron chest. A dark aura surrounds it, crackling and hissing with arcane energies. You note several runes and glyphs etched into the lid, their shapes crawling and twisting as if refusing to let their true forms be known.

590

You detect a stale, musty odour as you descend into the darkness. Your own eyes quickly attune to the gloom, noting that the ground below is littered with jagged fragments of shell – eggs. Caul mutters a curse, his hand groping for your shoulder. 'How d'you see in here? I'm going back for my lamp.' He starts to turn, but you urge him to wait.

'Relax.' You reach out with your mind, touching the dreamscape and drawing on Nanuk's power. The magic courses into you, searing your veins with its burning chill. Raising your arms, you let the cold fire spill from your fingertips, coating both of your weapons in a pale green light. The radiance blossoms outwards, filling the chamber – and illuminating Caul's astonished expression.

'How'd you do that?' he gasps.

'Magic,' you grin.

You turn back to your surroundings, prodding one of the serrated egg pieces. It appears that all the eggs have cracked open; whatever creatures were inside have long since hatched. You cast your light over the fragments, noticing a number of black scales amongst the debris. They remind you of the creatures that you fought at Bitter Keep.

'Smells like a drake.' Caul wrinkles his nose.

You look back at him expectantly.

'I was part of a hunting crew once, down south in the pine mountains. Some creature had got loose, was causing all kinds of havoc. Two heads, spitting acid and fire . . . savage thing it was; took ten of us to kill it.' He shakes his head as he looks around at the dozen or so eggs. 'Now, if each one of these was a drake . . .' He lifts his eyes, the pupils mirroring the ghost-fire from your weapons. 'We're in trouble.'

'Not the most inspiring speech, Caul.' You turn towards the room's only exit, a carved stone archway that leads through into a large spacious chamber.

'They're crafty beasts,' warns the hunter, putting two hands to his spear.

'Indeed.' You cross the room, boot heels cracking loudly through the carpet of egg shards. 'Let's hope they're also hard of hearing.'

The chamber is a vast hall, the walls and ceiling carved with angular designs. A row of wide square columns cut across the centre of the room, each one trailing black-iron chains across the ground. The nearest one ends in a large collar-shaped device, crusted with blood and grime. Whatever creature was tethered here, it had to be of an immense size . . .

You advance with caution, your light picking out the deep-gouged claw marks that rake the ground and run across several of the pillars. One wall looks like it has been melted by a terrible heat, the angular carvings now frozen in fluid, wax-like patterns.

Caul grabs your arm abruptly, pulling you to a halt.

You don't need to ask what has startled him. You hear the shuffle of feet, the clink of chain. The shadow comes into view before the creature – a hulking silhouette of darkness that stretches out from behind one of the pillars.

When the beast finally moves into your line of sight you discover it is not the draconian monster you had been imagining, but a hunchbacked giant. It lurches around the pillar, dragging a malformed foot behind it. The creature's body is half-covered in scales – the rest is a weeping mass of blisters. Tufts of hair sprout from its ridged skull, where a pair of horns curl in opposing directions, both broken and ending in toothed splinters.

The beast turns to face you. For a moment, its sorrowful appearance stays your weapons – but then the creature raises one of its stumpy arms. The scaled flesh ends in a reptilian head, a living creature with burning red eyes and wide gaping jaws. Somehow the two have become melded together; a horrible union of giant and drake.

The jaws crack open and a torrent of fire belches forth. It is time to fight:

	Speed	Brawn/Magic	Armour	Health
Drake keeper	5	5/3	5	70

Special abilities

♦ **Drake fire cannon**: At the end of each combat round you must take damage equal to the Drake keeper's current *magic* score, ignoring *armour*. (When rolling for a damage score, the Drake keeper uses his *brawn*).

♦ **Stalker's spear**: Caul adds 2 to your damage score for the duration of this combat.

If you manage to defeat this hunch-backed horror, turn to 625.

591

For defeating Instructor Barl you may now help yourself to one of the following rewards:

Instructor's faceguard	Cloak of defiance	Iron hand
(head)	(cloak)	(talisman)
+1 speed +2 magic	+2 speed +1 magic	+1 speed +3 health
Ability: deflect	Ability: overload	Ability: immobilise

When you have updated your hero sheet, turn to 444.

592

You leave the store and head back out into the snow-whipped gale. (The White Wolf Trading Post is no longer available – you cannot visit this location again during Act 1 of your adventure and any items that were stored in your locker are now lost.) Make a note of the keyword *ashes* on your hero sheet, then return to the quest map.

593

The monk opens out his meaty fist, showing you his five stones. This forces you to reveal your own. 'A Queen's Wave, double crowned

– beats your fool,' he declares with a toadish smile. 'The One God shines on me again. I win!'

Remove the word *scripture* from your hero sheet, then turn to 697.

594
Legendary monster: Gjoll the gaoler

The ground shakes at the giant's passing, his black steeled boots thudding deep into the cracked earth. Your eyes rove across the malign runes carved into his flame-red skin, each one rippling and crawling over the slabs of hard muscle.

'We can't hope to defeat it.' Anise draws back behind the boulder as the giant stomps past, making his circuit of the cauldron-shaped basin. In each of his meaty fists he carries a warhammer, their stone-carved heads bigger than an ox-cart.

You need no more convincing. 'This is folly. Let's go . . .'

'Wait! We can't let this suffering go unpunished.' Skoll's eyes haven't left the dragon, chained by runed manacles to the floor of the canyon. The sorry-looking beast is writhing in constant agony, flames and lightning roiling across its tortured form. Many of its scales are broken and seeping with decay. A milky film covers one eye. Teeth are missing, a horn broken.

And yet, even in its tortured state, the dragon is still an awe-inspiring sight. Its size dwarfs even that of the giant – its black-scaled form stretching nearly a hundred metres from head to tail, its wings arching back to obliterate the skies.

'I was a prisoner once,' says Skoll, looking to you for support. 'Those chains are Dwarven, bound by powerful rune spirits. They are trying to break the dragon's will – to force it to serve the witch. Not all their kind choose to ally with such evil.'

Lightning courses over the dragon's body, forcing it to jerk and convulse. You are immediately reminded of the chains that the einherjar used to restrain you, when you first sought an audience at Vindsvall. The chains that bind the dragon are twice their size, the runes worked into them of a far deadlier precision.

And they have given you an idea.

'Okay, keep the giant busy.' You are already moving before Skoll can reply, using the rock-cover to get closer to the dragon. Behind you, a barbaric battle cry rends the air as Skoll leaps atop the rubble, banging his twin axes together. The giant's head snaps round, a torrent of flame billowing from his nose.

Skoll's distraction has worked. The giant issues a ground-trembling roar, then charges the Skard. Your way is left clear. Quickly, you hurry across the dusty canyon, towards the manacles that hold the dragon prisoner. If you can break them open, then perhaps they could be used against the giant . . .

All of a sudden, each of the manacles starts to glow – the air around them distorted by magic.

Four spirits coalesce into being around the dragon – the rune spirits that have been bound into the evil irons. The largest is some beast of fur and ice, with a bestial face riddled with fangs. Another is fashioned from threads of flame, its thin body resting on four splayed legs. The third is a shadowy figure, almost humanoid-looking, with serrated blades for arms. The final spirit is a bloated pig-like creature, its devilish form obscured by a cloud of pestilent decay.

You glance back towards the giant. The beast is roaring and bellowing, trying to catch Skoll and Anise, who are dodging around the giant's blows, issuing taunts and keeping him busy. You know they won't be able to hold the giant's attention for long.

The rune spirits surge towards you, four deadly adversaries each with their own potent powers. You realise you will need to overcome these prison guardians in order to break their manacles. It is time to fight:

	Speed	Magic	Armour	Health
Gjoll	14	15	14	130
Sephix (*)	11	6	6	50
Raurg (*)	11	6	6	40
Anod (*)	10	5	5	30
Wendigo (*)	10	5	5	30

Special abilities

● **Prison guardians**: (*) Each prison guardian has an ability. Once a prison guardian is defeated, their ability no longer applies. The abilities are:
  - Sephix's pestilence: You must lose 2 *health* at the end of each combat round.
  - Raurg's fires: You must reduce your *armour* by 1 at the end of each combat round. (You cannot regain lost *armour* until the combat is over.)
  - Anod's reflection: Each time your damage score / damage dice inflicts damage to an opponent, you must take 2 damage in return (per opponent struck).
  - Wendigo's chill: You must lower your *speed* by 1.

● **Shackle the giant**: Each of the prison guardians (Sephix, Anod, Raurg and Wendigo) is guarding one of the manacles holding the dragon prisoner. If you defeat a prison guardian, you gain control of their manacle. This can immediately be used on Gjoll to help you defeat him. The manacle abilities are as follows:
  - Sephix's manacle: Gjoll is inflicted with pestilence and must suffer 5 damage, ignoring *armour*, at the end of every combat round (starting with the round after Sephix is defeated).
  - Raurg's manacle: Cruel fires melt through Gjoll's *armour*, reducing it to 4 for the remainder of the combat.
  - Anod's manacle: Gjoll's hammer becomes a shadow of its former strength, reducing the giant's *magic* to 4 for the remainder of the combat.
  - Wendigo's manacle: Ice encases the giant, reducing Gjoll's *speed* by 3 for the remainder of the combat.

● **In it together**: Abilities that strike more than one opponent can be used on Gjoll and the prison guardians as normal. All opponents are viable targets for such attacks.

To win the combat you must defeat Gjoll. Once Gjoll is defeated, any remaining prison guardians are also defeated. If you manage to overcome this ferocious giant, turn to 739.

595

Raising your hands you trace the circular patterns with your fingers, connecting the lines and whorls with the magic that now flows through you. The runes start to flicker and then glow, illuminating a trail to the centre circle, where purple energies crackle above the podium. For a brief moment you glimpse some creature trapped within the bright maelstrom – a writhing ball of shadow, with tentacles whipping out through the air – then it is gone. The energy sparks out and the runes dim.

When you walk over to the podium you discover that your item is now sparking and hissing with trapped shadow magic. (Congratulations! Your chosen weapon/item of equipment now has the *darksilver* ability.) When you have updated your hero sheet, turn to 684.

596

You manage to pass through the web unscathed! The dragons are less fortunate, however, slamming through the web and ripping it from its island tethers. The ragged threads catch around their bodies, sending crackling bolts of magic ripping into their flesh. Shrieking with anger, the dragons twist and shake to free themselves of the glowing netting – but not before they have suffered significant wounds from its evil magic. Record the word *frazzled* on your hero sheet, then turn to 773.

597

The topmost branches of the tree curl inwards, meeting at the centre of a wooden platform where a man hangs suspended from their grasp. He is naked, save for the tattered remains of a loin cloth and a few strips of leather that may once have been a shirt. He dangles by his feet, body twisting and writhing in agony. Every inch of his flesh has been scoured with deep gashes, forming channels that run from his feet to his scalp. A steady stream of venomous ichor drips from the branches, sizzling and steaming as it courses down the lacerated markings, inflicting great pain and torment to the captive prisoner.

'Skoll!'

It is unmistakably the Skard warrior you were sent here to find – his huge, muscular body and the long golden hair match the entombed half-giant you saw at Vindsvall. The manner of his torture is nightmarish and cruel, his deafening screams ringing like thunder in your ears.

You push past the knotted branches and step out onto the platform.

'Rata-rata-tosk!'

The giant squirrel scampers out in front of you, its head flicking from side-to-side as it sizes you up. 'Strong as ironwood. Yes, yes. But you climb before you can walk, rata-rata-tosk!'

'Out of my way,' you snarl, taking an angry step forward. 'Are you responsible for this?' You gesture to the tortured prisoner.

Ratatosk flexes his shoulders, dark claws extending outwards from his paws. 'The witch has dominion here, rata-rata. But I'll be generous, that's my nature. I'll let you leave, take word – whisper, whisper – back to Vindsvall. Tell them of what you have seen. Tell them all, rata-rata, of what befalls those who seek to hinder the witch's plans.'

'This is your last chance.' You raise your weapons, magic flickering around your tensed body. 'Out of my way!'

'So be it,' snickers Ratatosk, stalking around you. 'Stubborn as oak, fiery as the buckthorn. You would have been wise to listen to me, rata-rata-tosk!'

'Likewise.' You charge the creature, who dodges swiftly, diving past you in a red-brown blur. He scampers up the nearest wall, leaping over you as you charge in again, your weapons cutting futilely through the air. Spinning round, you spot the creature digging into one of his many pouches. With a flick of his clawed hand Ratatosk lifts a grey acorn to his shoulder, then throws it hard at the ground. There is a flash of dark light and then a twisted shape starts to emerge from the smoke, its gnarled limbs snapping and creaking as they unfurl. Within seconds you find yourself facing a spider-like tree with crimson eyes glowing from its soot-coloured bark.

With a hellish shriek the summoned creature lurches towards you on tentacle-like roots while Ratatosk lopes to a safe distance, rummaging in his pouch for more enchanted seeds. It is time to fight:

	Speed	Magic	Armour	Health
Ratatosk	7	6	5	80
Shadow sapling	5	4	1	5

Special abilities

♥ **Rat-a-tat-tat**: Ratatosk continues to sow more of his dark seeds, summoning minions to his aid. At the start of each combat round, roll a die. On a result of ⚀ or less, two new shadow saplings enter the combat (with the same attributes as the sapling shown above). If the result is ⚁ or more, only one new shadow sapling enters the combat.

♥ **Thorn fingers**: At the end of each combat round, you must take 1 damage (ignoring *armour*) from each shadow sapling currently in play.

If Ratatosk is defeated, the *rat-a-tat-tat* ability no longer applies. You must defeat Ratatosk and all shadow saplings currently in play in order to win the combat.

If you manage to overcome this rascally rodent, turn to 143.

598

You weave between the snapping beaks and raking talons, using the advantage of speed to give you the edge over the cumbersome creatures. Finally the last of the nightwings goes flailing backwards against the battlements, its wings torn and useless. Before it can find its feet again you swing your weapons in a savage arc, severing the beast's head in a spray of blue-black blood. Just like in the storybook, you have bested the vile monsters and saved the day!

You may now take one of the following rewards:

Fallen angel	**Skyhawk**	**Talons of the tower**
(cloak)	(main hand: crossbow)	(gloves)
+2 speed +1 magic	+2 speed +3 brawn	+1 speed +2 brawn
Ability: phantom	Ability: piercing	Ability: revenge

When you have updated your hero sheet, turn to 444.

599
Legendary monster: Quelertang the Hailstorm

Tracks in the snow have brought you to the edge of a pit, where wind chimes made of bone sing eerily from the withered trees. Their dry, cracked bark leak an icy-blue sap, which oozes in thick rivulets down into the base of the crater. There a small child, no older than seven, stands shivering from the cold. He grips a spear in his pale frost-bitten hands, gawping in fear at the dark opening in the opposite wall.

You notice the child is lame – one of his legs is misshapen, probably from disease or a broken bone that was never set properly. Glancing round at the tracks cutting through the churned snow, and the singing bone charms arranged around the pit, you suspect this is some Skard ritual – or punishment. Any sign of weakness is frowned upon in the north. A child that cannot hunt for his tribe is no longer of any use.

Your boots scuff through the snow as you step up to the lip of the pit. The child's head snaps round in your direction, frost glistening off his chapped lips and the snot frozen to his face. He looks so weak and afraid – and innocent. A mirror-image of yourself at that age.

A bone-chilling howl reverberates from the hole. The child gives a startled yelp, his attention flicking back to that impenetrable pool of darkness. He raises his spear and starts to limp backwards.

The wind picks up with a sudden fury, the bone chimes filling the air with a discordant din.

You draw your weapons, calling on Nanuk to pass his strength into you, heightening your senses and your spirit powers. Then you leap into the pit, landing in a crouch just as the monstrous apparition comes pouring out of the hole.

At first it seems to be a confusion of smoke and mist – a dust cloud that refuses to settle. Then you see the shards of ice spinning about its ethereal body. You manage to grab the boy, pushing him to safety as a flurry of ice is hurled in your direction at frightening speed. Twisting aside, you manage to dodge the worst of the bullets, but the force of the wind blows you back against the wall.

You barely have a chance to recover before the demon is surging across the pit, its body growing bigger as its whirling form picks up more ice and rocks to hurl in your direction. It is time to fight:

	Speed	Magic	Armour	Health
Quelertang	8	4	6	90

Special abilities

- **Hailstorm**: At the end of each combat round, the hail bullets automatically inflict 1 damage, ignoring *armour,* for every 10 *health* that Quelertang has remaining. (For example, if Quelertang had 65 *health*, the hailstorm would inflict 6 damage.)
- **Buffeting gale**: If you have the *insulated* ability you can reduce Quelertang's damage score by 2.
- **Body of air**: Quelertang is immune to *bleed, decay, disease* and *venom.*

If you manage to defeat this chilling maelstrom, turn to 742.

600

You must use these ancient defences to defeat the four advancing stone guardians. The diagram on the facing page shows a map of the hall. The circles represent locations where you can place an orb. Each orb has a different magical power – by choosing their locations carefully, you can combine their magics to devastating effect. Will you be able to defeat the guardians before they can reach you?

1. The four guardians begin on the first arrow at the top left of the diagram. (You may want to copy this diagram onto paper and use numbered counters to represent each guardian. The diagram is also available to download and print from www.destiny-quest. com.)
2. In each combat round, the guardians all move forward one square.
3. Each time the guardians move into a new square, they immediately activate the orb/s that have been placed next to that square. (See below for orb effects.)

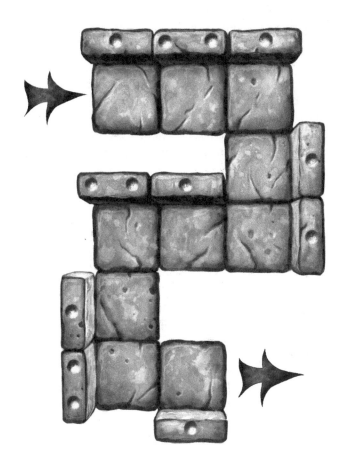

4. When a guardian reaches the final arrow (at the bottom right), it will engage you in normal combat with the *health* it has remaining.

	Speed	Brawn	Armour	Health
Guardian	5	5	7	150
Guardian	5	5	7	150
Guardian	5	5	7	150
Guardian	5	5	7	150

You find in the room three *frost orbs*, three *shadow orbs*, two *tremor orbs* and one *lightning orb*. You may have collected additional orbs on your travels, which you can also use. Each orb does the following:

Frost orb Slows one guardian, meaning it stays on its current square for an extra round instead of moving to the next.

Shadow orb Inflicts a curse on one guardian, inflicting 10 passive damage at the end of each turn for the duration of the challenge / combat. (Each guardian can only be affected by this once.)

Tremor orb Inflicts damage depending on how many guardians are in the square. (One guardian = 100 damage, two = 50 damage each, three guardians = 30 damage each, four guardians = 20 damage each.)

Lightning orb Reduces one guardian's *armour* to 2.

Decide where you want to place your orbs (using a symbol or colour to denote each type). Once placed, orbs cannot be moved. Their magic can only be used *once*. When the orbs have been placed – the challenge begins! (Remember, you cannot engage the guardians in ordinary combat until they have reached the final arrow.)

If you manage to defeat these powerful guardians, turn to 642. (Special achievement: If all four guardians are defeated before they reach the final arrow, turn to 513.)

601

A man knocks into you, seemingly by accident. You draw away as he grunts an apology, then you feel the sharp pain coming from your arm. Looking down you see a cut and black blood oozing out onto your sleeve.

The man stops, a burly-looking figure swathed in furs and leather. He lifts a knife to his nose, sniffing the blood on its blade. 'So, I found ya,' he says gruffly. He shifts round, his bearded face glistening with frost. A pair of black glasses cover his eyes, mirroring your surprised expression. 'Yeah, no mistakin' that stink – and corpse blood too.' In various straps and belts you see an array of weapons – pistols, daggers, short swords.

'You have me mistaken,' you reply, taking a step away. Your eyes scan the rest of the alley. All of a sudden it has gone quiet – empty. You can smell trouble.

'White Wolf Trading Post,' he scowls, tossing the knife aside. 'You're the one who dusted old Jackson. Bounty on yer 'ed now – and I'll be the one takin' it.' The man draws two short blades from his trappings, then springs forward with surprising speed, slicing his weapons through the air. It is time to fight:

	Speed	Brawn	Armour	Health
Bounty hunter	7	4	3	60

Special abilities

🥄 **Daring duellist**: If you use a speed or combat ability, roll a die. On a ⚀ or ⚁ result, the hunter deflects your attack. This cancels your ability (it can no longer be played during this combat) and inflicts 1 die of damage to your hero, ignoring *armour*. Passive and modifier abilities can be used as normal.

If you manage to defeat this mean mercenary, turn to 201.

602

Skoll turns his head, taking in the extent of the destruction. Deep cracks now run across the ground, having torn through the panelled floor. The left side of the hall has collapsed inwards, the ceiling little more than a skeletal framework of toppled beams. Wisps of snow fall from the exposed winter sky, dusting the wreckage with a glistening sheen.

'Drokke.' Aslev falls to one knee, his head lowered in reverence. He speaks in Skard, his words guttural and sharp. You sense their meaning, an apology for having failed his leader – for breaking his vow to protect Vindsvall.

Skoll answers in common, perhaps for your own benefit. 'Silence your words, einherjar – save them for the songs of this day. Look around. I see only stone and wood. This is not the flesh of our people. This is not the blood of the Ska-inuin. We have lost nothing to cause us shame.' He strides past the kneeling einherjar, his gaze shifting to the struggling figure trapped beneath the statue.

'What is this?' he barks with contempt.

'Gurt Bloodaxe, my lord,' slobbers the flabby man. 'I lead the einherjar – if it wasn't for my actions, this hall would have fallen long ago. My bravery, my skill has . . .'

Skoll lifts a hand. 'Silence!' His thick fingers explode into golden light. With a flick of his wrist the wooden statue is sent flipping through the air, shattering to pieces against the far wall. The freed warrior lies panting and sweating on his back, eyes bulging from his piggish face.

'Th . . . thank you,' he dribbles. He struggles to get up, his legs kicking feebly beneath his rotund belly.

'You are free to leave,' says Skoll coldly. He glances back at Aslev. 'This one is nameless. Be sure he does not return to Vindsvall or I will hang his craven soul from the tree.' He continues to the doors of the hall, his crowned helm glowing with runic script. 'Walk with me, prince of Valeron.'

Ignoring Gurt's squeals of protest, you fall into step beside the half-giant warrior. 'I will take my leave also,' you state quickly. 'My task here is done.'

You follow Skoll out onto the glacier. The warrior stoops, cupping his hands into the nearest drift of snow. He lifts it to his face, scrubbing the sweat and grime from his scarred face. 'Is it finished?' he asks, taking a deep breath of the chill air.

It takes a moment for you to grasp his meaning. 'I came because of Sura. I wanted to help.'

'But these are not your people,' states the warrior. He looks back at you, then his eyes flit to the hall, and Anise – who is still standing in silent reflection over the demon's body. 'You will name her,' he says matter-of-factly.

'Her name is Anise,' you reply, frowning.

'That is not a warrior's name.' He lifts another handful of snow, watching it spill between his open fingers. 'And what of you, prince of Valeron? That is not a true name. Not a name earned in battle. A name should sing of great deeds. I would call you Bearclaw, for I see you have the spirit of Nanuk.'

He rises to his feet, drawing himself to his full imposing height. You note the dark welts cutting across the warrior's pale skin – a reminder of the terrible wounds he suffered in the Norr. 'Understand my words. The witch will not spare your people or my people. The blows she has dealt us, they are as nothing to what is coming. Her mind is set to dark purpose, to free Jormungdar, the world serpent. When that happens, our realm – your kingdom – will be split asunder.'

You stare incredulously at the Skard. 'Do you really believe such a thing exists?'

Skoll continues. 'Once I knew only despair. I thought the battle lost. I travelled to the Norr to find answers, to find a way of matching the witch's strength.'

'Fimbulwinter,' you nod, remembering back to the broken shield.

'Yes. It was forged by the Titans in the frost fire of Mount Skringskal. If remade, it might be the weapon to defeat the witch. If we do not do this – if our courage fails – the cost will be more than our lives, Bearclaw. It will be the end of everything.'

Will you:

Ask about the witch's origins?	654
Ask about the Titans?	544
Ask about Jormungdar?	452
End the conversation?	326

603

You head deeper into the hive, the tunnel twisting and bending past numerous side passages. Concerned you may have led yourself into an endless maze, you finally catch sight of a light ahead: a sickly yellow glow, accompanied by the sour stench of rot and decay.

The tunnel opens out into a large cavernous chamber, its walls and floor heaped with large bloated maggots. They are all hungrily chewing on various remains – both animal and humanoid. The yellow hue is coming from the maggots themselves, seeping out of the spiracles along their bulbous bodies.

You pass over the sea of squirming shapes, aiming for a tunnel in the opposite wall. However, as you reach the centre of the chamber you hear a revolting squelching noise coming from below. Something is rising up out of the detritus, pushing itself past the layers of writhing maggots. A giant head emerges, eyeless and scarred, its yellow flesh dripping with filth and rancid secretions.

It is too late to swerve aside. The colossal monster lifts itself straight into your flight path, the head splitting open to reveal a cavernous maw of teeth. You are left with no choice but to battle your way past this disgusting abomination. It is time to fight:

	Speed	Brawn	Armour	Health
Maggorath	12	11	8	100

Special abilities

🖤 **Infestation**: Once you have taken health damage from Maggorath's damage score, you are immediately inflicted with infestation. You must lose 2 *health* at the end of the first combat round you are infected. This damage increases by 2 every round for the duration of the combat.

🖤 **Fire at will**: You may use your *nail gun* or *dragon fire* ability in this combat.

If you manage to defeat the giant maggot, turn to 748. (If you are defeated, remember to record your defeat as normal on your hero sheet, then turn to 770.)

604

A confined metal space filled with flame and exploding glass – not an appealing prospect. You decide to leave the store and head back out into the snow-whipped gale. (The White Wolf Trading Post is no longer available – you cannot visit this location again during Act 1 of your adventure and any items that were stored in your locker are now lost.) Make a note of the keyword *ashes*, then return to the quest map.

'Think I'd fall for that one?' growls the guard, snatching you by the collar. 'She ain't got a tab 'ere, the ladies ain't payin' for nothing. And you're a dirty liar.'

There are gasps and cries from the party-goers as they watch the guard drag you back into the taproom of the Coracle. He gives you a final shove before turning and heading back into the private room. It appears your attempt to get inside the cellar has failed. Turn to 80.

606
Quest: The crossing

The north has become a land of extremes. Its howling winds remain as cold and savage as ever, pushing against you every step of the way, seeking to grind you into submission.

And yet, all around you is desert.

There is no snow or ice, only a dry red dust. In places the ground is warm underfoot, as if some terrible heat is throbbing below the surface, eager to break free. Perhaps it is the serpent – the creature known as Jormungdar.

For days you have sighted no other living creature, only bones. Some were goblin, others larger – perhaps giant or troll. You wonder if the same fate will be shared by your companions. The barren desolation offers up no food or water. The few pools that you have come across have been filled with stagnant, acrid water. Anise and Skoll are suffering. You can see it in their drawn features, their weary stumbling strides. The last of the food has run out, and it seems there is little hope of finding more.

At last the seemingly endless plain breaks into a boulder-strewn slope which continues to rise, forming a high cliff wall. You climb it with difficulty, the rock constantly crumbling and sliding beneath you, until you finally reach the summit – a thin edge of bare ground, dotted with scraggly bush.

Squinting in the torpid light, you find the new elevation provides a perfect view over the low-lying clouds, to where a single mountain looms high in the distance – a huge peak of red-coloured rock. A greenish light flickers around its summit, almost like a candle-flame or a beacon.

'That's it . . . Mount Skringskal.' Skoll is still puffing from the climb, but he manages a contented smile. 'At last, we can remake the shield.'

Then the wind shifts direction, gusting the clouds eastwards, thinning them to ghostly ribbons. An act of nature's cruelness perhaps, as the true scene before you is gradually unveiled.

The three of you stare, blank and hopeless, at the colossal rift that has swept away the land. Rocks and larger bodies of earth hang suspended in the void, floating as if trapped in time, blown skywards and then frozen in situ. They form a chain of islands stretching for miles across the chasm, to where the mountain itself hovers in the empty space, its foundations ripped free from whatever land had once existed here, leaving it detached and unreachable.

'No . . .' Skoll shakes his head, disbelieving what his eyes are seeing. 'The mountain . . .'

You stare at him accusingly.

'It wasn't like this,' he breathes. 'The land . . . the tremors. Everything has changed since last I was here.'

You look back at the distant mountain, floating in the air by some act of magic. 'Evidently.'

'We've come too far.' Anise sags to the ground with exhaustion. 'We have to find a way. There must be a way . . .'

If you have the *captain's conch* and wish to summon *Naglfar*, turn to 671. If you have the *dragon's horn* and would prefer to summon Nidhogg, turn to 759. If you have neither item, then you currently have no means of navigating the rift. Return to the quest map to continue your journey.

607

Sura takes the staff from you, tossing it into the snow. 'No need for that. Now, step into the circle.'

You follow the woman's instruction. As you take your position at the centre of the runes, you feel a sudden prickling along your skin. It is as if a door to the Norr has been flung open and its freezing chill has flooded into you, turning your limbs to ice. You give a startled gasp, your throat clicking as it involuntarily constricts.

'Calm yourself!' Sura takes a step away, a sudden wariness to her manner. 'Find Nanuk, the link that makes you as one. Then pull him in. Let him inside!'

You reach out with your mind, sensing for the bear. Then you feel his shadow pass over you, a rush of energy so fast and powerful that it throws you to your knees. Your jaws are wrenched open, a gargling scream dying on your lips – becoming a thunderous, echoing roar.

You feel yourself blacking out, losing yourself to the agony that spears into your soul.

'Fight it!' You hear Sura shout desperately.

You shake your head, trying to release the pain, the throbbing agony. Black hairs are bursting up out of your skin – you feel your jaw bones stretching forward, fangs ripping from your gums. As you scrabble in the snow you see fingers becoming claws, the palms widening into massive paws.

'Control it! The bear is inside you – do not lose yourself to him!'

You throw back your head as your spine rips out from your armour, bulging with thick bands of muscle. Then you fall forward once again, landing on four powerful paws, their huge claws sliding deep into the snow.

You give a whining growl, pushing your mind forward – taking control of your body once again, slipping into it like a hand inside a new glove.

Sura nods approvingly. 'The old tales return. A were-bear. Like the first warriors of Helvsgard. Truly, you are the one to lead us.'

The were has the following special abilities:

Shape shift (co): Instead of rolling for a damage score, you can let Nanuk take full control of your body, shape shifting into a bear. This raises your *brawn* by 3 and restores 4 *health* but also lowers your *armour* to zero for the remainder of the combat. While in bear form, you cannot use combat abilities but you do benefit from *blood frenzy* (see below). Once you have shape shifted, you cannot change back until the combat is over.

Blood frenzy (pa): If a *bleed* effect is in play then you may raise your *speed* by 1.

You release the magic, shifting back into your human form. You lie shivering in the snow for some minutes, curled in a ball, still racked with shock.

'It will get easier,' says Sura, her tone taking on its usual cold detachment. 'But only use your power when needed. Else you may change and never find your way back.' She reaches inside her robes, producing a knotted chain of rune-etched bear claws. 'Take this talisman. It will help you to channel your power.'

If you wish, you may take the following item:

Altered beast
(talisman)
+1 brawn +2 health
Ability: bleed

Once you have updated your hero sheet, turn to 197.

608

The tongue snaps around your arm, pulling you in towards the deadly array of spines. Using its own momentum against it, you throw yourself into a sprint, charging the creature. At the last moment, you spring up into the air, using one of its root-like legs as leverage to sail over the top of its head. The tongue tries to detach itself but you grip it tight, swinging yourself behind the creature, then circling it until the thorny vine is wrapped tight around its spindly body.

The creature struggles to free itself, spinning and twisting in confusion – like a cotton reel trying to unwind itself. You watch its continued torment with a cruel smile, flowing magic into your hands and along the length of your weapons. Waiting for your moment.

The creature staggers dizzily towards you. In one swift movement you swing your shoulders, weapons and magic scything through the air.

An ear-shattering shriek.

The body splinters in two, showering you in chips and globules of green ichor. The head rolls to a halt at your feet, but the legs are still moving, carrying the other half of its body on a crazy, blind dance

– before it runs into a wall, then finally crumples to the ground in a further spray of slime.

If you are a warrior, turn to 515. If you are a rogue, turn to 408. If you are a mage, turn to 473.

609

'Lost my sled to a crevasse, only had a few belongings with me – some hides, weapons, food. They got left behind when I was attacked. Prefer to keep a hold of my life, if given the choice.'

'Perhaps we can go back and get them,' you add encouragingly. 'Do you remember the way?'

Caul scratches his cheek, leaving a bloody smear. 'Perhaps I might. The caves get real twisty. I'm a good tracker, got a sixth sense when it comes to direction – but not done me much good in here. I swear, it's like . . .' He shudders, hugging himself against a sudden chill. 'It's like the caves just want you to . . . stay.' His eyes dart nervously from side to side. When he catches your stare, he smiles awkwardly. 'You think me crazy, I know. But you'll see.'

Will you:

Ask what he knows about the caves?	498
Ask why he thought you were a ghost?	481
Ask if he will accompany you?	384

610

You drop down into a smooth stone passageway. Behind you, the shaft is clogged with broken rock – evidently the cause of the obstruction. The lift rattles away out of sight, coming to a halt above you with an echoing boom.

Hoping you haven't become trapped by your hair-raising efforts, you hurry along the passageway – relieved when it finally opens up into a small, rectangular chamber. An archway in the far wall leads through to another tunnel.

The room you have entered appears to be some sort of storage room or vault – but one that has already been ransacked. Wood and metal lie strewn across the ground, the scraps hinting at chests and weapon racks. There are also some splinters of rune-covered stone, which may have once been Dwarven spell tablets.

Rifling through the debris, you manage to scrape together 25 gold crowns. You also uncover a small bronze box. It looks of Elven design, rather than Dwarven, with suns and lotus flowers adorning the sides. Someone has tried to smash the lock, damaging the lid but not succeeding in opening it. If you have a *skeleton key*, turn to 649. Otherwise, you have no means of opening the box. Left with no other choice, you leave the box behind and head onwards. Turn to 2.

611

'Skoll believed you would have answers – the whereabouts of the last shield fragment.' You look upon the strange woman, questioning your own wisdom in trusting such a being. 'He believes the witch has a plan, to release a monster from the underworld.'

He speaks the truth. Aisa has many agents. Queen Melusine, the witch, was once like you. Her thread mirrors your own. Loneliness. Betrayal. Revenge. Aisa has pushed her down a very dark path.

'And the shield?' you persist. 'We need to find the last piece.'

The woman glares at you mutely. *The demon has it. The one that holds you in thrall. I tried to safeguard it. I tried to keep it from her, but Aisa is too powerful now. You must defeat the demon. Take it from him and return to your world. You are not safe here. Not safe.*

(Return to 713 to ask another question or turn to 760 to end the conversation.)

612

You place the 'three of snakes' on the discard pile and pick a new stone from the bag. You have gained the 'three of crowns'.

You have the following stones:

The monk takes his turn with an almost wearisome air, tossing the stone that he picked back onto the discard pile. You wonder if he's already got a winning hand or is simply bluffing. It is now your move.

Will you:

Play your current hand?	593
Discard the one of crowns?	522
Discard the three of swords?	487

613

It is almost impossible to keep up with the fleet-footed Skard – he shifts his weight expertly, sending you stumbling and sliding over the ice in your attempts to hit him. Frustration gets the better of you, your attacks becoming more impatient and ill-timed, until you leave yourself wide open to a counter-attack.

Desnar brings his staff up and under your guard, the antlers grappling your legs and throwing you up into the air. As you crash down onto your back the ice splinters beneath you, and then you are falling – hitting the chill waters with a thunderous splash.

For several panicked moments, you lose all sense of direction. The light refracts through the mantle of the lake, turning the waters into a sparkling, blinding assault. Desperately you kick in the direction you believe will lead you to the surface, your head slamming against a hard wall of ice. You swing your weapons, hoping to break through, but the water makes your movements sluggish, taking the strength out of your blows.

I cannot drown, you remind yourself. But the knowledge is cold comfort as you beat and claw at the ice, finding no way through. Your panic only intensifies – the thought of being trapped in this blinding, ice cold prison fills you with terror.

Then you see a shadow blotting out the light. Something hits the ice, cracking it. The water vibrates with the pounding blows. Another crack, then the ice is spilling away. A hand reaches down, knotted with muscle, settling around your arm and yanking you upwards. You grapple onto the edge of the ice, levering yourself the rest of the way.

You lie dripping on the surface of the lake, eyes tightly closed against the painful light. A shadow looms across you once again. You look up to see Desnar, his staff held tight in both hands, ready to bring it down in a fatal strike.

'I yield!' You cough, heaving a torrent of frigid water onto the ice. 'I yield.'

Desnar nods, looking satisfied. 'Halstek mine,' he states, as if the matter is now concluded. He turns and heads back across the ice, evidently not caring if you stay or follow. Shakily, you find your feet and start after the Skard, your mind picturing Sura's disappointment when she learns of the outcome. Turn to **578**.

614

The first mile is a chaotic scramble as racers desperately attempt to pull ahead whilst defending themselves from their opponents. There are explosions and screams. The broken wreckage of a sled spirals past, one of its razor-edged runners missing your head by scant inches.

You veer away from the crowd, avoiding the bottlenecks where the sleds have become bunched together, spikes and armour sparking as they meet. You are about to take an early lead –when a crevasse streaks out of nowhere, cutting across your path.

Your dog-team react instinctively, pulling your sled into a tight turn. The crevasse sweeps round to your left as you knife through the snow to reach safer ground. That's when you experience the teeth-jarring thump as another racer slams into you.

'Time to take a dip, rookie!'

You look round to see a fellow racer pulling alongside – a mast of stretched seal-skin giving his sled added momentum. With a triumphant howl he slams into you once again, forcing your sled nearer to the crevasse. As you skirt along its edge, you catch a worrying glimpse of the cold dark waters waiting for you below.

You will need to take a challenge test using your *toughness* attribute:

	Toughness
Early dive	14

If you are successful, turn to 248. Otherwise, turn to 198.

615

Leaping over the severed tentacles, you plunge your weapons into Caul's chest. The trapper gives a monstrous screech, his face twisted into a mask of painful torment, then he vanishes – leaving you staring dumbfounded at the empty space.

'*I WAS THE ONE WHO LED YOU HERE, MORTAL. THESE ARE BUT MY SLAVES. MY GHOSTS.*' The voice thunders all around you, shaking the very walls of the cavern. '*THEY WERE WEAK. USELESS TO ME. BUT YOU! WITH YOUR MAGIC I WILL TRULY BE REBORN. FAFNIR WILL LIVE AGAIN!*'

There is a terrible ripping sound. Ice rains down from above, forcing you to cover your head from the deluge. When you are finally able to look up again, you see that the drake is clambering down the far wall, its huge talons tearing into the ice.

You contemplate running, your eyes scanning back to the tunnel that Caul made with his dagger. But the reptilian monster is already rushing across the ice towards you, its twin heads dripping with a foul, black ichor. There is no escape – it is time to fight:

	Speed	Brawn	Armour	Health
Drake head	5	4	4	40
Drake head	5	4	4	40

Special abilities

♥ **Frost fire**: At the end of each combat round, you must take 2 damage from each surviving opponent, ignoring *armour*. (If you have the *insulated* ability, this damage is reduced to 1 per opponent.)

If you manage to defeat this ancient terror, turn to 680.

616

You raise your hand, sending a torrent of magic into the venom-dripping branches. Their dry bark withers and snaps under your assault, dropping the warrior to the ground. He lies, huddled and shivering, his lacerated body still steaming from the poison.

You kneel at his side, pulling the matted blond hair away from his face. 'Skoll?'

The half-giant's eyes snap open with a sudden fierceness. You manage to lurch away just in time as his wide hands grapple for you.

'I came to save you,' you state quickly, keeping a wary distance from the disorientated warrior. 'I am not your enemy.'

The warrior struggles to his knees, the scoured marks under his eyes weeping venomous tears. 'A hundred years,' he rumbles. 'A hundred years of pain.' He clenches his fists, cording the thick veins along his arms. 'You are not a Skard.'

Without pause, he pushes himself to his feet. You back away, taking in his full height – almost seven feet tall, his imposing body ridged by slabs of hard muscle. 'Vindsvall . . .' His eyes narrow as if suddenly remembering some long forgotten purpose. 'The shield . . . Fimbulwinter. I must return her. The Ska-inuin need me.'

If Leif is with you, turn to 772. Otherwise, turn to 400.

617

The three of you advance cautiously through the deep snow, bound to one another by a length of rope. Skoll leads the way, carefully testing the ground with his spear for any hidden crevasses. At last, after several hours of hiking, the ground becomes firmer underfoot, gradually turning from rock to ice as you near the intimidating wall of the North Face.

'Are we meant to go around this?' you ask, squinting up at the summit thousands of metres above you. Up close you realise that the entire edifice is leaning forward, its upmost tip curling over like a breaking wave. The ice walls are sheer, offering little purchase for a climber. Reaching the summit appears nigh on impossible.

Skoll shakes his head. 'Going around – that would take many days.'

Anise is sat on her pack, already exhausted from the long march. 'I can't climb,' she gasps despondently. 'Please, I can't.'

'We don't have to,' replies Skoll. He points to a symbol etched into a nearby boulder. 'There is a passage through. Dangerous. But it is the only way.'

As you continue to scan the great ice barrier, you notice a winged shape wheeling in circles overhead. At first you assume it is a bird, but the wings are too large – the body hinting at more human-like dimensions.

'Is that Habrok?' you enquire doubtfully, shielding your eyes from the glare of the surrounding ice.

Skoll follows your gaze. 'I sent him south to gather my people. He would not come here . . .'

The shape continues to wheel above you, the sunlight catching on the claws of its feet, the spines that protrude from its broad, scaly shoulders. Then realisation dawns.

'It's the demon!' you cry, remembering back to the Wiccans' ambush and the strange creature that saved your life. 'He told me to run – back when I was attacked, before I came to Bitter Keep.'

Anise puts a hand to her sword. 'Does that make him a friend or foe?'

You frown. 'I don't know. I just remember what he said – something about the fates setting me on this path.'

'The fates?' Skoll raises an eyebrow. 'He may know of the weaver.'

You raise a hand, igniting it with magic to form a glowing beacon. You then proceed to wave it back and forth, hoping to grab the demon's attention.

It is difficult to tell if you have been spotted; the creature has started to gain height, its silvery-white wings blurring as they beat faster. Gradually the demon grows smaller and smaller, until he is lost to the shadows beneath the curling summit.

Skoll gives a dismissive snort. 'Come – we must keep moving.'

He helps Anise to her feet then takes up her pack, shouldering its weight along with his own. Together they head up the slope, following the direction marked on the boulder. You hold back for a moment, pensively watching the skies – wondering what has brought the demon this far north. You reach for Nanuk, questing for answers. None are forthcoming.

Grudgingly, you snuff out the beacon. 'Friend or foe,' you mutter. 'Pray it is not the latter, demon.' Tugging down your hood, you turn and head after your companions.

You may now turn to **551** to begin the Act 2 green quest, *Angels and demons*.

618

Talia turns to leave, then pauses. 'Okay, okay, you won me over.' She reaches for one of her swords, tugging it free from the scabbard. 'You know, I wouldn't normally part with my favourite toy, but for you, sweet pea, it's all yours.' Talia offers out the weapon, its transparent blade still glowing with magic. 'Venetia glass. Holds a note better than I do – I can teach you, if you'd like.'

You may now take the following item:

Dusky sonnet
(main hand: glass sword)
+1 speed +2 brawn
Ability: sure edge, bleed

You may also learn the bard career. The bard has the following special abilities:

Good vibrations (co): Turn your swords into vibrating blades of death. This doubles the *brawn* modifier of any glass swords you have equipped, for one combat round only. This ability can only be used once per combat.

Deadly dance (sp): Goad your opponent with a series of dodges and feints. This automatically lowers their *speed* by 2 for one combat round, but raises their *brawn / magic* by 1 for the remainder of the combat. This ability can be used twice in the same combat, but each time it is used your opponent's *brawn / magic* is increased.

When you have made your decision Talia blows you a kiss and then departs, leaving you alone in the secret laboratory. Turn to **747**.

You skid down the sandy slope, magic flashing from your weapons. Below you, Nanuk and the wolf are rolling amidst a dark cloud of dust, the thick air affording only momentary glimpses of teeth, fur and thrashing limbs.

Your bolt of magic takes the wolf in the chest, sending it scampering away with a howl. Nanuk swings round, his anger readily apparent. His mind pushes against your own, insisting you return to the others.

You note his wounds – the bite marks along his torso, the skin and fur hanging from his throat. The great bear's breathing is laboured. He may have weight and strength on his side but the wolf is an agile opponent, using speed to whittle down his opponent's stamina.

'We fight together, Nanuk,' you insist. 'Old friend.'

Nanuk snorts, but you sense his grateful acceptance.

The wolf has dropped back onto its haunches, its head raised to the whirling crimson skies. Then he issues another howl – a mourner's wail. Within seconds, you hear the padding of feet. You turn to see a pack of dark shadows streaming towards you; wolves with bodies fashioned from mist and darkness, their eyes burning with fire.

'Wolves,' you remark grimly, putting your back to Nanuk's. 'Why does it always have to be wolves?'

Nanuk gives a bellowing roar in answer, his massive paws swiping through the air, trying to keep the wolves at bay. The pack closes in, forming a circle around you, heads low to the ground, drool spilling over their cruel fangs. Your eyes scan back to the spirit wolf. A name forms in your mind: *Sleet*. You meet his gaze – a single yellow eye.

He snarls.

You bare your teeth, issuing your own animal-like growl. Then you both spring at one another, a bestial rage fuelling your strikes. It is time to fight:

	Speed	Magic	Armour	Health
Sleet	13	8	6	80
Shadow warg	12	6	5	20
Shadow warg	12	6	5	20
Shadow warg	12	6	5	20
Shadow warg	12	6	5	20

Special abilities

🛡 **Tendon ripper**: Each time you take health damage from Sleet's damage score, you must lower your *speed* by 1 for the next combat round.

🛡 **Slashing claws**: At the end of each combat round, you must take 1 damage from each opponent remaining in combat.

🛡 **Bear power!**: Nanuk adds 2 to your damage score for the duration of this combat.

If you manage to fend off your savage attackers, turn to 758.

620

For besting Desnar and becoming leader of the bear tribe, your bond with Nanuk's spirit has strengthened. You have also gained the following special ability:

Recuperation (dm): Gain 1 *health* at the end of each combat round for the rest of the combat. This ability can only be used once per combat.

When you have updated your hero sheet, turn to 721.

621

Hands wrestle hold of your arms and shoulders. Angrily you try and break free, twisting your head to see two stern-faced guards standing either side of you.

'You're under arrest, traitor,' barks one.

'For crimes against the throne,' snarls the other.

Before you can react, the guards shove you forward.

The scene dissolves as you are propelled at speed. Wind rushes past you, stinking of death and rot, and then you slam hard into a stone wall. Recovering quickly you spin round, only to find yourself trapped in a stone shaft with walls on either side. Above you, the shaft rises a hundred metres or more towards a red sky, torn by fast-moving cloud.

'She wants me to keep you, as a plaything,' whispers the voice in your ear. 'But you are proving troublesome. More powerful than we thought.'

'Let me go!' you snarl angrily. 'Face me, coward!'

There is a wet-sounding slurp. Then you find yourself slipping . . . sinking.

The ground has become a fetid mire of mud and dirt. Maggots, worms and other crawling insects squirm out of the dank soil. You are gradually being pulled under, the mire sucking you down into its clammy, wet depths.

'The dead should stay in the ground,' hisses the voice, 'don't you agree?'

Mocking laughter fills your ears. Desperately, your hands scrabble against the smooth stone, trying to gain leverage and stop your descent. But you are sinking fast, the worm-ridden filth already rising past your waist.

If you have the *silver acorn* and wish to use it, turn to **381**. Otherwise, turn to **7**.

622

You regret the outcome of your actions, but it was the only way of stopping such a dangerous weapon from getting into the wrong hands. Searching Talia's body, you find 50 gold crowns and a *chipped emerald* (simply make a note of this on your hero sheet, it doesn't take up backpack space).

You rip up the formula, then begin a search of the secret laboratory. Turn to **747**.

(Note: You must have completed the orange quest *The crossing* before you access this location)

If you have the keyword *survivors* on your hero sheet, turn to **644**. Otherwise, read on.

A dark spire of smoke draws you to the island. A cooking fire, perhaps – or a distress signal. Certainly a hopeful sign of life amidst this scattered archipelago.

As you sweep down across the wind-blown plains, it quickly becomes apparent that you will need to make landfall – the streaming currents of dust make it impossible to discern the true nature of the terrain, and its potential dangers.

You set down on the far side, then head inwards to find the source of the smoke. Swathed in thick cloaks and scarves, hoods drawn low, you stumble through the whirling sand, guided only by the wan light of the sun – so distant and small amidst the storm-laden skies.

As you near the centre of the island, you sight a tumble of ruins. Several walls and a tower loom out of the mist, their edges blunted and crumbling by the driving wind. The smoke is coming from something large lying behind the tower.

A boom and a flash of light.

The ground at your feet explodes, throwing up shards of stone. You grab Anise and pull her down behind a scatter of rocks. Skoll drops beside you, squinting towards the tower. There is another boom. Something glances off the rock beside you, leaving a charred strip.

'Get back,' calls a gruff voice. 'I don't cares what magic yer got, or any fancy weapons. I got the future, right 'ere in me mitts. And it'll blow you back into that abyss if yer give me cause.'

You twist round, peering over the rock.

Skoll puts his fingers in the charred ash, licks them, then grimaces. 'What is this magic?'

'Gunpowder,' you reply grimly. 'There must be a sniper in the tower.' Your eyes scan the bleached ruins, focusing on a window near the tower's summit. Sure enough, there is a figure standing there.

'We mean no harm!' you call back.

Another blast of light, this time from the doorway of another building. You feel something whistle past your ear, its passage blowing your hood back from your face. You scowl back in anger. 'Stop this! I told you, we mean no harm!'

'Well, we do,' barks the sniper in the tower. 'Now, turn that ugly face of yours and get yer gone. Those were just warning shots; believe me – we won't miss again.'

If you have the keyword *repentance* on your hero sheet, turn to 55. Otherwise, turn to 10.

624

'What – you born yesterday? This is a trading post, go find me skins - furs. Then we can talk gold. Otherwise you're just wasting me time.' A pause – then a click of a tongue. 'Humph, okay. Maybe there is something. If you're headed north, perhaps you could keep an eye out for a friend of mine. Old trapper, veteran – been at it long as I've been 'ere. His name's Bullet, on account of the buckshot lodged in his brain. Made him a little crazy, I think – but I like a little crazy.'

'Where will I find him?' you ask, shrugging your shoulders. 'The north is a big place.'

'I dunno – what you think I am, a soothsayer?' He waves his gun barrels back and forth. 'Can't you track or something, sniff the air, follow prints – whatever you darn trappers do? He was looking for a mammoth. Not an ordinary one, mark my words – 'cos this is Bullet and he don't do anything by halves. No, this beast is a legend in these parts. A giant. They say his pelt's so big he could decorate every home in Valeron. Rich pickings, I think yer'll agree.'

(Make a note of the keyword *tracker* on your hero sheet.)

Will you:

Ask another question?	450
Discuss something other than news?	685
Leave?	Return to the map

Your weapons cleave through the beast's arm, sending the drake head spinning across the chamber in a spray of black blood. Caul steps in, ducking beneath the giant's remaining arm, and drives his spear through its midriff. The drake keeper gives a gurgling cry then topples backwards, taking out half of a pillar as it smashes through the black stone. After a few heaving, wheezy breaths, the creature finally lies still.

You examine the corpse, wondering what cruel magic could have been responsible for creating such a pitiful monster. Perhaps the same magic that created the Nisse – the scaled horrors that assaulted Bitter Keep.

For defeating the fearsome drake keeper, you may now help yourself to any two of the following rewards:

Drake scales	Drake fire cannon	Keeper's collar
(special)	(left-hand: unique)	(necklace)
Use on a cloak, chest,	+1 speed +2 armour	+1 brawn +1 magic
gloves or feet item to	Ability: drake fire	Ability: shackles
increase its *armour* by 1		

When you have updated your hero sheet, turn to 494.

You follow the ledge until you are directly beneath one of the fleshy appendages. Its trunk-like form stretches across the gulf, forming a crude but navigable bridge. You can feel the oppressive heat emanating from its cracked skin, but with no other choice you scale the rock wall and leap onto the tentacle.

Tentatively you start for the other side, where the strange tentacle merges with a tangle of others, climbing up into the dusty haze. You are halfway across when you hear a screeching clamour coming from behind you.

Glancing back, you startle when you see a host of shadowy demons crawling out of the darkness. Their shape and number are indistinct – at times they seem many, humanoid in shape, then they merge, flowing together into a single confusion of grasping limbs.

The shadows move with speed, flowing around the tentacle like some virulent disease. With no chance of outrunning them, you hold your ground and prepare to fight:

	Speed	Magic	Armour	Health
Abyssal shadows	14	7	4	100

Special abilities
🌑 **Tide of darkness**: At the end of any round where you do not play a speed or a combat ability, you must immediately take 5 damage, ignoring *armour*, as the shadows start to surround you.

🌑 **Fell heat**: At the end of each combat round you must suffer 1 damage, ignoring *armour*, from the molten-blooded tentacle.

If you manage to defeat this shadowy swarm, turn to **154**.

627

The light fades, leaving you jerking and kicking, a pained cry issuing from your lips.

Eyes snap open. You see a wall of black rock, inches from your face. You shift, trying to move, but your arms are tied. A rough blanket scratches at your chin.

Trying to remain calm, you wait for the spasms to pass, then quickly set about freeing yourself. The shield fragment is still in your hands, its sharp edge providing the perfect knife. Within minutes the cords are broken. You kick off the blanket and slide off the stone bench.

You are in a small natural cave. A few candles are lined on a rock shelf, casting the room in a flickering pale light. Thankfully, you are still dressed in your armour, and your weapons lie wrapped in furs nearby. You quickly retrieve them and stalk out of the cave.

Following the sound of voices, you navigate a short series of tunnels to arrive at a much larger cavern. Black-robed figures stand around a blazing set of coals stacked in a shallow pit. The dancing flames illuminate the pale faces beneath the cowls – each one disfigured by runic markings.

Pillars of rock are scattered throughout the cave, an iron brazier burning next to each one. You use them for cover, moving from pillar to pillar until you are afforded a better view of the strange gathering. It appears they have prisoners – two bodies, chained to rune-carved boulders. A girl and a half-giant . . .

'Let me go!' Anise pulls against her shackles, kicking back with her feet.

There is still some fight in her, unlike Skoll – whose body hangs limply from his own manacles, blonde hair trailing over his face. The runes in the iron flash with dark magics. Dwarven magic. They remind you of the manacles the einherjar used to sap your magic and your will.

One of the robed figures steps up to the young girl.

'Enough! Hold your tongue.' A woman's voice, cold and whip-sharp. 'Be grateful, my love. I could have killed you while you slept. But I have other plans for you. I'm going to break you, like we did the dragons. Turn you into a willing servant.'

'Arran, where is Arran?' Anise tugs again at her chains, crying out as magic crackles across the irons, making her convulse with pain.

'Do not worry about him.' The female acolyte turns and motions to one of her followers, a younger man who is holding an iron brand in the coals. He lifts it out, its pointed tip glowing white with heat. 'The witch has given your precious prince to Insidious, as a plaything. When that devil's done with him, I doubt you'll want to see what is left.'

The woman takes the brand, then steps closer to Anise. The girl whimpers, trying to draw herself away from the hot tip. 'The runes cut deep, my dear. They'll burn that weakness out of you, fill you with a new strength. Power. Yes, then you will be worthy – to join our ranks and stand at her side.'

You creep around the pillars, eyeing up your opposition. There are six acolytes in total, each armed with a dagger – and probably some magic to protect themselves. You contemplate your best course of action. Perhaps something you are carrying might aid you.

Will you:

Disguise yourself (requirement: coven robes)?	516
Create a diversion (requirement: explosives)?	187
Take on the whole of the coven?	375

628

You place the 'four of hearts' on the discard pile and pick a new stone from the bag. You have gained the 'two of moons'.

You have the following stones:

The monk opens out his meaty fist, showing you his five stones.

As you reveal your own hand, his look of smug elation turns quickly to one of surprise. 'It can't be, your Queen's Wave beats mine . . . the three of crowns,' he slams his hands on the table like a petulant child.

I hope you're a man of your word,' you grin, retrieving your gold (you have gained 50 gold crowns). You nod to the book. Grudgingly, the monk removes the chain from across his shoulder and hands it over. You have gained *Judah's Book of Canticles* (simply make a note of this on your hero sheet, it doesn't take up backpack space. Also remove the word *scripture* from your hero sheet.) You are also rewarded with the following special ability:

Gambit (pa): Each time you play a death move special ability, roll a die. On a ⚁ result you may also regain a *speed* or *modifier* ability that you have already played – allowing you to use that chosen ability again any time during the combat.

You bid farewell to the sulking monk, leaving him to drown his sorrows in ale. Turn to 80.

629

You reach out and take the spear. Desnar grins, evidently pleased with your choice. 'Victar!' He turns and raises his arms to the crowd. There are some approving grunts from his men, but few others. You sense that Desnar is no more liked than yourself – or perhaps the Skards are not ones to show their emotions easily. Nevertheless, you worry that Desnar already considers the test won.

You are both handed bone javelins and a collection of barbed traps fashioned from hunks of bone and metal splinters. 'What are we hunting?' you ask Sura.

'Whatever the land decides,' replies the shaman. She bows her head. 'May the ancestors be with you, southlander.'

'You aren't coming with us?' You look around at the watchful crowd.

Sura frowns. 'This is a test, a feud between yourself and Desnar. Only one of you will return with victory. This is a test of the hunter. The trophies you bring back will speak of your triumph.'

The crowd part, leaving you a clear path to the edge of the camp where the ocean of snow sweeps away in rippled waves. Desnar gives you a sly grin then breaks into a run, sprinting into the wasteland. You realise this is a race as much as it is a test of skill. Gritting your teeth, you narrow your eyes to the horizon and push forward into the snow. Turn to 738.

630

You put the vial to the girl's lips, watching as the viscous blood pours out, trickling scarlet trails across her cheeks. You tip it back until the vial is empty, watching and waiting.

Nothing. You feel your eyes burn as they stare upon hers, looking for some flicker of life. But they remain vacant, fixed on the heavens, where a chill wind howls past the broken ruins. It wails mournfully around the chamber, beating at you with its bitter cold – but not cold enough to expel the aching pain.

'No . . .' You lower your head, admitting defeat – feeling cheated by your own foolish belief in the paladin's faith. *I have failed everyone. Nanuk. Skoll. Anise . . .*

A wet gasp draws you from your reverie. You look back at the girl, almost sure you saw her eyelids flutter.

'Anise . . . ?'

You lean close, convinced now that it was a cruel trick of the wind. Perhaps a reflex action, nothing more. *I'm a fool. This isn't some storybook—*

Suddenly, the girl spasms, her body arching, legs kicking at the ground.

You draw back, startled and afraid; no longer sure what ill you may have caused by giving her the blood. You go to grab her hand, but the heat rising from it forces you away. A holy heat, like the sword that always repelled you. Like the paladin's inscribed skin . . .

A white glow rolls across her body, softening its dark bruising to a pale unblemished white. You continue to watch transfixed as the hands of time are wound back – flesh folds over bone, limbs reset, wounds close. Her eyes sparkle, a sudden light blossoming from their depths.

She sits up, chest heaving as she sucks in great lungfuls of air.

You can only stare at her, feeling frozen in that wondrous moment, a flood of emotions racing through you. Relief, amazement . . . love.

The girl's hands go to her throat, tracing the raised line of a blue-grey scar. The only mark to remain on her perfectly healed body. Her eyes meet your own. And her smile, crooked and wan as always, is perfect.

You have gained the title *The Redeemer* and the following special ability:

Salvation (pa): Each time you use a *heal*, *regrowth* or *greater heal* ability you can increase its *health* benefit by 1.

You may now return to the map or advance to the final boss monster encounter by turning to 717.

Searching through the wreckage, you find 60 gold crowns. You also discover a party invitation inside one of the guest's waistcoats. The invitation is for a private function organised by Lord Edward Eaton, to be held at The Coracle on Ryker's Island. You may take this *party invitation* (simply make a note of it on your hero sheet, it doesn't take up backpack space).

As you turn to leave, you make another discovery – a small metal casket lying underneath one of the sledges. You quickly retrieve it, hearing the rattle of coins sliding around inside. If you have a *skeleton key*, turn to **413**. Otherwise, you are unable to open the chest. If you wish, you may take this item with you, in the hope that you will discover a means of opening it. (The *hunters' chest* takes up one backpack space.) Return to the map to continue your journey.

632

You look back across the dusty plain to where the great serpent lies motionless – its scaled body stretching for over a mile until it is lost to the darkness of the abyssal rift. The edge of the world.

Aslev joins you, a smile turning his lips. 'We won a great victory, my Drokke.'

'No.' You turn your head to the wind, letting the chill currents rush through your body, filling its emptiness with a familiar, numbing cold. 'This is only the beginning. I am Drokke – but I am also king. The rightful king of Valeron. I will win back my throne, unite north and south. One people.'

You glance at Aslev, awaiting his response, expecting rebuttal.

The einherjar continues to grin back at you. 'Then you'll be needing this.' He offers you the warhammer – the runed weapon that Skoll had given Aslev as a symbol of his return.

'Surtnost.' You take the warhammer into your spectral hands, feeling its weight – its power.

'And you'll be needing these.' Aslev steps back, gesturing to the assembly of Skards, still nearly a thousand strong, the sunlight sparkling and flashing off their spear-heads and axes. 'We will take back your throne, Drokke. No army of southlanders can stand against our might.'

You raise the warhammer into the air. Magic sparks from your fingertips, coursing along the runed handle, awakening the trapped spirits that have been bound within it. A bear, and a wolf, an eagle, a stag – and others: muttok, seal, petrel, sabre cat. You feel them pressing against your consciousness, filling you with their primal energies.

Animal spirits. One for every Skard tribe.

Golden light bursts from the hammer, trailing bright ribbons into the azure blue sky. You lift back your head, eyes closed – listening to the cheers of the assembled Skards.

And in your mind's eye you picture Cardinal Rile, sat upon the throne of Valeron – your throne. The demon's words nudge at your memory.

Seeking to win back the throne of Valeron . . . it will not bring you peace, Arran. I am sorry.

'I do not seek peace,' you intone, speaking into the blustery gale. 'Only the vengeance that I am owed.'

Aslev turns his head, surveying the broken wasteland. 'How do you plan on reaching your homeland, Drokke?'

You meet his gaze with a smile. 'If we cannot go over . . .' Your eyes shift to the dark abyss, scything across the horizon. 'Then we will go under. Will your people walk such dark paths with me?'

Aslev flashes another grin. 'If it will make a song worth singing, my Drokke, we would follow you to the very gates of Hel.'

Your eyes remain fixed on the abyss, watching the smoke still steaming from its depths. 'I will hold you to that promise, Aslev. For that is where destiny may lead us.'

Congratulations! You have now reached the end of this adventure and have earned yourself the additional title *The Serpent Slayer*! You may now turn to the epilogue.

Using the open hatch, you wriggle through into the store area. It is much larger than you anticipated, extending back over thirty metres to a rock-hewn wall. Unfortunately, much of the space is on fire. A crate of whisky and other spirits has gone up in flames, not to mention a pile of sackcloth and a stack of hides. The flames are spreading quickly, trailing along lines of spilt oil and whisky towards a set of barrels.

Not wishing to remain here any longer than necessary, you quickly look around for items of value. At your feet lie the remains of Jackson, a middle-aged man with thick long hair and a wispy moustache. His clothes reek of filth and alcohol, and his body is almost black from grease and grime. It is a grisly task, but you quickly set about searching his corpse for anything useful.

You find 15 gold crowns and up to two of the following items:

Smoking buck shot	Titanium turncoat	Clerk's signet
(talisman)	(chest)	(ring)
+1 brawn +4 health	+1 speed +2 armour	+1 brawn +1 magic
Ability: charm	Ability: iron will	Ability: persuade

The barrels explode, showering the room in oil and blazing shards of wood. Covering your face from the heat, you hurry through the thickening smoke, looking to grab as much from the store as you can. (You have gained two *muttok pelts* and a *yeti pelt*. Simply make a note of these on your hero sheet, they do not take up backpack space).

A wall of shelving topples down, stopping you from progressing further into the store. Instead you scramble back the way you came, the smoke and debris making it increasingly difficult to navigate. Luckily you manage to reach the hatch. As you do so, your eyes catch on a small metal locker lying amongst the wreckage. Flames are raging around the box, but the item itself appears unharmed.

Will you:

Risk grabbing the locker?	691
Leave it and escape through the hatch?	592

You slip into one of the alcoves, shuffling around the table to get a good view of the taproom.

If you have the keyword *scripture* on your hero sheet, turn to 63. If you have the keyword *covert* on your hero sheet, turn to 373. Otherwise, turn to 457.

You pass beneath the arch into a large colonnaded courtyard filled with wildflowers. It is exactly as you remember it: high trellises steeped with vines, statuary peering between trees and bushes, a row of wooden benches lining the straight cobbled pathways. You look for some flaw in the scene, but it is perfect – save for the blurry edge at the far end of the courtyard, where steps would have led down to a boating lake.

You are almost lost to the beauty and the solitude, your mind racing back to days long past – then you hear the boots and the tapping of steel. A gruff cough announces the instructor's arrival as he steps around a trellis.

Instructor Barl. The royal weapons master. The man who had taught your two brothers to fight – and had doggedly persisted with your own training, on your father's insistence.

He glares back at you, his look mingled with disgust and pity. 'You're late,' he growls. 'As always. Too busy reading your books, I presume.'

You go to answer, but your words are cut short as the instructor raises his sword, striking you with the flat of the blade. The blow catches you across the shoulder, knocking you against one of the benches.

'Show me what you have learned, boy!' he snaps, regarding you with a grim smile. 'Come on, you puny wretch.'

You feel a weakness come over your body. Gritting your teeth, you struggle to take the weight of your weapons. It is as if time has wound back and you are that same sickly boy once again, too feeble to even wield a blade. Instructor Barl seems unconcerned by your plight. He flings himself at you, his blade raining blows with an intent ferocity. He uses the flat side once again, knocking you to the ground. He stalks around you, laughing.

'That was your last chance, wretch. Next time, I come at you with the edge.'

Desperately you fight to lift your weapons as the instructor steps in, his sword cutting powerful and deliberate strikes. It is time to fight:

	Speed	Magic	Armour	Health
Instructor Barl	9	7	5	60

Special abilities

♥ **Enfeeblement**: You cannot play any speed abilities for the duration of the combat.

♥ **Short temper**: At the start of the fifth combat round, if Barl is still alive he will go into a fit of rage. This will raise his *speed* by 1 and *magic* by 3 for the duration of the combat.

If you manage to defeat the bullying Barl, turn to 71.

636

'We are not settlers,' explains Sura, gesturing to the blocks of ice that form her shelter. 'It is in our blood to travel, to follow the hunt, the paths of the beasts, and live as best we can off the land. Our tribes are scattered. Like the four winds we are blown to the furthest reaches, but we are still the Ska-inuin. The people.'

Sura closes her eyes, taking a deep breath. 'Vindsvall is our meeting place. Where all tribes become one under the Drokke. He is the one who leads us all – the one who speaks words that cannot be questioned.' Her eyes flutter open as she releases a heartfelt sigh. 'Vindsvall is to the north. A hall of wood and bone, the most precious we have. The rarest of buildings, for we live beneath leather and ice – and these things are cheap, and not for a Drokke.'

'And the shamans you spoke of . . . the Asynjur, they serve this . . . Drokke?'

Sura lowers her gaze to the pipe, watching the thin tendrils of smoke curl up from the bowl. 'They serve him, yes. They serve him in both body and soul.'

Will you:

Ask about the current 'Drokke'?	461
Ask about the bear necklace?	545
Ask what 'vela styker' means?	587
End the conversation?	575

637

You leap over the final set of runes, feeling the air crackle behind you, the flames from the drake heads washing you in heat. For a second your vision is obscured by smoke, then you are stumbling forward into the chamber beyond, the cold that greets you a welcome relief.

Turning back you see the flames splutter then go out, leaving your view clear to the other side. Caul is pacing back and forth nervously, his spear tapping against the ground. He stops, his body tensing. He looks about to run . . .

'Wait!' You notice a small rune on the wall next to the corridor. You quickly put a hand to it, pushing your magic into its design, connecting the glyphs to activate its power. There is a distant humming sound, followed by a click. When you look back into the corridor you see that the flames are no longer burning inside the carved heads. 'I think I did something – try it now.'

Caul rocks back on his heels then pitches forward into a run, high-stepping across the runes. They spark and crackle angrily, but without the flames at his back, Caul is able to dodge them with ease. He finally catches up with you, his boots barely singed.

'I never want to do that ever again,' he pants, putting his hands to his knees.

'At least our daring has paid off.' You look around at the stone tablets stacked on shelves around the chamber. Most have been smashed, but a few remain intact. You set about examining the stones, looking for those that might contain useful enchantments.

You may now help yourself to two of the following items:

Glyph of strength	Rune of healing	Glyph of power
(special: glyph)	(special: rune)	(special: glyph)
Use on any item to add 1 *brawn*	Use on any item to add the special ability *heal*	Use on any item to add 1 *magic*

When you have updated your hero sheet, you leave the chamber through a doorway in the opposite wall. Turn to 726.

638
Quest: The dead and the damned

(Note: You must have completed the orange quest *The crossing* before you access this location)

The reading room shimmers around you, its curving walls becoming hazy mist at the edge of your memory. It is almost perfect, as much as you can remember of your favourite place, the hideaway that you always ran to to be alone – away from the politics and pressures of court. You shift your weight on the window seat, allowing Nanuk to rest his head on your lap. Smiling, you push a hand through his coarse grey hair. He seems much older now, his skin and muscle sagging a little from his thinner frame. It pains you to know that you are the cause – that your magic comes from him, keeping you alive in your dead body.

'Why, Nanuk?' You tousle his hair. The bear glances at you sleepily with his pale, amber eyes. He doesn't answer, merely stretches open his jaws to yawn.

You look back at the reading room, shifting your thoughts to the table, correcting a mistake in the scroll-work along the legs, adding details to the chairs. In the Norr, it seems, anything is possible. Memories can become reality, if you only concentrate and work the magic. But holding it, that is the difficulty. As you focus on the table the walls flicker and begin to fade, melting away to reveal the bleak wind-scoured landscape once again. The chair reverts to a slab of rock, scoured by the claws of some demonic creature.

You breathe in deep, enjoying the taste of the dead, cold air. A young and virulent heart beats fast against your breast, your lungs rising and falling. Just a memory. As fake as the library you had painstakingly built with your mind. But even the imitation of life is welcome – better than the dead body that awaits you in the real world.

Nanuk raises his head, sniffing the air. He gives a throaty growl, swinging round to eye the wasteland. You casually draw your weapons, expecting another demon. Following the bear's gaze, you fix on a shadow slinking past the stunted columns of rock. Its movements are slow, predatory. Not a demon. Another animal.

You slip off the boulder, crouching next to the bear. 'What is it? What do you see, Nanuk?'

In your mind you are given an impression of hair and teeth. And the stink of death.

The shadow passes around a lump of fallen masonry, its shaggy head edging into the pale half-light. A wolf. For a brief instant you fear it is the witch's spirit, Fenrir. But this wolf is smaller, leaner – yet no less intimidating. One eye is shut closed, little more than a fleshy stump of scar tissue. The other shines bright, yellow and piercing.

Nanuk is bounding forward before you can stop him.

You move to follow, but immediately feel a jolt as the bear pushes you away; trying to send you back to the waking world. You struggle to resist, failing to understand the reason for his rejection.

'We fight together,' you protest, trying to throw up walls to block his energy.

There is a pull on your shoulder. A voice.

Wake up. Don't sleep.

Angrily, you shrug it off. The bear and the wolf are circling each other, hissing and snarling. You want to stay, to fight beside Nanuk's side. But another tug forces your surroundings to blur.

Wake up!

'I'm not going back!' You snarl with rage, spinning round to find the source of the voice. It seems familiar, but that was another life – surely. There is only the Norr, the here and now. 'I have to stay,' you blare at the darkness. 'I don't want to come back!'

You are thrown into spasm, legs kicking into the dirt. A hand is gripping your shoulder. You knock it away, rolling awkwardly onto your side, knees tucked to your chest as you continue to shake and convulse.

'We cannot sleep here, Bearclaw. The Norr is too close. Much danger.'

Skoll is knelt beside you, looking for all the world like a corpse himself. Bedraggled hair hangs across his pale, pinched face. Stubble has turned to an uneven beard, scraggly and patched with grey. His eyes are sunken, encircled by dark rings. The scars that criss-cross his body seem all the more vivid in the blue torchlight.

Skoll stands and moves away, leaving you to beat and kick at the ground, gouging great holes out of the crumbling red stone. 'A wolf,' you hiss, trying to spit the words past clenched teeth. 'There was a wolf.'

Skoll looks back at you, eyes widened. 'Fenrir?'

'No.' You crawl onto all fours, taking a moment to let the last of the shivers pass. 'Something else. But I sense it is of this place. The mountain.'

Skoll shakes his head. 'I told you, do not go to the Norr. We are shaman. We cannot sleep here.' He gives a ragged sigh, his shoulders slumping. It is evident there is nothing more he would rather do.

'Come. I have something to show you.' Skoll moves to the far wall, his torch throwing light across an intricate carving. Just one of the hundreds that litter the caves and halls. 'What do you make of this?'

You struggle to your feet and start to hobble over. Looking down, you realise your left leg is dragging. Furiously you push magic into the joints, teasing it around the muscles, reconnecting the nerves. Grimacing, you flex your toes, then put the leg straight, feeling it take your weight. 'Each time it gets harder,' you grumble, taking a tentative stride. 'I fear I will not last much longer.'

Skoll is still staring at the carving.

You join him, your eyes searching the shapes and lines, looking for meaning. 'Nine worlds,' you whisper, passing a finger over the nine orbs lined in a circle. 'And this, I don't know.' At the centre of the circle is a symbol, almost rune-like – two crescent moons joined by a crossbar.

'Balance,' says Skoll. 'It's the rune for balance.'

You nod. 'And the flame?' You point to the symbol drawn beneath the rune, evidently indicating a fire of some sort.

'The forge.' Skoll raises his torch higher, illuminating the peak above and the curling flames that reach to the ceiling. 'The Titan forge, where we must remake the shield. It is above us, at the top of the mountain.'

Your eyes drift to Anise, curled in a tight ball beneath a fur blanket, head resting on her rolled-up cloak. Her breathing is shallow, her features grey. No food or water for days.

'We have to leave her.'

Skoll's words startle you. For a moment you fail to find words. 'We . . . we can't,' you splutter, half in shock and half in desperation.

'The girl slows us down.' Skoll speaks firmly, holding your stare.

'We can't . . .'

'It is the only way.'

'No, Skoll! That's the Skard way. To leave the weak behind. Throw them aside. I won't have it. Anise is one of us.'

'She was a Skard. She will understand.' There is a savage look to his eyes, no doubt fuelled by weariness and hunger. The last days have been hard, forcing him to draw on every last ounce of strength. He has muscle and endurance. Anise only has you.

You kneel by her side, pulling up the blanket and tucking it beneath her chin. A smile crosses her ashen lips as your fingers brush against her cheek. So soft.

'I was having a nice dream,' she whispers. Her eyelids flutter for a moment. 'We were in the kitchens . . . Segg was being all grumpy. Old Segg. You were helping me bottle the . . . wine. Do you . . . remember . . . ?'

'Yes, yes I do.' You stroke a lock of hair, watching it curl around your finger.

'You're a . . . good man,' she sighs. 'You were . . . kind to me.'

You choke on your reply, unable to speak past the pain.

'We have to move.' Skoll is almost pleading in his insistence. 'This place is not safe, Bearclaw.'

You snap round in fury. 'Do not call me that! My name is Arran. Prince Arran!'

Skoll takes his turn to startle at your words. His hand moves to the heft of his axe, hanging from his belt. You read his action, calling magic to your fists.

Then you hear a deafening screech from the adjoining chamber – a bird-like cawing, followed by the slap and squelch of something being dragged and hit against the stone.

Anger is quickly forgotten. Skoll takes up his axe and hurries into the passage. You draw your weapons and follow. Turn to 246.

Hal flips open the lid of a small box, revealing a number of vials and gourds carefully packed between wads of cloth. 'I can spare a few of these. Fofty shinies each.' He glances at your face, pulling a grimace. 'Although, for some of you, might be a little late in the day for tonics.'

You may purchase any number of the following for 40 gold crowns each:

Flask of healing	Elixir of swiftness	Flask of might
(1 use)	(1 use)	(1 use)
(backpack)	(backpack)	(backpack)
Use any time in combat to restore 10 *health*	Increase your *speed* by 4 for one combat round	Use any time in combat to increase your *brawn* or *magic* by 3 for one combat round

You may now ask to view Hal's weapons (turn to 728), inspect his treasures (turn to 674), trade your own items (turn to 95) or leave and return to the quest map.

640

Flames and smoke start to obscure your vision. Frantically you struggle to maintain your speed, seeking to stay ahead of the dragon's breath. The circle of daylight grows larger, its bright light competing with the flames and smoke – then you are finally free of the tunnel, hurtling away from the island as fast you can. Behind you an entire section of the hive explodes outwards in a fiery tumult, raining fragments of charred rock across the gulf.

Unfortunately, you don't have enough momentum to outrun the blast. Caught in a cloud of debris and fire, you suffer significant damage. (You must lower your transport's *toughness* and *stability* by 4.) Turn to 729.

641

Sam produces a pair of picks and sets to work on the lock. Within seconds, the storage locker is open. After Sam has taken his cut of the treasure, you are left with 50 gold crowns. (Remove the *locker* from your hero sheet.) If you have the *hunters' chest* and wish Sam to open it, turn to 8. Otherwise, you continue your journey. Turn to 563.

642

Your hands move across the console, activating the runes and throwing the orb's magic against your advancing opponents. They stumble through the onslaught, their enchanted stonework blasted and pummelled by the energies channelled against them. As the surviving statues near your location, you vault over the balcony and charge into the fray, using your own weapons to finish off their crumbling forms.

Amongst the smoking rubble, you discover glowing fragments of stone imbued by the magics that have been unleashed. If you wish, you may now take one of the following special rewards:

Frost spark	Earth spike	Shadow noose
(talisman)	(main hand: sword)	(necklace)
+1 magic	+1 speed +2 brawn	+2 brawn +2 magic
Ability: silver frost	Ability: fatal blow	Ability: vanish

When you have updated your hero sheet, turn to 737.

643

The rush of cold is sudden and fierce, punching through your chest, freezing your heart and stealing your very last breath. It fills you, numbs you, a coldness so intense that it burns the stone beneath your feet, cracking it to frozen splinters.

If you wish, you may now learn the revenant career. The revenant has the following special abilities:

Creeping cold (co + pa): Instead of rolling for a damage score, you can cast *creeping cold* on one opponent. This does 1 damage at the end of every combat round. For each ⚅ result you roll for any subsequent damage scores, *creeping cold* increases its damage by 1. This ability can only be used once.

Malefic runes (mo): For each opponent you defeat (reduced to zero *health*), you may raise your *magic* score by 1 for the remainder of the combat.

When you have made your decision, turn to 677.

644

The ruins are deserted and Hal's peculiar balloon is nowhere to be found. You can only assume that the explorer was able to repair his ship and has now headed back south – away from the destruction and the chaos. As you huddle deeper into your cloak, braced against the wind and the constant barrage of dust, you can't help but feel a pang of home-sickness, wishing you were on board that ship, headed home at last. (Return to the quest map to continue your adventure.)

645

Desnar raises his staff and gives a barking cry of victory. 'Taulu nost weak et vall. Desnar herat gost hastnet!'

His own warriors break into smiles and laughter – a few echoing his words. The rest of the gathering remain reverently silent. All eyes turn to Sura.

'The ancestors have spoken,' proclaims the old woman. She frowns at you, her disappointment evident. 'Desnar, son of Grendel Innervek – you have been chosen to lead us.' The old woman offers out the end of her staff. Desnar unhooks the bear necklace and places it over his head. You can't help but glower jealousy at the band of claws and teeth – the necklace that Taulu had entrusted you with. Part of you wants to rip it free and take it for yourself. Nanuk's anger is palpable, prickling like thorns in your mind.

But then you hear the Skards' chanting. Each and every person in the crowd – man, woman and child – has put a hand to their breast, speaking some vow or mantra in unison. There is hope written on their faces. And trust. You realise these people need a figurehead; someone to lead them. Perhaps Desnar will deliver the strength and courage that they need to see out this cruel winter.

The young boy steps forward, peeling back the hide bag he is carrying. You see that it is filled with treasures. Desnar puts his hand into the bag, helping himself to a golden talisman. His eyes meet your own, his lips curling into a conceited grin as he fastens the trinket to his chest.

'No southlander will ever lead the bear,' he snaps coldly. 'Nanuk made mistake in choosing you. Weakling.'

You go to draw your weapons, but a hand settles quickly on your shoulder, gripping it tight, urging restraint. It is Sura.

'No,' she whispers. 'The choice is made. And it cannot be undone. You are no longer protected by vela styker. Turn against one, you turn against all.' Turn to 721.

646

You place the 'one of crowns' on the discard pile and pick a new stone from the bag. You have gained the 'three of crowns'.

You have the following stones:

The monk takes his turn with an almost wearisome air, tossing the stone that he picked back onto the discard pile. You wonder if he's already got a winning hand or is simply bluffing. It is now your move.

Will you:

Play this hand?	734
Discard the three of snakes?	446

Several of your dogs take a tumble, slamming into the front of your sled and dragging other members of your team with them. The sudden collision forces your sled to lurch out from underneath you, sending you flying across the ice. You crash down in a bruised heap, the remains of your sled showering down around you.

Unfortunately, you have failed to complete the race and are now disqualified from the tournament. Replace the keyword *rookie* with *underdog*. Return to the map to continue your adventure.

648

The moment you pick up the book, you hear a grating sound from the walls of the room. Suddenly the floor begins to lower, carrying you past the surrounding bookshelves and down into a dark, cobwebbed recess.

With a sudden lurch you come to a halt, facing an immense door of black stone. Three large keyholes stare vacantly back at you from its face, inviting you to insert a key. The table begins to sparkle with motes of magic then, in a flash of dark brilliance, the books are swept away to be replaced by three rings of keys. All around you other keys start to appear, on the floor, on the chairs, on the table.

You recognise the puzzle from the storybook, but there is one element missing . . .

Then you hear the hissing sound from above.

The ceiling has become a whirling mass of dark smoke, and from it seven giant snake-heads are stretched forward, their mouths held open to reveal venomous black fangs. The smoky mass descends towards you, promising a painful death unless you can open the door in time to escape.

Quickly, you grab the three rings of keys. Each key has a number engraved on its head. You remember from the book that in order to solve Theomus' puzzle, the hero had to work out which key was missing from each set.

Set one:	21	29	27	35	33	?	39
Set two:	?	211	223	227	229	233	239
Set three:	1	8	27	64	125	?	343

Work out the missing number from each sequence (represented by the question mark). Add up the three separate numbers to give you an overall total. Turn to this entry number to see if you solved the puzzle. If the entry you turn to is incorrect, you must immediately roll on the death penalty chart (see entry **98**) and then turn to **444**.

649

To your surprise the bone key fits the lock perfectly. After a few twists and turns, there is a click and the lid comes open.

Inside the box you discover two clay gourds wrapped in cloth and an odd-shaped metal device, flickering with magic. If you wish you may take any / all of the following items:

Flask of healing	Elixir of swiftness	Moon dial
(2 uses)	(1 use)	
(backpack)	(backpack)	(talisman)
Use any time in combat to restore 10 *health*	Increase your *speed* by 4 for one combat round	+1 brawn +1 magic Ability: time shift

Pleased with your finds, you retrieve the *skeleton key*, then continue your journey. Turn to 2.

650

You place the 'three of swords' on the discard pile and pick a new stone from the bag. You have gained the 'four of stars'.

You have the following stones:

The monk takes his turn, then waits for you to make your next move.

Will you:

Play your current hand?	593
Discard the one of crowns	245
Discard the four of hearts?	212

651

It is a long and gruelling battle, but your dogged persistence pays off – the dragons' magic is finally dispelled. You watch with relief as their rotted bodies collapse into clouds of bones and dust, which plume away into the darkness below.

Congratulations! For defeating the dragons, you may now help yourself to one of the following rewards:

Cadence	Zombie cage	Corrupted eye
(left hand: horn)	(chest)	(ring)
+2 speed +2 brawn	+2 speed +2 armour	+1 brawn +1 magic
Ability: piercing	Ability: thorn armour	Ability: disease
(requirement: warrior)		

If you are sailing on the *Naglfar*, turn to 48. If you are flying with Nidhogg the dragon, turn to 542.

652

The herd follow an instinctive pattern. They run for several hundred yards, looking to put distance between themselves and their perceived threat. But once this has been achieved they settle back to grazing. By watching Desnar lay his traps ahead of where he thinks the mut-tok will run, you begin to understand the Skard's tactics. He uses his javelins to take down weaker members of the herd, sending the muttok into flight once again. He then races alongside the startled animals, looking to take down as many as he can with his javelins while the hidden traps lame the forerunners, making them easy prey.

This hunting challenge is played over seven rounds. Each round has two stages:

- ♥ **Hidden traps**: Decide if you will place your traps to the east, west or south of the herd. Decide where Desnar will place his (using one of the two remaining locations). Then roll a die. On a ⚀ or ⚁ result, the herd go west; ⚂ or ⚃ the herd go east; ⚄ or ⚅ the herd go south. Whoever's traps were placed in that direction, roll a die to discover how many muttok fell victim to the traps. (If you are a trapper you may add 1 to this result.)
- ♥ **Race the herd**: Using your javelins, you sprint along the flanks of the herd, looking for any stragglers to bring down. Roll two die and add your *speed* score to the total. For each result over 10, you spear one muttok. (If your total was 15 you would have speared 5 muttok.) Results of 10 or less means you were unsuccessful. Repeat this for Desnar, using a *speed* of 6.

Keep a running tally of how many muttok you and Desnar have hunted. At the end of the seventh round, the hunter who has the most muttok kills has won the challenge and will be attacked by the Muttok elder – his antlers presenting the greatest hunting trophy.

If you win the challenge, turn to 475. If you lose the challenge, turn to 270. (If the challenge is a draw after seven rounds, continue with the hunt until a winner emerges at the end of a round.)

653

Further into the city the streets are warded with runes – invisible to the naked eye, but to your magic-attuned senses they glimmer brightly, like spider's webs laced with frost. You doubt they are the witch's work; more likely one of her coven, as their crafting is weak and easily broken.

But they serve their purpose – to slow your progress.

Another pattern of runes hiss and spark as you unravel their weave. Raising your hand you draw your fingers through the air, leaving your own trace of magic behind, this one visible – a shimmering bear's claw for your companions to follow.

You've almost reached the centre of the ruins when the tremor hits. Your first warning is a faint drumming beneath your feet and the clink of rocks, dislodged and skittering down the hills of rubble.

Then there is an explosion of sound. A deafening thunder as everything begins to shake violently, throwing you from side to side. You hear walls toppling, the crack and splinter of the earth – in the distance, an entire row of towers simply disappears, dropping away from the horizon, leaving only thin whispers of dust to mark their passing.

You lurch across an open plaza, aware of fissures forming beneath your feet, branching and then widening, leaking a sulphurous smoke. Dodging a shower of falling rock, you find yourself taking cover inside the pillared colonnade of a vast hall. Symbols have been carved into the exterior stonework – nine orbs, arranged within a complex weave of crisscrossing lines. An open archway leads inside.

Arran.

A woman's voice, beckoning.

Your instincts tell you to turn and flee, but the urge to enter becomes overpowering, like an invisible thread reeling you in. Unable to resist, you find yourself entering the hall. Turn to **49**.

654

'We know little,' grunts the Skard. 'The tales speak of a Mordland princess, a sorceress who was married to a cruel king. He did not love her. They say he tortured her, made an example of her to his men. It was his unkindness that set her on the dark path. She went mad with a desire for revenge – murdered her king and fled north on a whaler's schooner. It sank during a storm. All on board were killed – save for the witch. The only one to survive.

'Now, she dwells in the ancient Titan city beyond the North Face. I have been there, only once. We believed ourselves stronger than her. I chose the best men. Ten of the strongest warriors from every tribe stood at my side. But every one fell to the witch – her gaze can turn flesh to ice. Only Fimbulwinter, a shield from the great hoard of Vindsvall, could protect me from her wrath. I was close . . . so close to ending her life. A hair's breadth from plunging my sword into her breast. Then the shield was taken from me, ripped from my grasp by one of her minions; a demon. His claws shredded the shield like it was paper. I tried to get it back – we struggled and fought on the very edge of the Well, a gateway to the shroud. The demon fell in and took the shield fragments with him. I had no choice but to flee. Without the shield, I could not look upon the witch.'

Skoll is silent for a moment, clenching and unclenching his fist.

'I still hear her voice, the screams . . . I do not think there is anything left of the woman that is human. The demons have taken her over, and together they work as one: to free Jormungdar and destroy our realm.'

Return to 602 to ask another question or turn to 326 to end the conversation.

655

You catch up with the thieves in the dark alleyway. They have the monk surrounded, backing him up against one of the walls. The leader, a tall lean man with a hooked nose and tattoos snaking around his arms, brandishes a pair of daggers.

'Leave him,' you bellow, striding forward whilst drawing your own weapons. Their magic rages to life, flooding the alleyway with their stark brilliance. The thieves draw back, momentarily blinded. The monk has started to sob, sliding down the wall into the mud and filth.

'What's it gotta do with you?' sneers the leader, squinting to get a better look at you. He starts forward, nodding quickly to his three companions. They are young, but have a confident, reckless air about them – evidently believing strength in numbers will give them the advantage. You decide to prove them wrong. It's time to fight:

	Speed	Brawn	Armour	Health
Sabin	7	4	2	40
Ruffian	6	4	2	20
Ruffian	6	3	2	20
Ruffian	6	3	2	20

Special abilities

- ♥ **Knives in the dark**: For every ⊡ you roll for your hero's attack speed (before or after a reroll), you must automatically take 2 damage, ignoring *armour*.
- ♥ **Outnumbered**: At the end of each combat round, you must take 1 damage from each surviving opponent, ignoring *armour*. This ability only applies while you are faced with multiple opponents.

If you manage to defeat these rash hoodlums, turn to 678. If you are defeated, record the defeat on your hero sheet, then turn to 69.

656

The shaven-headed Skard kneels beside you, the stench of his unwashed body filling your nostrils. As he leans close you see he is missing an ear, the white lines of scar-tissue cutting a ragged line to his upper lip. He puts a hand to your chin, pushing it back – then raises his axe.

'Berg vegger!' His eyes widen in surprise. 'Vegger!' You feel him tug something from your chest – the silver hound pin that Everard gave you. Boots crunch across the gravel as the other hunter takes it, turning it in his hand. He steps closer to you, his huge frame filling the sky.

'How you get this?' He kicks you in the side, then holds the pin out between his fingers.

It takes several moments for you to realise you understood him – his words are thick and guttural, but they are in the common tongue. A sudden hope rises within you – a chance at last to tell your story. The events of the past few hours spill out in a fervent ramble.

He looks at you incredulously as you describe the attack on the keep, the earthquake and Everard giving you the token. You don't know how much the Skards can understand, but you repeat everything a second time, looking from one to the other.

When you have finished there is a heavy silence, broken only by the sighing of the wind. The shaven-headed Skard gives a growl, then raises his axe again. 'Drap han han,' he barks, in his rough, harsh language.

'Nen!' The other hunter raises his hand, halting the fall of the axe. You quickly assume he is the leader – perhaps the necklace of bones he wears is some symbol of authority. He kneels beside you, scowling as he looks over your body and its many wounds. 'Dead meat,' he says, prodding his fingers into your grey-white flesh. 'You of the witch?' His gaze returns to the silver pin. He waits for your answer.

'I don't know what you mean. I come from the keep – I was the only one to survive.'

The leader clenches his jaw, working the muscles in his cheeks. 'Everard a good man,' he nods at last. 'We come for help. To the keep.' He points to his two companions, the giant and the short weasel-faced Skard. 'Our tribe weak. We feel badness of place. Wrongness. You understand this?'

You nod, even though your mind is still racing. 'There is nothing left,' you explain again, wincing as you try and rise. 'The keep has gone.'

'Nisse.'

It is the first time the giant has spoken. He stands a head taller than the leader, his mane of hair hanging in greasy ropes across his broad face. Every inch of him – indeed, every inch of all three of the hunters – appears weathered and scarred. He kicks the body of the creature lying on the ground next to him. 'Nisse.'

You gather it is their word for these scaled beasts. 'They attacked the keep,' you nod quickly. 'Did they . . . did they cause all this – the earthquakes?' Your eyes flick to the leader, hoping that your words are understood.

You are surprised when he shakes his head. He shifts, pointing behind him. 'The north witch. White witch. Makes earth . . .' He struggles to find a word you will grasp. His eyes catch on one of your open wounds, muscle and bone protruding from the cavity. 'Bad. Rot.'

You flinch uncomfortably. 'Perhaps there is a cure,' you add grimly.

The Skard strokes his necklace for a moment, studying you with a deep interest. 'We bear clan. You understand? Bear.' He pats his chest. 'Taulu.' His gaze shifts to his two companions. 'Hale. Ninvuk.' He nods to the giant and then the shaven-headed Skard.

'Arran,' you put a hand to your chest, mimicking his own gesture. 'My name is Arran.'

He leans forward, pinning the silver token back onto your jerkin.

'We get help. Keep gone. We go west. Find seals, seal clan. Put together, yes?' He clasps his hands in some show of unity. 'We move. You follow. Walk or die.' His eyes fix on your own. 'Everard's hound. Yes?'

He stands without waiting for an answer, arching his back to crack the bones. Then he turns and heads down the slope, retrieving his javelin from the downed Nisse. His two companions fall into step behind him, not sparing you another glance.

You are left lying in the dirt.

Walk or die.

A simple rule. And one that seems fitting to these solemn, predatory hunters.

You stumble to your feet, feeling no pain from your numerous wounds, only a discomfort each time you move. But you are still alive – and it seems, for now, the Skards are content for you to join them. After retrieving your weapons, you hurry as best you can to catch up. Turn to 698.

657

Searching through the wreckage, you find one of the following items:

Desecrated earth	Double cross	Web of lies
(talisman)	(necklace)	(chest)
+1 speed +5 health	+1 speed +1 armour	+2 speed +2 magic
Ability: decay	Ability: trickster	Ability: webbed

When you have updated your hero sheet, turn to 755.

658

Weapons are soon forgotten, giving way to fists and spectral claws – slashing, punching, cutting. Black blood covers you both head-to-toe as you tumble across the ground, locked together like savage pit bulls. One of Sable's claws drives into your side, parting the flesh and ripping through dead and useless organs. You try and struggle free but the prince now sits astride your chest, towering above you. His single eye is feverishly bright, glowing with victory.

He smiles, opening his mouth to say something.

But the words become a gurgling gasp as the point of a sword pushes its way between his teeth. His wolfish eye widens, then rolls back into his head ... blood gushes over his chin, then he slumps forward.

Anise stands over him, the hilt of the sword gripped in her white-knuckled hands. She steps away from the corpse, too exhausted to withdraw the weapon. She leaves the blade protruding from the back of the prince's head.

You push the body away, grimacing as you attempt to move your cut and ragged limbs. Nanuk's magic attends to the worst of the wounds, knitting the broken bones and dead flesh back together again, but most of your body is beyond redemption. A ruined husk. You touch your face, feeling the pulpy wetness along one cheek, the sagging flesh hanging loose from below your ear . . . Your hand probes a little higher. No ear. Torn loose.

Anise turns away, half-stumbling and half-falling into Skoll's arms. The Skard looks down at you, his grim-set features saying everything words cannot.

Slowly, sluggishly, you get to your feet, relieved that your legs are still strong enough to support you. Searching the prince's body, you find 50 gold crowns and one of the following rewards:

Warg crown	Dark fall	Sable's shadows
(head)	(chest)	(feet)
+2 speed +2 armour	+2 speed +2 magic	+2 speed +2 brawn
Ability: barbs	Ability: blind	Ability: rebound

When you have updated your hero sheet, turn to 720.

659

A wooden pier hugs the rocky shoreline, where a variety of different-sized ships lie at anchor. The most impressive looking are the whaling vessels, their immense prows plated with huge iron sheets engraved with runes. You assume these 'icebreakers' are used to cut through the ice as the ships make their way north. Beside them, almost like gnats in comparison, are a couple of flamboyant merchant ships and what you assume may be pirate schooners. Between them, the grey waters of the ocean are flecked with floating islands of ice, thumping and cracking against the ships' hulls.

Two buildings dominate the pier. One is a warehouse, or what remains of one. It has been built of wood, but part of a wall and an entire section of the roof have gone. Makeshift awnings of leather have been erected to keep dry what little stock remains. Two guards keep a wary eye on passers-by, while inside you see a short man in a thick moleskin coat grading a batch of furs.

Next to it is a more robust stone building, extending out from the sheer dark cliff. Light dances from its arched glass windows, where shifting shadows suggest a busy crowd. An oval shaped boat is netted to one wall. Next to it, a sign reads 'The Coracle'.

Will you:

Talk to the warehouse clerk?	104
Enter 'The Coracle'?	80
Head back along accident alley?	27

660

Anise trails behind you, swaddled in her cloak. Since leaving the mountain she has said little to anyone. You wonder if Maune's death still plays on her mind – as it does yours. When pressed she has not given voice to any dissent; nor has she complained or questioned your decisions. Instead it seems Anise has drawn inwards, becoming silent and melancholy, favouring her own thoughts for company. You cannot blame her – what she has endured since the fall of Bitter Keep, battling weakness and starvation, the enormity of the task you all face . . . You wonder if it is still love or something else that drives her onwards. Perhaps it's the realisation that there is no longer a choice – if the witch's plan is not thwarted, there will be nothing left to go back to; nothing worth saving.

At what cost, Anise? If we win, at what cost . . . ?

You watch her with an aching heart. Longing for it all to have turned out differently. With the paladin's supplies running low, you fear Anise is only headed for her own death.

'No!'

You jerk round, to see Skoll standing atop the ridge. The burly warrior stumbles back from the buffeting gale, shielding his eyes as he stares ahead at something you cannot see.

Keep it together. You force your numb limbs into action, stumbling and crawling over the last of the rocky scree, the wind growing stronger the higher you climb. Turn to 228.

661

The corridor ends at a T-junction. To your left, where a blood-spattered sign reads 'security wing', you see a metal door blocking the passage. Two burly-looking guards are leaning against it, armed with crowbars. You decide to avoid a confrontation and head right instead, finding yourself in a large room.

This appears to have once been a medical wing. Light spills through the barred windows to illuminate the twisted remains of beds, torn sheets and broken containers. Glass and wood crack underfoot as you cross the room and pass through an opened door. Beyond, a set of stairs take you down into what may have been a storeroom. It is now empty, save for some shattered trunks along one wall, the remains of a fire and some empty bottles.

If you have *Judah's Book of Canticles*, turn to 579. Otherwise, you find nothing of interest here. You retrace your steps and leave the prison. Turn to 426.

662

The tattoos are arranged to suggest some sort of code or message. On one side of a patterned scroll days of the week have been written in a neat row, and next to each day there is a symbol. You crane your neck to view the design:

Sol – cross
Ullir – star
Dilain – heart
Woden – snow flake
Jove – mountain

Unfortunately, the man shifts in his sleep, settling himself into a position that obscures the rest of his tattoo. Nevertheless, you wonder if the information you have gleaned might prove useful later.

Will you:

Approach the cellar?	**724**
Leave and return to the taproom?	**80**

663

You remove the skeletal hand from your backpack, gripping it tightly as it attempts to break free. With effort, you force the grisly appendage into the hollow, pushing it against the handprint depression. You hear the clink of the poisoned fangs hitting the bone, trying to stab and bite their way into the hand – but you maintain your grip, pushing it harder into the space.

You hear a hiss and then a creak from behind you. Looking back over your shoulder, you watch as the thorny bars of the cell retract back into the ceiling. The branches around the Skard warrior are also retreating, leaving him to drop to his knees, gasping for air.

Leaving the hand inside the hollow (you may remove *clackers* from your hero sheet), you hurry to the man's side. As you crouch next to him, you notice that the dagger has vanished – evidently an illusion to torment the warrior.

'Did ... did Skoll send you?' he gasps, rubbing at the scratches around his neck.

You frown, shaking your head. 'I'm here to rescue him – who are you?'

The warrior explains that his name is Leif, an einherjar who shared Skoll's gift for spirit-walking. Leif accompanied his great leader into the Norr, to help him find the means of defeating the witch – but they were both captured.

'I have been here for an eternity,' he sighs. His wearied gaze takes in the confines of his cell. 'Every minute, every second – I have wished for revenge. This place is *her* work. The witch.' He reaches for the horn hanging at his waist. 'I will lend you my strength. For we must climb – to the very top of the tree.'

Leif agrees to accompany you on your mission. For the remainder of this quest, you benefit from the following ability:

Leif's song (mo): Leif can blow his ancient horn to boost your powers in combat. You may use this ability any time in combat to raise your *brawn* or *magic* by 4 for one combat round. *Leif's song* may only be used once per combat.

Together, you follow the passageway as it continues to ascend through the tree trunk. Turn to 6.

664

You come awake in Anise's arms, shuddering as the life returns to your dead body. Gradually, the cave blurs into focus – then Anise's gaunt face sharpens into view. Tears are rolling down her cheeks.

'The others. I heard fighting,' she says, in a tight voice.

You both struggle to your feet, using each other as support as you head up the slope. From deeper in the mountain you can hear cries and the crackle of magic. As strength returns to your limbs you pick up the pace, the trail of blood teasing you down dark passageways.

When you finally emerge in a pillared hall, you find Skoll and Maune fighting a monstrous creation – a gigantic golem, fashioned from the body parts of various creatures. Its most recent addition appears to be the paladin's eagle, its severed head now sitting atop a brawny pair of shoulders.

Thankfully, the pair have the upper hand; the paladin's magic and the Skard's axe are making short work of the abomination, lopping off its bloodied limbs and appendages until all that is left is a grisly pile of body parts. Turn to 733.

For defeating the ancient wind demon, you may now choose one of the following rewards:

Tumult	Spin cycle	Quel's daggers
(main hand: axe)	(left hand: shield)	(necklace)
+2 speed +2 brawn	+2 speed +2 armour	+1 speed +1 brawn
Ability: frenzy	Ability: roll with it	Ability: bleed

The demon's heart still pulses with elemental energy. If you wish to absorb the demon's magic, you may learn the storm carl career. The storm carl has the following special abilities:

Hurricane rush (co): Give into your fury and become a reckless whirlwind of death! This ability inflicts 2 damage dice to each opponent ignoring *armour* (roll separately for each), but for every opponent you hit you must take 1 damage in return, ignoring *armour*. You can only use this ability once per combat.

Spin shot (co): This ability inflicts 2 damage dice to your opponent ignoring *armour* – plus 1 extra die for every *speed* point difference you have over your opponent in this round. (If your hero has a *speed* of 7 and your opponent has a *speed* of 5, you would roll 4 damage dice in total.) You can only use this ability once per combat.

When you have made your decision, return to the quest map to continue your adventure.

Unable to stop yourself, you charge up the steps and make a wild swing for the cardinal. Your blow should have cut him down in seconds. Instead your weapons grate across the hard, spiny flesh of a demon. The cardinal has assumed his true form, a reptilian giant coated in a thick mantle of crimson scales. Your hatred turns to fear as you prepare to take on this demon in combat. It is time to fight:

	Speed	Magic	Armour	Health
Cardinal	10	7	8	60

Special abilities

🖤 **Reflect damage:** Each time your damage score / damage dice cause health damage to Rile, you must take the half the damage you have inflicted (rounding up) as damage to your own hero, ignoring *armour*. (If Rile loses 14 *health*, you would lose 7.)

🖤 **Dark hate:** You must take 2 damage at the end of every combat round, ignoring *armour*, from the cardinal's deathly aura.

If you manage to defeat this devilish trickster, turn to 774. If you are defeated, remember to record your defeat on your hero sheet, then turn to 621.

667

Raising your hands you trace the circular patterns with your fingers, connecting the lines and whorls with the magic that now flows through you. The runes start to flicker and then glow, illuminating a trail to the centre circle, where blue-black energies crackle above the podium. For a brief moment you glimpse some creature trapped within the bright maelstrom – a spinning tornado of dust and rock, with two crimson jewels for eyes – then it is gone. The energy sparks out and the runes dim.

When you walk over to the podium you discover that the elemental is now trapped inside the orb, filling it with a powerful magic. (Congratulations! You have now created a *tremor orb*. If you wish to take this, simply make a note of it on your hero sheet, it does not take up backpack space.) Turn to 684.

668

You are pitched forward, flailing through a shower of ash to slam into a cracked stone pillar. The pain is relished, like an old companion. A reminder that you have left your dead body behind.

You draw your weapons, your body twisting round to scan the bleak nightmarish landscape of the Norr.

A circle of stones mark the edge of a mountain pinnacle. Beyond them there is nothing but cloud, streaking past at a vertiginous speed, a single crimson sun caught on their currents. It blurs overhead, speeding through a repeated arc, its garish light casting blood-soaked shadows across the carved circle.

So, this is where it ends . . .

A growl rumbles from the shifting darkness. The bear edges into view, circling warily. You sense his confusion. His questioning.

Your eyes lock with his own, glistening amber and then red in the flickering light. You try and speak but the words choke you. A pain presses against your chest, weighing heavy on your heart.

Love. Regret.

'You gave me life . . . old friend.'

Dirt crunches beneath your boot-heels as you follow the bear, the two of you moving inexorably around the circle like the hands of a clock.

The bear lowers his head, snuffling at the ground, emitting a regretful whine.

'You know it has to end this way. You know what's at stake.'

Every word pulls at your soul, cutting like razors. 'It's the only way, Nanuk. I need your magic. My body is gone, broken. It is time, old friend.'

Silence, save for the whistling of the wind filling your nostrils with its death.

The bear stops. You stop. Both stand rigid, facing one another.

'I'm sorry. Please understand—'

Snarling.

The bear launches itself forward; an explosion of fur and teeth, and claws that are suddenly a blur, leaving glimmering trails in their wake. All regret, all pain is gone in those few seconds – your mind snaps taut, as does your body, weapons spinning and blocking the bear's frenzied assault. A last battle together, a last glorious moment to be shared, remembered . . . It is time to fight:

	Speed	Magic	Armour	Health
Nanuk	13	9	8	80

Special abilities

🛡 **Basic instinct**: Nanuk rolls two dice to determine his damage score.

🛡 **Spirit link**: At the end of each round, roll a die. If the result is ⚄ or less, you must lose 4 *health* and Nanuk gains 4 *health*. (Note: this cannot take Nanuk past his starting *health* of 80.)

If you manage to defeat the ancestor spirit, turn to **51**.

669

Every thread a life. Every thread a hope. The woman's pale eyes flick across the coruscating cords of light. *The twining. The pattern of all existence. The course of fate.*

You pull an incredulous frown as you look down at the thread you are balanced upon, trying to imagine how this thin web-like strand could possibly represent a life. You follow it as it sweeps underneath you, spiralling around past other strands, intersecting, knotting together, twisting into thicker cords as several flow together.

This was once order. A destiny assigned to every being. Gabriel wove the plan, the great work. I only spin the thread, but he would decide its destiny, the length of life and day of death. Destiny could not be changed.

The woman scratches at her head again, leaving ugly welts where her nails have broken the raw skin. *Only discord now. Only discord. Do you not hear it? The weave should play a symphony. It should all meet the plan. But now. It grates, it bores, it tears at me.* She closes her eyes, nails raking back and forth as if trying to prise her very head open. *All her fault. All her fault!*

(Return to **713** to ask another question or turn to **760** to end the conversation.)

670

(If you have already entered the tournament, turn to **341**. If you have the keyword *underdog* on your hero sheet, turn to **192**.)

'Ah good, good!' The man beckons you over. 'You'll need a sled and the entry fee, ten gold crowns, then I can register you and make it all official-like.'

'What's the prize?' you ask, scanning the list of names on the chart. You note there are already twenty-nine other racers signed up for the competition.

'Best prize ever,' grins the man, his ratty face leaning closer. 'The money's all well and good, three hundred gold ones, but that don't outshine the Winter Diamond. Bigger than my hand, it is – and perfectly flawless too. So they say, 'cos I never actually seen it. But Ryker's got it under close wraps up in that fortress of 'is. Only way you're gonna swag the prize is by winning the races.'

If you have a sled and 10 gold crowns, you may enter the tournament (turn to 329.) Otherwise, turn to 106 to explore the rest of the compound.

671

You raise the captain's conch to your lips and sound a single, trumpeting call. The air above you starts to shimmer and distort, rippling outwards in undulating waves. They spin and swirl, moving around a single pinpoint of light. The brightness steadily widens, drawing itself back into a long tunnel, growing larger, spinning faster and faster – until there is a sudden spray of dazzling light as the corpse ship rolls out of the portal, magic breaking like surf around its dark prow.

The *Naglfar* rocks to a halt by the cliff side.

A ghostly crew member appears at the rail, hailing you with a cry. Then a rope ladder is flung over the side, slapping against the twisted nails and knots of hair that form the substance of the vessel's body.

'If the mountain won't come to us, we'll go to the mountain,' you grin, gesturing to the ladder.

Skoll looks at you incredulously, then he explodes into laughter. 'Of course! We will sail, Bearclaw. We will sail!' Bolstered by this change of fortune, he grabs hold of the ladder and climbs it with speed. Anise is less enthusiastic, eyeing the corpse ship with dread.

You hold out your hand. 'All aboard,' you smile.

'It's a thing of death,' she says, glaring at you sharply.

'As am I,' you reply. You gesture again, taking her reluctant hand and helping her onto the ladder. Once on deck, you see that Skoll has already taken the wheel of the ship. He is looking up at the unfurled masts, already filling with wind.

'Do you know how to sail her?' he calls to you. 'These are strange tides we must navigate, for sure.'

You close your eyes, reaching out with your magic. The ship has a presence, a dark pit of chill emptiness where the souls of the drowned sailors scream in torment. You push your magic into that pit, filling it with power – driving life into the hungry vessel, just as you would one of your own dead limbs. The deck rocks beneath you, the stays snapping tight as a ghostly wind, directed by your own magic, packs into the dark sails.

With a creaking groan the ship starts to lurch forward, gaining speed as it banks round towards the rift. You open your eyes, your pale gaze fixing on the mountain.

'How fast can it go?' shouts Skoll eagerly.

'Let's find out.' Your mind directs the surging currents of magic, blasting them into the sails. Within seconds the ship is tearing across the desolate plain, accelerating so fast that the crew are now clinging to the rigging and the rails. Then the ground drops away and you are flying out across a dark nothingness, your magic managing to keep the ship airborne.

As captain of the *Naglfar*, you have now gained the following special ability:

Nail gun (co): Instead of rolling for a damage score, you can use the nail gun. This inflicts 2 damage dice to a single opponent, ignoring *armour*. It also reduces their *armour* score by 2 for the remainder of the combat. You can only use the *nail gun* once per combat.

You may use this ability, in addition to your own hero abilities, for the duration of this quest. When you have updated your hero sheet, turn to 224.

As you retrace your steps you see a swarm of dark shapes hurtling towards you along the passageway. They have the appearance of floating pulpy brains, their undersides trailing a number of thin pale tentacles.

Caul skids to a halt, his spear-point held out before him. 'Those are the things that attacked me,' he growls. 'Watch them, their armour is strong – and their tentacles will shred you, given half the chance.'

You note each creature has a shell-like carapace curving back over their bulbous bodies. Black scales glitter in the glow of your weapons and the ghoulish lightning that flickers between the four brains. As one they sweep in, tentacles lifted to reveal hundreds of tiny serrated claws. It is time to fight:

	Speed	Magic	Armour	Health
Drakaloth	5	4	5	30
Drakaloth	5	4	5	25
Drakaloth	5	4	5	20
Drakaloth	5	4	5	20

Special abilities

◗ **Hive mind**: At the end of each combat round, you must take 1 damage from each surviving opponent, ignoring *armour*.

◗ **Stalker's spear**: Caul adds 2 to your damage score for the duration of this combat.

If you manage to defeat this dastardly swarm, turn to 40.

The skeleton key fits the lock perfectly. Flipping open the lid, you are met by the bright glow of gold. This must have been Jackson's money locker and now the wealth of the White Wolf Trading Company is in your hands. You have gained 100 gold crowns. After pocketing the coins, you hurry back to the hatch. Turn to 592.

674

'The rift walls are full o' caverns and tunnels. Dangerous places, but you never gonna come out empty-handed.' Hal opens up one of the crates, lifting out some braids of black hair to reveal a pair of rune-carved tablets.

Maune wrinkles his nose, taking hold of the tangled hair. 'Troll?'

Hal grins. 'Yeah, little memento from those critters you laid to rest. Never waste anything, I says.' He lifts up his cloak to reveal the tresses sown into the cloth. 'Warm as me wife's embrace. I'll sell 'em to yer too, if you want.'

You may purchase any of the following for 100 gold crowns (Note: you can only purchase one of each item):

Rune of healing	**Troll's tresses**	**Rune of nightmares**
(special: rune)	(special)	(special: rune)
Use on any item to add the special ability *heal*	Use on a cloak, chest or boots item to add the special ability *insulated*	Use on any item to add the special ability *fear*

You may now purchase first aid supplies (turn to 639), view Hal's weapons (turn to 728), trade your own items (turn to 95) or leave and return to the quest map.

675

As you hurtle along the earthen tunnel you see the wall ahead crumble, then start to topple inwards. You dodge around the raining debris, glancing back over your shoulder to see what may have caused the cave-in. A huge scaled foot pushes through the hole, tearing and ripping with its claws. You bank away down another tunnel, seeing a distant circle of daylight ahead.

'Faster! They've found us!' calls Skoll.

The tunnel starts to collapse behind you, raining down a torrent of rock and sand. A skull-like snout spears through the billowing cloud, green eyes illuminating the darkness.

You aim for the end of the tunnel as fast as you can. Behind you there is a deafening roar, followed by a sharp intake of crackling breath. Suddenly a violent heat is at your back, rushing along the passageway and threatening to engulf you in flames.

In order to outrun the dragon's fiery breath, you will need to pass a speed challenge using your transport's speed:

	Speed
Wrath fire	14

If you are successful, turn to 715. If you fail, turn to 640.

676

Caul strides over, shaking his head. 'It's just a pretty decoration. There's better ones, at the end of that tunnel.'

'A lot of effort for a pretty decoration . . .' You squat down next to the carved head, running a hand over the cold stone. In place of the serpent's eyes, there are two large hollow depressions. You wonder if some sort of object should be placed within each of these, to activate whatever secrets it might hold.

If you have two *flawless emeralds* and wish to use them, then turn to 690. Otherwise, you are unable to interact with the carving. Grudgingly, you are forced to leave the chamber and follow Caul into the tunnel. Turn to 775.

677

The circle starts to fade. You reach out, grasping for the gossamer thread that links your spirit to your old life and your dead body. Then you are travelling, streaking across the chill wasteland, your body trailing sparks of frost in its wake. The light ahead grows bright, blinding in its brilliance . . .

Eyes snap open. The wind and dust blast against your face. Anise is pulling at your sleeve, tears in her eyes. With a gasp she snatches her hand away, its leather mitten now cracked with ice.

Her voice carries fear. 'Arran! What have you done?'

A giddy laughter issues from your lips. 'Reborn. I'm reborn . . .'

Nanuk's magic fills every pore of your being. The cold of the Norr pulses through you, searing away the dead skin, consuming the deceased organs, the muscle, the tissue – melting away your very bones.

You stumble, falling forward, barely catching yourself before you hit the ground. As your fingers splay in the dirt, hands stretched out for balance, you see that they are now translucent, infused with a green luminescence. You turn your head to watch as your corpse finally disintegrates to dust – whipped away on the wind, leaving your clothes and armour to drop in a tangled mess onto the rocks.

You turn your hands over, eyes moving along your arms, across the bunched muscles to your broad chest. Everything is now alight with a green radiance – throbbing with the graven cold of the Norr.

Anise stumbles away, horrified. She finds Skoll's arms. 'Help him,' she begs.

The Skard is silent, equally transfixed by the sight before him. His face is unreadable, its many welted scars made ghoulish by the green light.

You rise to your feet, hands gesturing towards your armour. The pieces rise up on currents of magic, spiralling towards your body, where they snap into place around the glowing limbs. Within moments you are clad as you once were, but between the chinks of armour and the trim of your clothing the green light continues to spill into the haze.

'No flesh or bone can pass. But a ghost . . .'

Your voice is different. It sounds like the old Arran, but with a deeper resonance. A commanding tone. You turn back, to face the surging wall of stone and sand. 'I will destroy the source of this magic; then I will create safe passage for you. Heed my sign.' You raise your fingers, drawing them back through the air. Their path leaves a glittering trail of lights: the claw-marks of a bear.

'Arran, please! Stop!' You hear the scuffle of boots – Anise trying to break free.

You do not look back. With your gaze set firmly ahead, you march into the eye of the storm. Turn to **85**.

The fight is short and easily won. Three thieves lie dead, sprawled in the mud. The last, the tattooed leader of the gang, turns and makes a run for it. Phantom claws leap from your hand, piercing straight through his exposed back. When the claws retract back into your fingers, his lifeless body drops to the ground.

You turn your gaze on the monk, who is still lying amongst the bloodied snow.

'What . . . what are you?' he gasps, his horrified features illuminated by your weapons.

'Death,' you hiss, standing over him. Your eyes flick to the book of scripture, hooked by a chain around his neck. 'Yours. Unless you give me what I want – the book.'

With trembling hands, the monk lifts the chain over his head and holds it up to you. 'Yes, yes, take it!' he splutters, averting his gaze as if the hurt of losing his prized possession is too much to bear.

You snatch the book, then step away. 'Now, run along and pray to your god. Pray for my soul, if you think it's worth saving.'

The monk scrambles to his feet, then beats a hasty retreat.

(Congratulations! You have gained *Judah's Book of Canticles* – simply make a note of this on your hero sheet, it doesn't take up backpack space.) Turn to 659.

Turn to 659.

679

To the astonishment of the crowd you throw your trophy onto the ground, glaring around at the circle of surprised faces. Desnar bows his head, his expression pained by the chorus of gasps and exclamations from the assembled Skards.

'The ancestors have spoken,' proclaims Sura, a smile cracking her aged lips. 'Nanuk's strength is with you.' The old woman offers out the end of her staff. You unhook the bear necklace and place it over your head. The moment the chain rests proudly across your chest each and every Skard puts a hand to their own breast, speaking some vow or mantra in unison.

Then the young boy steps forward, peeling back the hide bag he is carrying. You see that it is filled with treasures.

'These belonged to past chiefs,' states Sura, noting your awkward confusion. 'You have the right to claim what is yours.' If you wish, you may now take one of the following rewards:

Chieftain's spirit	Chieftain's strength	Chieftain's guile
(talisman)	(main hand: spear)	(necklace)
+1 magic +2 health	+1 speed +3 brawn	+1 brawn +2 health
Ability: shatter	Ability: skewer	Ability: trickster
(requirement: mage)	(requirement: warrior)	(requirement: rogue)

If you are a warrior, turn to 620. If you are a mage, turn to 302. If you are a rogue, turn to 240.

680

Nanuk's magic floods into you, powering your strikes with a savage frenzy. As the last of the beast's heads goes sailing across the ice, showering the ground in black blood, you notice the creature on the slab start to convulse, as if experiencing some sort of pain. Fearing it might break free of its shackles, you jump up onto the ice, straddling the monster's body with weapons raised.

The stone mouth cracks open, emitting a wheezing gasp. *Stay your hand, mortal. I am Fafnir. Last of the Titans.* The chain links rattle as the creature tries to lift its arms. *I left my brothers. I wouldn't make the sacrifice. The Dwarves needed me. We had to stand together, against the horrors from the shroud. I had to defend them, defend the land.*

Your magic pools into your hands, running along your weapons and sparking in the chill air. 'They used your blood, didn't they? Mixed it with the drakes to make a race of . . . monsters.' You can still picture the horrific creatures that assaulted Bitter Keep.

The Nisse. We had to be stronger. We had to . . . survive.

'You call this surviving?' You glance over at the mangled remains of the drake. 'They used you, the dwarves. They bled you dry.'

I put my soul into the stone. Old stone, from another age – another world. Veins of it, brought to the surface by the cataclysm. We thought the magic within would be the power to defeat the demons. The Dwarves took the blood, yes – but they wanted it all. And when I refused, they shackled me.

'So you tried to escape. You put your soul into a new body . . . the drake.'

The dwarves left the city. Corruption . . . the magic . . . It twisted them. Twisted their minds. They went deeper. The dark places below. Left me here . . .

'Left – but now they're back. The Nisse have resurfaced.'

The Titan pauses before speaking again, its voice weaker, barely more than a rasp. *They know what is coming. They know and they . . . fear . . . .*

'What is coming?' You put your weapons to the Titan's chest. 'Tell me!'

The creature opens its mouth, giving a last wheezing sigh, then there is silence. Angrily, you hammer against the cold stone, demanding further answers – but whatever life force was beating within the Titan, it has now departed.

If you are a warrior, turn to **411**. If you are a mage, turn to **296**. If you are a rogue, turn to **543**.

681

The creature unfolds itself, limbs creaking and grating as they stretch out one by one. The circular disc, which was once the centre of the circle, flips forward to rest on a spindly body, revealing a head that is little more than a cluster of stake-like prongs. With a screech, the creature drags itself out of the hole, a multitude of roots serving as its legs.

You can see no eyes, but the monster has obviously sensed you. Tilting its head, it launches itself into a full-on charge, the crown of spikes lowered like a bull's horns. You manage to dodge aside, leaving the creature to rocket past. As it skids round, you sight a mouth-like aperture at the centre of the crown. Suddenly, a thorny vine whips out of the hole – a tongue that is attempting to wrap itself around you. Again, you manage to sidestep the attack, preparing yourself for the monster's next charge. It is time to fight:

	Speed	Magic	Armour	Health
Hyperbole	7	5	4	60

Special abilities

🌿 **Crown charge**: If Hyperbole rolls a double for its attack speed, it automatically charges you with its pronged crown. This does damage equal to its current *armour* score, ignoring your *armour*. (Note: This damage is in addition to any further damage Hyperbole might cause by winning the round.)

🌿 **Thorn tongue**: At the end of each combat round, roll a die. On a ⚀ or ⚁ result, you are hit by the creature's tongue and must take 2 damage, ignoring *armour*. This also lowers your *speed* by 1 for the next round of combat only. A result of ⚂ or more means you have dodged the attack.

If you manage to defeat this frenzied thicket, turn to 608.

682

Skoll leads the charge, an axe in one hand, magic in the other – chopping and blasting through the bodies that block his way. Behind him Anise hollers a defiant cry, swinging her sword to sever heads from bodies, clipping limbs and frozen weapons, leaving a trail of ice and writhing corpses in her wake. Turn to 761.

683
Quest: Eye of the storm

(NOTE: You must have completed the blue quest *The dead and the damned* before you can access this location)

You drag your wrecked body over the rocks, blinded by the whirling red dust. All around you the incessant heat presses close, a wrongness that seeps from the dead, cracked earth. Through the crimson veil, you can dimly make out Skoll. The Skard is pulling himself up the last of the tumbled boulders, his grit and determination driving him ever onwards – ever north.

Since abandoning your transport and advancing on foot, your body's deterioration has become worryingly evident. Your arms and legs drag like lead, wracked with frequent convulsions that leave you kicking and squirming in the dirt. Black blood continues to stream from wounds that refuse to heal, whilst torn muscle and cracked bone throw even the simplest movements into dizzying lurches.

Your body, your dead body, is finally giving up – the magic that once nourished it no longer able to stave off its inevitable decay.

Keep it together. You hiss the mantra through cracked lips while your rictus-hardened fingers scrape across the rocks, futilely attempting to pull you across the endless desolation. You look back, reminding yourself of your one last hope – the inspiration that keeps you going . . .

If you have the keyword *repentance* on your hero sheet, turn to 31. Otherwise, turn to 660.

684

You move to another circle, hoping to call on its power. However, despite your concentrated efforts you cannot influence or fortify the runes. Whatever magic was once held in the summoning circles has now been spent. You acknowledge defeat, much to Caul's relief.

He enters the room, stepping warily around the runic carvings. 'That was . . . interesting.'

You heft your weapons, then start for the exit. 'I have a feeling that was just a taste of the magic that still dwells here.' Turn to 732.

685

'Wait, you hear that?' The eye roves back and forth behind the peep hole. 'Scratching. Scratch, scratch . . . You hear that too?'

You shake your head, frowning.

'Hmm, maybe just the wind then.' The eye continues to flick around in a paranoid fashion. 'Always gotta watch the angles, sonny. Skards can creep up outta nowhere. Crafty ones, those north men.'

Will you:

Ask to see his wares?	151
Ask about trading?	327
Ask about his 'precautions'?	549
Ask if he has any news?	450
Trade items? (requirement: permit)	730
Leave?	Return to the map

686

As you take your position at the centre of the circle, you feel a sudden prickling along your skin. It is as if a door to the Norr has been flung open and its freezing chill has flooded into you, turning your limbs to ice. You give a startled gasp, your throat clicking as it involuntarily constricts.

'Relax.' Sura nods to the staff she gave you. 'Try and push it into the staff. The totem will hold your magic.'

Your hands are shaking as you fight to turn your head, to look down at the finely-carved bone staff. The head is sculpted into a bear's paw, the claws curled inwards. Gritting your teeth, you raise the totem and let the chill magic of the Norr pour through your body and into the staff. It blossoms into a bright green light, the claw snapping open as if coming alive.

'Yes!' Sura cackles with delight. 'Now, do it again – and this time, step out of the circle. You are strong enough. I see it.'

You continue to practise under Sura's instruction, learning to channel the magic of your ancestor spirit to power various spells and enchantments.

You may now equip the following item:

Phantom claw
(left hand: totem)
+1 speed 2 magic
Ability: boneshaker
(requirement: mage)

The shaman has the following special abilities:

Power totem (co + pa): (requires a totem in the left hand.) Instead of rolling for a damage score you can imbue your totem with magic. This costs 1 *magic* to activate (your *magic* is restored at the end of the combat). Once activated, *power totem* inflicts 1 damage to all opponents at the end of each combat round – and also heals you for 1 *health* at the end of each combat round – for the duration of the combat. *Power totem* can only be cast once per combat.

Totem blast (co): (requires *power totem* – see above) Instead of rolling for a damage score, you can invoke a totem blast. This causes two dice of damage to all opponents, ignoring *armour* – but cancels the effects of *power totem.*

Once you have updated your hero sheet, turn to 197.

687

'Well, that's a real shame, honey.' The woman settles back in her chair, absently playing with a stray lock of hair. 'Not often my charms fail to win over a gentleman, but then you are something special, aren't you? Hmm, if you change your mind, then you know where to find me. I see you're a thinker – you need to mull it over, work out if you can trust me. I like thinkers. Means you're smart. And that also means you'll be back.'

You rise from the table, readjusting your weapons. 'I'm not here to make friends, Talia.'

'Oh, who said we have to be friends, honey?' Her eyes follow you as you edge past, the corners of her mouth twitching with amusement.

'You talk a good game, I'll give you that.'

'Oh, I like games. See, you're curious.' Talia waggles a finger at you. 'You'll be back. Until then, stay out of trouble for me, won't you, handsome? Wouldn't want that pretty face of yours getting ruined.' The woman raises her mug in a toast, cocking her head. 'To absent friends.' (Record the keyword *covert* on your hero sheet.)

Will you:

Talk to the barman?	420
Listen to the conversation at the bar?	534
Leave?	426

688

'It is rare, but once or twice in a lifetime we find a child who is called by the dreams. One who sees the signs, who can enter the spirit world.' Sura takes a long pull on the pipe, sucking in the smoke then releasing it through her nose. 'The spirit world is like our own. Made of both good and evil. That is why we have spirit guides, good spirits who aid us and give us their strength, their wisdom.'

'And Nanuk is one of these spirits?' The pungent smoke has started to make you feel nauseous. At the back of your mind you feel the bear's presence awakening, his curiosity aroused. 'You have this power also?'

The woman grins, her eyes glowing bright in the haze. 'We have totems, magic that lets us focus our minds, make our bond with the spirits stronger. When we have mastered our spirit, we go to the Hall of Vindsvall to complete our training. Every tribe has one shaman. To act as guide, mediator, teacher. The others become Asynjur and must remain at the hall. It is their duty to serve, to perform the Solkning – the spirit hunt.'

Will you:

Ask about the Hall of Vindsvall?	636
Ask about the bear necklace?	545
Ask what 'vela styker' means?	587
End the conversation?	575

689

You put your fingers to the girl's throat. Closing your eyes, you start to draw on your reserves of magic, lifting it out from its well of darkness and pouring it through your fingertips – letting it fill her body, taking the dead limbs and working them back to life. The effort is draining, the task more difficult than you had expected. (You must lower your overall *health* by 5 permanently.)

Finally, with your magic spent, you remove your hand and drop back, watching and waiting.

Nothing. You feel your eyes burn as they stare upon her own, looking for some flicker of life. But they remain vacant, fixed on the heavens, where a chill wind howls past the broken ruins. It wails mournfully around the chamber, beating at you with its bitter cold – but not cold enough to expel the aching pain.

'No . . .' You lower your head, admitting defeat – shamed by your own foolish belief in the macabre act you were willing to perform. *I have failed everyone. Nanuk. Skoll. Anise . . .*

A wet gasp draws you from your reverie. You look back at the girl, almost sure you saw her eyelids flutter.

'Anise . . . ?'

You lean close, convinced now that it was a cruel trick of the wind. Perhaps a reflex action, nothing more. *I'm a fool. I cannot bring back the dead . . .*

Suddenly the girl spasms, her body arching, legs kicking at the ground.

You draw back, startled and afraid, no longer sure what your dark magic may have set in motion. You grab her hand, feeling its graven chill against your own. A cold that burns fiercer than any fire.

'Anise?'

A green glow rolls across her body, softening the dark bruising to a pale, mottled grey. You continue to watch transfixed as the hands of time are wound back – flesh folds over bone, limbs reset, wounds close.

She jerks upright, a dark light blossoming behind her eyes. Shadows hug the contours of her face, its porcelain white now lightly dusted by a green and ghoulish pallor.

As she leans forward, clumps of hair fall loose from her scalp. She cups them in trembling hands. Locks as red as fire. Bright as blood.

You can only stare at her, frozen in the moment, no longer sure what you feel. 'Anise, I'm sorry.'

Her dark eyes meet your own. From her lips, a hoarse-sounding croak – words struggling to find voice. 'My . . . love,' she finally gasps.

Anise falls into your arms. You hold her close, basking in her chill radiance. 'I will never let you go, Anise. Never.'

You have gained the title *The Everliving* and the following special ability:

Bloody maiden (mo): You may add 2 to each die you roll for damage for one combat round. This ability can only be used once per combat.

You may now return to the map or advance to the final boss monster encounter by turning to 717.

690

To your surprise, the emeralds fit perfectly into the hollow depressions. As they lock into place you hear a grinding screech, like stones scraping against each other. Suddenly, the floor of the chamber starts to tilt and then lower. Spinning round, you see that the coils are descending at different speeds and angles, turning the chamber floor into a spiralling pathway. Caul drops into a battle stance, his eyes wide with fear. 'God's teeth – this isn't good!'

There is an echoing boom, then silence.

The snake coils have formed a winding slope, leading down past the snake head to a chamber below. You look to Caul with a triumphant smile. 'Told you it wasn't for decoration.' Turning back to the carving, you try and prise the emeralds loose, but to your annoyance they are stuck fast. (Remove the two *flawless emeralds* from your hero sheet.)

'I bet this was locked for a reason,' says Caul. His eyes shift to the far wall, where the tunnel is now teasingly out of reach. 'Pity . . .'

You draw your weapons, then start down the newly-made path. 'No turning back now. May as well see what this serpent was guarding.' Turn to 590.

691

You reach into the blazing wreckage to grab the box. Roll a die and consult the following chart:

⚀ or ⚁ Your clothing has caught on fire. You must remove one item from your head, cloak, chest, gloves or feet locations. This item is destroyed and can no longer be used. (Remember to update any affected attributes.)

⚀ or ⚁ Your cloak has caught on fire. You must lose the ability associated with the cloak item you have equipped.

⚄ You have been singed by the fire. You must lower the attribute of a head, cloak, chest, gloves or feet location by 1.

⚅ You are unharmed by the flames and suffer no penalty.

The box is hot to the touch, blistering your skin as you struggle to prise open the lid. To your annoyance, you discover it is locked. If you have a *skeleton key*, turn to 673. Otherwise, you are unable to open the locker. If you wish, you may take it with you, in the hope that you will discover a means of opening it. The *locker* takes up one backpack space. When you have made your decision, turn to 592.

692

'No one messes with Ryker. After the break-out, he was the one who suggested the prisoners stay; take this place as their own. He was a criminal lord – got connections. Rich ones, too. He's made this place what it is. Don't believe what they're sayin', that Ryker ain't in charge, that someone else is pulling the strings and using that name. I know he's got a mage up there, gives him tonics – potions. Keeps him looking young.'

'Have you ever seen Ryker?' you ask sceptically.

'Not for a long time, I'll admit,' he says. 'The guy's a recluse – stays in the prison. But he's got eyes and ears everywhere, so always show 'im the proper respect. After all, look at what he created – a settlement out of nothing. Whalers use the island as a stop-over or to winter down for the season. We get smugglers and fur traders too, and of course, those who are on the run want to keep a low profile. No one stands in judgement over anyone at Ryker's. The past don't matter – it's all about today.'

Will you:

Ask about work?	469
Ask what he has for sale?	709
Take a seat in one of the alcoves?	634
Listen to the conversation at the bar?	534
Leave?	426

Footfalls echo back along the passages, then a cry followed by the ring of steel and a crack of magic. When you finally emerge in a pillared hall, you find Skoll and Maune facing off against a monstrous creation – a gigantic golem, fashioned from the body parts of various creatures. Its most recent addition appears to be the paladin's eagle, its severed head now sitting atop a brawny pair of shoulders.

'Back to the shroud with you, abomination!' Maune sends another bolt of holy magic into the creature's misshapen body while Skoll hacks away with his axe, ducking and weaving to avoid the monster's fists and scaled tail. Drawing your weapons, you hurry to aid your companions. It is time to fight:

	Speed	Brawn	Armour	Health
Eagle's head	12	9	5	40
Troll's arms	13	10	7	50
Drake's tail	13	9	9	40

Special abilities

- **Eagle's cry**: At the end of each combat round that the eagle's head is still alive, you must lower your *brawn* and *magic* by 1. This cannot be restored until the end of the combat.
- **Regeneration**: While the troll's arms are alive, all of your opponents heal 2 *health* at the end of each combat round. (NOTE: This cannot take an opponent's *health* above their starting scores.)
- **Tail lash**: If you roll a double for your attack speed (before or after a reroll) you must automatically take 5 damage, ignoring *armour*, from the drake's tail (providing it is still in play).
- **Blood 'n gore**: Your opponent is immune to *bleed*.
- **Grit and valour**: Maune and Skoll add 2 to your damage score for the duration of this combat. (If you are an einherjar, you can add 3 to your damage score instead.)

If you manage to take apart this vile abomination, turn to 462.

694

Your opponent gains the upper hand, her dog-team having maimed several of your lead hounds. You start to lose ground, watching in frustration as the girl-racer pulls away, crossing the finish line in first place. You follow shortly after, managing to grab second.

Whilst disappointed that you didn't win, you have still qualified for the final race. You also receive a prize of 150 gold crowns for your second place ranking. (Replace the keyword *rookie* with the word *veteran*.) Return to the map to continue your adventure.

695

You scrape and bump across the ice, looking to close the gap with the other racer – a scrawny-looking man dressed in ragged furs. He reaches for something at his belt and then leans back, his arm stretched out behind him. It isn't until the clouds shift and the sun's light sparkles across the ice that you notice a bright rainbow of oil.

Snickering to himself, the racer summons a flame to his fingertips then sends a jet of fire lancing into the oil. Within seconds a wall of flame is rushing towards you, eating through the ice and splitting open a widening crevasse.

To avoid this hazard, you will need to take a challenge test using your *speed* racing attribute:

	Speed
Fire and ice	10

If you are successful, turn to 753. If you fail, turn to 198.

696

The shock of your injuries leaves you drained of strength, your broken body buffetted by the strong currents. It is only when you feel yourself being sucked down, deeper and deeper into the churning pool, that you start to kick desperately, willing your limbs to move.

Somehow you manage to find the surface, where a pair of hands settle around your flailing arms, and pull you – with tremendous strength – onto the stony banks. You lie on your side, your dead chest heaving as you try and force the water out of your lungs. A glimmer of magic flickers across your body, knitting the bones and mending the worst of your injuries. At the back of your mind you feel Nanuk, his strength flowing into you once again.

Wiping the salty water from your eyes, you look up at your rescuer. 'Caul!'

The trapper appears unharmed, looking down at you with a half-smile. His clothes look as dry as bone, his appearance barely dishevelled.

'How – how did you survive?'

The trapper hoists you to your feet. 'I have my ways. Come, there is a tunnel over here – shall we?' He retrieves his spear then makes for an opening in the rock lit by a cluster of phosphorescent fungi. You hesitate, giving Caul a suspicious frown. Clearly, this trapper is not all that he appears – is he really an ally, or another of the cave's sinister tricks?

Along the banks of the pool you spot a number of items, which must have been washed up by the swirling currents. If you wish, you may now take one of the following:

Grotto grappler	Ground zero	Glacial teeth
(left hand: grapple)	(feet)	(necklace)
+2 speed +2 brawn	+1 speed +2 magic	+1 brawn +1 magic
Ability: stagger	Ability: insulated, focus	Ability: barbs
(requirement: rogue)		

You shoulder your pack, keeping a wary eye on your companion as you follow him into the tunnel. Turn to 726.

697

The monk downs his last mug of ale, then squeezes himself out of his seat with an audible grunt. After scooping his winnings into a leather sack, he waddles through the crowds towards the front doors. Immediately you spot a group of men peel away from the bar, four in number, with stern faces and a murderous gleam to their eye. You recognise one of them, possibly the leader, as the man that was beaten by the monk and lost all of his gold. They follow him out into the chill outdoors.

Will you:

Follow the ruffians?	**655**
Stay in the taproom?	**80**

698

The stench of death. Black flies crawl over the rotted corpses. As you follow the Skards into the ruins a group of crows startle in alarm, leaving their grisly feast to rise cawing and screeching into the air. There are bodies everywhere – men, women, children ... and the black-scaled bodies of Nisse.

It has taken half a day to reach these ruins, perched on the edge of a bleak rocky plateau. A few pillars, a cracked stone floor and some crumbling walls are all that remain of some ancient temple, or other structure from antiquity. The wind has become fierce, blasting cruelly against this exposed ridge, bringing with it a true northern cold. Even you feel it, biting at your hands and face, scouring the pale skin to leave it blistered and raw. Clumps of snow cling to the hollows of the surrounding rock. Beyond the ruins, where the bluff sears off into a drop of a hundred metres or more, you see a glittering expanse of snow and ice, stretching as far as the eye can see. The true north. The frozen north.

The seal tribe had evidently made this spot their temporary home. Hide shelters have been left flapping in the wind, the remains of cooking pots and other equipment lie discarded amongst the rocks. As well as the human bodies, you see the remains of animals – goats and dogs, and some bovine creatures covered in thick white hair.

The hunters are silent as they pick amongst the ruins, turning over bodies, kicking over rubble, scavenging anything that might be useful – weapons, tools, armour. There is no sense of loss or show of regret in their hard faces. You wonder if such scenes, such horrific suffering, are commonplace out here in the wilds.

But you feel it. And your eyes start to see it.

Everything here is touched with a green veil, glimmering in the fading light – a magical sheen that reminds you of the dreamscape. At the back of your mind you feel Nanuk's presence pushing forward, more powerful than before. From the dead lying around you, motes of light drift towards you, coalescing around your body and then sinking into the deadened flesh. A cold energy begins to fill you, growing steadily more intense the longer you remain in the ruins.

Feeding off the dead. The thought sickens you, but you are almost sure it is true – somehow, the barrier between this place and the shroud, the place of the demons and the dreams, is thin. The magic of that other world is seeping through, giving you strength and power. You also wonder, with a sudden pang of dread, what else might be able to slip through . . .

Soul charge: Your body has been able to heal. You may now remove three defeats from your hero sheet or one death penalty effect. If you are inflicted with *rift rot*, this disease is also removed.

The leader of the hunters, Taulu, is standing alone, his head bowed. You join him, your eyes wandering to the corpse sprawled against the nearby pillar. A man, broad and muscular, with dark hair blowing across his scarred face. A pile of Nisse bodies lie in a circle around him, their black blood spattering his seal-skin clothing. He accounted well for himself, a noble last stand.

'Drungen.' The hunter lifts his head, looking out across the ruins to the ice plains beyond. Then he begins to sing. A deep, sonorous melody filled with every emotion these hard men seem unwilling to show. The words are Skard, but you feel them, the sadness and the reverence in their tone – and know that they honour their heroes, their fallen.

A scuff of boots. You turn to see the others joining you – Hale and Ninvuk. They glance at the dead warrior, silent in death, and then they add their own voices to that of their leader, eyes staring off into whatever places, whatever thoughts, the words now take them to.

Then it is over. And in the distance, a different chorus. Taulu cocks his head to one side. The baying of wolves sounds across the cliffs and valleys, mournful and desolate. The sound makes you bristle in alarm, your weapons finding their way into your hands. You are reminded of your previous encounter with wolves, and do not wish to repeat the experience. Nanuk brings a wary growl to your lips.

'Varagan.' Ninvuk, the shaven-headed Skard, has started to sniff the air, looking alert.

You glance at the leader, sensing that they now share your unease. 'Wolves?'

Taulu looks around, eyes scanning the ruins. 'Dead place. Brings spirits. Witch. Much danger . . .'

The hunters quickly find positions, ducking behind cover, their attentions focused on the same area of cliffs to your right. A pale green mist is now curling over the broken rocks. You feel Nanuk's agitation growing, his mind shifting inside you, urging you to seek safety.

A giant wolf prowls out of the thickening fog.

This is no earthly creature – you see its body is translucent, edged with a faint green glow. The wolf moves quickly, its huge strides eating up the distance, muzzle hanging low as if tracking a scent. Then it lifts its head, the green-flecked surface of its eyes glowing with a sudden vigour.

'Fenrir.' The word is spat like venom into the air. Taulu gives you a look – and for the first time you see real fear written there. 'The witch's hunter.'

The wolf's jaws crack open, green spittle hanging in drooling strands from its enormous teeth. You half expect it to give a dread howl – one designed to put terror into your hearts. Instead the beast appears to convulse, its flanks arching back, the head swinging to and fro in painful discomfort. A blackness starts to swirl in the beast's stomach, slowly winding itself together into something large – solid.

Suddenly the throat bulges, the jaws locking wider as a pair of black hands emerge from inside the wolf's mouth. They grab hold of the front teeth, dragging the darkness out into the pale light.

The shadow slides like spittle from the beast's jaws, pooling on the frost-webbed ground. You watch transfixed as the dark matter bubbles and hisses then starts to stretch, rising up to form a vaguely humanoid shape with a myriad of tentacles sprouting from its black body. Each one ends in a tooth-like fang, flickering with magic.

The shadow streaks towards the ruins, the fangs blurring as they slash back and forth. Behind it the wolf throws itself into a bounding charge, finally emitting a deep-throated howl that seems to still the very world and announce its ending. It is time to fight:

	Speed	Magic	Armour	Health
Fenrir	5	3	4	40
Jaws of Fenrir	4	2	3	40

Special abilities

- **Corrupted claws**: Each time you take health damage from Fenrir you must lower your *brawn* and *magic* by 1 for the duration of the combat.
- **Jaws of Fenrir**: At the end of each combat round you must take 4 damage, ignoring *armour*, from the shadowy fangs. Once the jaws are defeated, this ability no longer applies
- **Baiting the beast**: The hunters' weapons seem ineffective against your ghostly enemies, unlike your own. However, they are able to distract Fenrir and his minion. If you lose a combat round, roll a die. If the result is 🎲 or less, your enemy is distracted and does not roll for damage. 🎲 or more and the combat round proceeds as normal.

If you manage to defeat both enemies, restore any affected attributes and turn to 712.

699

Boots scuff through the dirt. You look up to see Maune stumbling towards you, his body leaning to one side, favouring his left leg. The glow of his scripted skin is barely visible through a thick film of dirt and blood. It flickers, like a dying flame.

He drops to his knees next to you, mail and plate clattering against the stone. From his brow a deep cut runs back across his pale scalp, the blood already congealed into a dusty paste. Spittle hangs from his cracked lips, swaying with each rasping breath.

He doesn't speak, merely looks at Anise and then to you. His bloodied fingers reach for his belt, tugging something loose. He offers it out, a metal vial attached to a silver chain.

You take the vial from him, surprised at the heat emanating from within – the same heat which rises from the paladin's body.

'Martyr's blood,' he whispers. 'Will give . . . life.'

His head lolls forward, his shoulders slouching. He remains kneeling, as if in prayer, the light from above pooling over him, illuminating the last weak flicker of his magic.

You lift up the vial, turning it over in your hand. Martyr's blood – said to be drawn from the holiest of the One God's disciples. Your mind races back to the attack on the road, and the Martyr who tried to kill you. Can such a gift be trusted?

Will you:

Use the Martyr's blood?	630
Refuse the paladin's gift?	550

700

You send the girl sprawling onto the ice – just as you pass between the fluttering banners that mark the end of the race. Above your head, the bright yellow lights of the canaries zip back and forth, no doubt sending pictures of your accomplishment back to the prison.

Congratulations! You have won the ice sled tournament and receive a prize of 300 gold crowns. When you return to Ryker's you are met by a deafening crescendo of cheers – and people chanting your nickname 'ghost'. You have gained the following special ability:

Ice slick (mo): If you roll a ⚁ for attack speed, you may roll an extra die. This ability can only be used once per combat.

An entourage of men, each as ugly and mean as the last, escort you through the prison to a lush office where a small unassuming gentleman reclines on a chaise lounge. Unlike the scruffy prison uniforms of his men, Ryker is wearing a white suit trimmed with ermine. His ears and fingers are adorned with gold jewellery and gemstones.

He makes no attempt to speak, merely waves to the low table at the centre of the room. There are maps and what looks like a small model of a mine, but what really captures your attention is the large white diamond resting on a cushion. Lifting it up, you turn the jewel towards the candlelight, marvelling at the coruscating colours that seem trapped within it, almost like blue-green flames.

'Take it.'

A thin reedy voice. You glance back towards the door, where another man is standing. You recognise him instantly as the vagabond thief you first met when you entered Ryker's. But now he is dressed in an opulent robe of crimson velvet, decorated with runes and charms.

If you wish, you may now take the following special reward:

Winter diamond
(backpack)
A flawless crystal
imbued with frost fire

Before you have a chance to ask questions, you are roughly escorted out of the prison – and deposited back onto the dark, filthy streets of Ryker's Island. Return to the map to continue your journey.

701

You look back across the dusty plain to where the great serpent lies motionless – its scaled body stretching for over a mile until it is lost to the darkness of the abyssal rift. The edge of the world.

Through the shimmering haze, you pick out a lone figure. Their clothes hang in tatters from their body, a spear in one hand and a sword in the other. Both blades drip with blood, spattering a trail across the wasteland.

A girl.

No. A warrior.

'Anise.'

She stops at the foot of the ridge, swaying slightly with weariness. 'It is done.' Her eyes find your own, lips crooking their familiar smile. 'Did I earn my name?'

You grin back at her. 'You will always be my Anise.'

She tilts her head, nodding with satisfaction. 'Queen Anise. I could grow to like that.'

Aslev appears at your side. He takes a long, deep breath – as if savouring the air. 'We won a great victory, Drokke.'

'Indeed.' You turn your head to the wind, letting the chill currents rush through you, filling your emptiness with a familiar, numbing cold. 'But this is only the beginning. I am Drokke – but I am also king. The rightful king of Valeron. I will win back my throne, unite north and south. One people.'

You glance at Aslev, awaiting his response, expecting rebuttal.

The einherjar simply nods. 'Then you'll be needing this.' He offers you the warhammer – the runed weapon that Skoll had given Aslev as a symbol of his return.

'Surtnost.' You take the warhammer into your spectral hands, feeling its weight – its power.

'And you'll be needing these.' Aslev steps back, gesturing to the assembly of Skards, still nearly a thousand strong, the sunlight sparkling and flashing off their spear-heads and axes. 'We will take back your throne, Drokke. No army of southlanders can stand against our might.'

You raise the warhammer into the air. Magic sparks from your fingertips, coursing along the runed handle, awakening the trapped spirits that have been bound within it. A bear, and a wolf, an eagle, a stag – and others: muttok, seal, petrel, sabre cat. You feel them pressing against your consciousness, filling you with their primal energies.

Animal spirits. One for every Skard tribe.

Green light bursts from the hammer, trailing bright ribbons into the azure blue sky. You lift back your head, eyes closed – listening to the cheers of the assembled Skards.

And in your mind's eye you picture Cardinal Rile, sat upon the throne of Valeron – your throne. The demon's words nudge at your memory.

Seeking to win back the throne of Valeron . . . it will not bring you peace, Arran. I am sorry.

'I do not seek peace,' you intone, speaking into the blustery gale. 'Only the vengeance that I am owed.'

Aslev turns his head, surveying the broken wasteland. 'How do you plan on reaching your homeland, Drokke?'

'If we cannot go over . . .' Your eyes shift to the dark abyss, scything across the horizon. 'Then we will go under. Will your people walk such dark paths with me?'

Aslev puts a hand to your shoulder, gripping it tight. 'If it will make a song, my Drokke, we would follow you to the very gates of Hel.'

Your eyes remain fixed on the abyss, watching the smoke steaming from its depths. 'I will hold you to that promise, Aslev. For that is where destiny may lead us.'

Congratulations! You have now reached the end of this adventure and have earned yourself the additional title *The Serpent Slayer*! You may now turn to the epilogue.

702

Desnar heads eastwards, bringing you to the banks of a vast frozen lake. To your surprise his steps do not falter, his confident strides taking him straight out onto the sparkling ice. When he senses your hesitation, he turns and gestures for you to follow.

'An ice lake? This is your choice?' You glower at the grinning Skard, trying to shield your eyes from the glare of the sunlight.

Desnar walks to the centre of the lake, then spins his staff in his hands, the antlered head whipping through the air in a white-grey blur. 'Vestek nan Hur,' he spits. The butt of the staff cracks down onto the ice, sending cracks branching out across the lake.

You step onto the ice, almost losing your footing the instant you put weight on its slippery surface. The ice creaks beneath your boot heels as you take another tentative step, and then another. The mantle is thin, threatening to break at any moment.

Desnar moves swiftly, taking advantage of his lighter frame. Before you have even found your balance he is running towards you, his staff spinning above his head. Unable to block the strike in time, you find yourself being knocked to the ground, a follow-up swing sending you sliding forward across the broken ice. Fresh cracks fork outwards as you scrabble desperately to your feet. Desnar throws back his head and laughs – finding evident amusement in your awkward recovery.

You hunker down, trying to spread your weight, conscious that the ice around you is unstable, the cracks continuing to spread with each vibration of movement.

'Winter take you, southlander!' Desnar comes striding in again, staff whirling about his body. Clenching your teeth, you prepare to meet his deadly assault. It is time to fight:

	Speed	Brawn	Armour	Health
Desnar	6	5	4	60

Special abilities

🛡 **The ice vice**: Create a copy of the diagram above. This represents the ice lake. Your hero is represented by the circle on the fifth column. You may wish to use a counter or die to represent your position.

🛡 **Losing ground**: Each time you lose a combat round and take health damage from Desnar, you are forced back one column. If you win a round, you may advance a column (you can't advance further than the starting column, on the far right.)

🛡 **Cracking ice**: At the start of each combat round, the cracking ice advances one column (so at the start of the first round it would move to the 1 column, at the start of the second round the 2 column, and so on.) If your hero ends a combat round by standing on cracked ice, roll a die. If the result is ⚀ or less, the ice gives way and you plunge into the lake. This automatically loses you the combat. If the result is ⚁ or more, you manage to maintain your footing and the combat continues.

Surefooted: Desnar is immune to the cracking ice – he must be defeated in combat for you to win the challenge.

If you manage to defeat Desnar, turn to **714**. If you lose the combat, record your defeat on your hero sheet as normal, then turn to **613**.

703

By midday you are afforded your first glimpse of the North Face, a huge edifice of rock ranging across the entire horizon. Even from a distance it presents a formidable sight – one that only grows more daunting the nearer you get.

The width of the elevation is soon matched by its height, a vast summit of smoothed ice, sculptured by a millennia of northern winters. Its shadow stretches for miles across a tumbledown plain of boulder-strewn scree riddled with dangerous fissures and pitfalls. Progress is slow and wearisome, the chill wind lashing against you as if seeking to drive you away.

It isn't until you reach the higher slopes that the first of the tremors hit. Skoll drops to the ground, urging you both to do the same as the earth roils and shakes, ripping fresh crevasses out of the rock. Above you, great slivers of ice break away from the ridge, spearing down into the snow at its base. The rumbling continues, but as it grows in volume you realise it is no longer the quake that is causing it – a great weight of snow has started to roll forward, gathering speed as it ripples and smokes down the slope.

'Avalanche!' cries Skoll, scrambling to his feet.

'To higher ground!' You grab Anise, pushing her towards a tumble of boulders.

Desperately, the three of you clamber over the rocks, gaining height as quickly as you can. The rumbling gets louder and louder . . .

Suddenly the white flood breaks around you, smashing flecks of snow high into the air. You cling to the rocks, body pressed tightly against them, while the raging current surges past, threatening to rip you free.

Then the rumbling subsides – only to be replaced by the bellowing roar of some nightmarish creature. You pull yourself up onto the shelf of rock, where Skoll and Anise are standing back-to-back, their heads turned to follow the course of the swirling snow-storm. It ripples around the foot of the island then bursts skywards in a brilliant-white geyser, picking up boulders and ice from the ground. For a second the cloud hangs still in the air, then it sweeps down with a furious boom, moulding itself into a pair of colossal fists. It is time to fight:

	Speed	Magic	Armour	Health
Avalanche	9	5	6	40 (*)
Ice elemental (*)	8	4	4	25
Rock elemental (*)	8	4	5	20
Rock elemental (*)	8	4	5	20

Special abilities

🛡 **Break down**: When Avalanche is defeated (reduced to zero *health*), its body splits into three elementals (an ice elemental and two rock elementals). You then have three rounds of combat against these elementals. At the beginning of the fourth round, they re-join to form a new Avalanche (with 40 *health*). You must defeat Avalanche again, before it will release the elementals (with the *health* they have remaining) – giving you three rounds to fight them before another Avalanche is formed. This cycle repeats until you have defeated all three elementals.

🛡 **Enchanted elements**: Avalanche and the three elementals are immune to all passive abilities, including the passive damage from *frost hound* and *vital artery*.

🛡 **Skards' might**: Skoll and Anise add 2 to your damage score for the duration of this combat. (If you are an einherjar, you can add 3 to your damage score instead.)

(Note: When fighting Avalanche, the elementals cannot be harmed. You can only attack and apply damage to the elementals once Avalanche has been defeated each time.)

If you manage to defeat this dread behemoth, turn to 757.

704

You pick apart the folded moth wing and hold it up to the light. As the beams dance across its silken surface, you notice glittering patterns start to form. They intensify, glowing brighter, the silhouette created by their radiance casting a long shadow on the ground. To your surprise, you realise it is a magical glyph.

You hear the snapping of wood behind you. Turning, you watch as another hollow widens outwards in the side of the trunk, revealing a shimmering bridge of rainbow light. It stretches away into the cloudy fog, its shining radiance pushing back the haze to reveal a floating island.

Will you:

Cross the bridge to the island?	**589**
Decide to leave the chamber and continue onwards?	**509**

705

Anise steps around you, shaking her head. 'When you boys have done posturing, we still have a problem. A very big problem.'

You follow her gaze to the dragon.

Skoll retrieves his axes, then strides towards the dragon. 'Old one. We have need of your aid.'

The beast continues to lick at its wounds. Droplets of smoking blood spatter onto the ground.

You glance at Anise. 'This was a mistake,' you hiss through clenched teeth.

Scales creak as the dragon's neck swings toward the warrior. Then its presence fills your mind. A sentience both powerful and ancient.

Blood of the brood. Of Titan and stone. Know I am Nidhogg.

The dragon's words are like echoes, ringing back from some deep, fathomless dark.

Skoll halts before the giant beast, then drops to one knee. 'Great Nidhogg. I am Skoll, Son of Brunil Frostgrieve, Drokke of the Skards.'

You smell of fear. Brave or foolish. I do not know which. The dragon tilts its head, regarding the three of you with its crimson orbs.

'We did what we had to,' you reply quickly, gesturing to Skoll and Anise. 'All of us – we know what it is to suffer at the hands of the witch.'

Anise nods vehemently. 'We have to put an end to this evil!'

Melusine. The dragon's eyes narrow. *My brothers and sisters. All fallen to her power. They were not so strong. Unable to resist.*

The beast's attention has moved to the horn that Skoll is holding, wrested from the giant's helm. You realise the hollowed bone was once a dragon's – the same as those that still adorn Nidhogg's crest.

They were weak. They were not given a choice. Their fate was to fall.

Nidhogg gives a slow shake of his head. Then his eyes drift skywards.

All save one. He went to her willingly. Betrayed us all. Anger rattles from somewhere deep within the dragon's being. *Seethe will feel my wrath.*

'Yes, yes!' Skoll takes a hopeful step closer. 'Dragons. Mortals. No more will suffer – if you will only help us.'

The dragon's neck curls round, his gaze flicking back to the horn. *Let that be my call. A single note will carry to my ears. Then revenge will be taken.*

Nidhogg unfurls his great black wings.

'For revenge.' Skoll raises the horn.

The dragon springs forward, wings beating to give it lift. Skoll drops to his knees as the gigantic beast sweeps overhead, its shadow turning day to night.

Skoll shifts round, meeting your gaze with a look of relief and excitement. 'Put doubts aside,' he calls. 'The dragon lends us his strength. Now we will be unstoppable!'

Congratulations! You have gained the *dragon's horn*. This gives you the power to summon Nidhogg. (Simply make a note of this item on your hero sheet, it doesn't take up backpack space.) The dragon has the following attributes (record these on the second part of your hero sheet. You will be told when to use them.):

	Speed	Stability	Toughness
Nidhogg	9	8	12

Once your hero sheet is updated, return to the map to continue your adventure.

706

Melusine is agile, using her dancer's grace to weave around your attacks, the two of you falling into a deadly performance of blows and counters.

All around you the chamber has started to shake, the ground bucking beneath you, stones showering down from above – yet you remain oblivious to the destruction, focused solely on Melusine, trapped in an instant where thought has become instinct. You almost move as one, gliding through stances – chasse, heel-turn, closed change – spinning and turning, back and forth. A dance at the end of time.

Melusine hums, her music filling your ears. It reminds you of a lullaby Molly often sang to you to calm you after a bad dream. Back and forth. Sidestep. Spin. Turn. Its sonorous notes weave a powerful charm, locking you into a cycle of repeated steps. You start to forget your purpose . . . lost in the dance.

But something flutters against your consciousness. A memory. A face.

The crooked smile of a kitchen girl, who stole your heart.

Movements falter as you struggle to remember. A foot slips, streaking blood across the dark stone. Blood that trails to a girl's body.

Dance, Arran. Dance for me. My last great performance – oh, hear them applaud.

'No!' In an instant you snap out of the dreamlike trance.

Your weapons break rhythm, the cold steel whipping round in a swift arc. The blow passes through Melusine and continues through its stroke. You finish kneeling, the witch's head falling one way and her body the other. Shreds of her veil flutter down around you. The final curtain.

If you are a warrior, turn to 389. If you are a mage, turn to 744. If you are a rogue, turn to 504.

If you wish, you may purchase a locker for 5 gold crowns. You may store any extra backpack items or items of equipment in the locker during Act 1. If you swap equipment (weapons, backpack items etc.) during your adventure, you may put the item you are replacing in your locker by turning to this entry number. This will prevent it from being destroyed. You can only keep a maximum of four objects in your locker:

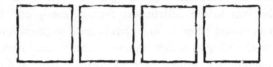

You can re-equip items from your locker whenever you visit this entry number between quests in Act 1.

If you wish to conduct further trade with Jackson, turn to **685**. Otherwise, return to the quest map to continue your adventure.

708

You take a blast to the stomach. The next thing you know, you are falling backwards – the cold ice rushing up to meet you with a thwack! The landing is painful, but not as painful as watching your sled pull away with the other racer in tow.

Without a sled you have been disqualified from the race. Replace the keyword *veteran* with *underdog*. Return to the map to continue your adventure.

709

'Watered-down ale and cockroach stew. Tastes as bad as it sounds, I'm afraid.' The barman nods to one of his servants as they walk past, their tray laden with steaming bowls of gruel. 'Funny really, all the best meat goes to the dogs. Keeps 'em strong and healthy for the races – you should see what those mutts can get through.' He shakes his head with a bemused frown. 'Out here, we learn to make the best of it. Trust me, by the end of winter we'll be serving up old boots for supper.'

If you have the keyword *Bowfinch* on your hero sheet, turn to 173. Otherwise, return to 420.

710

You suspect that the bars of the cell will open if someone places their hand over the print, but you do not wish to suffer more pain by doing so – your hand is already swollen, your body feeling weaker from the toxins that are now surging through it.

If you have *clackers* in your backpack, turn to 663. Otherwise, you have no means of interacting with this magic. You can either attempt to chop through the cell door (turn to 439) or leave and continue your journey (turn to 6).

711

By some miracle you are able to guide your transport through the sizzling barrage of magic, taking only minor damage (You must lower your transport's *stability* by 1.) Before the towers are able to discharge another assault you ramp up the speed, putting as much distance as you can between yourself and the towers' limited range. Turn to 492.

712

Hale is the first to fall. The giant warrior throws himself repeatedly against the might of the shadow fiend, trying to close inside the whirling tentacles and set to work with axe and knife. But the fangs are too quick. He is left stumbling back against a pillar, with two of the shadowy teeth broken and stuck fast in his chest. Their darkness spreads out from the wounds, eating him alive, his pain-racked curses cut short as his clothing and armour drop to the ground, empty.

Ninvuk falls victim to the wolf, dodging one clawed paw only to be hit by another. His body is shredded in two, leaving a crimson mist where he had once been standing.

It quickly becomes apparent that the hunters' weapons are no match for these magical adversaries, their blades and spears leaving no noticeable wounds. Only your own weapons, glowing with a green magic, seem to draw pain from these creatures, sending glittering blood spraying through the mist.

You dismember the shadow, leaving its tentacles roiling uselessly on the ground, then drive your weapons and magic into its black body, exploding it into shreds of darkness. Only Fenrir is left, snarling as the beast swipes its paws at Taulu, who is trying to fend it off with his javelin. He is forced to retreat, stumbling over the body of a fallen Skard in his haste. He drops onto his back, his javelin-point raised in the hope of spearing his over-eager opponent. The wolf sees the danger, twisting at the last moment, its teeth locking around the javelin and tearing it from the Skard's grip. You hurry to Taulu's aid, seeing that he is now defenceless against the wolf's teeth and claws . . .

All of a sudden something rushes into view, bounding over the rubble and corpses. It moves impossibly fast, a huge ball of muscle and fur, slamming into the wolf and sending it rolling onto its side. The wolf finds its feet quickly, skidding through the dirt, teeth snapping. Its howl is met by a thunderous roar.

'Nanuk!'

The bear rears up on his hind limbs, magic sparking around the translucent ghostly image. Then the two beasts charge at each other, biting and clawing, their bodies like gigantic constellations against the darkening skies. Taulu watches in bewildered fascination, a half-smile playing about his lips.

The two warring animals roll through the dirt, locked to each other in a deadly embrace. You see the danger before they do – the edge of the outcropping looming ever nearer. Nanuk tries to break free, its paws batting the wolf away, but Fenrir has its jaws locked around a hind-leg. Together they go tumbling over into nothingness.

'Nanuk!' You race for the edge, but when you look over there is nothing to see save for the green mist, swirling thickly around the jagged rocks below.

You reach out in your mind, feeling for the bear. He is distant, just a flicker of life at the brink of your awareness.

'Saviour.'

You turn to see Taulu staggering towards you, his clawed birthmark glowing in the green-tinged light. Its bright radiance is reflected in his triumphant gaze. 'You have ancestors with you. Spirits.'

You frown, confused. 'You mean the bear – Nanuk?'

'He hunt with you. I see behind eyes. Bear. Strength.' He reaches around to the back of his neck, his hands settling on the tie of his necklace. You realise that the bones hanging there must be the claws and teeth of a bear. 'You lead now. I follow. We go to hall. You free.'

He never finishes the sentence. A green blade punches out of the front of his chest. His eyes look down in shock, blood suddenly blossoming through the leather of his tunic. He gives a rasping sigh as the blade is withdrawn, then he drops to the ground, his necklace of bones rattling by his side.

A ghostly apparition hovers above Taulu's body, a wand-like weapon grasped in long spidery fingers. The body is slim and curved, like a woman's, but the face glaring at you is a monstrous mask, as if some bulbous parasite has taken over. From the pulpy flesh, hooked barbs form a mockery of a crown, their tips ending in glittering fronds that hang down the ghost's back like a wedding veil.

I have waited for you. The words are like fingernails, scratching across the surface of your mind. *My corpse prince. Blood of Leonidas.*

'You know me?' Your hands tighten around your weapons. Nanuk nudges you with his presence, still weak – but the knowledge he is alive fills you with a sudden courage.

I know a good many things. The woman's gown ripples around her narrow frame, its lace edging and woven pearls hinting at a dress that was once regal and lavish, but is now mottled with age, its edges tattered. *I know your heart, fledgling. I feel its emptiness, its cold.*

'You're the witch,' you venture, taking a tentative step backwards. 'The Skards spoke of you.'

The ghost flickers and starts to fade. *I wait for you in the north, fledgling. Come, I have much to show you, much for you to learn . . .*

The ghost reaches out a thin, pale hand, the fingers grasping for you – then the ragged body draws back into the mist, fading quickly out of sight. A few moments later the fog starts to dissipate, bringing the corpse-strewn battlefield back into view.

Searching the ruins, you find one of the following items:

Twilight's end	Rime raiment	Kaiptaq
(main hand: sword)	(chest)	(talisman)
+1 speed +2 brawn	+1 speed +1 armour	+5 health
Ability: piercing	Ability: frost guard	Ability: sixth sense

You also find two *muttok pelts* (simply make a note of these on your hero sheet, they do not take up backpack space) and a roll of greased animal hide. On one side are the words 'White Wolf Trading Company' and a stamp of a wolf's head. You open out the hide, flipping it over to reveal a basic map scrawled in a variety of coloured inks. The map-maker has used symbols rather than labels to mark locations, but the map may prove useful in helping you to navigate these wilds.

As you prepare to leave, your thoughts drift back to Taulu. The bone necklace still lies in the dirt, only inches from his bloodied fingers. He was offering you the trinket, before the witch ended his life. Perhaps it has some meaning, some greater significance than the grisly teeth and claws threaded onto the sinew. You reach down and take the necklace, feeling a power thrum from each of its bones. Nanuk's spirit suddenly grows stronger, filling you once again with his vital strength.

You place the necklace around your neck and tie it in place. Then you fix your eyes northwards, at the cold expanse of ice and rock. (Return to the map to continue your adventure.)

713

Momentarily blinded, you are aware of falling. Your hands reach out to slow your descent, fingers brushing against something fine – like silk. You find yourself bouncing and flipping, your body rolling over a series of soft flexible cords, perhaps a net.

Your vision starts to return. Bright shapes arch past, patterned like spiders' webs. You continue to fall, slipping between the criss-crossing bands, bouncing off others strong as rope – twisting and spinning.

Your dizzying descent makes it difficult to discern your surroundings. There is blackness, flashes of light, distant stars. From somewhere below comes a grinding clatter; some sort of machinery. You reach out again, hands snapping around one of the cords. It feels cold to the touch, burning like ice. Gritting your teeth, you try and ignore the pain, swinging your feet to catch another thread for balance.

You hang in the web, rocking sickeningly back-and-forth, your head turning in every direction to try and absorb what your eyes are telling you.

This is a web. A giant web of sparkling flex, extending all around you. The size is incomprehensible – there seems no end to it, the strands reaching out into the void of twinkling stars.

The sound of the machinery continues to beat beneath you. Looking down, you notice a confusion of wheels spinning in a fast-moving blur, whilst all around them pointed spindles extend like the minarets of a castle, catching the threads of silvery flax and winding them into glowing reels.

There is no ground to speak of – between the spokes of the wheels you see only more glittering weave, dropping away to a vertiginous darkness.

You hang like a fly, trapped in a web.

The cord you are holding starts to shake, as if disturbed by a weight. You notice other nearby threads vibrating, leaving an after-image of light shimmering against the darkness. With difficulty, you push yourself onto an adjoining section of the weave, turning your head to study the surrounding area. It is then that you see the woman clambering across the web, her legs bowed to the side like a spider, two long grey-skinned toes clutching the narrow threads with ease.

She moves gracefully, her thin body forming bony ridges beneath her tattered robes. The face is human, a woman of indeterminable age, with grey leathery skin and a bald scalp raked with bleeding abrasions.

'Where am I?' you ask, your voice echoing back to you from a great distance.

The woman stops, her elongated fingers spread across the single cord that balances her.

'You're the weaver,' you gasp. 'The one Skoll spoke of.'

The woman's almond-shaped eyes regard you curiously. When she speaks the words are heard in your head, but her ashen lips remain tightly closed.

Mistaken, yes. But some truth. Gabriel was the weaver. I am the spinner. The spinner.

The woman scuttles closer, passing effortlessly from one thread to the next. She stops, eyes staring once again. A hand scratches at her baldness, the nails adding fresh cuts and opening up old wounds.

I don't like the sound. Do you hear it? The discord. The discord. Her head twitches from side to side as she continues to scratch distractedly, like a cat trying to rid itself of a flea.

'What is this place?' You look down at the spinning wheels, clattering endlessly as they add fresh thread to the distaff spindles. 'Is this part of a dream?'

Not a dream. A demon has you. Strong and old and wise. I protect you here. Only a short time. A short time.

The woman's long toes bunch around the thread as she swings herself down, grabbing hold of a thread below her. She points to the spinning wheels. *I am life. I give life. Three of us. The fates. We were spun and nine norns with us. Our tasks were known. To make. To protect. Nine worlds our charge. And only one now remains.*

Will you:

Ask about the fates?	478
Ask about the norns?	743
Ask about the weave?	669
Ask about the nine worlds?	735
Ask about the shield, Fimbulwinter?	611

714

Your magic lifts the Skard off his feet, sending him spinning back onto the ice. As he crashes down the ice splinters beneath him, his body slipping through the widening hole into the chill waters beneath.

Dropping onto all fours, you scramble over to the hole. 'Desnar!' The water laps at the jagged edge of the opening, but there is no sign of the Skard. Then you hear a pounding against the ice. You see a shape flailing beneath the surface – a glimpse of a face pressed against its underside, bubbles streaming from an open mouth.

You draw back your hand, summoning Nanuk's spirit into your body. As bright claws flicker into being you drive them into the ice, cutting through the thin mantle. A head bursts up through the newly-made hole, gasping for breath. You reach down and grab the Skard's shoulders, helping to pull him back onto the ice. His staff is still gripped tightly in his right hand, its antlered headpiece dripping with frost.

You quickly find your feet, snatching up your discarded weapons. The Skard makes no move to attack, still coughing and spitting water onto the ice.

'Yield!' You hold a weapon to his throat, the tip breaking flesh and drawing blood.

The Skard nods quickly, offering up his staff. 'Take, southlander. Ancestors deny me – I am beaten.'

Congratulations, you have bested Desnar in the challenge of the fighter. If you wish, you may now equip the following item:

Winter prime
(main hand: staff)
+1 speed +2 brawn +2 magic
Ability: slam, silver frost

Record the word *triumph* on your hero sheet, then turn to 578.

715

Flames and smoke start to obscure your vision. Frantically you struggle to maintain your speed, seeking to stay ahead of the dragon's breath. The circle of daylight grows larger, its bright light competing with the flames and smoke – then you are finally free of the tunnel, hurtling away from the island as fast you can. Behind you an entire section of the hive explodes outwards in a fiery tumult, raining fragments of charred rock across the gulf. Thankfully the deadly shower falls short of reaching you, your speedy manoeuvre having carried you to safety. Turn to 729.

716

The spiralling pathway grows tighter and tighter as it twists around the mountain's peak. None of the other racers have made it through the rock fall and for a moment you wonder if you might be the last man standing – but then you catch a shower of sparks spewing along the trail ahead. There is another sled, but one of its runners has been damaged and is now dragging along the ground. Your dog-team are tired, struggling to make it up the steep and slippery slopes, but you urge them to make a final effort, knowing that the finish line can't be far away.

The path becomes even narrower, but you risk swerving alongside your opponent, trying to ignore the vertiginous drop to your left. To your surprise you discover your fellow racer is the girl with the blue-dyed hair. As you start to pass she makes a desperate leap for your sled, drawing a pair of daggers from her belt as she lands.

'Only one winner,' she cries over the roar of the wind. 'It's the first racer across the line, not their sled! And I'm taking this one!'

The girl goes to kick you, but you catch her boot, throwing her backwards. She makes a futile swipe with her daggers, but a lurch of the sled sends her reeling sideways. By some miracle, the racer manages to recover, coming at you again with only one thing on her mind – victory. It is time to fight:

	Speed	Brawn	Armour	Health
Blue Angel	7	4	3	70

Special abilities

💧 **Eyes on the prize**: You cannot use special abilities in this combat.

💧 **Competitive spirit**: At the end of each combat round you must take 2 damage, ignoring *armour*, from the girl's slashing daggers.

If you manage to beat this deadly racer, turn to 700. If you are defeated, remember to record the defeat on your hero sheet, then turn to 378.

717

Boss monster: Jormungdar the World Eater

It starts with a distant echo. A thrumming persistent beat. Then it rises, becoming louder, rippling across the chamber. You look around wildly, wondering if the dread demon has somehow come alive, but its pulpy flesh remains blackened with frost, unmoving – its tentacles reduced to a fine white ash, snaking across the cracked rock.

You watch the dust vibrate, shifting in patterns as each beat causes the ground to shudder. Louder and louder. Until there is a deafening crack of thunder. Your instinct is to look up, fearing the sky has been ripped asunder – but it is the ground that is now moving, throwing you to your knees, the stone crumbling. Falling away.

For a horrifying moment, it is as if the world has become undone. The walls blur, swaying away from you at an impossible angle. The floor rises, the ceiling finally breaking open like a cracked egg to blind you with shards of painful light.

And the drumming crashes around you. So deafening it has now become a single assault of white noise, like a furious tide swallowing you up in its rapids.

You are sinking, the stone fragments fracturing to dust, leaving you spiralling into a void. The ground has gone – and you are freefalling. Darkness and light reel past, merging into a grey madness. Then twin suns blossom into being, blazing towards you.

Eyes. Set either side of a giant reptilian face.

It streaks past. You hit something, flipping over, dimly aware of a forest of deadly-sharp spines, then scales – luminous blue and flecked with silver – rushing beneath you at impossible speed. Disorientated, you find yourself sliding and tumbling over the fast-moving surface. You reach out, claws spreading from your hands – trying to find purchase.

Sparks fly across iron-hard scales, your claws leaving trails of flickering brightness. You are falling further and further back, until a curved spine passes within reach. Desperately, you stretch out towards it – your magic transforming your claws into ghostly tentacles. They coil around the spine, finally halting your haphazard descent.

You pull yourself up, clinging to the spine like a drowning sailor as you are dragged and jolted through the whirling dust. The creature continues to hurtle forward at speed, taking you higher and higher, until the sky breaks above you: a vast dome of cobalt blue, peppered with purple cloud. Almost beautiful, serene. Twisting your head, you see the cracked wasteland far below, the ruined city little more than a few buildings and towers hugging the edge of a great abyss.

And then there is the beast itself, a vast serpentine creation streaming out of the darkness, its miles of scales and ragged spines sparkling in the dawn light. Its size is almost impossible to comprehend, each dizzying second revealing more of its gargantuan form.

If you have the title *The Mourner*, turn to 482. Otherwise, turn to 425.

718

The monk opens out his meaty fist, showing you his five stones. This forces you to reveal your own. 'A Queen's Wave, double crowned,' he declares with a toadish smile. 'The One God shines on me. I win!'

Remove the word *scripture* from your hero sheet, then turn to 697.

719

Raising your hands you trace the circular patterns with your fingers, connecting the lines and whorls with the magic that now flows through you. The runes start to flicker and then glow, illuminating a trail to the centre circle, where white-blue energies crackle above the podium. For a brief moment you glimpse some creature trapped within the bright maelstrom – a thin and spindly humanoid, its pale limbs coated in jagged icicles – then it is gone. The energy sparks out and the runes dim.

When you walk over to the podium you discover that the frost magic is now trapped inside the orb, filling it with a powerful magic. (Congratulations! You have now created a *frost orb*. If you wish to take this, simply make a note of it on your hero sheet, it does not take up backpack space.) Turn to **684**.

720

Maune joins you at the edge of the fire pit. Despite a few burns across his arms and face, the prince's magic does not appear to have done any lasting harm; his body still shines bright with holy scripture. You notice the fluttering green flames draw away from him, as if repelled by his light.

Skoll holds the three fragments of the shield. His mouth works nervously as he holds them over the flames. A shake of his head. He steps back, dropping his arms to his sides.

'He was right. The fire is wrong. Corrupted.'

You look around at the runes encircling the dais. They remain dark.

Then you notice something else . . .

Sculptured lines stretch away from the pit's edge, forming a bigger design that reaches as far as the circle of columns. You turn, trying to piece together the image – two crescents, linked by a crossed bar.

'Balance,' you nod, remembering the carving in the lower caves.

Skoll glances sideways, his brow furrowed. 'Eh?'

You study the green flames, billowing out of the pit. 'We have to restore balance to the forge. Cleanse the flames.'

Anise is sitting at the foot of one of the statues, tilting the last of the water from a canteen into her mouth. She lowers it, swallowing, then looks at you darkly. 'We wasted our time, didn't we? All this . . . for nothing.'

Skoll shifts round, his eyes coming to rest on the paladin. 'What about you?'

Maune tightens his mouth. 'This is evil magic. There is nothing I can do.'

Skoll continues to glare at the paladin. It takes a moment for you to understand the true intent of his question. Maune's magic glows bright as a beacon. His whole body is blessed by the holy light, a living library's worth of scripture carved into his flesh. His heat repels you, as it does the flames.

A sacrifice will have to be made, boy. Only you will be able to choose, life or death.

Maune glares at the Skard suspiciously, then meets your gaze. 'I cannot cleanse the flames. Short of throwing myself in . . .'

A silent pause.

His hand goes to his sword. 'No!'

'We have to remake the shield.' You take a step closer.

Maune regards you with contempt. 'You'd put your faith in three hunks of ancient metal? Is that what a life is worth?'

You lower your eyes. 'You are right, this is madness. We will have to find another way.'

Skoll rounds on you. 'We cannot face the witch, not without the shield! She is a demon, her very gaze would freeze you where you stand – I have seen it. I have lost brothers, good men, to her evil!' He shakes the broken shards at you. 'Don't be weak. We need the Titans' magic!'

You bristle at his words.

Maune is backing away from the dais. 'Fear is weakness. We can fight this witch together – isn't that why I was sent here? My God sent me.'

Skoll's head snaps round, the veins on his throat bulging. 'Winter's teeth! To die, you fool – to throw yourself into the flames!'

Maune draws his sword. 'Who are you to decide my fate? You are not my king, savage.'

'No,' spits the Skard. 'But he bloody is.' He stabs a finger at you.

Will you:

Sacrifice the paladin to the fire?	416
Save the paladin and let him join you?	496

721

Sura takes you by the arm and leads you away from the crowd. 'I have something to ask of you, southlander.'

You stand together at the edge of the camp, the snow spinning on the gusting eddies. The storm has engulfed everything, leaving no sense of sky or land. It is as if the world has been erased, and in its absence there is only a cold grey nothingness.

'What troubles you – is this day not one for celebration?'

The woman looks even frailer than you remember – little more than a jumble of knotted bones, her weathered face made even smaller by the thick swaddling of furs around her shoulders.

'My time is passing,' she states. Her bright eyes stray to an unseen horizon. 'My apprentice, Maya, has returned from Vindsvall. She will take over when I am gone. I had hoped there would be news from the asynjur. But Maya's tale was the same as I've heard sung winter after winter. Skoll, our Drokke – the leader of all Skards – is still lost to us. The asynjur are not strong enough – they are no closer to freeing his spirit, no closer to bringing him back.'

There is silence.

'You want me to go to Vindsvall?'

Sura looks back at you. 'Taulu left the tribe to find help. He was even willing to meet with our enemies, the southlanders behind the walls of stone. We cannot hope to survive. The witch – her magic will destroy everything. We have to stand against her or all will be lost.'

You flinch beneath her hard stare. 'What can I possibly do? I'm an outsider. Your people are strong – there's no reason why the tribes can't come together. Unite. You have warriors, hunters . . .'

Sura snorts. 'Our chieftains bicker. They have not the sense to listen to counsel. They are equals and would lose face to let another of their number lead. Only a Drokke can bring the Ska-inuin together. Only Skoll.'

'And you're asking *me* to rescue your leader?'

'He sought aid, like Taulu.' The woman speaks softly, but her words carry above the wailing of the gale. 'His journey was one of spirit, to the Norr. He sought the fates – the keepers of our destiny. Only they would know how to defeat the witch.'

Sura's face tightens with an inner pain, the sunken hollows painting a ghoulish visage. 'He never returned to us. The asynjur believe the witch holds him prisoner – torturing his spirit, keeping him from ever returning to his body. But you . . . you have the power of a shaman; a dream-walker. Nanuk chose you for a reason. Please, do right by our ancestors. The witch must be stopped, or your lands will suffer her wrath as surely as our own.'

'You believe I can do this?' You speak with a quiet pride, touched by the woman's belief in your abilities.

'If you can't, then no one can.' Sura puts a hand to your back, turning you to face the might of the storm. 'Winter is your ally, boy; you are its vengeance and its fury. Now go – to Vindsvall, the golden halls of our Drokke, and bring him back to us.'

'But what of your tribe – will they be safe?' You look round, but the woman has gone. You are alone, surrounded by the raging blizzard, its ice driving hard into your numbed skin. Tugging down your hood, you take a moment to calm yourself – to reach for Nanuk, finding comfort in his familiar presence, his strength.

I am winter. I am its vengeance and its fury.

With a bitter smile, you stride into the storm. (Return to the quest map to continue your adventure.)

722

You straddle the beast's brow, feet splayed to either side as the serpent-like head bucks and twists beneath you. 'Now!' Skoll screams into the wind, his axe still chopping his way through the deadly spines.

You raise your weapons then, with a deft spin, you reverse them – plunging their blades between the ridges of bone. You push down hard, powering your strike with the last of your magic.

Deeper they go.

The beast swings back its head, hissing and screeching in pain. The thrashing body whips through the ranks of Skards. You hear screams and shouts, the cries of the dying. Somehow you manage to stay with the bucking beast, hands frozen tight to your weapons.

There is no blood. No fountaining of ichor. Instead there is a blackening, like some dark bruise, which quickly starts to spread, turning flesh to ice. The head rears back, almost throwing you into the air. Another piercing scream fills the heavens with thunder.

You twist your weapons. Grinding. Back and forth. Your own screams of exertion mingling with the serpent's pain.

Then it is falling, fast.

Below you Skards are running, seeking to escape the widening shadow. Some make it – many don't. The beast crashes down onto the wasteland. You are thrown into the air, spinning through the dust. Scales and broken spines hurtle past you, a sled spirals overhead, its tangled lines dragging the broken bodies of a wolf pack. Everything becomes a surreal, dream-like haze – flying, falling . . .

You hit the ground, the dust washing over you to break against an outcropping of rock. Another body tumbles next to you with a cry. You feel something splatter across your armour. Blood.

You rush to the Skard's side, his body twisted – two immense broken spines speared through his chest. He coughs and chokes, fingers digging into the dusty earth as he writhes in pain.

'Skoll . . .' You crawl to his side, eyes drawn to the terrible wounds. The warrior's eyes are already glazing over. He struggles to speak, bloody phlegm bubbling from his mouth.

Somehow he finds strength to lift his arm. He grabs your shoulder, pulling you close.

'A song . . .' he grunts, then manages a wheezy laughter. 'Make sure they sing a bloody song of this.'

You nod your head, unable to speak.

'Take it.'

You frown, uncertain what he means. Your eyes search the ground, looking for his axe – wondering if he seeks an end to his suffering.

'The crown,' he gasps, eyes starting to close.

You look upon the stone-grey helm that still rests atop his brow, its rim masterfully worked into a circle of runed spines. The Drokke's crown.

'I cannot.' You draw back, aware now of the shapes emerging from the settling dust. Skards. They slowly start to surround you, heads bowed. You quickly scan their faces, realising that these warriors must represent the different tribes of the north. Some are clad in armour fashioned from bone, others simply wear fur and animal hide, their skin daubed in brightly-coloured paints. You search for those who may be familiar to you – and your eyes come to rest on Aslev, the einherjar. He has removed his helm, his snow-white locks braided and banded with gold. And next to him, Desnar of the bear tribe. His piercing blue-eyes meet your own, bright with a hunter's cunning.

Skoll gives a groan. 'I was wrong about you,' he whispers weakly. 'You will always be of the north. You are a Ska-inuin.' He grunts, trying to lift his arms. With effort, he manages to put a hand to his crown. 'Will you take this bloody thing off me!'

You reach forward, helping him to slide the helm free. 'Good . . .' His hand drops to his side, leaving you holding the crown.

'You are Drokke,' he gasps. 'And you will lead my . . .' A spasm of pain steals his words, forcing him to kick and squirm in the dirt. 'Your people . . .' he grins through bloody teeth.

Then his eyes lift, staring past your shoulder. They mirror the great winter sky as he breathes his last.

A crunch of dirt. Aslev moves to stand over you, Desnar at his side. The einherjar is holding Skoll's warhammer, the huge rune-forged weapon known as Surtnost.

You realise you still are clutching the crown. Your eyes lift to Aslev, and for the briefest of moments you see surprise pull at his features. When you left Vindsvall you had been a man – at least something of flesh and bone. Now you are a ghost, a spectre – bound within a prison of frost-coated armour.

You offer him the crown, but he shakes his head.

'I heard the Drokke speak. You have been chosen.' He nods to the crown.

You rise to your feet, aware of the crowd watching you – and more joining them, a sea of heads, a gathering of people. Your people. You climb the side of the outcropping, stepping over the jumble of boulders until you are at its summit, looking out across the assembled Skards.

There are many tribes, standing shoulder to shoulder. Men and women from the four corners of the north, reunited because of a shared vow. A single purpose.

To serve the Drokke.

You place the crown upon your head.

Aslev is the first to kneel, followed by the others around him. The movement ripples outwards, as hundreds and hundreds of Skards bow their heads to their new leader. Only one remains standing. Desnar. The wind whips at his bear cloak, his hands gripped tightly around his spear. Ribbons dance in his hair, their bone charms rattling.

You meet his gaze, sensing the heat of his challenge.

He studies you, tongue working thoughtfully around his mouth. Then he breaks a smile.

'Ancestors with you.' He offers you a grudging nod before dropping to one knee, his dark hair falling across his narrow face. 'My Drokke.'

If you have the title *The Mourner*, turn to 632. Otherwise, turn to 701.

723

You realise you will need to convince Jackson to leave his post. 'Tell me, what hides have you got left – any mammoth? I'll buy them off you for a good price.' You fold your arms, awaiting an answer.

'I don't sell hides, I buy,' mutters Jackson incredulously. 'You lost your mind?'

'Actually, no. Winter's here and you won't be seeing another trading ship for a while, so the fur isn't earning you anything right now, is it? How about you check out back and see what you got. I'll pay double.'

You hear a grumbling curse, then notice the gun muzzles go slack as footsteps go clanging away over an iron floor. When you are sure he is no longer at his post, you take the seal blubber from your pack (remember to remove this item from your hero sheet) and stuff the greasy mixture into the two barrels, packing it in tight. When you have finished, you step back across the line and draw your weapons.

The guns jump to attention as an eye reappears at the peep hole. 'Got no mammoth, but how about a . . .' He stops. 'What you doing? Put those away at once.' He rattles his guns at you. 'No weapons, didn't you read the sign outside?'

'What sign?'

'Darn Skards must have taken it – or wind blown it down. No matter, put your weapons away or I'll blow you back out into the snow. You hear me?'

You take a step forward.

There is a noisy intake of breath followed by a blustery outpouring of anger. 'Get back I tell you! Back, back! No one crosses the line!'

'I just did . . .'

There is a click as triggers are pulled. Then there is an explosion, loud and powerful enough to send you flying backwards across the room. At first you fear you've been shot and your plan has backfired, but then you see the smoke and flames billowing from behind one of the service hatches. It has been blown open in the blast. You hear glass shattering and another explosion. Clearly there was something highly flammable and volatile in the storeroom.

Will you:

Beat a hasty retreat?	604
Risk entering the blazing storeroom?	633

724

'Cellar's outta bounds to everyone except staff,' bellows the guard, his sneer revealing gold and silver teeth. 'I knows you ain't staff, so don't even try it. Already had one fool sneak in and drink half the stock dry.'

'I was sent here,' you lie, glancing back across the room. 'I'm a footman on an errand – and it wouldn't do to disappoint my superiors.'

'Yeah?' The guard suddenly looks uncertain. 'Well, can't let you take stuff for free. I'd get it in the neck for that. Herta behind the bar will give me a right tongue lashing.'

Will you:

Ask to put it on Lord Eaton's tab?	438
Ask to put it on Baron Fromark's tab?	265
Ask to put it on Lady Hawkers' tab?	605

725

With the spectral guardian defeated, you may now help yourself to one of the following rewards:

Monstrous beast	Tekk's trumpet	Plainstrider
(talisman)	(left hand: horn)	(ring)
+1 speed +5 health	+2 speed +2 brawn	+1 armour
Ability: bleed	Ability: stampede	Ability: haste

When you have updated your hero sheet, turn to 339.

726

The tunnel you are following joins a much wider passageway cutting through the stark black rock. As you advance the walls fan outwards, the ceiling lifting higher until you find yourself walking along an immense vaulted hall. Thick beams of ice are now visible in the rock – trickling water into glittering mirror-like pools that pockmark the paved floor.

'The glacier is melting.' You glance at Caul, wondering if he will agree or refute your statement.

He merely shrugs his shoulders. 'The Skards say that when the ice of the north vanishes, the great serpent will rise from the underworld. Its coils will rip the land in two, its poison will turn the oceans to blood. It will be the end of all things.'

'Of course,' you remark wryly. 'And here was me, worried about wet boots.'

You pass along a row of finely-carved statues, each set on an angular pedestal jutting from the walls of the chamber. They look like Dwarves, resplendent in rune-carved armour – several have long braided beards, sparkling with gemstones. There are no marks or script on the pedestals to denote who they might have been – you wonder if they are merely decorative, or were put here to venerate ancient kings or heroes.

It isn't until you have passed the first set of statues that you hear the flaking rustle of crumbling stone, followed by a series of sharp echoing cracks. When you look back, your eyes widen in horror as you see several of the dwarves coming to life, ripping free of their pedestals.

'More blasted traps!' Caul scuttles away from the nearest statue as it jumps down from its pedestal, the ground cracking and splintering beneath its immense feet.

Another three statues are also moving, a sudden fiery light blossoming from the jewels sunk into their eyes. You sense that these mighty stone guardians are far too powerful to defeat. You glance at Caul, who reads your expression – then you both turn and run.

The world seems to reel and shake as the statues pursue you down the hall, their heavy limbs pounding against the stone. Thankfully their movements are slow and ungainly. Within minutes they are lost to sight as the hall turns a corner and then another, forming a snaking pathway. More pedestals blur past you – but instead of statues they are supporting stone columns topped with circular rings. Some appear to have glass orbs resting inside. Others are empty.

'Look – just ahead!' Caul points with his spear, picking up the pace.

The light from your weapons falls on a set of stairs leading up to a stone balcony. Behind it is an immense wall of ice, bulging into the hall. A runic door has been carved into the glacier's surface, but there seems no way of opening it or passing through.

You hurry up the stairs, looking desperately for an alternate means of escape. Caul immediately moves to the balcony rail, where a stone plinth overlooks the hall below.

'Over here!'

You hurry to join him, surprised to discover that the stone has a number of runes engraved onto its surface. They follow a snaking pattern, which mirrors the winding pathway you have followed through the hall.

'What's it do?' asks Caul. 'Will it get us through that?' He glances back towards the wall of ice.

'No, I think these are defences.' You touch one of the runes, pouring your magic into its grooves and channels. A second later, the rune-shape flickers and then bursts into a bright crimson glow – kindling further lights along the hall as a selection of the stone rings pulse with magic. Only those that contain orbs have lit up. The others have remained dark and lifeless.

You spot several glass spheres lying next to the plinth, each one radiating a different coloured glow. 'The orbs . . . Perhaps we can use them to defeat the guardians.'

Caul pulls a confused frown. 'I'll leave that up to you. I'll work on the door.' He reaches inside his furs, producing a dagger of black stone. Dwarven runes are etched along its length, sparkling with silver light. 'A Skard gave it to me. They call them Atataq – the wonder fire.' He places his thumb and forefinger over the runes, producing a spark and then a flame from its tip. 'Do what you can to hold off those guardians.' The trapper dashes over to the ice wall and begins cutting into the frozen door with the heated stone of his dagger.

You turn back to the rune-covered console, trying to fathom its purpose and how you can use its power against the advancing statues. Turn to 600.

727

Ignoring Ratatosk's fervent protests, you draw your weapons across his throat, ending his life. You may now help yourself to one of the following rewards:

Crimson vair	Tawny paws	Shadow tail
(feet)	(gloves)	(left hand: club)
+1 speed +1 brawn	+1 speed +1 armour	+2 speed +2 brawn
Ability: critical strike	Ability: agility	Ability: rake

When you have updated your hero sheet, turn to 616.

728

'Found these on some bodies, Skards by my guess.' He shifts his gaze nervously to Skoll, who is hovering by the entrance. 'There's Dwarf work in the horn and totem, real nice rune crafting. The sword, though, that's something else. Almost tempted to keep it.' He snorts, scratching at his bristly chin. 'Nah, take it. Less weight, more speed.'

You may purchase any of the following for 200 gold crowns:

Vibrato	**Bone clef**	**Siren's maxim**
(left hand: glass sword)	(left hand: totem)	(left hand: horn)
+2 speed +4 brawn	+2 speed +4 magic	+2 speed +3 brawn
Ability: sweet spot	Ability: weaver	Ability: windblast, fear
(requirement: rogue)	(requirement: mage)	(requirement: warrior)

You may now purchase first aid supplies (turn to 639), view Hal's treasures (turn to 674), trade your own items (turn to 95) or leave and return to the quest map.

729

The floating mountain is only a few miles ahead – but your pursuers are much closer, and gaining fast. Caught out in the open, you watch as the two decaying dragons sweep past in a flurry of wings. The largest of the two opens their jaws, belching a cloud of noxious green gas into the air. The other hisses the words of a spell, surrounding you in a black miasma of magic – a cursed aura that saps at your strength, leeching away at your precious reserves of magic. With no chance of outrunning these dogged foes, you have no alternative but to fight:

	Speed	Magic	Armour	Health
Tiamort	12	7	5	60
Luicris	12	6	6	70

Special abilities

♥ **Aura of enfeeblement**: While Tiamort is alive, you cannot use speed abilities.

♥ **Choking cloud**: You must lose 2 *health* at the end of the first combat round. This damage increases by 1 each round up to a maximum of 5. Once Luicris is defeated the cloud decreases in damage by 1 in each subsequent round, until it reaches zero.

♥ **Rough ride**: If you have the keyword *frazzled* or *rocked* on your hero sheet, you may lower both opponents' starting *health* by 10.

♥ **Fire at will**: You may use your *nail gun* or *dragon fire* ability in this combat. (Note: If your transport's *stability* has been reduced to zero, you can no longer use its associated ability.)

If you manage to defeat the two zombie dragons, turn to 651.

730

'Go on then, big shot, let's see what you got. Remember, I got a good eye for a good hide, so don't be expecting winter prices for any summer skins. You can keep those for yer long-johns.'

The trading post will purchase the following items from you:

Item:	Payment (in gold crowns):
Seal blubber	15
White fox pelt	30
Muttok pelt	50
Yeti pelt	70
Sasquatch pelt	120
Mammoth pelt	160

Remember to remove any sold items from your hero sheet. (If you have the *trapper* career you can increase the value of each pelt by 5 gold.) When you have updated your hero sheet, return to 685 to ask another question or return to the quest map to continue your adventure.

731

You edge further into the shadows, pulling down your hood to conceal your face. The last thing you wanted was to draw attention to yourself, but now you feel eyes upon you – curious and questioning.

Talia notes your nervousness with a smile. 'Relax dear, I don't bite.' The bard tosses her hat onto your seat, then takes the chair opposite. 'You're new around here, aren't you?'

Your silence draws an amused smirk from the woman. 'Silent type, huh? Well, I'm Talia – a ray of sunshine around this bleak forsaken dirt pile. What about you, handsome?' She takes a delicate sip of her ale, her eyes focused intently on the shadows beneath your hood.

Her accent is cultured, the jewellery sparkling on her fingers and in her ears calling to mind the high-born women from court. 'You draw a lot of attention,' you hiss, glancing over her shoulder.

'Yes, I do have that effect. And around here, it's not necessarily a bad thing. Distraction can work wonders, especially on these simpletons.' She arches an eyebrow. 'Do I distract you, handsome?'

You pull back your hood.

Talia leans back in her seat. 'Well, lookee there – hmm, you do have a certain cadaverous charm, I'll give you that.'

'What do you want?' You tug your hood down as the barman walks over and places a tankard of watery ale in front of you. He glances at Talia thoughtfully, then returns to the bar.

'I'm on a mission,' the woman says, once he is out of earshot. 'A dangerous one.' She drops her voice, edging closer to the table. 'And you look like the kind of man I could use right now.' She lifts her chin, eyes peering over at your weapons and armour. 'Yes, you're positively perfect.'

Will you:

Agree to help? (This begins a red quest)	585
Politely refuse?	687

732

A smooth stone corridor angles downwards for several hundred metres before levelling off into a wider corridor lined with carved heads. They appear reptilian, like the Nisse you fought at Bitter Keep, with blue fire flickering in the hollows of their eyes. Their light bathes the black-stone passage with a cold luminosity, picking out a series of glittering runes running across the floor and ceiling.

Caul stops you before you take a step. 'It's a trap,' he whispers. He takes one of his knives and throws it down the corridor. As the spinning blade passes each of the drake heads fire gouts from their nostrils, filling the passage with billowing flame. The knife brightens with the heat, leaving a smoking trail as it arcs down the corridor to finally rattle down onto the rune-covered floor. As it comes to rest the surrounding glyphs immediately ignite, triggering a flurry of lightning bolts. The knife is thrown back into the air, where the flames continue to bake it in a fierce heat.

A few moments later and the corridor is silent, the fire having receded back into the carved heads. You are left staring wide-eyed at the melted pool of metal on the ground – all that remains of Caul's knife.

The trapper shifts nervously beside you. 'Still want to risk it?'

Will you:

Retrace your steps and find an alternate route?	672
Run the gauntlet of the 'corridor of doom'?	526

733

For a while, the only sound is your flapping footfalls as you follow the long, winding passageways. They slope ever upwards, taking you higher and higher into the mountain. Occasionally the walls recede, leaving you to stumble out into vast empty spaces. The paladin's glowing body and Skoll's torchlight are the only flickers of life amidst the encroaching gloom; even your heightened senses struggle to penetrate the furthest reaches of the halls. There is a sense of age here – and of ancient power. Statues and carvings leer from the dark like ghostly apparitions, depicting giants and dwarves and sometimes humans. The ground underfoot becomes grooved and uneven, suggesting some sculptured design marked into the stone – but you do not pause to investigate. Instead, you follow the bobbing lights of your companions, moving ever onwards, ever upwards . . .

You feel the rush of night air, cold against your skin. Another twist of the passageway brings you to a chamber flooded with light, its ceiling open to the sky. Columns of stone curve around its edge, forming a circle. Nine columns, each carved with a figure facing inwards, their hands clasping a glowing orb.

At their centre, a stepped dais of rune-carved stone encircles a bonfire of green flame which gutters and dances in the wind, streaking long ribbons across the twilit skies.

Skoll and the paladin have paused at the edge of the columned circle. A man stands on the steps of the dais, his body in silhouette against the bright green flames. It isn't until you join your companions that you are able to make out more of his features, your sharp vision parting the veil of shadow.

His body is encased in plates of dark iron, enamelled with bands of ivory. The shoulder-guards bristle with a cruel array of spikes, framing a fanged helm designed to resemble a snarling wolf.

He has a hand raised to his eye-line, studying the golden feather he is rolling between his fingertips.

'It is a wondrous thing, the apollo eagle.' His voice is dry and sharp, like the crackling of leaves. 'Such a beautiful creature, exquisite. My father had an eyrie at the castle; he found much pleasure in showing off his fine eagles. He would feed the prisoners to them. And make us watch.' He releases the feather, letting the gusts of wind carry it away. 'I was four when I attended my first feeding. I still hear the woman's screams.'

Maune draws his sword, muttering something beneath his breath. He is tensed and looks about to charge, but something holds him back – perhaps the sudden turn of the man's head, finally revealing the face beneath the helm. It might have been human once – a handsome face, piqued cheeks and an aquiline nose, suggesting someone of noble birth and bearing. Before the scarring and the ruination; before the bulbous tumour had taken hold, snaking out of a blackened eye-socket to wrap beneath his chin. The fleshy appendage appears to extend between his plates of armour, ending in a crab-like claw where the warrior's left hand would have been.

His single yellow eye glitters back at you. Cunning like his wolf's.

You leave Anise by the columns, then push past your companions to get a better glimpse of the face. The horror written on those grim features is almost captivating, a mirror of your own.

'What are you, that you would oppose us?' Your voice sounds muffled, as if the words are being fed into a great void. When the man answers, it is shrill and cutting in comparison to your own.

'You would not know me, Arran, but we are brothers of a sort. We share much.'

'Spare me the riddles,' you growl, eyes narrowing. 'I do not know you.'

'My mother was a Mordland princess, the youngest and most beautiful of the emperor's children. After the first shadow war, Valeron and Mordland sought unity. My mother was married to one of your kings, a marriage of convenience – a symbol of that unity. My mother was not given a choice. She had a duty.'

You frown, your mind picking through your knowledge of royal family trees. The first shadow war was a thousand years ago, the brief treaty with Mordland a hundred years later. That would mean . . . 'Your mother was Queen Lin?'

The man nods.

A sudden realisation forces your eyes to snap wide. Queen Lin was a figure of hate around the courts of Valeron; a woman who was imprisoned for witchcraft, who murdered her husband in cold blood. A woman forever branded 'The Witch Queen . . .'

The man attempts a smile, but the scarring turns it into something more grotesque. 'Go on.'

You continue to recollect what you remember from the dusty tomes in the palace library. 'She was imprisoned, with her only son. The heir. But they were never heard of again – there was no public execution.' You shake your head in bewilderment. 'You cannot be him. It's impossible.'

The man turns and starts to pace, his black cloak hardly seeming to stir around his armoured frame. 'He was a cruel man, my father. Twisted. Evil. My mother acted out of self defence.' His hand moves to his ruined eye for a moment. 'Imprisoned, you say.' He makes a sound between a snort and a chuckle. 'They put us in the Crucible, with the murderers and the lunatics. Those not even worth a hangman's noose.' He turns on his heel, pacing again.

Skoll shifts next to you, his tongue working inside his mouth. A killer, seeing his opportunity to remove a threat. You put a hand to his arm, urging restraint.

'You will never know . . . never know what it was like.' The man stops, brushing away the fluid leaking from his one yellow eye. 'What she had to do to protect us both; me – a seven-year-old boy. But we were lucky, we had our chance, escaped – and came north.' He tilts his head. 'I am Prince Sable Moran. What you see is what *they* made me into. The Church. Your feuding nobles. The scheming politicians. Sounding familiar yet, prince?'

'You know nothing about me,' you hiss.

'No I don't, but my mother is a prophet and a seer. And knows much. You'll perhaps know her better now as Melusine, the witch.'

Skoll makes a rumbling sound in his throat.

'Get out of our way,' you demand fiercely. Weapons find your hands, their magic sending slivers of light gusting on the wind. 'Or I promise you a death long overdue.'

The man barks a shrill laugh.

'Oh, what fine heroes,' he mocks. 'What did you come here for, the forge? It is corrupted. The Titans' magic is undone.'

'Lies!' Skoll leaps forward, torch and axe sweeping round in a furious swathe. Somehow the prince meets him with sword drawn, although you never saw him move, its blade so black it seems like another shadow. The slim blade cuts, strong and powerful strokes. The man barely shifts his posture but Skoll is already on the ground, fighting against some unseen pain that assaults his body.

Maune lifts a hand, pooling light into his palm.

The prince merely looks at him, unafraid. 'Thrones, kingdoms. What do you fight for, paladin? Your faith?' He gives a sad frown. 'You are no better than I.'

Maune springs at the prince. There is a blinding flash as light meets darkness. You stumble back, trying to make sense of the whirling shapes. Both men are fighting, frighteningly quick, moving fluidly like a performance long rehearsed. You start forward to try and aid your companion, but the spinning blades and magic make it impossible to pick one opponent from the other.

In your mind's eye you see Nanuk and witness a similar play unfolding – the bear is wrestling with the wolf again, both animals flipping and twisting through the black sand of the Norr.

The paladin is knocked back. He slams into one of the columns, crumpling to his knees, head bowed. He is feigning weakness, you can tell he is ready to spring again. But the shadows around the column thicken and rise, wrapping themselves around the man's body. There is the stink of burning flesh as they press against his glowing skin, eating away at the light. He screams in pain.

The prince barely looks out of breath. He stands, solid and immoveable, a darkness against the green fires of the forge. 'And you, Arran. What do you still cling to? Revenge? Against those who wronged you?' Another smile forms on his malformed lips. 'Think you will make a better king than your father? A better ruler than the cardinal?'

An eyebrow arches above his one remaining eye.

'I am here to end this – this chaos.'

'Ah, yes . . .'

From the chill darkness you hear a vast and terrible rumble. It is coming from all around you, the land groaning in agony, rock and stone crumbling away – seized by another chain of tremors.

' . . . the serpent.' The prince nods, gesturing with his blade to the impenetrable night beyond the columned circle. You cannot imagine the destruction being wrought there, but even the foundations of the floating mountain are trembling with its wrath. 'The great leveller, Jormungdar. The last seals of his prison weaken. Soon he will be set free.'

'To wreak *your* vengeance.' You scowl with derision. 'This is not the way; to release demons from the dark. To see everything fall to ruin.'

'You speak of endings.' The prince raises his dark sword, turning its edge to face you. 'We see beginnings. Man is corrupted. We are base and evil creatures, Arran, no better than the demons. But where we differ – the demons know exactly what they are. Monsters, fit only for destruction.' He snorts. 'They do not lie to themselves, swaddle their murderous sin in ideals of faith, duty . . . revenge. Surely, with our wisdom and enlightenment, we should have strived for higher purpose.'

'Then practise what you preach. End this mindless evil!'

Sable shakes his head. 'Beginnings, Arran. I want to see our taint cleansed from this land. Let the shroud take us. A ninth world ends, and a new cycle begins.'

He turns his blade, letting the light from the flames shiver along its darkness.

'Tell me. What joy do you carry in that stilled heart of yours, Arran?' His one eye flicks to Anise, who is leaning against a column, eyes closed, breathing shallow. 'Is it love, Arran? Is that the false hope that lends you purpose?'

You move at the same time as Skoll finds his feet, diving forward, axe-blade cutting towards the prince's leg. You hear the scrape of metal as his blow is deflected, but it gives you enough of an opening to close with the dark prince.

Sable meets your strikes with effortless skill, his blade moving as swiftly as the dancing shadows. 'Come then, Arran,' he snickers. 'For my mother foresaw this, and I welcome death.'

If you have the keyword *brothers* on your hero sheet, turn to **101**. Otherwise, turn to **751**.

734

The monk opens out his meaty fist, showing you his five stones. This forces you to reveal your own. 'A Queen's Wave, double crowned – beats your King's Table,' he declares with a toadish smile. 'The One God shines on me again. I win!'

Remove the word *scripture* from your hero sheet, then turn to **697**.

735

They have fallen to fire, shadow, chaos. Each one touched by her, Aisa. The destroyer. Only one remains. One worth saving. The world of Dormus. Your world.

'But what of these . . . other worlds?' You try and recall ever having read anything of such places. 'The shadow legion, the sky elves . . . they came from other realms, didn't they?'

They are lost children. Broken threads. They cannot be mended. At least, not that I see. The woman turns to look upon the weave, her eyes dancing over it as if reading some hidden meaning captured in its many strands. *Gabriel believed the last world was the key. The centre of the balance. If Dormus could be saved, then hope – the plan – may yet be restored.*

(Return to **713** to ask another question or turn to **760** to end the conversation.)

736

You sink deeper into the mire, the thick waters now lapping against your chest. As you struggle onwards the smoke grows thicker, its caustic toxins making your eyes burn and your head spin with nausea. (Add two *defeats* to your hero sheet.)

With persistence you manage to reach a tangle of dark roots, bobbing on the surface. Several are glistening with magic, their charcoal bark etched with malign runes. If you wish, you may take one of the following items:

Tainted root	**Brackenfell**	**Hanging tree**
(left hand: totem)	(necklace)	(left hand: noose)
+2 speed +2 armour	+1 brawn +1 magic	+2 speed +2 brawn
Ability: poison cloud	Ability: thorns	Ability: choke hold
(requirement: mage)		(requirement: rogue)

You must now decide if you will risk continuing to the centre of the pool (turn to 125) or wade back to shore and leave the chamber (turn to 303).

737

Caul has cut a block from the ice door and is now using his feet to push it inwards. He gives the block a final shove, sending it sliding away on a film of melted ice.

He clambers back to his feet, brushing ice from his furs. 'The old ways are the best ways.'

You drop to all fours and crawl through the space into the room beyond.

At first you find it difficult to comprehend the immensity of the chamber. It has been cut from the heart of the glacier, its smooth iced surfaces sparkling in the eerie green light. Your eyes fall on a slab of carved ice at the centre of the cave, where some creature is lying manacled to its surface. It looks like it was fashioned from the black rock of the mountain, veined with the green magic that Reah showed you in her shard. Grooves have been carved into the slab, leading to channels that snake across the ice to hollowed depressions. Each channel is stained with a black residue – perhaps blood.

'Is this their Titan?' Caul crouches next to one of the black stains, putting a hand to the cold ice. 'Whatever it was, looks like they were draining it of something – blood?'

'Titan blood . . .' You step around the slab of ice, taking a closer look at the creature. It is humanoid in appearance, but instead of flesh and bone there are simply chunks of glowing rock, sculptured and fitted together like some bewildering jigsaw. The legs and arms are bound by black-iron chains, sunk deep into the ice. Runes flicker along their length – their power still evident. You assume the creature was bound here to leech it of its blood. You look back along its body. The creature appears lifeless, its spirit fled. The face has been chiselled to look almost human, its eyes staring vacantly up at the ceiling.

As your gaze moves across the cavern, you catch a flash of colour in the ice wall ahead. Curious, you walk over to investigate, noting other shapes held within the ice. As you get closer, you feel a sudden dread knotting your stomach; Nanuk's presence shifts and tugs at you, bringing a nervous growl rumbling into your throat.

A body is suspended inside the ice. A woman in furs and leather. The stitched badge on her clothing reads: *Reah*.

You put a hand to the ice, brushing away the loose flecks. The face staring back at you is the same explorer you met in the canyon, her eyes vacant and lifeless like those carved into the stone creature. You scan the wall as you back away, your gaze flicking from one body to another – maybe a hundred or more, all trapped within the ice. There are human bodies and other creatures – goblins, trolls, giants, even dwarves. You see Jerico, the man that was wounded in the tent. Diggory, the man who asked you to come here – to rescue his team. You remember the haunting desperation in his voice, the words now given new and sinister meaning.

Please, give us peace.

'What is this place?' you gasp.

You note Caul is standing next to one of the bodies, his mouth moving but struggling to find words. 'I . . . it can't be . . .'

'Did you know them?' You hurry to his side, squinting at the body held inside the ice. It is a man, broad of shoulder, clad in tanned furs. His blond hair is plastered across much of his face, but there is no mistaking who it is – a perfect mirror image.

Caul is frozen in the ice.

You look back at the man standing next to you – his own expression one of horrified bewilderment. 'I'm dead,' he whispers. 'I'm dead.'

You step away, hands tightening around your weapons. 'If it's any consolation, I know how you feel.'

Caul turns to you, his pale face still slack with shock. 'I didn't . . . I don't remember . . . I must have . . . I died here . . . I died . . . *I DIED*.' His voice deepens, becoming something different, alien. His lips pull back from his teeth, his expression taking on a menacing ferocity. '*I WAS BETRAYED. ME! FAFNIR! THEY TOOK MY BLOOD, MY BODY . . . BUT THEY WILL NEVER HAVE MY SOUL!*'

Flakes of ice shower down from above. Your eyes are drawn to the ceiling, where a black shape is moving across the ice – a gigantic scaled beast, its two reptilian heads displaying a worrying assortment of jagged fangs.

Along the ridges of its back, some growth has taken root: a monstrous parasite of corpulent flesh, its many weeping sores oozing long, pale tentacles. Some are hooked into the ice, trailing to the bodies that hang suspended there. Others are flowing down, like streamers, their ends snapping with tiny black teeth.

The monstrous drake opens its twin mouths and emits a bellowing screech, one that is also echoed by Caul as he lunges forward with his spear. It is time to fight:

	Speed	*Brawn*	*Armour*	*Health*
Caul	6	5	4	40
Tentacles	5	4	2	25

Special abilities

- **Hunter's guile**: If Caul rolls a double for his attack speed, he automatically wins the round, even if your result was higher. You cannot use reroll abilities to alter this outcome.
- **Fafnir's embrace**: The tentacles are trying to latch onto you and drain your life force. At the end of each combat round roll a die. If the result is ⚂ or less, the tentacles have latched onto you. This

immediately lowers your *brawn* and *magic* by 1 each time. If the result is ⸬ or more, you have managed to avoid them, suffering no penalty. (If the tentacles are reduced to zero *health*, this ability no longer applies. However, you cannot restore your lowered attributes until the end of the combat)

If you defeat your devious opponents, restore any lowered attributes then turn to **615**.

738

You follow, quite literally, in Desnar's footsteps – shadowing his trail by placing your feet in the depressions he has already made. The Skard sets a tireless pace, maintaining a constant speed and presenting you with only a distant black smudge against the endless white expanse.

As the morning lengthens, sunlight breaks through an opening in the clouds, bathing the landscape in a sparkling sheen. To your sensitive eyes, its incessant glare is a constant pain. You tug your hood down as far as it will go, concentrating on the immediate line of footprints that lead you further into the wastes.

The canyon appears from nowhere. The ground banks steeply, then drops away into a steep-sided gorge. Thankfully, there are a number of shelves and ledges meandering down to its base: a huge plain, studded with black rock and scraggly-looking scarlet grass. A large herd of animals are packed closely together, resembling white-furred deer. They are using the thick coarse hair hanging from their necks to brush the snow from the ground, revealing more stumps of grass to chew on.

'Muttok,' you grin. These relatively docile animals are highly-prized for their winter pelts – if they can be caught.

Desnar has already reached the canyon floor, creeping towards the herd with a javelin resting against his shoulder. You scramble after him, not wishing to be left behind. However, you have barely started your descent before you hear a barking call ring out across the canyon. Perhaps it was the skittering of loose stones that gave away your position, or a sudden shift in the wind.

At the centre of the herd, one of the animals has raised its head - a grey-haired muttok with a pair of large barbed antlers branching from its forehead. The beast gives another barking call. The rest of the herd are now looking around, sniffing at the air, eyes wide and startled. Then, as one, they start running, filling the canyon with the thunder of their hooves.

Desnar spins round angrily, his eyes casting daggers. 'Skoja Pah!'

With a snarl the Skard sprints after the fleeing herd, moving with a startling speed across the uneven ground. You pull a javelin from your holster and follow his lead once again, realising that it will take considerable skill to best this practised hunter and bring down the fleet-footed muttok. Turn to **652**.

739

There is a thunderous roar as the power of the runes assault the giant, coating his body in flickering waves of torturous agony. He stumbles back, wobbles, then teeters forward, dropping to his knees. Spectral claws blossom from your fingertips as you leap onto his back, slashing away like a frenzied animal.

The giant belches a torrent of angry flame, then his life-spark dulls to darkness. He slumps forward into the dust, smoke pluming from around his dented helm. Skoll picks himself up, his skin and clothing caked in dirt and blood. He leans forward to spit out a tooth.

'That was a good fight, Bearclaw. There will be songs sung of this day.' He steps forward, settling his hands around a splintered horn on the giant's helm. With a grunt he rips it free, holding it up. 'Trophy.'

Nanuk's bloodthirst has yet to abate. Extending your claws once again, you proceed to cut and slash with a bestial vigour. A few moments later, you have the giant's spinal column dangling from your hands. You give an answering smile. 'Trophy.'

If you wish, you may now claim the following item:

Giant's backbone
(backpack)
Sticks and stones won't
break *these* bones

If you are a warrior, turn to 206. If you are a mage, turn to 576. If you are a rogue, turn to 399.

740

You look down at the musket barrels and a plan starts to form. If you could somehow block the barrels, then there might be a chance the guns will backfire – taking out Jackson and giving you access to his store.

If you have *seal blubber* on your hero sheet and wish to use it, turn to 723. Otherwise, you have no means of blocking the gun barrels. You may now continue trading and discussing news (turn to 685) or return to the quest map to continue your adventure.

741

You join Talia in the secret basement. The woman is already rooting through a pile of papers scattered across a table top. Your own attention is drawn to the cadavers chained to a set of beds. Their skin is hairless and translucent, stretched taut over their skeletal frames.

You lean in close to the nearest of the corpses, wondering what has kept the body from decaying. Suddenly you jerk back as the cadaver's eyelids flip open. With a hoarse-sounding groan, the creature starts to kick and tug, struggling to free itself.

'This one's alive!' you gasp in revulsion, drawing away from the writhing body.

'Then put it out of its misery,' says Talia matter-of-factly.

Your hands move to your weapons – but, with some relief, you see the body has stopped moving and is now lying limp against the bed, its eyes closed once again.

'What . . . what went on here?' You glance around at the charts and arcane equipment.

'Isn't it obvious?' Talia clicks her tongue in annoyance as she moves to another table, pushing away flasks and vials to rummage through more papers. 'They were test subjects. Mandaleev was working on a virus.'

'A what?' Your eyes fall on a row of cages, stacked against one wall. A few are open and empty, others contain dead rats. 'But you said he was obsessed with creating a superhuman, a mutant?'

Talia shakes her head, her attention still focused on her search. 'He started out with that intention, yes. But his objectives changed – wait, what have we here?'

Suddenly you hear a sickening squelching sound coming from above. Nanuk's instincts spark into awareness, alerting you to danger. Quickly you jump aside, just as a green fleshy tentacle swings down, grappling for you.

Talia draws her blades, her eyes lifted to the ceiling. There, spread out across the bare rock, is an oozing mass of rotted flesh. And at its centre, a mockery of a human face, snarling with contempt.

'Mandaleev!' gasps Talia.

The creature releases itself, dropping to the ground in a glutinous heap of pulpy decay.

Swiftly Talia tugs down her scarf, then presses her lips together to produce a low droning hum. The sound sets the bottles and equipment to rattling – filling the cavern with a ringing vibrato. When it rises in pitch, you notice her twin blades start to vibrate and glow, like they did back in the taproom.

Meanwhile the mound of flesh has begun to swell, pushing jagged bones out of its back to form a set of spines. Loose flabby folds lift and stretch, revealing a toothless maw dripping with slime. From this mockery of a mouth, you hear a garbled slurry of noise, almost an attempt at language – then the air is spattered with mucus and blood as slippery tentacles rush out of the monster's skin, seeking to envelop you both in their sticky folds. It is time to fight:

	Speed	Brawn	Armour	Health
Mandaleev	8	6	4	70
Tentacle	7	3	3	10
Tentacle	7	3	3	10
Tentacle	7	3	3	10

Special abilities

- 🛡 **Miracle grow**: At the start of every round (after the first), Mandaleev grows another tentacle, with the same attributes as the previous ones.
- 🛡 **We got chemistry**: At the end of every round, you must automatically take 1 damage, ignoring *armour*, from each tentacle currently in play.
- 🛡 **Good vibrations**: For every double you roll for your attack speed, Talia's energised blades will cut through one of the tentacles, reducing it to zero *health* (you may choose which tentacle is defeated).

Once Mandaleev is defeated, any remaining tentacles are also automatically defeated. If you manage to best this mutated horror, turn to 393.

742

The crater is lit by staccato flashes as your enchanted weapons strip apart the demon's body, leaving it slowed and weakened. You ignore the plaintive begs for mercy, your blows raining down with remorseless precision, each strike eliciting further shrieks of agony from the monster. At last the demon crawls before you, whimpering as it attempts to escape your fury.

'I am a prince of Valeron,' you hiss. 'And all your kind will kneel before me!'

With a bestial snarl, you drive your weapons into its exposed back, scattering the demon's remains across the floor of the pit.

Once the last rock has settled, there is silence. Save for the soft ringing of the bone charms.

Your blood-hungry eyes meet those of the child. He stumbles out of hiding, his face bunched into a grumpy scowl. His reaction takes you aback. You had been expecting some show of gratitude for having saved his life. Instead, he glares at you in disgust – as if you'd robbed him of his victory, or perhaps his death.

For a moment you wonder if the Skard's anger will drive him to attack. He takes an awkward step forward, his spear levelled at your chest. But then his resolve crumbles. He turns and lopes away, heading into the tunnel. You watch him disappear, swallowed by the inky dark of the underworld – and at that moment, you find yourself understanding his decision. The boy has no home or life to return to – no future in this harsh, bitter land. Now he seeks only death. You sense it won't be long in coming.

If you are a warrior, turn to 665. If you are a mage, turn to 763. If you are a rogue turn to 362.

743

Nine guardians. One to protect each world. The woman turns her head, gazing off into the starlit void. *Eight worlds have fallen. Only one remains. They went to protect it. To save it. They hold the Well of Ur closed. They gave what was left of themselves. To protect.*

'Wait, you mean the Titans; the norns are Titans.' You remember back to the stories that Skoll told you, of the eight stone guardians that stand in the witch's citadel, holding the rift to the shroud closed. And the ninth that chose another path . . .

Yes, Fafnir. The woman completes your thought. *He wouldn't make the sacrifice. He couldn't give up on those who needed him. Alas, he is lost to us. His star has faded.*

(Return to 713 to ask another question or turn to 760 to end the conversation.)

744

For defeating the witch, you may now help yourself to one of the following rewards:

Tainted veil	Even fall	Black horizon
(head)	(chest)	(ring)
+2 speed +3 magic	+2 speed +3 magic	+2 magic
Ability: deflect	Ability: blizzard	Ability: wind chill

When you have updated your hero sheet, turn to 538.

745

You lift the conch from the ashes of the defeated captain. A ghoulish glow blossoms around the black shell as you lift it to your lips and blow a long, shrill note into the air. The remaining crewmen freeze, then abruptly lower their weapons.

One of their number steps forward, bowing his barnacled head. 'The *Naglfar* is yours, captain. Blow the horn and she will come – we'll sail her to wherever you command, sir.'

You lower the conch, your gaze sweeping past the crewmen's faces to finally rest on the ship's wheel – a gruesome artefact, crafted from bones and skulls. A smile slowly spreads across your lips. 'My very own pirate ship. This could get interesting.'

If you are a warrior, turn to 454. If you are a mage, turn to 377. If you are a rogue, turn to 260.

746

You skilfully make your way through the rock belt, taking only minor damage (you must lower your transport's *toughness* by 1). The dragons have fared less well; their large bodies have been pummelled by rock and stone. Nevertheless, they are still on your tail and gaining fast. Record the keyword *rocked* on your hero sheet, then turn to 773.

747

Searching through the worktables, you find a few labelled potion bottles that might come in useful. You may now take any two of the following:

Flask of healing	Elixir of swiftness	Pot of cleansing
(1 use)	(1 use)	(1 use)
(backpack)	(backpack)	(backpack)
Use any time in combat to restore 10 *health*	Increase your *speed* by 4 for one combat round	Use any time to remove two defeats from your hero sheet

If you have the *chemist's notes*, turn to **484**. Otherwise, with nothing else of interest here, you decide to leave the prison. Turn to **426**.

748

The maggot's maw sweeps down, engulfing you inside its mouth. With a blast of magic, you smash through the membranous flesh before its inner jaws can take hold. The creature gives an agonised squeal as you rip out of the ruptured hole, making for the safety of the tunnel.

Squirming in pain, the giant maggot throws itself bodily at the wall of the cavern, raking the fetid earth with its immense bulk. You narrowly avoid being crushed by the blow, accelerating away as fast as you can while the tunnel behind you fills with dirt and dust.

For escaping the clutches of the vile maggot, you have gained the following reward:

Maggorath's rot
(backpack)
A patch of skin dripping
with vile corruption

When you have updated your hero sheet, turn to **675**.

749

The snow is fine and powdery, making visibility poor as the other racers' sleds whip up a blinding spray, obscuring the sharp rocks and other hidden dangers that could wreck your craft. Your only option is to risk a burst of speed, to try and get ahead of the pack and out of the dangerous whiteout.

You will need to take a challenge test using your *speed* racing attribute:

	Speed
Snow blind	13

If you are successful, turn to 103. Otherwise, turn to 647.

750

You try and retrace your steps back to the main cave, but the twisting maze has left you disorientated and lost. After several tiring hours, you finally emerge from the tunnels into a larger cavern dominated by a pool of melt water. You decide to make camp on its banks and resume your journey once the others have rested. Turn to 467.

751

The prince is light on his feet, moving deftly from stance to stance, parrying your attacks and countering with his own. You quickly lose ground to his skilful onslaught, the green-tinged flames getting closer to your back. To your surprise they give off no heat, only a fierce burning cold. But the fire's pit is deep and sheer, its shaft stretching away to darkness.

'I expected more from you, Arran. A prince with your learning, the best weapon masters, the best tutors.' Sable's black blade cuts across your cheek. You lean away, slashing for his midriff, but the prince has anticipated your blow, sidestepping it, his boot slamming into your knee. You stagger, thrown off balance.

'So disappointing.' Sable raises his sword, threatening a powerful overhead swing . . .

Skoll shoulders into his side. The two of them roll and slide down the dais. The Skard comes out on top but Sable is quicker, snatching

Skoll's throat in his clawed hand while the pommel of his sword smashes hard against the warrior's skull.

Skoll slumps off the prince, dazed.

But the Skard has bought you time to recover. Finding your feet, you take a moment to reach for Nanuk. The bear is biting and tearing at the wolf. He has the upper hand, but the wolf is proving a wily foe.

Sable rolls, then springs to his feet – in time to meet your charge. As your weapons clash and spark together, you find yourself inches from his malformed face. 'The wolf and the bear,' he sneers with relish. 'Let's see who has the sharpest claw.' It is time to fight:

	Speed	Magic	Armour	Health
Sable	13	10	7	100

Special abilities

🟣 **Might of chaos**: Each time Sable wins a combat round, roll a die to determine the nature of his attack:

⚀ or ⚁ Sable heals himself instead of rolling for a damage score, restoring 10 *health*. (This cannot take him above his starting *health* of 100.)

⚂ or ⚃ Sable rolls for a damage score as normal.

⚄ or ⚅ Sable inflicts a curse on you. This causes three dice of damage to your hero, ignoring *armour*, and stops you playing any speed or combat abilities in the next combat round.

🟣 **Fang and claw**: Roll a die and add 2 to the result. This is the number of combat rounds that it will take Nanuk to defeat Sable's wolf. (If you rolled a ⚃ then the wolf would be defeated at the end of the sixth combat round.) Once the wolf is defeated, Sable's *magic* is reduced by 2 and he immediately loses 10 *health*.

If you manage to defeat the dark prince, turn to **658**.

752

'Then we have a problem,' sighs the bard.

In a single blur of movement, the woman draws a sword and presses the tip to your throat. You feel the air humming around the blade, the runed glass still infused with some resonance of magic. 'Now, I like you, honey – a lot, as it happens. But I didn't drag myself to this flea pit just for the company. This is business. And you're getting in the way.'

You jerk sideways as her blade jabs forward, then leap back to avoid her downward cut.

'Impressive moves,' she says, arching an eyebrow. 'Shall we dance?'

You circle one another, eyes locked with intent. Then your weapons sweep together in a blaze of frenzied magic. It is time to fight:

	Speed	Brawn	Armour	Health
Talia	7	7	4	60

Special abilities

♥ **Gift of the gab**: The bard taunts you throughout the battle, seeking to distract you. All your ⚁ results when rolling for attack speed must be rerolled.

If you manage to defeat this taunting temptress, turn to 622. If you are defeated, remember to record the defeat on your hero sheet and turn to 56.

753

You make it round the glacier and onto the home straight – the walls of the prison now less than a mile to the south. Unfortunately, the other racers who cut through the glacier are too far ahead to catch, but you can still battle for fourth place with the scrawny racer who tried to fry you.

Cracking your whip, you urge your dog-team alongside his sled, looking to overtake. In desperation, he swings his sled into yours, the spikes along his wooden frame cutting gouges out of your own. His thin, malnourished hounds snap and bite at your dog-team, looking to maim your strongest runners.

You will need to take a challenge test using your *toughness* attribute:

If you are successful, turn to **512**. If you fail, turn to **647**.

754

You manage to beat a path through the cloud of frenzied insects, focusing your blows on the queen. Once she has fallen, the remaining drones scatter in confusion – the loss of their queen clearly throwing them into disarray. Blasting your way past the last of the stragglers, you speed inside another tunnel, hoping it will lead you out of this peculiar hive.

For successfully defeating the queen and her drones, you have gained the following reward:

Drone razors

(special)

Use on a gloves, boots or chest item
to increase its *brawn* or *magic* by 1

When you have updated your hero sheet, turn to **675**.

755

'Wake up, Bearclaw.'

You pivot round, raising your weapons, believing it to be another demon. Instead, you see the ghostly outline of a man drifting between the ash-covered wrecks. 'Find your way home, Bearclaw. Wake up!'

You frown, trying to place the figure. He seems familiar somehow. 'Skoll?'

He steps closer. 'You're in too deep. This is the shroud. Come back.'

A sudden panic grips you. 'I can't!' Your mind reaches out, grasping for Nanuk. You feel his energies, but they are weak, distant.

'Focus!'

The spirit's outline grows brighter, then solidifies into flesh and bone. Strong arms grip your shoulders. 'Listen to me. Find your anchor. Think of what is most precious to you!'

'I have nothing,' you gasp hoarsely. Again you reach out for Nanuk, begging for his aid. 'I have the bear . . . only the bear.'

'No!' The voice cracks like a whip. You feel yourself being shaken. 'Your old life. Anise. Think of her now. Try and remember!'

Anise.

'You love her.' The man's face seems torn by some inner pain. 'I know this – she is yours.'

Suddenly, you can picture her face. The crooked smile, the play of light over her cheeks. The way her hair hangs just so, tangled and messy, but still perfect. Then other senses wash in, the smell of her leathers, a perfumed sweat, the sound of laughter, crying . . . anger.

'I . . . I remember, you were sleeping . . . we were in the caves.' More images rush in, painting the scene back at your camp. 'The caverns of ice, the North Face . . .'

'Good!' booms the warrior. 'Follow your vision, let it take you back.'

In an instant your mind is set free, and you are hurtling towards the warmth of a blinding white light. Turn to 627.

756

Unable to steer a safe course, your sled pitches and rolls towards the edge of the ice. Quickly, you draw your weapons and hack through the harnesses, allowing your dog-team to scamper to safety.

Just as you are about to follow their lead your sled pitches over the edge, taking you with it. (Roll immediately on the death penalty chart – see entry 98 – and apply the effect to your hero.)

Unfortunately, you have failed to complete the race and are now disqualified from the tournament. Replace the keyword *rookie* with *underdog*. Return to the map to continue your adventure.

757

As the debris rains down, pock-marking the ground with hundreds of tiny craters, you also notice a few magical artefacts glowing amongst the rubble. You clamber down from the rock to take a closer look.

You may now help yourself to one of the following rewards:

Flood gate	Mass effect	Snow fall
(ring)	(head)	(feet)
+1 brawn +1 magic	+1 speed +4 health	+1 speed +2 armour
Ability: torrent	Ability: might of stone	Ability: knockdown

When you have made your decision, turn to 254.

758

The wolf turns tail and runs, magic spilling from its many wounds. You consider giving chase, but a tug on your cloak forces you to hesitate. Nanuk pushes a thought into your mind, *danger*, accompanied by a fleeting image of Skoll and Anise. *Return. Be by their side.*

The bear is already bounding across the sand, following the wolf's paw prints.

'Be safe, brother.' You lower your gaze to the smouldering corpses. For defeating the wargs, you may now help yourself to the following reward:

Shadow fleece
(special)
Use on a cloak, head or chest
item to give it the special
ability *warg strike*

Closing your eyes, you feel for the thread that links you to the waking world, using it to pull you back towards the light. (Record the keyword *brothers* on your hero sheet, then turn to 664.)

Skoll raises the dragon horn to his lips and sounds a series of blaring notes. You scan the skies, but see nothing save for the ragged yellow clouds and floating hunks of rock.

'There!' Anise is the first to spot something. In eagerness, she quickly finds her feet and points behind you. 'The dragon!'

The pale sun is blinding to your eyes, forcing you to wince as you try and focus into the light. You can dimly make out a blot of darkness moving closer, growing bigger. The light is soon eclipsed, snuffed out by the giant reptilian body that rises before it, wings stretched wide as they beat at the air. A deafening screech fills your ears.

'Nidhogg!' Skoll waves his arm towards the beast.

A rush of wind sends dust swirling, the force almost knocking you off your feet. The dragon sweeps overhead, its scaled underside displaying the torturous wounds that it suffered at the hands of the rune spirits. The dragon banks, sweeping round in a wide arc. The wings straighten, forelegs reach forward . . .

The three of you scamper out of the way as the dragon glides in to land, claws snatching hold of the rock, ripping deep into the earth. Through the whirling dust you see the dragon arch back its long neck, the long snout snapping wide. Then flames burst from its mouth, bright and red and angry, surging around the sharp yellowed fangs.

We ride to war. The voice booms inside your head. *Climb onto my back.*

You glance at the others in disbelief, wondering if only you heard the strange order. But Skoll is already rushing to the beast's side, using its wing to lever himself onto the dragon's torso. Anise starts forward, then stops. She chews her bottom lip.

'Riding a dragon . . . I have to be dreaming this.'

'It sure beats walking,' you grin.

Together you clamber onto the dragon's back, settling between the high ridges of bone. As soon as you have found your place the dragon springs up into the air, wings beating rapidly to gain height.

My sight is not what it once was. The dragon's voice thunders. *The torture I endured has made me weak. I will link minds with you, corpse walker. You will be my guide.*

You feel a quickening of power flowing through your being, then spreading outwards to fill that of the dragon's. You can hear its heart beating, feel the rush of the wind as it courses across its wings, the taste of sulphur on your tongue.

To your amazement you realise that the dragon has bonded itself with you, allowing you to use its flight and powers to help navigate the rift.

You have now gained the following special ability:

Dragon fire (co): Instead of rolling for a damage score, you can blast your opponents with dragon fire. This inflicts 3 damage dice to a single opponent of your choosing, and 1 damage die to all other opponents, ignoring *armour* (roll separately for each). You can only use *dragon fire* once per combat.

You may use this ability, in addition to your own hero abilities, for the duration of this quest. When you have updated your hero sheet, turn to 224.

760

The woman leans back, looking round in sudden agitation. *He's here. He's found you.*

Suddenly your surroundings start to change. From out of the darkness stone columns and walls rise up, the ground flowing beneath your feet to form a blood-red carpet. It runs the length of the hall that is steadily building around you, piece by piece, high-arched windows shimmering into being. Their faceted light falls on the throne set atop a stepped dais – your father's throne.

Listen to me! The woman's voice echoes urgently in your mind. *A sacrifice will have to be made, boy. Only you will be able to choose, life or death. Do you hear me? Do you hear?*

Within seconds, all trace of the woman and the sparkling weave are gone. You are standing in the main courtroom of the palace. Ghostly figures flicker at the edge of your vision; richly dressed courtesans, all looking down at you with imperious arrogance.

Cardinal Rile sits on the throne.

A small, unassuming man with sallow features and flat dead eyes.

His scarlet robes rustle as he leans forward, a finger scratching at his chin. He is wearing your father's ring.

You stride down the red carpet, weapons brandished. A dark anger has taken you.

'This is a dream, demon,' you hiss between clenched teeth. 'Show your true form, or are you afraid to face me?'

There are titters of laughter from the surrounding court. The cardinal meets your eye with a sly smile. 'Well, the wayward son has finally come home. And we thought you dead. Oh, wait . . .' His smile widens.

Your steps falter as you approach the dais. You can feel the power radiating from the cardinal. It seems to only grow stronger, as if feeding off your hate.

'This is not real,' you growl angrily.

'Are we having bad dreams, Arran?' The cardinal gives a mocking gasp. 'Perhaps you need your wet-nurse.'

A hand settles on your arm. You spin, driving your weapons into the shadowy form of your nursemaid, Molly. Her wizened old features crease with pain as she stares back at you in startled shock, then her body vaporises.

You resume your march towards the throne, rage seething through your body.

The cardinal stands, appearing to loom larger than you remember, his languid eyes suddenly goading and sinister. 'Yes, you want revenge, don't you, boy? I feel it. Take it.'

The man's body starts to swell, muscles bunching beneath his scarlet robes. 'Or are you still a boy, Arran? Too scared and frightened, hmm?' He wrinkles his nose as you approach. 'You stink of animal. You are an unholy abomination.'

Magic pulses along your weapons as you drive yourself forward, eyes narrowed and set on those of the cardinal. You have wished for this moment for what feels an eternity, to wreak revenge on the man who plotted against your family. The man who now sits the throne that is yours by birthright.

'Yes, hate makes you powerful,' grins the cardinal. Pools of shadow are starting to coalesce around his body, crackling with arcane energies. You sense his power growing with every step you take. 'Come, Prince Arran. Fight me. You know it's what you've always wished for!'

761

Within minutes it is over. A grey fog hovers over the melting ice, filling the chamber with a noxious odour of death. Skoll crouches next to one of the broken bodies, lifting up the severed head of a Skard. The ice has melted away, exposing the grey mottled flesh. A single eye glares back in defiance, the mouth stretched open, frozen in its final scream.

'Hemel the Hound's Tooth, son of Brinrik Yule.' Skoll shakes his head. 'He stood by my side, all those many winters ago. He had a wife, five sons.' With a grimace he tosses the head away, wiping his palms against his jerkin. He sniffs the air. 'She was here.'

You look back towards the balcony but, as you expected, Melusine has gone.

Lowering your weapons, you turn to Anise. Her red hair is plastered to her cheeks, her shoulders sagging from exhaustion, but she is smiling all the same – with the elation of victory.

Your eyes meet. And in that instant the smile is gone, replaced by something else. Uncertainty. A fear.

'Anise.' You sheathe your weapons and start towards her, wanting to hold her – to find comfort. Perhaps for the last time.

But suddenly, the world is sent spinning.

Another tremor.

Like all the others, it arrives without warning, blowing you back across the hall.

Desperately you try and find something to hold onto, anything to break you out of your dizzying tumble, but the stone has become like liquid, rushing away from you, sliding out of reach. Screams rend the air, cries, an ear-splitting crack from above. You reach out into the chaos, hands grasping. 'Anise!'

Stone rains down. You look up to see dust and a fiery red sky – and an angel descending through the maelstrom, silver wings outstretched, obliterating everything beneath its shadow. Turn to **584**.

762

You place the 'one of snakes' on the discard pile and pick a new stone from the bag. You have gained the 'two of moons'.

You have the following stones:

The monk decides to play his hand. Turn to 593.

763

For defeating the ancient wind demon, you may now choose one of the following rewards:

Cyclone	Whiteout	Sleet siren
(left hand: totem)	(head)	(necklace)
+2 speed +2 magic	+1 speed +2 magic	+1 speed +1 armour
Ability: wind chill	Ability: blizzard	Ability: immobilise

When you have made your decision, return to the quest map to continue your adventure.

764

Distance is hard to judge out on the ice. As you gradually near the glacier, what had once been a large pinnacle of ice has now become a colossal mountain blotting out the sky. Swallowed beneath its shadow, you bounce over the steel-grey foothills and head straight into the fissure.

Almost immediately you find yourself skimming through shallow pools of water, the howls and yelps of your dogs echoing back from the high walls of ice. The tunnel broadens, throwing you out into an immense grotto. One of the racers immediately veers to the left, plunging into a side tunnel which twists and banks like a tight corkscrew. The others have opted for a slope that rises up to form a winding high ledge. Both options look intimidating and treacherous.

Will you:

Brave the corkscrew?	210
Take the high wire?	112

765

It appears the trapper was right about the confusing nature of the cave system. The tunnel you are following soon branches, and then branches again, offering a myriad of icy corridors to follow. You put your trust in Caul, who leads with apparent confidence, occasionally pointing out the nicks in the ice where he has marked his previous forays.

Eventually the tunnel you are following widens, the ice receding into bare black rock. Its surface is smooth and faceted, occasionally shot through with the same green-glowing magic that you saw in Reah's stone.

'Any idea what this is?' you ask, putting a hand to the chill stone.

Caul screws up his face. 'Do I look like one of them geo ... geo-thingies?'

'Geologist?' you supply helpfully.

'Was gonna say geomancers. Them mages that do all that weird stuff with stone. Probably their doing. Magic.' He spits at the ground. 'No good ever comes of it, trust me. Now keep it down, we're almost there.'

Ahead the ground becomes a series of uneven stairs, which circle round into a small cave. Caul insists that his belongings lie just ahead.

However, you also notice a smaller side-tunnel to your left – more a cleft in the rock, tight and narrow-looking. It may be a trick of the wind, channelled down the many melt holes that pepper the caves, but you are almost sure you can hear a ghostly whispering coming from that direction. You try and discern if there is any meaning or hidden message to it, but the words, if any, are too faint to be heard.

Caul notes your hesitation and shakes his head. 'Stay out of those places,' he says, cutting a hand through the air. 'Seen things I never want to see . . . Let's get my weapons and supplies, then I'll show you a better route.'

Will you:

Follow the whispering?	**565**
Head down into the cave?	**474**

766

Searching through the wreckage, you find one of the following items:

Dream haze	**Guilt spike**	**Insidious knives**
(talisman)	(main hand: spear)	(necklace)
+1 speed +5 health	+2 speed +3 brawn	+1 speed +1 armour
Ability: heal	Ability: deep wound	Ability: revenge

When you have updated your hero sheet, turn to 755.

767

The moment you pick up the book, you hear a grating sound from the walls of the room. Suddenly the floor begins to lift up, carrying you past the surrounding bookshelves. You continue to rise, the ceiling of the room vanishing to be replaced by the red-flecked clouds of the Norr. The table begins to sparkle with motes of magic then, in a flash of dark brilliance, it is transformed into a mounted crossbow – just like the one Skyhawk uses in the book during the Siege of Mentorac, to fend off an attack of . . .

A piercing scream fills your ears.

You race to the edge of the battlements, looking out across the bleak wasteland that stretches into infinity. A staccato flash of lightning reveals the shapes, moving at speed towards you. Giant winged reptiles with oily-black scales and metallic-looking beaks. Nightwings.

You count four of the creatures – hardy beasts, each capable of ripping entire battalions apart. Only Skyhawk could stand against them. And in that instant, you know exactly what you must do. Rushing back to the crossbow, you swing it round, feeling its magic pulsing along the enchanted flight groove. Just like in the storybook, this crossbow will fire magical bolts. You relax your hand on the trigger, leaning against the sight to target the advancing beasts. They are moving fast – unless you weaken them quickly, they will soon be upon you at full strength. It is time to fight:

	Speed	Magic	Armour	Health
Nightwing	10	5	4	40
Nightwing	10	5	4	40
Nightwing	9	4	4	40
Nightwing	9	4	4	40

Special abilities

🌩 **Shoot 'em up**: You have five combat rounds before the nightwings reach the tower. They cannot attack you during this time, but you are able to fire at them using the magic crossbow. In each round, roll for speed against a chosen opponent as normal. If you are successful, you have hit them with a crossbow bolt. This inflicts 4 dice of damage, ignoring *armour*. If you lose, the round ends and the next one begins. At the start of the sixth combat round, the remainder of the combat is fought as normal.

🌩 **Ranged combat**: For the first five combat rounds, you cannot apply/use any abilities. Once the sixth combat round starts, abilities can be used as normal.

🌩 **Outnumbered**: Once you are in regular combat, each opponent inflicts 1 damage, ignoring *armour*, at the end of each combat round. This ability only applies while you are faced with multiple opponents.

If you manage to blast these winged horrors out of the skies, turn to **598**.

You misjudge the angle and hit the side of the web. The magic threads tangle around your transport, sending crackling bolts of magic ripping along its length. (You must lower your transport's *toughness* and *stability* by 2.) Thankfully, your momentum breaks through the sticky webbing, stopping you from becoming entangled. However, your collision has ripped a sizeable hole in the structure. Your two pursuers are able to pass through unscathed. Turn to 773.

769

Animal hides have been raised across one side of the camp, stretched taut between a line of mammoth tusks. They act as wind-breakers, taking the brunt of the storm's fury as it blasts across the snowy plain.

You help Desnar to drag the wolf into the centre of the camp. A horn blast fills the air, followed by shouts and hooting calls. Gradually the Skards emerge from their shelters, like haggard ghosts materialising from out of the storm. They gather around the pair of you, looking expectantly from yourself to Desnar, awaiting the outcome of your test.

You spot Sura moving through the crowd, aided by a younger girl with red hair shot through with streaks of white. As the old woman comes to a halt at the edge of the circle, you see she has the bear necklace wound around her staff. Behind her a boy holds a leather bag in both hands, the many bulges and lumps suggesting it is filled with objects. He grips it tight to his chest as if fearful the wind might snatch it from his grasp.

'Well,' says Sura, raising her voice above the buffeting gale. 'Who has been chosen?' (If you have the word *triumph* on your hero sheet turn to 679. Otherwise turn to 645.)

770

The maggot's maw sweeps down, engulfing you inside its mouth. With a blast of magic, you smash through the membranous flesh before the inner jaws can take hold. The creature gives an agonised squeal as you rip out of the ruptured hole in the beast's side, making for the safety of the tunnel.

Squirming in pain, the giant maggot throws itself bodily at the wall of the cavern, raking the fetid earth with its immense bulk. You are caught by the blow, sustaining significant damage to your transport. (You must lower your transport's *toughness* and *stability* by 4.) Luckily you are able to regain control, levelling out of your spin and accelerating into the tunnel before the enraged maggot can strike again. Turn to 675.

771

You rip the mirror from the demon's face, revealing a single bulbous eye surrounded by a pulpy mass of scarred tissue. Drawing back your weapon, you plunge it into the eye, pushing and twisting until the air rings with the creature's anguished shrieks. When you finally withdraw your blade the demon staggers, black ichor pouring from the gaping wound, then it hits the ground, its bony body collapsing into red sand.

'Sweet dreams,' you spit with derision.

In your hand, the mirror glows softly for a moment, then begins to change shape and appearance, becoming a smaller fragment of dulled metal – the last piece of the broken shield.

If you are a warrior, turn to 766. If you are a mage, turn to 657. If you are a rogue, turn to 370.

772

The Skard einherjar drops to one knee, his head bowed. 'My Drokke.'

Skoll glares down at the man, confusion turning to surprise. 'Leif . . . ?' His face softens into a smile. 'Leif . . . I thought you were lost – the witch had taken you. This is good news, indeed.' He pats the man's shoulder, his grin widening. 'We will drink deep of your deeds in the great hall – of your bravery, my friend. I will have the bards make a song of it.'

The warrior's expression remains solemn. 'My duty is done,' he states, rising slowly to his feet. 'My spirit is freed and now I will pass on.'

Skoll shakes his head, bewildered. 'We can go back. I can return to my body – the same for you, Leif, I am sure of it. We will fight again, as brothers.'

Leif shakes his head. 'I do not feel it – I see no path. My spirit here is unbound. Only my will has kept me alive – my body has . . . is no more.' He removes a ring from his gloved finger, then turns and offers it out to you. 'With your aid, friend, I have found peace at last.' He nods to the glowing band, its green metal worked with runes and glyphs. 'Please, take it – this ring was given to me on my naming day. My grandmother said it was crafted by the Dwarves, before they fell to ruin. It is all I have left to give.'

If you wish, you may now take the following item:

Leif's lantern
(ring)
+1 armour +2 health
Ability: regrowth, blind

The warrior's body starts to fragment, like the pieces of a shattered mosaic. They gradually drift apart, thinning to wisps of smoke which curl away between the twisted branches of the tree.

Skoll is silent, his jaw held tight. When he finally speaks, it is with a furious anger. 'He was a good man. Leif Lysander. Song of Dawn's Light. The witch . . . she has taken too much.' Turn to 400.

773

The mountain is getting nearer, but the distance is still significant – and the dragons are catching up with you once again, their screeching calls and beating wings filling the air with panic. Ahead of you is another island of rock, spinning slowly above the empty chasm. Its flanks are pockmarked with holes and fissures, as if the rock had been beaten by a shower of giant hailstones. It isn't until you get closer that you realise the island is actually a giant hive; the holes are tunnels snaking away into the innards of the rock. Just large enough for you to pass inside, but too small for the dragons.

A chance of escape.

You dive down towards the island, aiming straight for one of the openings.

Realising your intention, the dragons put on an extra burst of speed. They sweep in on either side of you, almost knocking you off course with the frantic beating of their wings. You spare a glance at one of your pursuers, finding yourself staring straight between a set of gigantic widening jaws.

'Faster!' screams Anise. 'Or we won't make it!'

The dragon's head reaches forward, its half-rotted teeth descending, looking to crunch straight through your transport.

With an extra nudge of speed you lurch away, passing into the tunnel opening – and leaving the dragons to smash forcibly into the side of the hive. You can still hear their screams of rage as you continue to hurtle along the tunnel.

'Close,' shouts Skoll above the rush of the wind.

'Hold on,' you call back, 'we're not out of this yet!'

The passage has widened, leading towards what appears to be a giant chamber. You can hear the droning buzz of insectoid creatures coming from that direction. Smaller openings whip past on either side, offering a possible alternate route.

Will you:

Continue into the main chamber?	107
Take one of the narrower tunnels?	603

774

This creature is growing stronger off your hatred, but even so it proves no match for the relentless barrage of attacks that comes its way. Screaming out for vengeance, you pummel the demon to its knees, showing no mercy as its black blood sprays across the stone. You know it isn't really the cardinal, but it no longer matters – your desire for revenge powers your strikes and makes you unstoppable.

As you deliver the killing blow the demon's body flickers and fades, replaced by the blood-spattered form of your nemesis. He looks up at you with those same expressionless dead eyes, muttering a final prayer to his god. Then he slumps against the throne, his hand leaving a crimson smear across the velvet seat.

For defeating the cardinal, you may now help yourself to one of the following rewards:

Cardinal sin	Betrayer's kiss	Cardinal's biretta
(special)	(ring)	(head)
Upgrade a main hand or left hand +1 *speed* weapon to a +2 *speed* weapon	+2 brawn +2 magic Ability: critical strike	+1 speed +4 health Ability: command

When you have updated your hero sheet, turn to 621.

775

The passage slopes, taking you down into a small square room with one other exit in the opposite wall. Caul moves to the left-hand wall, where a large stone carving covers most of the space. The image depicts eight tall humanoids, their features mimicking natural formations of rock and ice. Several have clusters of crystal protruding from their shoulders and arms, while others have icicles dripping from their noses and fingers. These strange creatures are shown standing around an oval slab of stone, set into the wall. Their arms are outstretched towards it, palms raised flat. You notice that the slab glows with a soft emerald sheen of magic.

'I wanted to show you this,' says Caul excitedly, passing his spear point across the stone guardians. You notice that each one has a rune-shaped mark carved into their chest. 'I don't know what it means – but has to be here for a reason, don't you think?'

If you have the *History of Skardland*, turn to 129. Otherwise, you are unable to make sense of the strange carving. After several attempts to try and open the portal, you finally give up and resume your journey. Turn to 494.

776

The rules of 'Stones and bones':

1. All stones are placed inside a bag. Players pick a stone. The player with the highest rank is the 'king' and may play first, with the player on their left taking the next turn, clockwise around the table. The order of ranks are as follows (lowest to highest):

| Skull | Snake | Heart | Cup | Sword | Moon | Star | Crown |

There are four stones in each rank. For example, a one of skulls, a two of skulls, a three of skulls and a four of skulls. All four are known as a house.

2. Stones are returned to the bag. Each player then takes five stones, keeping these hidden from opposing players. This is their hand.

3. Players take turns to decide if they will play their hand (reveal the stones to other players and force them to show their own hands) or discard a stone and take a new one from the bag. The goal is to match numbers (e.g. two of skulls and two of hearts) or build up an ascending hand of numbers (e.g. one of skulls, two of hearts, three of cups, four of snakes). Crowns cannot be used to build a hand, but they can be added to a hand to crown it (see step 7).

4. The goal is for players to create the best hand possible, and play it before their opponents can get an upper hand.

5. Bets can be made at the end of each round. The gold goes to the player with the best hand at the end of the game – or is split in the event of a tie.

Winning hands are as follows (highest to lowest):

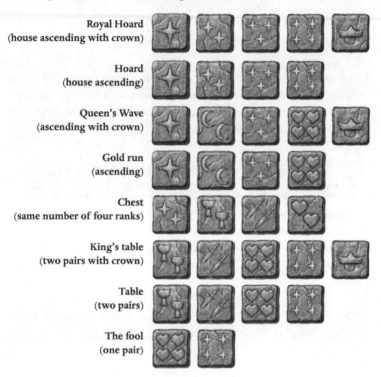

Royal Hoard (house ascending with crown)	
Hoard (house ascending)	
Queen's Wave (ascending with crown)	
Gold run (ascending)	
Chest (same number of four ranks)	
King's table (two pairs with crown)	
Table (two pairs)	
The fool (one pair)	

6. If players show the same hands (e.g. they both have one pair), the player whose hand features the highest rank is the winner.

7. Hands that feature a crown are known as 'crowned' hands. These hands rise in rank based on their crown. For example, a Royal Hoard with the two of crowns would always beat a Royal Hoard with a one of crowns.

777

The beast continues to gain height, spearing straight into the heavens. 'I was too late,' you realise hopelessly. 'The seals were broken. Jormungdar is freed.'

Suddenly the body jerks backwards, then begins to thrash madly. It is all you can do to simply cling onto the spine while you are thrown in all directions, the sky and ground lurching back and forth.

The air is split by an almighty screech – one seething with anger and torment. Another flick of the body. You realise the demon is wrestling against something; seeking to free itself.

You look to Skoll with a questioning frown.

The warrior shakes his head in confusion.

A shudder runs along the body, then the beast starts to plunge downwards, hurtling through the clouds. The crimson wasteland streams towards you – its hills and valleys swarming with ant-like specks.

An army.

Horns and whooping calls rise up from the throng, accompanied by a screeching cacophony of high-pitched caws. Battle standards flap in the wind, their structures of bone towering over the glittering brightness of raised spears. And overhead a flock of birds sweep in at incredible speed, their curved beaks flashing plates of razor-sharp iron.

Leading them is a white-feathered eagle – Habrok.

'They came!' shouts Skoll, laughing in jubilation. 'They answered my call!'

The land rushes up, closer and closer.

Jormungdar shows no signs of stopping, his gargantuan body curling like a dark rainbow over the land – overshadowing the vast Skard army. As you get closer you can make out sleds pulled by packs of dogs and wolves; the winged helms of einherjar; painted warriors astride giant boars; shamans glowing with auras of green magic . . .

So close now you can make out their panicked faces.

The beast's scaled body slams into the earth, the resulting shockwave ripping through rock and stone and blasting a cloud of debris across the wasteland.

Hundreds are caught amidst the deadly rain, dying in seconds – a bloody haze left in their wake. But as the dust settles, horns take up the clarion call once again. Lines of warriors rush in, leaping over fallen comrades, sending spears and rocks showering against the scaled hide. Habrok and the eagles dive, their shrieks merging with the wind's keening wail. They set upon the demon with a hungry vigour, their beaks and talons ripping through scales, tearing at flesh.

You hold on tight as Jormungdar starts to rise again, its body coiling back towards the rift. It gives another earth-shattering screech as it thrashes and beats against the ground, gripped in the throes of some violent seizure.

'It can't free itself!' You shout back to Skoll. 'One of the seals must have held!'

'Then we have a chance!' The warrior reaches back to his belt, tugging loose his axe. 'The head . . . get to the head!'

Your eyes follow the curved spine of the beast, past humps of bone where long fleshy appendages whip back and forth, their vibrations filling the air with a discordant rattle. Beyond them a wall of spines form a daunting collar, each barbed tip dripping with a black steaming venom.

Then there is the head itself.

You stare at it in disbelief, your spirit quaking at its immensity – a serpentine horror of chitinous scales and curved horns, its jaws stretched wide to display glittering fangs the size of mountains.

Below you, the Skards continue to pepper the body with spears, occasional balls of flame erupting against its flanks. From the beast's fanged maw, a black stream jets out across the milling chaos. At first you take it for some venomous spittle – but the blackness moves with a volition of its own, spreading out and then falling on the Skards like rain.

There are terrible screams.

In horror, you realise the black cloud is alive – a deadly swarm of winged creatures. They move quickly across the army, their black claws taking apart armour and flesh with equal abandon. As they continue to feed, you notice a magical glow flickering around the demon's body. Spears that were once embedded deep into its flesh start to tremble, then pop out of the wounds. The ruptured skin closes quickly, scales growing back to form a coat of luminous blue armour. It seems with every death caused by the dark swarm the demon is able to heal itself.

You rise shakily to your feet, taking a moment to find balance as the body bucks and shifts beneath you. Then, with weapons bared, glowing bright with magic, you are running – leaping and dodging around the spiked ridges, making for the beast's head.

While Jormungdar's body remains trapped, the demon is not at full strength – affording you a slim chance of besting this world-ending adversary. It is time to fight:

	Speed	Brawn	Armour	Health
Jormungdar	13	10	18/8 (*)	120
Black miasma	14	8	7	50
Dread rattles	13	6	6	60
Spine collar	13	6	8	50

Special abilities

- **Black miasma**: At the end of each combat round, Jormungdar heals 5 *health* (this cannot take him above his starting health of 120). Once the black miasma is defeated (or Jormungdar is reduced to zero *health*), this ability no longer applies.
- **Dread rattles**: While the dread rattles have *health*, you cannot play any speed abilities. Once the dread rattles are defeated, you no longer suffer a penalty and you may use speed abilities as normal.
- **Spine collar**: (*) At the end of each combat round you must take 2 damage, ignoring *armour*, from the creature's deadly spines. Once the spine collar is defeated, this ability no longer applies and Jormungdar's *armour* is lowered by 10 for the remainder of the combat.

Allies' abilities

(Each of the following abilities can be used once during this combat.)

- **Rousing blast (mo)**: The einherjar horns boost your spirit and fill you with renewed strength. You may increase your *brawn* or *magic* by 4 for one combat round, and restore 4 *health*.
- **Habrok's flock (mo)**: The birds' persistent attacks distract Jormungdar and provide you with a welcome respite. Use this ability to immediately restore one speed or combat ability that you have already played, allowing you to play it again.
- **Storm of spears (co)**: The Skards launch their spears at the beast. Use this ability instead of rolling for a damage score. This inflicts 2 damage dice to each opponent, ignoring *armour*. Roll separately for each.
- **_Naglfar_ and Nidhogg**: If you have the *captain's conch* and/or the *dragon's horn* you can summon these allies to aid you in the battle,

giving you access to their associated ability (*nail gun* and / or *dragon's breath*) once each during the combat.

Once Jormungdar is reduced to zero *health*, you have won the combat (even if other opponents still have *health*).

If you manage to defeat this monstrous demon of the underworld, turn to 722.

778

The creatures are surefooted across the ice, unlike yourselves. Sadly, your fumbling efforts only serve to increase their lead. Determined not to give up, you follow the svardkin into a winding maze.

The pathways are tight and narrow, twisting and crossing back on themselves in an infuriating manner. Soon you have lost all sense of direction. Of the Svardkin there is no sign, save for the distant ticking and scraping of their claws, the echoes giving no bearing to their course.

'We should go back,' pants Anise. 'Whatever they took isn't worth breaking our necks over.'

You raise a hand for silence, straining to detect the fading echoes.

'This way.' You choose a side-passage – and immediately stumble upon a bundle of discarded cloth lying on the ice. Scooping it up, you unravel the cloth to discover that it is a hooded set of robes with an insignia of a red eye stitched onto the chest. You assume the Svardkin dropped it, believing the cloth was of little worth.

'That's the sign of the witch,' says Skoll, gesturing at the red eye. 'All of her coven wear them.'

(If you wish to take the *coven robes* simply make a note of them on your hero sheet, they do not take up backpack space.)

You are about to turn away when a sudden movement catches your eye – a ball of yellow light is hovering in the passageway, darting quickly from side to side. It almost looks like an eye. Before you can alert the others the wisp zips away, heading down an adjoining tunnel.

Will you:

Follow the yellow light?	**285**
Return to the miners' bodies?	**750**

779

You may now help yourself to one of the following special rewards:

Dark storm	**Tomb life**	**Witched walkers**
(cloak)	(head)	(feet)
+2 speed +3 brawn	+2 speed +2 armour	+2 speed +2 armour
Ability: splinters	Ability: greater heal	Ability: freeze

When you have updated your hero sheet, turn to **514**.

780

The men avert their eyes as you scan their line looking for a sparring partner. Since besting Rutus, few have wanted to match themselves against you – partly out of loyalty to Rutus, and partly out of fear. The trainer grins when he sees you standing alone, shunned by the others.

'A soldier can work a long time to get your kind of rep.' He points the end of his riding crop towards the training dummies. 'Don't let success get to your head. Those maids need some lovin'. So get to it, eh?'

You glare at the mock faces painted onto the straw heads. Somehow they seem more insulting than the glares and smirks from the soldiers.

'What's the matter, too good for sack-cloth and straw now?' The trainer folds his arms, his brow creased in a heavy and disapproving frown.

'I have no taste for it today.' You turn and leave, wincing at the jibes and sniggers that follow in your wake. Return to **113** to continue your exploration of the keep.

Epilogue

L ight whipped across the dark space. Threads of silver unravelling at breakneck speed. Each tear, each split drew more blinding pain. The spinner covered her face, fingernails raking back and forth. *Make it stop! Gabriel, I beg you. Make it stop!* The symphony of the plan, the great work, had come undone. Its sharp crashing notes cut like murderous knives, growing louder and more insistent as the silver tracery writhed in chaos. Lives. Millions of fates were suddenly cast adrift without purpose or end.

The spinner could not weave the web. She could only give it life. Gabriel had been the weaver. The one who knew the purpose of the plan, as it had always been since the beginning of creation. He had decided the fate of every being. Every destiny had been known. But Aisa had ended all that. For she was the changer. She was death.

The music stopped. Silence.

An absence more deafening than the previous cacophony.

Then the threads began to move again, tangling together in knotted patterns, forming a bright maze across the starlit ether. A new pattern was quickly taking shape, the matrix of the weave striking up a different melody.

The spinner heard its song.

Crawling between the laced threads, her eyes scanned each shivering beam of light. The symphony was still discordant. The harmonies were straining against the confusion. A few chords lifted in sonorous rhythm only to be drowned by the drumming din of chaos.

Gabriel. What have you done?

The spinner lifted her arms to touch the brightest thread. It was warm, unlike the others, its heat radiating a sad and lonely refrain. *Gabriel . . .*

The spinner arched her neck, following the pattern of light as it speared to the centre of the weave. Only one light such as this had come before. Gabriel had sacrificed himself to the weave. His essence, his being, was now part of every thread, seeking to bring together the plan – to put destiny in the hands of those who were bound to it. Some threads had only the merest hint of that greatness, others were shadows – barely discernible against the void. Those threads sowed disorder, and there were many now. Too many. But this one . . . this one lonely thread, beating with the light of hope . . . outshone them all.

A great prophet. A teacher. A messiah.

Who is this, burning bright as Judah? Do you send them another messenger, Gabriel?

The spinner put her ear to the thread and listened.

*　*　*

The stone walls dripped with shadows, their malign forms seeming to feed on the man's torment. A ring of metal. The hammer came down a second time, striking the nail deeper into the blackened hand. A burning, acrid stench filled the room.

Caeleb watched, silent and grim as the shadows.

The torturer stepped away from the table, his naked torso glistening with sweat. He looked to Caeleb for approval, but the warrior's eyes were focused solely on their captive.

The man's broken face was already healing. The shadow magic bound into the brands that wound about his left arm had not been entirely spent.

Caeleb took a step closer, scrutinising the man's features. They were sharp and hard, accentuated by the half-light. His eyes, dark and inscrutable, reminded Caeleb of the one he hunted. The Nevarin.

'Tell me where he is. The betrayer.' Caeleb worked to keep the anger out of his voice – to keep himself under control. It was an effort. It was always an effort when he was faced with a horror such as this. A shadow spawn. An affront to everything he now believed in.

His shaking hand settled on the knife at his belt. He wanted to use it. To see how far he could go before this monster's healing gave out.

'He's gone, I told you!' The prisoner snapped with defiance, his body straining back from the nails driven through his hands. Their holy magic hissed as they continued to burn at his flesh. 'Lorcan. It's Lorcan now.'

Caeleb ground his teeth. His left eye twitched. 'My patience is wearing thin. Tell me where I can find this . . . Lorcan.'

'And if I tell you?' The prisoner's eyes flicked to the open leather case spread out on the table before him. Knives and needles glinted in the torchlight. 'You won't release me, I know it. You won't pardon me for my sins. What good is your god if he cannot forgive?'

Caeleb sprang forward, his fists coming down hard on the nails, grinding them deeper. The vaulted chamber rang with the man's deafening cries.

Caeleb breathed in the pain, like the scent of some half-remembered summer's day. 'I can do this for as long as it takes. You think yourself immortal. You can heal. But know this. Here, in the dungeons of the inquisition, we can make such a gift a curse.'

Caeleb leaned forward, the muscles of his neck standing rigid like cords of iron. When he spoke it was barely a whisper. The prisoner flinched all the same.

'Show me his face.'

The prisoner trembled, shaking his head.

'I know you can do it. Your kind all share that power, I have seen it.'

'Please, I don't have the strength.' The prisoner licked his lips, looking down at the nails driven into his hands. 'Perhaps, if you'd release me I'll . . .'

'SHOW ME!'

Caeleb raised a fist, the fresh inscriptions burnt into his knuckles flaring into life. He pulled back his arm, ready to strike – the white light illuminating his own tormented visage. 'Show me,' he breathed.

From the branded sigils on the prisoner's arm an answering glow washed along the winding brands. Then his body started to change, shifting and remoulding itself. The chest and arms grew thinner, more gaunt, the spine bent, shoulders rounding, the once tangled mane of hair receding into clumps of coarse white bristles. Within a matter of seconds the man seated at the table had aged fifty years, his once handsome features now those of a scarred, hunchbacked old man.

'This is Lorcan,' gasped the prisoner, his head slumping forward with exhaustion. 'This is the one you seek.'

Caeleb straightened, nodding thoughtfully. 'Yes, he is the one.' His glowing hand moved to the scarlet rose pinned to his white cloak. 'Where will I find him?'

The prisoner struggled to raise his head. 'The sands. You should seek the desert sands.'

Caeleb snorted. 'That's your answer?

The prisoner was silent.

'Not good enough.' Caleb shot a glance to his companion. 'He's all yours.'

The torturer cracked his knuckles. 'As you say, brother. There'll be no pardon for this one?'

Caeleb had turned to leave. He looked back, his gaze piercing. 'He is a shadow spawn. The One God does not pardon such evil.'

The torturer twisted his mouth, forming a semblance of a smile. 'Then I'll put him to the question.' He stepped up to the open case, his stubby fingers playing across the grisly instruments. Back and forth they ran, until finally stopping on a bone-handled saw. 'I'll do my duty, brother Caeleb. For the One God. For Valeron.'

'For Glory,' recited Caeleb. He gave the prisoner a last, disdainful scowl, then swept from the chamber.

*   *   *

Black sand whirled across the hellish plain, forming rippling clouds against the blood-stained skies. The demon crouched at the edge of the burnt, bone-scattered canyon, his blazing eyes fixed on the structure before him. A vast edifice of twisted metal, its innards thrumming with dark energies.

Slowly his wings spread back, their silver veins painting a bright afterimage through the dusty air. His muscles tensed, ready to spring. For him, the hunt was over.

The edifice was rising now, each fiery blast shaking the rocks and sending fresh cracks snaking through the parched earth.

Yet the demon paused, his eyes shifting – heightened senses warning him of another presence. Here in the shroud, that could mean only one thing . . .

He spun round, snarling, his clawed hands summoning balls of deadly magic. But the figure striding towards him, impervious to the whirling maelstrom of dust and sand, was no monstrous fiend. It was a man.

'How did you find me?' The demon closed his fists, snatching away the magic before it could fully form. 'Your powers have grown.'

The man laughed, halting some metres away. Beneath the brim of an iron helm his green eyes shone with a pale brilliance. 'The heart of a demon has many powers,' he jibed. 'Jormungdar and I are still getting to know each other.'

The demon scowled. 'I didn't ask for your aid.'

'I'm not giving it.' The man tilted his head to view the metallic structure. It was rising faster into the sky, its vast immensity throwing a mountain of shadow across the bleak landscape. 'Is that where you'll find him? The Lorcan that you seek?'

The demon straightened, his wings folding back across his shoulders. 'My visions have led me here. What you see, Arran, is the herald of our end. Melusine, Jormungdar, I knew such evils would be overcome. But this future . . . this web spells our ultimate doom.'

Arran moved to the demon's side, absorbed by the sight before him. 'You still speak in riddles, prophet. Tell me true. What is this . . . thing?'

Green lightning was flickering about the structure, illuminating the glowing rods that spiked across the metal plates. From its underside the thrumming blasts of heat had grown in intensity, punching through the air in roiling explosions of noise. Sand rose and fell in angry waves, the dry rock beneath splintering into chaotic mosaics.

'This,' roared the demon, raising his voice above the sudden din, 'is the true ending of the nine worlds, Arran.

'This is Ragnarok.'

Glossary:
Special Abilities

The following is a list of all the abilities associated with special items. The letters in brackets after each name refers to the type of ability – speed (sp), combat (co), modifier (mo), passive (pa). Unless otherwise stated in the text, each ability can only be used *once* during a combat – even if you have multiple items with the same ability (i.e. if you have two items with the *piercing* ability, you can still only use *piercing* once per combat).

Acid (mo): Add 1 to the result of each die you roll for your damage score for the duration of the combat. (Note: if you have multiple items with *acid*, you can still only add 1 to the result.)

Aftershock (co): Use instead of rolling for a damage score to inflict 1 damage die to two opponents (they must be next to each other on the combat list), ignoring *armour*. Roll separately for each. This ability can only be used once per combat.

Agility (mo): Use to change a ⚀ result to a ⚁ when rolling for attack speed. This ability can only be used once per combat.

Anguish (pa): Allows you to play *curse* and *fear* twice in the same combat.

Arcane feast (co): Use instead of rolling for a damage score to lower your opponent's *magic* by 2 and raise your own *magic* by 2 for the remainder of the combat. This ability can only be used once per combat.

Armour plating (pa): For every 2 points of *toughness* that your transport has remaining (rounding down), you may increase your hero's *armour* by 1 for the duration of a combat. (If your transport had a *toughness* of 9, you could increase your *armour* by 4.)

Barbs (pa): You automatically inflict 1 damage to all of your opponents at the end of every combat round. This ability ignores *armour*.

Best laid plans (pa): (see entry 547 for full description.) This ability can only be used once per combat.

Bleed (pa): If your damage dice/damage score causes health damage to your opponent, they continue to take a further point of damage at the end of each combat round. This damage ignores *armour*.

Blind (sp): (see *webbed*). You can only use *blind* once per combat.

Blind strike (co): If you play a *blind*, *immobilise*, *knockdown*, *stun* or *webbed* ability, you can immediately inflict 2 damage dice to the affected opponent, ignoring *armour*. If you have won the round, you can still roll for a damage score as normal. This ability can only be used once per combat.

Blizzard (co): Instead of rolling for a damage score, you can cast *blizzard*. This causes 2 damage dice to two opponents, ignoring *armour* (they must be next to each other on the combat list). Roll separately for each. At the end of the next combat round, each opponent also suffers an extra die of damage, ignoring *armour*.

Blood frenzy (pa): If a *bleed* effect is in play then you may raise your *speed* by 1.

Blood oath (mo): Sacrifice 4 *health* to roll an extra die for your damage score. This ability can only be used once per combat.

Bloody maiden (mo): You may add 2 to each die you roll for damage for one combat round. This ability can only be used once per combat.

Boneshaker (mo): Use this ability to reroll all of your opponent's speed dice. This ability can only be used once per combat.

Brittle edge (pa): Each time an opponent wins a combat round and rolls for a damage score, your opponent immediately takes 2 damage, ignoring *armour* (whether they cause health damage or not).

Chaotic catalyst (co): (see entry 484 for full description.) This ability can only be used once per combat.

Charge (sp): In the first round of combat, you may increase your *speed* by 2.

Charm (mo): You may reroll one of your hero's dice any time during a combat. You must accept the result of the second roll. If you have multiple items with the *charm* ability, each one gives you a reroll.

Choke hold (mo): If you play a combat ability and cause health damage to an opponent, you can immediately use *choke hold*. This inflicts 2 damage dice to your opponent (in the case of multiple opponents, you can choose your victim) and also lowers their *speed* by 1 for the next combat round. This ability can only be used once per combat.

Cleave (co): Instead of rolling for a damage score, you can use *cleave*. Roll 1 damage die and apply the result to each of your opponents, ignoring their *armour*. You can only use *cleave* once per combat.

Cold snap (mo): Reroll any die for damage, adding 2 to the result. This ability can only be used once per combat.

Command (co): When an opponent wins a combat round, use *command* to instantly halt their attack, allowing you to roll for damage instead as if you had won the combat round. This ability can only be used once per combat.

Corrode (co): (see *rust*). You can only use *corrode* once per combat.

Corruption (co): If your damage score causes health damage to an opponent you can inflict *corruption* on them, lowering their *brawn* or *magic* score by 2 for the remainder of the combat. This ability can only be used once per combat.

Counter (co): If your opponent wins a combat round, you can use *counter* to lower your opponent's damage score by 2 and inflict 1 damage die back to them, ignoring *armour*. This ability can only be used once per combat.

Coup de grace (pa): When an opponent is reduced to 10 *health* or less, you can immediately use *coup de grace* to reduce them to zero *health*. You can only use *coup de grace* once per combat.

Crawlers (sp): Cover your opponent in creepy-crawlies, forcing them to itch and scratch their way through the combat. This lowers their *speed* by 1 for two combat rounds. *Crawlers* can only be used once per combat.

Creeping cold (co + pa): Instead of rolling for a damage score, you can cast *creeping cold* on one opponent. This does 1 damage at the end of every combat round. For each ⠿ result you roll for any subsequent damage scores, *creeping cold* increases its damage by 1. This ability can only be used once.

Critical strike (mo): Change the result of all dice you have rolled for damage to a ⠿. You can only use this ability once per combat.

Cruel twist (mo): If you get a ⠿ result when rolling for your damage score, you can use *cruel twist* to roll an extra die for damage. This ability can only be used once per combat.

Crystal armour (mo): (see entry 431 for full description.) This ability can only be used once per combat.

Cunning (mo): You may raise your *brawn* score by 3 for one combat round. You can only use *cunning* once per combat.

Cure (-): Use at any time to remove two defeats from your hero sheet.

Curse (sp): (see *webbed*). You can only use *curse* once per combat.

Dark pact (co): Sacrifice 4 *health* to charge your strike with shadow energy, increasing your damage score by 4. This ability can only be used once per combat.

Darksilver (mo): Sacrifice 2 *health* to raise your *speed* by 3 for one combat round. This ability can only be used once per combat.

Deadly dance (sp): Goad your opponent with a series of dodges and feints. This automatically lowers their *speed* by 2 for one combat round, but raises their *brawn/magic* by 1 for the remainder of the combat. This ability can be used twice in the same combat, but each time it is used your opponent's *brawn/magic* is increased.

Decay (pa): You automatically inflict 1 damage to all of your opponents at the end of every combat round. This ability ignores *armour*.

Deceive (mo): (see trickster). You can only use *deceive* once per combat.

Deep wound (co): You can use this ability to roll an extra die when determining your damage score. You can only use this ability once per combat.

Deflect (co): (see *overpower*). You can only use *deflect* once per combat.

Disease (pa): If your damage dice/damage score causes health damage to your opponent, they continue to take 2 points of damage at the end of each subsequent combat round. This damage ignores *armour*.

Distraction (mo): (see *feint*). You can only use *distraction* once per combat.

Dodge (co): Use this ability when you have lost a combat round to avoid taking damage from your opponent's damage score. This ability can only be used once per combat.

Dogged determination (mo): You may reroll any/all of your hero's speed dice, accepting the result of the rerolled dice. This ability can only be used once per combat.

Dominate (mo): Change the result of one die you roll for damage to a ⚅. You can only use this ability once per combat.

Dragon fire (co): Instead of rolling for a damage score, you can blast your opponents with dragon fire. This inflicts 3 damage dice to a single opponent of your choosing, and 1 damage die to all other opponents, ignoring *armour* (roll separately for each). You can only use *dragon fire* once per combat.

Drake fire (co): (see *dragon fire*). You can only use *Drake fire* once per combat.

Dry ice (co): (see entry 484 for full description.) This ability can only be used once per combat.

Evade (co): (see dodge). You can only use *evade* once per combat.

Eviscerate (dm): Use *eviscerate* to automatically defeat all opponents with 5 *health* or less. This ability can only be used once per combat.

Exploit (pa): For each ⚀ result your opponent rolls for attack speed you automatically inflict 1 damage back to them, ignoring *armour*.

Fatal blow (co): Use *fatal blow* to ignore half of your opponent's *armour*, rounding up. This ability can only be used once per combat.

Fear (mo): Lower your opponent's damage score by 2 for one combat round. This ability can only be used once per combat.

Feint (mo): You may reroll some or all of your dice, when rolling for attack speed. This ability can only be used once per combat.

Finesse (mo): Use *finesse* to reroll one die for damage, adding 2 to the result. This ability can only be used once per combat.

First blood (pa): Before the first combat round you can automatically inflict 4 damage to an opponent of your choosing. (Note: This will also inflict any harmful passive abilities you have, such as *bleed* and *venom*.)

First cut (pa): Before the first combat round you can automatically inflict 1 damage to an opponent of your choosing. (Note: This will also inflict any harmful passive abilities you have, such as *bleed* and *venom*.)

Focus (mo): Use any time in combat to raise your *magic* score by 3 for one combat round. You can only use this ability once per combat.

Freeze (mo): Use any time in combat to ignore the passive damage you would ordinarily suffer at the end of a combat round for two rounds. You can only use this ability once per combat.

Frenzy (sp): Increase your *speed* by 3 for one combat round. You can only use *frenzy* once per combat.

Frost burn (mo): Use any time in combat to add 2 to your damage score. This ability can only be used once per combat.

Frost guard (mo): Use any time in combat to raise your *armour* score by 3 for one combat round and lower all your opponents' *speed* by 1 for the next round only. You can only use this ability once per combat.

Frost hound (dm): (requires Syn's heart) When you defeat an opponent, you can transform the corpse into a frost hound. The hound will immediately attack another single opponent, inflicting 2 damage per round (ignoring *armour*) for the duration of the combat. You can only use this ability once per combat, to summon a single hound.

Frostbite (co): If your damage score causes health damage to your opponent, you can also cast *frostbite*. This lowers your opponent's *speed* by 1 for the next two combat rounds. This ability can only be used once per combat.

Furious sweep (co): Instead of rolling for a damage score, you can use *furious sweep*. Roll 2 damage dice and apply the result to each of your opponents, ignoring their *armour*. Your *speed* is lowered by 1 for the next round only. You can only use this ability once per combat.

Gambit (pa): Each time you play a death move special ability, roll a die. On a ⚁ result you may also regain a *speed* or *modifier* ability that you have already played – allowing you to use that chosen ability again any time during the combat.

Getaway (pa): If you are defeated in combat, roll a die. On a ⚁ or ⚃ result, you do not need to record the defeat on your hero sheet.

Gouge (co): Increases the damage caused by the *bleed* ability by 1.

Greater heal (mo): You can cast this spell any time in combat to automatically restore 8 *health*. This ability can only be used once per combat. If you have multiple items with the *greater heal* ability, each one can be used once to restore 8 *health*.

Gut ripper (mo): (see critical strike). You can only use *gut ripper* once per combat.

Haste (sp): You may roll an extra die to determine your attack speed for one round of combat. You may only use this ability once per combat.

Heal (mo): You can cast this spell any time in combat to automatically heal yourself for 4 *health*. This ability can only be used once per combat. If you have multiple items with the *heal* ability, each one can be used once to restore 4 *health*.

Heart steal (pa): Whenever you use *piercing* or *deep wound* in combat, you may automatically roll an extra die for damage.

Heavy blow (co): (see *deep wound*). You can only use *heavy blow* once per combat.

Hooked (mo): Use this ability to save one die result from your attack speed roll to use in the next combat round. You cannot change or reroll the saved die. *Hooked* can only be used once per combat.

Hurricane rush (co): Give into your fury and become a reckless whirlwind of death! This ability inflicts 2 damage dice to each opponent ignoring *armour* (roll separately for each), but for every opponent you hit you must take 1 damage in return, ignoring *armour*. You can only use this ability once per combat.

Ice edge (pa): Any ⚃ result for your damage score will lower your opponent's *speed* by 1 in the next combat round.

Ice hooks (pa): Scale sheer and treacherous surfaces with these sharp climbing claws. You will be told when you can use this ability.

Ice mantle (pa): You may permanently raise your *armour* by 2. You are also immune to any effects/abilities that would lower your *armour* in combat.

Ice slick (mo): If you roll a ⚃ for attack speed, you may roll an extra die. This ability can only be used once per combat.

Immobilise (sp): (see *webbed*). You can only use *immobilise* once per combat.

Immolation (co): Instead of rolling for a damage score, you can cast *immolation*. Roll 1 damage die and apply the result to any two of your opponents, ignoring *armour*. This also lowers their *armour* by 1 for the remainder of the combat. You can only use *immolation* once per combat.

Impale (co): A penetrating blow that increases your damage score by 3. In the next combat round, your opponent's *speed* is lowered by 1. You can only use *impale* once per combat.

Insight (mo): Cast any time in combat to lower your opponent's *armour* by 2 for two combat rounds. You can only use *insight* once per combat.

Insulated (pa): This ability will protect you from some opponents' frost attacks. See combat descriptions for when you can use this ability.

Intimidate (mo): Use to reroll all dice for attack speed, for both yourself and your opponent. You must accept the rerolled results. You can only use *intimidate* once per combat.

Iron will (mo): (see *might of stone*). You can only use *iron will* once per combat.

Knockdown (sp): (see *webbed*). You can only use *knockdown* once per combat.

Lash (co): (see cleave). You can only use *lash* once per combat.

Lightning (pa): Every time you take health damage as a result of an opponent's damage score / damage dice, you automatically inflict 2 points of damage to them in return. This ability ignores *armour*. (Note: If you have multiple items with *lightning*, you still only inflict 2 damage.)

Malefic runes (pa): For each opponent you defeat (reduced to zero *health*), you may raise your *magic* score by 1 for the remainder of the combat.

Malice (mo): You may raise your *brawn* score by 3 for one combat round. You can only use *malice* once per combat.

Mangle (pa): For each ⚁ you roll for your damage score, you can add 2 to the result.

Mental freeze (mo): Use any time in combat to lower an opponent's *magic* score by 3 for two combat rounds. You can only use this ability once per combat.

Might of stone (mo): You may instantly increase your *armour* score by 3 for one combat round. You can only use this ability once per combat.

Mind flay (co): Instead of rolling for a damage score you can cast *mind flay*. Roll 1 damage die and apply the result to each of your opponents, ignoring their *armour*. For each opponent that takes damage, you may restore 2 *health* to your hero. This ability can only be used once per combat.

Mortal wound (mo): You may raise your *brawn* score by 4 for one combat round. You can only use this ability once per combat.

Murder (dm): Use to inflict 1 damage to a chosen opponent at the end of every combat round, and lower their *speed* by 1 for the remainder of the combat. You can only use this ability once per combat.

Nail gun (co): Instead of rolling for a damage score, you can use the nail gun. This inflicts 2 damage dice to a single opponent, ignoring *armour*. It also reduces their *armour* score by 2 for the remainder of the combat. You can only use the *nail gun* once per combat.

Necrosis (-): (see entry 98 for full description.)

Overload (co): You can use the *overload* ability to roll an extra dice when determining your damage score. You can only use this ability once per combat.

Overpower (co): This ability stops your opponent from rolling for damage after they have won a round, and automatically inflicts 2 damage dice, ignoring *armour*, to your opponent. You can only use *overpower* once per combat.

Pain barrier (mo): Heal yourself for the total passive damage inflicted to a single opponent in the current combat round. (For example, if an opponent was inflicted with *bleed* and *disease*, you would be able to heal 3 *health* – 1+2). This ability can only be used once per combat.

Pain sink (pa): (see *freeze*). You can only use *pain sink* once per combat.

Parasite (mo): Use this ability any time in combat to automatically raise one of your attributes (*speed*, *brawn*, *magic* or *armour*) to match your opponent's. The effect wears off at the end of the combat round. You can only use *parasite* once per combat.

Persuade (pa): When selling items to vendors (such as pelts or jewels), you may increase the cost of the item by 10 gold crowns.

Petrify (dm): (see *murder*). You can only use *petrify* once per combat.

Phantom (co): Instead of rolling for a damage score, you can summon a phantom. Your phantom has a *health* of 8 and will absorb any damage that would normally be applied to your hero at the end of a combat round. Once the phantom is reduced to zero *health*, it is banished and any outstanding passive damage is then passed back to your hero. This ability can only be used once per combat.

Pick 'n' mix (mo): When you use this potion, roll a die. On a ⚀ or ⚁ result, you restore 2 *health*. On a ⚂ or ⚃ result, you restore 4 *health*. On a ⚄ or ⚅ result, you restore 6 *health*.

Piercing (co): Use *piercing* to ignore your opponent's *armour* and apply your full damage score to their *health*. This ability can only be used once per combat.

Poison cloud (co): Instead of rolling for a damage score you can cast *poison cloud*. This inflicts 1 damage to two opponents at the end of every combat round for the duration of the combat. (Your chosen targets must be next to each other on the combat list). This ability can only be used once per combat.

Power totem (co + pa): (see entry 686 for full description.) This ability can only be used once per combat.

Protection (mo): Use any time in combat to turn an opponent's ⚅⚅ result for their damage score into a ⚀. This ability can only be used once per combat.

Punch drunk (co): When your opponent's damage score causes health damage, you can use *punch drunk* to increase your *armour* by 4 for the *next* combat round only. This ability can only be used once per combat.

Quicksilver (sp): Increase your *speed* by 2 for one combat round. You can only use *quicksilver* once per combat.

Radiance (sp): Lower your opponent's speed by 2 for one combat round. This ability can only be used once per combat.

Rake (co): Instead of rolling for a damage score, you can *rake* an opponent. This inflicts 3 damage dice, ignoring *armour*. (Note: You cannot use modifiers with this ability.) You can only use *rake* once per combat.

Rallying call (co): (requires a horn in the left hand) Instead of rolling for a damage score you can issue a rallying call. This instantly restores 6 *health* and raises your *brawn* by 2 for the next combat round only. This ability can only be used once per combat.

Reaper (mo): For each 5 health damage that your damage score inflicts on an opponent in this round, you can heal 1 *health* (rounding down). For example, if you inflicted 19 damage to an opponent, you could heal 3 *health*. You can only use *reaper* once per combat.

Rebound (co): When your opponent's damage score causes health damage, you can use *rebound* to increase your *speed* by 2 for the next combat round only. You can only use *rebound* once per combat.

Recall (mo): Cast any time in combat to restore a modifier ability that you have already used. You can only use *recall* once per combat.

Recharge (dm): You regain a speed or modifier ability that you have already used in combat – allowing you to use it again. *Recharge* can only be used once per combat.

Reckless (sp): Use this ability to roll an extra die for your attack speed. However, if you lose the combat round your opponent gets an extra damage die.

Recovery (dm): Immediately restore one modifier ability that you have already used. You can only use this ability once per combat.

Recuperation (dm): Gain 1 *health* at the end of each combat round for the duration of the combat. This ability can only be used once per combat.

Regrowth (mo): You can cast this spell any time in combat to automatically restore 6 *health*. This ability can only be used once per combat. If you have multiple items with the *regrowth* ability, each one can be used once to restore 6 *health*.

Resolve (mo): Cast this spell any time in combat to raise your *armour* by 4 for one combat round. This ability can only be used once per combat.

Retaliation (co): When your opponent's damage score causes health damage, you can immediately retaliate by inflicting 1 damage die back to them, ignoring *armour*. You can only use this ability once per combat.

Revenge (co): When your opponent's damage score causes health damage, you can immediately retaliate by inflicting 1 damage die to *all* remaining opponents, ignoring *armour*. You can only use *revenge* once per combat.

Roll with it (mo): If you win a round, you can use the result of *one* of your attack speed dice for your damage score (adding your *brawn* as normal). You can only use this ability once per combat.

Rust (co): If your damage score causes health damage to your opponent, you can lower the same opponent's *armour* by 2 for the remainder of the combat. This ability can only be used once per combat.

Salvation (pa): Each time you use a *heal*, *regrowth* or *greater heal* ability you can increase its *health* benefit by 1.

Savage call (co): Instead of rolling for a damage score, you can utter a *savage call*. This will automatically raise your *brawn* score by 2 for the remainder of the battle.

Savagery (mo): You may raise your *brawn* score by 2 for one combat round. You can only use *savagery* once per combat.

Scarlet strikes (dm): Automatically inflict damage equal to the *brawn* of your main hand and left hand weapons to all remaining opponents, ignoring *armour*. *Scarlet strikes* can only be used once per combat.

Sear (mo): Add 1 to the result of each die you roll for your damage score for the duration of the combat. (Note: if you have multiple items with *sear*, you can still only add 1 to the result.)

Shackles (sp): (see *webbed*). You can only use *shackles* once per combat.

Shadow thorns (dm): Summon barbed roots to rip and tear at your opponents. This causes 1 die of damage to each opponent (roll once and apply the same damage to each). *Shadow thorns* can only be used once per combat.

Shape shift (co): Instead of rolling for a damage score, you can let Nanuk take full control of your body, shape shifting into a bear. This raises your *brawn* by 3 and restores 4 *health* but also lowers your *armour* to zero for the remainder of the combat. While in bear form, you cannot use combat abilities but you do benefit from *blood frenzy*. Once you have shape shifted, you cannot change back until the combat is over.

Shatter (co): If your damage score causes health damage to your opponent, you can also *shatter* them. This reduces their *armour* by 2 for the remainder of the combat. You can only use *shatter* once per combat.

Shock blast (co): (see *revenge*). You can only use *shock blast* once per combat.

Shoulder charge (co): Use the result of one of your speed dice for your damage score (adding your *brawn* or *magic* as normal). This ability can only be used once per combat.

Sidestep (co): (see *dodge*). You can only use *sidestep* once per combat.

Sideswipe (co): (see *retaliation*). You can only use *sideswipe* once per combat.

Silver frost (mo): Use *silver frost* to 'freeze' your opponent's attack speed result, forcing them to use the same dice result in the next combat round. You can only use *silver frost* once per combat.

Siphon (pa): All of your opponent's ⚁ results become a ⚀ when rolling for their damage score.

Sixth sense (mo): (see watchful). You can only use *sixth sense* once per combat.

Skewer (co): Instead of rolling for a damage score, you can *skewer* your opponents. Roll 1 damage die and apply the result to each of your opponents, ignoring their *armour*. This also lowers their *speed* by 1 for the next combat round. You can only use *skewer* once per combat.

Slam (co): Use this ability to stop your opponent rolling for damage when they have won a round. In the next combat round only, your opponent's *speed* is reduced by 1. You can only use this ability once per combat.

Sneak (mo): You may change the result of one of your opponent's speed dice to a ⚀. This ability can only be used once per combat.

Sound the charge! (sp + co): (requires a horn in the left hand) Roll an extra die for your attack speed. If you win the combat round, you may also roll an extra die for your damage score. This ability can only be used once per combat.

Spin shot (co): This ability inflicts 2 damage dice to your opponent, ignoring *armour* – plus 1 extra die for every *speed* point difference you have over your opponent in this round. You can only use this ability once per combat.

Spirit breaker (co): Once you have successfully used *take the bait*, you can play a *spirit breaker*. This can be used in any subsequent combat round instead of rolling for a damage score. This inflicts three damage dice, ignoring *armour*, and reduces your opponent's *armour* by 2 for the remainder of the combat. This ability can only be used once per combat.

Spirit call (co + pa): Instead of rolling for a damage score after winning a round, you can summon a bear spirit to fight by your side. The bear spirit causes 2 damage at the end of each combat round to one nominated opponent. This ability can only be used once per combat.

Splinters (co): (see cleave). You can only use *splinters* once per combat.

Stagger (co): If your damage score causes health damage to your opponent you can *stagger* them. This lowers their *armour* to zero for the next combat round only. You can only use *stagger* once per combat.

Stampede (co): Instead of rolling for a damage score, you can summon a stampede! Choose an opponent on the combat list – they immediately take 3 damage dice, ignoring *armour*. The next opponent below them on the combat list takes 2 damage dice, and any remaining opponents below them on the list take 1 damage die, ignoring *armour*. This ability can only be used once per combat.

Sure edge (mo): If your hero is equipped with an axe, sword, dagger or spear, you can use *sure edge*. This adds 1 to each die you roll for your damage score for the duration of the combat.

Sweet spot (pa): Before a combat begins, choose a number 1–6. Each time your opponent rolls this number, they automatically take 2 damage.

Tactical manoeuvres (co): If your transport has a *speed* of 5 or greater, you may use *tactical manoeuvres*. This allows you to avoid taking damage from your opponent/s in a single combat round and increases your hero's *speed* by 2 for the next combat round only. This ability can only be used once per combat.

Take the bait (co): (see entry 382 for full description.) This ability can only be used once per combat.

Thorn armour (co): Use this ability to raise your *armour* by 3 for one combat round. It also inflicts 1 damage die, ignoring *armour*, to all your opponents (roll once and apply the same damage to each opponent). This ability can only be used once per combat.

Thorns (pa): You automatically inflict 1 damage to all of your opponents, at the end of every combat round. This ability ignores *armour*.

Tormented soul (mo): You may sacrifice 4 *health* to instantly restore a speed or combat ability that you have already used. This ability can only be used once per combat.

Torrent (mo): When using *cleave*, *lash* or *shadow thorns*, you can roll two damage dice instead of one. This ability can only be used once per combat.

Trickster (mo): You may swap one of your opponent's speed dice for your own. You can only use *trickster* once per combat.

Twin blade (co): Use instead of rolling for a damage score to inflict the total of your attack speed dice to two opponents, ignoring their *armour* (they must be next to each other on the combat list). This ability can only be used once per combat.

Unstoppable (mo): When an opponent wins a combat round, you may spend 5 *health* to automatically win it back and roll for damage. You can only use *unstoppable* once per combat.

Upper hand (dm): You automatically win the next combat round (without needing to roll for attack speed). *Upper hand* can only be used once per combat.

Vanish (co): (see *Dodge*). Use *vanish* to turn invisible for several seconds, avoiding your opponent's damage. You can only use *vanish* once per combat.

Veiled strike (pa): Each time you use *evade*, *sidestep* or *vanish* in a combat you can immediately inflict 1 damage die to a chosen opponent, ignoring *armour*.

Venom (pa): Your opponent loses 2 *health* at the end of every combat round for the remainder of the combat. This ability ignores *armour*.

Vital artery (co + pa): Instead of rolling for a damage score after winning a round, you can use *vital artery*. This inflicts 1 damage die to a single opponent, ignoring *armour*, and does a further 1 point of damage at the end of each combat round for the duration of the combat. You can only use this ability once per combat.

Vortex (co): Instead of rolling for a damage score, you can cast *vortex* – a spinning whirlwind of dark energy. At the start of each subsequent combat round, roll a die. On a ⚀ or ⚁ result, you have been hit by the vortex and must lose 2 *health*. A result of ⚂ or higher, each opponent is hit instead and must lose 2 *health*. Once cast, the *vortex* stays in play for the rest of the combat. The die result cannot be modified.

Warg strike (co): Instead of rolling for a damage score you can go for the jugular by casting *warg strike*! Roll 1 die to determine the outcome. On a ⚀ or ⚁ result, your opponent takes 2 damage dice, ignoring *armour*. ⚂ or ⚃, your opponent takes 3 damage dice, ignoring *armour*. ⚄ or ⚅, your opponent takes 3 damage dice and must take an extra 1 damage at the end of every combat round for the duration of the combat. You can only use this ability once per combat.

Watchful (mo): Use any time in combat to change an opponent's ⚅ result to a ⚀. You can only use this ability once per combat.

Wave (co): Assault your enemies with a wave of psychic energy. This does damage equal to your current *magic* score, ignoring *armour*. You can proportion this damage amongst any/all of your opponents, but no single opponent can take more than half of your *magic* score, rounding up. You can only use *wave* once per combat

Weaver (pa): Each time you play a combat ability, you may heal 2 *health*.

Webbed (sp): This ability reduces the number of dice your opponent can roll for attack speed by 1, for one combat round only. You can only use this ability once per combat.

Wind chill (pa): Each time you play a speed ability, all opponents must automatically take 2 damage ignoring *armour*.

Windblast (sp): (See *webbed*.) You can only use *windblast* once per combat.

Windfall (co): When your opponent's damage score causes health damage, you can use *windfall* to restore one speed ability that you have already used. You can only use *windfall* once per combat.

Wither (co): Instead of rolling for a damage score, you can cast *wither*. This inflicts 2 damage dice to a single opponent, ignoring *armour*. It also reduces their *brawn* or *magic* score by 1 for the remainder of the combat. You can only use *wither* once per combat.